Henry was born and grew up in South Africa.          o passions, the love of animation and writing, but he also had a fascina.      r Ancient Egypt. After a number of career changes, he found employment at the Durban Natural History Museum as staff artist/technical assistant. While working on the mummy exhibit, his interest in Ancient Egypt led him to do some more research. The plot for a historical fictional novel slowly developed.

After another career change, and while commuting to and from work, he started to write the novel. The final manuscript was completed in 2017.

To my wife, who had shown great patience with my writing and researching the material.

Henry Neville

# IN THE SHADOW
# OF PHARAOH

AUSTIN MACAULEY PUBLISHERS™
LONDON • CAMBRIDGE • NEW YORK • SHARJAH

A CIP catalogue record for this title is available from the British Library.

ISBN 9781788788366 (Paperback)
ISBN 9781528956222 (ePub e-book)

www.austinmacauley.com

First Published (2019)
Austin Macauley Publishers Ltd
25 Canada Square
Canary Wharf
London
E14 5LQ

# Foreword

Few other royal families had generated so much controversy and debate as the five kings and queens of the latter part of the Eighteenth Dynasty. This period is fraught with mystery and intrigue and is still subject to much debate among scholars of Ancient Egypt.

Was the Dowager Queen Tiye involved in the separation of Akhenaten and Nefertiti and the subsequent disgrace of the latter queen? Nefertiti disappeared off records soon after Queen Tiye's arrival.

The theory that Nefertiti had died in year thirteen of Akhenaten's reign, does not ring true. A Pharaoh who had loved his wife as much as Akhenaten did, would not have desecrated her memory if she had died, but would rather have honoured her. Objects have been found in the Northern palace bearing Nefertiti and Tutankhamun's names, *after* the obliteration of her name and images, proving she must still have been alive at that time.

Did Akhenaten and his brother and co-ruler, Smenkhare, have more than a family relationship?

The intimate relationship between Akhenaten and Smenkhare had never been proved, but many scholars believe there was a homosexual connection between them. The love poem I have included in the tale is creative writing and based roughly on a poem by Meritaten.

*'Before his reign was over, Akhenaten was keeping Smenkhare—a youth in his teens—close to himself for a year or so...there is also preserved a sculpture of Akhenaten embracing and kissing Smenkhare, a young boy sitting on his lap'* (Oedipus and Akhenaten—Velikovsky).

An inscription on the gold foil covering the mummy of Smenkhare reads *'Beloved of Neferkheprure Waenre'*. Neferkheprure Waenre was the throne name of Akhenaten.

Was there a plot to overthrow Akhenaten?

My account of the trial and execution of Tutu is pure fiction but historians are convinced he had been involved in subversive activities. The discovery of the "Amarna letters", found in the remains of a reed basket in the ruins of Akhet Aten's record storehouses, seemed to indicate that he had contact with the enemy king Aziro.

Was foul play involved in the deaths of Akhenaten, Smenkhare and Queen Meritaten who died within a year of one another?

Some scholars believe all three: Akhenaten, Smenkhare and Meritaten were murdered, but about that period, plague swept through Egypt, during which two of the younger princesses also died. They could also have succumbed from disease.

Were Tutankhamun's mother, Khiya, and the young king himself, murdered and was Nefertiti's father, the High priest and Vizier, Ay, involved in any of these deeds?

At one time, it was believed Tutankhamun had died from a blow to the back of his head, but more recent tests seem to prove the young king succumbed from blood poisoning or gangrene after infection from a thighbone fracture. A recent documentary on the mummy of Khiya, King Tutankhamun's mother, suggested the fracture on the back of her head had been caused by a severe blow and that she was most probably murdered.

Did Tutankhamun go to war?

Historical records do not mention a war during the reign of the young king, but a chest, found in his tomb, depicts Tutankhamun in a war chariot and shooting an arrow at a foe. His armour also shows wear-and tear, which would not have been caused, had the young king worn them during ceremonial occasions. There is also an inscription in the tomb of Horemheb, where he promises to "Guide His Majesty's footsteps" during battle. As the Egyptians did not mention any of their defeats, one can only assume the conflict had been lost, or as in my novel, ended in a stalemate.

Why did Tutankhamun's young widow approach the Hittite King Shubbiluliuma, Egypt's enemy, to beg for one of his sons in marriage? Who was involved in the ambush and slaying of the king's son, Zannanza?

Sixty five years old Ay was not of royal blood, and in order for him to claim the throne, it was necessary for him to marry into the Royal Family. Tutankhamun's young widow was about twenty eight, and, naturally was not looking forward to marrying her own grandfather. The accounts of her desperate attempts to secure one of the sons of Shubbiluliuma as a husband, is documented in the writings of his son, Mursil, the older brother of Zannanza. The young prince and his party were waylaid and killed en route to Egypt. Tablets, found more than a century ago, from a Queen Dakamun begging the king for one of his sons, was most probably from Ankhsenamun.

This novel is my attempt to explain and unravel the puzzling events at the court of that time.

Some liberties have been taken with factual events and historic characters to fit the pieces of the puzzle together in a coherent form.

Henry Neville

# Chapter One
## Massacre

Slowly, as the darkness left him, he became aware of a throbbing headache. He was lying face down in the sand, his head against a boulder. He tried to lift his head to see what was tugging at his tunic, but a severe pain shot through his shoulder blade and down his back. He cried out in agony. At the sound, the vulture hopped back a few paces, then stopped, watching him.

He reached over his left shoulder and could just feel the shaft of an arrow. With an effort he rolled over on his side and more pain seared down his lower back. A second arrow was lodged in the small of his back. His futile attempts to remove either, proved too painful.

Struggling into a half-sitting position, he squinted against the glare of the early morning sun, already bright and hot. He touched his head. There was a gash on his temple, and blood from it had clotted. A smear of dried blood on the rock suggested he must have hit his head against the rock when he fell. A vulture was watching him from a safe distance, its cold, red eyes unblinking.

He waved at the bird with his good arm but the action only brought on more stabs of agony and dizziness. 'Be gone, stinking, evil Eater of the Dead!' With raucous, guttering sounds and heavy flapping, it hopped away a little further. He kneaded his painful shoulder and glared at the vultures. 'I am not ready for you…yet!'

He raised his hand to his head. Semi-congealed blood, with sand stuck to it, caked his hair. It felt sticky and gritty. His tunic, soaked in blood, clung to his skin.

With an agonising effort and gritting his teeth, he got onto his knees. Some distance away, other vultures were gorging themselves on bodies of dead soldier, tugging, ripping on the corpses. One stopped feeding and watched him warily.

Stabs of pain made him wince as he struggled to his feet and he felt a warm trickle down his back as the wounds started bleeding again. His vision blurred and he shook his head to clear it but this just brought on more excruciating pain. He again reached over, grabbed the arrow shaft and gently tried to ease it out but the intense pain made him abandoned the effort.

All around him were the dead bodies of men, with birds continuing their gruesome feast.

What had happened here? He had no recollection of a battle, but from their garments, they were soldiers. From the manner they wore their hair and beards, they appeared to be Hittites, Egypt's enemy. His enemy.

Except one. This man was an Egyptian. Judging from the fine fabric of his tunic and his broad gold and lapis lazuli collar, he seemed to have been important. Probably an official.

Dimly, he recollected this man waking him. He remembered warning shouts and screams. Men roused and grabbed weapons. Panic all around. Vaguely, he remembered joining them in battle. Fighting alongside Hittites—but why would he be fighting *with* Hittites, Egypt's sworn enemy? His dulled mind was confused. Were they attacked by bandits?

Nearby lay the body of a young man, probably in his early or mid-twenties. He wore a rich purple tunic. This dye, obtained from Autha, was usually reserved only for royalty as only the very wealthy could afford it. He also wore costly jewellery—two gold rings on his fingers, one with a large green stone. Around his neck he had a heavy gold chain. If they were attacked by robbers, why would these treasures be ignored?

This young man and the faces of the slain Hittites somehow looked familiar. Why would he know them? He shook his head, puzzled, and grimaced as pain stabbed into his head again and looked away as more vultures arrived to glide down to tear at the bodies.

'Get away, vile carrion-eater! Away...away!' he waved as a bird hopped closer. In this desolation and badly wounded, no one survives very long. With a screech and wings spread wide, it hopped away to where other vultures were tearing at a body. The feeding bird, with wings out-stretched and uttering guttural calls, jutted his body and head forward in an aggressive attitude at the intruder. A short altercation between the two birds followed. The interloper retreated to find an easier meal

\*\*\*

The man's sword lay on the ground close by and, in spite of the pain he reached down for it. 'I will not die in this place,' he murmured and stumbled away from the carnage as more vultures circled overhead to join those already feeding.

Footprints of men, horses and chariot tracks had churned the area around the dead. Wheel furrows overran those of the horses indicating the direction the bandits took when they left the scene, heading south, towards Egypt. The man headed in the opposite direction. He had no wish to meet up with the men who attacked them. He had not the strength to defend himself.

\*\*\*

The relentless heat, his throbbing head and the searing pain of his wounds made his going agony. He struggled on and on. The noonday sun blazed straight down. The heat was unbearable and the scorching sand burned through his sandals. With no shade, and craving for water, he had no choice, but to go on. His mouth was dry, his tongue swollen and his lips cracked. He sucked on a pebble to generate moisture, but it did not work and his mouth remained parched. He had to find water, had to find help.

How far he had stumbled along, he was not certain, but eventually, as his own shadow was creeping up the eastern dunes, and growing longer, he realised that it was late in the day. Soon darkness would fall.

The severe pain in his back and head continued to burden him. The wounds had stopped bleeding, but the dried blood caused the tunic to adhere the injury, and every time he stumbled, which was often, the fabric pulled and tugged where it stuck to the wounds, making him wince.

He craved for just a single drop of water to ease his parched mouth. He tried to lick his lips, but his tongue, like a dried piece of bark, only scraped painfully over his swollen, cracked lips. There had been water where they had camped, but in the need to distance himself from that place of carnage, he had not thought about bringing any, an action he now regretted, but he vowed not to return to that place.

On and on he plodded. The action of putting one foot ahead of the other had become almost automatic. The sand seemed to grab and hold onto his feet. Every step was an effort. Finally, he reaching a hard, flattish stretch between the dunes, possibly a caravan route, and it made his going a little easier. There seemed to be no tracks on the rough rock-strewn ground.

More than once, he saw an oasis in the distance. Water shimmered and glistened invitingly, but vanished as he approached. He knew these false visions well…depraved attempts by the evil Seth to taunt mortals and derive malicious pleasure from the suffering of man. He tried to ignore these visions.

Presently, more hazy shimmering visions appeared on the horizon. Dark, ghostly spirits that hovered and danced just above the ground. He wondered if these were the *ka* of long-dead travellers.

He plodded on and on and the spirits kept coming closer. He would ignore them. They were not real; he kept telling himself. They were taunting him, trying to entice him to join them in the next world. Just more of Seth's deceitful visions. The figures remained before him, mocking him.

He squeezed his eyelids together as another wave of giddiness flooded over him. He stumbled again, tried to get up, but with failing strength he fought against the darkness that threatened to overwhelm him.

A distant soft tinkling of metal rang in his ears. Little bells, like those tied around the legs of dancing girls. Has he gone *west?* Reached the afterlife? The place where the ka, the spirit, dwells?

Then he heard voices. Hands were shaking him, tugging at him, lifting him. Slowly, the darkness faded and he saw visions…faces, blurry at first. He blinked again, several times. He could make out vague shapes. A vessel was held to his lips and he drank greedily. Some of the cool, precious liquid spilled and ran down his chin and neck.

'Do not drink so fast, Egyptian,' a man's voice said. 'Sip slowly!'

Giggles issued from women. Merry sounds…and low chattering.

'Silence, women! This is not amusing. Can you not see the man is injured?'

His vision started clearing and he could make out his rescuers. They were nomads. Bedu, as they called themselves. Dwellers of the Desert.

He tried to rise.

'Hold still, Egyptian. You will do yourself more harm,' the robed man turned to his party, 'Afsar, Hayata, assist me. We must remove the arrows from his back and attend to his head wound! Sarike, bring fabric strips and ointments.'

'Arrows?' his voice was raspy. For a moment, he seemed confused.

'Yes, two. Fortunately, neither very deep but they must be removed.'

'Oh, uh…yes.'

'Sarike, wrap a stick with cloth and place it between his teeth.'

The woman did as her husband ordered and held the stick to his mouth.

'Bite on this.'

He complied and was turned over. Using a knife, the Bedu woman, Sarike, started cutting into his flesh to remove the arrows. He cried out in pain and sank into darkness again.

***

Smells of roasting meat, incense and lamp oil flooded his senses as consciousness returned. His head and back were still aching but the arrows had been removed and the wounds dressed. He opened his eyes and looked about. He found himself inside a tent, that of the *nemau sha*, those who traverse the sand. A heavy curtain divided the tent in two and cooking smells issued from the other side of the curtain.

'Where am I?' his voice was hoarse.

'You are in my *House of Hair*, my tent. How do you feel?'

'In pain, but comfortable, thank you.'

'I am Honami, Sheikh of this clan. We are eight and twenty, including children. These are my sons, Hayata, my first-born, and Afsar, the youngest. They helped me bring you here.'

The man nodded a greeting.

The Sheikh, about sixty years old, had a strong tanned face, wrinkled and leathery and his beard almost white, with traces of black and grey still visible. His eyebrows were white and bushy. Hayata, the eldest, looked to be about thirty years of age, slightly younger than himself. He had a full, black beard and his skin, was deeply tanned after years in the sun and from the harsh desert climate. Afsar, the youngest, was beardless. His skin was still smooth and soft.

The man wondered about the big difference in the ages between the eldest and the youngest son. Perhaps, the Sheikh had several daughters between the births of his sons. Daughters are of no importance to these people…or perhaps, he had others sons that had left the clan, or died.

The young Afsar had an open, honest face. His widely spaced alert eyes never missed anything. He also showed intelligence, far beyond his limited schooling and age. He had a pleasant smile and a hint of amusement always played around the corners of a wide mouth.

All wore flowing robes and the headcloths of the men were secured with cords. The long trailing ends of the headcloths, draped around their chins and over the shoulders, were used to protect their mouths and noses from the sand during frequent strong winds or sand storms.

The women were more mysterious than Egyptian women. Unlike them, they dressed in loose flowing robes and were all heavily veiled.

'I am grateful for your kindness and hospitality. Thank you…I am…uh…' the man pinched his eyelids together and frowned, trying to remember, 'I…I cannot remember my name!'

'It matters not, it will return before long. The blow on your head probably caused it. Until then, we will call you Asti; our name for Egypt. From your garments and that medallion about your neck, I deem you be Egyptian?'

'Yes, I am. From No-Amun, in Upper Egypt.'

Honami gestured to the women. 'This is my wife, Sarike. She has great skills with a knife and it was she who removed the arrows from your back. She also washed you and provided you with clean clothing.'

Asti noticed the blood-smeared arrows lying on a table. They appeared to be of Egyptian construction. The bandits must have been Egyptian, but why attack people this far from Egypt? The ambush had taken place between Feka and Djahi, well away from Egypt.

'I am grateful you saved my life. I thank you for your kindness and for the garments,' Asti indicated the robe he was wearing. 'I shall repay you the moment I am able.'

'My son Hayata provided that. This is Tekele, the wife of my eldest son. She tended and dressed your wounds.'

Asti thanked her and Tekele acknowledged with a nod. The women have not yet spoken a word, and remained seated behind the men. The Sheikh turned back to him.

'You were lucky. If the one arrow had been but the span of four fingers to the side and a little deeper…' he did not need to complete the sentence.

'Come, you must be hungry.' A large carpet covered the floor and cushions were scattered around a low table. Honami seated himself on the floor at the end of it, cross-legged. Hayata, his eldest son sat on his right and Afsar on his left. Asti hesitated, waiting to see where the women will sit. The Sheikh noticed this. 'Women do not eat with us here in the *mag'ad*,' he explained. 'They will have their meal in the place of women, once we are sated. Come, you can sit here,' he gestured to the place next Hayata, then clapped his hands. 'Bring the food. We will eat now.'

The two women rose and hurried from the tent. A moment later, they reappeared, carrying jars and platters and placed the food onto the table, then retreated.

A platter of roasted meat, cut into small pieces had been placed in the middle. The meat was surrounded by rich gravy. Other vessels contained dates, goat milk, fish, bread and cheese.

'We slaughtered a sheep for tonight's feast. It is not often we have a guest,' Honami picked up a piece of meat, dipped it into the gravy and bit off a piece. 'Come, partake of the meal,' he proceeded to chew.

Asti thanked him again for his kindness, but winced as he tried to stretch out his left hand for some meat.

'No!' Honami held up his hand. 'Use only your right hand for food—the left one is unclean and is used for…other things.'

'I beg your forgiveness. I have much to learn.'

Puzzled, Asti copied the others. He picked up a piece of meat and dipped it into the gravy, wondering what "other things" his host referred to. He was soon to learn.

Water, scarce in Feka, the arid Turquoise land had to be collected at the Oases, and used only for cooking and drinking. According to their custom, the left hand, used for all body cleansing, was therefore unclean.

'We will teach you our customs. It seems you will be with us for some time,' Honami broke off a piece of bread and dipped it into the gravy. 'We have been to Pursath, on the coast, to trade. Our caravan is now heading back into the Feka interior to collect more copper and turquoise from the mines. That is our trade.'

'How long will you journey?' Asti asked.

'As long as it takes. Perhaps six months, who knows? Can you remember who attacked you?' Honami asked as they ate.

'No, I have no memory of that. I just remember there was a battle…'

'You said you were attacked while fighting *with* men from Khatti, but you are Egyptian!'

'I cannot explain.'

'There are many bandits along this route. Pursathi often attack caravans, and then we, the Bedu, get blamed for their evil deeds.'

'No, I do not think they were bandits!'

'How can you be certain when you said you have no memory of the attack?'

'One of the Hittites was still wearing his costly garments and had gold rings and a gold chain on his person. Another body had a gold collar. Also, all the weapons were left behind. Bandits would never leave anything of value.'

'True, but why would anyone have slain your party,' Honami reached for a piece of cheese, 'if robbery was not intended?'

'Why? Why was I with the Hittites? And who was that other Egyptian?'

***

Several months passed and Asti's wounds healed. He had had adapted well to the ways of the family who had rescued and treated him. He was doing his share of the work, herding their sheep and collecting trade goods. In Feka, they visited several mines and he met other Egyptians who had been collecting turquoise. This stone was sacred to the Goddess Hathor, Lady of the Turquoise, and it was often set in jewellery in honour of her. They traded some of their livestock for these stones, which in turn, would be traded on the coast for other items, each time making a slight profit. Thus, slowly they would build up their wealth, which would then be shared between them, and Asti also got his share.

Asti and Honami were enjoying a honey-sweetened drink that Sarike, Honami's wife, had served them, in the cool of Honami's tent.

'Our livestock have been replenished and we will be returning to the coast soon,' Honami took a sip of the sweet drink. 'We will be travelling away from Egypt, and you are well enough to leave us now, Asti,' Honami said. 'You must surely be eager to return to your home and your countrymen?'

'Would I be a burden, should I wish to stay?' Asti had grown fond of his rescuers and wished to remain with them. 'After all,' he told them, 'I have no recollection of a home, family or friends in Egypt.'

'No, you are no burden to us. You are welcome to remain. Afsar will be pleased.'

Just then Afsar lifted the flap of the tent and entered, beaming.

'I overheard. The news gladdens me.' He turns to his father, 'I can learn much from him—he is teaching me the Egyptian way of constructing bows, layering and gluing several strips of wood across the grain.' Afsar makes himself comfortable on the mat next to Asti.

'How is it you can remember the construction of weapons, when you cannot remember anything else, like your name, not even about that pendant of Isis you wear about your neck you are always fondling?' Honami asked.

'I do not know.' Asti fingered the medallion again. 'The inscription on it, *forever,* means naught to me…and the likeness on it is not of the Goddess Isis, but of Menefer. Maybe it is easier to remember a craft—' he stopped abruptly. 'Menefer! What made me suddenly remember that name?'

'It would appear your memory is returning,' Afsar replied. 'That is the first name you remembered since you came to us!'

'It suddenly appeared in my mind…but, as yet, I do not know who this Menefer is, or was!'

\*\*\*

The string of asses, mules and camels were loaded. Honami, as head of the clan, mounted a camel, gave a signal and with a jingling of bells and complaining groans from the camels, the caravan started on its journey. Older men and women who can no longer walk, rode on animals, while the younger members of the tribe, plodded alongside.

The caravan followed the ancient route travellers had used for centuries. Asti led his donkeys and a few camels, laden with trade goods and personal items. He had been with the Bedu for three years, and during that time, he acquired his own pack animals and a fine tent.

'What will you do with your share of the profits when we have traded our wares?' Honami asked. 'There are many taverns with dancing girls. For a small fee, you can visit the temple of Hathor…the priestesses are very comely and willing.'

'No, I will save my earnings and invest in more sheep and camels.'

'Perhaps you are thinking of taking a wife?' Honami hinted. 'There are many eligible maidens in the clan…'

'No, not yet. If this Menefer is, indeed my wife, it would not be fitting…perhaps once my memory returned and I am certain…'

But Asti's memory remained obscure. They had visited Egypt twice already, but his mind remained locked, his past still a mystery. He had become prosperous, had acquired household goods a large flock of sheep and some camels, but his memory was wanting.

Their journey led them to the south-eastern coast of Uatch-ur, the Great Green Waters, then they turned south again at Negba. They dared not risk travelling too far north. Djahi and Amurra were too dangerous. Constant battles still flared up in those areas.

15

They finally arrived at market place of Theb-en, Egypt. The colourful garments of people in the crowd made an ever-changing tapestry as customers weaved around the noisy stalls. It was particularly busy at this time and they all did well. Asti had gone off on his own to find a particular garment he needed while Honami, Afsar and Hayata finished their trading and shopping and were waiting for him at a pre-arranged location where they would meet before returning to the caravanserai just outside the city.

The pungent aroma of cooking tempted the senses and Honami sniffed appreciatively. It made him hungry. 'Afsar, did Asti say when he would return?'

'No father, he just said he had some business to attend to—I think he wants to purchase a new cloak.'

'The hour is late...he should be returning soon.' He tried to ignore the grumbling in his belly and tried to think of other things. 'And you, Hayata, how did you fare this day?'

'Very good, Father.' He patted the purse tied at his side and hidden under his voluminous garment. 'I paid twelve copper deben for twenty-one asses. They are in the pen this very moment.'

'Excellent. We will easily get one deben of copper each at the mines and make a good profit.' Afsar had also done well, which pleased the Sheikh. 'Tonight, we will slaughter a goat to celebrate our good fortune.'

Hayata nodded towards the crowd. 'Here comes Asti now.'

'Asti! You must have found what you were seeking! Your smile is as wide as that of a crocodile!' Afsar called out.

'Yes, I found an excellent garment. There was also a big demand for turquoise today. I sold my entire stock,' then he added, 'a big event is approaching—a celebration. I heard talk of a great feast.'

'No, it is not a celebration. Did you not hear the news?' Hayata asked.

'News? No, what news?'

'The Egyptian queen has died. There is to be a Royal funeral. It is for this funeral feast they are preparing.'

'Egyptian queen?'

'Queen Ankhsenamun!' Afsar reminded him.

'Ankhsenamun—' Asti repeated the name. 'That name seems to have significance...an important urgency...for me!'

'Now why would Queen Ankhsenamun be important to you?' Honami asked.

'I know not, but I see her face before me...it is vague, as in a smoke. I feel I know her, personally.'

'You, personally, know the wife of Pharaoh Ay?' Afsar asked.

Asti's face clouded. 'Did you say *Pharaoh* Ay?'

'Yes. He was crowned more than three years ago,' Honami explained. 'Soon after the young Pharaoh Tutankhamun was entombed.'

Asti's face suddenly paled. 'I...remember! I remember her now!' he exclaimed, excited. 'Queen Senamun!' He raised his hand to his head. 'It is all coming back to me.' He looked the medallion around his neck. 'Menefer! It was Menefer who gave me this talisman...the day Queen Tiye arrived in Akhet Aten all those years ago. Menefer is—was the woman I was to marry.'

'That is indeed wonderful news!' Honami clasped his hands together. 'Your memory is returning!'

'What else do you remember?' Afsar urged.

'Everything is coming back to me…three years of darkness—and now I wonder,' Asti's eyes took on a far-away look, 'I wonder, would she be waiting still?' Suddenly, his expression changed. A pained expression replaced his elated one. 'My mission…I had failed my mission!'

'Mission?' Honami asked. 'What mission?'

'Three years ago, Queen Senamun was being coerced to wed Lord Ay! She sent me to Khatti on a desperate mission to *prevent* this marriage…and I failed her!'

All three of Asti's listeners spoke at once. 'Tell us!' 'What happened?' 'How could you prevent this marriage?'

Asti explained, 'Since the death of Pharaoh Smenkhare, Vizier Ay had coveted the throne, but it went to Tutankhamun instead. When Tutankhamun died, Ay demanded Queen Anksenamun to marry him. As the father of Queen Nefertiti, he was eligible to the throne and had a royal connection. By marrying the widow of the young Pharaoh, he could claim it, but the queen had no desire to marry the old man! My mission was to persuade King Shubbililiuma to allow one of his sons to become the windowed queen's husband. He agreed, and our convoy was escorting Prince Zannanza, his youngest, back to Egypt for that purpose.'

'So, that was why you were amongst Hittites.' Afsar was now very intrigued. 'Go on.'

Asti paused, recollecting his returning memory. 'We were nearing an oasis and about to set up camp when we were ambushed. Everyone was massacred; I alone escaped.' Asti wrung his hands in despair. 'The body of that young man I saw, the one in the purple robe, must have been that of Prince Zannanza. The Egyptian I mentioned, was Hanis the queen's envoy…'

The pain on Asti's face showed his remorse. He blamed himself for failing to prevent Queen Senamun's reluctant marriage to Ay.

'Do not reproach yourself. You were not responsible for what happened,' Afsar tried to cheer him. 'Just be grateful you survived, Asti!'

'Rakhmet…my name is Rakhmet!' Suddenly, he looked at Honami and his eyes grew wide. 'The arrows in my back were Egyptian, because the assassins were *Egyptians*! I—I recognised one of them—the face of Sothis, the Royal Treasurer! He was in the employ of—' Rakhmet's throat tightened and his voice grew hoarse. '*I now know who was behind the massacre*!'

Afsar had never seen Asti lose his temper or showed anger before, until now.

Rakhmet, the man they had known as Asti, suddenly rose. A look of rage had changed his once gentle expression to one of hatred. His eyes became hard and cold, like orbs of granite.

'I must leave! Honami. You have shown me nothing but kindness and treated me like one of your family, and, therefore I give you my pack animals, my House of Hair and all my goods within. Take it as payment for your hospitality. Do with it what you will.'

He turned his gaze towards the South, his eyebrows drew together and his voice grew determined. 'I must return to Egypt, to No-Amun immediately!'

'Yes, go and find this Menefer,' Honami urged. 'She is surely still…'

Rakhmet's expression darkened, as if a cloud had cast a shadow over it. 'I have another mission—a much graver one! Revenge!'

# Chapter Two
## Pageant of Empire

**Nineteen Years Earlier**

From every part of Kemet they came. The arrival of the Dowager Queen Tiye in Akhet Aten was such a great event, Pharaoh had proclaimed it a feast day, named the *Pageant of Empire* festival, in her honour.

The wharf, near the *sownet*, the market-place, had been specially prepared for the Royal barge to dock. It was much larger than the landing-place at the palace, and would enable more citizens to see the procession. The foreshore was packed. Eager spectators, some having arrived before dawn, awaiting the arrival of the golden barge. Foreign visitors, wearing strange and exotic garments, browsed around the *sownet*, sampling the local fare, acquiring keepsakes or purchasing other local-made goods. Merchants and vendors were doing a brisk trade.

Djenna folded her arms, annoyed. The few minutes she had been waiting here by the temple gate, seemed like hours. Impatiently, she drummed her fingers on her arm. The pylon hardly cast a shadow to protect her from the blazing noonday sun. It was well into the season of Proyet, the winter season, but at mid-day it was still uncomfortable.

'Where are you, Menefer?' she muttered to herself and looked around. The noisy, milling crowd and their smelly animals made it even more unpleasant, adding to her misery and discomfort. Acrid smoke from food-vendor's cooking fires, smells of roasting meats and other foodstuffs, mixed with the odours of animal dung and urine, was overpowering. Djenna wrinkled her nose, sniffed contemptuously and scowled at the shuffling, pushing crowd.

Nearby, a merchant whipped a stubborn ass. The animal brayed and kicked, sending a spray of dust in her direction. Djenna ducked sideways to avoid the dirt. She cursed the man and his animal and moved further away, brushing her garments for any possible grime.

Her new wig, specially made for today, would soon be covered in red dust and sure to spoil it. Her appearance had always been most important.

Djenna had always been conscious of her good looks. She shaded her eyelids with malachite powder and lined her large eyes with kohl. Juice of berries coloured her lips, and she had her hands and fingernails stained and decorated with henna.

Her friend, Menefer, on the other hand, never bothered with her appearance, which was a pity. Menefer was very pretty, in a simple, innocent sort-of way, Djenna thought. Most women painted their faces, but not Menefer. She could not remember how often she had tried to persuade her friend to enhance her looks but she had always ignored her advice. *What a pity,* Djenna thought. She was such a pretty girl who could so easily improve her appearance if only she'd make an effort. She wore no jewellery either, except for one plain silver ring, left to her by her grandmother.

'Smearing powdered stone on my eyelids or lining my eyes were not to my liking,' Menefer would answer.

Both girls were well-known in noble society and should always make a good impression. Menefer's father, Thutmose, was the Royal Sculptor. When Pharaoh built his new city, Akhet Aten, Thutmose was given the task, and he made it a wonder to behold.

Djenna's father, Lord Nakht, was the Royal astronomer and advisor to His Majesty. He and his family had accompanied Pharaoh from No-Amun, or, as it was now known, Waset, to here, Akhet Aten, Pharaoh's new capital.

Both men and their families would be important guests at that night's feast, and Djenna was determined to make the most of the event, showing off her new wig and tunic. After all, apart from Royalty, all the *mariannu,* the nobility, would be present, and she was most eligible for marriage—a good marriage, befitting her status.

A faint breeze stirred the banners and pendants hanging limply from their masts on the nearby palace pylons, but it did not reach Djenna. She shifted her weight from one foot to the other and dabbed lightly at her face with a kerchief so as not to spoil her elaborate make-up.

'Where could Menefer be?' she muttered to herself. It was most discourteous of her to keep her waiting. She narrowed her eyes against the glare and surveyed the crowd. For the daughter of Lord Nakht to be loitering in this place was most unseemly...so...so common!

'Djenna!' Menefer's voice rang out thinly above the noise.

Djenna searched the crowds and saw her friend hurrying towards her past the row of sphinxes that lined the avenue leading up to the temple.

'Menefer! What took you so long? I've been waiting for ages! Look at my garments...filthy already!'

'Sorry, Djenna,' Menefer explained, out of breath, 'I ripped my tunic accidentally and had to go and change. A sure sign that something bad is going to happen.'

'Oh, you and your superstitions, Menefer! Let us be gone. The crowd is getting thicker. Hurry!' Djenna started moving off and Menefer had to walk briskly to catch up.

'What's the hurry, Djenna? The barge is still a long way away. The sentries in the hill above Maru Aten are yet to give the signal!'

'That is not the point!' Djenna replied over her shoulder. 'I want a good position before they are all taken.'

'No fear. Last night, Rakhmet promised to provide us with one.'

'Rakhmet?' Djenna stopped and glared at her friend. 'He did not mention this to me! I saw him but yesterday midday!'

'He supped with us last evening and told me he would arrange a good viewing position.'

'Oh, really? Why would he visit you?'

'He and my father had some…uh…business to discuss,' she dared not tell her friend the real reason for the visit—yet.

'Now what business would he have with a sculptor? Is he contemplating a likeness of himself?' Djenna scoffed.

'Oh, he often visits and we had become very close friends,' Menefer answered coyly.

Djenna scowled, waiting for her to say more, but Menefer turned and continued towards the riverbank.

Menefer was dying to tell Djenna that Rakhmet had been courting her, but she and her friend had been rivals since childhood. Every male friend she had ever had, Djenna had always managed to lure away. She was well aware Djenna had cast her eyes upon Rakhmet and had, more than once, remarked that an ambitious young officer with a secure future, would need a fitting and fashionable wife to present to high officials at court and other nobility, and that she, Djenna, would be the most suitable.

'There he is! At the chariot bay, tending the horses,' Menefer pointed. 'Rakhmet!' she called out as they hurried over to meet him.

'Menefer, Djenna!' Rakhmet greeted them and beckoned. 'Come. I have selected an ideal vantage point for you.'

He escorted them to a shaded area close to the royal pavilion. 'From here you will be able to see the events clearly.'

The area had a makeshift barrier around it. Several other people had gathered here already and Menefer recognised a few well-known citizens among them and nodded her greetings.

'How thoughtful of you, Rakhmet,' Djenna gushed. 'And so close to the Royals. I was hoping…'

'Yes, thank you, Rakhmet,' Menefer interjected. 'It is perfect.'

'I'm glad you are pleased. This area has been selected and prepared for only a few privileged spectators. It took a bit of persuasion…and bribery,' He winked slyly. 'But I managed to get permission for you two to be here. Enjoy your day. I must leave you now. I have duties to attend to.'

He was about to leave when Menefer took hold of his arm. 'Wait, Rakhmet! Before you go…' she reached into her waist-band pouch and removed a blue faience pottery talisman with a leather cord affixed to it.

'I have something for you…just a little token I fashioned, of my…uh…our friendship,' she handed him the trinket.

'How delightful, thank you,' He examined it. 'An image of Isis?'

'Oh, no, that is forbidden, as you know,' Menefer said, and then added shyly. 'It is supposed to be a likeness…of me.'

'Wonderful! Yes, I can see it now. It is you! And the blue glazing is most fetching…and costly!'

'Yes,' Menefer giggled. 'Ipuky scolded me for using it without his permission, but when I told him it was for you, he forgave me.'

'It is beautiful! Thank you, again,' he turned it over. On the reverse were four inscribed symbols—a zigzag line, the sign for water; a serpent; a bread loaf and a bar with three dots. Together they form the word *N-tchet,* meaning *Forever.*

'I will treasure it...*forever*,' Rakhmet said, reading the inscription aloud, then he kissed her.

'Allow me.' Menefer took the medallion and placed the cord around his neck.

He embraced her and kissed her again, a more lingering kiss. 'I shall keep it...here,' he put his hand to his chest 'close to my heart. Forever!'

Djenna glared at them. Her face, hot with resentment. 'Well, this is rather unexpected!' she sneered. 'What is going on?'

'You will know in due time, Djenna,' Rakhmet smiled. 'I must leave you now. Duty calls. I will see you both later at the banquet.' He turned to Menefer, 'Meet me by the gate of the Great Temple tonight afterwards. I have something important to tell you,' he gave Menefer another hasty kiss, then hurried to the stable.

'Is there something between you and him I ought to know about?' Djenna asked.

Menefer smiled, 'No, nothing...that concerns you.'

Djenna scowled, her eyes narrowed as she watched Rakhmet make his way through the crowd towards the chariot bay.

'He never showed *me* that much affection!' of all the young men suitable for a husband, he was the most eligible. His career would bring him great wealth and power one day. She wanted him for herself and dared not let him get away.

Suddenly, from upstream, came a great roar from the crowd. The sentries had spotted *The Aten Gleams* and were flashing copper mirrors to alert the sentinels at the palace. A moment later the royal barge appeared and entered the channel between the riverbank and the island. The expectant crowd rushed forward to get a first look. The barge, it's burnished copper cladding glistening in the sun like a jewelled floating pavilion, made its way slowly and gracefully towards the landing place.

Djenna had momentarily forgotten her ambitions, and turning towards the river, she stepped off the hard-packed area into some soft mud, 'A curse upon this place!' she muttered and tried to scrape the muck from her sandal. 'Why would they choose *this* jetty here at the marketplace? The Palace has a much better dock for the barge to moor. Now look at my sandals. They are ruined!'

'Perhaps,' Menefer suggested, 'they chose this place so more people get to see the Great Queen's arrival, rather than crowd them into the smaller space between the jetty and the palace.'

'Yes, but now I will have to wear *this* for the rest of the day!' She held up her foot. 'People are sure to notice, and I cannot go home and change, now.'

Djenna's whining was interrupted by troupe of women musicians approaching the pavilion. They were clad in diaphanous tunics and wearing lotus blossoms in their hair. They danced past Menefer and Djenna, and continued towards the ramp, shaking sistrums, strumming lutes and blowing flutes.

The crowd surged forward, but were pushed back by the guards, away from Djenna and Menefer's vantage point. Rakhmet had chosen well, and the guards had been instructed to keep the area clear, except for those authorised to be there.

A blare of trumpets and an excited murmur from the crowd, announced the arrival of Pharaoh and Queen Nefertiti. Ay, High Priest and Vizier, acting as *kheri heb, He who has charge of the Festival*, preceded the royal couple as they emerged from the temple. A leopard skin, the ceremonial cloak of office, was draped over his shoulder, and he kept flicking a zebra-tail fly whisk back and forth, more out of habit than to chase flies.

The king and queen were followed by the five princesses, in the charge of Lady Mutnedjmet, the queen's sister.

Djenna was ecstatic to have the royal family walk by so close.

'Oh Menefer, this is so exciting!' She clasped her hands together and whispered, 'Look, Her Majesty's tunic…is it not magic? The weave is so fine, one can almost see through it. See how the silver threads woven into it, sparkle in the sun?'

They watched, entranced, as the Royal family mounted the pavilion and took their seats.

Moments later, they were again distracted by gasps from the crowd. Queen Tiye's barge appeared, and was slowly rowed up to the pavilion and steered alongside the pier. On board, standing underneath a gilded canopy, were Queen Tiye, a sour-faced woman in her early fifties, her daughter, Pharaoh's sister, ten year old Baketaten, and behind them, the king's seventeen year old half-brother.

Djenna gasped, 'That must be Prince Smenkhare! Is he not absolutely beautiful?' Then in a breathless whisper, she added, 'Would it not be magic if he should notice me?'

'Djenna, cease your ardent chatter!' Menefer giggled, and for once, got her own back. 'He is a *prince* and you, a commoner. He would not give the likes of you a second glance.'

Djenna flashed her a fierce look. 'You forget,' she hissed in a hushed voice. 'The Great Queen Tiye was once a commoner herself!'

The barge docked and as it was secured to the posts, a fanfare sounded as the Dowager Queen and her royal entourage disembarked.

Ay stepped forward. 'All hail Queen Tiye!' He bowed low with palms raised and held forward in the Royal salute. 'Great Wife of the God, Great of Favour, Mistress of the South and North, the Lady of the Two Lands. Life prosperity and health to the Daughter of the Sun. The people of Akhet Aten welcome you.'

'Daughter of the Sun?' Menefer whispered. 'Is she a worshipper of Aten?'

'Yes,' Djenna answered in a low voice. 'Did you not see the name of the barge, *The Aten* Gleams? It was a gift from her husband, the Old Pharaoh, the Third Amenhotep.'

'But I heard rumours she is planning to convert Pharaoh *back* to the Old gods.'

'My father says her visit was to try and stop Pharaoh from desecrating Amenhotep the Third's memory,' Djenna leant closer and whispered, 'The King father's name contained the hated name of *Amun* and Pharaoh had it erased from public buildings.'

'Yes, I know—my brother Nebaten had to change his name as well, from Ne-b*amen*, but it seems Prince Smenkhare is defying his brother's decrees. Look!' Menefer whispered back and pointed to where Smenkhare's chariot was being brought ashore.

The vehicle, of silver, and decorated in black and red, had a golden Horus with wings stretched out across the front shield. Emblazoned on either side, were two cartouches, bearing the name Amenhotep!

Menefer looked up to see if Pharaoh had noticed the prohibited name, but the king's gaze rested upon the young prince. His Majesty had last seen his brother, eight years earlier and the prince had grown into a comely young man, since.

Unexpectedly, Pharaoh stepped forward, embraced and kissed his mother, sister and brother. Queen Tiye was taken aback by this breech of protocol but quickly regained her aloof stance.

'Did you see that?' Djenna asked, shocked.

'My father is used to this Royal Family's familiarity,' Menefer said. 'He says the king often shows affection and kisses the queen and the princesses. My father says Pharaoh wants his subjects to accept him as he really is, a caring husband and father, and not merely a figurehead.'

'But not in public!' Djenna sounded quite shocked. 'I still think it is not appropriate!'

'Shh,' Menefer warned. 'Not so loud. People might hear you.'

After the brief welcoming ceremony, the royals were escorted to their various means of transport. The king, queen and Prince Smenkhare would each drive their own chariot. Queen Nefertiti was often seen, driving her blue and electrum chariot by herself around Akhet Aten, trailed by a string of guards, trying to keep up.

The princesses and other ladies would be carried in sedan chairs. Queen Tiye and Princess Bekaten mounted their own litters. The queen's carry-chair, made of ebony, with poles of sesnedjem wood and sheathed in gold leaf, had accompanied them from Waset.

When all were mounted and seated, and with another fanfare, the procession started for the palace. The crowd waved and cheered as they passed. The nobles followed in chariots, with guards and Medjay, the local police, marched alongside or behind.

*****

Menefer and Djenna strolled back to Menefer's father's house and workshop which was much closer to the markets than Lord Nakht's house, south of the city.

'Look! There...next to the temple wall!' Menefer called out excitedly and pointed. The tent of a seer! Oh, let's find out what the future holds.'

Djenna looked to where Menefer was pointing and grunted. 'I hope it will not take too long.'

'Oh, do cheer up, Djenna. Come, it will be fun.' Menefer was eager to know about her and Rakhmet's future. She had such high hopes, and had always dreamt of a happy life and a big family. She hurried towards the tent.

Djenna shrugged and reluctantly followed her. 'You don't really believe in the prattle of those old hags, do you?'

'Don't scoff. Not all are frauds. You believe in magic yourself. Are you not convinced that kohl around the eyes will protect them?'

'Eye make-up *does* protect the eyes!' Djenna pursed her lips. 'But soothsayers are a waste of time! Your money could be used for something much more useful,' she studied Menefer's face. 'I saw the most beautiful blue-green stones that would make an excellent colouring powder for your eye-lids.'

Menefer did not reply, and Djenna continued, 'You really should try some face-paint. It will improve your appearance double fold.'

As the two girls approached the fortune teller, the flap of the tent lifted. A very comely young woman appeared and bade them enter. She looked no-where near an old hag they had expected. Long black lashes bordered her heavy-lidded dark eyes. A heavily decorated head cloth covered her head and dark tresses flowed from underneath the cloth and cascading over her shoulders. She wore clusters of large earrings that tinkled as she moved her head. From her robes and adornments, Menefer judged her to be from Pars, a mysterious country beyond Mitanni and Babal.

'Come,' the seer invited, 'and learn what the future holds for you!'

'What is your fee for such a consultation?' Menefer enquired, cautiously.

'I will make you a special fee. For the two of you I can...'

'No,' Djenna gestured negatively. 'Only my friend here believes in your prattle.'

'Ah, a disbeliever. Perhaps I can convince you otherwise?'

'Some other time, soothsayer. Just throw your bones!'

'What payment will you take for your services?' Menefer asked again. 'I have but one piece of copper, worth three senyu...'

'That silver ring you wear... For that as payment, I can tell you much more!'

'You will take *just* the copper piece!' Djenna offered rudely. 'Get on with your telling.'

'Please enter, mistresses,' the fortune-teller gestured and lifted the tent flap for them.

'Phew, it really smells ill in here!' Djenna screwed up her nose. 'What is that vile stuff?'

'The entrails of a goat, sacred herbs, oils and strained fluids from a...'

'Stinking rotten animals parts!' Djenna looked around disgustedly, holding her nose.

'There is nothing rotten here!' the woman replied indignantly. 'It is all fresh. It came straight from the altar of the temple and had been blessed by a priest this very morn!'

Menefer gave the woman her copper token. 'I wish to know...uh...about my future...' she suddenly felt awkward, conscious of Djenna's attention and she could not bring herself to ask about Rakhmet.

The seer accepted the copper piece. 'Ah, yes, I know what all young maidens desire. Love and romance, yes?'

'Yes, tell me. What does my future hold? Will there be...' she glanced at her friend, but Djenna's attention was elsewhere. She was engrossed in all the paraphernalia in the tent and in a low voice, asked, 'will there be a happy...marriage?'

The seer walked over to the table containing a cloth-covered bowl on a tray. She moved her hands mystically over the bowl and mumbled some strange incantation, then removed the cloth, revealing a pile of revolting animal intestines. She tipped the entrails onto the tray, then sprinkled some powders onto the liquid that was seeping out.

'Ah, a vision is shaping... I see nought of weddings, but there is sorrow... Great sorrow.'

A chill seemed to grip Menefer's heart. 'Sorrow? Are you certain?'

'I see shadows…four, no, five shadows, five Great Houses! You are walking in these shadows,' she leans over the table, fans her fingers and waved them over the vile heap. 'Now a light appears…it issues forth…from you.'

The soothsayer looked up at Menefer, her voice husky, as she continued, 'This light, it will cause a shadow to be cast…a long shadow. It overshadows those before it!' She stirs the entrails again, then sighs, 'The vision dims…it is gone!'

'What does it all mean?' Menefer asked, confused and disappointed. 'I need to know more. You said you saw sorrow…? Is it…did you not see a wedding?'

'For that silver ring, perhaps more will be revealed…'

'Charlatan! You demand too much for your nonsense!' Djenna hissed and turned to her friend, 'She is deceiving you, Menefer! She is holding out for more payment. She will just talk in more riddles. Come, before she bleeds you dry and you will still be no wiser.'

Djenna had to just about drag Menefer away from the seer's tent.

'But Djenna…' Menefer protested. 'I need to know more. My questions have not been answered.'

'That is what they do, Menefer. They never tell all. They hold out for more payment then give just enough for you to want more.'

'But, what she said,' Menefer persisted. 'What does it mean, Great sorrow, five shadows, five Great Houses? It makes no sense. I am so confused.'

'Do not fret over the prattle of some soothsayer. It means naught,' Djenna decided to change the subject. 'What are you going to wear tonight for the feast? I have something really exceptional and Prince Smenkhare is certain to notice. We are to be seated close to the royal dais, my father said.'

Menefer was not really listening; her mind was still on the prophesy. She had such hopes for her and Rakhmet's future together. She needed to know if they would be happy together, but the prediction had left her concerned.

'*Five Great House*s,' she muttered to herself. In the words of the tongue of Egypt "*Great house, Per-O*", is Pharaoh. *I will walk in the shadows of five Pharaohs. Which five Pharaohs?* The prophesy means naught. Perhaps Djenna had been right, after all. It's all nonsense.

# Chapter Three
## The Banquet

A dais had been erected on the new parade ground in front of the Great Temple for the feast. Slender, wooden columns, painted blue and trimmed with gold, supported a beautifully decorated canopy over the raised platform where the Royal family would dine. Oil lamps and torches illuminated the area. Nobles and citizens of distinction were escorted to their seats around the dais, and others of lesser status, were making themselves comfortable around the outer perimeters.

Excited guests were already enjoying the music and dancing, and cast hungry eyes towards the food. Tables, laden with roast waterfowl, fish, roasted venison, sweetmeats and honey-cakes; fruits from exotic places and breads with chopped dates and nuts, made up some of the dishes. Decorated with bowls of floating water lilies and fragrant flowers, the tables were placed all around the banquet area. Naked servant girls, wearing only beaded belts and heavy wigs topped with scented wax cones, were already serving beer and other drinks to the guests.

Curious citizens who were not invited to the banquet, but those who had come to gawk at the arriving guests, lined the King's Way, the road, which ran between the temple and the banquet area. After finishing their offerings to Aten at the Great Temple, the Royals would make their way along this road to the feast. Everyone hoped to catch a glimpse of the Great Queen Tiye, Egypt's living Goddess.

The sounds of temple bells and chants of the rites, heard above the hubbub of the crowd, indicated that the offering ceremony was still in progress.

As the guests arrived, most foreigner dignitaries had brought gifts for the Dowager Queen, and the crowd gazed on in awe. A tall black man, the chief of a province in Punt, passed by wearing a gold-studded leopard-skin cloak and a necklace of lion claws. His headdress, fashioned in gold, glittered with multi-coloured gems affixed to it. A cloud of dyed ostrich feathers, sprouting from the crown, swayed and nodded with each step. His entourage of half-naked warriors led strange animals rarely seen in Akhet Aten. One animal had a very long neck, and another, an antelope, flourished great spiralling horns. Bearers carried elephant tusks, hides of zebra, leopard and lions and chests of fragrant and costly myrrh and other spices.

The procession was directed to a waiting locale alongside the banquet area where officials received them, and then escorted the guests to their places of honour.

Menefer and her parents arrived and Thutmose, her father, went off to talk to an acquaintance.

'Menefer, over here…' Djenna called out. Her voice almost lost over the music and noise of the crowd.

'Go along, dear,' Mutnames, urged her daughter. 'We will be along shortly as soon as we know where we are to be seated.'

Menefer made her way to where Djenna waited. 'May Nut smile on you, Djenna.'

'Greetings, Menefer. You look charming. Is that a new kalasiris?'

'Yes. My mother made it.' Sheath dresses fitted Menefer's slim figure well, whereas they tend to stretch and fold slightly on Djenna, who was a little more curvaceous.

'That style suits you. What a pity you are not wearing something special to enhance it. A nice collar would have given it a bit more colour, don't you think?'

Before Menefer could reply, Djenna continued. 'What do you think of my new tunic? It was woven from haik muslin and it took three women two days to stitch the garment,' Djenna spun around to show off the finely pleated garment that clung to her body and outlined her figure provocatively. A pleated shawl was tied to a cord around her waist, and then draped over her shoulders.

'You always look very beautiful, Djenna.' Menefer knew, from experience, her friend would spend hours, grooming herself.

Newly arriving guests were draped in garlands of flowers and given perfumed wax cones to wear on their heads and Djenna secured a cone for herself. 'It smells wonderful, just magic, Menefer. Try one.'

'No, thank you. I dislike grease melting and running down my back. The perfumed oil I rubbed on my skin is quite adequate.'

'Well, personally, don't think…' she was interrupted when Menefer's parents strolled over. They exchange greeting.

'Kheruef had just informed me we are to be seated with Lord Nakht and Lady Susmaat,' Mutnames announced. 'You and Djenna will then be together.'

'Seated by *us*?' Djenna exclaimed, annoyed, but then quickly added. 'Uh, how nice! After all, Thutmose, you too, are important to His Majesty.'

Thutmose ignored her insensitive remark, 'Come, this way.'

They made their way through clouds of incense, to their chairs as directed.

'I have not yet seen your parents, Djenna,' Mutnames remarked as they took their seats. 'The ceremony is about to start.'

'As His Majesty's advisor, his services were needed. They are accompanying the Royal family.'

'He must have many duties to perform,' Thutmose remarked.

'Yes, he has to calculate the most auspicious day for the opening ceremony of the two temples that Pharaoh had erected for Queen Tiye and Princess Baketaten.'

'Ah, yes. Neb told me about it. He and Ipuky are to decorate them. I trust…'

'Yes, your sons' crafts are highly valued at court. Will they be attending the feast tonight?' Djenna interrupted.

'No. They have gone south, with Bak, to a newly located quarry to look at some red granite. Pharaoh wants only the best stone for his project. He had…'

Thumose was interrupted by a fanfare of trumpets and they all turn toward the dais. Vizier Ay, carrying a staff and the ever-present fly whisk, mounted the platform, tapped his staff three times and in a loud voice, addressed the assembly.

'All kneel!' As the guests knelt, Ay raised the staff, 'Hail, His Majesty, Per-O, Great House, Lord of the Two Lands, King of Upper and Lower Egypt, Nefer kheperu-ra Ua-en-ra, Who Liveth in Truth, Lord of the Crowns, Akhenaten, Son of the Sun, and Queen Nefertiti…'

'Windbag!' Thutmose grunts as he struggles to kneel, muttered under his breath. 'He does go on and on.'

'Father!' Menefer cautioned. 'Hush, someone might overhear your remarks.'

'Well, he does. I do not trust him. He changes his allegiances like the weather,' Thutmose whispered.

'…Great Royal Wife, whom he loveth,' Ay continued. 'Lady of the Two Lands, Nefer-neferu-Aten, Nefertiti, Beloved of the Gods, Who liveth in Health and Youth Forever and Ever…and hail the Great Wife and Widow of Neb-Maar-Ra, Queen of the South and North, Queen Tiye…may they live Forever.'

Another fanfare preceded the entrance of Akhenaten and Nefertiti. They were closely followed by Queen Tiye and the younger royals.

Menefer noticed that Djenna's eyes were upon the young prince. She smiled at her friend's impossible and lofty ambitions.

The royal family took their seats. With a slight gesture, Pharaoh signalled Ay, who invited everyone to rise and be seated, and for the banquet to commence. The royals were served first, then a horde of servant girls entered, carrying platters laden with food and drink for the guests.

Lord Nakht and Lady Susmaat, who had arrived with Royals, had been waiting at the entrance to the banquet area until Pharaoh had been seated. They were then permitted to enter. They took their seats and exchanged pleasantries with Menefer's parents.

'Menefer, did you see that?' Djenna whispered. 'The prince was looking in our direction! I am sure he noticed me.'

Mutnames, Menefer's mother, smiled at her remark. She leaned over to her and whispered. 'Well, apart from the princesses, you are certainly the most striking young woman here tonight, dear!'

Djenna, flattered, dropped her eyes demurely. Mutnames winked at Menefer who beamed broadly.

Thutmose, chewing on a sweetmeat, leaned over. 'Have you had a chance to talk to Rakhmet today, yet, Menefer?'

'Oh, just briefly, father. We will, later tonight, though. We are to meet in front of the pylon of the Great Temple, after the banquet!'

'Good. He has a surprise for you.'

Mutnames and her husband looked at each other knowingly. 'I am certain you will be pleased,' Mutnames whispered to Menefer.

Djenna scowled. She had noticed their clandestine exchanges, and Rakhmet and Menefer's behaviour today had made her suspicious. Is there something going on that she is unaware of? She will confront Rakhmet and find out exactly what his intentions are. She got up. 'Please excuse me a moment, I need to attend to something,' she hurried past a group of dancers and left the banquet area. 'She is so fussy,' Susmaat sighed. 'Always trying to look her best.'

But it was not her appearance that concerned Djenna. Menefer and Rakhmet's recent intimacy had been nagging at her. She hurried over to the where the guards were feasting. She had to speak to Rakhmet and find out exactly what it was.

Benches and tables had been placed randomly behind the royal pavilion and banquet area for the guards.

After they had escorted the Royals to the temple, most of the soldiers were given leave to relax and partake in the festivities, except for the bodyguard, the few who are still on duty, had to attend the Royal party after the feast. Horemheb, their commander, had threatened all of them with severe punishment for rowdiness and misdemeanour.

The soldiers had been conducting themselves well…thus far, but after a little too much beer, their self-control lapsed. A soldier, his mouth filled with roast waterfowl, looked up as Djenna approached.

'A pleasant evening, lady…coming to entertain us?'

Guffaws and lewd comments followed his remarks, followed immediately by a sharp reprimand from a junior officer. 'Behave yourselves!' He turned to Djenna. 'Young lady, this is the soldier's quarters. It is no place for the likes of you.'

'I…I am looking for an officer…Rakhmet. Is he here?'

The soldier rose. 'He would be in the tent near the chariot bay. I will call him. Who shall I say is asking after him?'

'Djenna, daughter of Lord Nakht.' She glanced around at the interested men, then added, 'It is urgent!'

'Wait here,' the officer disappeared into the darkness beyond the torchlight.

The other soldiers continued their feasting and quiet conversations, but kept glancing at Djenna. She had always enjoyed the attention of young men, but so many eyes on her, especially from half-inebriated soldiers, made her nervous and their stares made her uncomfortable. She kept shifting her weight from one foot to the other, trying to keep her composure. She now wished she were back at the banquet.

A short while later the soldier returned. 'Rakhmet sends his greetings, but cannot speak with you now. He will see you on the morrow.'

'But…did you tell him who it was, wanting to see him?'

'Yes, mistress Djenna, but he was adamant. He will not see you now.'

Never before had she been scorned. How dare he treat her thus? Offended, and with a disgruntled humph, she spun around and stomped away.

'Who does he think he is?' she muttered under her breath. 'He is not Commander-in-Chief yet…to treat the daughter of Lord Nakht like a common servant. This is an insult, Rakhmet. Believe me, I will get even!'

In a black mood, she made her way back to the banquet hall and rudely pushed her way through the crowd, back to her seat.

***

Eventually, Rakhmet joined his men to have a meal. He was still on duty, and had been too busy tending the chariots, earlier, to think of food. By the time he finally arrived at the tables, most of the best dishes had already been consumed and he had to pick through what was left.

'Your little friend was not too happy about you, Rakhmet,' one of the guards remarked.

'Yes, she was most upset. I do not think she will have many kind words, or anything else for you, later.' Another laughed.

Intoxicated, one soldier was showing a lack of restraint. 'Yesh, Rakhmet…I c'n shee her (hic) chasin' you down the shtreet, with you wearing nothing but a sh…(hic) shenti. Ha ha ha!'

Rakhmet cautioned them on their bawdy remarks.

'Wha's the matter…' another slurred. 'Afraid she'll chastise you later? You have to be…(he burped loudly)…firm with these fillies. Keep your women in line, I always shay!'

'She is not *my woman*, Batu,' Rakhmet replied angrily, 'and keep your voice down, soldier, and sober up! You are drunk! I think you've had enough emmer.'

'C'mon Rakhmet,' he slurred. 'This is a special occasion…have a drink with ush!'

'No thanks…and stop breathing your sour breath in my face.'

Grabbigb hold of Rakhmet's neck, 'It will not tarnish thish pretty little trinket.' He reaches forward, but lost his balance. As Rakhmet reached out to steady him, Batu snatched the talisman and yanked it free.

'Oops…look, it came away in my hand…'

'Return it, immediately!' Rakhmet reached for it.

In spite of being drunk, Batu moved swiftly. He ducked out of reach behind a table, keeping it between himself and Rakhmet.

'Not so fast, officer, I jush want to look at it…'

'Give it here!' Rakhmet lunged at him. 'I warn you…'

Batu laughed, dangling the medallion just out of Rakhmet's reach. Some of the other soldiers, all a little tipsy, joined in the merriment.

'Give that back, Batu!' Rakhmet demanded again. He was starting to lose his temper with the soldier.

'Come'n get it…' Batu giggled. Urged on by other soldiers, he dodged Rakhmet's attempts to get close to him. Their goading and chanting became louder and the noise of their laughter and jeering, reached the banqueting guests.

'Give me the medallion, you miserable desert rat!' Rakhmet shouted. 'You spawn of Seth!' He leaped over a table, upsetting it. Platters of food, goblets and cups of beer crashed down.

'What is going on here?' A voice demanded, sternly.

'General Horemheb!' Batu suddenly sobered up. 'I…I was merely admiring this medallion…'

'Rakhmet!' Horemheb scowled at the officer, sprawled on the ground covered in left-over food and scattered platters. 'I did not expect this from you! The Royals had been disturbed by the noise, and Pharaoh is most displeased!'

'But General, I…'

'Silence! Your conduct was inappropriate…no, it was way beyond that! You had disgraced the unit and me. This brawl is going to cost both of you dearly. Consider yourselves under arrest. I will deal with you later.'

He stretched out his hand. 'Hand over that trinket.'

'Please, General, it's a…'

'Enough! It seems to me *this* was the cause of the trouble, so I will remove it. Present yourselves to my quarters within the hour,' fuming, Horemheb turned abruptly and marched away.

\*\*\*

The banquet was done. Wrestlers and jugglers had performed for the bored banqueters, but they abruptly halted their conversations when black dancers from Kush arrived. To a wild and furious pounding rhythm, the energetic dancers writhed and leapt in unison. Perspiration covered their half-naked glistening bodies and the guests watched, enthralled. The primitive dancing drew gasps and outcries of astonishment from the onlookers as the troupe performed daring and astounding acrobatic feats.

But Queen Tiye looked bored. She had seen it all before. She yawned, then leaned over and spoke to Akhenaten. He had to cup his hand over his ear to hear what she was saying over the drumming and whistling. He nodded, and beckoned to Ay.

Ay held up his hand and immediately the thumping drums were silenced. 'All rise!' Everyone rose and faced the dais expectantly.

'Their Majesties thank you all for attending this great occasion, and the magnificent welcome you gave to Kemet's Living Goddess, the Great Queen Tiye, and all the honours and tributes she received this day. Long may she live and prosper. His Majesty invites you to continue the feasting.'

With a fanfare the Royal party rose and left the dais. Only the Princesses, Meritaten and Baketaten, and Prince Smenkhare chose to remain. The dancers regrouped and continued their performance.

Menefer turned to her parents, 'Mother, Father, I beg your leave. I must go and meet Rakhmet. He will escort me home. I will see you later.'

'Be not too late, Menefer. Take care. I will see you in the morn.'

Djenna, still morose, nodded. 'I will see you tomorrow, Menefer, or will you be keeping Rakhmet company? Menefer, about to reply with a sarcastic remark, changed her mind and smiled sweetly.

'Of course. We have much to talk about. Till then, Djenna, Lord Nakht, Lady Susmaat, stay in peace.'

'Go in peace, Menefer.'

\*\*\*

'Where are you, Rakhmet?' Menefer muttered and looked around, impatiently. She had been waiting by the pylon of the Great Temple for quite some time. The soldiers had all been dismissed some time ago and Rakhmet had not yet arrived.

The feast ended and drunken revellers were weaving their home down the darkened street, dimly lit by torches affixed to the wall of the nearby temple pylons and that of the King's House along the broad King's Way. A few soldiers staggered past Menefer, singing and laughing, on their way to the military barracks behind the King's House.

Some of the torches around the banquet area had gone out and had not been re-lit. The hour was late, but still no sign of Rakhmet.

A shooting star flashed across the sky and a chill went through Menefer. An omen—a falling star was always an ill omen.

She was just about to try the soldier's area to find Rakhmet, when a figure approached from the darkness. 'Rakhmet! What kept you?' Her joy was short-lived as she recognised the approaching man. 'Oh, General Horemheb! Good evening. I was expecting someone else.'

'I am sorry for keeping you waiting, Menefer, but I had only just finished my duties. I was told Rakhmet was to meet you here but. He has been…detained, and asked me to come.'

'Had something happened to him?' Menefer asked, alarmed, and then had another thought. 'Or…is he too drunk to…'

'No…! No nothing like that…he has been confined to his quarters.'

'Oh, will he be long?'

'Yes, I'm afraid so…he has been involved in an incident.'

'Was it serious?' She asked again, dismayed. 'We have a…'

'Yes. He will be in custody for quite a while. He had committed a serious misdemeanour.'

'We have important matters to discuss.' Menefer looked anxious. 'When will he be released? When can I see him?'

Horemheb looked uncomfortable and nervously adjusted the shoulder strap of his leather uniform. 'You may see him—in the morning…come to my quarters at the military barracks tomorrow morning.'

***

Rakhmet's court-marshall was brief. No serious crime had been committed and there was no need for a trial, but because he and Batu had caused a disturbance, they had to be disciplined. Both men were allowed visitors before they were led into court and Menefer was able to see Rakhmet for a few moments.

She was not present during the hearing. Both pleaded guilty. Horemheb, as General of the armies and Royal guards, presided over the court. His verdict was swift—both men were sentenced to serve a year at an outpost, starting immediately. After the sentence, no visitors were allowed, but later, Horemheb told Menefer she could see him again, the following morning at the landing dock, before he left.

'I…I don't understand,' Menefer was puzzled. 'The landing dock?'

'It's from there he will depart,' Horemheb explained. 'For Sesibi, where he is to serve out his year's sentence.'

'*Sesibi*? But…'

'Yes. It's an outpost in Kush.'

Kush, a land well beyond the southern border of Egypt, was also the most distant centre for the worship of Aten. The priests there had the task of converting the black-skinned people to Atenism, but the inhabitants mostly resented it and the priests had been attacked. Soldiers had to be sent there to defend them, but they were there against their will and often deserted. Most soldiers sent to replace them were serving sentences for wrong doings.

'But…a year? A whole *year*?' Menefer asked, stunned.

'If you wish to see him before he leaves, you'd better do it tomorrow, the boat leaves for Upper Egypt at sunrise!'

# Chapter Four
## Banishment

With harsh *kiree-kiree-kiree* cries, a flock of ibises greeted the dawn. They flew over the rooftops, circled a reed-overgrown swampy area and glided down onto the mud.

These birds were sacred to the god Thoth, Keeper of Records, because of their habit of searching for food by scraping their long beaks in the mud, leaving marks which the people believed to be sacred writings.

The sun was not yet visible in Akhet Aten, but the hills on the western side of the Great River were already glowing pink with its first rays. Menefer had left home very early. The eastern sky had just started to lighten when she rose and headed for the docks. Some boats were already on their way and she quickened her pace. This would be the last time she would see Rakhmet before he is being shipped off to that lonely outpost.

She hurried past small cultivated fields that lay between her home and the city of the Sun. She reached the King's Way. It ran the entire length of the city and passed through the market place, in front of the Small Temple. Immediately inside its walled forecourt, she turned left towards the river and the docks, and passed colonnades of sphinxes that lined the city's market place. The landing place lay before her, just beyond the gates. She and Djenna had passed through this very place to see the arrival of the royal barge, just the day before yesterday, but it seemed like an age ago.

The market place, usually bustling with shoppers, was almost deserted at this early hour, save for a few merchants, busy setting up their stalls, displaying their wares and getting ready for the approaching day.

Even at this hour, the docking area was busy as trading boats arrived and departed almost continuously. Several vessels were moored at the main jetty and, looming high above them all, Queen Tiye's barge, *The Aten Gleams*.

The first rays of the sun appeared over the distant hills and bathed the tops of the temple and palace pylons in its golden glow, a signal for many of the vessels to hoist their great rectangular sails to prepare to depart.

Horemheb had allowed her to briefly visited Rakhmet yesterday, and she hoped, this morning, she would have a few moments longer, alone with him while the vessel was being loaded. It would be distressing for her to see him shackled, but she was determined not to appear too anguished. It would only upset him more.

Her thoughts turned to yesterday, when he had taken her in his arms. 'Menefer, I am sorry this had to happen. I had planned to tell you so much. I have made so many plans for us, since your father's permission for us to marry.'

The pain on his face was heart breaking when he had to express his need for her, and she returned her longings for him, but how much more wonderful it would have been, in a more appropriate atmosphere, rather than there, as a prisoner.

'The surroundings matter not, just those words I had hoped to hear,' she had whispered.

'I had wanted to arrange our betrothal to be, perhaps on your sixteenth birthday, but now...my plans had all been for naught.'

'No, not for naught, she had sobbed. 'Now we both have something to look forward to.'

'It would be a year before we could resume our relationship. Promise me you will wait.'

She had promised she would wait. The year would pass painfully slowly, she knew, but it would pass, and they would be together again.

Then they had kissed. A long and passionate embrace to last their year of separation. Then Horemheb had entered and they were torn apart.

Menefer wiped her eyes as she remembered yesterday's meeting. Marriage suddenly seemed an eternity away. There was no point in dwelling on things that could have been, she thought, as she searched the assembled vessels to find the one carrying the prisoners. She could not find it.

A robed merchant in a curious headdress struggled by, dragging a reluctant donkey loaded down with bags, casks and bundles that contained samples of his wares. He cursed the animal and its ancestors for not producing a swifter and more obedient beast.

'A moment please,' Menefer called out to him and touched his sleeve. 'Which one of these boats will be going to Kush?'

The merchant, annoyed at the interruption, turned and glared at her. 'Kush? You want to go to Kush?' he asked in disbelief. 'Why would you want to go there?'

'No, I...I'm seeing someone off.'

'Oh!' he said, and then turned to the ass tugging at the reins. 'Hold still, you Mother-of-fleas!' He turned back to Menefer.

'Kush?' he repeated thoughtfully, looked at the boats, then scratched his stubbly chin. 'No. I cannot help you.'

Menefer thanked him and turned away as he tugged at the reluctant animal. She next approached a man, tying some packages together and repeated her question.

'Only one boat travelled south this day, to the port of *This*. I think it carried soldiers.'

'Yes, yes, that is the one!' she answered.

'You are too late.' He turned back to his task. 'It left well before dawn.'

Stunned, her eyes started to moisten and she suppressed a sob. 'Oh...' she said in a small voice, her hands starting to shake.

'Are you all right?' the man asked as he glanced back. 'You look unwell.'

'I...I am fine,' she lied. 'Are you certain it had already left? Perhaps you're mistaken...?'

'No, no mistake. There was only the one vessel. It was loaded, and I heard someone say there was no need to delay.'

She quickly turned away for him not to see her tears. As she walked away, she consoled herself that, at least, she had a chance to see him the previous day. She bravely lifted her chin and headed home—her vision blurred. She wiped her eyes and blinked a few times.

Thin spirals of smoke issued from village dwellings as morning meals were being prepared in the cooking areas. A haze had formed and hung over the city like a ragged shroud. It would soon dissipate as the rising sun heated the air.

By the time Menefer arrived home, her parents were already up. For them, this day would be the same as every other day…but for her, it was a day of sorrow. Her dreams had been shattered and a lonely year lay ahead.

Mutnames immediately noticed her daughter's distress and went to comfort her, but Menefer rushed past her mother to her bed chamber, fell upon her sleeping couch and burst into tears. Mutnames entered and sat down next to her daughter.

'The year will pass swiftly, dear,' her mother assured her. 'Keep yourself busy and it will go by quickly, it will be gone before you know it.'

'Oh, mother, why did this happen…now…just as we were to be betrothed?' she sat up and they hugged.

'Since the beginning of time, people have been asking that very same question, whenever misfortune befalls them, child.' She pressed her cheek to her daughter's head. 'But we must trust and believe that everything happens for a purpose. When someone departs, those left behind feel an emptiness no one can fill. This is the time to reflect. When the one you long for, is away, you will appreciate him all the more when he returns.'

Mutnames squeezed Menefer's shoulder and stood up. 'Remember the time when you were ill, and we had to give you that aloe potion? How bitter your mouth tasted? But then, we gave you some honey afterwards to drive the bitterness away and the honey tasted all the more sweet? Joy is like the honey. It is much more intense when you have experienced sorrow.'

As Mutnames left the room, she had a last word for her daughter.

'Cheer up, I have a little surprise for you later.'

*** 

Menefer had cried herself to sleep, and it was well past midday when she awoke. She felt better and was curious to find out what surprise her mother had prepared for her. Maybe Ipuky and Nebaten had returned from the quarry. She missed her brothers, especially Ipuky.

After a light midday meal, her mother escorted her to her father's workshops next to the house. Noise of hammering and chiselling from the carvers' workplace echoed through the foyer. Apart from painting and sculptures, the studio also produced vases, perfume jars and ornamental pottery, gold and silver objects for the wealthy and even furniture for the palace.

The main workshop lay at the far end of the hallway. This was where her father and brothers worked. Large tanks with water and clay lined the walls opposite the main entrance. Rows of figures and busts, likenesses of royalty and many of the nobles, in various stages of completion, stood on shelves behind the tanks. Some had been cast; other had been fashioned in clay. There were also numerous small likenesses, these were usually fashioned first, then stone workers would take measurements and chisel larger copies of them in sandstone, granite or, for those who could afford it, costly alabaster and marble.

Thutmose had been working on a statue group of a seated man and a woman with their arms around each other. She recognised the figures immediately. They were of Djenna's parents, the Royal Astronomer, Nakht and his wife, Susmaat. The likenesses of the figures were uncanny. They were fashioned in the old style. Her father refused to break with tradition, unlike Ipuky, whose panels of the king and queen outraged many traditionalists.

Ipuky had depicted the queen, striding forward with feet apart, and the king with his feet together—exactly opposite to what tradition dictated. He also showed the Royal family with exaggerated, almost comical elongated features. He also depicted the king caressing his wife, playing and kissing the princesses, and the queen, eating and drinking. This was also a divergence from the custom. Many had considered it inappropriate, but it pleased Pharaoh Akhenaten. His policy of Living in Truth, would even apply to the arts.

Thutmose looked up from his work as they entered. 'Menefer, child,' concern wrinkled his face. 'Did you manage to see Rakhmet before his departure?'

'No father,' tears blurred her vision again and she quickly wiped her eyes. 'I...I was too late. The boat left early.'

'I'm most sorry, but it happens sometimes,' he nodded. 'They have to abide by the winds. When they are ready to sail, there would be no reason to tarry.'

'Thutmose, I brought Menefer here for a reason,' Mutnames interrupted. 'I believe you wish to tell her yourself...you know? What we talked about?'

'Oh? Oh yes.' He dipped a cloth in some water, squeezed it and then wrapped the damp fabric around the clay figure he was working on to keep it from drying out.

'As your wedding will be postponed for a while, I thought...actually it was your mother's idea that, as you will be idle for a time...and, well...' Thutmose wiped his clay-covered hands and scratched the side of his neck anxiously. 'You know my feelings about women working at a craft. It is not fitting! A woman's place is in the home. So, instead of you weeping and lamenting like a love sick...'

'Get to the point, Old Man!' Mutnames demanded, then scoffed. 'Humph! And you complain about *Ay* being a windbag!'

'Yes, yes...of course,' He smiled. 'Menefer, I have prepared a workroom for you. I wish you to join us.'

'Me?' Menefer clasped her hands together, expectantly. 'Work here?'

'Yes. Ipuky told me about the talisman you fashioned for Rakhmet...apparently it is of very fine craftsmanship.'

'And,' Mutnames added, 'you always craved working in clay, or carving images, rather than weaving, cooking or stitching...'

'Yes, I love creating and fashioning things...'

'We do need more skilled people. We have been so busy, working on decorations and carvings for Pharaoh's city,' Thutmose continued, 'the wants of the people had been neglected. We have fallen way behind in supplying ushabtis. People need these likenesses of friends and servants to accompany them into the next world, but we had to have them fashioned in Waset or Mennufer and transported here, which had become rather costly. So, I was thinking…perhaps you could help out? Fashion some of them here?'

'Oh father, that is wonderful. Yes.'

'Mind you, you might tire of it. It can be tedious.'

'Oh no! I would love to do it,' she replied eagerly.

'I must add that it will be a temporary assignment only, until you have overcome your despair and ready to move on. I am not comfortable with the idea of a woman working in a workshop.'

'Yes, father, I understand.'

'Come. I will show you to your workplace.'

*** 

The journey to Kush could take two weeks or more—just the trip to No-Amun would take over five days. Sailing upstream, the boat had to depend on wind from the north to make any headway. They would sail only during the day, as it was dangerous to travel in the dark. Where there is a watercourse one day, there might be a sandbank the next and the boat-pilot had to be wary at all times to instruct the helms and oarsmen. They had seven rowers on each side, but from time to time it was necessary for the boat to be towed along the shore, using oxen or asses and then they would manage just five atur a day.

All the prisoners, fourteen altogether, were soldiers. Those with more serious offences were shackled together, and sat huddled on the deck, in the shade of the large rectangular braided papyrus sail.

Rakhmet, one of those privileged to move around, was leaning against the mast when Batu walked up.

'You were born in No-Amun, I hear. I am from the far north.'

'Tell it to someone who cares!' Rakhmet answered with a scowl. He turned away from the soldier, and seated himself on the side of the boat.

Batu shrugged, and without another word, returned to his original spot.

Rakhmet watched the changing scenery for a while, then busied himself doing a variety of tasks to forget his plight. His depression and moodiness of the first few days, passed. After the initial self-pity and anger towards Horemheb, he managed to come to terms with his misfortune. After all, he had brought this on himself. As an officer, he should have shown more self-control.

His main regrets were being away from Menefer, just when they were about to announce their betrothal, and the loss of the medallion. He had made Menefer a promise to keep it close to his heart, and he had already lost it. Horemheb had promised he could have it back on his return.

They were approaching Waset, previously known as No-Amun, the former capital city. It had been abandoned by Pharaoh, when he had his new capital, Akhet Aten, built. Akhenaten had also insisted, as it contained the hated name of Amun, be renamed Waset.

Rakhmet was sitting on the deck with his legs dangling over the side when Amseti, the overseer of the guards, escorting the soldiers, strolled up.

'Well, soldier, enjoying the trip thus far?'

'No complaints. How long will we remain in No-Am…uh…Waset?'

'About a day to unload and reload. We leave tomorrow evening.'

'Evening? I thought the boats did not travel at night?'

'They don't…we will travel only another atur upstream for more supplies, then sail the morning after. Planning on going sightseeing?'

'Are we not confined to the boat?'

'Not you. Horemheb told me your misconduct was not serious. And as an officer, you value your career too much to abscond. Unlike some of the other prisoners, you will be allowed to disembark tonight while we load supplies for rest of the journey.'

'Thank you.' Rakhmet was grateful for the opportunity to visit family and old friend.

'But, just be back before nightfall tomorrow. Will your companion accompany you?'

'Companion…? Oh, you mean Batu.' Rakhmet's voice took on an edge, 'He is not my companion!'

'I noticed you avoiding him.'

'I have my reasons!' Rakhmet turned to watch the landscape glide by.

They remained silent for a while.

'Do you know why Egypt is called Ba-ti?'

'Uh… Sorry, I was not paying attention.'

Amseti nodded towards the shore. 'During *Akhet*, the month of the inundation, the rain wash the fertile black top soil from Kush and Punt, then the Nile deposits it along its banks, so Egypt is called Ba-ti, the Black Land.'

'Yes, I know.'

'I'm often ask about it, so I usually explain,' Amseti gestured. 'Just habit, you know.'

The city of *No-Amun-of-a-hundred-Gates*, or Waset, was in the Fourth Nome, or *sepat*, a district at the southern end of a great bend of the river. As the vessel approached the eastern bank of the city, Amseti left Rakhmet and made ready to berth. 'I better go and see to the other prisoners.'

'Thank you, again, for allowing me shore-leave,' Rakhmet called out.

The boat, now on a slight south-western course, approached the Great Temple of Ipet-isut. The wind had died and rowers were needed to dock.

Dusk approached. To the west, in the distance, the great mortuary temple of Amenhotep III, father of Pharaoh Akhenaten, stood silhouetted against the dying day. Two huge statues of the deceased king, like sentinels, guarded the temple gate. To the south, just visible in the gloom, rose the palace of Malkata, now, all but deserted since Queen Tiye, Prince Smenkhare and Princess Baketaten had left.

Behind it loomed the darkening purple-grey of the western hills. Here, on *The Peak of the West,* its highest point, dwelt the *Lady of the Peak* or *Lover of Silence*, the dreaded serpent goddess Meres-Ger.

Rakhmet remembered a rhyme his mother taught him when he was but a child:
'Beware Meres-Ger,
The Goddess of the West,
She strikes without warning,
When you disturb her rest.'

The boat docked and Rakhmet went ashore, taking a wrap with him as the heat of the day faded. The nights can often be quite chilly.

Instead of visiting a tavern, as the captain had suggested, he was ferried across the river and made his way to Mat, the village where he grew up.

Already dark, he had to use a torch to seek out the homes of family and old friends. To his dismay, he found that almost all had left the city. He reached the house of Asi, his boyhood friend. There were of the same age, nineteen, and looked as if they could be brothers. Both were tall, heavy-browed, dark eyed, and had the same well-built physiques. They also kept their hair, fashionable for men of rank, neatly trimmed to just below ear-level.

He knocked, wondering if he too had gone, but soon footsteps approached the door from within.

'You've come back, Rakhmet!' Asi cried out as he opened the door. 'You've come home!' He wept like a child as they embraced. 'How I've missed you, old friend! It has been many years.'

'It's good to see you too, Asi,' Rakhmet replied as Asi wiped his eyes and led him inside.

'You look well, Rakhmet. How have you been?' His words tumbled out. 'Have you come back to stay? I can arrange…'

'Slow down, Asi,' Rakhmet interrupted. 'No, I am just passing through. I leave again tomorrow eve.'

Asi led the way to the parlour where they seated themselves on some couches and Asi summoned a servant, 'Prepare extra food, Marsi, my guest will sup with me tonight…and prepare a room for our guest,' the servant nodded and returned to the cooking area. Asi turned to Rakhmet. 'You will be staying, of course? We have ample room here. My parents are visiting relatives in another Nome.'

'Just for tonight, thank you. I would appreciate staying overnight. Sleeping on the deck of the boat is not all that comfortable.'

'Why not stay a while longer, surely you can…' Asi persisted, but Rakhmet then explained the reason for his journey, then asked about other friends and family.

'All gone. It is all the doings of that criminal in Akhet Aten!' Asi spat out the words. 'That accursed Akhenaten!'

'Careful, Asi,' Rakhmet warned. 'Do not voice your anger. Pharaoh has ears everywhere.'

'I know what you mean.' Asi nodded towards the kitchen where two servants were preparing the meal. 'Come, let us talk where it is safer.' He led Rakhmet to an enclosed courtyard at the back of the house.

The pleasant garden had a fish-pond with lotuses rising out of the shallow water. There were several mud-brick seats under some trees. During the heat of the day, they provided cool shade, but it had now turned cold and Rakhmet pulled his cloak around his shoulders. The moon had risen early and bathed the garden in a soft light.

'Do you also worship Aten, Rakhmet?'

'No, I am still faithful to the Old Ones, but, like everyone else, we must do it covertly.'

'You saw the destruction of the temple on your way here?' It was more of a statement than a question.

'No, it was too dark to see clearly. The light from the torch did not reach that far.'

'We will go there tomorrow and you will then see for yourself what Akhenaten's decrees had wrought. The priests have become beggars.'

They sat in silence for a while.

'Many houses seemed deserted...my parents' house is empty and neglected,' Rakhmet said.

'Your father was a follower of Hathor, I believe?'

Rakhmet nodded, 'She is still worshipped in Bau-kem, in Kush.'

'Pharaoh's claws had not reached there yet?'

'No, but I wonder for how long. That is why I am being sent to there. The Aten priests were attacked when they tried to convert the people.'

'You will prosecute, maybe even kill those who oppose that Criminal's edicts?'

'It is my duty. My personal feelings cannot interfere in my task. You are a Medjay yourself, Asi, *One Who Keeps the Peace*. Did you not, in the line of duty, at one time or another, apprehend a friend or a family member?

'Yes, I suppose you are right, but here in No-Amun the feeling against Pharaoh is very strong,' he sighed and shook his head slowly. 'If the Nubian people feel as strong, you will have it hard in Sesibi!'

The servant appeared at the doorway. 'The meal is served, master!'

Asi and Rakhmet went inside, and after a sumptuous repast, they reminisced about their childhood until late.

\*\*\*

The next morning, Asi had to wake Rakhmet, who slept well beyond his usual night's rest. After the earlier uncomfortable nights on the ships deck, he felt pampered and relaxed. They broke their fast with course bread, cheese and emmer, a thick sour millet beer, sweetened with honey.

'When you are finished, I will show you what deeds were done on the orders of Akhenaten...unless you prefer to rest. We can spend the day relaxing.'

'No. I wish to see the city again. It has been many years.'

Asi led him to his favourite barber where they were both shaved, a morning ordeal that all men had to observe. Very few sported facial hair, and even Pharaoh's beard, a mark of authority, was false, and was worn only at certain times.

They crossed the river to the eastern part of the city. Signs of desecration and destruction were everywhere. The once beautiful temple of *Ap-Apit*, the temple of Amun Ra, lay in ruins.

'Both the temple and sanctuary of *Per neter tuaut* had been destroyed and the priests and priestesses banished,' Asi explained. 'But Mut is still worshipped in *Ipet-Isut* and *Ipet-resyt* and, for some reason, her temples has been left unscathed.'

'Perhaps,' Rakhmet explained, 'it is because the Lady Mutnedjmet, sister of Queen Nefertiti, once served as priestess there.'

'That must be the reason,' they continued their walk.

Large areas of the city looked desolate. Pylons, obelisks and stellae had been attacked and destroyed. Everywhere the name of Amenhotep the Third, the God-king and father of Pharaoh, had been erased.

'Even *Per nesu*, the house of the former Pharaoh, had been…cleansed,' Asi remarked, his voice bitter. 'The old God-king was revered here and in the Fourth *Sepat*, the people resent Akhenaten for desecrating his name.'

They stopped at another temple. 'Look yonder,' Asi pointed. 'Remember the great bronze doors of the temple? Gone!'

Rakhmet nodded.

'Worshipping at the temple is prohibited and no offerings are made any more. The priests, the few that remained, were starving and forced to beg alms at the gates of the city. Fearing reprisals if they assisting the former servants of Amun, the people would not help, so the priests resorted to stripping the temple doors of the bronze cladding to sell for food.'

All day Asi and Rakhmet toured the city visiting many of their former haunts. The day drew to a close. Strolling along the waterfront, they watched two fisher-men paddling a reed boat, the prow pointing homewards.

'It is time for me to return to the boat,' Rakhmet said and looked towards the western hills. 'It grows late.'

Purple shadows lengthened and crept eastward. The breathtaking view of the temple pylons and an obelisk lay before them, glowing in the late afternoon sun. They went to a tavern for a last drink.

'It was pleasant to see you again, Rakhmet. I hope you will call again, on your return.'

'I will seek you out, Asi. I promise. I am just sorry I did not get to see your parents. Give them my blessings.'

'I will. This day passed much too swiftly. May that never happen to our friend-ship.'

'Nothing can ever change that, Asi. We will always be friends.'

'Yes. Friends forever.'

Asi accompanied Rakhmet to the docks where he boarded the boat and re-mained on the wharf until well after the vessel had sailed and the figure of his friend was no longer visible in the growing gloom.

Batu, who had also been allowed ashore under guard, was drunk again and staggered towards Rakhmet, then nearly fell overboard as he doubled over to vomit into the darkened water. Disgusted, Rakhmet stomped past the retching soldier.

By the light of a flickering torch fixed to the stern, Rakhmet fumbled through his belongings that he had stored on the deck next to the mast, removed a straw-filled bag, covered himself with his cloak and lay down on the bag to sleep. 'For-ever,' he whispered the words again. Both Menefer and Asi had spoken that word.

'Friends forever,' Asi had said, but Rakhmet was not to know, that their next meeting would be anything but friendly.

# Chapter Five
## Royal Appointment

The news thrilled everyone in the workshops. Awed servants talked in hushed tones. Something like this had never happened before, and Menefer was just as excited and thrilled at the news. Queen Nefertiti was to visit the studio. Usually, the sculptor would have to go to the palace to fashion the likenesses of the king or queen. They would pose for a portrait bust in their own surroundings, but not this time.

Ipuky took the news in his stride. He had sculpted the king and queen often and was used to being in the presence of royalty. To him, this day would be no different than any other.

'But Ipuky,' Menefer gushed. 'This is different. She is coming *here*! She will be a guest in *our house*!'

'Not exactly in our house, Menefer,' he shrugged, 'just the studio.'

'You know what I mean.' She feigned annoyed at his indifference. 'How can you be so...so...' she stammered, trying to think of a word, then snapped. 'So unruffled!'

'The queen is just another woman...with a crown.'

'Oh Ipuky, you are impossible!' She knew he was only teasing, but it infuriated her. He just laughed.

Menefer had missed her brothers, particularly Ipuky, while they were away and she was so happy to have them back home again. Ipuky was three years older and closer her own age. Nebaten, the eldest, at twenty-five, seemed more mature and often behaved more like a parent than a brother.

They had returned from the quarries just two days earlier and brought with them blocks of alabaster, marble, serpentine and limestone for the fashioning of statues and vases. Their father, Thutmose, needed the limestone for the queen's intended portrait-bust.

***

Ipuky had been instructing Menefer on the finer points of glazing, when a breathless servant rushed into the small studio.

'She has arrived, Master Ipuky!' he announced, excitedly.

'Queen Nefertiti?' Menefer looked up expectantly.

'Yes, mistress.'

'Thank you Ramu,' Ipuky turned to his sister, 'Sorry Menefer, I must go, I have to prepare father's tools to use on our special visitor's likeness. I will continue our lesson later.'

'*Special visitor,* Ipuky? Did you not say she was just another woman, with a crown!' Menefer teased. Ipuky chuckle and gave a sly shrug as he rose.

'Wait a moment, I am coming too!' Menefer jumped up. The look of alarm on Ipuky's face made her giggle. 'Oh, don't be so concerned, I will go only as far as the hallway.'

Ipuky proceeded to the main workshop and Menefer joined other craftsmen and servants that had lined up along the wall in foyer. They chattered excitedly among themselves in anticipation. The queen would pass right by them. To be this close to Royalty would be a thrilling experience.

The Overseer of the Workshop entered the hallway from the main studio where he had been supervising the tidying up in preparation for Nefertiti's visit.

'Silence!' he commanded. 'Those of you who wish to stand and gape at Her Majesty, may do so, but in an orderly way!' He waved his hand imperiously. 'Line the passage properly and stand upright. When she passes, salute with a slight bow, your palms up and forward, raised to shoulder height—thus!' He demonstrated, then straightened. Scowling, he then gave them a final warning. 'And...no talking!'

'Mistress Menefer,' one of the workmen whispered. 'Show yourself. He did not recognise you. You deserve a more privileged position.'

'No. I am one of you,' she whispered. 'Just another worker. I want no...'

'I said *silence*!' the overseer called out, glaring at them. 'One more word from any of you and I will send you *all* back to your workplaces!'

Queen Nefertiti and her entourage arrived in the courtyard behind the house. The queen drove her own chariot. She alighted from the platform and waved away a guard who tried to assist, but allowed them to take care of the vehicle and horses. She and her escort proceeded to the pillared porch of the workshop building where Thutmose awaited his Royal guest.

Kheruef, the queen's Chief Steward, preceded the Royal party. 'Make way for Her Royal Majesty, Neferneferu-Aten, Queen Nefertiti!' he announced, waving the gaping spectators aside.

Thutmose led the queen along the hallway. She smiled and nodded to the assembled workers as Thutmose chatted. 'Your Majesty, everything is in readiness. I managed to acquire some quality limestone from the hills near Waset that should serve splendidly. It is of the finest quality, personally selected by my sons...'

The group disappeared into the main studio. The Overseer of the Workshop ordered everyone back to their workplaces and Menefer returned to her tasks. She had been fashioning a set of four funerary jars for a *marianni*, one of the nobility. These jars, each with a stopper in the images of one of the four sons of Horus—Imsety, Duamutef, Hapi and Qebehsenuef, were assigned to protect the vital organs of the diseased.

She had almost finished the fourth, the falcon-headed Qebehsenuef, the guardian of the intestines, but, still daydreaming about Queen Nefertiti, could not concentrate on her work. Her Majesty had been so close she could have reached out and touched her garment.

Ipuky entered. 'Busy?' he asked, seeing her gazing wistfully out the window.

'Uh…no, I was just…uh…'

'Never mind. Get yourself ready,' he gestured to her clothing. 'You look a mess. You are wanted in the main studio.' He started to leave.

'Me?' Menefer asked, puzzled. 'Why?'

Ipuky stopped, looked at her and shrugged, 'Don't know, but it's important. Hurry.'

Menefer quickly removed her soiled protective over-garment, glanced into a copper mirror, smoothed her hair and turned to follow her brother. He leaned over and wiped a smudge of clay from her chin. 'Missed a spot.'

They entered the chamber and Ipuky gestured her to wait by the door. The queen sat on a chair on a low dais, attended on either side by handmaidens. Kheruef, the queen's Chief Steward, stood behind her. Ipuky went over to him and indicated that Menefer had arrived. He beckoned to her and she approached him nervously, wondering why she had been summoned.

'Don't be frightened, child,' he smiled and steered her to the queen. 'Your Majesty, the sculptress Menefer.'

Nefertiti turned smiled and waved her closer. 'Menefer, my dear. I have heard much about you.'

Menefer did an awkward obeisance. '*Me*?' she stammered and quickly added, '…Your Majesty?'

'I have been told much about your skills. Your father has high regards for your work.'

Menefer glanced at her father who gave her a wink.

'I have something here…something you fashioned.'

Nefertiti signalled to Kheruef who handed the queen a small object. Menefer reacted in astonishment and apprehension when she saw what it was, the talisman she had fashioned for Rakhmet. If the queen assumes the image on it to be that of Isis, she could expect severe punishment.

'This is a fine piece of work,' Nefertiti said softly and Menefer trembled visibly. 'You certainly have great skills. It would be a great pity…'

Oh, oh, here it comes, Menefer thought and dropped her eyes.

'…if your skills are wasted,' Nefertiti continued, 'I believe your engagement here, at this workshop, is to be only a temporary one?'

'Yes, Your Majesty,' Menefer answered, her eyes still downcast.

'May I make you an offer—of a more permanent one?'

Menefer looked up, surprised.

'I wish you to join the Royal household, as a tutor!'

Amazed, Menefer just stood there, her mouth open, for a moment, too dumbfounded to speak.

'As…as Your Majesty commands,' she finally stammered in a weak voice.

'No, it is not a command but a request. It is for you to decide. Two of my daughters show great interest in crafting, in clay and painting, but I am certain *all* the princesses will benefit from your skills. Think it over. I do not expect an immediate answer.'

Menefer, overwhelmed and flattered, glanced at her father. He smiled and nodded his approval. 'Yes, Your Majesty,' she replied eagerly. 'I accept!'

'You do not wish to think it over? Discuss it with your family first?'

'There is no need, Your Majesty,' Menefer replied. 'My family is sure to approve. It will be an honour and privilege to serve Your Majesty.'

'I am pleased.' Nefertiti turned to her steward, 'Lord Kheruef, please make all the arrangements, and see that suitable accommodations be prepared.'

Kheruef bowed slightly and nodded. 'I will see to it immediately, Majesty.'

'And, Lord Kheruef,' Nefertiti added. 'See to it that the amulet is returned to the young officer from whom it was taken,' she turned back to Menefer. 'I shall see you in due time.'

'Yes, Your Majesty. Thank you, Your Majesty.' Menefer saluted as she had been instructed earlier, with her palms raised towards the queen and with head bowed, she backed towards the door.

'Now, Master Thutmose,' Nefertiti rubbed her neck. 'I have interrupted you long enough. Let us continue. This helmet is getting heavier every moment.' She adjusted the headdress and resumed her pose.

***

For the rest of the day, Menefer found it difficult to concentrate on her work. Her thought kept returning to the queen's offer.

She could hardly wait to tell Djenna the wonderful news. Djenna, a keen royal follower, would be greatly impressed. That evening after *mesit*, the evening meal, Menefer rushed over to the house of Lord Nakht.

Lady Susmaat saw her coming up the steps, welcomed her and led her into the reception room. Like those of others of the wealthy, it was impressive. Eight colourful and highly decorated pillars supported the ceiling. Along two of the walls, cushion-covered brick benches, as well as a number of wood-and-thong chairs, provided seating. Susmaat bade her to make herself comfortable. She called to Djenna, informed her she had a visitor then went into the *rekhes* to prepare refreshments.

Djenna entered and they exchanged greetings. 'Guess what, Djenna,' Menefer bubbled. 'I am to join the Royal staff at the palace.'

Instead of being surprise, Djenna frowned. 'You? What would *you* be doing there?'

'I have been offered the task of teaching the princesses! Is that not wonderful?'

'What could you possible teach them?' Djenna seemed unimpressed. 'Anyway, I too, have great news!' Djenna hesitated a moment for effect, then continued. 'My father had managed to secure a position for me at court as well! I am to join Queen Tiye's entourage as Robe Mistress!' Then she added smugly. 'Caring about one's appearance and following the latest court fashions as I do, has its benefits, and Queen Tiye obviously noticed. More than once I saw her looking in my direction during the banquet.'

'I thought you said it was Prince Smenkhare who had been looking at you.'

'Uh…well, uh…he did,' Djenna stuttered, 'but so did Queen Tiye.'

'It is indeed great news, Djenna,' Menefer smiled and grasped her friend's hand, affectionately. 'I am glad for you.'

'When will you be going?'

'I am to report to Lord Hatiay, Overseer of the Royal Household, as soon as I have finished the task my father gave me.'

'I know Lord Hatiay,' Djenna replied haughtily. 'I assume you will keep company with the princesses only? *I* will, of course, be with Queen Tiye!'

Susmaat entered with some refreshing drinks of pomegranate juice sweetened with honey. 'I overheard your news, Menefer, I am so happy for you. It is a great honour.' She noticed her daughter's scowl and quickly added, 'for both of you!'

The older woman returned to the kitchen as Djenna gushed on about the garments she had ordered. 'I have women stitching garments for me this very moment. Colourful fabrics are very popular these days, you know…and I am having my wigs cleaned and re-plaited.' She looked Menefer up and down, 'I trust you will be getting new garments as well. One must be well-groomed at all times, especially in the presence of Royalty and nobility.'

Djenna droned on and on but Menefer did not pay much attention. Her friend's remarks and lack of support for her was disappointing, but it was typical of Djenna. She should not have expected much more.

*** 

Menefer had completed the four funerary jars and also some ushabti figurines. Her father was pleased with her assistance and the skill she had demonstrated, and was actually disappointed to see her go.

'The workshop will lose a fine craftsman—uh—crafts-*woman*, Menefer, and my clients had already expressed their regrets about your leaving. They were all pleased with your fine work and wanted you to remain, but your mother and I wish you well with your new position.'

Menefer had been packing her clothing into a woven reed chest, and paused a moment. Just two weeks had passed since she first started working for her father and Menefer could hardly believe that so much had happened in such a short time. She looked about her small bedchamber where so many happy years of her life had been spent. Those times would be missed, but a new life awaited her. She would be leaving home shortly, but planned to visit her family every ten days, which was one Egyptian week.

She finished packing and dragged the clothing chest to the door. Ipuky promised he would deliver it to *Per nesu*, the Royal residence, later.

With mixed feelings, she bade her parents leave and set off for the King's House. Ipuky wanted to accompany her, but she wanted to be alone. It was almost an hour's walk along the dusty road, but it gave her a chance to rehearse her lines for when she arrived.

The King's Way, the main road, dissected the city and separated *Per nesu*, the King's House, from the palace. Water-carriers and food vendors, pushing hand-carts, sold their wares along the way. Traders, pack-animals, citizens and chariots crowded the wide street and kicked up dust that settled on everything. Bread often contained grit from sand, blown onto the dough.

She soon reached the King's House. A bridge straddled the King's Way that connected it to the palace. Three passages allowed traffic to pass underneath. Directly over the middle passage was a large open balcony, the Window *of Appearance,* where the Royal family regularly appeared to the public.

The King's House and garden inside the walled enclosure, were on raised grounds, much higher than the road, and steps and a ramp led up to it. The guard at the gate to the house had not been informed of Menefer's arrival and she was directed across the road, to a side gate of the palace wall, the entrance to *per-hemt,* the House of Women!

Disappointed, Menefer crossed the road. She had hoped she would not be housed here where Pharaoh's concubines and harem boys were quartered. She approached a guard at the gate. 'I wish to see Hatiay…I am here at the request of Her Majesty, Queen Nefertiti.'

He grunted, turned and called out. A rather portly man appeared from a small kiosk. 'I am Minares, Scribe and Keeper of the Gate. You must be Menefer, the sculptress?'

'Yes, I am here to…'

'Yes, yes I know. I have been expecting you…come!' Menefer followed him. They passed the harem and went up the ramp to the bridge.

'Will I be staying here, in the House of Women?' she asked, apprehensively.

Minares, more accustomed to sitting down, puffed his way up the steep slope. 'No!' he replied, a little breathless. 'Most of the staff is quartered at the far end of *Per nesu*, beyond the garden.' He waved a pudgy arm in the general direction of the living quarters. The flabby underarm fat waggling with the action.

'The King's House?' she asked, relieved. 'I will be staying there?'

'That is what I just said!' he answered curtly, then regretting his rudeness, continued in a more friendly tone. 'It has pleasant surroundings. The garden has a pond with fish and pens with animals. You will like it there.'

'Animals?'

'Gifts to His Majesty. Envoys from far-countries often present Pharaoh with wild animals. The tame ones are kept there.'

Halfway across the bridge, they passed the open balcony she saw earlier. 'This is the *Window of Appearance.'* Minares gestured with a sweep of his forearm. 'During the New Year Upit festival, Pharaoh and Queen Nefertiti show themselves to the people and bestow rewards upon those who had pleased them during the year,' he puffed breathlessly.

'Fascinating,' Menefer responded, enthusiastically. 'To actually be here, where their Majesties often trod.' She knew about the ceremony, but did not wish to offend the fatigued man.

They descended the ramp into the precincts of *Per nesu*. Minares directed Menefer's attention to a building on the left, situated on the upper level of the terraced garden. 'That is the *Sbau, the Place of Learning*, where you will be instructing the princesses.' He then waved his hand to a large pillared building on his right. 'That is the Royal residence. The Princesses' bed-chambers are over there,' he pointed, 'and those, Their Majesties' quarters on the far side.'

They entered a courtyard in the lower garden. Rows of shade trees lined a number of paved pathways, and at the far side she saw the animal pens.

An official approached them. 'This must be the sculptress?'

'Yes,' Minares gestured. 'Menefer, this is Lord Hatiay, Overseer of the Royal Household.'

'Welcome. I will show you to your quarters.'

Menefer thanked Minares and he returned to his post at the Gate. Hatiay led Menefer along a raised Pillared walkway running the full length of the Royal Residence. 'Have you any baggage?'

'My brother, Ipuky, will deliver them later.'

'Ah yes, Ipuky!' He gestured towards a large doorway. 'His Majesty's Audience chamber is through there. The walls contain some of Ipuky's works. He is a very good craftsman, don't you think?'

'I do not care too much for his likenesses of the king and queen,' Menefer admitted.

Hatiay leaned over and in a conspiratorial whisper, answered. 'To tell the truth, neither do I, but let us keep that a secret, eh!' he laughed, a deep rumble from his belly.

Menefer liked him almost immediately. They chatted as he led her past the animal pens. She had heard the sounds of waterfowl and birds as they came down the ramp, but as they approached, she was amazed at the variety. Most of them were not from Egypt and the colours and songs impressed her greatly. Small tame antelope grazed on the lush grasses between the shade trees. One pen had a cheetah, an animal she had heard of, but had never seen.

'I'm afraid,' Hatiay wrinkled his nose and rubbed it with the knuckle of his first finger, 'the smell can be a bit strong at times. I hope you will not be too discomforted by it.'

Menefer chuckled. 'Not really, my sleeping chamber at home, is close to our ass' stable and goat pens. I am used to it.'

They passed through another gate in a wall behind the pens into a smaller garden containing a large circular pond.

'Those buildings over there…' he gestured to two rows of box-like dwellings facing each other, 'are the quarters for the female staff. Males are housed behind them.'

He directed Menefer to the first building on the east-facing row. 'This one will be yours.'

The spacious room had a small window and a reed door. A woven-reed mat covering hung down on the inside of the window to keep out the heat of day, and flies and night-insects. The sparse but adequate furniture consisted of a small table, stool, and an *aft*, a sleeping couch, not quite as comfortable as her one at home, but better than a pallet, on which many of the servants had to sleep, and, on the wall, a few pegs to hang her clothing.

'Does Djenna live here as well?' Menefer asked, hoping her friend might be nearby.

'Djenna?' Hatiay hesitated for a moment. The name sounded familiar, but he did not immediately place her.

'Yes, Queen Tiye's new Mistress of the Robes.'

'Ah yes, Lord Nakht's daughter. No. Queen Tiye now resides in her own house; the one His Majesty had built for her. Djenna would be there.'

'And Prince Smenkhare…is he there also?'

Hatiay laughed that rumbly belly laugh again.

'Oh, now I see where your thoughts are going. No! The prince is housed in the Great Palace…and well away from the House of Women!' Hatiay laughed again.

'If there is anything you need, do not hesitate to ask. Make yourself comfortable.' He showed her where the ablution chamber was and where the servants had their meals. 'The *rekhes*, the cooking place is over there. *Ash-t-f meter-t* is at noon. After you have eaten, I will send someone to call you to meet your Royal charges,' with a wave, he departed.

Ipuky duly arrived at a side gate with her baggage. After she had unpacked, she decided to call on Djenna. Queen Tiye's house was but a short walk away, and she would be back before *meter-t,* in time for the midday meal.

'So, your dwelling is at *Per nesu*!' Djenna sneered after Menefer told her of the day's happenings. 'I suppose you will now consider yourself better than *me*, stuck in this house.'

Taken aback by Djenna's remark, Menefer quickly explained, 'No, Djenna— I…I'm in the staff's quarters.'

'Oh. Servant's quarters? Yes, I suppose that is understandable. She waved her hand in abroad gesture. Serving Her Majesty's person is a bit more…noble than being merely a *mena mesu seru*!'

'I am not a child-minder,' Menefer replied indignantly. 'I will be an *instructor* to the princesses.'

'Same thing!' Djenna scoffed. 'At least, I wait on Her Majesty's person! But, uh, Menefer…' Djenna hesitated. 'Is there a place where I can come and visit you—other than in the servant's quarters?' Djenna sniffed contemptuously. 'After all, it would not be fitting for someone of my standing to be seen there!'

'I suppose we can meet in the garden. It is quite lovely.'

'Well, that seems a bit more appropriate, I suppose.'

Djenna's insensitive remarks appeared to be more spiteful than usual, but Menefer ignored them. Djenna was just being… Djenna.

# Chapter Six
## The Quarrel

The princesses were charming. Setenpenre, the youngest, at six, amused Menefer and kept calling her Mellifer. Ten-year-old Neferure, called "Nefer", was still being groomed by Hentaneb, her nurse, when Menefer arrived, but came rushing in a few moments later, all breathless, and apologised profusely. Slightly older, at twelve, Nefertiti the Younger, Neferneferure ta-Sherit, or "Sherit" for short, was a bit shy at first.

The two older princesses, fourteen-year-old Senpa, short for Ankhsenpaaten, and Meritaten, or "Merit", seventeen, a year older than Menefer, arrived later. Both were delayed, making special offerings at the temple ceremony.

After the *Greeting of the Aten* ceremony, Lady Mutnedjmet, Queen Nefertiti's sister, accompanied them from the temple. She had heard of Menefer's skills and was curious. When they arrived, Menefer's apprehensions of the Royals being formal and stuffy, turned out to be exactly the opposite. Lady Mutny, as she was called, was a warm, jolly lady and she and Menefer immediately became friends.

At their first meeting, Lady Mutny, noticed Menefer's nervousness, and immediately put her at ease. 'I don't know if you like rising early, but personally, I do not.' She leaned over and whispered, 'It is rather tedious but, like it or not, we all have to attend the dawn ceremony at the Small Temple.'

'I don't mind getting up early,' Menefer said. 'But I thought the ceremony was at dusk. I heard chanting last evening.'

'We have two every day, a dawn one, welcoming the sun, and the dusk ceremony, when Aten is put to rest, and a third, at noon, during Aten festivals.'

Senpa, Menefer discovered, had a wonderful flair for drawing. Hatiay tutored them in reading and writing, both in *metcha-t*, the formal monument script, as well as *sekh shat* or simpler writing used mainly for writing manuscripts. Merit and Senpa, looked forward to their first lessons in *nechit*, drawing in colours. Her first lessons were in the grinding of different minerals for the pigments, then mixing it with a variety of animal fats, egg-white or vegetable resins and water to make a paste or ink.

'Colours are important and have meanings,' Menefer explained, and held up some gypsum powder. 'This one, white, *shesep*, is for purity, cleanliness or something sacred. Black, *kem*, is made from soot or charcoal,' she pointed to a container with black powder, 'and is made by burning animal bones or wood. It is the symbol for death, but as Egypt is called *kemet*, the "Black Land", it is also life giving, as the black mud, deposited by the waters of the Nile, provide new fertile soil, used for planting crops. We also use black for writing and to outline drawings. Red, *desher*, is made by grinding these stones,' she points out the different coloured minerals—iron oxide and cinnabar.

'Blue, *intiu* and *sbedj*, and green, *wadj*, are more precious, as the stones from which it is ground, are costly and must be brought from distant places. Use them sparingly.' Then Menefer holds up a dish with a yellow pigment, 'This is yellow, *khenit*, and used to depict gold, and symbolising something eternal or indestructible, but be very careful,' she warns. 'This powder is very poisonous. Wash your hands carefully after using it.'

'Today's lesson will be mainly the grinding the stones, and mixing of the various powders to create a variety of colours. Then we'll mix them with the oils and gums to make the paints and ink. Tomorrow, I will show you the technique of making brushes and pens to draw and apply the colours.'

Each girl was given a pestle and mortar and they had to grind the stones into powder. No one liked this part of the lesson. It was messy and tedious.

The next morning, Menefer woke to a blast of distant trumpets. With a jolt, she sat upright on her sleeping couch. This was her second day here, and for a moment, she was disorientated. She was expected to join the Royal Family for the Temple ceremony from today. The sun had not yet risen but the pink of pre-dawn was visible through the woven mat covering of the window. She gathered the bedclothes around her shoulders. Proyet, the season of Emergence, the winter months, can be chilly in the early hours.

A knock on the door. Adia, a servant girl, sent by Hatiay, brought Menefer a garment of pure white linen to wear for the ceremony. Menefer thanked her, dressed hurriedly and after performing a quick ablution, hastened to the forecourtyard as instructed. Kheruef, the Royal Steward, rushed back and forth, organising the procession. Members of the court were lined up in pairs and Menefer took her place alongside the others. The thin garment did not warm her, but as the others were braving the cold, so she would also.

After a short wait, sounds of tambourines, flutes and sistrums floated from within the Royal quarters. A moment later, the vizier Ay appeared, followed by the Royal family, then high officials and the Royal handmaidens. Djenna and lesser servants joined Menefer's group. She noticed that Prince Smenkhare was missing. He was not a worshipper of Aten, and did not attend.

Ay, led the chanting procession through the gates to the temple. Even at this early hour, crowds lined the street, eager to get a glimpse of the Royals.

The procession moved down the King's Way, then entered the Small Temple through the two pylon gates and proceeded to the altar. Panehesy, the High priest of the temple, welcomed them. His duties included the opening of the doors every morning, and closing them at night when the god rose or went to their rest.

The altar, shaded by awnings, supported by wooden pillars, stood just inside the gates of the first courtyard of the temple. The Royal party stopped at the altar to give offerings. The twilight hours, just before sunrise and immediately after sunset, called the *In Between Time*, was believed to be the time that the earth died, and it was Panehesy's task to make offerings and incant prayers until this perilous time had passed. After a brief ceremony and offerings, they continued towards a second gate.

The chanting procession entered the second court where more offering tables were located. More offerings were made. The altars were heaped with contributions; legs of oxen, wildfowl and venison, urns of grain, fruit and vegetables, bowls of flowers, jars of honey and wine and smoking sticks of frankincense were offered daily. The priests and priestesses feasted well afterwards.

Servants and officials took their places along two sides of the temple wall and the Royals continued into a third court, then all, but Akhenaten and Panehesy, remained there. Only Pharaoh and the High priest were allowed to continue into the *Holy of Holies*, the most sacred place in the temple.

The rays of the rising sun touched the tops of the pylons, and Meryre, a secondary priest, appeared. His head was shaved and he was bare to the waist. A number of priestesses, shaking sistrums and played lutes, followed him. They formed two rows, one on each side of the altar. All worshippers raised their hands in salute to the sun, and Meryre, in a sing song voice, started reciting the Hymn to the Sun, the chant Pharaoh Akhenaten himself had written.

*'Thou risest beautifully in the horizon of heaven, Oh living Aten who created life!*

*When though risest in the eastern horizon, though fillest every land with thy beauty. Thou art beautiful, great, gleaming and high over every land. Thy rays, they embrace the lands to the limits of all thou have made. Thou art Re and brightest of them all, thou bindest them for thy beloved son.'*

It had eleven verses altogether. He continued to chant on and on and the lengthy hymn seemed to go on forever. By the time it finished, the sun was already above the distant hills and it started getting very warm and uncomfortable. As everyone lowered their weary arms, Meryre held aloft a sceptre towards the sun, then, followed by the novice and chanting priestesses, they filed back into the inner sanctum.

The High priest and Vizier Ay appeared, followed by Panehesy, old and very overweight and carrying a bowl of fragrant sacred water. Muttering incantations and breathing heavily from the exertion of the ceremony, he led Pharaoh and the other Royals and again stopped by the main altar. Panehesy gently and reverently placed the bowl upon it, dipped a feather into the water and sprinkled it around, blessing the temple and worshippers.

The procession then returned to *Per nesu*. The ceremony was over for the morning, but will be repeated again that evening. Menefer changed her clothes, and, escorted by Adia they went to the *rekhes*, where other court servants were already seated at benches for *ash-t-f tuat*, the break of the fast.

\*\*\*

Their lesson for the princesses this day, was the making and using of reed brushes. The ends of the reeds were hammered and frayed, then trimmed to the required shape for the project. While everyone was busy working at their brushes, Menefer and her students were getting acquainted. The princesses were curious about Menefer's life before she joined them. She explained briefly about her father needing her assistance and the sculptures she fashioned for him. Then, about the queen seeing the medallion, and Queen Nefertiti's suggestion she teach the princesses.

'We know all about that already. Tell us about Rakhmet. How did you meet?' Princesses Meritaten asked.

'Yes, what's he like?' Ankhsenpaaten added. 'I suppose you'll miss him, won't you?'

Menefer was momentarily taken aback. 'You know about him?' she asked, surprised.

'Merit told me about him,' Ankhsenpaaten explained. 'She heard about him after he was sent away.'

'Actually, Senpa, I learnt about him in a round-about way,' Merit corrected her sister, then turned back to Menefer. 'When our mother saw the craftwork on the talisman, she told me the circumstances that led to you being here.' She leaned forward, eagerly, 'Tell us all about *him*…'

'Yes, I think it's so…romantic. Tell us *everything*. What is he like, where and when did you first meet, what attracted you to each other.' Senpa leaned forward, expectantly, her chin cupped in her hand with a half-finished brush poised clasped between her fingers, 'And don't leave out any details. When did he first kiss you?'

Menefer's romantic anecdotes entertained and delighted the princesses, then Menefer mentioned her friend and their conversation turned to Djenna.

'She has a passion for rich garments and fine jewellery. That is how she caught the eye of Queen Tiye and Princess Baketaten.'

'Oh yes,' Senpa added. 'She is the daughter of Lord Nakht, is she not?'

'That's right. He secured her a position at court, as Queen Tiye's Mistress of Robes,' Menefer told them.

'Mistress of robes?' Merit giggled. 'Did she tell you that? She is but one of Queen Tiye's garment stitchers!'

'Really?' Menefer's eyes widened with surprise. 'She made me believe otherwise, that her style and knowledge of clothing impressed Queen Tiye!'

'One does not achieve the status of Robe Mistress overnight. It takes many, many years of faithful service, moving up step by step to the top rank,' Senpa added, sniggering. Menefer felt guilty gossiping about her friend, but savoured the satisfaction she had just learnt regarding Djenna's boasting.

The princesses finished their tasks that first day. Apart from making a variety of brushes and pens, Menefer and the girls learned much about each other and they became good friends.

The following day, their lessons were about the preparing papyri, stone slabs for drawing, and shards of broken pottery for practice, as better material were costly. They also prepared pieces of slate and slabs of damp clay. Only, once they had mastered their craft, could their works be done on primed surfaces.

*** 

Several days later, after the sunset temple ceremony and *mesit*, a meal of honeyed fruit-loaf, marrow, beans and onions washed down with barley beer, Menefer decided to visit the raised garden. She had passed it a few times but had never strolled around it.

She took a wrap with her against the chill of the early evening. The songbirds had retired to their perches for the night, but the sounds of frogs and crickets around the pond, made it a peaceful place to sit and reflect on the day's events. The moon rose and cast a soft light over the garden and only dappled light reached the area where she sat. Relaxed and deep in thought, she did not hear the approaching footsteps.

'A pleasant evening, Menefer!'

Startled, she looked around. 'Oh! Your Highness!' She quickly rose and saluted Prince Smenkhare, surprised he knew her name.

'Lady Mutny mentioned you were now living in *Per nesu*.' He sat down opposite her and gestured for her to be seated again. 'It is peaceful here, is it not? I often come here to relax.'

'Yes, it is, Your Highness.' She fiddled nervously with the end of her girdle-cord, 'I... I was not aware this is a private garden. I shall leave immediately.' She started to get up again.

'No, no. You are very welcome. Please stay,' he gestured again for her to sit. 'The garden is for anyone here at *Per nesu*,' he paused and leaned forward slightly. 'I heard you started your teachings. The princesses are most charmed by you...and are enjoying your lessons'

'I am glad to hear it, Your Highness...'

'No need to be formal. When we are alone, you can call me by my name.'

'Thank you Your...uh...Smenkhare. You say you come here often? To this garden, and not the one at the Palace? I hear it is quite beautiful.'

'Oh, it is fine, but it's frequented by the women of the harem. It is not fitting to be seen with my brother's concubines, although, I have become good friends with Lady Tadukhipa and Lady Khiya. I enjoy talking with Lady Khiya's little son. He is such an intelligent little boy.'

'Akhenaten has a son? I did not know. I thought he had only daughters.'

'Yes, Tutankhaten. He was born two years after the death of Princess Mekhetaten. Being the son of a concubine, like me, he is all but ignored by the Royal family.'

They sat in silence for a while listening to the sounds of the night.

Then they both spoke at once.

'I am glad...'

'Do you miss...?'

Menefer giggled, embarrassed. 'I am sorry...uh, Smenkhare. You were saying...'

'I was about to say I am glad I finally met you.'

'Me, Highness?' incredulously, Menefer searched his face.

'Yes. I noticed you the night of the banquet.'

Again surprised, Menefer smiled. 'I...I am flattered, Highness.' *So*, she thought, *the Prince had looked at me that night, not Djenna*. She turned her eyes away, wondering how her friend would react at the news.

'I was surprised at how much you and your mother looked alike. At first, I thought you were sisters.'

'Thank you, Your Highness. She will be so pleased to hear it. We are often told that we look alike,' Menefer searched for something to say. 'Uh…you lived in the Palace of Malkata, in Waset, before coming here, Highness?'

'Smenkhare,' he reminded her. 'Yes, in the *House of Women*…with my mother Mutemwaya.'

'I suppose you have left many friends behind…'

'No, none. I was Ignored by Baketaten and my three other older stepsisters. I do not have the liberty to roam about on my own. When I came here, I hoped for a little more freedom, but once again I am confined to the palace or *House of Women*.'

'But surely your brother…uh, His Majesty is…'

'Mph! Akhenaten doesn't even know I'm alive. I haven't seen him at all since the day we arrived.'

'But you and Princess Meritaten are…'

'Merit! Yes. We are sort of…betrothed. It was all arranged when we were very young. A political move. Neither of us was involved in the planning. We had hardly spoken since my arrival. I'm sure…' He stopped, cocking his head. 'Shhh! Someone's approaching.'

A man's voice drifted over the darkened pond and footsteps were coming up the steps.

'I cannot do it! I cannot just send her away!' the man said.

'Yes, you can!' A woman sounded angry. 'She is a troublemaker. She is disruptive and overbearing. Ever since her arrival, she's been trying to bring about changes!'

Smenkhare looked at Menefer and shrugged. In the darkness, even with only filtered moonlight illuminating his face, she could see he was puzzled.

He leaned over and whispered. 'Do you know who they are?'

Menefer shook her head and shrugged. 'I do not know many people at *Per nesu* yet,' she whispered back.

'She is my *mother*!' the man said, anger in his voice.

'I don't care! I want her gone! She should return to Waset, where she belongs!'

'There is trouble there, as you know. She came here on a visit.'

'You mean, to change your severe decrees…to relax your laws…She blames you for the trouble in the East.'

Menefer and Smenkhare looked at each other and both immediately realised who they were. Pharaoh Akhenaten and Queen Nefertiti!

'We should not be here!' Menefer whispered, alarmed.

'Shh!' Smenkhare cautioned and leaned back, deeper into the shadows.

'My decrees have nothing to do with it. The trouble in Phoenicia is an old one. Khatti and Amurra have been trying to get their hands on our Eastern territories for years! You know as well as I that Abdashirta had repeatedly attacked Katna and Tunip even when *Amun* was still being worshipped, so she can't use religion as an excuse!'

'Your mother had always been over-friendly with those Eastern potentates— can't you see they are using her to get to you to interfere?' Nefertiti sounded annoyed. 'The trouble in Asia is a matter between Aziro of Amurra and…what's his name…the Governor of Gebal?'

'Ribaddi!' Akhenaten answered.

'Yes, Ribaddi! Let them sort out their own squabbles!'

'My mother is convinced that great harm will befall us by being passive. She wants me to take up arms against Aziro. He is a threat to Egypt. Perhaps I should do something.'

'Aziro is not the issue here. He has always pledged loyalty to you. You have letters to prove his fealty. Do not make war against an ally.'

'Aziro is Abdeshirta's son. Why should he not continue his father's battle?' Akhenaten explained. 'Aziro is a traitor and must be subdued…his continual harassment was halted only by force. Since then, peace was kept only by continual vigilance. As soon as Aten replaced Amun, the attacks started again. Had you not been so fanatical about Aten, you would have realised that.'

'Fanatical! *Me fanatical?*' Nefertiti exploded. 'Who exiled the Amun priesthood? *You!* Who had their temples destroyed and banned the mere mention of the name of Amun? It was *you*, Akhenaten! You went too far!'

Menefer and Smenkhare glanced at one another in the dark, their eyes wide in astonishment.

'It was *you* who introduced me to the worship Aten in the first place, Nefertiti! You converted me. Now that I'm devoted to Aten, you're blaming me for the troubles.'

In a calmer tone, Nefertiti replied. 'I merely *introduced* you to a more gentle religion,' then, in a more accusing voice, added, 'Amun is a cruel deity! You forget your ancestor, the second Amenhotep, sacrificed human beings to Amun—clubbed prisoners to death before Amun's image.'

After a pause, Nefertiti continued, her voice, soft again. 'Aten is gentle. His religion is a beautiful one… I thought you understood, but then, suddenly, you wanted to change the world. You emptied the city coffers to build this city.' She spread her arms wide in an all-encompassing gesture, '*That's* the reason for so much hardship and the discontent among the people, not the worship of Aten.'

'I did not empty the *city* coffers. Much of the riches were confiscated from the temples of Amun. Their priests had become too powerful and greedy…*they* became wealthy at the expense of the people.'

'Now your mother wants you to restore Amun. Is she not an Aten worshipper, herself? She lives in the past. She craves to recapture her former status and the glory she once had…to be a worshipped as a goddess again! It was you who tried to discourage that, Akhenaten! You are the one who had chosen the adage *Living in Truth.* Now *live* by it!'

Akhenaten sighed, 'It seems no matter what I do, there will be trouble. If I restore Amun, the priests will prosper and the state coffers will dry up. If I do not, rebellion will break out in No-Amun…'

'Waset!' Nefertiti corrected him. 'There are uprisings there already!'

'Either way, the trouble in Asia will escalate!'

'Do what you think best, but do not allow your mother to influence you.' Nefertiti drew her wrap closer about her shoulders. 'We were happy here before she arrived. Can that not be so again?' she shivered. 'It is cold. I am going inside.'

The queen turned and went down the steps back to the house. Akhenaten pondered their argument awhile, then turned and followed.

Once they were out of earshot, Menefer sucked in her breath sharply. 'I would never have guessed…I always assumed His Majesty introduced the Aten-worship.'

'Oh, no. Aten was worshipped even during my father's rule and Tiye was a strong supporter, but the veneration of the Disk had always been just a minor religion. Only now, since Akhenaten's reign, had it become all-powerful.'

'Just how much influence does Queen Tiye have? Will she really be able to turn Pharaoh's head?'

Smenkhare looked at her and sighed. 'I don't know. No one confides in me. I really don't know where all this will lead. My step mother is a very strong-willed woman. We will just have to wait and see.'

# Chapter Seven
## The Spy

The trip from Waset to the first cataract was uneventful. They stopped frequently to load and unload wares. Ten days later, they reached Yebu. The city, situated on an island in the first nome, was the most southern port of call before the rapids. Only flat-bottomed boats of a shallow draft could proceed further south during the full-river season, but as the Nile was low this time of the year, they could not proceed by river.

Located at the crossroads on main caravan routes, Yebu, in Lower Nubia, became the main gathering place for trade between the distant Eastern Sea, Egypt, Kush and the land of Punt. Cargoes were transported from here to all of Egypt or its neighbours, and the docks were stacked with all manner of goods.

Apart from ivory, for which Yebu, the name means "elephant", was famous, was also well known for another trade—slaves. Black captives, brought here mainly from Punt by Asiatic dealers, could be seen everywhere. Most were naked, but a few wore *shenti* or loincloths, all were heavily fettered. Copper clamps, of four *nemset* in weight, were fastened around their ankles. Any attempt to escape and swim to freedom from the island, would be impossible. The heavy fetters would drag them down and they would drown.

After their supplies, to be taken back down-river, were loaded, they sailed to the small fort of Iken on the western bank of the river. The rest of the cargo, mostly military goods, was unloaded onto the already busy dock. The boat would return to the north, but for its passengers and for the next stage of their journey, they would have to travel overland.

Rakhmet stood on the dock holding onto his belongings. The other soldier detainees joined him, all looking bewildered. There was hardly any space left for additional cargo on the already crowded wharf. Rakhmet was still wondering where he would put the stuff, when some men, dressed in the garb of *an-tiu*, those who transverse the desert, approached him. The man was accompanied by a small entourage and a number of pack-animals, asses and one horse. The man, that seemed to be their leader, looked around, searching.

'I wish to see the master of this vessel,' he demanded brusquely.

Rakhmet pointed to the bow of the boat where the captain was giving instructions some men.

The man turned and shouted to the men, 'Okay, you can start loading the boat.'

'I am Nehesew,' he said, turned back toward Rakhmet. 'I am to conduct all of you across the next stretch of your journey,' he nodded towards the animals. 'Those are the asses you will need to carry your stuff. Choose one each, but choose wisely.

*You* will be leading him and will be responsible for the beast and the goods,' he laughed and walked off towards the horse.

Rakhmet had wondered why he thought it was funny, until they started loading their animals. The stubborn beasts milled and pranced about, kicking up dust that seemed to hang in the air forever. There was much confusion and cursing as the soldiers tried to steady the reluctant animals.

Finally, the caravan was organised and ready to depart. Rakhmet had secured his belongings, holding his beast's tether firmly in his grasp. He looked back, briefly, towards the boat that had been his home these past twenty days.

'Do you want something to drink?' Batu offered him an ox-bladder pouch freshly filled with beer. 'Ahead lays a hot dry trip through the desert.'

Rakhmet shook his head. Batu had been trying to befriend him ever since they left Waset, but he had no desire to acquaint himself with the man who was the cause of his dilemma.

'As you wish!' Batu shrugged and took a swig from the wooden spout. 'All the more for me.'

He plugged the opening with a stopper and slung the bag over his shoulder, resting the pouch on his hip, gave it an affectionate pat, grabbed the reins of his provisions-laden ass and started after the slow-moving caravan.

The hard-packed earth of the riverside area was soon left behind as the caravan made its way along a dirt track up a small hill. Beyond the ridge, they headed into the rocky terrain of the desert and gradually the stony ground gave way to sand. Nehesew came up, riding on horseback. Rakhmet stared in wonder. No one in Egypt, certainly not in the north, would *ride* on these animals.

'Why not *ride* the donkeys?' he laughed. 'That's what they're for!'

Horses were used to pull chariots but to sit atop of one, or an ass, was unheard of. Earlier, Rakhmet had been so busy trying to steady and load the animal, he never noticed, until now, the caravan leader riding the animal.

Nehesew shouted instructions for stragglers to move faster. 'Make haste…the hour is late!' he turned and headed for the front of the train.

Some of the men tried, tentatively, to mount the asses, but failed hopelessly, at first, but eventually, after many attempts, and falls, most, including Rakhmet, finally managed.

The going proved much more difficult than Rakhmet had anticipated. Walking on the soft sand was heavy going for man and beast. After hours of marching, they had covered just over an atur. The sun, already low when they reached a small hill, would soon be gone. On the hill, an outcrop of rock, a well-known landmark, in the shape of a toad, loomed ahead.

'The *Rock of Offerings*, sacred to Khnum,' Nehesew explained. 'He is the God of the Cataract.'

Rakhmet nodded and peered up the hill. Nehesew shouted a command, the caravan halted and spread out and prepared to camp for the night. Thorn-tree branches were collected and fashioned into crude, but serviceable fences against wild animals, lions, especially, abounded in these parts.

Rakhmet, grateful for the rest after the tedious journey, dismounted painfully and stretched his aching back.

'Kushites and Nubians call this area *Land of the Ghosts* and fear travelling alone,' Nehesew explained as they prepared the camp. 'They would often join caravans for safety. Merchants are often robbed, so they seek each other's company and camped together for the night,' he gestured to a group of men. 'There are several accompanying us. They joined us at Iken.' He then pointed to a lone traveller. 'That one is a tax collector. He is ostracised by most of the travellers and, although he camps with us, he will be on his own, well away from the others.'

Camp fires had been lit. It was not yet dark, but they were needed for warmth and light to organise the camp. Many huddled together around the fires, exchanging gossip. Some merchants, close enough for Rakhmet to hear their conversation, were showing off their wares and comparing their goods. One trader proudly displayed his cargo of sea sponges.

'These were brought all the way from *Uainn*, the land beyond *Uatch Ur,* the Great Green Waters.'

'Yes,' his companion answered. 'They would fetch high prices in Nubia.'

'Sponges?' A third enquired. 'Of what use would they be in a dry land?'

'They are used in the gold-workings there,' the first merchant explained. 'Some of the finest gold comes from Nubia. Even the name *Nubia*, comes from the Egyptian word, *nub* for gold.' He took a sponge from his supplies to demonstrate. 'The gold ore is crushed and powdered, water is washed over it to remove the unwanted material, and the gold dust, being heavier, would settle on the bottom of wooden sorting tables. The sponges are then used to extract the remaining mud and water, leaving the gold dust behind.'

'Yes,' the second merchant announced gleefully. 'We are sure to make a very handsome profit from them.'

Nehesew came over to where the soldiers were camped. 'This is a place for offerings. If any of you wish to pay homage to your gods, go up to that rock,' he announced, pointing to the rocky outcrop. 'When you have done, hasten back to the shelter as soon as possible. It is not safe here.'

Rakhmet had no wish to pay homage to any gods, but went up to the rock anyway. He wanted to stretch his aching legs after that uncomfortable ride, and also to study the surrounding terrain before it became too dark. The rock was covered with countless inscriptions from earlier travellers and even bore the names of a few kings. The name, Amenhotep, had been added to them, but it had been defaced.

'Even here!' he muttered bitterly to himself. 'Even here Akhenaten's troops of destruction had been!'

Far in the distance, on the eastern side of the hills, the Nile wound its lazy way to the sea. Just visible in the dusk, the dark shape of the island of Yebu could be seen. Thin curls of smoke rose from countless cooking fires, and spread out like a ghostly shawl, over the city. The high cliffs on either side of the river contained the acrid air, preventing the smoke to dissipate.

His thought turned to Menefer, and he wondered what she would be doing at that very moment—helping her mother with the evening meal perhaps? Would she be thinking of him as well?

Some of his fellow travellers were still at prayer at the rock and he caught a few phrases from the Hymn to Aten. From the camp fires, the faint fragrance of roasting meat wafted up to him. He sighed and started back towards the camp.

'Didn't come here to worship, did you?' Rakhmet turned to see Batu watching him.

'No!' Rakhmet answered curtly and again started for the camp.

'Rakhmet, I've been trying to speak to you before, tried to apologise, but you have been avoiding me. I know I did wrong. I know it was my fault for getting you into this mess, but give me a chance to make amends.'

Rakhmet looked at him coldly without answering. Far in the distance, a hyena gave a hysterical whooping laugh, a perfect response to Batu's words.

'Rakhmet, please. I am sorry for what had happened. I was drunk and—'

'That seems to be your condition most of your waking hours!' Rakhmet sneered.

'I know.' He dropped his head and his entire body seemed to sag, 'For this too, I am sorry.'

'Look, Batu!' Rakhmet jabbed a finger into Batu's chest. 'You bring misfortune. I do not wish to have you near. We have been sentenced…banished, to serve in the same god-forsaken place. I hope to make my term there as agreeable as possible so it will pass speedily.' He stabbed at Batu with his finger again. 'With you around, it will not! I therefore wish to avoid your company. Is that clear enough? If you want to please me, then do the same!' Rakhmet straightened and strode down to the camp.

Before dawn the next morning, a soul-shaking blast from a ram's horn trumpet roused the camp, which quickly came to life. After a hasty meal of gritty bread, goat's milk cheese, onions and dates, the men razed the camp, rounded up and packed the complaining animals and carts, with only a few braving riding again. Most of the men, including Rakhmet, chose to walk this time. The caravan set off on its way again along the ancient road south-west, veering away from the river. The going became a little better now, as the road had been paved in places in earlier times.

\*\*\*

After a hasty meal mid-day, Menefer hurried to the *Sbau*, the place of learning. Her first session had finish just before noon, but she wanted to prepare some tablets for her next lesson. Minares, the Scibe of the Gate, the *Sbai*, the instructor, was getting his lessons ready for his afternoon session, teaching the princesses reading and writing.

'I'm sorry to interrupt,' Menefer apologised. 'I just was to get a few things ready that I had forgotten.' She collected some brushes and packed them into a small woven basket.

'Go right ahead,' Minares said, rearranging some tablets. 'I hear your lessons are most popular and the princesses love them. Their skills with line-work and proportions had greatly improved since you started.' He unpacked some scrolls and tablets from a sturdy leather case, his pudgy arms jiggling with the action. 'Why don't you join us for our session? If you have nothing else to do…?'

She had just consented to stay a while, when Minares's pupils arrived.

The two younger princesses, Sherit and Nefer, also attending Minares's lessons but were not very skilled yet. They were given simple symbols to copy. Minares would draw a symbol on a shard, and the princesses would copy it in red, not always too successfully. The older girls were made to copy text from classic works in *sekh shat*, a stylised form of script, much simpler than the elaborate Holy Script used on temples and monuments.

Menefer, remembering her own schooling and the endless text she had to copy, took pity on the Princesses. It was not always pleasant. It took her five years to learn just the basics, but she was lucky. Not all Egyptians know how to read or write. Schooling can be costly and only those with means can afford to send their children to school, and even then, school was mainly for boys.

Instead of sitting idly, waiting for Minares to complete his instructions, she decided to see if the paints were ready. For her next lesson, after Minares', the princesses would work in *nechit*, painting in colours. She had taught them how to grind and prepare the paints and inks, but to save time, she had requested someone to prepare them for her. She was told to approach Khay, the Royal Scribe, who had offered—or was instructed—to mix the paints.

Minares directed her to the Audience Chamber where she found Khay at the foot of the dais, his usual place, preparing some clay tablets. He was much younger than she had expected. Instead of a middle-aged man, like Minares, Kay was about twenty years of age. His head was shaved and he was bare-chested with a simple collar around his neck. He wore a white kilt of a stiffened material, and sat on a flat cushion with his legs crossed, stretching the skirt with his knees to create a very functional working table. A little woven reed table next to him served as a place for his tools. He had been reading some clay tablets, with strange wedge-shaped symbols on them, and was about to reply to them on prepared damp-clay tablets, when she interrupted.

Khay smiled pleasantly as she approached. He had a very wide, attractive smile. 'You must be Menefer. I hear all about you.' She greeted him and stated her reason for her visit. 'Oh, yes,' he replied with a sly smile. 'The colours! For a moment, I had hoped you had come to seek my company.'

Menefer laughed softly. 'We had never even met, until now.'

'Well, I hope, now that we had, we can see more of each other,' he handed her a woven reed basket containing a number of stoppered pottery jars with the ready-mixed paints.

'Yes, I would like that,' she said, taking the basket and started back, 'as soon as I have free time.'

'Go that way!' he called out, directing her to a side door. 'It is shorter.'

She nodded and started walking along the passage. It was the very one Hatiay, Overseer of the Royal household, had spoken of, when she first arrived. Every wall was covered with paintings. She recognised Ipuky's style—almost comical elongated figures of the Royal Family with exaggerated bean-shaped heads, balanced on long spindly necks. To her, they looked so odd, compared to her father's elegant, traditional style.

Minares had finished his lessons by the time she arrived and the princesses were taking a short break before their drawing and painting lessons with Menefer would start again. A large basket was delivered, that contained a pile of broken shards of pottery, broken plates and tiles, for practice drawings.

They had three session daily. In the first, Menefer taught them how to draw the correct proportions of figure. It was very important to keep every object to their correct proportions. A figure was drawn first, then onto it, a grid was drawn. This grid was also used to enlarge the drawing and copy it, exactly to scale, onto a wall.

A human figure measured three Royal cubits, and this scale was used as measurement for the drawing. The bottom of the feet to the hairline was subdivided into an eighteen unit grid. When the figure is drawn, the knee would always be drawn on the sixth line from the bottom, the chin on the second line from the hairline, the elbow would be on the sixth line from the hairline, the waist on the seventh, and so on.

That morning, each student had to draw a figure, in charcoal, on shards of pottery and broken plates and tiles. Each figure was then copied onto thin slabs of slate. Senpa did an excellent job, and obviously had a talent for drawing. Merit was good, but struggled a bit with fine detail, but the others were just messing around and just enjoyed themselves, doing their drawings their own way. Setenpenre's figure was merely a stick-figure and her "grid" was a complete failure. She gave up after discarding several shards of pottery, and then amused herself by just scribbling.

That afternoon, the elder three students busied themselves, outlining their drawings carefully in a light coloured ink, then paint it in full colour, and lastly, outline it in black ink. The charcoal would then be wiped off, leaving the neat completed image.

The princesses were pleased with the results and looked forward to more lessons in painting in colours.

***

The first ten days, Menefer's first week as tutor, passed quickly. She was eager to see her family and hurried home for her break and her family was interested to hear all about her experiences. During the evening meal, she related, in great detail, little incidents that occurred during her first week, amusing them with little anecdotes, like Princess Setenpenre calling her Mellifer; her meeting with Prince Smenkhare and the tiresome temple ceremonies. Then, as she mentioned the quarrel between the king and queen, Thutmose suddenly became very interested.

'Royal quarrel?' he urged Menefer to try and remember more of the details.

'Now, why would you be interested in hearing about other people's quarrels?' Mutnames scowled at her husband. 'Everyone disagrees at one time or another, why should not Royalty? Do not pry!' She started cleared the table and carried some platters and goblets to the cooking place.

'Old woman, it is more serious than you think,' he called after her, then turned to his daughter. 'Tell me about it.'

Menefer gave a brief account of the argument. Thutmose looked around to make certain the servants were not within earshot and leaned over. 'Lord Nakht mentioned certain happenings at court. He suspects someone is conspiring against Pharaoh and heard rumours that someone, other than Pharaoh, was writing to Aziro. He tried to investigate but it had come to naught. I think he would be most interested in hearing about what you heard.'

Thutmose then invited Lord Nakht to come over, telling him he had some news that the Court Advisor might find interesting. Nakht arrived shortly, breathless and curious.

'I am sorry that Thutmose dragged you over, Nakht,' Mutnames apologised as she let him in. 'I am sure he is making a big thing out of nothing.'

'Let Nakht judge for himself, woman!' Thutmose replied, annoyed. They seated themselves and sent for Menefer to join them. 'Nakht, Menefer overheard a quarrel between Pharaoh and Nefertiti, and they mentioning Aziro and Ribaddi!'

'We keep getting conflicting stories about Aziro,' Nakht explained after Menefer had joined them and they greeted each other.

'Tell me as much as you can remember, child.'

She repeated all she could remember.

'Yes,' Nakht rubbed his cheek. 'I was present when Pharaoh received those letters, but was not able to read them myself. Apparently, Aziro claims to be loyal to Pharaoh, but, from other letters, it seems he had attacked some of our provinces! No one seems to know the truth. We can only go by what Lord Tutu says. I have no proof of Aziro's loyalty and cannot get access to the tablets. Lord Tutu, as Overseer of Foreign Affairs, has them in his care.' Nakht hesitated, deep in thought for a moment. 'If I can just get my hand on the actual letters—Lord Tutu's translations always seemed rather vague, and as the letters are written in the script of the East, not everyone can read them.'

'You are a high court official. Why cannot you just ask to see them?'

'That is not as easy as it seems, Thutmose. Tutu receives all foreign correspondence. He translates them for Pharaoh as His Majesty cannot read their strange wedge-shaped writings, they are then stored in a vault at the records offices. Only he, and those directly involved in the business of Foreign Affairs, may enter. We can only go by what he chooses to tell us.'

'What about the scribe? It is his duty to store the tablets. Could you not approach him?' Menefer asked.

'Yes, but I still need a good reason to inspect them, Menefer. Khay is under a strict oath. If I show interest in foreign correspondence that does not concern me, he will be suspicious and...' Nakht pulls the corners of his mouth down, and shrugs, splaying his hands.

'I see him frequently. He prepares the inks and paints for my lessons and we have become friends, maybe I can persuade—'

'No, no. Out of the question! You cannot just obtain official documents through *persuasion*. He will get suspicious and alert someone. Whoever is plotting against Pharaoh could suspect someone is investigating and—who knows...' Nakht again, did not finish the sentence and everyone could guess what might happen. He gave another helpless shrug.

'No, it is much too dangerous.' He waved his hands in a negative gesture. 'All I can ask is that you keep your eyes and ears open. Perhaps you might stumble onto something that could help us uncover the conspiracy, if indeed there is one.'

'I will do what I can to help, Lord Nakht. What about Djenna? I heard Queen Tiye had corresponded with Aziro. Would she not be able to...?'

'No, I'm afraid she would not be of much help,' he shook his head. 'Queen Tiye's house is well away from the official chambers, and the queen's dealings with Aziro had been during the reign of the third Amenhotep. From Djenna, we hear only servant's gossip, nothing of any importance.'

'When I saw the scribe recently, he had some clay tablets and he seemed to be writing a reply to one of them…in that same strange wedge-type writing of Asia you mentioned…'

Nakht suddenly brightened. 'Yes, those must be some of the letters!' He clenched a fist in the air before him. 'If only I can get my hands on some of them.'

'Do you read *metu ra en Kamp-t*, the *words of the mouth* of the Asians, Lord Nakht?' Thutmose asked curiously.

'I do. Read and speak it. I studied the stars under the guidance of an Eastern prophet from *Aamt-t*. He taught me much…but,' he turned to Menefer, 'as I said child, do not do anything. It is much too risky. Just watch and listen—no more. I will be most pleased to hear of anything of interest.'

'I will do so, Lord Nakht. I promise not to do anything foolish.'

*\*\*\**

On her way back to *Per nesu*, Menefer's thoughts were on the clay tablets. She had decided to do more than just watch and listen. There must be a way to secretly get hold of one of those clay tablets…but how?

An opportunity arrived sooner than she had expected. Princess Merit had expressed a desire to learn how to fashion figurines in clay and Menefer, again, approached Khay for some of the material. He had been looking forward to seeing her and was most eager to assist.

'Certainly. It will be a pleasure. I keep a ready supply.' He held up a thick cylinder of rolled soft clay which he was about to slice into cakes. 'You can have some of this,' as he prepared the clay for her, softening it with water and kneading it, she noticed he had some letters ready to be fired.

'Are those your replies?' she pointed.

'Yes. I was about to wrap each in a thin envelope of clay and press a seal into it. No one can read them without breaking the seal.'

'Oh, how clever!' she exclaimed, and flattered, he smiled broadly.

She noticed two tablets with their broken envelopes, lying on a tray on the table. He saw her looking at them and answered her unasked question.

'I see you are interested in the tablets,' Khay smiled and gestured. 'These are recent letters we received. I have already replied to them, so they are ready to be stored in the magazine vault.'

'Oh…uh,' Menefer had to think of an excuse to handle them. 'Uh, yes! I'm curious about that writing—it is very strange. I have never seen anything like it before.'

'It is a much simpler way to write than ours,' Khay took a piece of soft clay and pressed a shaped stick into it, making several combinations of the wedges. He held it up for her to see.

'Your name, in the *words of the mouth* of Amurra!'

'Fascinating.'

She took the clay impression. 'Can you teach me to read this?'

'It is not that simple. You need to learn the language before you can understand the writing.'

While he was explaining, she casually kneaded a piece of clay he had given her. She kept asking questions for him to explain, to distract him. She picked up one of the letters, ostensibly to study it and quickly pressed the clay onto it.

'How long will it take to learn?' she asked as she examined the original tablet. 'I really wish to learn this form of writing. It looks so very…elegant, don't you think?'

He agreed and, as he showed her a few more examples, she quickly pocketed the piece of clay with the imprint into a fold in her tunic when he had his head turned away and replaced the original tablet.

'I would love to come and see you again so we can talk,' she gathered up the clay he had prepared for her and started to leave. 'Unfortunately, I have to get back. The princesses are awaiting my return.'

Khay smiled that wonderful broad smile again and happily helped her with her load. 'Yes, I would like that very much. I'm looking forward to it.'

Khay had always considered himself rather plain, and to have a beautiful girl, like Menefer, paying him so much attention, flattered him. Up to that moment, he had only dreamt of someone, like her, seeking his company. Now his dream had seemed to come true and he eagerly anticipated their next meeting.

He smiled to himself and pressed his hand to his chest, where he could feel his heart beating wildly. He was totally enamoured of the young artist.

Menefer too, smiled to herself. Things were working out fine and Lord Nakht would be so pleased. Being a spy was much easier than she had imagined.

# Chapter Eight
## The Belly of Stone

The ancient overland route lay beyond the first cataract. It led them well west of the river then turned almost due south where the river curved away to the east. The territory between the first and second cataracts had been the buffer zone between Kush, Punt and Egypt. Nubians and Kushites needed special permission to travel this road. Egypt had to enforce this rule strictly as the Black Land had once been invaded by Hittites. Nubian kings sat on the throne of Egypt for generations afterwards until, one hundred years earlier, Pharaoh Thutmose drove them back. Once again, an Egyptian Pharaoh ruled Egypt and he made an oath that Kemet will never again be ruled by them.

To prevent another such an invasion, a series of forts had been built along the route on both sides of the river. Traffic, both on land and water was strictly controlled. Only those with official business or on special trading missions were allowed to pass. Accompanying this caravan, were several Kushites who had traded at Yebu and were now returning home with their wares.

In spite of the cold season, it started getting very hot as the blazing sun rose higher.

'The heat from the ground is burning through my sandals. I envy the Kushites,' Rakhmet complained, watching those walking just ahead of him. 'They wear no shoes and yet seem not to feel the heat.'

'Yes,' Amseti, the Overseer, agreed. 'I marvel at how they can cope with the hot sands. I often wonder how they fared in the season of Shomu when the sun is at its full fury.'

'Perhaps, from countless journeys, their feet had become hardened to these harsh conditions,' Rakhmet spread his arms wide, 'and can walk through these burning sands with apparent ease.'

Suddenly, he noticed a change in their demeanour. It had not been the hot sand that had disturbed them and their animals, but something else. 'The beasts seemed agitated.'

Then the *An-tui*, the Dwellers of the Desert, hurriedly undid some of their bundles and removed lengths of cloth. They gesticulated to the other travellers around them to do the same. Their distant voices sounded anxious and there seemed to be an urgency in the tone, but they were too far way and Rakhmet could not hear what they said. One of the Kushites raced towards them, shouting and gesticulating wildly. Only when the man pointed to something behind the soldiers, did one of them turn. His eyes widened.

'Sandstorm!' Amseti shouted.

Rakhmet spun around. Bearing down on them was an immense orange-yellow cloud that stretched from horizon to horizon.

Then pandemonium broke out as others too, saw the approaching storm. The warning shouts of the men, alarm cries of the beasts, banging and the clanking of cooking utensils and tools, dulled any other sounds as the men rushed to get clothing, scarves or heavy fabric to protect themselves and their animals. The beasts, already frightened by the approaching storm and sensing the sudden alarm of the men, became more agitated and panicked. They milled around, causing confusion and chaos. Some broke free and bolted, scattering their cargo as they went, pursued by cursing men.

Nehesew, the caravan leader, knew of such storms and was prepared. He removed several lengths of fabric and cloth-bags from his belongings and gave some to Rakhmet and Amseti.

'Get to high ground,' he urged. 'But avoid the highest areas. Find a boulder and shield behind it,' he instructed the travellers, 'try and get the pack animals to lie down. Place a bag or cloth over the head of the animal and sit on its lee side.'

There was some confusion as men struggled with their protesting beasts for a while, but finally they were able to calm the panicked animals.

'Now, wrap the cloth about your heads…thus.' He went up and down the caravan, instructing and assisting his charges.

Everyone quickly followed suite. Eventually they succeeded and took refuge behind their prostrate animals.

The first gust of wind tugged at his clothing, it was followed immediately by a blast that nearly blew off his cloth hood. The wind seemed to die down, then started up again with a vengeance. It increased in strength until it howled around him like a soul in torment. The panic-stricken cries of animals and shouting of men were lost in the furious wail of the storm. The ass struggled to rise but Rakhmet forced it down again. The swirling sand had completely obscured Nehesew and the rest of the caravan and he couldn't see anything but the blinding, shrieking yellow haze around him. The sand seemed to get into his eyes, nose mouth and ears and he closed the gap in his hood.

Articles that were not secured were blown away. A heavy copper vessel rattled off down the road but Rakhmet dared not look as sand stung his face. Men, who left their secure positions to retrieve their possessions, were blown off their feet. Rakhmet was almost winded when someone collided into his back, then tumbled right over him, arms flailing. The man grabbed at him, frantically clawing for a secure hold. Unable to see, his attempts were futile and he was propelled along helplessly.

The fury of the wind drove the sand with such force that all exposed skin stung, but Rakhmet dared not move to cover any bare areas. He covered his face and head with his arms, as, even with the wrapped cloth around his head, sand still penetrated. He had to pinch his eyelids and lips tight to prevent sand from getting in.

The relentless blast of sand continued for what seemed like an eternity. Gradually, as sand built up against his body, the stinging sensation against his bare skin eased until sand-drifts almost covered him. He wondered if anyone had ever suffocated, buried beneath the sand. He understood why someone would panic and run, as he too, was beginning to feel anxious.

The storm seemed never-ending. He was beginning to wonder just how much longer it would last, when, just as sudden as it had started, the wind dropped and the wailing ceased. The storm had passed.

For a while no one moved, expecting the fury to start afresh. The howling became a distant roar. Slowly, yellow-grey, like spirits rising from their graves, men and beast emerged from their individual drifts. Sand had managed to penetrate everywhere, in their hair and inside their clothing. Nostrils and ears were clogged and even managed to get into some eyes and closed mouths. It poured forth from garments, as they were unfastened. Everywhere, men and beast coughed and sneezed.

Once they had rid themselves, their baggage and clothing, of sand, they went to retrieve their scattered possessions. Whoever had rolled over him during the storm, remained a mystery, but Batu emerged from a pile of sand on the other side of the road, ten cubits away from where he had crouched down before the storm struck.

The orange-yellow cloud receded into the distance towards the south-east, but the roar was no longer audible. The effect of the sandstorm had changed the scenery. Drifts of sand had piled high against boulders and new dunes had formed that completely obscured the road.

The pack animals were once again loaded and baggage secured. A quick assessment was made of any injuries that might have occurred, and the caravan started moving again. The going was difficult in places as the travellers' feet sank deep into the soft sand that now covered parts of the paved road.

Lower Nubia was a bleak, inhospitable place. All about them were bare granite boulders and sand.

Rakhmet sighed and mumbled to no one in particular, 'I long for home. This place is fit only for lizards, snakes and scorpions.'

'I agree.' Nehesew looked about him, 'But I am accustomed to it.'

'Do you not long for the green valleys with groves of palms, willow and sycamore trees, forests of papyri along the river, waving their plumes in the breeze; villas, with enclosed courtyards, gardens with shrubs, fruit trees and flowers?' Rakhmet waved his arm about. 'Here, nothing grows.'

'I do, sometimes, but I make a good living. I like the solitude, the open spaces, rather than being confined in crowded cities.'

'How much further before we return to the river? It has been two days since the storm.'

'Soon.' Nehesew pointed to some low hills in the distance. 'The caravan should be turning towards the river any time now. That is where the Nile and this track, the *Great Nubian Way* once again meet.'

As they neared a pass through the hills, the animals could smell water and started moving faster. The soldiers too, became more light-hearted and looked forward to the boat journey. The last part of their march to the river proved a little rough. The caravan wound its way along a narrow wadi down the cliff, past boulders and down steep banks. Soon the river lay before them, like a giant silver snake, slithering between the boulders and cliffs towards the Great Green Waters far to the north. A small village, surrounded by a few scattered palms trees, hugged the shore, and just beyond, two boats lay at anchor.

'Are those for us?' Rakhmet asked Amseti, and nodded his head towards the river. 'The boats we will travel on?'

'Yes, they are squatter and wider than those used further north, these are almost as wide as they are long. They have no keel and have a very shallow draught, to make it easier for us to manoeuvre over the cataracts.'

'Manoeuvre? You mean, we are to drag them ourselves?'

'Yes, except them!' Amseti jerked a thumb towards the merchants. 'They're paying passengers.'

The caravan reached the village and the boats were loaded.

A few merchants, the tax collector and a government envoy, and of course, Amseti, would accompany the soldiers by water, but some of the other travellers remained with the caravan train. After a brief rest, Nehesew bid them a good journey, and leading the caravan, headed inland again to continue along the route to an oasis.

The next few days were uneventful and the dull scenery made the boat trip monotonous. Sand dunes, granite cliffs, boulders and more sand dunes slid slowly past. Occasionally a tiny village or temple would come into view, then recede into the distance behind them.

At Faras, a town close to the second cataract, they broke their journey for cargo to be off-loaded and fresh provisions brought on board. The passengers had a chance to stroll around the small marketplace and enjoyed the opportunity to stretch their legs on solid ground. Amseti allowed the soldiers some freedom, as here, there was little likelihood of any of them deserting—there was just no place to go. The boats were rather cramped and afforded little room for exercise, except for the soldiers' occasional stint at the oars when the wind dropped.

The next morning, they boarded the boats again and continued upstream. By late afternoon they reached the second cataract, a place called the "Belly of Stone". In past ages, great boulders had broken free from the towering cliffs and crashed into the river, strewing the riverbed with rocks.

'This is where we will have to start hauling the boats over them,' Amseti remarked. 'When the river is low, as it is now, navigation around the rocks are hazardous and in places, impossible to skirt the obstructions,' he started to strip. 'You best do the same,' he suggested. 'Wear a *qerf-t* to protect your head from the heat of the sun. It gets hot.'

Rakhmet stripped down to his *shenti*. While he was binding the head-cloth, more soldiers arrived. They were mostly Nubian.

'This area is notorious for bandits,' Amseti nodded towards the cataract. 'These soldiers are for extra protection and to help with the boats. They are from the nearby garrison of Argin.'

Their weapons were the normal cowhide shields and spears, but they also had strange bows made from antelope horns. The soldiers stripped naked for the task and so did many of helpers that came with them. Not very much later, Rakhmet regretted his decision of not stripping completely. The rocks were slippery and falls were frequent. Soon, from the soaking and scraping against the rocks, his shenti had been shredded. He removed it and he tied it around his head for protection from the blazing sun. Woven cloth was not cheap, so instead of discarding the torn garment, he hoped that, somehow, later, he could mend it.

Hauling the boats was hard work. More often than not, it seemed that for every five cubits forward, the boat dragged them back three. The going was slow, the water cold and cuts, bruises and scrapes, common.

At sundown, they had only travelled halfway through the second cataract. Another four lay ahead. The air had become cold by the time they made camp on the riverbank. After changing into dry garments, the men huddled together around camp fires for warmth. Only the paying passengers were in a merry mood. Almost everyone else complained of aching muscles, sore limbs and scraped skin. Those who had foolishly worn garments during their labours, hung them, wet and torn, close to the fires to dry. They will not do so again the following day.

Wood was scarce and only small fires could be built, but not enough to keep them warm for very long. A cold wind sprung up and Rakhmet folded his blanket double for extra warmth, drew his legs up and wrapped himself in it. Batu, sitting opposite him, on the far side of the fire, had nothing to cover himself.

Rakhmet, trying to take his mind of his aching limbs, closed his eyes to dream of better days. Every muscle felt like it had been pummelled raw. A cold wind blew down his back, making it difficult to fall asleep. Amseti was already asleep, nearby, and snoring loudly.

Then the image of Batu, shivering, invaded his thoughts. That vision made it worse for him to sleep. He tried to force himself to think of other things— Menefer—it would be her sixteenth birthday soon, the day their betrothal would have been announced. Again, Batu's image intruded and he opened his eyes.

Batu looked pathetic. *Serves him right*, he thought. *He deserves it.* He closed his eyes again, wondering if Batu had also been torn away from a loved one? *But why should I care? Batu had brought this on himself!*

Through the weak flames of the dying fire, he again watched Batu's miserable form and gave in to compassion.

'Batu!' he called out, a little angry at his own weakness.

At the call of his name, Batu looked up and stared, amazed, as Rakhmet opened his blanket into a single layer and signalled to him to come over.

Batu hesitated a moment, bewildered, and Rakhmet signalled again. He went over, and accepted the offered portion of the blanket, but, still apprehensive, kept his distance.

'If you move closer we will both be warmer.'

Batu huddled closer and with their combined body warmth, managed to ward off most of the biting cold from the steady blowing north wind.

'Where are your things, your sleeping mat?'

'I lost all my possessions during the sandstorm. I was unable to find anything afterwards,' Batu wiped at his eyes. 'I did not expect any kindness from you for what I have done. You are indeed a good friend.'

'Batu, I pitied you because of your discomfort and will share what I can with you, but I am *not* your friend, do you understand!'

'I… I understand,' hurt, but grateful for Rakhmet's deed, Batu vowed to repay him, somehow, for everything. He closed his eyes and fell into a fitful sleep.

\*\*\*

The house bustled with servants preparing food and drink, and Thutmose and Mutnames were constantly interrupted for advice—they were asked to judge the quality of the wines, the consistency of the beer, the freshness of the waterfowl, the perfume of wax cones or the fragrance of oils that guests would rub on themselves.

At sunset, the feasting began. A fire had been lit in a central fireplace against the cold of the night air. Soft music from flutes, harps and a lute floated on the air, heady with incense. As the chamber heated and became more comfortable, the merry-making increased. Naked dancing girls performed and servants rushed back and fro with trays of food and drink. Guests sated themselves on the variety of delicacies and beer and many soon became sick from over-indulging, which was considered a great compliment to the host.

'Behold, my daughter, Menefer,' Thutmose announced proudly. 'On this, her sixteenth year, she had become indeed, a fine young woman. With her appointment with Their Majesties, she had already fulfilled all our hopes and dreams, and can only improve on it. After the births of our two fine sons, Nebaten and Ipuky, we longed for a daughter and my good wife made an offering to Bes.'

He gestured to Menefer, 'Bes accepted her offerings and granted our prayers, and tonight, the twenty fifth day of the month of Phamenat, sixteen years later, we celebrate our daughter's coming-of-age. She is now a woman full grown. Her childhood toys will be packed away and she will be given a dowry.'

Her father continued extolling her virtues, but Menefer was not listening. Her thoughts were elsewhere—*speaking to herself without words*—reflecting over what could have been. She was thinking of Rakhmet again, and it brought tears to her eyes. She quickly wiped them away lest her parents or guests should see.

'Menefer?' Mutnames seemed concerned and touched her daughter's arm lightly. 'You seem far away. Are you all right?'

'Yes mother. I am fine,' she lied.

'Lord Nakht and his family had arrived.' Mutnames and Thutmose greeted their guests and escorted them to a wall-bench. Djenna led Menefer to a secluded corner and Djenna immediately started to glorify her position at court.

'I'm sorry I've not been so visit you yet, Menefer, my chores of looking after Queen Tiye's garments is a full-time task. I wish you could see…'

Menefer nodded and thought, *Yes, it must be such a task, stitching and mending all those garments*. Then out loud, 'Yes I wager it must be.'

'Well, Her Majesty had ordered another complete wardrobe change for the next season. Shomu and Akhet are far too hot for her here, she said, and all her garments are…'

'Excuse me, Djenna, I must talk to your mother and father for a moment.'

'Oh! Yes, certainly. I'll amuse myself…somehow,' miffed at being snubbed, Djenna went off to find Ipuky.

'Welcome, Lady Susmaat, Lord Nakht. I'm sorry Djenna dragged me away so quickly. I'm glad you could attend.'

'Menefer! Aten's blessing upon you,' Susmaat answered.

'And may the gods smile on you,' Nakht added as Menefer greeted them.

'Lord Nakht, could I see you privately?'

Nakht excused himself and Menefer directed him to the roof, a favoured retreat where the family could escape the heat of summer. Lord Nakht had made himself comfortable on one of the couches. 'Well, what have you heard? Anything of interest?'

'Not heard, but I have something for you.'

From a hiding place behind an urn, Menefer removed a clay object, wrapped in a piece of cloth and handed it to him.

Carefully, he unwrapped it and studied the clay tablet.

'This is wonderful!' his look of delight turned to concern.

'I told you not to try and get one of these…it is much too dangerous. How did you…?'

Menefer laughed softly, interrupting him.

'It's a copy. I made an impression of a section of the original, and, when it had dried, I used that to make this positive image, then had it baked in one of our kilns.'

'Amazing. Yes, it is a part of a letter.' He tilted it to read in the light of the moon, but found it too difficult and took it over to the stairs where a torch was burning in a sconce. In the flickering light, he read the letter and frowned.

'Is the impression clear enough, Lord Nakht? Some detail is usually lost when one makes copies.'

'Yes, I can read the message,' he gestures. 'It is not the quality that disturbs me, but the content…it is as I had suspected. I was present when Lord Tutu was discussing this incident with the king, but his translation of it, is not what is written here,' Lord Nakht inhaled deeply and looked up into the starry sky. 'Unfortunately, it is not the complete letter, but even so, this is very damning. He is deceiving the king…deliberately misleading him.'

'His Majesty needs to know about this.' Nakht turned and looked at Menefer, 'I will, of course, not reveal how this came into my possession.'

They returned to the feast and Djenna stormed up to Menefer.

'So!' Her face flushed. 'Ipuky told me something very interesting!'

'About what?'

'Have you nothing to say?' Djenna flung her open hands wide.

'I don't know what you are talking about, Djenna'

'You and someone else!'

'Someone else? …What do you mean?'

'Don't act all innocent with me, Menefer,' Djenna straightened. 'You have been seeing somebody, privately!'

Menefer laughed, making Djenna even more furious. 'Djenna, it is someone I need to contact for my lessons, that is all.'

'In the garden? At night…in the dark? What are you up to?'

'Uh…that!' she thought Djenna had been referring to Khay, but it seemed Ipuki had mentioned her meeting with Prince Smenkhare. 'I'm *up to* nothing! I happened to be in the garden when he arrived. Mere chance—nothing else!'

'Well, I certainly hope so!'

Djenna stormed off, leaving Menefer bewildered. Djenna must have thought she and Prince Smenkhare were meeting in secret. Would she really think there was something other than friendship, between them, a *servant* and a *prince*?

***

75

'What do you mean "Lord Tutu had not been honest" with me, Lord Nakht?'

Nakht straightened up after he had prostrated himself before Pharaoh, and smoothed his kilt.

'Your Majesty, your Royal Chamberlain told Your Majesty to ignore Ribbadi, calling him "a whining beggar", but Lord Tutu had seemed to cover up a very real threat from Abdeshirta and Aziru. Instead of "taking care" of the matter himself, as Lord Tutu suggested, he had made matters worse. Instead of gaining Your Majesty's support for the country's defence, he gave Ribbadi the impression that Byblos was unimportant and to be ignored. Then, when Simyra had been invaded, Lord Tutu made it appear that Ribbadi blamed Your Majesty for complacency and thus gave Your Majesty the impression that Ribbadi was the villain.'

Furious, Akhenaten immediately summoned a bewildered Lord Tutu before the council.

'Lord Tutu, I demand an explanation!' Pharaoh read Lord Nakht's translation.

Vexed at first, Tutu's calmed and composed himself and requested a brief respite before answering the accusations. He was a good Ambassador and also a very clever diplomat and could talk his way clear of any situation. During the council's brief recess, he instructed Kenti, his servant to retrieve the original tablet, giving him time to formulate his defence.

Presently, Kenti arrived. A council was resumed and Lord Nakht was summoned. Tutu approached King Akhenaten.

'Your Majesty,' he cleared his throat. 'I realise I did not translate the letter word for word. Briefly, Ribbadi, Your Majesty's vizier of Gebal was having trouble with one of the local princes and requested funds and stock to ease the situation.' He gestured towards Lord Nakht, contemptuously, '...as Lord Nakht can verify.'

Tutu held the copy of the tablet to the light. 'This copy of the letter Lord Nakht presented, is not complete, but most of the message is there. I will now read the original as it is written. Ribbadi writes...' He cleared his throat again and read the letter. '..."*Now Abdeshirta is marching with his brethren, March against him and smite him. This land is the land of the King. Since I have written thus, and you did nothing, the city of Simyra has been lost. There is no money to buy horses. All is finished. We are ruined.*"'

He turned to Lord Nakht and gave him the tablet. 'Is not what I have just read, the true contents of the letter?'

Nakht nodded. 'Yes, it is so.'

Tutu turned to Akhenaten triumphantly and smiled. 'Your Majesty, as I recall, I said it was a trifling matter, and I can deal with it. Aziro had, more than once, proclaimed his loyalty to Your Majesty. Yes, he and his father, Abdeshirta, *had* taken several cities in Phoenicia, but in *your* name, Sire. This he had done for Egypt,' he gestured broadly.

'These cities were breeding rebellion and he had crushed them. This letter from Ribbadi,' he waved the tablet around, 'is not so much concerned with the so-called fall of Simyra, as it is with Ribbadi's own treasury. All he wants are money, men and horses...for his own needs and protection for his own coffers!'

Tutu waves his hand in the general direction of Asia. 'Your Majesty knows how many others had begged for gold. The king of Mitanni believes that, in Egypt, gold is as common as dust and ours is a land of gold. They all *want*, but none *give*!'

He paused again for the words to sink in. Murmurs of agreement from the council encouraged him and he continued. 'I did not wish to burden Your Majesty with Ribbadi's begging request,' he lifted his shoulders and opened his arms wide in a supplicant gesture. 'Because, after all, Majesty, that is what they are! Beggars! I have therefore taken it upon myself, in Your Majesty's name, and dismissed their requests. That is all, Your Majesty…I have spoken.'

He bowed low and retired to his place in the council.

'Can you fault any of this, Lord Nakht?' Akhenaten looked at Nakht, sternly.

Nakht, not too familiar with foreign matters or of any detailed knowledge of the others correspondence, shook his head. 'No, Your Majesty.'

Akhenaten had heard the answer, but wanted to make certain everyone else did too. 'I did not hear you, Lord Nakht! Speak up!'

'No, Your Majesty!' he repeated in a loud voice. 'I do not fault any of what Tutu had said.'

'Then the matter is closed!' Akhenaten got up and walked off, briskly. Everyone scrambled to their feet and saluted.

Tutu glanced at Nakht, smirking, and left the chamber, leaving Nakht humiliated and embarrassed.

'You slipped through the net, this time, Lord Tutu,' Nakht muttered under his breath. 'But, the matter is not closed! I will be more vigilant in future! Be assured, I will yet discover the truth!'

# Chapter Nine
## Attack

The rapids were stronger and wilder than those of the previous days and hauling the boats became more difficult. The vessels were swept back many times in the strong current, dragging the struggling men across the boulders. With bodies scraped raw and their hands blistered from dragging on the ropes, they valiantly advanced southward, but progress was slow and torturous. The men, wiser now, had removed all their clothing and stored them on the decks. The least tattered ones would be mended later, and the ones beyond repair were saved for use to patch other garments when they reach their destinations.

Gradually, the scenery changed. The barrenness of the previous few days was replaced by greenery. Reeds and papyrus grew in scattered clumps in inlets and bays. Silt, washed down from the highlands and checked by the rocks, had settled, forming fertile banks where seeds took root and flourished. Behind the reed beds, further up the banks, fragrant shrubs grew and the occasional feathery tamarind or palm tree appeared.

The larger and denser reed and papyrus marshes attracted waterfowl and flocks of egrets floated overhead in search of feeding grounds. Lotuses grew in profusion in the sheltered bays along the banks between rocks. Here ducks darted in and out of the reeds to paddle among the water lilies.

They reached a stretch of shallow water and the men were given a brief respite before tackling the next obstruction of rocks. Rakhmet leaned against the hull of the boat, rubbing his aching arms and longingly watched the ducks. He wished for a throwing stick or his bow and arrows, stowed on deck. Waterfowl would add a nice change from the cooked grain, bread, onions and fish. Many Egyptians considered fish unclean. He did not mind them now and then, but roast duck would be very welcome.

A slight movement in the reeds ahead, sent the birds off noisily. A crocodile perhaps? No, the river was much too shallow and rocky. It could be an impala or other small antelope. Venison would be even more welcome. He had not tasted meat for a while.

He was still watching the spot to see what would emerge, when they were ordered back to their tasks. Reluctantly, he turned and grabbed hold of the rope, then noticed the tops of the reeds vibrating. Something was moving in the thicket where the first boat and its team drew level with the spot.

It was not an animal, as it did not flee. Rakhmet spat on his blistered hands and rubbed them together for a better grasp on the rope. Slowly the boat started moving forward. The first boat had cleared the rocks and the second was being eased over them.

He envied the paying passengers, and glanced back at them, comfortably settled on the deck. Suddenly, whooping cries came from the reed-thicket. A horde of blacks appeared and stormed the boats. The suddenness of the attack caught them unawares and before they could retrieve their weapons, the attackers were upon them. Spears and battle-axes flashed. Startled, most of the men slackened their holds upon the ropes and the force of the water started to drag them and the boats downstream again.

Contradictory orders were shouted: 'Secure the boats!', 'Arm yourselves!' and 'Take cover,' the soldiers scrambled to obey the orders. The confusion was exactly what the bandits had hoped for.

This was an ideal place for an ambush. Travellers were most vulnerable here as the large rocks slowed their progress. The river was fairly narrow and the reeds extended well into the shallows and had kept the attackers hidden.

The first wave of the attack was a signal for other ambushers. They appeared from behind every boulder and clump of papyrus, and swooped down upon the struggling men.

The experienced soldiers from the fort quickly manhandled the boats and rammed them against some rocks, preventing them from being swept away, and quickly armed themselves, then handed weapons to the detainees.

Rakhmet received a bow and arrows. At first, he thought the bow was broken and useless until he saw others with similar weapons and realised it had been fashioned this way. It was a curious shape. The middle was bent at almost a right angle. He would have preferred an Egyptian bow, but this was not the time to be selective and he quickly became accustomed to the use of this curious weapon.

Cries of pain and triumph echoed and bounced off the cliff face as arrows and spears found their marks as soldiers desperately tried to keep the foe at bay. Men cursed as they slipped and stumbled, searching for a foothold on the slippery rocks while spears clattered around them. The ambushers surrounded the two boats and arm-to-arm combat ensued. The surprised soldiers suffered heavy casualties during the first wave of the attack, but quickly recovered and defended themselves with more vigour. The clangour of metal and wood resounded down the narrow gorge, mingled with other sounds of battle—the dull thuds of a battle-axe biting into flesh and bone or a spear or arrow thrusting into a body. Cries of agony made an indelible impression on Rakhmet. He had been trained in battle, but had never experienced bloodshed before, and not in this kind of terrain.

Realising they too were in peril, the paying passengers joined in the melee, casting spears and shooting arrows from the boat decks. Rakhmet, about to notch an arrow, lost his balance on a slimy stone as a bandit charged. Still clutching the arrow, he instinctively steadied himself, but the man, with a club raised, was too close for him to load the bow. The attacker swung his club at his head, Rakhmet twisted sideways and thrust the arrow forward and up, driving it into the man's chest cavity just below his ribs. With a look of surprise on his face, poised, with the club raised and spurting blood, the man toppled forward clutched at Rakhmet, then slid down the rocks and into the river. It was Rakhmet's first kill.

For a moment, he stared at the corpse, fascinated, and did not see another Kushite bearing down on him with a spear. The attacker's cry of triumph jerked him back to reality and he fumbled for his sword, then he realised it was still on deck. He raised his arm to ward off the attack. Someone slammed into him from the side, sending him flying into the already crimson water.

He quickly struggled to his feet, unhurt and looked around for the person who bumped him out of the way, but the man who had saved his life, was not that lucky. The spear, meant for him, had pierced the man's shoulder and impaled him to the hull of the boat, his naked body hanging limply from the shaft.

Rakhmet went to free him, and gasped, 'Batu!'

In a rage, he scrambled towards the Kushite who had thrown the spear. Rakhmet wrestled a sword from the hand of a nearby floating body and lunged at the enemy. Just as the bandit turned to face him, he thrust the sword into the man's side. The Kushite grasped at the weapon and at Rakhmet's arm. Rakhmet thrust the sword deeper, then twisted it free. Clutching his side, the bandit sagged to his knees and toppled forward. Rakhmet went to Batu and worked the spear free. Batu was unconscious. Just as well, as it took some effort. The weapon came free and Batu slumped into his arms.

He lowered the limp body onto a rock. Nearby, a Kushite was wrestling with one of the soldiers. With a cry, Rakhmet flung himself at the enemy. He wanted to avenge himself on the entire band of bandits. With his club, the Kushite parried Rakhmet's blows. He smashed Rakhmet's sword from his hand but the momentum carried the man's arm forward and across his body. Rakhmet gripped him around the waist, pinning the man's arm between them. They struggled and both rolled into the water. Rakhmet forced the man's head down past the rocks and under the water. Off balance and flailing his arms, the man's fingers groped at the slippery rocks in a vain attempt to right himself.

Rakhmet held the man's head under water until his actions weakened, his clawing and groping ceased and his body became slack. When he had finally stopped struggling, Rakhmet relaxed his hold and the man slid into the water, then he watched, panting, as the current slowly carried the limp body downstream.

Satisfied he had avenged Batu, Rakhmet turn back to the fight and reached for his sword that was still lying on the rock. There was an explosion in his head and everything went black.

***

After the evening temple ceremony, Menefer went to seek Lord Nakht. She found him on a terrace at the palace complex. This was where he did his observations of the stars to calculate the most auspicious times for any upcoming events. It was dark. The moon had not yet risen, but a candle flickered on a table near where he was gazing at the heavens.

'Good evening, Lord Nakht!'

'Menefer!' surprised, he straightened up. 'I did not hear you approach.'

He greeted her and beckoned her to sit down. 'What brings you here?'

'Lord Nakht, I heard about the encounter with Lord Tutu…'

He looked depressed as he seated himself nearby. 'I failed, Menefer. Tutu is very clever. He managed to talk his way out of the situation. I was ill prepared and my evidence was not strong enough.'

'I could try again, Lord Nakht. Maybe I can get another—'

'No, no. Out of the question! I cannot allow you to endanger yourself. I am being watched. I would not be surprised if we are being observed at this moment.' He glanced around, suspiciously. 'It is best we leave it be. I will find another way.'

'Watched? Here? Are you certain? Perhaps you are mistaken…'

'No mistake. I saw Kenti, Lord Tutu's servant, earlier, concealed behind one of the pillars of the King's House observing me. Obviously to find out whom I have contact with, I might be putting you at risk. We ought not to meet…not here.'

'I don't see why not, our families are on friendly terms. We might merely be planning a family gathering.'

'I sincerely hope you are right, but be very careful, Menefer. You have done enough, but please, promise me you would do no more!'

'I will heed your warning, Lord Nakht.'

Menefer left and walked back to her quarters. *Could Lord Nakht be mistaken, perhaps there was no conspiracy after all. What if all the letters can be explained away as the one she had copied…but then, why would Lord Tutu have Lord Nakht watched if the contents of the tablets were harmless? If they were not, how would she know which ones were damaging? She must try and get another. After all, she made no promise to Lord Nakht, except to be wary.*

*Khay! He would know, but could she take him into her confidence? Is he loyal to Pharaoh? Could he be persuaded? He was interested in her, she was certain of that—perhaps she could make use of it…but it was against her upbringing, her very nature, to manipulate people. She wrestled with the thoughts until late that night, then finally came to a decision.*

'Forgive me, Rakhmet, for what I am about to do,' She muttered softly to herself, 'Watch over me, Oh Hathor. To achieve my goal, I must use my only weapon…my feminine charm.'

***

Khay was at his usual place next to the dais in the Audience Chamber, replying to another letter. Menefer greeted him warmly, 'I've been looking forward to your company, Khay.'

Again, he was flattered. Pleased by her interest. 'I have no clay prepared at the moment, but if you need some—'

'Not immediately, thank you.' She gave him a sweet smile. 'You are very kind. I hope I am not disturbing you.'

'No, not at all. I'm pleased to help…is there anything you need?'

'No, I just wanted to see you.' She feigned interest in what he was doing and gestured towards a clay tablet. 'Uh…is that another letter you are replying to?'

'Yes, it arrived this morn…from Asia.'

'May I have a look at it?'

Khay hesitated.

'I will not damage it, Khay.' She smiled coyly. 'I promise.'

'I am truly sorry, Menefer, but Lord Tutu urged that no one else handles the letters,' Khay seemed nervous. 'I am to see they are safely deposited in the vault.'

Dishearten, she looked at him, wide-eyed and feigning disappointment, then pursed her lips, 'You do not trust me?'

'Someone managed to access confidential material and brought it to the notice of Pharaoh,' he shrugged one shoulder. 'It was bound to happen. Too many are involved,' he waved a hand. 'Anyone could have—'

'Involved? It sounds like you are talking about something secretive.'

'I dare not say more. If word gets out—'

'Khay, is Lord Tutu misleading Pharaoh?' she asked bluntly.

With frightened eyes, he looked about. 'Yes…but I dare not comment further. I am under oath.'

'Are you loyal to Pharaoh, Khay, or to Lord Tutu? If there is a conspiracy, should you not expose it?'

'Menefer, you are making it very awkward.' He put down the wet clay tablet and looked at her. 'I could get into a great deal of—'

'You need not do anything yourself…but perhaps someone else, without your knowledge, could,' she leaned closer.

'Someone like you perhaps?' he laced his fingers and stared into her eyes.

'Yes. If there *is* a conspiracy and if you know something, it is your duty—' she toyed with the top of her tunic halter. 'If it were me, I will not hesitate.'

'It is much too risky,' he straightened and waved one hand in a negative gesture.

'Khay, I thought we were friends, but…' Menefer turned and walked out. Khay called out after her but she ignored him.

After she had gone, he sat brooding for a long while. If he remained faithful to his vow, he might lose the friendship of the one woman that seemed to care for him. Lord Tutu had been misinforming Pharaoh, but he, personally, had no interest in foreign affairs and just answered the tablets as directed, but, by doing so, *was* he involved in a conspiracy? Would he too, be implicated? He had no love for the king and would not regret his downfall, but, he wanted no part in treason.

Still wrestling with his conscience, he finished the reply he had been working on, gathered the tablets and headed for the vaults.

# Chapter Ten
## Istar

Rakhmet could hardly open his eyes. A severe throbbing pain pounded in his head. Confused and disorientated, distant voiced drifted to him, garbled and indistinct, as if coming through water.

Water! He remembered water, red water. He tried to lift his head but a sharp pain stabbed through it. He groaned and fell back on headrest. *Red water, why red*, he wondered. He moved his head again as a cool hand touched his brow. A woman's voice commanded him to remain still.

'Menefer?' he croaked. His mouth felt dry.

'No, I am Istar…do not speak. Try and drink this…'

He felt a cup at his lips and a warm liquid dribbled into his mouth. He took a few gulps. The broth, made from duck and some herbs, tasted good. Slowly he opened his eyes. He couldn't make out any details in the semi-darkness of the room.

'Where am I…what is this place?'

'You are in Buhen.'

Suddenly, he sat upright, his eyes wild. More stabbing pains and again he groaned. 'Kushites! We are being attacked!'

'You are safe.' She eased him down gently and seated herself on a stool next to the couch, 'They have been driven off. They were of the Wawat tribe and have been a problem for some time. Fortunately, the soldiers here were alerted and went to your aid. You were brought here late yesterday. The wounded are being cared for here, but the rest of your companions had to continue on upriver.'

Rakhmet lay back, relieved, that they were safe. Suddenly, he lifted his head again. 'Batu! He was wounded…is he?'

'I know naught of Batu. Sleep now, the sun has not yet risen.' She started to get up. 'I will find out on the morrow.'

He grabbed her wrist. 'Were many…uh…lost?'

'Yes, several, and many injured, some very badly. More might die…but you must rest. You are going to be all right.'

She caressed his forehead. It soothed him and he fell into a fitful sleep.

When he woke, the sun was streaming into the room. He was alone. His head still felt like a herd of animals stampeding around inside, but his vision had cleared and he had a tremendous thirst. He looked around.

The building, of sandstone blocks, was white-washed, and judging by the window-sill, the walls were very thick. The room was not exactly over-furnished, but had all the basics. Apart from the sleeping couch on which he lay had a stool and small table next to it, and a wooden clothing chest stood by the window. Some of his possessions were piled on it and his tunic, as customary in Egypt, other garments hung from wall-pegs. On the nearby table were a cup and a jar which probably contained water. He remembered he was thirsty.

Gingerly, he eased himself upright and sat on the edge of the bed for a moment until the throbbing in his head eased. He felt giddy, but determined to get to the water, he removed the bed covering. He wore no clothing. His tattered shenti had been draped across the clothing chest, but his needed for water was more urgent than to be clothed.

He stood up and reached for the table. The room tilted and the walls buckled and he sat down again holding his head in his hands. Slowly, the room settled and he tried to get up again.

'Get back to bed!' Istar's commanding voice was friendly but stern. 'You should not walk around!'

Rakhmet grabbed the bed covering to hide his nakedness. The room tilted once again and he went to sit down, lost his balance and landed heavily on the floor. Istar rushed forward and assisted him up onto the couch. He tried feebly to cover himself but was lying on top of the cover. Istar rolled him to one side and pulled the bedding free.

'No need to be shy. Who do you think cleansed you of the blood and grime?'

She leant over to cover him and tuck him in. He studied her face closely. She was not Egyptian. She had a light olive skin, and the most haunting eyes he had ever seen. They were large, and, unlike the dark eyes of Egyptians, hers were green, flecked with gold and ringed in a deep blue-green. Her heavy eyelids, not painted like those of Egyptian women, slanted slightly downward at the outer corners and gave her a sad, almost dreamy look. Her long dark brown hair was tied at the back.

'What are you doing here?'

'I'm helping you get comfortable and concealing your…modesty,' she laughed. It was a very nice laugh, almost musical.

'No, I meant—what are you doing here, in this place so far from…everywhere?'

'Oh,' she reached for the cup and water jar. 'My father is the commander of the garrison, the *Keeper of the Door of the South*. I was born and grew up in the village of Buhen. I come here, to the fortress, quite often to help him.' She filled a cup of water and offered it to him. 'They told me your name is Rakhmet.'

'Yes!' he said and took the cup. 'Why am I separated from the others?'

She gestured towards the clothing chest. 'From your uniform, I gather you are a Royal guard, am I correct?'

He nodded, 'Yes.'

'That was why you were not put with the other wounded.'

'I vaguely remember your name…Istar?' he sipped some water.

'Yes, named after the goddess Ishtar. She is our version of your goddess Isis.'

'*Istar*? You are not Egyptian, are you?'

'Not *pure*. My father is Egyptian but my mother is…*was* Mittanian, from Assur, in Mesopotamia. She died several years ago.'

'Do you have a family…apart from your father?'

'Brothers and sisters, or do you mean—am I married?' she gave a disdainful laugh. 'No. I'm an only child—and I have no husband. No one here will marry me. I am still considered an outsider, an enemy, by most Egyptians. I am shunned at the market place and taunted at the wells. That is why I prefer to help around here, at the fort. Soldiers are not as petty as the village women.'

'If all the enemy looked like you, there would never be wars.' He meant it. *How could anyone spurn someone as beautiful as this?*

Istar blushed and looked away, then quickly changed the subject. 'This friend you mentioned—Batu? I found him. He is seriously injured. We are trying our best but he is not responding.'

'Take me to him!'

Before Istar could reply, two men entered to chamber.

'No, in your present condition you should remain put,' one of the men replied. Around his neck hung a medallion with the head of the lion-headed goddess, Sekhmet, the symbol of a physician. 'That blow to your head probably cracked your skull. You must remain here and keep still for a while.'

'This is Nufer, the *sunu* here at Buhen,' Istar introduced the physician, then gestured to the second man. 'And this is Baka, my father, *Keeper of the Door of the South*. Father, this is Rakhmet, the officer I told you about.'

'My daughter tells me you are concerned for your friend!'

'Yes, he saved my life…and it almost cost him his.'

'Well, it still might. He seemed to have lost the will to live,' the *sunu* scratched his shaved head. 'Perhaps, with your encouragement, his condition might improve.'

'Then, can you bring him here?' Rakhmet asked

'Perhaps.' The physician turned to Baka, 'Would that be possible?'

'Mmm. I do not usually allow common *apir* in quarters reserved for officers.' Then to Rakhmet, 'Do you wish to share your accommodation with a common soldier?'

'I do not mind having Batu here.'

'Very well, so be it. I will arrange it.'

The physician smiled, 'I cannot guarantee your friend's recovery, but it cannot harm him any further…as long as you keep yourself still. All my care, medicines, spells and incantations will only work with your co-operation.'

Rakhmet promised to comply. A folding cot was fetched and placed next to Rakhmet's couch and Batu was brought in. He was unresponsive, pale and covered in perspiration, his breathing was weak and shallow. When they were alone, Rakhmet called out softly. There was no answer. Then he stretched out and patted Batu's arm.

'Batu, can you hear me?'

Batu's eyelids flickered, but his eyes remained closed, then in a feeble voice, he spoke.

'Is…that you, Rakhmet?'

'Yes.'

'I… I am sorry…' a look of distress spread over his face.

'Shh, don't talk. Just get well, Batu, just get well.'

Batu opened his eyes for just a moment but closed them again.

'Batu, it was a gallant thing you did, shoving me out of the way. You could have been killed.' Rakhmet hesitated, searching for words to thank him, 'I…I want you to get well, understand?'

A faint smile appeared and Batu opened his eyes, nodded weakly then closed them again.

'Now rest. We will talk more later, my…friend.'

\*\*\*

Khay could not concentrate. The image of Menefer kept intruding into his mind. Her delicate skin, her shiny black hair and those eyes haunted him. At night, as he lay on his sleeping couch, he wondered what it would be like to touch her— kiss her moist lips—inhale the fragrance of the perfumed oils she rubs into her skin.

It was true what she had said. Lord Tutu's translations of the correspondence from Asia, was not always as accurate as it had been written. On more than one occasion Khay had wondered if, perhaps, he should correct him, but had always dismissed the idea as political diplomacy.

His task, when replying to the letters, was to copy, faithfully, the words of Pharaoh or Tutu only, then he had to store the tablets. He also swore an oath, not to divulge any of the information. Nothing else. He had never before question any of it, till now.

After the altercation between Lord Tutu, Lord Nakht and Pharaoh, he had been urged by Lord Tutu to be more vigilant and not let anyone near any of the tablets. If Lord Tutu is immersed in a conspiracy, he had wished not to be involved. He had wanted no part in treachery, but now he reconsidered that demand.

What if he helped Menefer? It might hamper a conspiracy against Pharaoh— and should there be an investigation, would it not count in his favour?

Also, if he allowed her access to the vaults, she might return the favour, allow their friendship to grow, perhaps even lead to…more than just friendship!

\*\*\*

'Menefer, I have something for you. I hope you can forgive me…'

She had been relaxing in the garden at her favourite place when the scribe approached her. 'Why, Khay, thank you.' She untied the cloth wrapping. It was a little Babylonian figurine. 'This is beautiful. A *shesp* figurine from Asia!'

Shesp figurines were common in Egypt, a crouching lion with the head of a man, but this one was different. Apart from a full beard and long crinkly hair, it wore a tall cylindrical crown and also had wings. Only once before had she seen a winged sphinx. Queen Tiye had once been depicted as a human-headed lioness with woman's breasts and wings.

'You are pleased?

'Yes, of course, but why the gift, Khay? Upit, the *day of the open hand* is still a long way off.'

'You said you were interested in the writings and art of Asia, so I thought you might like this,' he pointed. 'See, it has an inscription at the base.'

'What does it mean?'

He took the figure and turned it over. 'It reads; *A gift for my father, Dudu.*'

'Who is Dudu?'

'Lord Tutu. That is what Aziro calls him.'

Menefer looked at him in surprise.

'I do not understand. Did you not say…?'

'I know what I said, but this is not a letter. Lord Tutu said nothing of figurines, except to get rid of it…but I kept it in the vault.'

'Will he not miss it? What if he wants it back?'

'It has no value for him. I thought it would do no harm to let you have it—as long as he is not aware of it.'

'Thank you again, Khay.' She leaned over and kissed him on the cheek. 'I am absolutely delighted with it. I will keep it in a safe place. You are very kind.'

'I am glad. Can we…be friends again?'

'Yes, of course! I was not aware our friendship was broken. I'm happy to be your friend.'

Khay fought to suppress the emotion that suddenly swept over him. He could not describe the feeling and had a sudden urge to abandon all his oaths, to ignore the pledges he had made to safeguard the items in his care. His responsibilities seemed trivial. To have her friendship and company seemed all important.

'Menefer, uh… I have decided to allow you access to the letters!'

Startled by his sudden change of mind, she could but stare in astonishment. Did her ploy work? Khay seemed suddenly so vulnerable. A feeling of guilt swept over her. She was not the kind of woman to use her allure to make someone yield to her wishes, yet she had done so. Were all women capable of using their wiles for their own gain?

Khay was not handsome, but good looking, in a masculine way. He was bare to the waist, his white plaited linen skirt, fastened about his middle, hung down to his knees. About his shoulders, he wore a broad collar of painted wooden wedges, separated by coloured beads.

His thick black eyebrows moved often as he talked, accentuating his every expression. Aged about twenty years old, he had a strong, fairly well-built body but due to his trade, he lacked physical exercise. He had a slight flabbiness around his waist, a feature many Egyptian women found attractive, and it was considered a sign of well-being and affluence.

'Khay, will you not get into trouble? You told me yourself you had been cautioned. What if your every move is observed? No, I cannot allow—'

'I have made up my mind. I *will* show you all you wish to see. Lord Nakht had been correct. Lord Tutu is deceiving Pharaoh.'

Menefer just stared at him, trying to think of a way she could respond. She wanted very much to get hold of the letters, but not if it would endanger this blameless man.

'Why are you looking at me that way?' He flashed his charming smile and his eyebrows arched.

'I had been…uh…thinking.'

'About what?' He leaned closer and tried to kiss her, but she gently pushed him away.

'Khay, you mustn't.' She dropped her eyes.

'Why not? You kissed me earlier…'

'I… I like you Khay…very much, but I am betrothed.'

'Really!' He sounded sceptical and raised one eyebrow. 'I have not seen you with anyone since you arrived here. Where is your so-called *betrothed*?'

'He is not here. He is away…in Kush.' She looked up into his dark searching eyes.

'Well,' he said, smiling broadly. '*I* am here…you can see and touch me. Is it not better to have someone close rather than someone that far away?'

He ran his finger up her arm, over her shoulder and slowly down to her breast. She gently pushed his hand away.

'No, Khay, you must not.' She didn't want to encourage his advances, but didn't want to completely discourage him either.

'We are friends; can we not just remain good friends?'

'Is there no way…we can be *more* than friends?' he ventured.

'I want our friendship to grow, Khay, but I cannot make any promises.' She was being coy. She needed his friendship and did not quite dismiss him, but also, she was careful not to commit herself to anything.

Khay's eyes lit up. He had not been rebuffed and it gave him courage. It would take time, he thought, but eventually he would succeed.

\*\*\*

Under Rakhmet and Istar's care, Batu improved rapidly. Rakhmet too, was healing fast and would soon be able to continue his journey south, but Batu, although the fever had passed, had become morose. His right arm was now useless in battle. The army had no need for useless men. He would no longer be of any use as an *apir*, a mercenary soldier. He would be worthless, even as a labourer, a mud-brick maker, stonecutter or quarry worker.

Once he had recovered, he would be dismissed. He had no skills or training in any other occupation. A soldier was considered the lowest of professions and recruits had to accept abuse and ill treatment almost daily during their initiation. He had entered the army as a last resort after his parents died. The wages were meagre, but he had friends, a place to sleep and fed regularly. Course bread, fish, onions and beer, the basic diet, was not much, but adequate. Now, crippled, he would most probably end his days as a beggar and even the meagre diet of a soldier would seem a feast.

'Rakhmet, you had been good to me during my recovery,' he answered, when Rakhmet questioned him about his gloominess. 'I do not wish to burden you with my problems.'

But Rakhmet insisted.

'With a useless arm, what future have I now? You have a prestigious occupation and will reach a status that someone like me can only dream of. When you can no longer fight, you will be given a pension and can retire in comfort, but what awaits me? I cannot read or write…'

'Batu that gives me an idea,' Rakhmet sounded enthusiastic. 'If, somehow, I could remain here in Buhen for the duration of my…uh, term. I can teach you! The basics, anyway. What do you say?'

Batu brightened. 'Could you do that?'

'Could do what?' Istar arrived with a tray of food and placed it on a table.

'Rakhmet said he would teach me to read and write!' Batu sounded enthusiastic. 'If he could—'

'I too, would like to learn,' Istar interrupted, eagerly. 'You could teach us both!'

'Only if I remain here, at the fortress.'

'What do you mean?' Her haunting eyes seemed disappointed as she searched Rakhmet's.

'I am to continue on to Sesibi once I recovered…unless I have an excuse to remain here.'

She brightened. 'We could use another scribe. Ours has gone to Yebu for a while. The bodies of the soldiers who had died in the attack had to be returned to Egypt. It was unthinkable for an Egyptian to be buried in a foreign land and the scribe had gone to arrange for the embalming and shipment of the dead.

'Nufer, our *sunu* had helped out where he could, but we have over two thousand combat troops here…too much work to keep records, as well as attend their ailments. An extra scribe would be most welcome. Perhaps, I can persuade my father…'

'He would never agree to that.' Rakhmet shook his head. 'My stay here is temporary, and I would have to return to my duties eventually.'

'Well, your recovery could take at least another month. How much can we learn in that time?'

'Not very much, but it would be a start,' he thought about it a moment. 'Let us see. Can you get me some tools? A slate and a drawing stone perhaps?'

'I can do better than that. The scribe left his extra tablets, brushes and inks behind. I will get them for you.'

She rushed off as Rakhmet and Batu finished their meal. Before long, she came back with a small chest. The box contained two ink tablets, one red and one black, reed pens and several brushes, a wooden palette with a hollow for mixing, and a jar with liquid gum used for binding the pigments.

Rakhmet explained that red ink was used for text headings and black for the text. He showed them how to grind and mix the pigments, add gum and water to the required consistency to flow easily, and how to hold the brushes. Then on a pottery tile, drew a vertical shaft with a plume on top.

'This is a drawing of a reed. The word for a reed is *aish* and the sound of this symbol is "*aee*".'

He then drew another vertical line with the top folded over.

'This is a fold of cloth, *sheshen*, the sound of "*ss*".'

He drew two more symbols, one, a half circle, flat on the bottom, and the other, a rounded wedge, tapering to points at the sides. 'The first is the symbol for a loaf of bread. It has the sound of "*t*", and next one, two lips, represents a mouth, the sound of "*rr*". When we read these sounds together, it sounds like this…' He points to each symbol in turn and makes the sound. "*Ee— ss— t— r*".'

Suddenly, Istar looks up amazed. 'It's my name!'

'Right, but to tell the person who reads this, that it's a woman name, we do this…' He drew a stylised kneeling female figure.

Istar grabbed the piece of pottery. She had never seen her name in writing before and was thrilled. She rushed off to show her father.

Rakhmet then showed Batu how to do his name. A leg, the symbol for the "*b*" sound, a vulture, for the "*ah*" sound, and when drew the loaf symbol, Batu immediately recognised it as the "*t*" sound, and a rope and noose—the sound "*oo*".

'Yes, well done. You are learning fast.'

When he had finished the name, he drew a figure kneeling on one knee, to indicate it is the name of a man.

Istar returned, accompanied by her father. She was as excited as a child with a new toy.

'My daughter tells me you are teaching them the skills of reading and writing?'

Rakhmet confirmed it, but stressed again that it takes time to acquire all the knowledge, as the writings can be very complex. A single sound can be written in many different ways.

The commander was silent for a while, thinking. He was aware of his daughter's affection for this young officer, a *mes-seru* the son of a noble family. Rakhmet was educated, had a good position and bound to rise to a high rank. He would make an ideal husband for his daughter and he wanted a good match for her, but in Buhen, that possibility had seemed very remote—until now. This was an opportunity he could not let go by. He too, had grown fond of Rakhmet. It would be in his favour to keep this soldier here and encourage the relationship between him and Istar.

'Rakhmet, I have been thinking,' he seated himself and continued. 'My scribe has gone to Yebu—'

'I already told him that, father.'

'Don't interrupt, Child. As I was about to say, I had just received word he had been taken ill and will not return for quite some time,' the commander cleared his throat, 'My physician had been helping out with my correspondence, but with so many injured soldiers here, has very little time for the additional tasks and my records are falling behind. If I can arrange for you and your friend,' he indicated to Batu, 'to remain here and you to take over as scribe, for the duration of your…uh…confinement, would you be interested in staying?'

Surprised, Rakhmet looked first at Batu, who nodded, eager to remain, then at Ishtar who could hardly contain herself. She clasped her hand together and pressed them to mouth. Her eyes were wide and expectant, and her body rocked back and forth in eager anticipation.

'Yes, I will be happy to remain.' Rakhmet remained cool and casual, but inwardly he whooped with joy.

Istar cried out in delight. The *Keeper of the Door of the South* rose and nodded.

'Then I will make the necessary arrangements immediately…your first duty as scribe will be to write to the commanding officer at Sesibi, and to your Superior in Akhet Aten to notify them. Once you have done, bring the documents to my chamber for my Seal of Office so I can dispatch them as soon as possible.'

Istar, overcome with joy, threw herself at her father, hugging and kissing him. 'Calm down, girl.' He brushed her away, feigning annoyance and indignation, but deep inside, he was pleased. 'Istar, come with me. Rakhmet will need papyrus scrolls and tablets on which to write. You can bring them to him.'

Rakhmet too, was pleased...very pleased. His stay here would be much more pleasant than in that dreaded place, Sesibi, where he was to have serve his punishment.

# Chapter Eleven
## The Scribe

'Menefer, it is good to see you again, but I cannot stay. I have made other arrangements for this afternoon.'

'That is no problem, Djenna; I have come to see your parents, anyway.'

'Oh?' Djenna had been sorting through her cosmetics. She stopped and turned to Menefer, scowling. 'Not here to see me? Your visits are getting so scarce these days.'

'I was told you would be busy today. I heard you are instructing some of the ladies in the skills of perfume making and…'

'Yes, and I am running late already,' Djenna closed her cosmetics box. 'I will see you later, perhaps?' She hurried to the door, stopped at the top of the steps and turned. 'By the way, someone saw you, again, meeting men in the gardens the other day, one was that scribe!'

'Oh… Khay!' Menefer suppressed her irritation with her friend. She already knew of her and Prince Smenkhare's encounter. It's obvious that Djenna was referring to her meeting with Khay.

'Yes, we have become good friends.' She gave a slight shrug, hoping to appear indifferent.

'More than good friends, it seems. You were kissing him!'

'Your informer is mistaken. It was a chance meeting, and I was just thanking him for a gift.'

'Another chance meeting? That excuse is getting rather tedious, Menefer—'

Lord Nakht approached from behind Djenna and overheard the conversation. He put his finger to his mouth, a signal to be cautious.

'—And are you accepting gifts from strange men now? That is not very fitting, you know!'

'Djenna, you should not be minding other people's business!'

Djenna spun around, startled. 'Father!'

'Greetings, Lord Nakht!'

'Good day, Menefer,' he greeted her in return.

'Menefer, we will talk again some other time. My friends are waiting,' Djenna rushed past her father and disappeared down the steps.

Lord Nakht sat down and beckoned Menefer to a seat.

'I love my daughter dearly, but unfortunately, her tongue sometimes controls her thoughts. Be very wary what you tell her, Menefer. Palace servants love to gossip and Djenna is only too eager to comply.'

'Yes, thank you for your warning, Lord Nakht.' It was obvious, Menefer thought, that someone at the King's House was watching her, and was informing Djenna of her every move. Her private, albeit casual chance meetings in the garden had been observed and, as usual, Djenna had misconstrued them. She would have to be more careful.

Menefer told Lord Nakht about her meeting with Khay, and his awareness of Lord Tutu's deliberate misinforming Pharaoh, and that the scribe had offered to help.

Nakht was pleased, but again expressed his concern. 'I still think it is too risky—tempting, but risky!'

'Khay told me it is not only Lord Tutu who is involved. There are others.

'Others? Who else could it be?' Nakht was silent for a while, staring at a wall, then turned. 'I know you will keep this to yourself, but you need to know. Pharaoh has many enemies—even in the palace—who would like to see him removed from the throne. These people are ruthless and will do whatever is necessary for their cause. They will stop at nothing; that is why I am concerned for your safety. Be very wary.'

'Why? Who would benefit from…?'

'Pharaoh has antagonised the priesthood of Amun. They were once powerful and would be eager to have him replaced with someone more sympathetic to their cause. There are still many followers of Amun who also wish to have this religion restored.'

'Other members of the Royal family?' Menefer asked. 'Queen Tiye perhaps, or—Prince Smenkhare? He still carries Amun's cartouche on his chariot.'

'No. Smenkhare or Tutankhaten could become just toys on a stick, pawns, like a game of hounds and hares, to be manipulated by someone ambitious for power.'

'But I know of no one who could—'

'Who stand to gain the most if Akhenaten is removed?'

'I can think of only one such a person—Lord Ay. As Queen Nefertiti's father and Queen Tiye's brother, he has a strong claim to the throne, but—'

Lord Nakht smiled and nodded.

Menefer gaped. 'The vizier?'

'He might be behind the conspiracy, but as I said, I have no proof. Anything you find out might be useful, but don't do anything drastic; and I'd prefer you not to involve Khay. Too many people embroiled could lead to disaster.'

Menefer had much to think about on the way back to *Per nesu*. There was no way she could find out anything about Lord Ay. He moves in royal circles, and cannot be approached. Her only contact would be Khay, but Djenna's remark disturbed her. She did not realise anyone had seen her kissing Khay and as Djenna found out, anyone else could too. It was disturbing. She will have to be very cautious.

\*\*\*

Menefer returned to the Kings House after the visit to her family and finished unpacking her bag. She emerged from her dwelling and found Khay waiting for her in the garden. He presented her with a cosmetic box of rare woods inlaid with silver and ivory. 'Khay, I cannot accept this.'

'I have displeased you? You are dissatisfied?' He looked hurt.

'No, on the contrary, I am very pleased. This is beautiful, but you cannot afford such a costly gift.' She held it out to him.

'I want you to have it. Please,' he pushed it back with both hands.

She hesitated, and looked around nervously. *Was anyone observing them?* They seemed to be out of view of the King's House and the walkway.

'Very well, I accept—but no more gifts, promise? It makes me feel guilty as I cannot give you anything in return.'

'But you *can*, Menefer. Break down that wall you have built around yourself. You say we are friends, but you still distance yourself from me and I cannot seem to get close,' they started walking slowly along the paved garden path.

'I don't know what you mean?'

'For one, you avoid my kisses…'

'I don't want you to get the wrong impression. I already explained about Rakhmet.'

'Menefer, I think I love you.' He stopped, took her by the shoulders and turned her to face him. 'No one has ever affected me as much as you. You have been in my thoughts day and night since you kissed me that time…'

'It was just a gesture of thanks, nothing more.' She backed away and he released her. 'I should not have done it. Someone saw us.'

'I don't care.' He waved his arms in a wide gesture. 'I want the world to know. I will do anything for you… I was even prepared to allow you access to the letters.'

'About that, Khay, I don't think it would be wise. I have decided against it.'

'Oh, that is no longer an option. Lord Tutu had demanded the return of all of the letters. I had to give them to him!'

'But—'

'I know what you're thinking—the letters are now beyond reach, inaccessible, right?'

'Uh, yes, I suppose so.'

'Yes, Lord Tutu has the *tablets*,' Khay chuckled, beaming that wide smile that lighted up his excited features, 'but, I have something almost as good!'

'I don't understand,' Menefer knitted her brows and shook her head slowly.

'I will show you. Meet me at the garden entrance tonight, after the temple ceremony!' He hurried away.

She stared after him, not understanding what he meant by "almost as good". She was puzzled. If the tablets have been removed, what else could it be?

\*\*\*

The magazine-vaults consisted of two low buildings facing each other, each with rows of secured storage chambers. Menefer and Khay entered one of the storage areas. Wood for shelving was scarce so rows of niched mud-brick walls divided the chamber into several narrow passages. The niches were stacked with a confusion of items. Baskets and urns containing scrolls, clay tablets and hundreds of figurines, piled everywhere.

'Well, this is the chamber where we keep all correspondence,' Khay gestured, sweeping his arm in a wide arc, then led her round the back to a far wall.

'This is where the tablets were kept,' he motioned towards the empty niches.

'I don't understand. If they had been removed, why bring me here?' Menefer was confused. She had brought with her a cloth bag, as he suggested, but if the tablets had been removed, there was no need for a container.

'Here.' He reached down to a niche in the corner and removed a loose mud brick. The concealed compartment behind it contained a woven reed basket. 'These are the items I kept for you.'

Her eyes went wide with amazement. The basket was half-filled with the clay envelopes from the tablets.

'Lord Tutu was quite satisfied to have the incriminating tablets in his own care, but gave no thought to their coverings, which he assumed, had been discarded.'

He removed one and showed her. 'The envelopes retained impressions of the writings. Not all are clear, and they are reversed, but in most cases are still readable. Will they do?'

Menefer was thrilled. 'I am certain I can make good use of them. I really appreciate it, Khay.'

He watches as she gently, started packing the pieces into the bag. 'You are pleased?'

'Yes! Thank you so much.'

'Do I get…anything?' Khay ventured cautiously. 'Some sort of reward, in return?'

Menefer hesitated. He had risked much to help her. Finally, after a moment, she conceded. 'Very well, Khay. Just one kiss.'

Eagerly, he put his arm around her waist and drew her closer. Her garment felt cool against his bare chest. As he kissed her, he moved his hand slowly up the soft folds of her tunic and under her arm. She did not resist when he cupped her breast. He grew bolder, slid his hand underneath the halter and stroked the mound of her nipple. His breathing became heavier. She started to tremble and drew back.

He took her face in his hands, drew it to him and kissed her again. His hungry lips explored her face—her cheeks, her eyelids, the tip of her nose. His passion rose with every kiss.

He put one arm around her again, fumbled at his tunic with the other and drew her even closer. His kilt dropped to the floor. He was wearing just his shenti.

She realised he had become aroused, checked herself and drew back, frightened. 'No Khay!' She pushed him away.

'But Menefer…' he protested.

'No!' she was emphatic. 'We have gone too far already…'

'I… I will go no further. Please…let me just hold you close. I promise I will not…'

'No! I must go.' She grabbed the bag and started for the door.

'Menefer, no, don't leave like this…not now!' He started after her and tripped over his garment. He quickly lifted the kilt and fastened it about his waist again. By the time he had done, Menefer was already out the door and gone.

'It is not the end of it, my lady!' he vowed. 'You toy with me, but I will get my reward, yet!'

Rakhmet's pupils were learning fast. They had already mastered some of the basics and could write and read simple names and text. Istar mastered the skill of writing quite quickly, but Batu was battling. His shoulder had almost healed but there was still stiffness in his hand movement. He would never again be able to draw a bow or throw a javelin and manipulating a brush did not come easy.

For two hours, every morning, Rakhmet made them practice, sometimes under protests, but this was the way he had been taught and he merely repeated what he remembered from his schooling. Istar had other duties to perform. He and Batu no longer needed nursing and they did not see too much of her during the day, so Rakhmet could explore.

He enjoyed strolling along the parapets of the great fortress. The season of Proyet had passed and the dreaded desert heat of the season of Shomu, was approaching. The days were already getting quite hot, but the early mornings and evenings were pleasant. During his evening walks, he often gazed across the river to watch the rising moon dance on the water. At that time of the day, a cool breeze often blew from the south-east.

The fortress of Buhen, an impressive stronghold, had a complex system of ramparts surrounded and protected by dry ditches, and even a drawbridge that moved on rollers. The surrounding bush, once in close proximity to the fortress, had been cleared to prevent approach from the cover of the trees.

Towering walls with round bastions gave protection to standing and kneeling archers who, through an ingenious triple loophole system, could inflict serious damage to any enemy who might be foolish enough to attack.

Buhen was not as large as Mirgissa, the fortress headquarters of the cataract district to the south, but was, nevertheless, immense. Many of its troops were stationed here permanently, and had families living in the village beyond its walls.

It had been another, rather hot day, and Rakhmet enjoyed his customary stroll in the cool of the late afternoon. He stopped to watch as great billowing clouds advanced towards him. Deep rumbling issued from within the dark mass.

The sky darkened. Lightning flashed and speared the desert. The whip-cracks and booms resounded from the fortress walls.

Thunderstorms were rare in Egypt and Rakhmet stood transfixed by the spectacle. Only when the rain came, like a great water curtain being drawn across the countryside, did he retreat inside to watch from a window.

From the roof of a small temple nearby, water started gushing through the mouths of stone figures. He had seen similar carvings on other buildings on his journey from Waset, but did not know their purpose, until now.

The water spouted forth in solid streams and splashed onto the paved walkway to form rivulets that poured through openings in the walls and frothed into the ditches surrounding the outer walls of the fort. Here they turned red from the soil and, joined by other streams, grew bigger and stronger, dislodging stones that were swept along towards the Nile.

All too soon, the sudden downpour stopped and the sky cleared. The late afternoon sun caught the receding rain curtain and a rainbow appeared; only the second one Rakhmet had ever seen. He was deeply moved.

Istar came over and stood beside him and he instinctively put his arm around her. She responded and moved closer.

'It is beautiful,' he said, still looking at the colourful arc against the deep blue-black of the storm clouds. 'The Nile of the Sky.'

'The what of the sky?' she was puzzled.

'Oh.' He turned to her. 'In Egypt, we call it the *Nile of the sky*, he gestured towards the storm. 'The rain, of course…not the coloured arc. It is early yet, but in about four months from now, in the season of Akhet, the rains in the south-lands will flood the Nile, bringing the gift of fertile soil once more.'

'Oh, speaking of gifts…I have something for you.' She held out a small wooden box. It had a cord tied around it and a clay seal covered the knot. The seal had an impression of a royal cartouche.

'It arrived earlier but we could not locate you. It looks important.'

'I was strolling on the sentry-walk,' he said as he broke the seal and tried to untie the knot. Patience was not one of his virtues and after a few tugs at the stubborn knot, he took his knife and sliced through the cord. A parcel, especially from the palace, was rare and Istar was curious to see what was inside.

The box contained two rolled sheets of papyrus as well as an object wrapped in cloth. This he unwrapped the parcel first, and almost dropped the box when he saw it, it contained the amulet Menefer had made for him!

Memories flooded his thoughts. His mind went back to Akhet Aten and the moment when Menefer placed the pendant around his neck.

Istar spoke to him, but he was oblivious to her voice. Only when she tugged at his arm, did he realise she had been speaking to him.

'I…I'm sorry. I was lost in thought.'

'I asked if the gift was from Pharaoh.'

'Uh…no…it is the one Menefer made for me.'

'Oh yes, the sculptress…your betrothed!' her voice sounded cool. 'But why the Royal cartouches upon it?' She nodded towards the broken clay seal on the box and the two scrolls, one of which also bore a royal name.

'It is the seal of Queen Nefertiti.' He unrolled the papyrus, with the queen's name, first, and read it, then read the second scroll. He looked up at Istar, 'Did any other letters come for me during the last several weeks?'

'Other letters? No, not as far as I know. Why?'

'This second one is from Menefer. She asked why I had not answered her earlier ones.'

'Perhaps they were lost along the way. It is a treacherous journey, as you know.'

Istar was not too keen to talk about Menefer and changed the subject. 'What about the other letter…the one with the Royal seal? It looks very official. It must be important.'

'It's from the queen…about the pendant. It was taken from me by General Horemheb. Remember? I told you how it was snatched from me and that was how I came to be sentenced. It somehow landed into the hands of Her Majesty. She was so impressed with the craftsmanship that, upon learning Menefer had made it, she was invited to join the Royal household. She is tutoring the princesses…' Rakhmet looked off into the distance, and almost to himself, 'I did not even know that.'

'That information must have been in a letter that went missing.' He turned back to Istar. 'Anyway, Her Majesty feels, as the talisman belongs to me, I should have it back and is returning it.'

'I am glad for her—Menefer, I mean—it is not often a woman gets a chance to achieve such a well-placed position on her own.'

Rakhmet read the official letter again, looked up at Istar and smiled. 'There is more. You will be pleased…I have official permission for both Batu and myself, to remain here at Buhen!'

***

Most of the outer-coverings of the tablets, had been broken but Menefer had managed to assemble and glue together some of the pieces. She then made positive impressions of one of these, and was eager for Lord Nakht to see it.

Nakht, the Royal astronomer, had been particularly busy. One of his duties was to calculate the exact dates for various festivals by consulting the positions of certain stars, the sun and moon. The *Feast of the good Soul*, the Day *of the Shining Ones* and the *Harvest Festival*, were due, and he was to calculate the most auspicious time for their feasts, and did not want to be interrupted.

'Lord Nakht still cannot see you!' The servant was polite but determined. 'He gave instructions not to be disturbed!'

Menefer had been barred twice. She explained she would take only a moment of his time, but the servant would not be swayed. 'It matters not. The sun does not pause while Lord Nakht is distracted.'

'I just want him to see this!' She held up the wrapped items. 'He is expecting these.'

He noticed Menefer's concern. 'If you wish, I will take them to Lord Nakht later.' He reached out to take them from her.

She could not risk leaving them with anyone. 'Uh…no. I need to give it to him personally.'

The servant refused and she reluctantly returned home to store them in a safe place. It would be another ten days before she could try to see lord Nakht again.

***

Menefer returned to *Per nesu* later that afternoon and as usual, went to the garden. She had collected some food scraps to feed the ducks. The garden was deserted. The hot afternoon sun had driven the birds to seek shelter in the cool of the reed bushes along the far side of the lake. After a bit of coaxing, some cautiously emerged to receive the titbits she offered them.

'I knew I would find you here!'

'Khay! I heard you had gone south with your friends. I thought—'

'I decided to come back early.' He seemed unsteady on his feet. 'I just arrived back from Akhmin. We had been celebrating the Feast of the Good Soul.'

'The fertility festival? I did not take you for someone who would seek that kind of celebration.'

'I do not indulge in anything of that nature, Menefer. It was just a good excuse as any to make merry with my friends!'

He leaned closer and Menefer could smell the sour smell of beer on his breath. He was not drunk, but obviously not completely sober either. He must have continued his celebration on the boat.

'I'm glad I found you here. I've been trying to speak with you since…you know! You've been avoiding me.'

She stood up and faced him.

'I am trying to forget the incident. I was also to blame, but I don't think we should…'

'Stop!' He held up his hand. 'I know what you are going to say, so don't! You haunt me day and night, Menefer. I cannot get you out of my mind.'

'Our relationship must end, Khay. I want it to finish. From now on, our meetings will have to be strictly official!'

'You mean you are going back on your word? I risked much for you, and now that you have what you wanted, I am to be discarded! Is that it?'

'I made no promises but made a mistake by allowing you to go as far as you did and things got a little out of hand…'

'Out of hand?' he laughed mirthlessly. 'I would say I had things well in hand!' he said grabbing her arm.

'No, Khay!' She backed away. 'What are you doing?' She twisted her body and tried to remove his hands. He got hold of the halter of her tunic and pulled her towards him. She struggled to free herself, clawing at his hands.

'Come on, Menefer. Let me hold you close as before…after all, it is the feast of sexual rites.'

Still clutching the halter, he put his free arm around her and pulled her close. He was strong and her efforts to wrench free were futile. She pushed against his chest with both hands. With a ripping sound the halter tore, exposing her breasts. Still clasping her to him, he started groping at her naked breast with his free hand. His closeness, his clammy, sweaty chest against her bare bosom, and his beer-sodden breath repulsed her and she renewed her struggles. She clawed frantically at his face and began weeping.

'What is the meaning of this?'

A stern voice behind them, made Khay release his grip and she broke free. Clutching her torn tunic, Menefer turned and recognised her rescuer. 'Your Highness!' She quickly bowed and saluted.

'For this, scribe, you will be whipped until your skin peels off your back!' Smenkhare was shaking with rage and raised his arm. Khay fell to his knees and covered his head with his one arm.

'No, Your Highness, please…' Menefer interjected.

'You are defending him?'

Menefer fumbled with the torn halter, trying to cover herself. 'No…no Your Highness, but…'

For a while, Smenkhare stood, staring first at the cowering man, then at Menefer. He then turned to Khay and waved him off. 'Be gone, Scribe, and be grateful for the lady's mercy!'

Khay scrambled to his feet and hastily fled the area.

'Are you all right?' Smenkhare's voice was soft and caring.

'I…I think so, Your Highness!'

'Smenkhare!' he corrected. 'We are alone.'

'Smenkhare… I am fine,' she repeated and futilely tried to mend the torn garment, but realised it was a hopeless effort. She abandoned the attempt and the halter fell away. It was not unusual for women to wear garments that exposed the breasts.

'You are hurt,' a red wield ran down from her shoulder almost to the nipple. Smenkhare stepped closer and gingerly touched the scrape mark.

She looked down and tried to dismiss the injury. 'Oh, it is nothing, just a scratch.'

'Come with me. I'll get someone to tend to it.'

'There is no need, Your…uh… Smenkhare, it is not serious.'

'It was lucky I happened to be near.' He led her to a bench. 'Are you certain you don't need care? I still feel the scribe ought to be punished.'

'I am fine…truly. I am to blame. Please, ignore the incident.' She changed the subject to dispel any further attention, 'I have not seen you for a while. You must be very busy.'

He led her to a bench and they seated themselves.

'No…uh…in fact, I have been rather idle. I am not allowed to wander outside the palace-grounds without an escort.'

Smenkhare picked up some pebbles and flipped them into the lake. In the awkward silence, Menefer tried desperately to think of something to say, but finally, it was the prince who spoke first.

'Menefer, I had decided you should teach me your crafts.'

She was surprised by his request. 'It would be an honour, Smenkhare, I am sure the princesses would love…'

'No, I don't wish to join them, I want you to teach me privately…in my chambers.'

'If that is your desire, Your Highness.'

'Yes, that is my desire. I want you to teach me…about everything,' he seemed nervous.

'I will do my best, Highness.'

'Excellent. I must go,' He got up and, without looking back, walked away. 'I will send for you soon, Menefer.'

She thanked him again for coming to her assistance, and watched him as he returned to the Palace, wondering what skills he wished to learn, and what he meant by *everything*.

# Chapter Twelve
## The Visitor

Another week had passed before Menefer was finally able to see Lord Nakht. He escorted her into the parlour and they sat down. She started telling him about her fortunate gain, but he quickly changed the subject with small talk.

'How are your parents?' He nodded towards a side entrance and Menefer realised his caution. 'I hope they are well?'

'Very well, Lord Nakht…oh, greetings, Djenna,' she called out cheerfully. Djenna entered and greeted her. She turned back to her host.

'Like yourself, Lord Nakht, my father had been very busy,' Menefer continued. 'He has almost completed the queen's likeness and she no longer comes to the workshop.'

'Yes. I heard she is rather unhappy lately,' Nakht said as Djenna joined them. 'She avoids company.'

'There is friction between Queen Nefertiti and my lady, Queen Tiye,' Djenna shrugged. 'But that is to be expected. Two queens in one palace—' she left the sentence unfinished.

'How is your relationship going with that scribe, what's-his-name?'

Djenna's blunt question caught Menefer slightly off-guard. 'Uh—there is no *relationship* between us, Djenna. He supplies me with materials for my lessons— only! Whatever you suspect, is flawed, as I've already explained.'

'That's not what I hear from some of the servants at *Per nesu*.'

'I have no idea what you mean, Djenna!'

'It seems you have been seeing him, secretly, a little more than necessary.'

Menefer again protested and tried to explain. Lord Nakht saw her discomfort, and aware of her true reason for seeing the scribe, he excused himself and slipped away to where Lady Susmaat busied herself in the *rekhes*. After a short discussion with his wife, Susmaat called out to Djenna to come and help her. Djenna protested, but at her father's urging, went to help her mother in the cooking place.

Nakht returned. 'Sorry about that, Menefer, I had to draw Djenna away. We are alone—for a while, what have you for me?'

She quickly explained about the tablet-coverings. 'I managed to gum together fragments of a letter-covering and made an imprint.' She carefully removed it from her bag, still wrapped in cloth for protection and handed it to him. 'I hope it is clear enough to read.'

He unwrapped the tablet and examined it. 'Yes, it is readable. "*Behold, Aziro has fought my chiefs, and my chiefs whom I dispatched to the city of Simyra*" …this next word is unclear… "*seized in the city. All the lands of the Amorites have gathered themselves. I need men to save the rebellion in this land. Give me soldiers"...'* he looked up. 'You have done well, Menefer. Thank you. Not much to go on though.'

'I have almost completed mending several others, Lord Nakht, but it is not easy trying to match the broken fragments.'

'I am pleased.' He wrapped it again. 'I am looking forward to the others. Perhaps they will reveal more.'

'I will get them to you as soon as I am done. It is slow going. Some are badly damaged. I will try and repair them as best as I can.'

'I am grateful for your efforts, but you are taking a great risk. You had done well beyond what I had expected.'

Djenna and Susmaat entered with some refreshments and Lord Nakht quickly changed the subject.

***

The air resounded to merriment and festivity in Buhen. The Feast of *The Day of Het-Hert* was not as popular as the great *Festival of the Voyage of Het-Hert*, in the month of the inundation, a fertility festival for the Goddess Hathor, but it was celebrated with much joy, dancing, song, beer, and love-making. After all, she was the patroness of festivals.

Soldiers with families in nearby villages had gone home for the festival, but others, those with no family, or families too far away, stayed at the fort and many remained on duty. They would get their break once the others had resumed their tasks.

Everyone, but Rakhmet, was in a jovial mood. A letter he had received the day before, had upset him—the letter, signed simply *from a friend*, had a faint fragrance of costly perfume on the scroll. It obviously came from a woman. He guessed it was from Djenna.

'What ails you?' Istar asked.

He was staring wistfully out over the distant wooded area, fingering the amulet about his neck.

'You seem far away.'

'Oh, uh…it is nothing.'

'Then your *nothing* is not a good thing. Your mood seemed to have changed since you received the scroll and trinket. This letter from Menefer should cheer you, but instead, you seem depressed.'

He turned and looked at the haunting eyes of Istar and her flashing smile. Could she, always so gay and bubbly, know anything of heartache?

'She no longer loves me!'

Surprised, Istar just started at him.

'The letter I received…' his head sagged. 'It is not from her. Her friend, Djenna, sent it. She wrote Menefer was seeing someone else.'

'Befriending someone else does not mean anything. It could be quite innocent,' Istar answered cheerfully. 'Are you not, also seeing me?'

'They have been seeing each other…in private. Djenna wrote someone saw them kissing.'

102

Istar shrugged. 'Perhaps, it was just a casual kiss. It could mean nothing. It could be—'

'It means something to me!' He pressed his hand to his chest. 'She had never done anything like this before.' Again, he turned, gazed out over the forest and flung his hands up. 'I had known her for a very long time. We grew up together, had grown to know each other's ways. We had been inseparable—until now!'

'But she loves you, does she not? She would not betray you.'

He placed his hands on the parapet wall and answered softly. 'We are betrothed.'

'Yes, but did you ever declare your love for each other?' She came and stood next to him. 'Not once did you mention that you loved her.'

'What is love, Istar?' He turned to her. 'I think of her every day, I miss her, wish to be near her. We have never been separated until now.' He turned back, gazing towards the distant trees and sighed. Istar was right. Neither of them had actually expressed their love. 'I am beginning to wonder if this separation was *meant* to be. Perhaps that invisible cord that had tied us together, broke, and released her true feelings.'

'Forget about the letter for now.' She took his hands and coaxed him inside, 'Come, join us for a while, after all, it is feast time…and the sun is setting and you are off duty.'

It was customary to become inebriated during the Feast of Het-Hert, and punishment for drinking on duty was severe, but after sunset, it was allowed for those off duty. *Ash*, a potent Sudani beer, wine and delicacies were in plentiful supply. All manner of foodstuffs for the feast were brought from the village.

Some time later, after several cups of wine and A*sh*, Rakhmet, feeling sorry for himself, had forgotten about the letter and the drink had started to make him feel jovial.

Istar was pleased to see his mood had changed. 'Do you know, this is also the feast time of Ishtar, our Goddess of love and fertility? It is in celebration of when she was resurrected from the underworld.' She filled his cup again.

'I can see the connection—the season of *our* goddess of fertility.' He took a sip of the brew. 'You have been well-named—like her, you certainly inspire love.'

Just then, Batu came hurrying past.

'Batu!' Rakhmet called out. 'Come and join us for some beer.'

Istar excused herself and went over to the food table.

'No thank you, Rakhmet. I no longer drink anything that will dull my senses.' He started for the entrance again.

Rakhmet was surprised. 'This is indeed a revelation. I have never known you to refuse a drink.'

Batu stopped by the door and grinned back at him. 'I no longer drink strong brews. My life has changed since we came here. The military can no longer use me, but the Commander has arranged for me to remain here, as scribe. He has already given me a task, to report on all Kushites that travel from the desert.'

'I am pleased for you, Batu,' he lifted his cup in salute for his friend.

'I know I still need to learn much, but I am determined to better myself. I will not jeopardise my future by drinking again.'

'In that case, I will not temp you.'

'But, you enjoy yourself, Rakhmet. This is an occasion to be merry. Anyway, I cannot stay; I am going into the village to meet someone, a local girl.' He again started to leave.

'Do I know her?' Rakhmet called out.

'I don't think so,' Batu stopped and turned. 'I met her but two days ago—at the market place.'

'I wish you luck, and…may she put on a wig for you.'

'She is not that kind of woman, Rakhmet,' Batu shook his head. 'I will not bed her until we have sworn troth to one another. No, she will not be putting on a wig for me.'

'Who is putting on a wig for whom?' Istar approached and stopped in the doorway, one hand on her hip, the other holding a tray with foodstuffs, balanced on one shoulder.

'Ah, the goddess Hathor has arrived. Just what we lovelorn soldiers need,' Rakhmet beamed.

'Is that what you need, Rakhmet? Love?' Istar frowned, but a crooked smile tugged at the corners of her mouth. Her heavy-lidded eyes fixed onto Rakhmet's face, her sparkling eyes hiding a smouldering fire beneath, like grey ash that look deceptively cool until stirred, then suddenly bursts into flame.

Slightly intoxicated, Rakhmet looked her up and down. She noticed his eyes caressing her body and coming to rest where the fullness of her breasts strained at the fabric of her tunic. She pulled her shoulders back to enhance the effect.

'I see hunger in your eyes, Rakhmet.' She watched his face intently. With all the allure she could muster, and in a low voice, she murmured, 'I brought some food, but I think your hunger is not for food…is it?'

Batu prudently excused himself and started to leave. 'I had better be going. It is getting late…and she is waiting.'

'Go in peace, Batu,' Istar bade him a good night without taking her eyes off Rakhmet. Batu left, and she sauntered over to Rakhmet in a slow deliberate manner, swaying her hips provocatively.

She held the tray of food in front of him. 'Do you see anything you desire?' Her voice was soft and sultry. Rakhmet's heart started thumping wildly. He stood up, and with slightly trembling hands, took the tray from her and placed it on a nearby table. 'Yes, Istar. I desire something. You!'

His arms encircled her slim waist. She leaned back a little and pressed her free hand to his chest and gently pushed him away. Still looking into his face, she gave a short mocking chuckle. 'Remember, Rakhmet, you are a betrothed man.'

'Perhaps…but not dead. My *betrothed* is enjoying herself on the other side of the world,' then, in an almost inaudible whisper, '…but my world is right here!'

His powerful arms crushed her to him and his hungry lips sought hers, exploring her face, her neck, and her shoulders. She closed her eyes and slid her arms up and around his neck. He caressed her body and she rested her head against him. Her long soft hair tumbled over her shoulders and against his bare chest. The sensation excited him.

The wine, her perfume, her hands caressing the back of his neck and her body pressed against him, awakened a passion he could not contain. She too, felt it, and her passion grew also. He picked her up and carried her to his bedchamber. He kicked the door shut behind them, and put her down next to his cot. Slowly and sensually, he removed her garment as she untied the cord securing his kilt. Then both allowed their garments slip down. He untied his shenti and it too dropped to the floor.

For a moment they stood, just holding each other tightly, flesh against flesh. Two lonely people, both hungry for love, hungry for each other. He picked her up again and lay her down on the sleeping couch.

***

Menefer followed the guard through the vast palace complex, past impressive pillars and along passages with wall paintings depicting duck hunting scenes. He marched ahead with long strides and she had to trot to keep up with him.

They entered a large chamber, used as a common room. It was well furnished with several couches and tables, some with board games. A faint perfume from aromatic herbs issued from two braziers and, through an open window, just audible, from the nearby *per-hemt,* the House of Women came a woman's singing, accompanied by harps and flutes.

Several rooms led off the chamber. The guard beckoned her to be seated, then went to speak to a servant. She was left on her own for a while. A moment later Prince Smenkhare appeared.

'Leave us, Dhaba.' As soon as they were alone, he turned to her. 'Welcome Menefer…please make yourself comfortable. I am most pleased you could come.' He sat down and she took a seat across a small table from him and placed the bag she was carrying, on the table.

'Your Highness, you did not mention whether you wished sculpture or painting instructions, so I brought material for both…' she started taking items from the bag.

'Fine,' he leaned forward. 'Whichever you wish, but not today.'

She was puzzled. 'I don't understand…'

'Today, we will just relax and talk.'

'Certainly, Your Highness, but—'

'Menefer,' he interrupted. 'I am no good at art. I have no skills or interest in anything in that direction at all.'

'But, Your Highness, I thought…' She stopped and looked at him.

'I'm afraid I brought you here under false pretences. I have selfish reason for inviting you here…it was for your company.'

'My company, Highness?'

'Is it so strange to wish for female company? I have the same feelings—same desires as any other man.' He paused and neither spoke for a while. 'I have watched you often as you strolled around the garden. Many times, I had wanted to join you, but it was not always possible.'

'Your Highness, I would be glad of your company, at any time.'

'I feel like a prisoner here. I cannot leave the palace or *Per nesu* without an armed guard. A palace wall not only keeps people out, but can also keep some in. I cannot go and meet people my age, as even the lowliest servant can,' he sighed and gestured. 'It can be very lonely. I envy those who can come and go as they please.

105

Being a prince has many drawbacks,' he looked at her intently. 'I need a friend, Menefer,' he reached out and touched her hand slightly. 'I want you to be that friend, someone who would wish to visit me for myself, not to be summoned or for official reasons.' He withdrew his hand. 'Can you understand?'

'I am honoured, Your Highness, and will gladly visit you whenever possible'

He got up and turned towards the window. 'I am naïve in matters of the heart and hoped you would be able to enlighten me.'

'Your Highness, I have no experience in the art of…that.'

He turned back to her and stood, leaning on the table. 'But, you are betrothed. I was so sure you would know…'

'No, Highness, I do not.' She leaned back and shook her head slightly, realising what he had meant by his earlier remark, teaching him "everything".

'Then, perhaps we can…learn together?' He came over and sat beside her on the couch. 'If I ask something of you, will you be offended?'

She shook her head, not certain what he meant.

'Good, then…then I wish…a kiss.'

'Highness, I am betrothed.'

He looked at her in silence for a moment. 'Am I then…to be refused? When I heard you and that scribe met a few times, and you and he…' he looked so bewildered, hurt, so helpless, she suddenly felt feel sorry for him. It seemed the gossip of her kissing Khay has reached his ears as well. She hesitated a moment, then leaned towards him and kissed him lightly on the cheek. He reached out, guiding her chin with his fingertips, turned her head towards him and kissed her on the mouth. It was not a passionate kiss, but it was a lingering one. She did not resist.

*** 

Alone once more, Smenkhare lay back on his sleeping couch, Menefer's image before him. She had left some time earlier, but he still seemed to sense her presence. He could still smell the faint perfume from her hair; still feel the soft smoothness of her cheek and her full, moist lips upon his. In his mind, he could still feel the warmth of her breath upon his neck when he held her close. Something deep inside, stirred, but he did not know what.

The urge, the longing to hold her again was overwhelming. She had been the first woman he had ever embraced…that way. He started to fantasise about her. Creating images of them together…he wanted her, more than anything.

He got up, disrobed, and walked over the ablution chamber, a small low-walled shower recess, with a raised, slightly inclining floor. It had a spout for draining off the water into a channel that emptied into a basin. Usually Dhaba, his servant of the bed-chamber, would pour water over him while he bathed, but this time, wanting to be alone, he had not summoned him.

He reached up and tilted the water jar to let the water run over his body, but the cold water did not cool his ardour. He could not dispel the thoughts of Menefer from his mind, and imagined her, in there with him. As he washed himself, his hand explored his body. The sensation in his groin caused a reaction he could not control. He was stroking himself when he realised someone was watching him.

He grabbed the drying cloth and covered his nakedness. 'Akhenaten! How—long have you been standing there?'

'Long enough.' A faint smile playing around the corners of Akhenaten's mouth as he looked his half brother up and down. 'You certainly have—grown up.' He crossed his arms and leaned against the door frame. 'You ought to have your man-servant stand guard—at times like this.'

'I sent him to get more water,' Smenkhare lied. 'Anyway, I do not need a guard in my own quarters,' the plait on one side of his head, the lock-of-youth worn by all Egyptian boys, was dripping water and he wiped at it with his free hand.

'Use the drying cloth,' Pharaoh suggested. 'No need to cover yourself from me.'

Akhenaten's surprise visit had stilled his passion. Smenkhare removed the cloth and started drying himself.

'I am honoured by your visit. Did you wish to see me for anything in particular?'

'No, just to talk. I have neglected you these last few months.'

'More than eight!' Smenkhare answered.

'That long? It did not seem so.' Akhenaten entered and sat on the edge of the sleeping couch. 'My duties keep me busy. I had hoped you would come and visit me.'

'Visit you? Without requesting an audience? Queen Tiye insisted that all visitors…'

'I am not my mother. I am your brother, Smenkhare.'

Smenkhare fetched a fresh set of garments from his clothing chest, laid them on the foot end of the couch and started dressing, conscious of Akhenaten's gaze.

'You have been seeing the sculptress in your chambers. How long has this been going on?'

'Today was her first visit.' He fastened his shenti and reached for his kilt.

'Are you having an image of yourself fashioned, or did she put on the wig for you?'

'Neither. We are friends. She came here merely for us to talk.' Smenkhare fitted the kilt and picked up a broad gold-and-blue girdle.

'Well, brother, we must certainly meet more often so we too, can…talk,' Akhenaten stood up, embraced his brother and headed for the door. 'I will visit you more often, from now on, I promise.'

Pharaoh left the chamber and closed the door behind him, leaving Smenkhare staring at the door.

# Chapter Thirteen
## Tiye Commands!

Menefer had been expected and Dhaba, the prince's personal servant, invited her in. The chamber was heavily perfumed. It was early evening just after the temple ceremony. Presently, Smenkhare entered. He had been practising his archery skills and had changed his grimy tunic for a fresh one. He and Menefer exchanged greetings and Smenkhare handed the servant the bow and quiver of arrows.

'Put these away, Dhaba, then leave us. We do not wish to be disturbed,' the servant took the weapons and backed out of the room, bowing.

Smenkhare turned to Menefer and waved his hands around the room. 'How do you like the new fragrance?'

She had been aware of the heady perfume, more a female's choice than that of a man, when she entered. 'It's wonderful, Highness.'

'You don't think it's too overpowering?' He walked over and sat down near her.

'It *is* rather strong, Highness, but very sweet-smelling.'

'It is jasmine, a flower from Asia. I had it brought here especially for you.'

'Thank you. It is very nice...you have been hunting, Your Highness?' She started unpacking the items needed for her instructions, wondering if again he wished to...just talk.

'No, I was just practising my marksmanship. There is not much to hunt around here.'

'There is always fowling.'

'Fowling? That is one sport I have not attempted. Do you go fowling?'

'I used to, with my parents, but have not done so for some time. We used mainly claptraps and snares.' She waved a hand towards the south-west, 'We often went to the reed marshes on the island. It is teaming with waterfowl.'

'Claptraps and snares, not bows and arrows?'

'No, but Ipuky, my brother uses a throwing stick. He is good at using it.'

'It would be difficult to retrieve a duck from the marshes that way.'

'Not really. We had a cat who did that for us.'

Smenkhare laughed. 'Nothing looks as funny as a wet cat. I can just see it wading through the reeds trying to find a wounded duck.'

Menefer laughed too, then awkward silence followed and Smenkhare noticed her slight frown.

'Is something bothering you? You look a little troubled?'

'It's the queen,' Menefer said. 'She had not attended any of the temple ceremonies lately. Is she ailing?'

He shrugged, 'No, but...there is tension in the house, I believe. I try not to interfere...'

'You are right, it's nobody's business. I was just concerned.' She removed a lump of clay from a container and he was watching her kneading and softening it. 'To change the subject, this is how to prepare the clay. It has to be just the right consistency. One rolls and kneed the clay to make the basic shapes.'

Smenkhare reached out and laid his hand on hers. 'I can't believe these little hands can perform such wonderful work.'

'Your Highness, I... I...' Menefer stuttered.

'We are alone. Call me by my name.' He nuzzled up to her and noticed her nervousness. 'Do not be so tense, I will not do anything to distraught you.'

'It is not that, Smenkhare. I...I don't want things to...to go too far... I...I'm not...'

'I'm sorry. I did not mean to upset you. I was just hoping...'

'Hoping? I don't know what you mean.'

'Nothing!' the prince leaned back. He looked ill at ease. 'Menefer, you are one of the few...no, you are the *first* woman I feel comfortable with.' He leant forward again and continued in a lower voice. 'I wish us to be *close* friends. Perhaps even—'

'Smenkhare, I am to be wed, as I told you already,' she tried to guard herself.

'You *were almost* betrothed. I am aware of uh...' He turned his eyes up, trying to remember the name, and his eyebrows knitted. 'Your friend?'

'Rakhmet.'

'Yes, Rakhmet—and that he had been sent away, but, should you no longer— uh—should your feelings for him changed, will you consider me?'

'Consider you?' she frowned. 'For?' She was puzzled.

'Menefer, I, uh—I need a friend. A really close friend with whom I can—share things.'

'You can share things with me. I'm willing to listen.'

'Well, uh, someone, not just to talk to, but...' Smenkhare wiped his brow. Menefer could see he was embarrassed...then suddenly she understood.

'Smenkhare, I have never been...with anyone.'

'I thought you'd know...about those things.'

'No. Smenkhare, I am...still a maiden...' now she was the one feeling uncomfortable.

'Oh! No, I was just hoping our friendship could be more...personal...you know? Not...not *that*!' Embarrassed, he changed the subject. Forgive me my ramblings...let us continue with the lessons.

The rest of the day continued as usual, but there was a slight tension between them. Both Khay and Prince Smenkhare had been hinting at advanced, if not intimate, relationships. She will need to be very cautious.

*** 

Several days had passed. Still lost in thought from her meeting with the prince, Menefer continued her lessons, but was often distracted, gazing out of the window. The princesses noticed.

'Everyone seems to be in a pensive mood,' Meritaten remarked.

'Everyone, Highness?'

'Not just you, but my mother and Mutny too. You all seem absorbed of late.'

'Yes, I noticed Her Majesty's absence—I trust she is well? She had not attended any of the temple ceremonies for a while.'

'She's not just pensive, she is upset over something,' Senpa interrupted. 'I found her crying in her—'

'Hush, Senpa,' her older sister reprimanded. 'It is a personal matter and we should not concern ourselves with it.'

Menefer, not wishing to pry any further, tried to distract them with her lesson when Queen Nefertiti and Lady Mutnedjmet entered. Menefer bowed and saluted. Neither had paid a visited to the *Sbau*, the Place of learning, before.

'I am going to spend more time here, with you, from now on,' Nefertiti announced when she saw their surprised reactions. 'Too long have I been neglecting my little ones.'

The princesses were delighted and were eager to show off their achievements.

'What a pretty bracelet, Merit,' the queen said, and bent down to examine the trinket on her eldest daughter's ankle. 'Did you fashion it yourself?' Nefertiti wondered if it had been a gift and had been aware of the rumours that Akhenaten had been considering taking Meritaten as a secondary wife.

'Yes,' Merit beamed. 'Menefer showed us how to stitch beads together to make patterns.'

'Very nice. I am delighted with your achievements.'

Queen Nefertiti seemed to show great interest in all the items the girls had fashioned, but she had an ulterior motive for her sudden visit. Too many whispered tales were flying around, and servants and the ladies at court seem suddenly to grow silent whenever she approached. By spending more time with her daughters, she hoped she might learn more.

Over the following week, the queen's visits became more frequent. She no longer attended the temple ceremonies, but instead, visited her own private shrine at *Maru Aten*, her Northern palace. It had become a common sight to see the queen drive her own chariot there and back.

The season changed and the heat of Shomu, the summer season, was upon them. The Royal women chose to put aside their hot wigs and went about with shaved heads and wearing light, diaphanous garments.

Nefertiti and Lady Mutny often met in the shaded part of the garden, but from the queen's mannerisms and lively gestures, their meetings were anything but relaxed. Menefer suspected there was a reason for the queen's change of behaviour, and all too soon, she would learn of it.

\*\*\*

'Menefer, a moment, please. I wish to speak with you.'

Menefer had been heading back to her quarters after a long day. Annoyed, she stopped and turned as Khay approached and she glared at him warily, her fists balled. 'I do not wish to speak with you, Khay! You dare approach me after that incident?'

'I am sorry about what happened, Menefer. I deeply regret my conduct and I wish to apologise.'

'Your apology is *not* accepted. Leave me be.' She started walking again and he trotted behind her.

'Please, hear me out. I went too far. I did not mean to lose control. I had been drinking, you see… I know I angered you, and I will understand if you wish our friendship to end, but…if there is a possibility, just the slightest likelihood that you can forgive me…do I…do I stand another chance to be your friend?'

She stopped, again, turned and looked at him for a long moment. He was flushed and cowering like a little boy that had been caught stealing and awaiting punishment.

The incident that caused her to break off her friendship with him was regrettable, but she needed the remaining tablet envelopes that were left behind in the storage vault. Also, her parents had taught her compassion, to forgive those who did wrong and who regretted their mistakes and show mercy to those are willing to repent.

'Well, Khay…' She paused, deliberately, to make him cower. 'I suppose I was just as much to blame. I should not have encouraged you.'

Pleased, Khay placed a hand upon her shoulder. 'Friends again?'

She removed it and forced a smile. 'Yes. But we must remain just that—friends.'

They hugged briefly then she noticed someone watching them from behind a pillar. Kenti was again spying on her, and she wondered how many other servants were also observing. She stepped back, guiltily. 'Khay, I meant what I said about us being friends, but for the moment, for a short while anyway, we should not be seen together.'

'What do you mean?' He searched her face for an explanation. 'I am not in the mood to play games. Either you want our friendship to continue, or wish it to end it. Which is it?'

'Do not pursue it further, Khay. Too many servants, and now Kenti has been watching us.' She gestured, with a slight tilt of her head in the direction of the walkway, 'It could mean trouble for you if we are seen in each other's company too often.'

'But Lord Tutu had removed all the letters. Why should he still—?'

'I know not, but let us not take chances, for both our sakes.'

'I still have some fragments of letter coverings for you. Do you still need them?

'Yes, of course I do.'

'Shall I bring them to you…or will you come and get them?'

She hesitated, not wanting to be alone with him again. 'I will be most grateful if you can bring them.'

'How grateful?'

'Please Khay, let's not go there again.'

'Very well. I will bring you the fragments.'

\*\*\*

Lady Mutnedjmet was awaiting Queen Nefertiti in the anti-chamber of *Per nesu* when Queen Tiye stormed in. Without even a greeting, her manner brusque and impolite, she demanded, 'I wish to see Nefertiti!'

'*Her Majesty* is not here,' Mutny answered, in the same curt tone.

'I can see that for myself!' Tiye snapped. 'Instruct *Her Majesty* to present herself to me and Pharaoh as soon as she arrives.'

Lady Mutny could not believe her insolence and gripped the armrests of the chair in which she was sitting, with such force, her knuckles showed white. 'I will tell her!' she replied in anger.

Tiye stormed out in a huff and closed the door behind her. 'Yes, O Great Royal Battle-axe!' Mutny snarled.

Instantly, the door opened again and Queen Tiye leaned in. 'We will await Her Majesty in the Great Hall.'

For a moment, Mutny thought Tiye had overheard her remark, but Tiye left without another word. 'That was close!' She exhaled noisily with relief and chuckled to herself.

'Did I miss a joke?' Queen Nefertiti asked as she entered.

'Yes,' Lady Mutny snickered. 'A Royal one—but she just left. Tiye almost caught me making a rude remark about her,' she told Nefertiti about Queen Tiye's demand.

'She summoned me to *her* presence? *Summoned* me, in my *own house*, like a common *servant*?' Nefertiti spluttered.

'Very disrespectful of her,' Mutny agreed.

'I can think of another word other than *Battle-axe* that would better describe her!' Nefertiti's expression became grim. 'More and more that woman is meddling in our affairs!' She headed for the door. 'I'd better go and find out what irritated her *this* time.'

*** 

The feast-day of the thirteenth-year reign of His Majesty, King Akhenaten, was approaching. These special celebrations always exited the princesses. They eagerly awaited their mother's visit to the Place of learning. She would be discussing and planning the coming event with them.

Under the supervision of Menefer, Merit and Senpa were fashioning clay figurines when Lady Mutny entered, smiling to herself. 'You look pleased, Lady Mutny,' Senpa wiped her brow with the back of a clay-soiled hand.

'Oh, just a private little joke.' She was still thinking about her impolite remarks to Queen Tiye, and changed the subject, 'Now, about the up-coming feast day. Any suggestions for the entertainment?'

The girls eagerly put forward their ideas, but the jovial atmosphere was short-lived when Queen Nefertiti arrived. She did not look too happy. 'Join me on the balcony,' Nefertiti beckoned and went out ahead of Lady Mutny. She pulled a sardonic face for the girls, shrugged and followed her sister.

'Do you know what she did?' Nefertiti fumed as Mutny joined her. Mutnedjmet shook her head.

'The *Window of Appearance* ceremony had always been a personal one, Mutny!' Nefertiti gestured. 'Akhenaten and I spent days planning the thirteenth year of his reign, but now *she,'* the queen flung her arm in the direction of the King's house, 'she wants to re-organise it! We had already selected those people to be honoured, but now she came forth with her own list!' her voice rose in anger.

Those inside the chamber tried not to listen but could not help overhearing. Menefer tried and draw her pupils' attention away from the queen's fury and proceeded to explain some technique of a craft, but the princesses were straining, not to miss a word of the conversation.

'Yes, I noticed,' Mutnedjmet replied. 'During the temple ceremony, Tiye walked *ahead* of Akhenaten. How could she have the effrontery to leading the procession? Akhenaten is Pharaoh, the living incarnation of Aten, and no one dares precede the god.'

'I am well aware of it.' Nefertiti tried to control her emotion. 'The worst thing is that Akhenaten *allows* it!' she turned, facing the garden and slammed her fist on the balcony wall to emphasise her words. 'That was why I chose not—*and will not* attend any more ceremonies of the Disk. Not until she is absent!' Nefertiti paused a moment and turned back toward Mutny. 'After a fierce argument, I told her it amounted to blasphemy, a downright insult to the Royal House and to Aten, but she scoffed, remarking that *she,* as a goddess, had a right,' the queen lowered her voice a little and there was a note of despair in it, 'Her influence over Pharaoh is getting out of hand. It has to be stopped, but what can I do? Akhenaten will not stand up to his mother!'

Menefer again tried to distract the girls from the conversation, but she herself was eager to hear more.

'Did you speak with him about the matter?' Lady Mutny sounded concerned.

'Yes, but instead of siding with me, he scolded me like a child!' The queen lowered her voice. 'He said I have shown great discourtesy to him and the Aten by neglecting my Royal commitments. When I reminded him that Tiye had taken over those duties and I might as well abstain from public appearances, he told me not to be petty.'

There was a lull in the conversation and only the sound of birds from the garden could be heard. Menefer made another effort to draw the princesses' attention to Senpa's clay figure, which she had finished and was now smoothing with a scrap of damp fabric.

The queen spoke again, in a lower voice, a quaver in her voice, and they all pricked their ears to hear. 'Tiye then added that "her son needs someone to support him and keep him happy." I told her we *had* been happy, that we had enjoyed life, once, but since her arrival we did nothing but quarrel.'

'How did she react to that?'

'Unfortunately, she does not believe it.' Nefertiti threw her hands up. 'She said I'm blaming her for our bickering…using *her* as an excuse to shun my duties.'

'*You*? Using *her*? That is ridiculous,' Mutnedjmet snorted.

'She then asked Akhenaten why he puts up with me,' there was a slight whine in Nefertiti's voice, 'She suggested he find someone in the House of Women to be by his side…someone more worthy…'

Lady Mutny gasped, 'She said *that*? That lowly daughter of a…a…' Mutny raged aloud, trying to think of an appropriate name for Queen Tiye.

'Shhh, keep your voice down.' Nefertiti, suddenly aware of their proximity to her daughters, dropped her voice, 'Then finally, Akhenaten defied her. He told her, very firmly, that he would not reject me and I would remain by his side to share his throne.'

'Good for him.'

'But by then, I had had enough. I told them I was done, and was going to see my daughters and I left.' Nefertiti paused, then her voice rose again as she recollected the argument. 'That insufferable woman! That low-born commoner who caught a king's eye and affection, ensnared him in her web, like a spider wrapping a fly. Amenhotep did her bidding, doted on her and granted her every wish—she shared his throne as an equal. He even elevated her status to that of a deity. Now she is trying to get that same status here in Akhet Aten. Did you know Akhenaten is having a temple constructed in her honour on the island?'

'Yes. I know…but she does not have him completely in her power. He did speak up for you.'

'Yes!' Nefertiti fumed. 'For once, he did.'

'She has rather an overpowering presence,' Mutny added. 'I try to avoid her whenever I can.'

'Akhenaten has changed, Mutny.' Nefertiti calmed down, her voice becoming almost emotional. 'I can see it in his eyes. He looks different. The husband I once knew is no more. She has changed him. Akhenaten no longer rules the Two Lands, *That woman* does!'

\*\*\*

Dhaba, Smenkhare's personal servant, entered the chamber. 'Lord, Pharaoh is on his way here!'

The prince had been busy replacing some flight feathers on his arrows. 'Quick, Dhaba, help me clear this mess.' Feathers, slivers of wood, gum and bits of cord were all over the place and he quickly started tidied up, but before either could do very much, Akhenaten entered.

'Am I interrupting something important?'

'No, just keeping myself busy… I did not expect you, I would have arranged a proper—'

Akhenaten seated himself. 'We are brothers, Smenkhare, there is no need for formality, is there?'

'No, you are welcome…any time.'

'Good, but I hoped you would also have visited me be now.'

'I tried, but you seem to be rather busy. The arrangements for your anniversary feast for one, your mother, Queen Tiye's visits…'

'That should not deter you. There are rumours that you are kept busy, frequently entertaining the sculptress in your chambers.'

'Menefer?' Smenkhare looked at his brother, surprised. 'I told you we were just friends…why?'

114

Akhenaten shrugged. 'I was just curious. Has she been putting on the wig for you, yet?'

'No!' Smenkhare replied, indignantly. He resented Akhenaten's implication. 'As I told you, we are just friends!'

'Do not make any arrangements for her yet. I have other plans for you...and Meritaten.'

'But... I heard that you and Merit are to be—'

'Do not pay attention to rumours, Smenkhare! Nothing has been decided. If you do decide to have this...the sculptress as a wife, take her as a concubine or a secondary wife.'

'I have made no plans regarding Menefer...she is betrothed.'

'Ah, yes. I recall...her betrothed was sent to Kush.'

'Why the sudden interest in my relationship with Menefer?'

'Just curious. My feast day is approaching and I will make an announcement then. I have decided you to be my heir, the future ruler of the Two Lands, and for that you need to wed a Princess Royal.'

Smenkhare gasped. 'Me? Your heir? But I—but what about your son...'

'Tutankhaten is still very young...and sickly. Pentu fears, regrettably, that the boy might not make it to adulthood and would join my dear Meketaten soon. I need someone strong to follow in my footsteps. After Setenpenre's birth, we came to accept that Nefertiti would bear no sons, nor, for that matter, any more children.'

'I regret to hear that about Nefertiti, and am honoured you want me to succeed you, Akhenaten. I am most grateful.'

'It is the will of Aten for her to have no sons. I will try again, but in the event I do not sire another son, you are to be my heir and I will make an official announcement soon. It is time you learn how to deal with administrations problems. You ought to be by my side during my audiences with officials.'

# Chapter Fourteen
## Letters

'Menefer!' Smenkhare called out and hurried over.

The weather was uncomfortably hot, and the high walls, surrounding the court-yard, retained the baking heat of the sun. She was looking forward to her usual cool pitcher-shower. She had finished her lessons for the day and was on her way to her quarters, when the prince called out to her. She stopped and waited for him to reach her.

'Your Highness,' Menefer greeted him with the customary royal salute.

'Come, let's sit down. The garden is cool, now that the sun has gone down,' he led her back along the path.

'Yes, it is pleasant here now, and the birds are particularly melodious as the evening approaches.' She took a seat on a bench opposite him and placed her basket of writing material on the seat next to her.

'Akhenaten again visited me. He brought me a poem he had written.' Smenkhare held up a papyrus scroll. 'Read this.' He handed it to her. 'It seems his interest in me has greatly increased since my arrival. He is finally taking more noticed of my existence.' He hesitated, then looked at her shyly. 'It is rather personal.'

She read the poem.

*'Oh my beloved, though makest me young again,*
*Thy sweet body makest me live.*
*And the world is good.*
*To love thee exeedeth the love of others.*
*I inhale the sweet breath that comes from thy mouth.*
*I contemplate thy beauty every day.*
*It is my desire to hear thy lovely voice,*
*Like the North wind's whiff.*
*Love will rejuvenate my limbs.*
*Give me thy hands that hold my soul,*
*I shall embrace and live by it.*
*Call me by my name again, forever;*
*And never will it sound without response.'*

'It's beautiful, and very personal...and rather amorous, Highness, but it's good for two brothers to bond.' She handed him the scroll and he placed it on the seat next to him.

'I am to be his heir!' Smenkhare declared. 'He is soon to make it official and plans to announce it during the festival.'

'That is wonderful news, Highness.'

'*Smenkhare* Menefer,' he corrected her. 'We are alone.' He hesitated. 'I—uh—I have two reasons for wanting to see you. Firstly, I wish you to do something for me…'

'Anything…Smenkhare.'

'I wish you to craft a small likeness of me, as a gift for…for Pharaoh.'

'I will be happy to, High…Smenkhare, but I will not be able to finish it before Pharaoh's feast day.'

'No, not his anniversary feast, it is for the Upit festival, the time of gift giving. Will that be sufficient time?'

'Three months from now?' She mentally calculated the time she would need. 'Yes. That should be sufficient time.'

After a pause, she asked, 'You mentioned *two* reasons for wanting to see me. What is the other?'

Smenkhare got up and sat next to her. 'Pharaoh is aware of your visits and is displeased.'

She looked up at him, surprised. 'I don't understand…there is nothing between us. Did you not explain we are just friends?'

'Yes, but he is still concerned. He said rumours breed like fleas, and is spread as easily.' He looked uncomfortable. 'He wants it to cease. You are aware of my feelings for you, Menefer, but—'

'I understand.'

'Akhenaten had again mentioned his plans for me to marry Merit.' He paused, 'I would rather wed someone I really care for, but for now, I must abide by his wishes.'

He stood up. 'I must go, he is expecting me. We will meet again, soon.'

She remained seated for a while after Smenkhare had left. She was aware of Smenkhare's feelings and in a way, she is grateful for Akhenaten's intervention. Her heart belonged to Rakhmet, only Rakhmet.

She stood up and picked up her basket, then noticed the scroll on the opposite seat where Smenkhare had forgotten it. She picked it up, preparing to return it to him later.

'Menefer!' The sudden voice behind her made her drop the scroll. 'Sorry, I did not mean to startle you,' Khay bent down and picked it up. 'Still trying to decipher the *words of the mouth* of the Asians?'

'Oh, uh…no. It is just a letter.' She reached out to take it from him, but he held it away from her.

'It is private,' she said, annoyed. 'A poem. May I have it back, please?'

'A poem? I did not know Rakhmet writes poetry.'

'It is not from him.'

'Oh? Another admirer? The prince perhaps? I saw you two snuggling up together.'

'It is not *from* him, it is *to* him…and we did not *snuggle*!' she snapped.

'You have been seeing a lot of him lately, have you not? You'd rather have a prince than a scribe, yes?'

She again reached for the document. 'Please Khay, May I have it. It is his property—'

'Why would you have his private letters?'

'It's a poem, as I told you. He forgot it on the bench. Do not make it appear anything more than…' as Menefer again reached for the scroll, she noticed the half obscured figure observing them. In a low voice, she added, 'We are being watched again.'

Khay turned and looked around. 'I see no one. You seem to see a spy in every shadow, Menefer.'

'I know what I saw.'

'You use that excuse every time we meet. It is getting tiresome.'

'I am not making it up. Someone *was* watching!'

'You are a very mysterious woman, Menefer. Secrecy seems to surround you— but I like mysteries.'

Then his demeanour changed and he shrugged. 'Very well, perhaps, if it is as you say, we had best be cautious. I brought you the remaining fragments of the tablet coverings.' He handed her back the scroll. 'I left them for you near your dwelling, hidden under the castor-oil bush.'

'Thank you, Khay. Thank you very much. I really appreciate it.'

*** 

That evening back in her quarters, Menefer lit a second oil lamp from one she kept lit all the time. It was easier than to light it from fire-stones. She changed the tunic she wore for the temple ceremony for a more casual one, and carefully hung it back on the peg.

She seated herself on a low stool, removed a sandal and inspected her foot where a sandal strap had caused a blister. The strap had broken and was mended, but she had done it hastily and the ridge had been chafing her foot. She'd have to re-stitch it again, she thought, but will need more care.

She looked about the room, and then her eyes fell on her basket with the scroll. The sandal was forgotten as she limped over to her sleeping couch and removed the scroll from the basket. Carefully, she unrolled it and re-read the poem again, then sat pondering for a while. It was quite beautiful and tender, but a love poem from Pharaoh to Prince Smenkhare? Had the king become enamoured of his brother? Could Smenkhare be that naïve, not to have recognised it as a love poem? Surely not. Perhaps the joy of his brother's attention had made him oblivious of the implications.

*** 

It was the day before the Feast of Pharaoh's Celebration. Menefer had been given leave to return home for the feast days. She had been browsing through the *sownet*, the great market place in the forecourt of the temple, when she saw Djenna and hurried to catch up with her and called out.

'Djenna!'

Djenna stopped and turned. It was very hot and she was wearing an *afen-t*, a cotton head-cloth instead of her usual wig.

'Menefer, it has been a while…'

They exchanged greetings and quickly brought each other up to date with trivial chit chat. The market place was crowded, and Djenna was not too pleased.

'The sownet seems very busy,' Menefer observed.

'And dusty and smelly.' She wrinkled her nose. 'Tomorrow is a great occasions and the merchants would do well.'

'Yes. That is why I came early. By now, all the best goods would already be sold.' Menefer held out a small jar studded with bright red seeds with black markings, 'It is supposed to bring luck. These seeds are called *lucky beans*.'

'Very pretty—I do not believe in lucky charms, but I've seen them, punctured, to make into beads and woven into wigs. You should try something like that.'

'You know I prefer my hair *neshu-t,* natural. It is so much more comfortable, and cooler than wearing a wig.'

'No need to be so smug, Menefer.' They walked in silence for a while. 'By the way, have you heard from Rakhmet lately?'

'Yes. I received another letter just two weeks ago, but very impersonal—almost like he was writing to a sister. He mentioned that his pupil, Batu, was doing well. Then he mentioned the weather, the land of Aahes…'

'No words of…anything else?' Djenna looked at her friend, expectantly.

'No. It's mostly about his work.' Menefer stared ahead. They had almost reached the city exit and her eyes following the road to the village.

'Or perhaps he now has other plans for his future,' Djenna smirked. 'People are fickle, you know.'

Menefer glanced at her and frowned, deciding not to answer. She changed the subject. 'That is a nice collar you are wearing, Djenna.'

'And costly! A gift from Queen Tiye,' Djenna stroked the necklace. 'A merchant from Tanis presented it to her, but she decided it made her neck too scrawny.'

'Serving the queen seems to have many advantages. I do hope you—'

'Look out!' A man's shrill voice called out above the clattering of horses' hooves.

Both girls spun around to see a driver-less chariot bearing down on them. With a cry, Djenna scurried out of the way but the chariot was heading straight for Menefer. Seemingly from nowhere, someone pushed her violently, sending her sprawling. She landed heavily on the dusty road. The pounding hooves and spinning wheels thundered past, just missing her, but a wheel caught the lucky-bean jar, shattering the gift she had bought for her mother.

Cries and gasps of concern came from the crowd and they rushed forward to assist. Menefer struggled into a sitting position and stared in dismay at the broken jar. The man who had knocked her out of danger's way, picked himself up from the dirt and helped her up.

'Sorry I had to push you out of the way. That was a near miss. Are you all right, Little One?'

'General Horemheb! Yes…yes I am fine, thank you, only a little winded.'

At that moment, Horemheb reminded her of Nebaten who also called her "Little One".

'You could have been badly injured—even killed.' His concerned eyes were upon her face. Horemheb was about three years older than Rakhmet, probably about twenty two years old, she thought, and slightly younger than her older brother, Nebaten.

Djenna came hurrying up, her face as while as her tunic. 'Menefer, are you hurt?'

'I… I'm all right, just a little shaky,' unsteadily, she started brushing the dirt from her garment.

'No, you *are* hurt!' Horemheb bent down and touched her ankle. 'Your leg—it has been grazed and there is a large bruise. Can you walk?'

Menefer took a few careful steps. 'Yes…I can manage, Thank you.'

'Your right arm!' Djenna called out in alarm. 'It's bleeding!' Menefer twisted it to see. Blood trickled down from a deep gash above her elbow.

'Let me help you to the temple gate…they can see to your wounds there,' Horemheb offered.

'No, it is nothing, really…'

The sound of approaching horses and a chariot made them turn. Mahu, chief of the *Medjay*, the local police, had secured the reigns of the runaway horses. 'We managed to stop them, General Horemheb, but they still seem agitated. If the accident happened in the market-place, it could have been much more serious.'

'Thank you, Mahu. Good work!' Then Horemheb noticed something. 'Uh-huh?' He walked over to the still skittish horses. 'This was no accident. Someone deliberately provoked the horses.' He leaned forward and pointed, 'Look. See, these gourd balls suspended from their tails? They are studded with thorns from an acacia tree. As the balls swing, they hit the backs of the horses' legs. The sharp spikes caused them to bolt!'

He removed the gourds and held them up to the gathered crowd. 'Did anyone see who did this?' Murmurs, perplexing looks and shaking heads answered his question.

He turned back to Mahu. 'Take the horses and chariot to your barracks and see if your Medjay can find out who owns them. I'm going to find the Overseer of the Royal Stables. Seti might know. I *will* find the culprit who did this.'

He turned his attention back to Menefer who was nursing her arm and dabbing at the cut and scrapes with a kerchief. 'Now, let's get you over to the scribe at the gate.'

With a slight limp, Menefer and Djenna followed him back to the temple gate. Menefer disregarded her injuries but complained bitterly about the broken lucky-bean jar.

***

General Horemheb escorted Menefer and Djenna home. Mutnames hurried into the courtyard to greet them. She stopped abruptly, alarmed, when she saw the bindings on her daughter's arm. 'Menefer, you are hurt!'

Horemheb declined Mutnames' invitation to stay. He had to return to his duties. They thanked him for his deed and help; he waved a parting salutation, turned his chariot around and headed back towards the city. She helped her protesting daughter into the house and to a chair, fussing around her the way all doting mothers do. 'Shall I summon a physician? I shall send a servant…'

'No need, mother. The injury is only slight.' She dared not mention Horemheb's suspicion of a deliberate action to do her harm.

'Oh, Mutnames! Your arm! It is also bound!' Djenna exclaimed. 'The same arm and the binding is almost identical to Menefer's.'

Menefer, still bemoaning the broken jar, had not even noticed, until that moment. 'Mother, what happened?'

'Oh, it's nothing,' Mutnames gestured indifferently. 'I was in the kitchen, helping prepare for tomorrow's feast, when I pressed my arm against a hot copper cooking pot. It's not serious.'

Djenna looked at Menefer, then at Mutnames. 'So much for your "lucky" beans Menefer! You both suffered matching injuries. It's uncanny.'

'People always say we look alike. Just as long as they don't think we did it deliberately, just to match each other's wounds,' Mutnames laughed. She stroked her daughter's bruised ankle. 'Are you sure we should not consult a physician? It might be painful to walk in a day or so, and could ruin the fowling trip you and your father had been planning.'

'I am certain I don't need a physician. I had already been tended to. I told you, Mother, the injuries are trivial. Please don't fuss.'

'Very well, but should you need one later, let me know.' Mutnames rose and went to prepare some light refreshments for the girls.

'Fowling?' Djenna asked when they were alone. 'It has been a long time since you last did that.'

'Yes. My father, Ipuky and I are going.' She rubbed her bandaged arm lightly. 'Did you know, the prince… Prince Smenkhare, had never fowled? I thought it was a popular Royal pastime.'

'Smenkhare? Then you are still seeing him?'

'Uh…Yes. We have become good friends. I am teaching him crafts. He is quite interested.'

'It might be his interests are *more* than just hunting.'

Menefer ignored Djenna's remark and changed the subject. 'I wager you have something special to wear for tomorrow's ceremony, don't you?'

'I'll be wearing this collar again, of course,' Djenna stroked the adornment. 'Queen Tiye is sure to notice. It will go well with that banded garment, the colourful one I recently acquired…oh, that reminds me, I better hurry home. My tunic-halter had come undone and I need to stitch it. I will see you at the gathering, then.'

*Djenna stitching her own garments? Very unlikely, she would most probably coerce her mother to do it*, Menefer thought, as her friend excused herself and left.

Her painful ankle forced Menefer to stay off her feet the rest of the day, but she did not mind. She used the time to assemble the remaining broken tablet-coverings. Lucky she brought the last of them home the previous week, she thought. They could also have been destroyed, like that pottery jar.

She had managed to glue together most of the pieces of two more envelopes. Checking to make certain the missing pieces were not among the fragments, she carefully made clay impressions of them and left them to dry. She would fire them and get them to Lord Nakht presently.

***

The day of the Feast of Pharaoh's thirteenth year had arrived. The morning temple ceremony, the *Ceremony welcoming the Rising of Aten*, was a special one for this great day, but Menefer's ankle was still a bit stiff and swollen and decided not to attend. Anyway, Queen Nefertiti no longer attended them. Queen Tiye had taken the queen's place for the Aten ceremonies, but Queen Nefertiti would be present for the *Window of Appearance ceremony* later that day. This was Pharaoh's great day, and the queen vowed to be by her consort's side, in spite of Queen Tiye's presence.

Djenna had positioned herself just below the Window of Appearance. She was wearing an ornately decorated wig despite it being hot. She fanned herself with a *khu*, an ostrich feather, set into a short silver handle.

The windows, where the Royals would appear, were open balconies on the bridge, overlooking the King's Way, just above the main thoroughfare. The street, usually reserved for carts, chariots and other traffic was, for now, closed, except for pedestrians.

Djenna was most surprised when Menefer arrived, as she had not expected her to attend. 'Greetings, Menefer. I did not think you would come. I was certain your injuries would have kept you away.'

'This is a special day for my family,' Menefer explained. 'My father and Ipuky both are to be honoured and I had to make an effort.'

'How is your foot?'

'My ankle,' Menefer corrected her. 'Not too bad. I'll live.'

'Large crowd today!' Djenna looked around.

'Yes,' Menefer said, following her gaze, then muttered under her breath. 'Curse him!'

'Whom are you cursing now?' Djenna whispered, trying to see whom Menefer was condemning.

'Don't look.' Menefer shielded her pointing finger with her other hand. 'Kenti. Watching us!'

'Kenti? Why?' Djenna glanced sideways.

'Uh…it's a long story. I'll just ignore him.'

'Another one of your suitor, perhaps?'

'Perhaps,' Menefer shrugged, not daring to tell her friend the real reason. She steered Djenna away to another area then looked about her. Kenti had not followed and she relaxed.

The crowd hushed as the Vizier Ay appeared on the balcony. He looked most uncomfortable and was perspiring profusely. His leopard-skin cloak and heavy wig only made it worse. Flies, attracted to the moisture, buzzed about him and this kept his zebra-tail fly-swatter busy.

'Rise and rejoice, people of Egypt!' he called out in a loud voice. 'Hail our beloved sovereign, Per-O, King Akhenaten, and his Great Royal Wife, Soother of the King's heart whom he loves, Queen Nefertiti.'

Akhenaten and Nefertiti appeared to the cheering crowd, holding hands, and followed by fan-bearers. Rumours of a Royal quarrel that had been spread by servants, and then the queen's absence from the temple ceremonies, had been widespread, but the dispute between them seemed to have been resolved.

Ay then announced Queen Tiye. She entered from the Palace side and took her place on Akhenaten left, the opposite side of Queen Nefertiti. The contrasts between the two queens were very obvious—Nefertiti, graceful and elegant, and always smiling, whereas Tiye remained aloof and stern-faced, and wearing a permanent scowl. The corners of her mouth were drawn downwards, and the deep lines on each side, made her appear she was smelling something unpleasant.

*I would sculpt her one day,* Menefer thought. Preserve that look forever in stone, for all the following generations to know her for the bitter woman she was.

Ipuky arrived and joined Menefer and Djenna. After mutual greetings, he was about to compliment Djenna on her elaborate wig, when the crowd hushed as the king stepped forward to bless the crowd.

'People of Akhet Aten. Aten's blessings be upon you. May he brighten your lives and bring you joy. May this, my thirteenth year, be a prosperous and healthy one and may you enjoy everlasting blessings. May your lands yield good crops, your businesses expand a hundredfold and may the Glorious Aten smile upon you.'

'Hah!' Ipuky hissed in a low voice. 'Of course he wishes our businesses to expand. This is also the time when our taxes are assessed.'

'Shhh,' Menefer cautioned in a whisper. 'Don't be so cynical, Ipuky!'

Akhenaten then announced his successor, Prince Smenkhare. A murmur arose from the crowd. Many had seen the prince's Chariot with the Amun name, and rumours were rife about the young prince's religious preferences.

After more tedious speeches, Hatiay appeared on the balcony and started calling upon those who were to receive honours that day. The first to be called was General Horemheb who was awarded a golden pectoral, which was placed about his neck. Then Huya, Superintendent of the Royal Household was next, followed by Kheruef, the Chief Stewart; Sethi, Judge and troop commander; Ranefer, Akhenaten's chariot driver. One by one, the men approached the balcony to receive their tokens of appreciation.

'Thutmose and Ipuky, Royal sculptors…' Hatiay called out.

Excitedly, Menefer pushed her brother forward. 'Go Ipuky! You have been summoned.' Father and son made their way through the crowd.

'Thutmose…Ipuky,' Pharaoh addressed them. 'For services rendered, a small token of appreciation to each of you,' Akhenaten passed down the objects to the sculptors. Thutmose saluted and stepped back to make way for his son. Ipuky received his award and they returned to their places in the crowd.

'Ooh, let me see what you received!' Djenna asked, curiously, and she and Menefer crowded around him.

'It is nothing special, just a copper armband,' he appeared indifferent. 'Just as the previous one I received.'

'But it is inscribed!' Djenna replied, awed, 'with Pharaoh's name! That makes it very special.'

'Yes,' Ipuky answered casually. 'Copper has some value—'

'Ipuky!' Menefer scolded. 'You are being—'

'Mistress Menefer, the Royal Tutor!' Hatiay called out.

Stunned, Menefer looked up, disbelieving. Had she heard correctly?

Djenna prodded her. 'Menefer, go, *Go*! You have been summoned,' Meekly, she approached the window.

'Mistress Menefer, for services rendered, a small token of our appreciation.'

Akhenaten passed the object down to her and she bowed in a Royal salute.

'What is it, Menefer? Let me see!' Djenna hastened forward as Menefer returned to her place.

'A beaded collar!' Thrilled, Menefer held it up for her friend to see. 'It was the one I saw Princess Merit working on, but never suspected it was meant for me!' She tried to place it around her neck, but her bound arm made it a little awkward.

'It is beautiful! Let me help you,' Djenna fastened it about Menefer's neck. 'Turquoise and lapis-lazuli beads. What a wonderful gift, Menefer. Jewellery *does* become you, as I had often said. I am truly envious.'

Elated by the honour bestowed on her, Menefer was also surprised by Djenna's comment. It was the first time ever that Djenna had expressed admiration about anything she wore.

'Good day, Mistress Menefer!' They all turned as Horemheb approached. 'Congratulations. I am pleased you have been honoured this day… How are your injuries?'

'Greetings General Horemheb, thank you. Yes, the award was quite unexpected, and thanks for your concern. I'm fine.'

'Well, you will need a few days to rest and heal. Shall I notify Hatiay—?'

'Rest?' She cut in. 'No, I am not going to sit idly at home. My father and Ipuky had planned to go fowling tomorrow and I am going with!'

'Fowling? I never thought you as being a huntress.'

'Oh yes, I taught her to use a throwing stick when we were very young. She is quite skilled…almost as good as me!' Ipuky bragged.

'A pity I will not be using it…' Menefer lifted her bound arm and gestured towards it with a nod, '…this time. I'll just use claptraps instead.'

'Where will you be going? I believe the reeds along the lake up north is good…'

'No, we'll be going to the island. The marshes there, opposite the Southern Pleasure Palace, is very popular. Hunting had always been very good, I believe.'

Pharaoh blessed the people and with a prayer to Aten, the ceremony wound to a close and the crowd dispersed. Djenna was eager to get home to rid herself of the hot wig and tight-fitting garments, and urged Menefer to hasten. Neither of them noticed the curious eyes watching the two girls depart. Someone who had eavesdropped on their earlier conversation, had been most interested in Menefer's plans.

# Chapter Fifteen
## The Hunt

Thutmose had been in a sombre mood throughout *mesit*. Only Menefer had joined her parents for the evening meal as Nebaten and Ipuky were in the workshop, finishing a task, and had their meals taken there.

'Why the long face, Thutmose?' Mutnames leaned one elbow on the table and gestured at Thutmose's untouched food. 'Are my honey-cakes not to your liking? Is the bread gritty, or the beer too sour?'

'No, no, Mutnames,' he drew his gaze from the two vacant seats and looked at his wife. 'Your cooking is as good as ever,' he took a deliberate bite from the bread and chewed. 'Old age comes too quickly. I was just remembering the past—when Nebaten was still called *Nebamun*, Ipuky still wore the lock-of-youth and Menefer was but a babe in swaddling clothes,' he sighed. 'How I wish for those days again.'

'This is a time to be merry, a time to rejoice. Our children are now grown. We live in a new time. Things change and we must adapt. We have both grown old and…'

'*You* have not!' he put his hand gently upon hers. 'You still look as youthful as ever. How often do people still mistake you for our daughter's sister? But, I feel my years. It is getting more difficult for me to chisel the stone—to do my task. I fear tomorrow's hunt will be my last.'

'Don't talk like that, father. You still have many years ahead of you…' Menefer reproached him.

'Yes. It is bad luck to say things like that,' Mutnames agreed. 'Your talk of doom and gloom is—'

'No, I merely meant that I am not as energetic as I used to be. The stiffness of age is upon me and my bones object to my every move. I am getting too old for hunting now.' Thutmose had that far-away look in his eyes, 'Remember the time when I used to leap from one skiff to another with ease? Now I can barely climb the stairs.'

'Yes,' Mutnames nodded and smiled. 'But I too, am no longer agile.'

'Remember when you knocked down a duck with the throwing stick on your very first try?'

'Mother!' Menefer asked, surprised. 'You? Hunting?'

'Yes, she used to love it,' Ipuky said as he entered, brushing at his dusty garments.

'It was just plain luck! Most of my other attempts failed,' Mutnames laughed. 'I missed almost every bird after that…and remember when I once tried to catch my returning throwing stick and fell in the water,' they laughed merrily together, reminiscing about their young days.

'You never came hunting with us when I was younger, why?'

'When you arrived, Menefer, I decided to give it up and remain at home. With a growing family, there was too much to do, even with servants helping.'

'Then why not go fowling with us tomorrow?' Menefer invited. 'We would love to have you along.'

'No, you go and enjoy yourself. I will stay and stitch you a garment to go with that new collar.'

'I think you ought to come,' Menefer insisted. 'If father is going to give up hunting after this one, you *should* go with him…for old times' sake.'

'The skiff is not big enough for all of us…' Mutnames explained.

'Oh, it will be… I was going to tell you. I've decided not to go,' Menefer announced.

'But you were so looking forward to it, Menefer.'

'At first, yes, but…but my arm has started to hurt, and my ankle feels rather sore and stiff.'

'But I though you said you felt much bet—' Ipuky started to contradict but Menefer gave him a fierce look. Then he understood.

'Oh…yes, Mother, she was limping around this morning and her arm was really acting up. Yesterday, she could hardly stretch out to receive Pharaoh's gift. I had to carry it home for her.'

'Ipuky!' Menefer hissed through clenched teeth. 'Don't overdo it!'

'Do you really want me to go in your stead?' Mutnames asked expectantly, contemplating the adventure.

'Yes, really!' Menefer and Ipuky both urged.

'Very well, I will go!'

'Are you certain, Mutnames?' Thutmose asked. 'You are no longer as young— uh—as spry as you—'

'Yes I am, Old Man!' she laughs, 'But are *you*?'

'Very well,' he said, pleased to have her company again.

Suddenly a flutter of wings and chirping startled them.

'A bird!' Menefer cried out as a bird flew into the house and over the table.

'How did it get in here?' Ipuky ducked as it darted back and forth in panic.

'Catch it, Ipuky!' Menefer looked around for something to snare it and reached for a large jar.

'You will never catch it with that! Try and chase it towards the door…it will get out by itself.'

'It's an omen!' Mutnames, eyes wide with fear, and she had a hint of a tremble in her voice. 'A bad omen!'

'It's just a frightened little bird, Mother,' Ipuky tried to pacify her.

'No. It's a sign of bad luck. Something dreadful as going to happen…I just know it!'

\*\*\*

A morning haze hung over the marshes when the hunting party reached the island. Mutnames was kneeling in the centre of the skiff, with Ipuky at the bow, guiding it along through the reeds by means of a barge pole. Thutmose, at the stern, was steering with a paddle. They navigated their way noiselessly so as not to disturb any birds.

'Ipuky, look,' Thutmose observed. 'Other fowlers had already set their claptraps here. I think we need to go elsewhere.'

'I was about to say the same thing,' Ipuky agreed. 'I know of a small inlet that would be ideal,' he pushed the pole into a clump of reeds and the skiff edged out into a canal.

'Oh look,' Mutnames exclaimed, pointing. 'A kingfisher. How beautiful. I have not seen one for years.'

'All manner of birds abound here that won't be found around the city,' Thutmose explained.

The skiff entered the inlet, disturbing a flock of ducks that took off noiselessly. 'Oh dear. We frightened them away,' Mutnames said, disappointed.

'No matter, dear, they will return shortly.'

'There!' Ipuky pointed. 'That is the place I told you about,' he started to manoeuvre the craft to the place.

'It looks ideal,' Thutmose conceded. 'It is sheltered, and there are no other hunters about.'

'It's nice here, so peaceful and quiet...and lush.' Mutnames looked about her and trailed one hand in the water. For the first time in many months, she felt relaxed.

'We will need to anchor. The river runs fairly deep and fast in the channel,' Thutmose looked around for a secure site.

'We are not completely alone. I just saw another skiff moving through the reeds over there,' Mutnames nodded towards the area.

'Well, it is not as crowded as the other place. It seems the entire hunting community is out there,' Ipuky said, steering towards a clump of reeds.

'We cannot blame them. Everyone is taking advantage of the holidays,' Thutmose remarked.

Ipuky carefully stepped on a knoll of papyrus to test its firmness, then went about securing the skiff.

Mutnames started to rise, causing the skiff to rock violently.

'Careful, Mutnames!' Thutmose cautioned. 'You're not as agile as you used to be, remember?'

The skiff steadied and stiffly Mutnames straightened up. 'The constant kneeling has given me cramps. I need to stand for a moment to stretch my legs.'

She turned in the direction of a whirling sound. There was a dull thud, Mutnames' legs buckled and, with a slight groan, she sagged.

Thutmose, assuming she was trying to sit down again, reached out to assist her, but she swayed away from him. 'Mutnames! Watch out!'

Ipuky spun around at his cry of alarm just in time to see his mother fall into the canal and disappeared beneath the water. Without a second thought, he leapt into the canal and started groping around the dark waters for her.

'Ipuky, find her!' His father's anguished voice rose in panic.

Ipuky continued to splash and dive beneath the skiff, searching blindly and groping around the tangled reeds. He would come up spluttering, then dive again and again, widening his search. His father, trying to steady the rocking skiff, watched helplessly, praying to all the gods who might assist.

'I beseech thee, O Hapi. You are the god of the Nile. Please return her to me. O Isis, O Horus, have mercy on an old woman who had always revered thee. O Osiris, do not claim her yet. She has many years yet.'

Ipuky surfaced again, panting heavily, his chest burning from the exertion. 'She *must* be around here… perhaps caught in the reeds!'

He dove again. Thutmose, fearing the worst, prayed again. 'O Nephthys, I call upon thee. If she had succumbed, only thee can revive her.'

He started calling out for help. They were in a secluded area and no other hunters were nearby. After a while, and only by chance, two hunters paddled by. Thutmose's calls for help reached them and they paddled closer, but the old man's explanations were garbled and they did not immediately understand. Only when Ipuky surfaced again, did they learn of the accident.

'Where did she fall?' one of them asked. Ipuky indicated to an area in the channel, but because he had disturbed the mud, the water had become murky. They could see nothing.

'The current is strong,' one of the other hunters remarked. 'She must have been carried downstream. We will search there.'

More fowlers were alerted and helped with the search, but after several hours, and still no sign of Mutnames, they started leaving.

'It is no use,' one remarked. 'We had searched the entire area. She is not here.'

'If she is not found alive,' another added, 'we must leave her. We cannot remove her body from the river anyway.'

Ipuky nodded silently. He knew the customs of Egypt. Those who had been claimed by Hapi must remain in the god's domain. It is sacrilege for a drowned person to be mummified and buried on dry land and it would incur the wrath of the god. He resigned himself to the obvious. 'I will take my father home.'

'No…no we must find her!' Thutmose voiced his alarm and again, for the umpteenth time called out. 'Mutname-e-e-esss!'

'Father, we have been here for hours. If she were here, we would have found her by now. She must have been swept downstream. The river flows swift, we know not where to look.'

'There! Ipuky, there she is!' Thutmose pointed, his voice shrill with excitement. 'Get her! Quick!'

Ipuky paddled over to something caught in a clump of reeds. He reached over and dragged it out. 'A curse on you, Seth!' Angrily, he cast the shredded rag into the marshes, then noticed something else floating nearby. A throwing stick had drifted against a clump of reeds. It did not appear to have been there very long. He picked it up. *Why would a hunter abandon a good throwing stick?* When it misses its target, it would return to the thrower, and if not, the hunter would retrieve it, together with its quarry.

The throwing stick had drifted from upstream, where they had been anchored, but all the hunters had been south of them this morning…except for the one they had glimpsed on a skiff earlier.

Absent-mindedly, Ipuky tossed the throwing stick into the basket and suddenly emotion overwhelmed him. The basket still contained the uneaten meal his mother had prepared for them that morning. There were sweetmeats, little honey-and-date cakes, a flask of home-made emmer beer, and an assortment of fruits. It had been the last meal she had made.

Then the full horror of the incident, the realisation that she was dead, struck him…his mother had been taken from them in the cruellest way. He will never again hear her voice, taste her food or feel her embrace.

Ipuky's cry of anguish, of despair and grief startled a flock of waterfowl and sent them flying noisily off into the late morning sky.

*\*\*\**

Stunned by the news, the servants crept silently about the house, wide-eyed and fearful. Others, those who had served the family a long time, threw dirt upon their heads and rent their clothing in distress and mourning. Everyone, aware that three accidents had already occurred, circulated superstitious stories that a fourth might follow. They glanced about, fearful that more might strike.

Ipuky kept reliving the grim event, repeating the episode over and over in his mind. Something was amiss, but, at first, he could not pinpoint what it was. Then, when a servant brought the traps and the basket of food from the skiff, he noticed the throwing stick! He picked it up and stared at it. A throwing stick had struck his mother—this throwing stick!

How else would she have collapsed so suddenly and fallen into the water? There had been no outcry, so she must have been stunned! His mind replayed the moment, and he remembered hearing a swishing sound and a dull thud just before she fell! At the time, he did not pay any heed to it, until now.

All three siblings were in a grim and depressed mood, but Menefer especially, was taking the news very badly. She blamed herself for what had happened. She had insisted her mother went on the hunt. Had she not feigned discomfort at her injuries, her mother would still be alive. She remained in her room all that day, weeping and lamenting.

'It is perhaps good that Menefer should mourn thus,' Ipuky remarked. 'She will recover quickly, but it is different with father. Since his return home, he has not shown any emotion and spoken not a word. He will not eat or drink, but just sits there, staring out the window. One, who does not express his sorrow, will take long to heal.'

'It is the god's way to calm his *ka*,' Neb agreed. 'His *ba* is wandering away from his body and his mind has been closed to the brutal reality.'

Menefer emerged from her chamber later that evening, her hair dishevelled and her eyes red and puffy. Without a word, she passed Nebaten and Ipuky and headed for the kitchen.

'Come, join us, Little One,' Neb invited, concerned.

'No, I must see to *mesit*,' she answered in a flat voice.

'No need. The servants will prepare the meal. Come, sit with us. At a time like this we need to be together.'

She took a seat near them. 'When I passed their bedchamber, I heard father talking to mother…as if she were there with him.'

'In his mind, she is,' Ned answered. 'His *ba* has left his body and dwells with hers. The physician told us there was nothing we can do. It might either never return, or it might happen suddenly. It is one of the mysteries of life.'

Thutmose the sculptor had nothing left to live for. The love of his life was no more. He will never again create another piece of artwork and the ones on which he had been working, would forever remain unfinished. The likeness of Queen Nefertiti, so close to completion, will remain incomplete for all time.

***

The princesses were summoned to Queen Nefertiti's chambers that afternoon and they immediately noticed their mother's distress. She hugged them close and the girls looked at one another, bewildered.

Nefertiti then, in a grave voice, told them the news. 'I had just been informed that…that our dear Menefer had…had been taken from us. She had drowned this morning!'

'What?' Merit asked, shocked. Senpa gasped.

'Yes, a great tragedy and loss, not only for her family, but for us as well. We must be brave,' there were tears in the queen's eyes as she hugged them.

'What about out lessons now…' Senpa leaned back and looked at Nefertiti.

'Senpa, this is not the time to speak of lessons!' Merit reprimanded.

'I'm afraid that has come to an end, Senpa,' the queen dropped her arms and shook her head slowly. 'No one can fill her place. We will have to go on as before…the way we did before she came here.'

The girls returned to their quarters feeling very depressed. They had come to love Menefer.

***

Sentu, Nefertiti's messenger arrived at Thutmose's residence bringing condolences from the Royal family. The queen had been shocked at the news, and had sent Sentu to express her sympathy. She grieved with the family over their loss and Her Majesty had stated that Lady Menefer would be sorely missed.

'*Menefer* would be sorely missed?' Neb repeated, mystified.

At that moment, Menefer appeared briefly. Sentu gasped, surprised. 'Mistress Menefer!'

'Sentu, you look quite pale.'

'Lord Nebaten…Her Majesty had…' Sentu stammered and pointed towards the family chamber where he had just seen Menefer. 'Her Majesty had been informed that Mistress Menefer had drowned, but…but who—'

'No, it was our *mother* who had died…' Neb glanced back but Menefer had already gone. 'Our sister, Menefer is very much alive.'

'Yes, I…I am now aware…I shall inform Her Majesty immediately,' Sentu bowed and hurried back to the city.

Neb returned to the family chamber just as Menefer entered. 'I suppose I will have to take over Mother's duties now,' her voice sounded flat and monotone.

'No need, Little One. Let the servants take care of everything here. Some of them had been with us for many years and know what to do. Perhaps you ought to go away for a while…visit father's sister in Waset—to be away from here.'

'No, I will return to *Per nesu*. My tasks will take my mind off things,' Menefer answered after a short pause. 'There is too much around here that reminds me of…Mother. I will return to my duties tomorrow.'

***

Kheruef escorted Kenti into the chamber where Queen Nefertiti was questioning a distressed Khay, his eyes were puffy and red from weeping. Kheruef directed Kenti to a place next to the scribe then stepped back. Kenti saluted and the queen turned to him.

'Master Kenti, my scribe had informed me earlier, of the drowning of the sculptress Menefer. He said he heard it from you?'

'Uh… Yes, Your Majesty, I ran into Khay late this morning and told him the news.'

'Where exactly, did you "run into" him?'

'At…uh…the servant's quarters, Majesty…'

'At *Menefer's* room, I was told.'

'Uh…yes, I think it was, Majesty!'

'Why there, specifically?'

'I…uh… I went there to see if she had something of mine, Your Majesty.'

'You were digging through her things!' Khay contradicted him. He then addressed the queen. 'I found Kenti rummaging around in her chamber, Majesty. I confronted him, and that's when told me of Menefer's death.'

'Is that true, Kenti? Going through someone else's things? That is a serious accusation. Explain!'

'Your Majesty, I went to collect something…uh…that belonged to my Master…' Kenti kept shifting his weight, looking very nervous.

'Your Master? You mean Lord Tutu?' Nefertiti rubbed her cheek with a finger.

'Yes, Majesty. When I learnt of her…when I learnt Mistress Menefer had drowned, I went to her room to get Lord Tutu's scroll…uh…before her family collected her things…'

'That's not true!' Khay hissed.

'Silence!' Kheruef commanded. 'Her Majesty was addressing Kenti!'

Khay apologised and the queen turned to Kenti again. 'This scroll…it is important, is it not?'

'To my Master, yes, Your Majesty.'

Khay glared at Kenti, shaking his head. Nefertiti noticed. 'You seem to disagree, Master Scribe.'

'Yes, Your Majesty!' Khay answered forcefully. 'The scroll he took, has *nothing* to do with Lord Tutu, Majesty.' He gave Kenti a piercing glance. 'It was a letter, Mistress Menefer told me, belonged to…someone else.'

'I will see this document. Where is it?'

'I took it from Kenti,' Khay explained. 'I put it in a place of safekeeping.'

Nefertiti demanded the document to be brought to her. Khay gave Kheruef directions where to find it, then Nefertiti continued.

'Now Kenti, about Mistress Menefer. You told Khay she had drowned?' Nefertiti sat back, steepling her fingers against her chin.

'Yes, Your Majesty,' Kenti looked uncomfortable.

'What would you say if I told you she is very much alive?'

Both Khay and Kenti gasped.

'It…it cannot be! It *was* her…she disappeared in the river and they searched for her for over an hour!' Kenti exclaimed.

'No, Kenti, it was not Menefer, but her mother that drowned.'

'No! I saw the binding on her arm! It was her.'

'You *saw* the binding? You were there?'

Kenti started to sweat. His eyes went wild and he looked around bewildered, then back at Nefertiti. 'No, Majesty, not me… I meant, a fowler saw the accident. He told me he saw her…being hit by a stray throwing stick. He saw her fall into the river.'

'A *fowler* informed you?' Nefertiti looked at him sharply.

'Uh…yes, Your Majesty,' Kenti wiped his forehead.

'This fowler…do you know his name?'

'I do not know his name, Majesty, we only meet occasionally, at the docks. I often get waterfowl from him for feast days. I only saw him today after some time.'

'How did this fowler know it was Mistress Menefer? Does he know her?'

'He has seen her before, Majesty…she had a binding around her arm…from an earlier accident.'

'Why would he come to you with this news?' Nefertiti leaned forward again.

Kenti swallowed hard, 'I ran into him, Majesty…at the market place.'

'Kheruef, go with Kenti and find this fowler!' Nefertiti watched them leave then dismissed Khay.

Kheruef accompanied Kenti to the landing place then the market, but the mysterious fowler was not to be found and no one seemed to know him. Suspecting that Kenti knew more than what he was telling him, he was taken to the Medjay headquarters for further questioning where general Horemheb joined them.

Mahu, the head of the Madjay, had discovered that the run-away chariot belonged to Lord Tutu, and he, Kenti, had been seen around it, moments before the incident in the street. Kenti, at first, denied the allegations. Lord Sethi, the judge, and Horemheb were both present in the Holding Chamber during the interrogation. Kenti was tied and stretched out on the floor, his arms above his head. After excessive "persuasion" with a flaming torch, he finally broke and confessed.

Yes, he admitted it was he who had alarmed the horses. He had directed them towards Menefer—to frighten her. When she escaped the chariot-charge, he was ordered to try again, but to make a better attempt the next time.

'Who ordered you, and why?' Sethi interrupted. Kenti's eyes, wild in their sockets, rolled around in fear. 'Kenti, *who ordered you*? Was it Lord Tutu?'

'Yes, Lord Sethi, it was Lord Tutu!' Kenti sobbed. 'He is my *Master* and I *have* to obey! Mistress Menefer had been causing trouble and he wanted her stopped!'

'Then what happened,' Mahu urged.

Kenti composed himself, took a drink from a flask offered to him and spilled some of the water. It trickled down is neck. 'The following day, at the gathering before the Window of Appearance, I overheard her telling someone she was going fowling, she even mentioned the time and place. I waited by the reeds.

'I saw her and two men arrived in the marshes I recognised them too—her father, Thutmose, the carver of likenesses, and her brother. When she stood up in the skiff, I could see her clearly. She still wore the binding on her arm from the chariot accident. Then I hurled the throwing stick at her and it had hit her head. I saw her fall into the water and disappear. I watched them search for her body. I only wanted to scare her...'

'Two attempts to *scare* her? Very unlikely!' Horemheb sneered.

Kenti broke down and sobbed. '...I then hurried away...back to Per nesu,' his arms still secured, he tried to wipe his tear-stained face on his shoulder. '...I went to her quar...quarters to retrieve the letter. Lord Tutu urged me to remove all letters she was holding. This was the one that she was particularly protective of. It was then that...that Khay showed up and took it off me!' He gulped loudly and sagged.

'You will repeat this confession in Lord Tutu's presence,' Lord Sethi told him.

Kenti went quite pale and his eyes widened in fear. 'No, he... I will be severely punished. He will take revenge...'

'You had already confessed to murder.' Horemheb's voice chilled him to the bone. 'For that, you will be punished. He can do no worse than what you will receive from the court!'

Kenti gulped again. 'No, Lord, I was merely trying to scare her. I did not mean to kill her... It was an accident!' he was trapped. There was no way out for him but to confront Lord Tutu!

# Chapter Sixteen
## A Traitor's Fate

Menefer had decided to return to her duties as quickly as possible. The sombre mood at home made everyone stressful, including the servants, who skulked around, keeping close to the walls as if trying to avoid bad spirits. At Per nesu, she could busy herself with her tasks and keep her mind off the recent tragedy.

She arrived a little tense, not knowing what kind of reception awaited her. The Princesses, overjoyed, hugged her and cried as soon as she arrived.

'Oh Menefer, it's so sad about your dear mother,' There was a slight tremble in Merit's voice. 'At first, we all thought it was you…'

'I know,' Menefer replied as they seated themselves. 'I heard about Sentu's confusion.'

'Well, Kenti confessed. He will be severely punished.'

'Punished? For what?' Menefer looked puzzled.

Merit waved a hand at her sister. 'Hush, Senpa!'

Senpa ignored her sister. 'For the deed of course…your mother's murder!'

'What? I…we thought it had been a tragic accident, but…but *murder?*'

'Yes. He deliberately—'

'SENPA!' Merit's stern voice cut her off abruptly.

Stunned, Menefer collapsed onto a couch and stifled a sob.

'Oh dear!' Senpa looked around at her sisters, bewildered. 'I did not think it—'

'That is your problem, Senpa. You never think!' Merit scowled at her sister and went to Menefer to comfort her.

'I'm sorry… I should not have mentioned it until—' Senpa started to apologise.

'I'm… I'm all right,' Menefer composed herself and wiped at her face. 'What did he say? What did he do?'

'You might as well know everything…now,' Merit glared at Senpa momentarily then told her the whole story, including the supposed accident with the chariot. 'Kenti said Lord Tutu is involved.'

'He tried to kill you, Menefer!' Senpa's eyes were wild. 'Why does he want you dead?'

'There is going to be a trial in a few days,' Merit added, 'then everything will be revealed. Lord Nakht was also summoned to appear before Pharaoh!'

Menefer dried her eyes and muttered a silent prayer. She thought about the two letters she 'delivered to Lord Nakht. 'I hope he—'

'Menefer! You're back!' Queen Nefertiti exclaimed as she and lady Mutny entered. They were both, just as pleased to see Menefer as the girls. They welcoming her back and expressing their condolences.

'I expected you to have at least a week off, Menefer, if not longer. Don't you wish some time away?'

'No, Your Majesty. As there will be no funeral and no preparation of the…of the body, the grieving time is much shorter. We held a small ceremony at the temple to pray and made burnt offerings.'

'We all feel so sorry for you. It was such a terrible blow. Did you hear about Kenti's…involvement?'

Menefer nodded, her mouth and eyes pinched to suppress more tears.

'So cruel, but rest assured he will be severely punished.' Sympathetic and understanding, and wishing not to dwell on the subject, the queen and Lady Mutny rose and started to leave, then Nefertiti stopped and turned. 'You are welcome to attend the trial, if you wish, if you are up to it, of course…'

'Thank you, Your Majesty. Yes, I would like that.'

'There is another matter I wish to discuss with you, Menefer.' Nefertiti laid a hand on Menefer's. 'But it can wait till later. I do not wish to concern you now, at a time like this.'

As they left, wondering why the queen wanted to see her. Will she be dismissed for her involvement in the business of the clay tablets?

***

The trial took place in the Great Hall of the palace. News of the hearing spread far and wide. Many officials attended, and it also drew a large number of curious citizens. The chamber was soon filled to capacity.

Kheruef entered the hall, tapped the floor with his staff then called for everyone to kneel. King Akhenaten and Queen Nefertiti were announced and they entered, followed by Ay and the judge Sethi. At a signal, everyone rose as they seated themselves.

'We are gathered here on a very serious matter. There has been, not only a murder in the city, but also a plot against the Royal House, and the welfare of Egypt is at stake. The trial will therefore, not only be handled by Lord Sethi, in the usual way, but will also to be presided over by His Majesty.'

Kheruef stepped aside. Ay rose then addressed the court. 'You Majesties, Judge Sethi…it has come to our ears that Kenti, the servant of Lord Tutu, had attempted to maim or slay a member of the Royal Household, the sculptress Menefer. When his first attempt failed, he tried a second time. He loitered in a place where he was certain the Lady would appear. But it had been the wife of the Royal sculptor, the lady Mutnames who had been slain instead. Kenti mistook her for his intended victim, and struck her down by a hunting throwing stick. The lady fell in the river and was drowned.'

Murmurs from the crowd were hushed and the trial continued.

Kenti was brought in and stood before Sethi, who cleared his throat. 'Kenti, during your interrogation, you confessed to the killing of Mistress Mutnames. Did you not?'

'Yes, my Lord. I ask for mercy,' Kenti pleaded.

'Do you think you deserve mercy?'

'It was not all my doing, Oh, Great One,' Kenti wrung his hands in anguish.

135

'Not *all* your doing? Clarify.'

'Please, Lord! I was ordered to do it!' Kenti sobbed, 'I am compelled to do my master's bidding.'

'Now you ask the court to grant you mercy?' Sethi asked.

Kenti nodded. 'Yes, Lord.'

'We shall see if you deserve it.' Sethi gave a dry cough. 'Is the person who had commanded you, present in the chamber, and if so, identify him!'

Fearfully, Kenti turned to where a scowling Lord Tutu stood, and pointed at him. 'It was him, my Lord...Lord Tutu.'

Tutu Spluttered with indignation. 'Lies! All lies!'

His words were drowned in the hubbub and the court had to be silenced. Once order had been restored, the proceedings continued. Kenti explained how he had been commanded to watch Menefer's every move. 'I reported to Lord Tutu that I had seen her with a letter. I was then directed to retrieve the letter. He said that the lady was a threat to "the cause" and need be "removed", and I had to see to it.'

'What "cause" was Lord Tutu referring to?' Lord Sethi asked.

'I am not certain, Lord. There had been rumours...'

'Rumours? Of what?'

'We are not concerned with rumours, Kenti. Only facts,' Ay interrupted. 'Why would Lord Tutu be interested in this document?'

'He learnt Mistress Menefer was in possession of certain letters. Lord Tutu feared she would hand it over to Lord Nakht. He said the—'

'They were official documents, Lord Ay,' Tutu cut in. 'Private—'

'Silence, Lord Tutu. You will have your turn later,' Ay turned back to Kent, 'Continue.'

'Some time ago, Lord Nakht had been given an official document,' Kenti explained. 'Lord Nakht was under the impression it contained information that could harm my Master, but it proved not to be so—'

'I remember the clay tablet,' Akhenaten interrupted, 'but why the interest over this particular scroll?'

Kenti bowed low and addressed Pharaoh. 'Lord, my master was convinced it was another official document. One that could cause great harm, if it should fall into the wrong hands.'

'Why? What could be so damaging to your master?' Sethi asked.

Kenti hesitated and looked around at Tutu nervously. He swallowed hard. 'I would receive mercy, my Lord? ...As you promised?'

Sethi looked at Akhenaten who nodded. 'Yes, you have the word of Pharaoh.'

'My Master, Lord Tutu,' Kenti glanced briefly at Tutu again, then turned back to the Judge and in order to save his hide, blurted out. 'Lord Tutu was...involved in a plot.'

The court erupted into an uproar. Tutu stormed forward shouting, but was dragged back. Because of the noise, no one heard what Tutu had said. The court was once again calmed and the trial continued.

Kenti looked at the floor, not daring to look at the furious Lord Tutu. 'They— they had plotted the overthrow of Pharaoh Akhenaten!'

'Liar!' Lord Tutu shouted.

Sethi called for silence and quelled the uproar. 'Lord Tutu, you will refrain from interrupting the court…'

'But I am being falsely accused!'

'You will have ample time to defend yourself later!' Sethi turned back to the accused and continued the questioning. 'Now Kenti, who are the "they" you spoke of?'

'I was not allowed in the chamber when Lord Tutu had his meetings. I do not know who the others were. I just caught a glimpse of them when I was given the tablets.'

'And these damaging tablets—where are they now?'

'All gone, Lord Sethi. Lord Tutu ordered me to destroy them all.'

Tutu crossed his arms and smiled, confidently.

'And this other letter, this scroll, where is?' Sethi asked. 'Was that destroyed as well?'

'No, Lord Sethi. It was given to Her Majesty, Queen Nefertiti.'

Sethi consulted with Pharaoh, then stood aside. Pharaoh crossed the Crook and Flail, symbols of office, across his chest. 'Kenti, you confessed to a very serious crime. For the attempted murder of the sculptress, and the murder of her mother, Mistress Mutnames, I find you guilty. The sentence is *"met-t mut"*. Death!'

Startled, Kenti cried out. 'No, NO! *Ur ser*! You promised me mercy!'

In a calm voice, Akhenaten replied. 'We *are* showing you mercy! You are a *nekenu*, a murderer and must die for your crime, but because of your full confession, your execution shall be swift and painless. Your cooperation saved you from a more severe one and spared you much suffering!' Pharaoh, held the crook and flail, the symbols of leadership and authority, and crossed them over his chest. 'Kenti, you have been found guilty of a most heinous crime. I hereby sentence you to be beheaded. Let justice be done. Sentence is to be carried out at sunset. Take him away.'

\*\*\*

The court adjourned until after noon. Lord Tutu had been detained since that morning and now his turn had arrived to stand trial. He looked smug and self-assured as they led him into the Audience Hall. They had no hard evidence to tie him to Kenti crimes, he made certain of that. All the incriminating tablets had been destroyed. He would claim Kenti's statements as fabrication and that Kenti would say anything to save his worthless hide!

The court reconvened and settled as Ay approached the accused, swatting imaginary flies. It was so quiet the swish of his fly whisk was clearly audible.

'Lord Tutu.' He cleared his throat. 'Serious charges had been brought against you by your servant, Kenti. He had confessed to the murder of Mistress Mutnames, and he confessed to the court this deed had been done under *your* orders!'

'Lies! Why would I want to have the sculptress killed? I do not even know the lady!'

'We were told Mistress Menefer obtained certain documents that could incriminate you and you wanted her out of the way.'

'It is true that the lady did manage to get an *illegal* copy of a letter, a *confidential* document, which, by itself is a misdemeanour and, for that, she ought to be charged. With that tablet, Lord Nakht tried to implicate me, before His Majesty, for collaborating with the enemy, but he failed,' Tutu gestured towards Nakht. 'His Majesty himself, declared me innocent!'

Sethi called upon Lord Nakht who was ordered to explain. 'Yes, it is true,' Nakht admitted. 'But, since then, new evidence had come to light.'

'What new evidence?' Lord Tutu's eyes grew large. All the tablets had been destroyed, as Kenti explained.

'Lord Nakht, you have accused Lord Tutu once before, and failed,' Akhenaten interrupted. 'Are you certain of your facts this time?'

'I am, Your Majesty.'

Akhenaten nodded and gestured for Nakht to continue.

'Lord Tutu,' Nakht held up a clay tablet. 'Do you recall this letter? It is from Ribbadi, Governor of Gebal.'

Nakht read it out loud. *'Behold, Aziro has fought my chiefs, and my chiefs whom I despatched to the city of Simyra. He has caused to be seized in that city. I need men to save the rebellion in this land. Give me soldiers.'*

And this one, *'It grieves me to say what he has done, this dog, Aziro. He cries peace unto the land and behold what has befallen the lands of the King. Behold what has befallen the city of Simyra, a station and a fortress of my lord. Men cry from this place, women weep. This violent man, this dog has spoiled the fortress.'*

Akhenaten sat forward, listening intently.

Tutu turned to him. 'As I said once before, Majesty, Aziro is a petty troublemaker and we can deal with him easily, but Ribbadi just wants—'

'Let Lord Nakht continue. I wish to hear all,' Akhenaten scowled.

Nakht turned to Tutu. 'So, you agree this Aziro is a problem and that we should crush him?'

'Yes, Lord.'

'Then, if someone here assists *him and Abdeshirta* in his attacks on Gebal, we should seek out that person and charge him with subversion?'

'Y…yes. He would be a traitor,' Tutu was nervous and started to sweat.

'This next letter is addressed to Dudu. Would that be you, Lord Tutu?'

'Yes, Lord Nakht,' Tutu swallows hard.

'It reads… *'Though art in that place, my father, and whatever is the wish of Dudu my father, write, and I will surely give it. Behold, though art my father and my lord. The lands are thy lands, and my house is thy house, and whatever thou desirest, write, and I will surely grant thy wish. Though sittest before my king, my lord, and my enemies have spoken slanders of me to my father before the King. Do not allow it to be so, my lord,'* Nakht finished reading and glared at Tutu.

*'You* are the *"father"* of whom he speaks. Your wishes are his commands. What do you say, Lord Tutu? Did you then, assist him?'

'Yes, my Lord, as I said, Ribbadi is loyal to Your Majesty and we should assist him wherever we can. As I said before, I dispatched two hundred deben of gold to aid his cause…to buy horses and get soldiers…'

'You sent the gold in respond to this letter, then, Lord Tutu?'

'Yes.'

Lord Nakht turned to Akhenaten and held up the tablet.

'You Majesty, you have just heard Lord Tutu confess that he sent a shipment of gold in response to this letter.'

'Yes, yes. I know about it. Go on!' Akhenaten was getting impatient.

'Your Majesty, Lord Ay, may I present the letter as evidence of Lord Tutu's betrayal. This letter is from not from Ribbadi, but *Aziro*, Egypt's enemy!'

A thunderous outcry resounded through the great pillared hall. It took Ay and Kheruef a while to restore order and to hear Lord Tutu's objections.

'I had been tricked and falsely accused. I claim the letter to be a forgery, all the originals had been destroyed.'

Once again, Nakht contradicted him. 'No, you had all the letters *removed* from the vaults, and had *ordered* your servant to destroy them. Kenti, suspecting they might come in handy later, did *not* destroy them but had them stored in another part of the magazines complex.' Nakht signalled and servants entered, carrying baskets filled with clay tablets.

Tutu gasped and turned pale.

'When I showed Kenti, copies of the tablets taken directly from their coverings, he had no choice but to reveal the location of the original. We retrieved them and carefully studied their contents.' Nakht paused for effect, and then pointed an accusing finger. 'Lord Tutu, you dealt with Aziro secretly, while misleading His Majesty with false information.' He lifted a tablet from the basket and held it aloft. 'These letters will support my accusations. Do you wish them to be read?'

'N... No, Lord,' Tutu answered, soft and meek. The evidence against him was overwhelming. He was doomed.

'You, Lord Tutu are a traitor! You acted against Pharaoh and the welfare of the Two Lands!'

Akhenaten glared at his former Foreign Minister who bowed his head and looked at the floor. 'Lord Tutu, I have been deceived. What have you to say?'

'Nothing, Majesty.' He inhaled loudly, almost a sob. 'I—I was trying to…hoping to restore balance to the land…'

Sethi, who had been listening intently, cut in, 'Lord Tutu, I believe there were others also involved in the plot…who are they?'

'There were no others, Lord Sethi.' He gave a quick, almost unnoticed glance in the direction of Vizier Ay.

'You know we have ways to persuade you to reveal all your secrets?'

'Yes, Lord, I am aware…there were no others.'

'Very well,' Ay interrupted quickly, 'we shall not press for an answer.'

'But, Lord Ay, we must find…' Sethi objected.

'No, Lord Sethi.' Akhenaten interjected. 'Under torture, he will confess to anything, whether it be true or not.'

'Yes, Your Majesty.'

Akhenaten leaned back and stared at Tutu a moment, tapping the palm of his right hand with the *heka*, the crook, the symbol of leadership, his expression troubled. 'Lord Tutu, it grieves me to pass sentence on you. You had been my advisor and confidant for a long time, someone I had trusted…yet you conspired against the State and the Crown. Once, I had defended you. I believed you to be innocent of such a treacherous deed, but now the opposite had been proved to be true.'

Akhenaten sighed and continued, disappointment visible in his eyes. 'You betrayed us. You brought me false information to mislead me, to cause our enemies to undermine Egypt's power and to do us harm. Through your actions, many had died and we had lost vast territories in the East. The city of Simyra had been lost because of it. There is no justification for your actions. I am not only grieved by your actions against your country, but deeply wounded that someone who had been so close to me, someone I had regarded almost as a friend, could commit such a deed.'

Akhenaten straightened up, picked up the flail and still holding the crook, crossed his arms. 'Have you anything to say before I passed sentence?'

'No, Your Majesty,' Tutu shook his head slowly.

'Lord Tutu,' Akhenaten spoke in a loud voice for the entire assembly to hear. 'You have been found guilty of the crimes of conspiracy and treachery…the sentence is death! You shall be taken from this place, to the Temple of Sobekh, and there, cast into the sacred pool.'

'Your Majesty!' Tutu's eyes grew wild and fearful. 'Please, let—'

'Silence!' Akhenaten's voice rang through the hall. 'You had your chance to speak.'

Pharaoh turned to Kheruef and gestured with the crook.

'Let the records show the crime and the punishment. Let it so be written, let it so be done!'

The doomed Lord Tutu sagged and he dragged his feet as he was led away, causing his escorts to support him.

To be cast into the Sacred Pool of Sobekh, the crocodile god, to be devoured by the sacred beasts, was the most severe of all punishments. It was reserved only for those who had committed the worst of crimes. The grand tomb Tutu had had constructed for himself, would forever remain empty. There would be no happy afterlife for him. His *Ka* would roam forever in the twilight world of the damned!

# Chapter Seventeen
## That Woman!

Menefer was again seated at her favourite place, a shaded bench in the garden. She had received another letter from Rakhmet this morning, but something about it, troubled her. Like his earlier ones, this one too, was formal and "distant". He expressed his regrets over her mother's death and her accident. He wished her speedy recovery, but nothing else. He made no mention of his feelings for her, no longing, no desire. He made no mentioned of looking forward to his return, or seeing her. He had never express his love for her, but had, before, talked of their life together—but in his recent letters, he made no reference to it, instead, he wished her a happy and contented life.

Queen Nefertiti and lady Mutny had noticed her melancholy, and approached her. Menefer quickly stood up and saluted. 'Your Majesty! Lady Mutny.'

Nefertiti took a seat and invited Menefer to sit next to her. Mutnedjmet seated herself on the opposite bench. 'How are you bearing up…after the recent events?' Nefertiti looked concerned.

'It all seems so unreal, Your Majesty.'

'I can only imagine what it must be like. With no funeral, there is no closure. We all feel so truly sorry for you and your family…and Thutmose? Any improvement yet?'

'No, Your Majesty. He walks around the house, calling my mother's name, expecting her to appear at any moment.'

'Dreadfully sad. I hope it will all pass quickly, and you can resume your lives again.'

'Thank you, Majesty.'

'Menefer, I hate to trouble you at a time like this, but there is another matter I wish to talk about.'

Menefer tensed. She had been anxious since the queen mentioned it earlier, and had feared the moment.

'During that dreadful affair, Kenti removed a scroll…this scroll.' She lifted her hand that held the rolled-up document. 'It was brought to me, and, at the time, I thought the contents had been more evidence against Lord Tutu, but I found it to contain a poem…a love poem.'

'Yes, Your Majesty,' Menefer sounded nervous, but, at least, the queen's concern is not about her involvement in the plot.

'A love poem, Menefer, how romantic,' Lady Mutny exclaimed.

'I recognised the style. This was written by the king, was it not?'

'Yes, Your Majesty.'

Mutnedjmet gasped and leaned forward. 'A love poem? From His Majesty?'

'Yes, Lady Mutny. It is from Pharaoh,' Menefer nodded, her eyes downcast.

'Menefer, I hold you no grudge, so do not be afraid to answer, but please explain why His Majesty would write you a love poem.'

'Oh, no, Your Majesty! It was not for me,' Menefer almost laughed with relief. 'The poem belongs to His Highness, Prince Smenkhare! His Majesty had written it for him. I was only given it to read.'

Nefertiti sat, silent a moment, eyebrows knitted in thought. Then she got up, thanked Menefer and, without another word, hurried away.

Mutnedjmet looked at Menefer and shrugged.

'I'm sorry, Lady Mutny. I seemed to have upset the queen.'

'No need to be sorry, Menefer, you did nothing wrong.'

'No, I mean, for having betrayed the Prince's trust. I should have taken better care of the scroll…'

'It is not your doing, Menefer. It was not your fault your privacy had been invaded.'

'I know, Lady Mutny, but I still feel bad about it. I still think I am at fault.'

***

Nefertiti approached the king's quarters. The guards saluted and opened the double doors for her. The air inside the chamber was already heavy with perfumed smoke, but Ahmose, Akhenaten's personal steward, was adding more fragrant bark to a smouldering brazier.

Nefertiti wrinkled her nose. 'I wish to see Pharaoh. Is he in his quarters?'

Ahmose saluted and bowed. 'He is, Your Majesty, but—'

'He cannot see you now!' Dowager Queen Tiye, Akhenaten's mother, entered from the doorway of an adjoining chamber and waved the steward away. 'Leave us, Ahmose.'

He saluted and quickly retreated.

'He *will* see me!' Nefertiti demanded and proceeded towards the king's bedchamber.

'He is unwell and is resting,' Tiye stepped forward, barring her way. 'What is the urgency?'

'It is a private matter…between Akhenaten and me!'

'You will not disturb him!' Tiye stood in front of her, arms akimbo.

'Get out of the way, Tiye!' Nefertiti rudely pushed her aside.

The bedchamber door opened and Akhenaten appeared. 'Is anything amiss?'

'Get back to your sleeping couch, my son. I will handle this.'

Nefertiti ignored Queen Tiye and waved the scroll in front of him.

'What is the meaning of this, Akhenaten?'

'Meaning of what?' He took the scroll and looked at it. 'Oh, the poem! How did you get hold of it?'

'That's not important. Did you write it?'

'Yes, I did.'

'Did you mean what you wrote?' She balled her hands into fists. 'Do you love him?'

Queen Tiye took the scroll from him and read it. 'Nefertiti, this is nonsense. A love poem means nothing. It is merely my son's expression of love for his brother!'

'This is more than an expression of brotherly love, Tiye,' Nefertiti snatched the document from her and waved it in front of her face.

'Of course it means more…' Tiye shrugged and seated herself on a nearby couch. 'Smenkhare is to succeed Akhenaten one day. That means a—'

'Read the poem again, Tiye, carefully, before making pointless comments!' Nefertiti stabbed at the scroll with a finger. She was furious.

'My comments *are* to the point,' Tiye glared at Nefertiti. 'Smenkhare is his heir. He will take the place of the son and heir *you* never produced.'

'That is not what he expresses in the poem, Tiye—'

'You are imagining things, Nefertiti,' She laughed mockingly. 'Get a hold of yourself. Allow my son some concessions, some little whims—'

'Whims, Tiye?' Nefertiti shook with rage. 'As you did…allowing your husband to dress in women's garments?' She fixed her eyes on Tiye. 'Oh yes, Tiye, I know all about it, the paintings of the *'Great Amenhotep… Amenhotep the Magnificent* dressed in women's garb.'

'Do not talk to *me* of unconventional portrayals, Nefertiti!' Tiye stood up and pointed. 'What about you? You had allowed depictions done of you, in the stance of a man, instead of standing *behind* the king, as befitting a woman and queen!'

Nefertiti hesitated, trying to find words to counter attack. It was true. She had been portrayed the same size as Akhenaten, not smaller and inferior to the king as convention dictates. The king's feet are shown together, in the manner of a woman, and hers, striding forward, in the manner of a man. Akhenaten himself had wanted it thus. He had wanted to show the people that he and his queen were equals. Somehow, that had been misconstrued.

Tiye used this moment of silence to attack Nefertiti again. 'I see my remarks had hit a tender spot!' She smiled smugly. 'I suppose, next you will be telling me you are ignorant of the king's harem boys!'

'I know of them,' Nefertiti nodded slowly. 'Many Pharaohs had had them. It is fairly common, but…harem boys are not…not…' She searched for the right words. 'No Pharaoh before had *proclaimed* his *love* for any of them!'

'Nefertiti, please. You do not understand,' Distressed, Akhenaten reached forward and put his hand on Nefertiti's arm, but she shook it off.

'Do not touch me! Do not come near me!' She turned on Tiye and jabbed a finger at her. 'This is all your doing,' Nefertiti gestured broadly. 'All this had happened since you arrived.' She straightened again, her voice husky with emotion. 'Why do you not leave us alone, Tiye? We were happy before you came. We were…we were…'

'I came here to talk some sense into the two of you,' Tiye turned towards Akhenaten and gestured. 'The country is falling apart, but you arc both so blinded by your faith in Aten…' she sat down again, and locked her fingers on her lap. 'You need to revoke your laws, you need—'

'Tiye, pack your travel chests and go home…' Nefertiti waved her hand towards the south. 'Go back to Waset!'

'Act like the queen you are, Nefertiti!' Tiye demanded, lifted her head and gestured imperiously. 'Not like some deserted lovesick little—'

'Not now, mother,' Akhenaten held out a hand to check her. He turned, stepped over to Nefertiti and took her by the shoulders. 'Nefertiti, why don't we try to—?'

She drew back from his grasp. 'Stay away, Akhenaten. Never come to me again!'

'You do not mean that, Nefertiti!' Akhenaten's voice was soft, pleading.

'Yes, I do. I hope you and your mother will be very happy together. You deserve one another!'

'You will regret that remark, Nefertiti. Regret it for the rest of your life!' Tiye interjected, her voice low. She turned to Akhenaten, 'Are you now convinced? I told you, make Khiya your queen.' Tiye fanned her fingers and gestured, 'She gave you a son. Yes, I am aware poor, dear Tutankhaten is sickly, but she could provide you with another, a healthier heir.'

Akhenaten nodded, and scratched his chin with his thumb, not answering. Tears welled up in Nefertiti's eyes. She turned and stormed out.

In the passage, half blinded by tears, she almost ran into the Vizier Ay. 'Daughter, you look upset. What ails you?'

It has been many years since Nefertiti had sought her father's sympathy, but now she had no one else. As they walked together, she opened up her heart to him.

'Khiya?' He stopped, placed his hands on her shoulders and turned her to face him. 'You say Pharaoh is contemplating replacing you with *her?* Making her his first wife and queen?'

'Yes!' Nefertiti sobbed.

'No, that will never be,' he shook his head. '*You* are Queen of Egypt and destined to remain so…no one else, certainly not the mother of a crippled boy.' He took her in his arms to console her.

'Queen Tiye is controlling his mind.' Nefertiti flashed her eyes in the direction of the king's chambers. '*She* will make it happen.'

'My sister has always been headstrong,' Ay remarked. 'Tiye wants neither Smenkhare nor Tutankhaten on the throne. Both Mutemwaya, mother of Smenkhare and Khiya, Tutankhaten's mother, are concubines.'

'She seems determined to have Akhenaten produce a legal heir!' Nefertiti answered and broke into more sobbing. 'I tried, father. I prayed. I've made offerings in the temples and worshipped Aten faithfully since we were wed, but I gave him only daughters…now I am to be discarded and replaced by Khiya, who *had* given him a son.'

'Tutankhaten will most probably never reach maturity.'

'That is why he is planning to make Smenkhare his heir.'

'Yes, I have heard the rumours—but never fret *Beautiful One,*' Ay stroked her head. I will not allow that to happen. I will take care of everything!'

\*\*\*

Pleasant sounds of the caged birds in the garden filled the air, but their songs did not soothe Nefertiti's troubled thoughts.

Mutnedjmet came hurrying over. 'Nefertiti, is it true? The rumours?'

'Yes, Mutny.' Mutnames noticed the traces of recent weeping, which cosmetics could not hide, on the queen's face.

'It has finally come to this. Akhenaten and I have parted. He plans to wed Khiya and make her his queen. I am to be a secondary wife!'

'That is…is so unfair!' Mutnedjmet seated herself next to her sister and patted her hand. 'What are you going to do? Maybe it is just a temporary thing…' she straightened up again and rested her hands on her lap.

'No,' Nefertiti shook her head slowly. 'Things will never return to normal.'

'That damned poem had brought this on!'

'No, it is not the poem. Things had gone awry long before that—ever since *she* arrived.' Nefertiti bobbed her head in the direction of Tiye's house. She was silent for a moment, then suddenly looked up with a determined expression. 'Mutny, I have come to decision… I am going to do something drastic. I am—'

A distant scream from the direction of the House of Women rent the air and both women turned around, startled. Then, over the noise of the street that separated the Palace and Per nesu, came more cries.

Mutnedjmet jumped up and hurried off, calling over her shoulder. 'I will go and find out what happened,'

Servants appeared from doorways along the walkway of the King's House and looked around, wide-eyed. Menefer and the princesses, also disturbed and frightened, came rushing out of the teaching chamber. Nefertiti beckoned to them. Upset and puzzled, they approached her.

'What has happened?' Merit asked, alarmed.

'It is probably nothing,' the queen tried to quell their fears. 'Mutny has gone to find out. Probably a serpent had found its way into the garden of Per-hemt.'

The princesses smiled wryly. Their quarters were fairly close to the women's quarters. Quarrels frequently broke out and they often heard loud noises coming from there. The women often quarrelled, but this had been different. The screams were not of anger, but that of fear or horror. They cast concern looks in the direction of the gate.

Presently, Lady Mutny arrived looking pale and distressed. Something serious had occurred. Breathlessly, she sat down, aware that everyone's eyes were upon her.

'Nefertiti.' She swallowed hard and laid a shaky hand on her sister's. 'An awful thing has happened.' She looked at the princesses as they searched her face, then turned back to her sister. 'It is Lady Khiya…she…has been murdered!'

Gasps and cries of disbelief came from everyone.

'Murdered?' Merit asked, horrified.

Lady Mutny just nodded, 'The cries we heard came from the woman who found her.'

'Oh, poor Tutankhaten!' Nefertiti exclaimed. 'The boy is now all alone.'

'What's going to happen to him?' Senpa ventured.

'He and his mother were always scorned by the other women,' Mutnedjmet explained. 'She was Pharaoh favourite concubine. She gave him a son, and because of that, they resented and ostracised her. They will now do the same to that poor little boy. Some of them can be vicious and cruel.'

'Did…one of *them* do it?' Merit asked fearfully. 'Out of jealousy?'

'Perhaps, who can say?' Nefertiti shrugged. 'Pharaoh had planned to make her his queen!'

'Mother, no!' Merit shouted. 'Why?'

Nefertiti decided to tell her daughters everything. They were of an age where they should know of the situation.

'Really?' Senpa exclaimed, surprised, when she had finished. 'I had no idea it was that serious.'

'But, will this murder change anything?' Merit ventured. 'Will he not be persuaded to choose another?'

'And if that should happen,' Senpa added. 'What will happen to you...to us? Are we to be sent to the House of Women?'

'No. I will never allow that! I have made other plans.' Nefertiti glanced at her sister. 'I was about to tell you, Mutny...just before this awful thing occurred.' She turned back to her daughters. 'Instruct your servants to pack.'

'Pack? Are we going back to Waset?' Merit asked. 'For how long?'

'No. We are moving to the North Palace. We are going to live there, *permanently*. We leave, just as soon as you are ready.'

***

The time of the inundation, the season of Akhet had come. Nefertiti and the princesses had settled into the Northern Palace and Menefer had been given quarters within the palace complex. This palace was more than twice the distance she used to travel, and she no longer went home as often, but it mattered little. She had no reason to, any more, anyway. Her mother had died and her father kept to himself almost all the time. Ipuky and Neb were always away, working on some project.

The surroundings of the North Palace were pleasant and she could go for long walks along the Nile or by the nearby pleasure lake. The palace, some distance outside the city and well away from its noise, made living there more peaceful. It suited her.

Lady Mutnedjmet decided to remain at Per nesu, but little Tutankhaten had been moved to the Northern Palace under Nefertiti's care. About the same age as Setenpenre, the young prince readily joined in their games and the three younger princesses enjoyed having him there.

Queen Nefertiti no longer attended ceremonies at the temples except those at her own temple at the North Palace. Panehesy, the old priest at the Great Temple, travelled to her palace for important religious ceremonies.

With less duties to perform than before, she had more leisure time and spent more time with the children. Lady Mutny became a frequent visitor. For entertainment, they playing board games or stitched garments for the girls and the young prince. These latter tasks would usually be done by servants, but they both enjoyed doing them and gave them ample time to talk or exchange the latest gossip.

The queen had been in the palace for about a week and Lady Mutnedjmet was again present, when a messenger arrived with an official letter.

'From Akhenaten?' Nefertiti was puzzled when she saw the seal.

'Pharaoh probably wants you to return,' Mutny remarked, jokingly.

'Never!' Nefertiti replied with determination.

'What if Tiye is leaving the city for good?' Mutny ventured.

'No. Not even…uh…perhaps then!' Nefertiti unrolled the papyrus, read it, then read it again and slammed the papyrus down on the table, startling Mutny.

'He is summoning Meritaten to Per nesu,' Nefertiti's face was flushed. 'He wants her to be present for the Feast of Aten!'

'Why her? What he is planning?'

'You mean what is *Tiye* planning! She is surely behind it.' Nefertiti gazed out the window to the distant Palace. 'Who knows what they have in mind.'

*** *

The Feast of the Birth of Aten, the twenty-sixth day of Payopi, in the season of Akhet, had arrived. In the distance, the blare of trumpets, and chanting could be heard. For this great occasion, the ceremony was to take place in the Great Temple.

Mutnedjmet had attended the early morning temple ceremony but would not be present at the main celebration. She had been a priestess of the vulture goddess, Mut, and had no particular concern with the Aten ceremony. It was midsummer, and wanting to avoid the hot and uncomfortable midday celebrations of this feast day, she went to the North Palace earlier than usual.

The atmosphere at Nefertiti's palace was peaceful and relaxed. The muted strumming of a harp and soft tones of a flute, issuing from somewhere in the place, was soothing. Perfumed smoke of burning herbs issuing from a container, floated on the slight breeze from the river.

In an adjoining room, came the sound of children. Tutankhaten and the two younger princesses were playing games. Menefer and Princess Senpa were at a table nearby, making bead jewellery.

Nefertiti and Mutnedjmet had just started playing *senet*, their favourite board game, when the messenger arrived and bowed. Nefertiti turned to face him. 'What news, Sentu?'

'Your Majesty, Pharaoh has declared Prince Smenkhare to be co-regent…'

'Co-regent?' Nefertiti looked around, amazed. 'I knew he been declared heir, but *co regent?* This is indeed news.'

'Your Majesty…' Sentu continued. 'He is to marry Princess Meritaten.'

Nefertiti nodded, frowning. 'So, that was why Akhenaten wanted Merit to be present. I should have realised.'

She addressed the messenger again. 'When is this to be?'

'During the *Pageant of Empire*, Your Majesty.'

'*Pageant of Empire*? Has it been a year already?' Mutny asked.

Nearby, Menefer, who had been working on a decorative beaded armband, looked up, surprised at the mention of the festival.

'Are they to celebrate the Pageant feast again?' Nefertiti asked, an edge to her voice.

'Yes, Majesty, it is to be an annual event…by decree of the queen.'

'The *queen's* decree? What insolence!' Nefertiti banged the senet game-piece down so hard, the peg snapped off. 'She is *not* queen! I am.'

'I humbly beg your pardon, Majesty, I did not mean…'

'No, not you, Sentu. I speak of *That Woman*! She has no authority to issue decrees…what of the king? What was his word on this matter?'

147

'His Majesty had agreed, Majesty.'

'He might as well deify her…again!' Nefertiti scoffed, 'Then declare it another *holy* day!' She dismissed the messenger, then, breathing heavily, turned to Lady Mutny. 'So, it has finally happened, Mutnedjmet!'

Mutny, who had started packing the game pieces away, stopped and looked at her sister. '*What* finally happened?'

'Did you not hear? *That Woman* now rules Egypt!'

'Have you not been aware of that, Nefertiti?'

'Not to *this* extent. She had been manipulating Akhenaten, yes, but never before had she issued decrees!' Nefertiti stood up, walked to the balcony and gazed over the city. After a moment of silence, she turned and spread her arms wide in a quizzical gesture. 'What next? I will not be surprised if she demands a crown and her own throne, next!'

# Chapter Eighteen
## Rakhmet Returns

Princess Meritaten had left for *Per nesu*, and Menefer had only one pupil left, Princess Senpa. The younger children had lost interest in the lessons and chose to amuse themselves. Menefer and Senpa had become close friends, but she missed Merit. Following suggestions by Queen Nefertiti, Lady Mutnedjmet had decided to move to the Northern palace. When not playing senet, they would often spend their leisure time with the princesses and the young Prince Tutankhaten. To allow the Royals, some private time together, or during her leisure time, Menefer would often take long walks along the bank of the Nile or the lake.

A grove of date palms grew along the banks of the lake. She would walk in their shade or sit and gaze at the boats gliding across the river, or watch waterfowl, gathering on the riverbank to feed. This had become Menefer's favourite place, her own little lonely world.

She longed to see Djenna again. One afternoon, instead of going to the lake, Menefer decided to stroll down to the house of Queen Tiye to see her friend. It had been months since their last meeting.

She was shown to a pleasant, spacious hall, with a large pillared balcony overlooking the Nile. No breeze disturbed the perfumed smoke rising from several incense-burners, and it drifted lazily about the room. She seated herself on a low *aft*, a cushioned couch with armrests, carved in the image of Queen Tiye as *shesps*, lions with the heads in the likeness of the queen. The servant went to fetch Djenna, who after a long moment, appeared.

Djenna did not exactly seem overjoyed to see her friend. 'So, you decided to exile yourself along with the ex-queen!'

'Greeting, to you too, Djenna,' Menefer replied, just as coldly, 'and Queen Nefertiti had not been exiled! She *chose* to move…and yes, I decided to go with her to continue my task of tutoring the princesses.'

'I heard the rumours about that poem that caused all this. You were involved, were you not?'

'I was not *involved* in anything, Djenna. Prince Smenkhare simply showed it to me, and in landed in the hands of the queen.'

'You and Prince Smenkhare seem to be very…uh…on very friendly terms!'

'We are acquainted only, Djenna. Do not make any more of it.'

Djenna's suspicions and jealousy was again beginning to show, Menefer thought.

'Do you not crave the company of someone older?' Djenna smirked. 'Being with children all the time must be very tedious.'

'Senpa is very mature for her age, and good company. Anyway, Her Majesty and Lady Mutnedjmet often sit with us.'

'The queen? Does she ever talk about the unfortunate death of lady Khiya?'

'She felt bad about it, but we don't discuss it. Why?'

'You have not heard the rumours? *She* was behind it!'

'What do you mean?' Menefer gasped. 'Are you inferring Queen Nefertiti was involved in…murder?'

'Those are the stories going around the House of Women. I thought you knew—Lady Khiya was about to replace Nefertiti. Removing that obstacle would be in her favour.'

'That…that is rubbish!' Menefer spluttered, angered at Djenna's remark. 'Think about it, Djenna. If she *was* to gain from Lady Khiya's death, why would she have left *Per nesu*?'

'Who knows? As I said, that is the story going around. No need to jump down my throat!'

Her visit to this palace was becoming unpleasant. Djenna made it very clear that everyone, even Lady Mutnedjmet, who had also moved away, were now regarded as outcasts and largely ignored by the rest of the Royal Family. Menefer felt most unwelcome. She had just made excuses to leave, when Queen Tiye's personal servant entered.

'Mistress Menefer, Her Majesty had been informed of your visit and wishes to see you.'

Curious, Djenna accompanied Menefer and they were escorted to the queen's chambers. They bowed and saluted.

'A pleasant day, Menefer,' Tiye's friendly greeting surprised her. She always saw her as being rather sour-faced and unpleasant.

'I know your brothers well,' Tiye bade them to sit down. 'In fact, I commissioned them to decorate my *per-neheh*, my house of eternity, in the valley west of Waset. They are both excellent craftsmen.'

'Thank you, Majesty—'

'But I believe you too, have a great talent.'

Menefer blushed at the praise. 'Your Majesty is very kind… I… I am flattered.'

'You are a very gifted family. You are surely all blessed by the gods.'

Again, Menefer thanked her for the compliments.

'I am happy you paid us a visit today. I have been looking forward to meeting you.'

'Me, Majesty?' She noticed Djenna's look of irritation.

'Yes, Menefer. I wish you to make a likeness of me, a life-size one, in limestone or granite, perhaps? You *do* tool in stone, do you not?'

Menefer confessed that she had only fashioned likenesses in clay or carved in wood, and had never attempted anything in stone.

'My father had been the master in those materials,' she explained.

'Your father. Yes. I know of Thutmose. What a misfortune. His works are well known. You have my deepest sympathy for the tragedy that struck your family. I too, have known sadness and loss,' Tiye sighed and had a far-away look in her eyes.

'But we must all move forward.' She collected herself again. 'About the likeness...perhaps just a small image first? To see if you can do it, then, if it pleases me, I will commission the larger.'

'Yes, Your Majesty, it will be a pleasure.'

'Thank you. When it is done, you will be greatly rewarded.'

Menefer returned to the North Palace, excited. Her visit, initially soured by Djenna's attitude, had turned out most promising.

*\*\**

The day dawned bright and rosy. Menefer stood on the balcony of her bedchamber and gazed across the city, still mantled by the purple-grey shadows of the Eastern hills. The Northern Palace, situated on elevated ground, allowed her to overlook and see beyond Akhet Aten where the Nile snaked past the city. Further south, her eyes strayed to the island, which will now, always hold painful memories for her. That was where her mother had been taken from her.

This view, although not as serene as that of the peaceful garden she had enjoyed at *Per nesu*, was much more interesting. Far to the south, beyond the island, the river curved gently around the bluff, the southern tip of the range of hills that surrounded the valley. Below these hills, just visible in the morning haze, lay Maru Aten, the King's Pleasure Palace.

The sun rose higher. The pylons and obelisks of the Great Temple and the palace, blushed as its first rays reached them. The river shone like a burnished copper ribbon, reflecting the dusky pink of the sky. Several boats, their rectangular sails hanging limp, glided across the smooth surface of the waters, hardly making any ripples, and pushed along only by the flowing current or oarsmen.

With shrill calls, a flock of egrets rose from the green cultivated patch of farmland between the city and the Northern Palace. They wheeled lazily over the papyrus thickets on the bank of the river, then settled again near a herd of cattle, grazing in an open field.

Faintly, a gong sounded, followed by the sounds of drums and chanting from Hat-Aten, the King's temple. The morning ceremony of the "Greeting of the Aten" had begun. *Merit would certainly be attending, walking obediently behind Queen Tiye,* Menefer thought.

Menefer's attention shifted elsewhere. She scanned the river expectantly and scrutinised every vessel as it came into view. Boats do not sail during the night hours. Many of those, voyaging from the Upper Nile, would have berthed overnight at Khusiya, a few hours to the south of the city, to set sail again before dawn. They would be arriving here, round about this time.

She had been watching the river every morning, for several days now. Ever since Horemheb had told her of Rakhmet's imminent return, she had been like a child, probing him for more details, but he kept changing the subject. He could not, or would not even tell her which day he would be arriving, just saying "any day now". Perhaps this would be that day.

She softly muttered a prayer. 'Oh my beloved, how I yearn for your embrace, dream of having you near. How often I have reached out for you and you were not there? How many times did I hear your voice, only to find it had been just the sighing of the wind in the trees? But now, you are coming home. Oh, to have you close again, to feel again your arms about me, your lips upon mine—and my dreams will be sweet again.'

She watched as a vessel approach the landing place. For a moment, it was obscured by the pylon gates as it moved behind the Great Palace. She waited for it to reappear, almost too afraid to blink.

The boat came into view again and neared the landing place alongside the Palace. Its oars were held in place in the water to slow its approach. She could just make out the helmsmen straining at the two great paddles that guided it.

The symbol of the nome, from whence the vessel had come, would be displayed on a pennant, affixed high on the mast. But, for the lack of a breeze, it hung limp and a bit too distant, so she could not identify it.

Queen Nefertiti had given her permission to send Sentu, the messenger, every morning, to await all boats due at the landing place. He would hurry back with any news of Rakhmet's arrival. Rakhmet had to report to his commander the moment he arrived and she would not see him immediately, but she needed to know that he had arrived.

The boat landed and the men disembarked but it was impossible to make out who they were. She scanned the road for Pentu. The King's Way ran parallel to the river. The road started at the king's palace, Maru Aten, south of Akhet Aten, dissected the city and continued north to Nefertiti's palace. It was starting to get crowded as early risers, hoping to be first for the choicest of produce, made their way to the market.

Then a figure, a man running, appeared. He was moving in the opposite direction of those on the road, darting in and out of the crowd, avoiding carts, ox-wagons and an occasional chariot.

With bated breath, she watched him. She knew he was running at a fairly steady pace, but, to her, seemed to be moving painfully slowly. He disappeared behind the pylon walls of the Great Temple, reappeared a moment later, much closer now, still heading north. As he passed the cultivated farmlands, she recognised him. Sentu!

Before he even reached the gates of the North Palace, she rushed to meet him, almost colliding with Lady Mutnedjmet. 'My apologies, Lady Mutny. Please forgive me…'

Mutnedjmet knew the reason for Menefer's excitement and haste. 'Good luck, Menefer!' She called out and smiled as Menefer darted around the great pillars of the foyer.

A few moments later, she returned, beaming, and hastened to Lady Mutnedjmet's quarters. 'He has come, Lady Mutny!' She cried, out of breath and flushed. 'Rakhmet has arrived!'

'Are you going down to the city to meet him?'

'No. He would be long gone before I get there. He would most certainly go to the barracks first, to report back. I'll await him here. Commander Horemheb is sure to tell him I now reside here.'

'Very wise. Never show a man you are too eager to see him. It will make him appreciate you all the more if *he* has to seek *you* out. A man appreciates the hunt as much, if not more than the kill.'

***

Several days passed. Menefer had been working on the miniature figurine of Queen Tiye, in ebony, a scaled version of the larger one she had been planning, but her mind, now elsewhere, made it hard to concentrate on her work.

The sound of a chariot entering the courtyard, interrupted her reverie. She waited, expected to be summoned, but after a while, gave up, shrugged and carried on working.

Some time later, Segi, her servant, entered and started tidying up around the work-bench.

They called her Segi, the Egyptian word for "mute". No one knew her real name. Years earlier, she was brought to *Kemet*, the "Black Land", as a slave. Her tongue had been cut out, probably to prevent her from revealing the atrocities she had witnesses. She was brought into Queen Nefertiti's household when the queen moved to the North Palace, months earlier, and the queen had then given her to Menefer as her personal maid.

Menefer could no longer contain her curiosity. 'Any visitors yet, Segi?' She asked.

Segi nodded that there was indeed someone. A tall man, she gestured, wearing a uniform, an officer. He came to see the queen.

Curious, Menefer called to a passing guard about the identity of the visitor.

'Commander Horemheb,' the guard answered. 'He is just leaving.

'Commander?' Menefer asked.

'He has been promoted.'

Menefer hurried to the gate and called out. 'Commander!'

Horemheb stopped and turned.

'Commander Horemheb. Congratulations on your promotion.'

'Thank you, Menefer,' he nodded and smiled.

'Uh, Commander, any other…uh…news?' she hoped he would tell her something of Rakhmet's return.

'Yes, there had been several changes at *Per nesu*. Huya had been appointed Superintendent of the Royal Household.'

Menefer nodded. *Is he again avoiding talking of Rakhmet?* she wondered.

'Vizier Ay has an additional title "Chief of the King's Works", and Lord Nakht is now Royal Chancellor and Chief Justice, probably for his part in exposing Lord Tutu's treachery.'

'I am happy for Lord Nakht. He had risked much to bring the justice to the conspirators.'

'But you too, did a great deal, and suffered much for your part in the affair.'

'Anything else?' she asked anxiously. 'What news of Rakhmet?'

'Has he not contacted you yet?' Horemheb seemed surprised.

'No.'

He searched her face. 'I don't know what to say… I will find out for you.'

***

Later that day, Queen Nefertiti invited Menefer to her chambers. After some trivial conversation, the queen became more serious. 'We, here in the North Palace,

153

are been scorned by those in *Per nesu*. Pharaoh no longer recognises me as his consort, and has declared the North Palace no longer part of Akhet Aten!'

'Your Majesty! But…but you are queen!'

'We have been ostracised, but it does not include you. You, of course, are free to enter or leave the King's House. I will understand, and therefore will not think badly of you, should you wish to return. Meritaten has few friends there and would love your company.'

'I will visit her there, Your Majesty, but have no wish to go back. If I may, I choose to remain here.'

'That pleases me.' Nefertiti smiled and stood up. 'You are welcome to stay as long as you wish. The little ones too, have grown fond of you and would not wish you to leave.'

The queen ventured a personal question, 'I believe you have spoken to Horemheb?'

Menefer nodded, 'Yes, Majesty. I am delighted with his promotion…and that of Lord Nakht.'

Nefertiti sighed. Menefer did not mention anything of her betrothed's return, and the queen decided not to urge her to talk about it. She would volunteer the information at her own convenience, so she directed the conversation to other things, asking her about the progress of the princesses and her relations with the young Prince Tutankhaten.

'Princess Ankhsenpaaten is doing very well, Majesty. She has a gift for delicate work, and the young prince seems very interested in adventure stories.'

Lady Mutnedjmet arrived and they spent the rest of the afternoon gossiping and playing board games.

*** 

Another four days passed and Menefer was again busy, working on the figurine of Queen Tiye. Segi entered and indicated that she had a visitor. Excited, but guarded this time, Menefer forced herself to remain calm. She put her tools down, taking her time to arrange them carefully. She stood up, smoothed and groomed her hair in a copper mirror, then unhurriedly, but with her heart pounding, strolled to the foyer.

Rakhmet had kept her on edge for almost a week, making her wait and agonise over his coming, so she too, will let him wait. She remembered Lady Mutnedjmet's words: "He will appreciate you all the more if he has to seek you out."

She rounded a corner into the courtyard and saw him. How handsome he looked in his uniform. Her soul had craved for him, had longed to hold him to her and have his arms around her. Her entire being, ached for his embrace.

But her great effort to restrain herself was for naught. She lost control and composure and the words of Lady Mutny forgotten. Unable to contain her emotions, she rushed to him, her arms wide.

'Rakhmet! It's been so long.'

'Peace be with you, Menefer,' he made no move towards her. His voice was even and emotionless.

She embraced him but he still did not respond, made no effort to return her caresses. Puzzled, she looked up into his face. He was looking over her shoulder. She turned. A woman was watching them from the shadow of a pillar.

'Rakhmet? What…?' puzzled, she dropped her arms to her sides.

The girl had an olive complexion and the most unusual haunting eyes. She walked over to them, slowly and deliberately.

'Who…who is she?'

'Menefer…' Rakhmet reached out for the girl as she approached. 'Menefer,' he repeated and put his arm about the woman's waist. 'I wish you to meet Istar…my wife!'

# Chapter Nineteen
## Smenkhare

For a long moment, Menefer just stood there, staring, her mind, numb. Her hands started to tremble. An unfamiliar feeling started building up within her—a feeling she had not experienced before—a feeling of disappointment, anger—and hate!

Her face felt stiff, like leather. She tried to smile, but the taut muscles would not allow it.

'Your…*wife*?' her quavering voice sounded thin.

'Yes,' he nodded. 'We married some months ago, after you—'

'How nice.' She cut him off, her voice cold. 'I hope you two will be very happy,' the last words had almost to be forced out.

She turned and, blinded by tears she could no longer hold back, ran back to her quarters. As she entered her bedchamber, her first thoughts were to fling herself on her sleeping couch and to sob her heart out, but her rage was the stronger emotion. She wanted to retaliate, hit back at him…at anything. Destroy.

For a moment, she stood at the door, undecided, then, in a frenzy of despair and anguish, she attacked her worktable. On it were her artwork in various stages of completion.

Blindly, she struck out at them, muttering curses under her breath. 'You desert Jackal!' Pottery and figurines went flying in all directions. 'Miserable belly-crawling viper!' Bowls and platters, perfume jars and cosmetic containers, which she had crafted and decorated with such care, crashed to the floor.

'May your offspring dwell with vermin!' she grabbed a pottery cosmetic-container and smashed it against a wall, 'and may your sleeping mats forever be crawling with fleas.'

The almost completed figurine of Queen Tiye was flung at a far wall, shattering it into fragments. She then attacked her clothing, hanging off pegs on the wall. She ripped her garments and flung her jewellery around the room, scattering beads across the floor.

Servants, startled by the commotion, came running to investigate. Wide-eyed, in shocked amazement and in disbelief, too afraid to enter, they crowded the doorway and stared at her destructive rampage. They had never known their mistress to show such temper.

Menefer, unaware of her audience, attacked her bed clothing next. Ripping the couch covering, she flung her headrest out onto the balcony. Finally, with nothing else to destroy, exhausted and her fury spent, she fell on her bed and sobbed, heartbroken.

Segi, aware of the reason for her mistress' anguish, signalled to the others to leave. She closed the door silently behind her and left the weeping, grief-stricken girl to herself.

*** 

The sun rose bright and golden the next morning and the people in the city went about their business as usual. Boats on the Nile plied their trade as always, and everyone continued their lives as usual, but Menefer.

With her face flushed, her eyes puffy from weeping and her tears spent, she surveyed the destruction in her room. Had she really caused that much damage? Her memory of the day before, after Rakhmet's visit, was vague.

She got up, and with a heavy sigh, started cleaning the mess. A moment later Segi arrived and started helping her tidy up, but Menefer ordered her away. She wanted to be alone to straighten the place herself. It would give her time to think and also amend her mind…and her shattered life.

She bent down and picked up the head of the figurine, the only fragment of the sculpture that was recognisable. She stared at the sour-faced queen. Once, Queen Tiye had also been happy, carefree and idolised by thousands, then she was a forgotten, lonely widow. The death of King Amenhotep must have left the queen as empty as Menefer now felt. With Tiye's husband gone, her glory and power went as well. Feeling discarded, Menefer now understood that queen's bitterness, she could empathise with the aged dowager queen.

She restored some order to her room, sat down on her couch and started mending her torn garments. A light knock on the door interrupted her and, as cheerfully as she could, bade her caller to enter. It was Segi. Menefer started to explain that she had already tidied up, but the servant waved her hand in a negative fashion and indicated outside. She had a visitor, and, from the way Segi signed—broad shouldered and strong, it was a man.

Menefer, her face a mask of determined arrogance, set down her mending.

*This time I will tell Rakhmet exactly what I think of him… I will heap such curses on him that all the waters of the Nile would not be able to cleanse him!* She stood up, smoothed her tunic and indicated towards the adjoining gathering room. 'Show him in, Segi,' she said, then proceeded there.

While she waited, she rehearsed the speech with which to greet him, her hands clenched so tight, her palms stung. She inhaled deeply at the sound of approaching footsteps and prepared herself.

'Khay!' Surprised, she relaxed. Her mood softened and she even managed a smile. 'What brings you here? I have not seen you for many months.'

He greeted her with that wide, attractive smile. 'I have been away, to Waset, to see to the restoration of the Malkata Palace. I had been kept rather busy with His Majesty's business. There just seem to be no end to it. Reorganising—uh—sorry. I did not mean to bore you with official business. I am here to apologise.'

'Apologise? For what?' She sat down, puzzled.

'For Commander Horemheb. He feels very badly about what had happened. He knew of Rakhmet's marriage…we both did, for some time…'

Menefer jumped up, furious.

'What? Did he send you?'

'Please,' he raised his eyebrows, pleadingly. 'No, he did not send me. I came of my own accord. You had to know the reasons why we had remained silent. Rakhmet's application for permission to marry had been an official document. Commander Horemheb and I were both bound by our oaths and—'

'But why…?' her voice was barely audible. 'Why did he not…let me know, somehow?'

'We had to wait until you had seen Rakhmet first. Before then, neither of us could tell you. Rakhmet wanted to tell you himself.'

Menefer remained silent for a moment, then muttered something.

'What?'

'Oh, uh… I…was just thinking aloud. Something Horemheb had said some time ago "*when circumstances had changed*" perhaps that was what he meant.'

Khay just stared at her, still puzzled.

'Uh… Forget it, Khay, it is not important.'

'Oh, yes…there is something else. Your brothers had completed their task in Waset.'

'You saw them? Wonderful! How did it go? Are they well?'

'You can ask them yourself. They are arriving in Akhet Aten, tonight.'

*** 

Menefer returned home, happy to see her brothers again after all these months. She greeted them warmly.

'My, how you have changed, Little One.' Nebaten hugged her. 'You suddenly seem all grown up.'

'It is good to see you too.'

'Yes, you have certainly turned into a comely and desirable young woman,' Ipuky observed as he greeted her. 'I will wager you must have many eager suitors…'

Neb gave Ipuky a warning look and shook his head for Ipuky not to pursue that line of conversation, then added. 'I might have some good news for you, soon. I have met someone…a lady.'

'Neb, that is wonderful. Who is she, what's her name?'

'Her name is Sarem, but I will tell you more, later, if things work out. Be patient. How is Queen Nefertiti coping with her self-imposed exile?'

'Quite well, I think. She gets a little upset now and then when she is not informed of new developments at *Per nesu*.'

'Has she said anything about the rumours?'

'Rumours?' Puzzled at first, then Menefer remembered what Djenna said. 'Oh, about Lady Khiya, you mean?'

He nodded.

'I don't think the gossip had reached her ears. She is certain to be devastated should she learn of it,' Menefer scowled. 'I cannot imagine anybody thinking such an unkind thought about her. It is not in her nature to have planned such a vile deed.'

'Let us say no more about this matter. It is not fitting even to think about it,' Ipuky agreed.

Thutmose came shuffling and Menefer rushed over to greet him. She hugged him and asked about his health, but he did not seem to recognise her, appearing as if she were not there. 'I must go and finish Her Majesty's likeness,' he said and looked around, dazed. 'Where are my tools? I mislaid my tools.'

He shuffled off and a servant led him back to his room. Once he had retired, Menefer and her brothers, sat down gloomily for the evening meal.

'He is like that most of the time,' Ipuky explained. 'One minute he wouldn't recognise any of us, the next, his mind would return. More than once he would call upon us not to talk too loud as our mother was trying to sleep, then at other times, he would walk around the house calling her name.'

Not to dwell on their father's condition, Nebaten turned the conversation to Waset. 'After we concluded the work on Queen Tiye's "House of Eternity", we spent a few days in Waset, waiting for a boat to bring us downriver.'

'There is much trouble in the city. Things there do not look good,' Ipuky shook his head, sadly. 'The people are very dissatisfied. They heard Smenkhare is to be co-regent and are calling on him, once he rules there, to restore the worship of Amun. Instead of Waset, they want the name of No-Amun to be restored.'

'If it does not happen soon, I fear rebellion is imminent,' Neb added. 'Even here, in Akhet Aten there are rumours of trouble.'

Nebaten could not have guessed how soon his observation would be realised.

***

The feast of Aset, the Goddess Isis, had always been celebrated during the winter solstice, but as the worship of that deity was no longer allowed, the *Day Aten returns from its Southern Journey* was being observed, instead.

Akhenaten had gone to Maru-Aten, his southern pleasure palace, to relax after the festivities. He sent for Smenkhare and Tutankhaten to join him. While they were enjoying the break after the celebrations, trouble was brewing in the city.

A group of protesters had gathered at the gates of *Per nesu*. They had come all the way from Waset to petition the king, unaware Akhenaten was not at *Per nesu*. When they were told the king would not see them until his return in a few days, the delegate then went to Queen Tiye, but their representatives were snubbed and the mood of the crowd turned ugly.

Later that afternoon, the two princes prepared to return to the city, and Smenkhare called for his chariot. Driving the chariot himself, and with Prince Tutankhaten standing at the front rail, he set off for the city at an easy pace. They were escorted by fifteen guards who ran ahead to clear the way. They were approaching *Hat Aten*, the small temple to the south of the city, when one of the officers ran back, waving his arms. Smenkhare reined in the horses.

'Your Highness, there is trouble ahead. It might be favourable for your Highness to return to the Southern Palace.'

'No one would dare attack a Prince. We shall proceed!'

The officer ordered his men to remain close to the chariot, arms at the ready. The excited Prince Tutankhaten, barely able to see over the chariot guard, watched wide-eyed as the soldiers positioned themselves protectively, alongside. As they approached the mob, the rebels, shouting and demonstrating, reluctantly withdrew to let them pass.

They entered the southern gate of the walled court of the small temple and approached the avenue of sphinxes. The angry throng hemmed them in all three sides. The guards were struggling to clear the way. Mahu, the Chief of police, and a small company of his Medjay, manned mostly by Nubian warriors from Kush, came forward to force a way through. The hostile crowd, objecting to being prodded with spears, reacted and remonstrated, with much arm waving and shouting.

The Prince's already nervous horses, not used to this kind of behaviour, snorted, whinnied and rolled their eyes in fear. Smenkhare's gentle words and soothing voice did nothing to calm them and he struggled to control them.

A man in the crowd, waving a banner with the inscription 'Hail Amun' painted upon it, stepped forward. He shouted to Smenkhare. 'Restore Amun! Give us back our god! Let us worship him in peace!'

Smenkhare paid no heed to the man and concentrated on his grip on the young prince and trying to control the horses. An officer in his guard grabbed hold of the reins to assist the prince. The agitated animals continued to stomp and whinny.

The man then ripped the banner from its mast, rolled it into a ball and flung it towards the officer. 'Hang that on the pylon of the temple!' he shouted.

The flag missed the officer, unfurled, and landed over the head of one of the horses. The panicked animal neighed in terror and reared up. The chariot jerked, causing Smenkhare to lose his balance. He grabbed the rail to steady himself, letting go of Tutankhaten. The chariot lurched again violently. Tutankhaten lost his balance and went flying off the platform, hitting his face against the chariot wheel and landing heavily, head first, on the road, blood seeping from his mouth and nose.

Smenkhare leapt off the chariot and cradled the stunned boy in his arms. 'He's dead!' he cried out in despair. 'The Prince is dead!'

The angry guard retaliated and loosed an arrow at the banner thrower. The arrow pierced the man's neck. He clutched at his throat and, with a gurgling scream, fell down, dead. Pandemonium broke out.

The closer demonstrators panicked and tried to retreat. Those at the rear pushed forward to attack, hurling everything they could lay their hands on at the soldiers, while those in front, tried to escape. The unruly crowd milled in confusion. The guards, slashing and stabbing with their short swords, struck at the crowd, trying to force them away from the accident scene.

The frenzied mob would not be calmed and their anger increased. More arrows were sent into the surging, screaming, stone-throwing mob. What had started as a peaceful demonstration, turned into a bloody carnage.

Smenkhare, oblivious of the commotion around him, picked up the limp body of the boy and Tutankhaten groaned. 'He's alive!' Smenkhare exclaimed. 'He's alive, thanks, O Lord Horus!'

'Back, Highness,' Mahu urged. 'Make haste! Get to safety! My Medjay will take care of this rabble.'

'I will take care of them, Mahu. I will get the princes to safety!' One of the officers offered. He then assisted Smenkhare, still cradling the groaning Tutankhaten, onto the chariot, then stepped upon the platform and turned the horses around.

He steered the chariot around the city, behind the military quarters and around the Great Temple. There was no road and they had to drive over a stretch of rough ground before joining up to a crude, wagon track through the northern suburbs.

Nefertiti and Mutnedjmet, who had been drawn to the window by the distant commotion in the city, watched as the lone chariot raced rounded the eastern wall of the Great Temple. As it drew close, they recognised the blue and electrum vehicle as Smenkhare's. When they saw him holding the boy in his arms, they realised something terrible had happened and, alarmed, raced to the gate to meet them.

The gates of the Palace were flung open as the speeding chariot approached. The driver did not stop until he was well inside the courtyard. Distressed, Nefertiti and Mutnedjmet arrived, just as the officer helped Smenkhare down, still carrying the young prince.

'Summon Pentu, quickly!' Nefertiti ordered. The servant rushed out to get the physician, and she and Mutnedjmet hurried to the injured prince's side.

'Thank you, Captain.' Smenkhare started inside, then turned. 'What is your name? I wish to reward you.'

'No need for a reward, Highness. It is a pleasure to be of service. My name is Rakhmet.'

The officer left and Smenkhare watched the departing man. He had heard that name before…somewhere. He dismissed the thought, went inside, laid the prince onto the couch then knelt down next to him. The boy's face had an ugly purple-black bruise on his left cheek. Blood still oozed from his nose and mouth and his lock-of-youth was matted with congealed blood.

*\*\*\**

Tutankhaten's left cheek had been broken when he hit the wheel, and two of his teeth were also shattered, causing the bleeding from his mouth, but apart from that, he was all right. Relieved, Nefertiti thanked Pentu.

The physician recommended the prince be kept still for a few days and to feed him only broth and millet porridge for a while.

'I will remain here, with him,' Smenkhare offered, 'until he has recovered.'

Lady Mutny thanked the prince, but assured him that she and Nefertiti would tend to the prince. 'Of course, you are welcome to stay. I will arrange quarters for you,' Lady Mutnedjmet clapped her hands and instructed her servant to see to it.

Smenkhare nodded, then on a table, noticed a small figurine of a seated woman. He went over and picked it up. 'Merit!' he exclaimed, delighted. 'What a wonderful likeness. Menefer's work?'

'Yes. She is quite a remarkable young woman,' Mutnedjmet replied.

'Remarkable indeed.' Smenkhare smiled. 'It is beautiful.'

'You may have it, if you wish,' Nefertiti offered.

'Thank you,' he nodded towards the queen. 'I will treasure it.'

It was not the likeness of the princess, Smenkhare desired, but rather the object itself, the handiwork of the sculptress, that he wanted to have close. 'I wish to compliment her. Where can I find her?'

'She had been visiting her family for the feast, but should be back by now. I have not seen her since her return. She often strolls along the riverbank or by the shores of the lake. You might find here there.' Mutnedjmet noticed the look in his eye as he left and understood. He was attracted to the young woman.

*** 

Smenkhare searched the bank of the river without luck. He then went to the lake. The surroundings of the place were pleasant and serene, but Menefer was nowhere in sight. Disappointed, he started back.

It was late afternoon, and she would surely return later. Then he noticed his arms and tunic still smeared with blood. The distressing events of the afternoon and concern for the young prince had made him ignore his own appearance.

He looked around. No one was about, so he stripped down to his shenti and strode down to the lake edge. He scrubbed his tunic as clean as he could, draped it over a nearby bush to dry, removed his shenti and then washed himself. The water was very cold.

When he had finished, and with his tunic still wet, he dabbed himself dry with the shenti, then shivering, put it on and lay down on the grass to dry in the warmth of the late afternoon sun. Soft footsteps behind him made him turn around.

Menefer saw him the instant he turned and for a moment both hesitated, then Smenkhare jumped up and reached for his tunic.

'Smenkhare! I… I am sorry… I did not realise you were here. Did I disturb you?'

'It's all right.' He struggled with the garment but it clung to his damp skin.

'No need to do that.' Menefer waved a hand. 'My brothers often wear loin-cloths around the house. It does not bother me…but it's a bit cold to go swimming this time of the year, though.'

He replaced the still wet tunic on the bush again and explained about the soiled tunic and his bathing.

'Blood? Did you injure yourself?' Alarmed, she searched his half-naked body for wounds.

He told her about the accident that afternoon, the unruly crowd, and the drastic action the soldiers and the Medjay had taken, but his recollection of the events were vague and could not give her all of the details. Then he noticed the concern in her eyes. 'Be assured, the young prince would recover. We managed to escape the rabble. An officer, Rakhmet, drove us to safety.' He suddenly realised where he had heard of the officer. 'Oh, I—I'm so sorry! I heard about your—about him.'

Emotion suddenly overcame Menefer again. It had been over a month since that fateful day. She had forced herself to remain composed and indifferent at home with her family, but this time she could no long contain the flood of tears. 'Oh, Smenkhare, I loved him so. Why did this happen? I thought he loved me.'

Smenkhare tried to comfort the distressed girl. As he embraced her, she wept on his shoulder. He allowed her to deplete her pent-up sorrow. When her sobs ceased and she calmed, he bent down and kissed her tear-stained face.

'Why, Smenkhare, why…why me?' she asked in a small voice.

'Because I love you, Menefer,' his voice was soft, almost a whisper.

'No, I meant…why did he do this to me? I don't understand…I…' she stopped and stared at him. 'What did you say?'

'I love you!' he repeated, his eyes burning into hers.

'But…but…you and Meritaten? I heard rumours…'

'Yes, we are to wed, but our marriage is a necessary one, reasons of State, as I mentioned before…but it is *you* I really want, Menefer!'

'But…what about Merit!'

'She will be my Great Wife, but I want you as my favourite wife. I tried to tell you that before, but you were betrothed. I did not wish to, uh…could not pursue the matter. Now, as Rakhmet is no longer…' he paused, searching for just the right words, '…in your life, you too, deserve happiness.' He bent his head and kissed her on the forehead. 'Will you allow me to make you…forget him?'

She looked up into his face, confused, 'Can you do that, Smenkhare? How?'

'Yes, I can.' He crushed her to him and stroked the back of her neck, then slowly moved his hand down, tenderly caressing her shoulder, her breast.

'No, Smenkhare. It…it is not fitting…' her protesting voice was small but she did not resist. He was encouraged.

'It is, Menefer. It is very fitting,' he whispered back, husky voiced. 'We are meant for each other. Do not shun me.'

'Meant for each other? What do you mean?'

'Had it not so been designed by the Gods? Had they not meant to cause the separation between you and Rakhmet? Had not the Gods, by their doing, intended for you to come to the King's House, the act that brought us together? Had the Gods not directed us here, to this lake, at this time? Does that not prove that we were meant to be together?'

'Yes. It *does* seem more than just chance…' She hugged him close. 'You are right! It all does seem to have been prearranged. Oh Smenkhare, hold me close—make me forget!'

Smenkhare eased the halter off her shoulders and her tunic dropped to the ground. He loosened and dropped his shenti and embraced her tightly. They both sank down onto the soft grass.

# Chapter Twenty
## Royal Wedding

News of the massacre in Akhet Aten soon reached Waset, sparking renewed outbreaks of violence there. The soldiers and Medjay could do little to quash the anger of the demonstrators and were hampered by the rest of people. Most of them sympathised with the protesters against *that criminal in Akhet Aten.*

Feelings against Pharaoh continued to rise. The people screamed for vengeance for those killed during the demonstration. Now, even more than ever, they wanted Amunism restored. They wanted the freedom to worship the deity of their choice, and nothing short of it will be accepted.

'The first delegation I sent to restore order there, failed,' Akhenaten paced back and forth in the Hall of Audience, waving his arms in despair. 'My spokesman was killed and other emissaries were driven from the city.'

Ay cleared his throat. 'Majesty, perhaps troops could accompany your delegation…'

'No, Lord Ay, sending an armed guard would seem like a threat,' Horemheb protested. 'It will antagonise them more.'

'I have to do something, but it could mean the death of anyone I send,' Akhenaten stopped, concerned, and rubbed his face. He sat down on the edge of the dais. 'I have to find someone *they* can trust, someone who can be very diplomatic…and someone who will go willingly.'

'Your Majesty, I will go.'

'You, Horemheb?' Akhenaten looked up, surprised. 'You realise it is a dangerous mission.'

'I do, Majesty, but I have family and friends in No-Am…uh…Waset. They know me, and will listen to my words.'

'I am pleased, but I am still concerned for your safety.'

'Majesty, *any* assignment, *anywhere,* has its risks, this will be no different.'

'But, as Lord Ay suggested, perhaps you will need an escort.'

'I will take one person with me. I will choose a trusted officer to accompany me, one who is well known in Waset.'

It did not take long to persuade Pharaoh.

\*\*\*

'But Rakhmet, is it not dangerous? Could the Commander not take someone else?' Istar looked anxious.

'It is no more risky than here, and I volunteered,' Rakhmet explained. 'Waset is my childhood home and I readily accepted the position there.'

'Is it not, perhaps, an excuse to avoid the sculptress?' She sounded cynical. 'You no longer wear the amulet she gave you, but you still keep it with your belongings.'

'I am not trying to avoid her. Whenever we meet by accident, it is always awkward, but it is *she* who avoids *me*. Did she not break our troth, as all those letters indicated? Did you not see her move across the street when we chance to be on the same road?'

Istar was not satisfied, but she was relieved to move away from Akhet Aten, as she too, felt awkward whenever she happened upon Menefer at the marketplace or in the street.

'I know you still care for her... I saw you glance at her whenever we encounter her. Perhaps this move will be good, will make you forget.'

He nodded his agreement, but Istar knew it was not going to be easy.

***

Menefer was not her usual self when she returned to the palace after a family visit and Lady Mutnedjmet noticed. 'Is everything well at home?'

'Ipuky and Nebaten are fine, Lady Mutny. Neb has met someone, but would not talk about it, yet. It is about time he marries...both my brothers are troubled. They are concerned about the escalating violence in Waset that seems to have reached us here, in Akhet Aten, but my concern is for my father. When I arrived home, he mistook me for my mother and called me *Mutnames,* my mother's name. Sometimes he wanders from room to room, as if searching for something. Other times he just sits and stares.'

'Time will heal all,' Mutny replied. 'Is there something else? You do not look well.'

'I... I have been feeling ill, lately, but I will be all right. Segi, the mute brought me some herbs that seem to help.'

'It is probably anxiety. Also, the winter season is ending. The change in the weather can also cause such a malady, but there is someone here who wishes to see you and might bring some cheer!' She directed her to the chamber where the princesses had gathered.

'Menefer!' Merit bubbled with excitement as Menefer entered and greeted her with enthusiasm.

'Princess Meritaten!' Menefer rushed over and they hugged. 'I'm so glad you are back. Are you just visiting or will you be staying longer?'

'Just a short visit, to bring some news. Smenkhare and I are finally betrothed!' She could not contain her joy. 'We are to be wed soon.'

'How wonderful, Your Highness,' Menefer squeezed her hands. 'I've been expecting this news for some time.'

'No date has been set,' they seated themselves. 'It should be announced in ten days' time. There is to be a feast in the Great Palace then the announcement will be made official. You will all receive formal invitations'

'Wonderful. When is the wedding day?'

Merit seemed not to hear Menefer's question, and excitedly, gushed on about the coming event, the dress she shall be wearing for the wedding feast and the gift she had planned for Smenkhare. 'Senpa had suggested a royal barge for us to sail to distant river ports, perhaps even to the Great Green waters beyond the Delta!'

'Oh, I just realised,' Senpa interrupted. 'What about our mother? She vowed not to return to *Per nesu*.'

Merit had completely forgotten about Nefertiti's vow. 'Oh dear. She did not mention anything when I told her and Mutny the news. Perhaps, in this instance, she would make an exception, perhaps...' She paused at a knock on the door 'Enter!' she called out.

'Highness, a messenger is here from His Majesty the King. He had sent a chariot and wishes Princess Ankhsenpaaten's company.'

Senpa looked up, surprised. 'Me? I wonder why?' She got up. 'I will return shortly.'

***

After the queen's sunset temple ceremony at her private temple, Merit and Lady Mutny joined her in her common chamber.

Menefer returned from her early evening stroll and had just entered the Palace courtyard when Senpa arrived back from *Per nesu*. She looked bewildered and unhappy as she stepped off the chariot.

'Senpa, is anything wrong?'

'I... I am to pack my clothing chests... I too, am to accompany Merit to *Per nesu*...on Pharaoh's orders,' she started for her quarters.

Menefer hurried and caught up with her. 'It is probably just for the feast they are planning for Princess Meritaten's wedding,' she tried to sound casual and cheery.

'Perhaps...but why did he request I pack *all* my belongings?' They reached the queen's chambers and entered. Queen Nefertiti was anxious to hear the reason her daughter was summoned.

'Perhaps he misses us, miss you, mother,' Merit suggested after Senpa had explained. 'You two had always been rather close. Perhaps, by having me and Senpa there, he hopes, from sheer loneliness or longing, you could reconcile your differences and you would return.'

Nefertiti scoffed. 'The suggestion is too far-fetched and very unlikely!'

But no one had any other explanation for the King's action. A command from Pharaoh cannot be refused. Senpa directed her maids to pack her chests and the following day, she and Meritaten left for *Per nesu*.

***

Several days passed. No word had come from *Per nesu*. Queen Nefertiti and Lady Mutnedjmet were, again, playing their favourite game of senet. Little Tutankhaten, whose injuries had mended well, was playing with the two younger princesses and Setenpenre laughed with delight at the antics of her six years old half-brother.

166

The blare of trumpets and sounds of drums and singing from the Great Temple, reached the North Palace.

'What's going on?' Nefertiti got up and walked onto the balcony. 'There seems to be some kind of ceremony. Surely not the announcement of Smenkhare and Merit's wedding.' She summoned a servant girl and sent her to find out what it was about, returned to her seat and she and lady Mutny resumed their game.

Menefer no longer taught her craft. With both the elder princesses gone, she was concerned her services might be terminated, but Lady Mutnedjmet had assured her she could stay as long as she wanted. There would always be something to occupy her, and her task now, could be to entertain the younger children. She amused them with stories and, for the fifth time that day, was asked to retell the story of the brave lion hunter.

'I like that story more than all the rest,' Tutankhaten said. 'One day, when I grow up, I too shall kill a lion, or maybe even two!'

She started the tale again, ignoring the distant commotion coming from the city. Only Nefertiti, concerned, looked up often.

'You miss the festivals, do you not?' Mutnedjmet asked, noticing her sister's interest in the goings on.

'No. We can still celebrate all the feast days right here. I need not be in the city.'

'Well I, for one, am curious to learn what it is all about.' They played the board game in silence for a while, then Mutnames moved a game-piece on the senet board, 'I win.'

The queen got up and went to the balcony again, noting the shadow of obelisk had moved some distance since she last looked. 'The ceremony, whatever it is, seems a lengthy one. Just what is going on, down there?'

Mutnedjmet reset the pieces for another game. 'Perhaps, what you said in jest has come about.' Nefertiti turned to her sister, puzzled.

'Tiye is being deified...again!' Mutnedjmet laughed and Nefertiti grinned widely, returned to the chamber and sat down, then gestured to the game. 'Your turn to start.'

After what seemed like ages, the servant girl returned, exhausted, ashen faced and trembling. 'Your Majesty...' she inhaled deeply to steady her speech. 'It is a wedding ceremony.'

'Merit and Smenkhare? So soon?' Nefertiti asked surprised. 'They have not even announced the betrothal, yet.'

'No, Your Majesty. His Majesty, Pharaoh Akhenaten is being wed.'

'Akhenaten?' Nefertiti and Mutnedjmet called out almost simultaneously, looking at one another. Nefertiti turned back to the servant. 'Whom is he marrying?'

The girl swallowed hard and nervously looked from Nefertiti to Mutnedjmet, obviously frightened.

'Come on girl!' Nefertiti demanded.

'Your Majesty... His Majesty has wed Princess Ankhsenpaaten!'

\*\*\*

The shock of Akhenaten's marriage was not the only one the queen was to suffer. Soon after the wedding, on Akhenaten's orders, teams of workmen set out to obliterate every trace of Nefertiti. Her name was erased from every monument, pylon and obelisk; her features hacked from the Royal Palace walls, and even at Hat Aten, the private royal temple. The destruction was particularly severe at Maru-Aten, Akhenaten's Pleasure Palace. Personal objects left there by the queen, her cosmetic jars, mirror and jewellery box, were also defaced or destroyed.

Statues of the queen were thrown down or disfigured. Cartouches bearing her name were over-painted or simply scraped off walls, even from the walls inside *Per nesu*.

This had not merely been an act of revenge; it had a much deeper, more sinister meaning, and to the queen, the final blow.

'I cannot believe he would do such a thing, Mutny!' Nefertiti's eyes were dry, but she was shaken and pale and her lips quivered when she spoke.

'He is denying me my afterlife! When I pass on to the West, I will have nowhere to reside. My *ka* will dwell in the shadows for all eternity. It will be destroyed!'

'No, Nefertiti!' Mutnedjmet comforted. 'I assure you, you will not be forgotten. Here, in the Northern Palace, your name shall remain. For every one Akhenaten destroys, we shall replace it with two!'

'What could have brought on this act of vengeance? Our love had now cooled, but it had endured for over twenty five years! Does that mean nothing to him? Could he have forgotten the happy times we spent together? Is Tiye's influence so strong that she could manipulate Akhenaten to this extent?'

Mutnedjmet watched her sister, helplessly. This time, she could not think of words to console the queen.

Nefertiti vehemently expressed her feelings for Pharaoh and retreated to her chambers where she remained, secluded, seeing no one, except for her sister and children. The palace had become a cold and cheerless place. The queen's distress affected everyone in the palace and the moods of all who dwelt there. No more laughter, no gay chatter or the friendly, lively conversations during their senet games, were heard. Frowns replaced smiles and grunts replaced greetings.

Few visitors came to the palace. The court at *Per nesu* had shunned the Northern Palace and virtually declared it off limits. Most felt reluctant to be seen entering the place for fear of the scorn of others. Only a few persons dared visit it.

Princess Meritaten was one of these visitors. She felt deep sympathy for the way her mother had been treated and had come, for a while, to comfort her. Her erstwhile happiness at *Per nesu* was short-lived since the Royal wedding, and she and Prince Smenkhare had quarrelled and drifted apart. The prince looked upon their betrothal and eventual marriage as a mere formality, a duty to the State.

She did not explain the reasons for their disagreement, and neither the queen, nor Lady Mutnedjmet wanted to pry. Meritaten will reveal it all in her own good time, but they guessed the cause.

Smenkhare, a strong supporter of Amun, had been planning to reinstate the god to his former glory in No-Amun. Merit, greatly influenced by her mother's pro-Aten views, was against it and this had caused a strained relationship.

A few days later, the North Palace had another visitor. Prince Smenkhare disregarded the adverse opinions of the court. Their opinions mattered little to him and he was not influenced by their petty attitudes. He was, after all, a prince, the Royal heir.

A sombre Lady Mutnedjmet managed a wry smile as she greeted him.

'Welcome, Smenkhare. I'm afraid we are not of good cheer these days. The palace is a rather gloomy place to visit.'

'I understand, Mutny, I will not intrude on Nefertiti's privacy. I came to speak with Merit.'

Mutnedjmet sent a servant to notify the princess of her visitor. Princess Meritaten arrived duly, but did not appear too pleased when she saw him. Mutnedjmet sensed the cool greeting, made her excuses and left.

'You wanted to see me?' Merit sounded aloof.

Smenkhare attributed her coolness to the atmosphere of her surroundings. 'Yes, Merit, I regret the actions of the King. It is unfortunate. I hope the Queen's disgrace will not…'

'Disgrace? What are you saying?' Merit's face flushed with sudden fury. 'It is not she who had brought dishonour upon the court. She was pressured into taking a stand. Anyone in her position would have done the same. *I* would have done so, too, if I were provoked!'

Smenkhare was taken aback by Merit's outburst. 'Merit… I did not mean it in that sense. I merely meant she had—'

'Why have you come, Smenkhare?'

'I…I wanted to see you. I thought—I thought we could make a new start—get to know one-another better…' he fumbled for the right words but he lacked the skill to express himself and felt awkward.

'Under the circumstances, I don't think it is wise,' Merit turned her head away.

'But we are to be wed soon, Merit…'

'Yet, while the preparations for our betrothal is being made, you went with *another woman*!'

He was taken aback. 'Perhaps I should not have told you, but… I only did so, so that there would be no secrets between us. Can you not understand…?'

'Yes! I understand you needed the company of someone else.' She turned and headed for the door. 'But you could have chosen a more appropriate occasion. Please excuse me, I must be with my mother and you can go back to your harlot!'

She fled, leaving him standing in the chamber, bewildered and undecided, then noticed Lady Mutnedjmet in the passage. 'Mutny!' he flushed.

'Forgive me, but I could not help overhearing. Your conversation was loud and carried into the corridor.'

'I'm…sorry… I did not realise…'

'No need to be concerned. I will talk to Merit. She will understand,' Lady Mutnedjmet turned to leave, then turned, puzzled. 'I will pry no further into your personal affairs, but…do I know the lady in question?'

Smenkhare looked about, uncomfortably, then flushing again and looked way. 'It is… Mistress Menefer.'

'Menefer!' Mutnedjmet, surprised, reacted back and grinning. '*You and Menefer?*'

169

'Please, Mutny. Someone might hear. You said sounds carry—'

Mutnedjmet steps closer and patter the prince's hand, whispering, 'I suspected it for some time. I will keep your secret safe, be assured.'

Smenkhare left for *Per nesu* and Mutnedjmet stared after him. 'Smenkhare and Menefer!' she muttered and shook her head, smiling broadly. 'Smenkhare and Menefer.'

***

To get away from the gloomy atmosphere of the palace, Menefer headed for her usual retreat, the lake. Lady Mutnedjmet noticed her leaving, and, eager to talk to her, followed. 'Menefer wait!' she called out. 'Would you like some company?'

Menefer stopped and waited for Mutnedjmet to catch up. 'Lady Mutny, yes. Please join me. I often stroll along the river bank.'

'I know. I have seen you go that way before,' they walked along in silence, listening to the waterfowl and the distant calls of fishermen on the river, guiding their skiffs along and boasting of their catches, as fishermen always do.

'Menefer, I'm concerned,' Lady Mutny tried to find words to get around to the subject. 'This illness of yours…I noticed you have not fully recovered yet.'

'No, I still feel unwell in the mornings. I might have to see a physician soon.'

'Could you tell me more?'

After a few more personal questions, lady Mutnedjmet was able to offer an explanation of Menefer's malady. 'Menefer, I think I know what ails you. It appears you are with child!'

Menefer stopped and stared at her in disbelief. Mutnedjmet smiled and put a motherly arm around her shoulders. 'First…please, would you confide in me? Consider me as your friend? You need to take me into your confidence. This is much more serious than you realise.'

After a little more persuasion, Menefer nodded an agreement and revealed she had a relationship.

'With Smenkhare?'

'Yes!' Menefer asked surprised, 'how did you know?'

'I am aware of many things. Oh, no need for concern, your secret is safe. He told me himself, after I overheard, quite by accident, when he and Merit were talking. I had also been curious why he had tried, unsuccessfully, to see you lately. But…' she shrugged, 'circumstances had made it rather difficult for him. He had obligations…the wedding for instance,' Mutnedjmet realised she had been rambling, and quickly returned to the subject. 'But, enough of that. Will you allow me to assist you during your…time? I am but a few years older than you, but believe me, I know about these things.'

'Thank you. I…appreciate your offer.'

They reached the shaded area in the palm grove. Mutnedjmet beckoned Menefer to sit down next to her on a grassy bank.

'A woman who bears a child out of wedlock could be in serious trouble,' she explained in a serious voice. 'She could be liable for severe punishment, and, in some nomes, could even be stoned to death!'

Fear gripped Menefer, but Mutnedjmet quickly put her at ease. 'Do not be concerned. I will arrange for your confinement at a place where you will be safe. No one, except a chosen few, will know of the birth of the child and, above all, we must keep the identity of the child's father confidential. Carrying a royal child is a great risk...to you and the babe. If this knowledge should fall into the hands of wrong people...' Mutnedjmet shrugged. There was no need to explain. 'We must handle this carefully. First, promise you will tell no one.'

Menefer agreed and Mutnedjmet continued explaining her plan. 'First, you must visit you family...soon, before any signs are visible. Explain that you will not be able to see them for some time...that you have been assigned to do some—uh—task—decoration work at the temple of Ipet-Isut, and will need to reside there for a while.'

'Ipet-Isut? Why there?'

'I was the High Priestess of Mut-Sekhmet before Akhenaten's reformation. Did you not know?' Menefer shook her head, surprised, and Lady Mutny continued. 'The priestesses there still regard me highly.'

She hesitate, pain showing in her face. 'I am going to tell you something that must remain between us. Only a few people know about it.'

Menefer promised to keep her secret.

Mutnedjmet had a far-away look in her eyes as she reminisced. 'When I was younger, perhaps a little younger than you are now, and just as foolish, I fell in love with a General...Nakhtmin. He was so handsome and kind...'

She blinked and returned to reality. 'Anyway, I...became with child and frightened, but the priestesses of Mut-Sekhmet understood and cared for me. Unfortunately, I had not been discreet. Akhenaten found out, and as the sister of the queen, he was most displeased. He had the unborn child murdered and Nakhtmin sent into exile. He returned many years later, we were married, and had two more children, a son Baraka, and Sitre, a daughter. We were happy, until I was summoned to Akhet Aten to attend to Nefertiti who was with child then—Setenpenre. I was instructed to divorce Nakhtmin, surrender my children to my husband's mother who raised them and I also had to relinquish my position as High Priestess. For that reason, I have no love for Akhenaten. This caused much strain to my relations with my sister.'

Menefer stared, surprised. She now saw Lady Mutnedjmet in a new light. Her respect and admiration for the lady suddenly grew.

'Enough of me, we are changing the subject—now, to your little—uh—problem. You will stay at Ipet-Isut until the child is born, then return here, after you have "completed" your decorating task. The child will remain there until we can find someone to adopt...'

'No! Please, I want to keep my baby.'

All Mutnedjmet arguments could not dissuade Menefer to change her mind. 'Well...' she said after a bit of thought. 'You can always adopt a *foundling* child yourself. You might even be praised for being kind and generous, for raising a deserted baby as your own.'

This plan suited Menefer and she agreed.

Mutny now sounded enthusiastic. 'Very well, yes, we can do just that. Now listen carefully to my plan and do not breathe a word to anyone. Walls have eyes and ears…and servant's tongues flap like banners in a breeze. This is what we'll do…'

# Chapter Twenty-One
## Wrath of Aten

Upit, the month of Thoth in the season of Akhet, was the time of the flooding. During the Great Inundation, the Nile-of-the-Sky would send its waters down to earth in the lands of Punt and Kush. It would swell the rivers, rush north and flood the land of Kemet, depositing its rich black soil.

Just as the river gave Egypt its gift, on this, the first day of the New Year, so too, the people gave gifts to each other, called the time of the *Open hand*. Everyone in the country had been preparing for the festivities of Upit, and the five feast days preceding the start of the New Year.

Nakht, the Royal Astronomer, had been particularly busy, observing the sun and the stars, to calculating the exact day when the sun would reach its Summer solstice. The star Sopet, that had disappeared from view, about two and a half months earlier, would reappear again at dawn on the day of Upit. It would be the brightest body in the heaven after the sun and the moon.

Satisfied with his calculations, he prepared to make his announcement on the morrow.

The designated day for the Upit ceremony arrived, and, as Pharaoh had decreed, Smenkhare and Merit were wed. This news of the marriage reached the North Palace, but again, the queen and Lady Mutnedjmet could only watch the procession from afar.

'First, the marriage of Senpa, now the wedding day of my eldest daughter, Merit's happiest moment, and I cannot attend!' Nefertiti lamented. 'Oh, Mutny, will it be thus from now on? Will I forever be denied all those important occasions?'

'It is a decision of your own choosing, Nefertiti!' Mutnedjmet reminded her. 'There is nothing preventing you from joining the crowd attending. It is only the ceremony from which we are barred.'

Nefertiti sighed and turned from the balcony. She sat down and idly busied herself threading beads. She had been fashioning gifts for Merit and Smenkhare, making each a matching pair of collars.

'No. I will not go! I will not look on alongside the common people, like some beggar, from the back of the temple.'

Princess Neferneferure entered the chamber. 'Mother, when is Menefer coming back?'

'She will be away for some time, Nefer, why?' The queen asked, without looking up from her bead-work.

'I miss her company, and Sherit is fighting with me again!' Nefer pouted, petulantly.

'You girls must really stop arguing all the time.'

'Come, Nefer.' Mutny got up and escorted the princess back to their chamber, 'I'll go and make peace and try and find something to amuse you.'

The festivities continued throughout that day and well into the night. Many important foreign visitors attended the celebrations. One such a visitor was King Burnaburash of Babal. During the Eastern conflicts, his country too, had been threatened by the Amorites. The king had allied himself with Akhenaten, and as a "token of his loyalty", offered his son, Prince Nijmat, as hostage, or *a long-term guest*, as they preferred to call it, as a gesture of faith.

In a jovial and generous mood, Akhenaten, delighted, made an announcement. 'Your Majesty, as a faithful valued ally, and as an additional and everlasting bond, I too will make an offer—my daughter, Neferneferure, as bride to your son, Nijmat.'

The fifteen-year-old Nijmat, surprised at the sudden gesture, could not reply. He had been at Akhenaten's court for a while and had not expected this sudden declaration. At a loss for words, he just gaped.

Burnaburash spoke for him. 'Your Majesty is most gracious and generous. It is a great honour and we accept your kind offer.' Then, fearing Akhenaten might have a change of heart later, quickly added, 'We will arrange the wedding forthwith.'

'Nefer is thirteen years old,' Akhenaten added. 'A good marrying age.'

'Excellent, excellent!' Burnaburash laughed. 'I did not wish to delay the alliance—and marriage.' He glanced at his nervous son and chuckled. 'I am certain Nijmat is pleased with the arrangement, yes?'

Queen Nefertiti had returned from her morning temple ceremony, and after their morning meal, joined Lady Mutnedjmet for their usual game of senet, when Sentu brought her the news of Pharaoh's latest act.

Sentu fled as the Queen exploded in fury and flung the game board at the door. 'Is there no end to his folly?' She screamed and jumped up, storming back and forth. 'Is it not enough for him to have removed my two eldest daughters and take Senpa as a wife? Must he now also deprive me of my Little Nefer? Without even consulting me? She is a mere babe! When is this madness going to end?'

Mutnedjmet, too stunned by her outburst to reply, could only stare. The *mere babe* happened to be thirteen, Nefertiti's age when she had married Akhenaten, but decided not to remind her angry sister of this fact. Nefertiti rushed into her daughter's quarters and clasped Neferure to her breast, weeping. The bewildered girl, not aware of her forthcoming wedding, hugged her mother. Prince Tutankhaten just stared, puzzled and fearful.

\*\*\*

Menteret, the High Priestess of Mut, waited at the landing place as Menefer disembarked, then escorted her to the temple. The complex of Ipet-Isut and Ipet-Resyt, North and South Ipet, turned out to be vast, much bigger than Menefer had anticipated. As they walked to the temple, Menteret pointed out various buildings of interest.

'Over there, on the right, is the shrine of Queen Hatshepsut.'

'Oh yes,' Menefer replied, eager to show off her knowledge. 'When her husband died, she dressed like a man in order to become Pharaoh.'

'Not exactly,' Menteret laughed. 'When Pharaoh Thutmosis III died, she became regent, as her step-son, his heir, had been too young to rule. Only after she had tasted power, did she decide to remain in control and to become Per-O. The people objected to having a female ruler, so she donned the *nemes*, the striped head cloth worn by Pharaoh, and the *khabes*, the ceremonial beard, for State occasions only.'

They continued past rows of *shesps*, an avenue of sphinxes, and entered the walled enclosure of the Temple precinct.

'There,' Menteret pointed. 'Straight ahead is the temple of the goddesses Mut, the dwelling place of the protective mother-goddess, over which I preside. The smaller one on the left is of Khonsu, her son, a moon-deity.'

They were joined by another priestess.

'This is Abina,' Menteret introduced her to Menefer. 'She is a priestess of Sekhmet and had been appointed to care for you. I must return to my duties for now, but am looking forward to hearing all the latest news and gossip from Akhet Aten, later, so I will leave you for now.' She turned to Abina, 'Watch over her, Abina, Menefer is a very special guest.' Menteret hurried off, and Menefer wondered how much the two women knew of her situation.

'I have arranged for your things to be brought from the docks. Come, I will show you to your chamber.' She gestured to a small cluster of buildings alongside the temple of Khonsu, 'These are the living quarters. It will be nothing like your quarters at the palace. We are but a humble order, but I will try and make you as comfortable as possible.'

'Thank you, I am certain I shall be happy here.'

'Do you like an occasional stroll? There is a sacred lake behind the temple,' Abina pointed to a curved lake, just coming into view behind the Temple of Mut. 'There are several footpaths to, and around the lake. We often go there for walks or to meditate.'

'Oh, yes, I would love it,' Menefer immediately felt at home.

\*\*\*

One month later, on the morn of the Feast day of Aten, Smenkhare was officially declared co-regent and proclaimed Ruler of the Southern Land with Waset as his capital. The coronation would take place as soon as a favourable date had been calculated.

The new co-ruler and his wife attended their first official duty, at the "Feast of Aten", held at noon at the Great Temple. The procession approached the inner sanctuary. All were dressed in white, the men, bare to the waist. Their skirts secured by broad blue-dyed leather belts and all wore broad necklace collars. The women wore pleated linen skirts and some were bare-breasted. All wore heavy perfumed wigs, each with a fragrant cone fixed to the top and decorated with a water lily bud.

The High Priest, Panehesy, the *Keri-heb*, "*he who hath charge of the festival*", met the Royals. He escorted Akhenaten and Smenkhare to the sanctuary and the

Holy of Holies. Smenkhare had not yet been crowned, and had to remain outside. Only the High Priest and Pharaoh could enter this most sacred place.

At precisely mid-day, as the sun reached its highest position in the sky, a ray of light penetrated an opening in a stone lintel above the altar in the holy of holies and struck the Golden Disk. Panehesy, reciting magic formulae and sprinkled holy water, reappeared, accompanied by Pharaoh, and gave a signal for the ceremony to begin.

A line of lesser priests entered the inner temple, carrying upon their shoulders a small boat covered in gold. On a raised platform in the centre of the boat, a smaller version of the Golden Disk of Aten had been affixed. From the disk projected rods, each ending with a tiny hand in a protective attitude. Garlands of flowers, draped over the barge, hung almost down to the ground.

The procession then moved onto *Gem Aten*, *the House of Rejoicing,* followed by chanting priestesses. Smenkhare, and the rest of the Royal Family, fell in behind the procession. They stopped at an altar, where Panehesy and the Royals made final offerings and made their way back to the gate. As they passed through and exited the temple, Panehesy blessed them, sprinkling holy water.

In the street, worshippers bowed and raised their hands in salute as the Royal party crossed the King's way, and continued to the Great Hall of the palace. A great cheer rose from the crowd…but not all of those who watched the procession, were pleased. Anger boiled beneath calm surfaces.

***

For most, the ceremony brought joyful feasting and celebrations, but for others, it had been a disappointment. Smenkhare had joined Akhenaten for the Ceremony of the Sun, a rite to venerate Aten. They did not take it kindly to his action. It appeared Smenkhare had accepted the Disk, they said, and had forsaken Amun.

To quell the protesters who had gathered outside the Palace walls, Smenkhare announced that Amun *would* be restored in Waset. Just as Akhet Aten and On were the seats of Aten, Bast in Bubastis, Yebu the place of Isis, so Waset will once again revert to its original name *No-Amun*, the place of Amun.

Amun worshippers were heartened. Their gods would be restored. Some, once again, painted the names and symbols of their erstwhile gods on their houses.

But in Akhet Aten, Aten followers were inflamed. They did not take it kindly to see blatant sacrilege against the Disk in the dwelling place of Aten.

"Leave Akhet Aten," they cried. "Go back to Waset!"

Tempers flared. Anything, bearing the name of Amun, was vandalised or destroyed. Mud was smeared over the offensive names or scraped away. The owners of damaged homes retaliated and in turn and images of Aten were disfigured.

Heated arguments turned into brawls, and brawls into battles. The Medjay had difficulty in keeping order, and the unrest grew worse. The followers of the Disk wanted all worship of other gods, other than Aten, cast from the city of Akhet Aten, and the *Horizon of Aten* cleansed.

Zealous Aten supporters, convinced of Akhenaten's support, would meet and strike at the homes of suspected non-Atenists. Images of the banned ones were confiscated or destroyed and the owners tortured to reveal names of others. Those, with grievances against their fellows, would denounce them. Neighbour turned against neighbour, friend against friend. Attacks against people and property occurred sporadically and without warning and many were slain. No one knew who, or were they would strike next and the army and royal guard were helpless.

Maids and other servants often gossiped among themselves and each tried to outdo the other with a story and many secrets were revealed.

'Don't tell anyone, but, the home and workshop of the sculptor, Thutmose, contain many such illegal images,' Djenna remarked casually when the servants discussed the subject.

'Really?' Queen Tiye's maid asked, surprised. 'Tell us more!'

Encouraged by the reaction and interest of her listeners and revelling in the attention, Djenna continued enthusiastically. 'I have seen them myself. Menefer's family had been fashioning likenesses of the forbidden ones for some time. Clandestinely, long before now, they had been fashioning images for those who worship them, knowing it was illegal.'

Her remarks, supposedly confidential, was repeated, and soon reached the ears of a dedicated Atenist group. The house and studio of Thutmose became a target. Stones were flung over the walls and fireballs, of oil-soaked straw, thrown into the buildings through open windows. Craftsmen, who toiled in the workshops, were threatened. Many, fearing for their lives and those of their families, fled the city.

Ipuky and Nebaten were also threatened and they too, decided to leave for a while, to return once the trouble had passed and order had been restored. Menefer would be safe in Ipet-Isut, but they needed to get their father to safety.

Nebaten arranged passage for three, on a vessel bound for Mennufer, the *City of the White Wall*, about halfway between Akhet Aten and the Great Waters beyond the North Land, but Thutmose refused to go. Nebaten and Ipuky's persuasion, begging and even threats could not change his mind.

'Mutnames is here. I will never leave her!' He did not comprehend, or accept that his wife was dead. 'She is away and will return, soon.' He argued, but could not explain where she went or when she would return. 'I will await her here!'

His sons could not leave him, and reluctantly decided, they too, would remain.

*** 

They came in the night, armed with spears, clubs, bows and arrows. In the dim light of a torch, a servant saw them stealthily creep along the shadows of the outer wall of the villa and quickly alerted others.

'Intruders,' she warned. 'We are being attacked and I think Royal guards are amongst them!'

'Royal guards? Are you sure?' The other servants asked, incredulously.

'I cannot be certain, the light was dim, but one looked familiar. I am almost certain he had been one of the guards who came here with Queen Nefertiti.'

A scream, followed by shouts and crashes startled them. Too frightened to find out what had caused it, many servants fled the building.

Nebaten and Ipuky, roused during the first wave of the attack, ran to the roof. They looked down into the street where the surging mob entered the courtyard through a gate, opened by the earlier intruders. They rushed to defend themselves and their property. Both brothers were artists, not warriors, and did not keep any weapons, but they had to arm themselves with whatever they could find.

The mob broke into the workshop studio, destroying everything they could lay their hands on. They toppled the columns in the great hall. The roof of the workshop that had rested on their stone architraves, collapsed, and brought down some walls as well. The wall of the room that contained the nearly completed limestone bust of Queen Nefertiti, collapsed, and buried the bust of the queen beneath the rubble.

The noise of the attack woke Thutmose. His bed chamber was close to the workshop. He hurried there, saw the men destroying his life's work and ran to stop them. A servant tried to get the old man to safety, but the sculptor, stubborn as ever, pushed him aside and charged at those bent on destruction. Thutmose was clubbed to death in the hall where he once received the queen.

At the other end of the building, Nebaten rushed to a work chamber where tools were kept. Armed with an adze, he was about to leave, when two figures suddenly barred his way. The adze would be no match against their curved swords and spears and he looked around for something else with which to defend himself.

A large decorative urn stood on a pedestal next to the doorway. He picked up the heavy container and, with all the strength he could muster, hurled it at the attackers. It hit the man wielding the spear, knocking him to the ground and the urn shattered against the wall. The second man, momentarily thrown off-guard, regained his balance and lunged at Nebaten with the sword. Neb warded off the sword's blow with the adze and dived sideways as the man struck. The momentum carried the man past Nebaten who grabbed his arm, twisted it behind the man's back and forced it upwards. The man's sword clattered to the ground. Behind the struggling pair, the dazed spearman recovered. Neb, struggling with the swordsman, had his back to him. It was a fatal mistake.

The spearman came up from behind the wrestling men. He thrust his spear with such force, it pierced Nebaten's body to protrude through his rib cage. Neb relaxed his grip on the swordsman's arm, and, with a look of surprise and bewilderment, clutched feebly at the spear tip sticking from his chest. He tried to say something but only managed a bubbling gasp. His eyes glazed over and sank, lifeless, to the floor.

The servants' quarters behind the workshops were ablaze. The dry reed-thatched roofs burned readily and the glow from the fires illuminated the faces of the fleeing, panic-stricken workers. A burst of arrows sailed into the escaping crowd and many sagged to the ground, some writhing in pain, others never moved again.

In the ruins of the workshops, Ipuky found the battered body of his father. He cradled the old man in his arms, but only for a moment, and had to flee as more attackers came storming through the house. Their blood lust, not yet sated, they were bent on slaying everyone in the household. As Ipuky fled through the ruined house, he almost stumbled over his brother's body. With a cry of anguish and almost blinded by tears, he stumbled on. His entire family, save for himself and Menefer, was now dead. He staggered on, groping in the darkened areas where the flames of destruction had not yet reached, found the gate and fled the house, never to return.

# Chapter Twenty-Two
## A New Life

Isheru, Ipet-Isut's sacred lake, curving around the temple of Mut, had several large willow trees growing along its banks. These trees were sacred to the god Osiris. The pleasant surroundings, and the lake's shaded grassy bank, became Menefer's favourite place.

Menefer had been placed in the care of Abina, one of her priestesses, and since her arrival, the kindness and care of the priestesses had been most welcome, but Menefer insisted on earning her keep. She was determined not to be a burden and offered to fashion and produce little figurines, to be sold at the temple kiosk.

Many of the figurines being traded around the market places, were crudely fashioned. The ones sold at the temple kiosk were better-crafted and in high demand, but as the statuettes were brought from far away, they were costly, and always seemed to be a short supply. Menefer's offer to add to their dwindling supply was greatly appreciated.

Images of some gods were still allowed to be fashioned. Sekhmet, Mut and Khonsu were, surprisingly, spared from Akhenaten's purge. Even though they were all closely associated with the hated Amun. Mut, or *Lady Asheru*, as she was also called, was regarded as one of the Pharaoh's "hallowed" parents. Mut, also closely associated with Nekhbet, the vulture goddess, adorned the front of Pharaoh headdress. Her worship was thus allowed. Khonsu, a deity whose image was not often on demand, was depicted as a child, with a *"lock-of-youth"* and swathed in funerary cloth. Regarded as the *Lord of Life*, he was also a god of healing. The symbol of life, the *Ankh*, was worn as his charm. The rays of Aten often ended with little hands holding the protective *Ankh* symbols, and therefore, he too escaped persecution.

So also the Lion-headed goddess Sekhmet, closely associated with Mut, and regarded as Pharaoh's protectress and supporter of the king, in his battles against the country's enemies. It is written that *"His arrows fly after his enemies, like the arrows of Sekhmet"*. She is also the goddess of healing, and was the reason why her image was popular, and therefore, the first figurine Menefer fashioned, was that of Sekhmet.

From the finished image, Menefer made a clay mould and from this, she cast copies, which were left to dry by the lake. She had no fear of someone stealing any of them as a high wall surrounded the complex. Abina would come regularly to collect the dried figurines to take to the furnaces to be fired. Soon they had a large collection. Her figurines proved immensely popular and she could not supply them fast enough. They were finely crafted and colourful and worshippers often queued to get them. The Priestesses were pleased, and their coffers filled quickly.

Menefer too, was pleased, and started adding other deities to their stock. Working here, by the crescent lake, had become perhaps the most enjoyable of all previous workplaces.

Some weeks had passed. Menefer had been adding some colour glazing to a figurine when Abina came hurrying over. Menefer looked up and smiled. 'This batch is ready, but where is your basket, Abina? You'll not be able to carry them all in your arms!'

Abina did not answer, but from her troubled look, Menefer realise that something was amiss. 'You look troubled,' she said as the priestess came and sat down beside her on the bench.

Abina reached out and laid her hand lightly upon Menefer's.

'Menefer... I... I have grave news,' almost tearfully, she continued. 'There had been more riots...in Akhet Aten.'

'There seems to be no end to it,' Menefer sighed and shook her head. 'When will it all stop?'

'Menefer...' Abina struggled with the words. 'It is...your family...they—' She choked back a sob. 'They were caught up in the unrest.'

Menefer's eyes grew large and her face drained of blood as a sudden fear gripped her. 'Was anyone hurt? My father...?'

Abina told her the news of that terrible night, of the destruction of Thutmose's house and workshop, and the deaths of her father and Nebaten.

With a cry of anguish, Menefer hunched over, her shoulders quivering, her hands over her eyes, and she wept softly. 'How...how did they perish?' weeping and wiping her eyes, Menefer enquired in a trembling voice.

'Servants found them the following day,' Abina explained and she put her arm around the girl to comfort her. 'They had both died instantly and did not suffer.' Abina did not want to tell her the way in which they were slain. That would only add to her sorrow.

'You...you mentioned my father and older brother.' Menefer suddenly looked up, distressed, her face tear-streaked. 'What about Ipuky? What...what happened to him?' she wrung her hands.

'All the servants knew, they were to leave for Mennufer on a boat, but only Ipuky managed to get way.'

Menefer stared at the ground. Still in shock, she slowly shook her head from side to side, still staring at a fixed spot on the ground. 'Neb had wanted me to go and see their handiwork. He urged me, as soon as I arrived here, in Ipet-Isut, I must visit the tomb he and Ipuky had prepared for themselves, but I had not been there yet.' She blinked hard and wiped at her eyes with the back of her hand. 'They had been overjoyed when Pharaoh gave him permission to build a *House of Eternity* for the two of them in the Valley.' Menefer looked up at Abina, her eyes red and glistening. 'It is a great honour, you know?'

Abina nodded. The Valley of the Dead had been reserved for Royalty, and only those, high in Pharaoh's favours or with his special permission, could be buried there.

'It is ironic, Neb was originally named Nebamun, but because of Pharaoh's decrees, he had to change his name to Nebaten…and died as a direct result of Pharaoh's decrees, but, he told me, when I go there, I will see on the walls of his tomb, and in defiance of the king, he had written his name as Nebamun!' Menefer gave a short mirthless laugh and continued, reminiscing. She gazed towards the horizon, not looking at anything in particular. 'On another wall, he had painted our garden. The pond filled with fishes and ducks, and lotuses, and where fruit trees grew in abundance—he too used to enjoy sitting in the shade by the water—he shall dwell happily there.'

Abina, not wanting to break her reverie, just nodded.

'Do you know we had fig trees, plums, olives and a nut tree?' Menefer turned and looked at Abina, her lips smiling, but her eyes showing pain.

'Very nice,' Abina said. 'I love figs.'

Menefer sat in silence for a while, then suddenly made a decision. 'I shall make ushabtis…of myself and Ipuky…and place them in the tombs at my father's and Nebaten's funerals.'

'No! You cannot go!' Abina cried, suddenly alarmed.

'Why? It is my duty… I have to farewell my brother and father!'

'Menefer, by the time of the burial, your condition will be very obvious. There will be many officials attending the ceremony…people who know you will be there. You cannot risk being seen. Questions will be asked. No one must know you are bearing a child. You must protect it at all cost, even deny yourself the last homage to your family. You could endanger yourself and the baby,' Abina showed genuine concern.

Menefer's whole being, sagged. She looked sideways at the priestess and wondered if she knew the baby was of royal blood. Does Menteret, the High Priestess, know? 'Yes, you are right… I was not thinking clearly.'

'I could arrange for a novice priestesses, from the temple, to attend the funerals, of both your father and Nebaten, in your stead. They could place the ushabtis for you.'

Menefer dwelt on Abina's offer for a while then finally accepted the suggestion. 'Yes, that…that seems the best solution.'

She would grieve alone, here, by the banks of the lake.

\*\*\*

'I am to blame for all this.' Smenkhare turned to Meritaten, 'I had chosen the wrong time and the wrong place to announce my plans to restore Amun in Waset.'

They were in the garden of *Per nesu*, sitting in the shade of the trees by the *House of Birds,* the place once favoured by Menefer. The fierce heat of the previous months had been replaced by more comfortable weather and made the late summer afternoon, quite pleasant. Even the birds were more lively and melodious.

''Tis not your doing.' Merit tried to sooth him. 'The people cried out for reform. By trying to satisfy one group, they had caused another to become troublesome. My father often said "A king cannot please everyone—it is like getting stuck in the mud. Lift one leg and the other is only pressed deeper into the muck".'

'What can I do to bring peace, Merit?'

'You are not yet an anointed and crowned king. Once that has happened, you will need to gather about you good advisors, a council of elders, who know the people.'

'Yes, you are right. This delay is causing people anxiety. They are restless and want change. I will need a vizier, someone like Lord Nakht. He is a good and wise man and would be a strong arm to rely on. I will speak of it to Akhenaten. He is sure to agree.' Smenkhare suddenly seemed to glow with new enthusiasm. His earlier concern had changed to a new hope, a brighter future. 'When we arrive in Waset, we will create a wonderful new kingdom. We will have monuments built as great as those of my father, the third Amenhotep. Maybe even greater.'

*** 

An early morning mist hung over Isheru, the crescent-shaped lake. Ducks and other waterfowl darted in and out of the clumps of reeds or dived underneath water lilies, searching for frogs and snails.

Menefer had all her things laid out ready to do some work, but was not in the mood for it this morning and stared, absent-mindedly, at the birds. Abina approached her, carrying a scroll and a small chest. Menefer gave a start as the priestess suddenly sat down beside her. 'Abina! …Sorry, I was deep in thought.'

'Day-dreaming?' Abina made herself comfortable. 'What about?'

'Oh, nothing in particular. What have you there?'

Abina handed her the chest and a scroll. 'From Akhet Aten. The chest is from Lady Mutnedjmet.'

The chest contained some magical objects, a *mesh,* an amulet to induce labour, a figurine of *Meshkent,* the goddess of childbirth, a blue faience hippopotamus, the sacred animal of *Taueret,* also a goddess of childbirth, and *Bes,* the curly bearded dwarf god with a grotesque tongue. He presided over the birth chamber.

Menefer's heart went out to Lady Mutny, and she praised her for her care and kindness. 'I hope I can repay the great lady one day for all she had done for me.'

'It is her nature to be kind and generous,' Abina agreed.

Menefer unrolled the scroll and read its contents, frowning, then giggled to herself. Curious, Abina waited for Menefer to tell her the news.

'It's from Djenna. She writes that several new buildings are being erected in honour of Smenkhare, including a palace. That caused more discontent in the city, as the people had been expecting him to rule from Waset, but it seems His Majesty, King Akhenaten wants him to remain.'

'There will surely be more trouble,' Abina shook her head slowly. 'What else? You were amused at something?'

'Yes, she wrote about Prince Smenkhare and Princess Merit's wedding. It occurred a while ago, but she had not had a chance to write about it until now. She said, at the feast, Queen Tiye had a little too much beer. She bent over a fruit table and her perfumed wax cone slipped off her head and landed in a bowl of figs. She bent over to retrieve it and fell headlong onto the table.'

Both women laughed. They could imagine the Great Queen losing her dignity. Acting out the scene, the two women tried to outdo one another to make the incident even funnier, each with their own version of the incident.

'I can just picture the Queen, with a face-full of crushed fruit…' suddenly Menefer clutched her belly. 'Ooh!'

Immediately Abina rushed to her side. 'Another pain?'

'Yes. I've been getting them all morning, but this one is more severe.'

'Shall I go and get help?'

Menefer assured her that it was not necessary, but moaned again as another spasm made her double over.

'Perhaps we had better get back to your quarters.' Abina helped her up and they returned to her room where Menefer was made comfortable on her sleeping couch. More contractions followed.

A chamber had been prepared in one of the larger rooms and they took Menefer there. She was given the *mesh* talisman to hold and some emmer, the popular, but sour beer, to drink to help dull the pain. When her time arrived, she was led to the *meskhen-t* a pair of birthing stones, decorated with images of Hathor and other magical symbols. They placed a mattress of straw between the stones, and two priestesses assisted Menefer to squat upon them, then held her arms to support her.

On the twenty-fourth day of Athyr, in the season of Akhet, in year fifteen of Akhenaten, Menefer was delivered of a boy-child, but for this birth of her son—of a prince—there would be no celebration. No feast day would be declared, no re-joicing in the streets, and no message of any kind, would be sent out to announce the great day.

According to custom, mother and baby were secluded for several days. A *mena*, a wet nurse, was found. She was called Maia, a woman who had recently lost her own child.

That evening, a special private ceremony took place in the temple of Mut. The altar flame was lit and sprinkled with incense. The placenta, considered sacred, was placed upon it as an offering. Then Abina brought forth a figurine of the cat god-dess, Bastet, and a talisman, an *Udjat*, the Eye-of-Horus.

Abina held the sacred objects in the smoke of the altar to purify them while Menteret, the High Priestess chanted incantations. These items were then held out toward the statue of Bastet. Menteret then blessed them and the magical items were then taken to the baby and placed next to him as protection.

*** 

All too soon, the time arrived for Menefer to leave Ipet-Isut and her baby, and return to Akhet Aten. She spent a last few hours with her son, holding him close. Abina entered. 'The boat is loaded and ready to depart.'

Reluctantly, Menefer called to nurse. 'Maia…it is time.'

The nurse took the sleeping child from her. Dewy-eyed, Menefer kissed him on his forehead. 'Stay in peace, little one. I wish you a good, healthy and prosperous life.'

Once they reached the docks, Abina assured Menefer that Maia would take good care of the child. Maia knows nothing of his parents, only that he was illegit-imate and to be adopted by a wealthy couple. She was not even told Menefer's name, nor who she was, except that the child's mother was "an important lady from the North".

Menteret and Abina accompanied Menefer to the landing place to farewell her. A close bond had developed between the women and they would miss each other's company dearly. Their parting was emotional.

'Menefer, we are always here for you. Call on us any time we can assist you,' Menteret offered.

The current caught the boat and took it downstream. The two priestesses watched and waved until it had disappeared out of view around the wide curve of the river. The High Priestess did not realise, at the time, that her assistance would again be needed one day, under much graver conditions.

# Chapter Twenty-Three
## Child of the Wind

Everyone welcomed Menefer back with great joy, and especially glad to see her, was Lady Mutnedjmet, who greeted her like a long-lost daughter. Even Segi became all emotional as Menefer hugged her.

The princesses and prince Tutankhaten were just as overjoyed to see her again. 'I missed your stories, especially *The brave hunter and the lion*. Can we hear it again?'

'Restrain yourself, child,' Mutny cautioned. 'Give Menefer a chance to settle first before badgering her with your requests lest she packs her bags and leaves again, just to get some peace.'

Wide-eyed, Tutankhaten hesitated. 'Will you do that? Leave us again?'

'Of course not, my little prince,' Menefer hugged him tightly. 'Lady Mutny was only jesting.'

Queen Nefertiti, had been aware of Menefer's arrival, but not wishing to interrupt her worship, she finished her evening prayers and offerings first, then left her private temple and hurried back to her chambers. From a distance, she could hear the children's gay laughter. Being cut off from the city and the Palace and *Per nesu's* social life, had made her long for any news from outside. She sent a maid to invite Menefer to her common chamber where she awaited her. Eager to see her as well, Menefer hastened to the queen's quarters.

'Menefer.' Nefertiti kissed her on the cheek. 'Welcome back,' she expressed her condolences for the loss of Menefer's family, and indicated her to sit. 'We were all shocked and troubled by that dreadful incident. So many people killed or injured. There is so much discontent in the land.'

Mutnedjmet joined them, 'What is the feeling in Waset?'

'The people there rejoiced when Prince Smenkhare and Princess Merit were wed, but turned bitter when they learnt Pharaoh had built him a palace, here.'

'We are puzzled as well. No one knows what Pharaoh has in mind,' Nefertiti sighed, looked Menefer up and down then observed, in a more cheerful tone. 'Your stay in Ipet-Isut must have been very agreeable. You have developed a fuller figure.'

'Yes…thank you, Your Majesty.' Menefer suddenly realised her breasts were straining against her tunic-halter. 'The priestesses took good care of me. I'm afraid I indulged in too many of their tasty delicacies.'

Mutnedjmet gave her a knowing smile. 'Yes, the people of Waset are very generous with their offerings and the temple of Mut is fortunate for having a large following.' She started reminiscing about her early life there, when Queen Nefertiti made excuses that she needed to go and rest, and left.

'Is she unwell?' Menefer was concerned. It was not typical for the queen to be tired that early in the morning.

'Let us take walk by the lake, then we can talk,' Mutnedjmet suggested. Once they were well clear of the building, she continued, 'My sister is troubled—and feels a bit guilty.'

Menefer gave her a puzzled look.

In a low voice Lady Mutny added, 'She dislikes me talking of my past at Ipet-Isut. I would not be surprised to learn it had been she, who had encouraged Akhenaten to rid me of my child and arranged my divorce. It had been Nefertiti who had urged Akhenaten to outlaw the worship of Amun, did you know?' Menefer nodded that she had been aware of that.

'Akhenaten can be influenced easily and it troubles her...this talk of Smenkhare reversing Akhenaten's decrees...she fears Tiye and Smenkhare might convert Akhenaten to Amunism.'

'But Smenkhare would rule in Waset...he plans to only restore Amun in that city, would he not?'

Lady Mutnedjmet shrugged. 'Perhaps, I don't know. I tried to tell her so, but why build this palace for the prince...?' she let the sentence hang. 'We can but wait and see...'

Menefer nodded and they walked along in silence, then her thoughts turned elsewhere. 'Lady Mutny...' she enquired anxiously. 'When is...when will I have my baby? When will he arrive?'

'Be patient, Menefer. All has been arranged. In a few days' time, two people will leave for Ipet-Isut...Pentu and Segi.

'They would pose as a wealthy childless married couple who would be adopting the baby. Maia, the wet nurse, had not been told anything else. She does not know who they are or where they are from. After the baby has been turned over to them, they would head south, to Waset, also to mislead her or anyone else. In Waset they would stay overnight, and only when they deem it safe, would they come back here.'

'But,' Menefer was still concerned. 'If a *mena* does not accompany them, how will the baby be fed?'

Lady Mutnedjmet laughed. 'We thought of that too. Pentu is a physician and has knowledge of these things. Fresh milk from a cow or goat would be obtained daily during their journey. They would feed the infant with a faience cup with a tiny spout that he had prepared. He assured me he had fed many an infant that way, whose the mother had died during childbirth, and whose families had no means to afford a *mena*.'

***

Time seemed to pass slowly. It had been more than a week since Segi and Pentu left. Then word reached Lady Mutnedjmet a boat was approaching a landing place further north. Menefer should not be seen anywhere near the North Palace when the child arrived, and Lady Mutny had arranged she visit Princesses Merit and Senpa during this time.

As arranged, a messenger arrived at *Per nesu* to bid Mistress Menefer to hurry back to the North Palace. Menefer made her excuses and, with her heart beating furiously, hurried back to the Palace.

A small crowd had gathered in the courtyard when a breathless Menefer arrived. They directed her to the chamber where Lady Mutnedjmet and Segi were caring for an infant.

'What is all the excitement?' Menefer asked, feigning surprise and curiosity.

'A woman had abandoned a little boy-child by the lake's edge,' Princess Neferu explained.

'She saw Segi approach and ran off,' Setenpenre added.

'The baby was brought here, and now we must decide what to do with him.' Mutnedjmet glanced at Menefer who had picked him up and was cuddling him.

'He's beautiful,' Princess Sherit remarked as she and her sisters fussed around the baby, making crooning sounds. A disinterested Prince Tutankhaten, after a cursory glance, turned his attention back to his toy bow and reed arrows.

'A foundling child!' Menefer stroked the sleeping infant, swaddled in a linen blanket. 'How could a mother find it in her heart to discard a baby?'

'We cannot judge her until we know all the truths. Who knows what circumstances would drive someone to do such a deed,' Mutnedjmet replied, resisting another glance in Menefer's direction.

'Lady Mutny, I know a couple who would gladly adopt the child,' one of the servants suggested. 'My sister recently lost a child,' the servant explained. Startled, Menefer looked up at her.

'Your sister?' Mutnedjmet studied the woman. 'The wife of Lord Sethi, the Judge?'

'Yes, Highness.'

'No, I wish to keep him!' Menefer said softly. 'He's my…' she quickly corrected herself. 'I… I mean, if I may, I would love to raise the child…as my own.'

'Lord Sethi still has to be informed,' Lady Mutny added. 'It must be done legally.'

Lord Sethi listened patiently as Menefer and Lady Mutny related the story.

'I have known you since you were in swaddling clothing. I know you will take great care of the boy…as if he was your very own…' he looked at her sideways and there was a hint that he knew more than he pretended. 'Is there anything you are *not* telling me? I must know the truth.'

Menefer was nervous and most uncomfortable. It seemed the judge could see into her *ka*, her inner soul and she looked at Lady Mutny for support.

'Menefer, I think we should take Lord Sethi into our confidence.'

'Do not fear, Lady Mutnedjmet, Menefer. I will not reveal any secrets…'

Lord Sethi was told the story again, but this time, the real story.

He smiled. 'I had deduced that you were the child's mother. I could tell—but a royal child? That *was* indeed a surprise. I think it is important the father also be informed.'

The two women whispered together, and Lady Mutny volunteered to tell Prince Smenkhare.

'Good. I will grant you full custody of the boy, but it is a very difficult task for a woman alone, so I will act as his guardian. When he is older, he will need a mentor, someone he and you can depend on—to seek out in time of need.'

Menefer agreed and Lord Sethi officially declared her to be the boy's adopted mother.

'What are you going to call him,' Princess Nefer-tasheri asked.

'Oh, uh...well how about...Mes-sheshen. *Mes*, for child, and *sheshen*, reeds, as he was found in the marshes.'

'That's too hard to say,' Tutankhaten shook his head, waving an arrow he was fashioning.

'Then instead of *sheshen*, what about *shu*, for wind or air. Mes-shu...or just Messu, for short. *Child of the Wind*?'

'That's a good name. Messu!' Tutankhaten agreed. 'Is he going to live here?'

'Only if the Queen and Lady Mutny approves,' Menefer replied. 'Then, in time, you will have a friend to play with.'

'Of course he will live here,' Lady Mutny replied.

'But he is too small! Babies can't play games,' Tutankhaten protested.

'He will grow, Your Highness,' Menefer assured him.

'I'm almost six,' Tutankhaten announced. 'When will he be six?'

'In six year's time!'

'Then we will be the same age!' Tutankhaten exclaimed happily.

'No, Tutankhaten,' Lady Mutny corrected him, smiling. 'When he is six, you will be twelve.'

'Oh.' Tutankhaten was not convinced. 'Well, then when he catches up, we will be friends.'

\*\*\*

Unrest once again erupted in Waset. To try and resolve it, Horemheb, who had been sent to the city, called a public meeting. A rowdy crowd greeted him as he mounted the dais. He had to call for order several times, and finally, with the help of the Medjay, was able to restore order.

'People of Waset...' his next words were drowned by shouts of "No-Amun!" from the crowd. Once again, he had to call for silence.

'People of No-Amun...hear me!'

This was greeted by shouts of approval and some laughter.

'People of No-Amun, I know what is in your hearts and I sympathise with you. Like you, I too, had to change my beliefs...but it was necessary.'

'Yes, to serve that criminal!' someone shouted.

'We all have to make sacrifices for the sake of making a living. Behold the priests of Amun!' He waved an arm towards the Great Temple. 'Those who would not change, now beg in the streets for food, or steal from others who earned their rewards honestly.' He paused to let the words sink in. 'Is it not better to toil for a taskmaster you dislike, and have a home to return to, to have clothes on your back and a full belly,' he paused again, '...rather than to turn your back on him and let your family suffer, or to have to depend on the handouts of others?' He pointed among the crowd. 'Craftsmen who continue to work, endure hardships, but eat and can clothe themselves!'

He looked around and waved a hand with the palm up. 'How many of you are farmers?' Many hands were raised. Horemheb looked at them, pointedly.

'You who work the lands, do you have good crops every year? No! There are times when the Nile does *not* flood the lands and your crops are poor. Do you condemn and shun the Nile for your strife? No! When plagues of locusts devastate your crops...do you give up farming to do something else? No! You struggle on. The land can be a hard taskmaster, but it can also be a generous one. You curse your lot, but carry one, taking the bad with the good.'

Some murmurs of approval from the crowd encouraged him to continue. 'You, fishermen! Do you come home with a good catch every day? Or do you sometimes cast your nets, day after day without any fish, and your families go hungry? Do you then decide to become a merchant...or a mason? No, you do the task you have always done, the one you know!'

'Why then do you ask me why I serve Pharaoh?' he scowled at the crowd and gestured broadly. 'Not all of us are satisfied with our lot, but we continue...and hope that things will change...and change *will* come. You accuse King Smenkhare for attending a temple of Aten, but it does not mean he had been converted. He did so, out of respect, a gesture to Akhenaten. He *will* rule here, some day, but we need to be patient.'

'We cannot wait very much longer. Pharaoh had married again. What if his wife bears him a son, a brat who will continue his father's decrees? He will replace Smenkhare and our lot will then not change...unless he is removed.'

'You speak treason! In Akhet Aten, you would be severely punished...even sentenced to death for such utterances! So curb your tongue!' Horemheb warned, shaking a fist. 'When Akhenaten was made co-regent with his father, Amenhotep, fifteen years ago, changes did not happen immediately. He waited for a fitting time. Smenkhare is not yet crowned. He will do the same when the time is apt. We must be patient.'

'When is the coronation to take place, then? Our patience is running low.' A chorus of others agreed with the man.

'That time too, will be decided. Reform *will* come, but only with your help!'

Shouts of "how?", "what help?" and "tell us" rose from the crowd.

'First, we *must* have peace!' Horemheb gestured. 'You must show that you respect the laws...there should be no more riots, no more dissidence or any kind of trouble here in No-Amun or in Akhet Aten, lest Pharaoh is enraged! Only then can I convince him that a change of policy will work.' He spread his arms wide, in an imploring gesture. 'Can I depend on you?' He was greeted with shouts of "Yes", "Good", "Let us do it" and "We give our word".

Horemheb smiled. He had succeeded.

\*\*\*

Horemheb entered Rakhmet's house, only to find him sitting on a sandstone block outside, dejected. 'Any news yet?' he asked.

'No. Amenia chased me out. She said I was not helping any by bothering them every few moments. A midwife is attending Istar.'

'Yes, that is my Amenia, all right!' Horemheb laughed and took a seat nearby. 'My wife can be rather dominant at times.'

'Perhaps it is because she has to live with *you*!' Rakhmet joked and smiled cynically. He got up and started for the house again.

'Sit down, Rakhmet!' Horemheb demanded. 'A child will be birthed when *it* is ready. Your impatience will not hasten it along.'

'But I wish to be near her.'

'No,' Horemheb shook his head. 'That is no place for a man. It is much better…much safer…to stay away. You will only antagonise the women.' He suddenly brightened. 'That reminds me…you should have been there. I had the crowd in my hands. I think I have won them over.'

'I'm glad,' Rakhmet nodded. 'All this unrest had made Istar rather upset. She is not used to it. She grew up in Buhen where it was relatively peaceful and—'

The front door opened and Amenia peered out. 'Rakhmet, I have… Oh, Horemheb! You are back…'

'Yes Amenia, my address worked. I had the people in—'

'Tell me later,' Amenia cut him short. 'I have much more important news. Rakhmet, you have a son!'

# Chapter Twenty-Four
## A King Is Crowned

Lord Nakht finally announced the most auspicious day for the coronation, forty days from the Feast of the Good Soul, the Harvest Festival. Nineteen days after the feast, in the fifteenth year of Akhenaten's reign.

Since the announcement, ships had been arriving from many countries for the coronation. Their strange shapes and sails made a splendid and colourful spectacle. Emissaries and dignitaries, dressed in magnificent costumes, brought tributes for the new king and had them carried openly for the gawking crowd to admire.

On the balcony of the Northern Palace, Menefer watched as yet another vessel unloaded its cargo and passengers disembarked. From whence they came, was impossible to tell. They were just too far away for her to see clearly.

She sighed loudly. Djenna would probably attend. Fine garments and costly jewellery attracted her like honey attracts a bee, especially since most of those arriving, were nobles or the wealthy. Menefer had not seen her since she arrived back from Ipet-Isut, but she did hear some disturbing news. Servants gossip among themselves, and word reached her that it was a remark, made by Djenna, that had caused the attack on her home which resulted in the deaths of her father and Nebaten. Djenna's loose tongue had brought her much pain and grief, but this time she will suffer the consequences. *He who grows thorny weeds, is sure to step on them one day*, as an old saying goes. For now, she no longer wish to see her erstwhile friend again. She is quite content to look after her little son.

***

Huya came to Queen Tiye's house to prepare the court for the coronation. All the servants of rank were assembled and he explained the protocol during the ceremony. When Djenna was told a place for her had been allocated at the rear of the hall, she huffed indignantly. 'Why can I not be in front?'

'The front rows had been reserved for Royalty, visiting Princes, Statesmen and Emissaries.' Huya explained in the most patient voice he could muster. 'The following rows are for High Officials, Viceroys, judges, physicians and scribes, then the Overseers of the Royal Household, and the heads of the various departments. Behind them, the personal staff of the Royals, the *Keepers of the Royal Bedchamber*; *He who washes the hands of his Majesty; Keeper of the Royal House of women* and so on, and then the remainder of the personal maids and servants. That is where you will be. At the rear, with the common servants.'

'But my father is Royal Chancellor and Chief Justice! Surely, that would entitle me a place near the front.'

'Your father, yes, not you!'

Comments from the other servants, "who does she think she is", and "what arrogance", although whispered, reached her ears. Djenna glared in their direction.

'Consider yourself fortunate, Mistress Djenna. Many others could not be placed and will have to watch from outside the Palace entrance.'

'And what about the sculptress, Menefer. Will she be there?'

'She is to be in the second row!' He had to restrain himself not to be rude to the girl. 'She is highly regarded by the Royal Family.'

'What! Why?' Djenna exploded, furious, 'because she nurses the Royal children and teaches them to scribble? I mend the Royal garments, I—'

'No,' Huya cut her off, aware of Djenna's tongue and vindictiveness. A faint, reserved smile played around the corners of his mouth. 'It was a personal request—from *King Smenkhare*!'

'But I too, have close contact with Royalty!' Djenna continued to protest. 'I tend to Her Majesty, Queen Tiye's person.'

'If *everyone* who has contact with royalty is placed in the second row, you might *still* find yourself at the rear, or even outside!' He inhaled loudly. 'There are many. Vying with one another for favours will only cause discord. This way, at least, your place is secure! Accept, or surrender you place for someone else!'

\*\*\*

The great day finally arrived. Temples and pylons were decorated, and the Great Temple of Per Hai Aten was particularly well adorned. Here, the newly crowned king would present offerings to Aten, and for the first time, would be allowed to enter the *Holy of Holies.* The great bronze doors were burnished until they shone like the sun. The pylons, pillars and walls were festooned with garlands of flowers and ribbons. At the Great Hall of the palace, where the coronation would take place, more ribbons and pendants fluttered from masts and the fragrance of incense and perfumed candles permeated every corner.

Sounds of chanting and music rose and fell on the breeze.

Menefer was reluctant to attend, at first, but it did not take Lady Mutny long to persuade her to change her mind. 'Menefer, Smenkhare is the *tef*, the father of your child. He is aware the boy is his son and had attempted to visit you, but had been unable. He is looking forward to seeing you. Do not let him down, on this, the day of his greatest achievement. He will be searching the crowd for you. For his sake, more than anyone else's, you need to attend!'

\*\*\*

Dhaba, Smenkhare's personal servant, met Menefer at the pylon gate and escorted her through the throng in the palace courtyard into the Great Hall. Its huge pillars, swathed in flowered garlands, many brought from the distant northern nomes, were vying to outdo the colourful garments of the nobility.

Dhaba, by Smenkhare's request, was also allotted a place in the second row, to attend Mistress Menefer. 'For a tutor to the Royal children, it is quite an honour,' Dhaba's remark was more in admiration than cynical. 'Prince Smenkhare must hold you in high regard.'

'We have become…very good friends, yes,' Menefer smiled

Summer had not yet arrived, but the days were already quite warm. In the crowded halls, the smoke from hundreds of candles and braziers of burning incense, made the air even more stifling.

Dhaba and Menefer were positioned slightly to one side in front of the dais on which four Royal thrones, and several lesser seats, had been placed. Each of the delicate four thrones, fashioned of ebony, had bands of gold around the curved legs and frames of the back rests. Fretwork-carved panels of intertwining lotuses and papyrus reeds, symbolising the joining of Upper and Lower Egypt, and bound with gold, served as stressers, holding together the front and back legs of the seats.

The Royals had not yet arrived and the crowd, hot and uncomfortable, moved about restlessly. Servants, with fast-melting perfumed wax cones on their heads, moved around the hall, topping up the incense burners.

'I wish they would cease adding fragrant bark to the braziers,' Menefer remarked. 'The perfume is already a bit overpowering and the smoke is—'

'Mistress Menefer?' She turned at the man's voice behind her.

'Lord Sethi!' She bowed her head slightly. 'Greetings.'

'How is your son?'

'He is well, Lord Sethi. I did not think it prudent to bring him along today.'

'Yes, it is much too hot and it would have been distressing for you both.'

'I wished for…' she looked around furtively. Dhaba was not within earshot, so she whispered. 'I wanted…*someone* to meet him, but I thought it better to do so when we are more private.'

'Very wise!' Lord Sethi knew the *someone* she was referring to.

A fanfare of trumpets interrupted her and announcing the arrival of the Royals.

A sudden hush fell over the crowd. Lord Kheruef entered, followed by the Vizier and High Priest Ay, using his fly swatter as a fan.

Kheruef tapped his staff three times. 'On your knees. Pharaoh comes.'

The Royals entered and took their places. Akhenaten and Ankhsenpaaten, looking radiant, took the two larger thrones on the dais. They were followed by Smenkhare and Merit who seated themselves on the slightly smaller ones on the right-hand side of Pharaoh. Queen Tiye, Princess Baketaten and Lady Mutnedjmet took their chairs at Akhenaten's left side of the dais. Only Akhenaten, at this stage, held the crook and flail symbols, and crossed them over his chest.

Then Akhenaten tipped the crook slightly towards the assembly and they rose to their feet again.

Both Pharaoh and the prince wore stiff white pleated skirts, bound with broad golden sashes which hung down in front. Each sash, of a broad triangular shape of stiffened material, had been finely embroidered in gold thread, decorated by a pair of uraeus serpents at each corner. Tails of leopards, the symbol of chieftaincy, hung from the backs of each sash. Both the Royal brothers wore fine white blouses enhanced by broad gold and blue collars which covering their shoulders. Their gold sandals and wristlets were inlaid with blue stones.

Akhenaten wore a *khepersh*, a blue warrior helmet of leather, with the *nebti*, the heads of Nekhebet, the vulture goddess, and Buto, the cobra goddess, symbols of Royalty. Smenkhare wore a *nemes*, a striped Royal headdress of cloth. The Buto and Nekhebet symbols were, as yet, absent.

Ay stepped forward and bowed low. A gong sounded and a line of priestesses, lead by the High Priestess of Aten, entered. A blue cloth had been draped over her hands which held a golden bowl. The bowl, containing sacred water, could not be touched by the naked hand. She bowed, raised the bowl and held it toward Ay.

Kheruef handed the High Priest a staff. He dipped the tip of it into the bowl, and turned towards Smenkhare. 'In the name of the Disk and the Glory of Aten...' he lightly tapped Smenkhare's forehead three times, 'I anoint thee, in the presence of this assembly.'

A gong sounded again, followed by a chorus of chants. Ay removed Smenkhare's *nemes* headdress and Lord Kheruef handed Ay the white *Sutenu* crown of Upper Egypt, a tall, bulb-ended crown. Affixed to this headpiece, were the symbols of Buto and Nekhebet. Kheruef then handed Smenkhare the two symbols of leadership and power, a crook and flail, which he crossed over his chest.

Ay raised the crown, first, towards the people, then turned back and held it to the left of Smenkhare's head.

'In the presence of Pharaoh and this assembly...in the name of the Disk and the Glory of Aten, I crown thee Lord of Upper Egypt. Ankhkheprure Mery Neferkheprure, Son of the Sun, Per-O. May thy reign last forever and ever.'

A gong sounded and a chorus of chants from the priestesses rose and fell, then ceased. Then Ay moved the crown to Smenkhare's right, and repeated the declaration. He then held it over Smenkhare's head, repeated the chant a third time, then lowered it upon Smenkhare's head. The chanting from the priestesses started again.

He raised his arms above his head and turned toward the crowd. 'People of Towy... People of vassal countries, behold. Look upon Pharaoh Smenkhare, Lord of Upper Egypt, Lord of Diadems,' he then turned and again addressed the new king. 'Life prosperity and health to thee. May thee live forever and ever and may thy reign be a long and peaceful one. May thee be fruitful and have many sons.'

The gong sounded again and Ay waved his hand towards Merit. 'Behold, his Great Royal Wife, Queen Meritaten, Beloved of Aten. May she live forever and ever.' He turned to the crowd again and gestured. 'Kneel and pay homage to thy King and Queen!'

The assembly knelt and chanted. 'Hail Pharaoh Smenkhare, hail Queen Meritaten.'

They were again asked to rise as Smenkhare stood up, still with the crossed crook and flail over his chest. He looked upon the sea of faces, then his eyes met Menefer's and for a moment, they locked. He smiled and gave a slight nod. Menefer beamed up at him. Smenkhare looked around the hall and the ceremony continued.

'I, Smenkhare, vow to be a fair and just king... I will rule with compassion, and to defend the boundaries of the land of Egypt. I will protect its people and slay its foes without an axe and shoot arrows without drawing a bow.'

Menefer leaned over towards Dhaba. 'What does that mean?' she whispered.

'It means he will overcome his enemies with diplomacy instead of force,' he answered in a low voice.

Smenkhare seated himself. Kheruef nodded to Ay, who stepped forward. 'Pharaoh will now accept the tributes,' Ay announced.

There was a rustling and shuffling as the envoys of the many lands made their way to the dais, each with an entourage, bringing the tributes. The procession continued in an almost endless line and seemed to go on forever. The assembly, sweltering and weary, started getting restless and there was much shifting about.

Finally, it was over. There were more brief speeches, thanking everyone for the gifts and for attending. The Royals then proceeded to the Great Temple to make their offerings, and the hall started to clear. After the stifling atmosphere inside, everyone welcomed the fresh air of the courtyard again.

'The ceremony was interesting,' Menefer remarked to Dhaba, 'but it was rather uncomfortable in there!' He agreed. She took her leave of him and returned to the North Palace, to her son and to rest.

The following day, a courier arrived, with a message for her from the palace. Segi led him to Menefer's day room where she had been amusing Messu.

'Mistress Menefer, Their Majesties, King Smenkhare and Queen Merit, request your presence and that of your son at your earliest convenience.'

***

The people of Akhet Aten rejoiced in the streets, but in No-Amun, the atmosphere was anything but jovial. The people had waited patiently, and did not demonstrate, as they had promised Horemheb, but the coronation came and went, and Smenkhare had made no attempt to change Akhenaten's decrees, nor did he announce any plans to return to No-Amun. Discontent surfaced and once again, renewed rebellion broke out.

Horemheb called upon the leaders of the rebels to come forth to speak with him. Several attended the meeting, led by Asi, the boyhood friend of Rakhmet.

'I wish to hear your grievances so we can put an end to all this displeasure. Now, you first.' Horemheb pointed to Asi, 'You had decided to break your promise to me. Why?'

'Commander Horemheb, we pledged to restrain ourselves and not protest against our Lord, King Smenkhare. You said he would return and restore Amun, and our choice of worship, yet, a palace had been built for him in Akhet Aten from where he now rules. Nothing has changed.'

'His Majesty's stay in Akhet Aten is a mere formality, a courtesy, a show of respect for Pharaoh Akhenaten,' Horemheb tried to be patient. 'It was Akhenaten, after all, who had made him co-regent. Allow Smenkhare more time. Things will be rectified, in time. Just be patient.'

'Patience! That was what you asked of us some time ago, yet here we are, still waiting for a sign that changes will come.'

'These things cannot be achieved overnight. We must all suffer the wait.' Horemheb's patience was beginning to wear thin as the same arguments seem to be repeated. 'Nothing has changed since we last spoke,' Horemheb argued.

'You seemed to have overlooked a few very vital changes, Horemheb!' Asi's disrespect for Horemheb's rank made the Commander tense. A muscle in his cheek tightened as he clamped his teeth.

'At his coronation,' Asi continued, 'Smenkhare was given his Royal Nomen, *Neferneferu-ATEN Mery Waenre.*' He emphasised *Aten* in Smenkhare's throne name. 'Is it not the custom for Pharaoh to add the name of the deity of his State to his name? If that is so, why then is he now called *The ever Beautiful ATEN*?'

An uproar followed as others agreed with him. Encouraged, Asi continued. 'Right after the ceremony, did he not then, proceed to the *Aten* Temple to make offerings?'

Horemheb was taken aback. He had not considered Smenkhare's coronation name, nor the temple ceremony, and realised they had a valid point.

'I am certain there is a reason for it. Let us not be too hasty. If you will permit me, I will return to Akhet Aten and find out, but you must understand, there will always be dissatisfaction. Not *everyone* can be pleased all the time.'

***

As promised, Horemheb took the people's grievances to Akhenaten's court.

'If they want a king, then give them a king!' Queen Tiye declared, but Akhenaten was not too willing to let the young king leave.

'No, mother! He is still too young, too inexperienced. He will remain here for a few years more and learn the duties of the court, especially with all the trouble in Waset.'

'Smenkhare is well aware that he lacks experience that is why he wants Lord Nakht as his vizier and advisor,' Queen Tiye answered. 'I too, will accompany them and act as mentor. You cannot say *I* have no experience. I have been governing since before you were in swaddling clothes!'

'But mother, I have built you a palace here. Why return to Malkata?'

'My task here is done,' Tiye gestured broadly, 'I had come to persuade you to allow the return of Amun worship, which Smenkhare is ready to do. Also, I came to make certain my own flesh and blood would rule Egypt.' She cast her eyes upwards. 'May the gods allow, through your marriage to Ankhsenpaaten, that that dream would be realised. Nefertiti is no longer a threat. She has been replaced, and I can now return to Waset. I am content.'

With a flourish, Tiye turned and left the chamber, to the murmur of the assembly.

# Chapter Twenty-Five
## Farewell to a Friend

Smenkhare was overjoyed when he finally held his son in his arms. The months prior to the coronation had kept him so busy, he could not arrange for Menefer and the boy's visit.

'He is a fine and healthy boy,' Smenkhare remarked as he looked down upon his son. 'He will grow into a comely young man, some day.'

Merit smiled when she saw Smenkhare's pleasure. He had been tense and anxious earlier, but now looked relaxed. 'How many know of Messu's…heritage, Menefer?'

'Your Majesties, we thought…' she hesitated.

'We are alone, Menefer,' Meritaten reminded her. 'You and I have been friends for some time. There is no need to be formal.'

'Thank you, Merit. Lady Mutny had warned me of the problems and dangers that could happen if word got out, so we decided it best to keep it a secret. Only Lady Mutny, Segi, my deaf mute servant, Pentu the physician and Lord Sethi are aware…and of course, Prince Smenkhare and yourself…I don't know about the two priestesses at Ipet-Isut or how much Lady Mutnedjmet told them. They never spoke of it.'

'Good. We will keep it that way for the time being until we are ready to receive you into our family,' Meritaten smiled at Menefer's surprised expression. 'Yes, I am aware, and willing for Smenkhare to take you as a second wife.'

'Hopefully that will not be too long,' Smenkhare said, bouncing the happily crowing baby on his knee. 'The Malkata Palace is being restored at this very moment. As soon as it is done, we can start making preparations.'

\*\*\*

In No-Amun, most accepted and abided by Horemheb's explanation of changes that will come, and were prepared to await the outcome, but there were factions impatient for change.

'Pharaoh is stalling!' one declared. 'It is not going to happen. It is all just talk and no action! Almost seven months had passed since his coronation, without change.'

'King Smenkhare is too young, too inexperienced and too naïve. When he does rule here, Akhenaten will control him, you will see…he will be a game-piece, a toy on a rod, for Akhenaten to manipulate him from afar, and things will remain as they are!'

'Let us not be hasty...let us wait and see what comes of it,' another said, trying to calm the agitated crowd.

'No! We have done so before. When we allowed Atenism to be introduced, we waited in just such a manner, and see what has befallen us?' he gestured towards the ruined temples with a sweep of his hand. 'We must not let this happen again. We need to be strong and force the change,' He punched a fist into an open hand. 'We must resist the king's schemes! Change must come soon. We will wait no more!'

Horemheb too, became troubled. To the dissatisfaction of those bent on causing mischief, there seems to be no plans yet for the young king to return to No-Amun.

To force Pharaoh's hand, bands of anti-Atenists roamed the streets at night, attacking anyone who might favour, or appear to aid Aten. Then they decided to bring strife and hardship to the Royal House by cutting off all trade to the city of Aten.

Boats and caravans, bound for Akhet Aten, were attacked and the cargo taken or destroyed. Medjay and private soldiers had to be employed to protect large caravan trains, and boats had to travel in a convoy, to be relatively safe.

'Stop these pirates! Execute their leaders!' Merchants demanded.

The city's bad reputation spread and discontents and robbers flocked to No-Amun. Caravans changed their routes in favour of Gebtu, a city to the north, and marketplaces suffered, as trade was lost.

Rakhmet was assigned to track down the ringleaders and bring them to justice, but failed in all his attempts. Most people, secretly in favour of the disorder being wrought on Akhet Aten, were reluctant to pass on any information, which could lead to the arrest of the outlaws.

'Goods bound for Akhet Aten attract bandits like flies. If we can disguise it somehow, they might ignore the traders,' Rakhmet commented. 'But where do we start?'

'Instead of disguising it, why not use it as a trap...to attract the flies and ensnare them?' Horemheb suggested. He explained his plan.

A few days' march north-east of No-Amun, at Bekhen, Rakhmet assembled his men, all seasoned soldiers. They were all dressed in the garb of *An-tiu*, dwellers of the eastern desert. Bekhen, a village on the caravan crossroads on the trade route from Quseir, on the Eastern Sea, and Qena, on the Nile, was chosen as being the most suitable place to start.

The men were ordered to enjoy themselves at this outpost. Casually, they would let it be known that their caravan would carry a costly cargo of rich spices, fine linen from the south, and precious stones and minerals from the turquoise and copper mines of Feka. They would pose as merchants of myrrh, frankincense, ebony and ivory from Punt, and other items bound for Akhenaten's court. The word quickly spread that a rich caravan would be travelling through the *sepat* or district.

The caravan assembled and started on its way.

The first few days passed without incident. The following night they put up camp in a wadi. Scattered tamarisk and acacia trees grew along the banks of a dried watercourse, and the "merchants" erected a boma of acacia branches around the perimeter of the camp. The thorn bush-enclosure would keep out most unwanted animals and visitors. The asses were fed and watered, and tethered to an acacia tree, in the middle of the camp.

After a camp fire had been lit, they prepared the evening meal. Their meat had not lasted long and had been consumed by the third day. They had no luck hunting hares or impala, so the men had to satisfy themselves with some dried figs, bread and onions, washed down with emmer. Then sentries were posted to keep guard while the rest sat chatting. It was late in the month of Athyr, the start of autumn, and the cold nights in the desert compelled the men to huddle around camp fires.

The sun disappeared and the desert grew dark, but for the west, where a faint smudge of pink still remained visible behind a black rocky hillock. One of the men, boasting about some of his adventurous exploits, suddenly halted mid-sentence and stared at the silhouettes of boulders and trees a short distance away.

'Come on,' a listener urged. 'Then what happened?'

'I saw something move,' the man nodded toward the west, 'There...among the rocks on that low hill.'

Some of the men turned and looked, but saw nothing.

'Could be just a wild animal,' Rakhmet remarked. 'But be wary lest it is not. Go about your usual business. If it is a bandit, he must not suspect we have noticed anything suspicious.'

Later, those not on guard duty, unrolled their sleeping mats, took to their beds and soon dozed off, lulled to sleep by the soothing sounds of the night. Their turn to guard the camp would come soon enough.

The night wore on without incident. The only sounds, occasional yip-yip of a jackal and the snoring from the sleeping men, disturbed the peace and a sentry drew his cloak tighter about him against the chill.

Night wore on slowly. A faint, almost indiscernible, sound of pebbles rolled down the sloping side of the wadi and alerted Rakhmet. He stiffened and turned his ear towards the sound. A moment later, he heard it again. It was slight, but it was there. Something or someone was approaching stealthily towards the camp. In the dark, he could not make out anything, save the black outlines of the acacias against the starry sky.

He alerted the sentry by flicking a pebble at him. He then called softly to a nearby man. The soldier did not respond and the sentry used his spear to gently prod the sleeping man. The startled soldier woke, mumbling.

'Shhh!' Rakhmet hissed, then whispered, 'someone is coming this way.'

The soldier rubbed his eyes and half rose onto one elbow and listened.

'I can't hear anything. It is almost dawn,' he yawned. 'No one will attack now. Let me sleep. We have a long march in the heat before...' a twig cracked somewhere in the small grove of acacia and he froze. Then he gently shook the sleeping man next to him, warning him to be silent. He in turn, woke the man on the other side of him, and one by one, the soldiers were alerted and silently removed their weapons from under their sleeping mats.

'Remain in your sleeping positions,' Rakhmet whispered, 'but be prepared and have your weapons at the ready.'

Stars still studded the western sky, with the silhouette of the low hill faintly visible, but in the east, a dirty yellow-grey smudge of pre-dawn appeared.

The prostrate soldiers, every muscle tense and alert, still pretending to sleep, scanned the dim outline of the trees and boulders.

Suddenly, a dim shape appeared against the backdrop of stars, then another…and another.

Somewhere, a baboon coughed his greetings to the coming day. Another, further away, took up the call. This is what the bandits had been waiting for. The sound of animals and birds of the early morn would muffle their approach. Stealthily, they hastened towards the sleeping "merchants".

The bandits had to clear a way through the boma. They worked cautiously and silently and soon, a hole was made where they could slither through. Noiselessly, they grouped on the inside of the fence, fifteen in all. On a signal from their leader, they spread out and crept up to the sleeping figures.

Rakhmet watched and waited, then gave a signal. Almost as one the "sleeping" men leapt to their feet, fully armed, catching the surprised bandits unawares. Confused, they panicked. Their well-planned attack had gone awry. Instead of scared and bewildered traders, they suddenly faced fully armed and seasoned fighting men.

A brief battle ensued. In a short time, several of the bandits lay dead or had been captured. The few who had managed to escape, made a hasty retreat back into the hills, pursued by soldiers who gave up the chase after a while. The bandits knew the area well and got away. In the dim light of early morning, the soldiers searched the area, but the rocky ground left no footprints to follow. They returned to camp, empty-handed.

Those they apprehended were bound and interrogated separately. Each unaware what the others would reveal.

Rakhmet wanted their ringleaders, but learnt that none were with this group. He was told they would meet, given orders, then disperse, each group would then carry out their mission, and return to the meeting places. The ring-leaders' identities and meeting places were not revealed.

Rakhmet had to know their names and their meeting places. He had to have this information soon, as those who had escaped would warn them. The prisoners refused to talk. Even drops of boiling oil on their bare skins could not loosen their tongues. Then Rakhmet had them stripped and splayed on the ground, their hands and feet bound to stakes.

'Scour the area and collect scorpions, as many as you can,' he ordered.

The sting of a black scorpion, although painful, was not very poisonous, but those of white ones could be lethal.

There was no shortage of these creatures, and soon Rakhmet had all he needed, both black ones and white. The scorpions were released near the bound men. At first, the confused creatures remained where they were dropped with their pincers open and their tails curved over their bodies in defensive attitudes, but as the sun rose higher and started to heat the sand, the scorpions became agitated and scuttled for shade. The soldiers blocked the creatures' escape, and they made their way to the only shade available—those provided by the prostrate men. They were guided to areas where the bodies were most sensitive—the necks, under their armpits and between their legs.

As the scorpions began to crawl under the men, the involuntary reactions of their muscles caused them to twitch, and the insects stung. Their stings were excruciating. The screams of those stung, soon had the others begging for mercy, their tongues quickly loosened and they talked.

All of them said the same thing. None knew the names of their leaders. They would use names like *Vulture of Vengeance*, or *Seth the Slayer* to identify each other. They could also, not identify them as their faces were always covered, but the locations of their meeting places were revealed, several secret caves in the cliffs near No-Amun. One, partly concealed by an egg-shaped boulder, balancing on its smaller end, was particularly important. The scorpions had done their work.

The bandits, because of their crime against the king, still had to be punished. They were untied, the right hand of each, was severed, and they were then released. Two of the prisoners were not so lucky. They had died in agony from the scorpion stings.

***

Rakhmet and the soldiers hastened back to No-Amun. They had to overtake those robbers who had fled, and arrived after midday. From the descriptions the prisoners gave them, Rakhmet had an idea where their meeting places would be. As boys, he and his boyhood friend, Asi, used to explore the western hills around and above the great mortuary Temple of Queen Hatshepsut, searching for items early tomb robbers had discarded or lost. He knew the area almost as well as he knew the back of his own hand. Several caves fitted the description he had been given. He had several detachments under his command, and he directed one to each of them.

Rakhmet sequestered several soldiers from their units, and after detailed instructions, set off for the western hills. He knew of a shortcut to one of the meeting places and they made good time.

The hills above and behind Hatshepsut's temple were considered sacred. Here, many kings and queens had their *Houses of Eternity* constructed. Also in this place, where so many past rulers of Egypt sleep, the enemies of Aten had made their gathering places.

Rakhmet had no great love for Aten, but he had sworn to defend it against those who made war on the worshippers of the Disk. He would defend anyone, friend or not, who was being threatened. He had a duty to perform. The bandits had broken the law, had killed and maimed innocents, and for that, they must be brought to justice.

There were many caves in these hills. Boulders, dislodged from the cliffs, lay scattered on the floor of the narrow valley. They made their way past these and soon found a cave that matched the description the prisoners had given. A cave with a great egg-shaped boulder, resting on its narrow point, partly concealing the entrance. The cave was empty, but appeared to have been used from time to time. There were unlit candles and torches around the walls and other signs of recent occupation.

Rakhmet directed the men to take cover, outside the cave, behind the boulders and in crevices in the cliff face. They waited all afternoon. Well after sunset, men started to arrive. A few appeared agitated. They gesticulated wildly and their behaviour seemed suspicious. Rakhmet crept closer and managed to hear snatches of their conversation.

'No, it did not go well!' one man explained. They were forewarned and had armed themselves.'

'We will have to be more cautious in future lest we are met by armed resistance,' a second added. 'Many caravans are now taking precautions.'

Rakhmet was convinced these were the men who had managed to get away that morning. The robbers still did not seem to be aware the "merchants" they had attacked, had been soldiers.

One of Rakhmet's men indicated that he was anxious to attack, but Rakhmet signalled back to hold off a while longer. These were not the men he wanted—yet. The soldiers had to await the arrival of their leaders!

It grew dark and lamps and candles inside the cave were lit. They were dimmed or shielded to prevent the glow from being seen from outside. The moon had risen and bathed the area in a soft light.

After what seemed a long wait, three more men arrived. They carried no torches but made their way by the light of the moon. Their features were obscured; all three wore *afen-tu*, head-cloths that also covered the lower parts of their faces in the manner of the Bedu, the desert dwellers. From their bearing, Rakhmet surmised these were men of importance, the ones he had been waiting for.

As the men approached, some snatches of their conversation reached Rakhmet and it seemed they were planning another strike, something big. The details were lost, but it appeared some cargo ships, bound for to Akhet Aten, were to be their next target.

The three glanced around cautiously, and entered the cave. A moment later, two men emerged and took positions outside, as sentries.

Rakhmet, hoping his instructions could be seen in the dim light, gestured to his men to take the guards without a sound. After a moment, dark shapes appear from behind the sentries, then a flurry of movement and the two sentries sagged silently to the ground. Good, the soldiers had done well. He signalled again and approached the cave with caution.

Once he had the entrance secured and escape made impossible, Rakhmet entered the cave. 'You are surrounded! Lay down your arms!' he commanded.

The startled men, caught completely off guard, instinctively reached inside their robes and drew their weapons. One of them charged at Rakhmet, but from behind him, an arrow hissed and the man sank down, still clutching his sword. The remaining bandits stopped in their tracks as two rows of archers with drawn bows took aim.

'Lay down your arms,' Rakhmet repeated, 'lest you too taste the sting of an arrow!'

He walked over to the three leaders who raised their swords defensively. They were prepared to fight to the end, but one held up his hand and motioned for the other two to desist. 'Let no more blood be spilled, friends. It is over,' they dropped their swords. Rakhmet reached over to pull the face covering away from the man.

'I am arresting you for treason against the king and the—' He froze as the face covering came away and revealed the man's features.

'Asi!' Rakhmet stared in disbelief at his boyhood friend.

'Surprised, Rakhmet? You ought not to be. You knew how I felt about Akhenaten and his policies,' Asi appeared calm and resigned to his fate.

'But Asi, why? The decrees against Amun are to be revoked. Smenkhare had promised—'

'Promises!' Asi scoffed. 'We got nothing but promises, and nothing has been done. We had hopes for Smenkhare, but he too, betrayed us. He now worships at the temple of the Disk, while we are persecuted, harassed. We endured hardships, even death these last eight years. Now the king wants us to accept his changes and accept him without a murmur—and show *gratitude* for his actions!' The word *gratitude* was spat out contemptuously. 'Tomorrow he might *again* have a change of heart, and everyone has to nod and smile and do his bidding, bow to his every whim,' he gestured. 'No, Rakhmet, we cannot let that happen. Not without demonstrating that we too, have feelings and needs and a right to live our own lives as we see fit,' Asi's voice became more determined, more harsh. 'The king must feel the sting of our resentment. We cannot rest until we have struck a blow that counts. That criminal has to be punished!'

More of Rakhmet's men entered the cave and started to bind those inside.

'No, Asi! Your band is no more. There will be no rebel armies to carry out your wishes,' he waved a hand. 'My *Meti-u* had been instructed to surround other such meetings and by now most of your followers would have been arrested. We will soon have them all,' his voice dropped to a hoarse whisper. 'It grieves me to say this, Asi, but your cause is lost.'

Asi smiled wryly, '*I* might be, and this small band, but we are many, there are some in high places…even in the Palace itself. No, we are not vanquished.'

\*\*\*

Horemheb was summoned back to Akhet Aten, where Sethi presided as *Shesmu,* judge at the trials of Asi and his companions and the other gangs of bandits.

The trials were short and the sentences varied according to each individual's involvement of the crime. Those who had participated during raids and attacks on caravans had their right hands removed. Those who were more deeply involved, who had injured or maimed, were sentenced to lifelong services in the gold or natron mines, or granite and sandstone quarries in the desert. For the leaders of the rebels and those that caused death, the sentence, the same for all. Death!

A reluctant Rakhmet had been assigned to escort two of the leaders to their place of execution, the crocodile pool at the temple of Sobekh. It included his boyhood friend, Asi.

'Do not grieve for me or blame yourself for my fate,' Asi said, as they stopped by the pool where the priests were waiting to perform the last rites. 'I do not hold a grudge. We each did what he had to do, Rakhmet. I knew what fate awaited me if I failed. Had I been in your place, I would have done exactly what you did. Good fortune to you my friend and may your son grow up in a much happier land. Farewell.'

Asi turned, and without looking back, marched towards the waiting priests…and the hungry crocodiles.

# Chapter Twenty-Six
## Return of the King

Akhenaten, agitated and angry, paced up and down his day room. 'How could this happen, Smenkhare? How can the worship of Aten, the "*One who Giveth Life*", whose protective rays should bring joy to all living things, cause such misery, violence and death?'

Smenkhare, sitting on a couch, was absent-mindedly stroking the gilded lion-shaped armrest. 'It is hard for the people to give up their beliefs…'

'I do not understand.' Akhenaten flung his arms up, helplessly. 'I already let it be known that you will rule in Waset, that their gods will be restored to them there. I disbanded the armies to show our enemies we are not a war-like people and we wish to live in love and friendship,' he waved his hand, expressively. 'For that, I am scorned. They call me weak, and took advantage of this to attack our borders.'

'Perhaps you should have kept the armies at the ready. We *must* have them prepared to strike at all times. We cannot become complacent.'

Akhenaten turned to face his brother and swept his hand wide again. 'Must we go to war…to enable us to live in peace? Must we smite our enemies to make friends?'

'Sometimes peace must be earned,' Smenkhare shrugged. 'We have to shed the blood of others to safeguard ours. It is the way of the world.'

'I know not what to do. This constant killing…I abhor it. How many have been put to death already to preserve peace?'

'Eight, from Waset, ringleaders of the rebellion. About fifty had been sent to the mines, and another hundred lost their right hands…I will give the people what they want. When calm is restored, we will know I have done the right thing.' He stood up and spread his arms wide. 'But why am I still here?' Smenkhare sat down again. 'Hasten my return to Waset, Akhenaten. I am needed there.'

Akhenaten rubbed his chin in deep thought and nodded an agreement. 'I will instruct Nakht to have Malkata readied as soon as possible. It had been neglected for too long.' Smenkhare did not tell him work had already begun on the palace.

\*\*\*

The major rebel band had been smashed and their leaders executed. The city slowly returned to normal and there were no more dissent gatherings, no riots or attacks that Nakht was aware of. As the Vizier of No-Amun, he then turned his attention to his next task, that of preparing the palace of Malkata to receive the new Pharaoh and his Queen, who would be arriving soon.

Nakht had planned a great welcoming procession for them. Every building would be decorated—even across the river, the Great temple of *Ipet-Resyt*, would be draped in garlands of flowers. After all, *Per-Amun* was the House of Amun. The entire population of No-Amun, the "Place of Amun" looked forward to their new king and queen.

In Akhet Aten too, an air of expectancy existed. Akhenaten's young queen, Queen Ankhsenpaaten, was with child. Since the announcement, the priests have been saying prayers and making offerings. Akhenaten had consulted an oracle who had seen an omen; He saw a boy-child wearing the double crown of the Two Lands. It could only mean one thing—the queen would have a son who would one day rule over the whole of Egypt.

Even though it meant the child would overrule him one day, Smenkhare rejoiced with his brother. He had been preparing for such news and it did not trouble him. He would be quite happy to reign over just the first nine *sepatu,* the nomes or provinces of the south.

Two months had passed and Smenkhare and Meritaten finally disembarked in their capital. The palace of Malkata had been repaired and the names and images of Smenkhare and Meritaten now graced its walls.

Great rejoicing greeted their arrival, and cheering crowds lined the way along which the Royals travelled towards the palace. Flowers and palm fronds were cast before them in the street.

They approached the palace where a great banquet had been arranged in their honour. It had been almost two-and-a-half years since his coronation, but finally the time to rule, absolutely, over Upper Egypt, had arrived.

*** 

All day long, the priests had been making offerings in the temples. They all agreed that, according to the oracle, Akhenaten would have a son. After muttering final incantations and burning offerings, Ay hurried back to the birth-chamber.

The tail of a hippopotamus, sacred animal to Taueret, the Goddess of Childbirth, was dipped into holy water, then gently stroked over the abdomen of Queen Ankhsenpaaten. Senpa called out in pain and clutched her distended belly.

'It is time!' Ay summoned the midwife.

In an adjoining room, Akhenaten awaited the birth, anxiety showing on his face. He had been through this ordeal seven times, but had yet to get used to the screams of a woman in labour. He knelt, facing the setting sun and bowed his head.

'I beseech thee, O Aten, Oh shining Disk, thee who giveth life to all creatures. All live and rejoice in thy blessings. Grant me a son, O Aten, and I will build thee a temple, mightier than any other.'

Senpa's cries stopped and all was quiet for a long moment, then the wail of a baby broke the silence. Akhenaten rose, quivering with expectation. The door opened and Queen Tiye, her face expressionless, appeared. Coldly, she approached her son and in a like voice, announced, 'You have another daughter!' Then, without another word, she turned and left the room.

Too stunned to move, Akhenaten stood, staring at the door from whence the child's cries came. Tears welled up in his eyes. 'Aten has let me down, again,' he muttered softly. 'Another daughter…another daughter!'

Ay appeared and bowed. 'Your Majesty, it pleases me to announce that her Majesty, Queen Ankhsenpaaten has borne Your Majesty a fine daughter which her Majesty has named "Ankhsenpaaten Ta-Sherit".' He gestured towards the birthing-room. 'Your Majesty may see your daughter now.'

Akhenaten did not respond. Ay straightened and stared at Pharaoh, puzzled. 'Your Majesty… Her Majesty expects—'

Akhenaten inhaled deeply. 'Another time, perhaps,' he replied and left the room.

Ay tried to communicate with him through closed doors, but Pharaoh rebuffed him.

'I wish to see no one!' Akhenaten shouted.

'But Your Majesty, Your Great Wife—'

'Go away!' Akhenaten shouted. 'I will not see her!'

For the next few days, he saw no one. He had locked himself in his bedchamber and refused entry to anyone, even Queen Tiye. Food taken to his quarters had been sent back, untouched. He did not attend any of the Aten ceremonies any more.

The king never saw his daughter. Several days after her birth, Princess Ankhsenpaaten Ta Sherit died.

*** 

Greatly distressed at the news of the child's death, Queen Nefertiti's heart went out to her daughter. She too, had once lost a child, but it saddened her that she had not been able to see her daughter's daughter, or that she could not be with Senpa in her hour of need.

Her anger and resentment against Akhenaten, rose, when she learnt of his stubborn refusal to visit his distressed wife. Ankhsenpaaten needed him more than ever, at this time.

'I do not understand his attitude,' she shook her head. 'He had never acted this way before. Six times I had given him only daughters, but he had loved them all, equally. Never once did he despair at the news of their births. Never before had the mention of a male child been raised,' her eyes narrowed. 'Until the arrival of Tiye!'

Lady Mutnedjmet paid Senpa frequent visits and Queen Nefertiti urged Menefer to do the same. 'You had been friends for years,' she said, and laid her hand upon Menefer's. 'I am certain she would love to see you…and Messu.'

Surprised and delighted to see Menefer again, and especially little Messu, Senpa hugged and kissed the boy, then indicated for them to sit. 'Did you not come by carry-chair?' Senpa asked, observing Menefer's dusty feet as she sank onto a couch.

'No, we walked. It was pleasant, but slow going. Messu wanted to explore everything along the way. Waterfowl fascinates him. When we passed the reed marshes, he wanted to watch the birds and I had to wait for him…then he wanted to pet every ass and goat we passed on the King's Way.'

Senpa suddenly burst into tears.

'Your Highness! Did I say something to upset you?' Menefer asked, concerned.

'No.' Senpa wiped away her tears. 'I was just thinking about my own little daughter. I will never have that pleasure, the joy of watching a little child grow up.'

'You will bear many fine children, yet, Senpa,' Menefer soothed. 'You are very young, still.'

'I need a son, Menefer. Nothing short of a male heir will restore the king's faith in me.'

'Do not despair, Senpa. Next time, perhaps…'

Ankhsenpaaten suddenly looked up with a renewed hope. 'Menefer, you have been to Ipet-Isut!' Menefer nodded and Ankhsenpaaten continued. 'The priestesses there, they all know you. Perhaps you could persuade them to do offerings for me, to Khonsu…I have heard that when the moon is in the quarter, it is the most auspicious time to give offerings to ask the god to ensure the birth of a son.'

'Yes, I was also told that…but only once you are with child. My mother told me of other ways. You must know your husband on uneven days of the month. You need to eat lots of meat, red meat, not fish or waterfowl, and you must also eat salty foods.'

'I prefer red meats to fish anyway, so that is no problem, but…the king refuses to visit my bed-chamber.'

'It will pass. He is just very disheartened at the moment. His black mood will change,' Menefer suddenly thought of something else. 'Oh, and you must avoid wearing red or yellow garments. Wear instead green, blue or brown.'

'I will do all those things. I just need to persuade the king to come to me again. He had finally allowed Ay, Kheruef and Khay into his presence for official reasons.'

'Khay?' Menefer asked, surprised. 'Has he not gone to Waset?'

'Not yet. He is to travel with Queen Tiye's servants, when she returns to Malkata.'

'Queen Tiye? Is she leaving?' Menefer glanced at Messu, who had been exploring the chamber and now fiddled with a sash. 'Messu, leave that. Come, sit here.'

Senpa ignored the curious boy. 'Yes, Tiye and the king had a quarrel. She blamed him for siring daughters. The birth of Senpa Ta-Sherit only caused strife between them.' She noticed Messu inspecting some flowers and she indicated to them, 'Khay brought me those after the birth of the baby. They are a bit wilted now and have little fragrance, but he said they would cheer me up…that was when he told me about the quarrel.'

'Messu, don't touch!' Menefer scolded. 'They're oleander flowers. Very colourful, but I believe quite poisonous.'

\*\*\*

Year Seventeen of Akhnaten's reign, was due, but no feasting had been arranged. He made no effort to celebrate. In No-Amun, Smenkhare sympathised and identified with his brother. Merit had also given birth to a daughter, several months after her sister, but the child had lived just long enough to receive a name—

Meritaten Ta-Sherit. He and Merit were still young, and there would be more children, but Merit was uneasy.

'I fear I will bear no more children, Smenkhare. So the physician had informed me. An evil presence hangs over our family. Never before had there been so much bloodshed and discontent, and I feel it is not done yet. I saw an omen. More deaths will follow...many more. I am frightened.'

Smenkhare tried to pacify her, but she continued.

'Had not my sister, Meketaten, died, just at the time when Aten replaced Amun? And now those changes were once again happening. The gods are angry and two more newborn Royal children had died.'

Smenkhare did not believe in omens or visions and scoffed at his Queen's words. 'Do not fret Merit. They are the beliefs of fisherman's wives, not of a queen. Many children die, at birth or soon after, it is just the way of things. We will have more children.'

Merit kissed him and thanked him for his comforting words, then, more seriously, she reminded him that he *had* a son. 'You should marry Menefer and declare the boy your heir, soon. In the event...my fears come to pass.'

He started to protest but she silenced him with a hand gesture. 'We are now established here in Malkata. Your *House of Women* is ready, but empty. It needs the laughter of children.'

Finally, after some persuasion, Smenkhare agreed.

On the third anniversary of his reign, Smenkhare would carry on the tradition of his predecessors. He would have a ceremony, similar to that of the *"Window of Appearance"* to honour those who had served him well. He would have a list drawn up.

Khay, the scribe, had arrived in No-Amun with Queen Tiye's servants, and the queen would follow, later. The trouble Khay had caused when he had attacked Menefer, had been forgiven, and Smenkhare treated Khay as if nothing had happened. He would make Khay Chief Scribe of his court.

But Khay still bore a grudge. He had not wished to be sent to Malkata, but was compelled to do so. He will never forgive, nor forget Smenkhare's threats to have him flayed, and, when Smenkhare summoned him, he grudgingly obeyed.

'You sent for me, Your Majesty?' Khay bowed as he entered the king's day room.

'Khay, first, I want you to write a letter, then to make me a list. Have you your writing things?'

'Yes, Majesty. I am prepared.' Khay always carried his tablet, inks, reeds and a knife with which to shape them, as well as rolls of papyrus and a few clay tablets, whenever his services were needed. He seated himself on a mat, and crossed his legs, stretching his stiffened skirt tight over his thighs to act as a flat surface.

Smenkhare made an effort to be pleasant. 'It always amazes me the way you scribes can utilise your skirts as tables.'

Khay did not smile. 'Yes, Majesty.'

'First, I wish you to take a letter. It is to go to Akhet Aten, to Mistress Menefer.'

At the mention of her name, Khay suddenly showed interested. Since she had adopted the child, he had hardly seen her as she rarely took her usual walks by the river or lake. He had gone there often, but she always busied herself around the palace to be near the child. Whenever he called upon her, she was almost always in the company of others, or tending to the child and refused to see him.

Khay readied his writing tablet and scrolls and waited for the king's dictation.

Smenkhare cleared his throat and wagged a finger, a signal for Khay to start writing. 'Menefer, at long last we are now able to send for you,' he paused to think of the correct words to use. 'We want you…no, it is our desire, you come to No-Amun. You will join our household as a second wife. We beg you hasten!'

Startled, Khay nearly spilt the container of freshly mixed inks.

'You wish to marry her, Your Majesty?' he blurted out. 'You wish to marry mistress Menefer?'

'Yes. Write!' He folded his hands behind his back and looked at the ceiling, thinking.

'Yes Majesty,' Khay continued writing, but his mood was black and his thoughts wandered. He had to ask Smenkhare several times to repeat the message.

'Until My Great Royal wife bears a son, our Messu will be proclaimed *rpat*, my heir…'

Khay stiffened. 'Messu is…is *your son*?'

'Yes…and, you realise this is confidential?' Smenkhare half-turned and waved a warning finger. 'If one word of this news leaks out before I proclaim it publicly, I will know who did it, and hold *you* accountable. Is that clear?'

Khay nodded and muttered his acknowledgement. Smenkhare continued.

'My Great Royal Wife, Meritaten is in accord and will welcome you both. Make all speed. Too long have we waited.'

Khay was asked to repeat what he had written. 'When the ink has dried, I will add my seal…then you are to dispatch it immediately…' he waited until Khay had done. 'Now, you will make a list of those to be honoured…'

\*\*\*

That evening Khay sat brooding over the letter, muttering to himself. He stared at the flame of small oil lamp nearby. 'So, Menefer's son…is his!' he clenched his fists so hard his hands hurt. 'I should have guessed…adopting a foundling, just after…' he calculated, '…after nine months' absence from Akhet Aten.' He smashed a fist onto a table, making the jars of inks rattle. 'The child should have been *mine*! *Menefer* should have been mine!'

A sinister grin spread over his face, and his eyebrows knitted into a scowl. His normally attractive smile took on a sinister appearance. 'Perhaps…perhaps she could *still* be mine…I can still win over. I can use the letter to my advantage and "persuade" her to marry *me*.'

Khay sat scheming late into the night. Well past the time, the oil in the lamp burnt away, the flame spluttered and went out.

# Chapter Twenty-Seven
## A Royal Funeral

Peace seemed to have been restored in Waset, now called No-Amun once again, but in Akhet Aten the unrest continued. The people there, many still faithful to the "Old Ones", also demanded to have the freedom to choose whom to worship.

'This rabble will never be satisfied,' Nefertiti sighed. 'The more we do for them, the more they want. Akhet Aten is the seat of *Aten*! When will they realise that? If they want to pursue other faiths, let them move!'

Nefertiti's personal servant knocked on the door, and entered. He bowed low and saluted. The queen acknowledged with a slight nod. 'Yes Sentu?'

'Your Majesty, the *Tjaty* is here and wishes an audience. He is awaiting your presence in the hall of Audience.'

Nefertiti and Mutny looked at each other.

'Father? Here? That is unusual.' She turned to the servant. 'I will be there presently.'

Nefertiti entered and greeted Ay coldly. 'This is a surprise! Are you here as Vizier, or is it a family visit?'

'It has been a long time, Nefertiti.'

'Yes, it has!' She gestured for him to be seated and she made herself comfortable.

'I am sorry. I have been very busy…' he started, but she cut him short.

'Yet, here you are. Are you not breaking his ruling now? We are off limits, you know!'

'Akhenaten has become very morose. He speaks to no one, save on matters of State. He no longer attends council meetings. Only Seti visits him regularly.'

'Sethi, the Judge and Chief of Archers?' She was surprised. 'Why?'

'No, *Seti,* your brother!'

'Half brother!' Nefertiti corrected him.

'Yes, half brother. Akhenaten and Seti had been on friendly terms for some time, but that is not why I am here. We need to talk.'

Nefertiti sniffed contemptuously. 'About what? Remember, I no longer exist, according to everyone in *Per Nesu!*'

'Nefertiti, the time of embalming is done and the little princess Ankhsenpaaten Ta-Sherit is to be buried soon. We need the presence of someone to represent the throne. Akhenaten will not attend, so I thought—'

'What about Senpa? Is she not queen? She is the mother of the child…'

'Senpa will attend, but needs someone to comfort her, someone for her to lean on. Akhenaten refused. He did not even attend the ceremony of his Seventeenth

Year on the throne. The Upit Festival is approaching and there will be no Royal attendance for the ceremony of the *open hand*.'

'Tiye would obviously be at the burial. I will not breathe the same air as that woman! Mutny can go in my stead.'

Ay rose wearily and sighed. 'It is a great pity. Senpa will need *your* comfort.'

'Thank you for your visit, father. I appreciate it, but I am not welcome! I pity Senpa and the misery Tiye and Akhenaten had caused her. He dragged her from my side and then he cast her aside like a worn sandal!' Nefertiti's demeanour changed and a look of contempt crossed her face as she shook a clenched fist. 'I wish to make him suffer the way he had made me suffer…and now my poor Senpa! Oh, if only it were in my powers to strike him down. I would smite him!' Nefertiti sagged and dropped her head.

'Be careful, Nefertiti!' Ay waggled a finger at her. 'Walls have ears.'

'What do you mean?' She looked at Ay as he turned and started headed for the door, stopped and turned. 'You know the old saying…*Wish not upon mischief, lest thy wishes be granted!*'

'Well, I meant it!' she called out as Ay left the chamber. 'I wish him dead!'

***

Smenkhare was perplexed. He has had no reply from Akhet Aten yet. It had been some time since he had instructed the scribe to send off the letter. He summoned Khay.

'Your Majesty, I do not understand,' Khay looked concerned, 'It should have been delivered already. Perhaps it was mislaid or lost…'

'Lost?' Smenkhare scowled at him.

'It does happen, Majesty,' Khay appeared nervous. 'Perhaps the scroll fell overboard and the messenger, fearing for his life, fled. Or perhaps he had been waylaid and robbed, or even slain!'

'I thought the bandits had been rounded up and punished and river journeys are safe!'

'Majesty, there will always be robbers, those aiming to fill their own coffers. A Royal dispatch can often mean valuables are being transported, a tempting cause for someone of ill repute to enrich himself—or perhaps the lady had decided not to respond immediately.'

Smenkhare did not question his answer, nor had it investigated. He will pursue the matter later, but for the moment, there were other businesses to occupy his mind. He was concerned for Akhenaten. His brother had never acted this way. It was unlike Akhenaten to ignore his duties. Perhaps he could visit him and rouse him from his melancholy. He shrugged and dismissed the scribe.

Merit too was distresses at her father's mood. 'He grieves,' she explained. 'He had suffered a great loss, but he will recover. When Meketaten died, he did not celebrate his Fourth Year of rule either…perhaps you are right. We ought to visit him.'

They made arrangements to travel to Akhet Aten within the week, but early in the morning, a few days later, Vizier Nakht called upon them. 'Your Majesties, I have grave news from *Per nesu*!'

Alarmed, Merit immediately thought of her sister. 'Ankhsenpaaten! She had always seemed frail. The birth of the child must have been a difficult one and she—'

'No, Majesty.' He turned from a troubled Meritaten to Smenkhare. 'It is not the queen…it grieves me to bring you bad tidings…His Majesty, King Akhenaten is dead!'

*\*\**

The death of Akhenaten left the people of Akhet Aten stunned. It had been so unexpected; many assumed it to be a hoax, a ploy to flush out those who opposed Pharaoh's policies. But elsewhere in the country, many received the news with joy and relief.

Songs were sung that the Criminal of Akhet Aten was no more, and with him had passed the cult of Aten. His Majesty, King Smenkhare, now ruled the Two Lands and named him "Restorer of the Faiths". The hated symbols of the Disk and all associated with it, could now be removed without the fear of reprisals—so they thought.

But Queen Nefertiti soon made it clear that Aten is anything but gone! The Medjay were ordered to patrol the streets and anyone caught raising a hand against Aten, was immediately arrested. This brought on renewed unrest.

Then rumours spread that King Akhenaten had not died a natural death, but had been assassinated. Even the death of little Princess Ankhsenpaaten Ta Sherit, also came under suspicion. 'Someone within the Palace is killing our Royal Family!' someone remarked. 'The followers of Amun had caused of all this!'

Rivalling factions were soon at each other's throats and trouble started all over again. Worshippers of Amun were targeted and Amun worshippers, bent on eradicating Aten, retaliated.

Panehesy, the old priest of the Great Temple, returning home from evening prayers at the temple, was attacked. He was severely beaten and died later that night. It inflamed the Atenists.

'Return to Waset, worshippers of Amun!' was the cry from the faithful of Aten. 'Leave us be to worship the Disk in the City of the Sun!'

To keep the peace, the Medjay were kept very busy.

*\*\**

A more urgent matter had to be attended to. The embalming and burial of Akhenaten. The priests had set up a large tent in the courtyard of *Per nesu* for the purification ceremony. A Royal Guard had been appointed to protect the king's body at all times. There would be no resurrection or afterlife for the king, should it be destroyed or lost.

Inside the tent, a table in the shape of a lion had been prepared and on this, they placed Pharaoh's body where it was washed and purified with lustral water while a priest chanted incantations. Then they dressed it in clean clothes, arrayed with decorations and jewellery, and placed golden sandals on his feet.

The king's body was then removed and taken to the "mesq-t", the *Place of the Skin*" on the western bank of the river. A group of priests accompanied it across the river on a garland-draped barge. These priests would perform the ceremony of embalming.

At the *Place of the Skin*, a priest was summoned to perform the first incision into the body. He cut open the left side of the abdomen with a special flint knife. As soon as he had done the task, the other priests turned on him and ceremonially, drove him from the mortuary for desecrating the dead king. The internal organs were then removed. The liver, lungs, stomach and intestines were washed and packed in natron, then the skull cavity cleaned out and washed.

The embalming of the body, a lengthy and thorough process, came next. Pharaoh's body, ready to be dried, was packed and covered in natron. They wrapped it in a *meska,* the skin of a bull that had been sacrificed in the temple. The *Mesq-t, "House of Skin"*, the "Place of Embalming" got its name from this skin.

For seventy days, the body remained in the bath of natron to dry. During this time, the inside and outer coffins, ushabti figurines and other funerary implements were prepared.

The king's tomb, as well as those of Nefertiti and their daughters, had been excavated in the eastern hills, during the construction of the city of Akhet Aten. During the seventy days of the embalming process, the king's "House of Eternity" was being prepared.

Once the body dried, a group of chanting priests carried out the task of wrapping the king. Symbolic jewellery, a *djed* pillar, a set-square and level and an *ankh*, the symbol of life, were wrapped into the fold of the linen coverings. A semi-precious stone *kheper* scarab, representing rebirth, was placed on Akhenaten's chest, but several other traditional symbols were absent. Because of Pharaohs, beliefs, the *Udjat*, the Eye of Horus, and the Girdle of Isis were not present.

A gold mask, fashioned in the likeness of Pharaoh, and wearing the nemes head-cloth bearing the symbols of the Two Lands, Nekhebet and Buto, the vulture and cobra goddesses, was placed over the head of the mummy. Then, on the chin, they affixed the khabes, the ceremonial beard and symbols of sovereignty. The Royal body was then reverently lowered into its inner coffin, then when it was closed, it was placed within an outer coffin. The two coffins, one inside the other, had both been covered in beaten gold and silver and inlaid with precious stones. Both coffins, as well as the golden funerary mask, were fashioned in the likeness of Akhenaten.

The most important ceremony, other than the actual burial, was the *"Opening of the Mouth"*. A large number of priests and priestesses, headed by Ay, wearing the leopard skin of office, arrived and surrounded the coffin that had been stood upright, just outside the Place of Embalming. They believed this important ceremony would enable the deceased to breathe, eat, drink and speak in the hereafter.

Ay placed an adze to the ears of the body. 'You are reborn from the dead and shall live forever and ever. Open thy ears, O Majesty, and let thy *ka* hear again.'

He then moved the adze to the eyes, nose and mouth, in turn, each time repeating the command, invoking the eyes to see again, the nose to breathe and the mouth to eat. A priestess fanned the mummy with an ostrich feather fan to breathe life into

213

the deceased. The mouth was touched and commanded to speak. It was again, followed by incantations.

Incense was again burned, and libations poured over the body, which was then invited to partake of the feast provided for the living. The ceremony was over and the priests and priestesses withdrew.

Then preparations for the final ceremony, that of the burial, was begun.

\*\*\*

As the Royal barge, carrying Smenkhare, now officially called "*Lord of the Two Lands*", and his queen, Meritaten, travelled north to Akhet Aten, people gathered along the riverbank to express their grief.

The sound of wailing women, shrill staccato ululating sounds made by rapidly moving their tongues from side to side, echoed from the cliffs and travelled with the Royal barge down the river throughout its journey.

Nefertiti had been persuaded to attend the funeral. 'You had been his queen and as such ought to be there.' After more coaxing by Mutnedjmet, Nefertiti reluctantly, agreed.

'I will go, Mutny, for the sake of my little Senpa and to see Merit again, but it will be awkward…should I meet up with Tiye.'

'It is her son's burial, Nefertiti,' Mutnedjmet remarked. 'Surely, on such a day she will not bear ill feelings.'

The day of the funeral arrived. Nefertiti had been preparing for the journey to the eastern hills, when Lady Mutnedjmet arrived with a message. Brief but clear, Queen Tiye had expressed the desire that Queen Nefertiti would not be welcome to attend the funeral of King Akhenaten! She had not been the king's wife when he died, and therefore could not claim the right to be present when he goes to his "*House of Eternity*".

Livid with rage, Nefertiti spluttered, 'this is the last insult I will endure from *That Woman*. I will get my revenge, Mutny! Mark my words. I will avenge myself!'

\*\*\*

From the balcony of her Northern Palace, Queen Nefertiti watched the precession she would not attend. In spirit, at least, she would be there, participating in the final ceremony for the man she had known and loved for twenty-three years. Akhenaten, the father of her six daughters, was gone forever. Silent tears welled up in her eyes and rolled down her cheeks. She made no attempt to wipe them.

The ceremony started on the west bank. A funerary barge awaited the two wooden coffins which were placed in a heavily decorated catafalque atop an ox-drawn sled. The horns of the oxen were gilded and their necks draped in garlands of flowers. Behind this, on a second ox-drawn sled and decorated in a like manner, were placed the urns containing the king's viscera.

The oxen dragged the sled toward the river, where it was loaded onto the barge. After more ceremony, the barge, with its precious cargo, and surrounded by chanting priests, cross the Nile to the eastern bank, where the mourners waited.

The procession started on its long journey east. Ay, swishing his zebra-tail fly swat, walked behind the ox-drawn sled. Dressed in the garments of his office, a leopard skin and wearing a heavy wig, he sweated profusely.

Queen Ankhsenpaaten and Queen Tiye, carried in litters, followed the priest. King Smenkhare and Queen Meritaten, in a chariot, came next, in their litters, came the princesses and Lady Mutnedjmet. Other dignitaries followed on foot.

Next, after the nobility and favoured royal acquaintances were Menefer and Djenna, who nodded greetings to each other but did not enter into conversation.

Behind them followed the rest of the priests and priestesses, all dressed in white and wearing white headbands.

King Akhenaten's personal belongings, his furniture, clothing, weapons and armour, war helmet, crowns and headdresses, jewellery, wigs and grooming tools, loaded onto ox-drawn wagons, came next.

For the enjoyment in the afterlife, baskets of fruit, urns of wine, bread and honey-cakes, jars of fragrant oils and honey, and bowls of grain, followed, carried by servants.

The grain would be placed in a wooden tray in the shape of Osiris, and dampened. This would be placed in the tomb. The sprouting grain symbolised the resurrection of the king.

Boxes of ushabtis, representing the king's favourites and court officials, fashioned during the embalming, were packed in boxes and were carried by servants.

Nefertiti watched the procession weave through the city and along a dusty road through the eastern suburban villages. The distant monotonous thumping of a drum, chanting and wailing rose and fell as the breeze carried the sounds to her. She could just distinguish some of the mourners from their mode of transport and dress.

Lines of professional mourners walked behind the cortège. They were easily recognised from those others who came to pay their last respects. These women would rent their clothing and cast handfuls of dirt over themselves, leaving clouds of dust in their wake.

Slowly, the procession disappeared from view. Nefertiti sighed heavily, turned away from the balcony and went inside. The internment of the body and the sealing of the tomb would be followed by a funerary feast, which could continue well into the night, but for her, the funeral was over.

# Chapter Twenty-Eight
## Plague

Before their return to No-Amun, Smenkhare and Merit invited Menefer and Messu to visit them, informally. They were delighted at seeing the three-year-old Messu again, who had grown into a fine, sturdy and very talkative boy.

'I want to be a soldier when I grow up,' he explained. 'I can shoot with a bow and arrow already!'

Both the king and queen again expressed their desire for Menefer and the boy to join their family. 'I had written, but never received an answer,' Smenkhare explained.

'Oh…I never received anything. When did you write?'

'Some time ago. Before…before Akhenaten's death. I fear the letter had been lost,' Smenkhare said. 'I was about to send another, but because of the circumstances, I…we…' he faltered.

'Yes, it was so sad. I'm so sorry. My heart aches for you,' Menefer understood their heartache after the loss of their child, so soon after Senpa suffered the same misfortune, then followed by the death of Akhenaten.

'Always in threes. These things always happen in threes,' she replied.

To change the gloomy mood, Smenkhare brightened. 'Preparations are being made for me to receive the double-crown. I wish you to be present and will send for you before the ceremony, I assure you,' Smenkhare promised.

Menefer nodded, but secretly, she was of two minds. 'There is no urgency for us to leave. Messu is attending *kap*, the Royal school. He enjoys being with other children, and had made some friends there. I well remember you telling me of your own loneliness while growing up in Waset, and do not relish the same solitude for Messu,' she explained.

'I understand…' Smenkhare said, but her answer disturbed him.

'He loves going down to the lake, hunting waterfowl with his toy weapons. He could never kill anything with them, but enjoys the chase. He is a boy of the outdoors.'

'There is a pleasure lake at Malkata,' Smenkhare replied, hopefully. 'It is surrounded by reed marshes where he can hunt with complete freedom any time he wishes, and I will join him often. I will not restrict him as I have been.'

'Oh yes, mother!' Messu interjects, 'I would love to go!'

Satisfied with Messu's response, Menefer shrugs and agreed, 'Very well, Messu seems happy to go, and I too, look forward to a new life there.'

'Wonderful,' Merit took her hand in hers and squeezed. 'It will be like old times, Menefer. I often look back at the pleasures we enjoyed together and look forward to your arrival. The palace had been rather gloomy recently, and once you arrive, there will be laughter and joy again.'

*** 

Another great welcome awaited the young king and queen. No-Amun had once again, been proclaimed the Royal Capital. Smenkhare now ruled the Two Lands and the people rejoiced.

With the court once again established in No-Amun and with the death of her son, Queen Tiye and Princess Baketaten, to the delight of Queen Nefertiti, returned to No-Amun. Her servants had already preceded her to prepare her quarters for her eventual return.

But the sight that greeted her upon her arrival at Malkata, dismayed Queen Tiye. The palace had still not been fully restored. Her pleasure lake, overgrown with papyrus reeds and after years of neglect, had become a swamp. It would take an army of workers to clear it.

'Tiye,' Smenkhare tried to explain, 'much work had already been done. Your servants and all available *hupsu* have been employed to work on the palace and temples. After the troubles we had, I do not wish to antagonise the unskilled labourers by pressing them too severely.'

'But,' Tiye waved her hand around, agitated. 'You were aware of my coming. My comfort should come *before* superficial decoration, that's why I sent many of my servants ahead. They've done *nothing*! Look at the lake, overgrowth and a cesspool of slime. I cannot sail my barge in that mire!'

'Perhaps you could sail on the river?' Merit suggested, annoyed, 'as we do. Once, when all other *necessary* repairs are done, we see to our own needs and—'

Not prepared to wait, Tiye ordered a workforce from outside the country be brought in, to have her pleasure lake cleared.

The following spring inundation, the Nile flooded into the cleared lake, and Tiye had the two Royal barges, her own *The Aten Gleam*s and that of Pharaoh, the *Skhai-t,* the *Crowned One,* brought into the lake.

Next, she had a pavilion erected by the shores of the lake. A fine diaphanous curtain had been affixed to an elaborately decorated canopy, which could be drawn around her couch to keep out unwelcome flies and other annoying insects. From here, cooled by the breeze or fan bearers, she could conduct her business, or relax and gaze out across the lake.

Tiye watched the two Royal barges, idly floating on the calm water. The *Aten Gleams* had been burnished and repainted, making Smenkhare's modest and smaller craft, alongside it, look almost mundane.

Beyond the lake, the river flowed placidly towards the far-off sea. A heat-haze hung over the river, tinting the distant temples across the river, a blue-grey. A few boats drifted slowly with the current, their rectangular sails hanging limp. Closer by, a large flock of pin-tailed ducks took off, disturbing the smooth surface of the lake. They formed a large wedge-shape in the sky as they followed their leader.

Then a flock of herons rose above the marshes, immediately followed by egrets and ibises, their harsh cries echoing back from the hills. Along the banks of the river, more birds took to the air until great swarms wheeled overhead.

Queen Tiye marvelled at the sight of such unusual behaviour and wondered what had caused the birds to take flight.

Then she felt it. A slight vibration shook the table on which some vessels, containing a honeyed drink, Tiye's favourite, stood. The cups rattled slightly, startling her, but she ignored it.

Lounging on a nearby couch was her daughter, now renamed Bakamun, after she dropped the name of Aten at the end of her name, dozing nearby. She surveyed the peaceful scene, satisfied. The glassy smoothness of the lake, had been disturbed by the tremor but quickly smoothed again, mirroring her barge, the surrounding by water lilies, lotuses and waterfowl. Its gold and copper trimmings shimmering in the sun.

Then she noticed some of the copper had tarnished to a dull greenish colour and immediately summoned more workers. 'I want the vessel cleaned, the copper burnished, and all the paintwork refreshed!'

The bored Bakamun, roused from her nap, half listened to her mother's complaints.

'Everything is left to me to organise,' Tiye continued, 'No one else seems to be aware of the many tasks to be done. If not for me, the whole country would fall to pieces.'

Bakamun yawned. She had heard it all before and gazed lazily out over the lake. Tiye glanced at her. 'Even your brother is neglecting his business. I have been urging him to start planning his tomb, but he just dismissed the thought. A king cannot ignore these things, especially something as important as planning for one's own House of Eternity!'

'He's young, Mother, there is still plenty of time for that!' Bakamun stretched a languid hand out towards a bowl of fruit and selected a large peach. She bit into it and a trickle of juice ran down her chin. Quickly, a servant rushed forward with a kerchief to dab at her face.

'Smenkhare ignores me!' Tiye complained. 'He says he has more important things to concern him.' She waved a hand, exasperated. 'I ask you, what is more important than caring for your own afterlife? Even I had a second, *better* tomb built for myself.'

'Yes, mother. I'll make sure you're buried in *both* of them when the time comes.'

Tiye glared at her insolent daughter. 'And it is time we find a husband for you, Bakamun. You are almost sixteen already, and the sooner you are wed, the better!'

Another tremor vibrated the ground and the Dowager Queen sat up, startled.

'Did you feel that?' she asked.

The mild earthquake caused no great concern, but the funerary temple and statues guarding the structure of the third Amenhotep, her dear departed husband, suffered some damage.

'More restoration work!' Tiye complained, when she was informed. 'Now we will need more builders to repair the damage! Why does it always happen to me?'

After the Feast of the Third Year of his reign, Smenkhare received the *Sekhemti*, the double crown of Upper and Lower Egypt. Meryre, the High Priest performed the crowning ceremony.

'Behold the King of Upper and Lower Egypt, Lord of the Two Lands, Ankheperure, beloved of Amun, beloved of Waenre, Smenkhare Djeserkheprure. We pay homage to your Divine being. We wish you Life, Health and Prosperity and your beloved consort, Great Royal Wife, who will be called Meritamun from this day forth. In the presence of this assembly, in the name of Amun and the glory of Ra, I crown thee *Per-O*. May thee live forever and ever.'

And thus Smenkhare became absolute ruler of the Two Lands, all its protectorates and suzerain states.

Queen Tiye too, was in her glory. Her stepson was a young man, fresh as softened clay that she could mould and shape to her will. 'With my knowledge and the experience I had gained, Smenkhare, you could become the greatest Pharaoh Egypt has seen. We must start immediately on your greatest monument. Your funerary temple shall overshadow even those of Hatshepsut and Amenhotep!'

The young king started to protest again, but she ignored him and continued. 'Remember, it was I who had pushed your father to greatness. Without me, he would never had been deified. I could do the same for you…make your name great as well!'

Smenkhare nodded and agreed. He knew of the power and strong will of this woman.

Tiye rambled on, lost in her own daydreams of what he could achieve—with *her* assistance. She omitted to tell Smenkhare that she plans to be the influence behind his throne. Through him, she would once again command the power, respect and reverence she had once possessed. She was back in No-Amun, back with the people who had once worshipped her as a goddess. She was home!

***

Peace appeared to have settled over the country. With Aten, worshipped in the cities of Akhet Aten and On, and No-Amun once again the seat of Amun, the people seemed content. As long as the one does not encroach on the territory of the other, there would be harmony.

In Akhet Aten, most felt strongly about Aten, but with Amunism now the official religion of the land, the worshippers of the Disk had to constrain themselves. Queen Nefertiti was an avid Atenist and still a powerful force. An uneasy peace reigned.

Nefertiti had decided to remain in her Northern Palace. She had grown fond of the place and declined suggestions she move back to the noisy, dusty and smelly city, but she frequently visited her daughter at *Per nesu*, usually driving her own chariot, and often accompanied by one or more of her children. The people had grown used to seeing the queen, wearing her tall blue-green helmet with its colourful ribbons, streaming out behind her.

To appease the citizens, she had also resumed visiting the Temple of Hat-Aten for the morning ceremony of the Disk. The worship of Aten had been neglected and it had disturbed her. By attending the temple every day, she hoped, the people would take heart and follow suit. Soon, the worship of the Disk had regained its former popularity in the City of the Disk, and Nefertiti rejoiced.

It had been several months since Smenkhare had assured Menefer he would send for her, but, kept busy with repairing the damaged buildings, he had forgotten his promise. She did not mind. Being Pharaoh was not be easy, and he must have had more pressing commitments. Messu, almost four years old, caused her much joy and contentment. He would become a handsome young man one day. He laughed often, and when out playing with the other children, his voice seemed to rise above all of theirs, a sign of a leader, Hatiay, the Overseer of the Royal household, had told her.

She occupied herself, mending Messu's torn tunics often. His clothing always seemed to need mending. She had been busy with this task, again, when a knock on the door interrupted her. Segi, the mute, bowed and indicated someone wished to see her. 'Who is it?' Menefer asked, puzzled.

Segi touched her face and shrugged, indicating she did not know the person. She then shaped her hands over her breasts and hips. It was a woman.

Perplexed, Menefer went to the courtyard. The woman was a stranger, about ten years older than herself.

'You are Menefer? From the house of Thutmose the sculptor?'

'Yes, I am the daughter of Thutmose.'

'I am Sarem... The name means nought to you, but I know of you. Nebamun spoke of you often. I am...was...Nebamun's betrothed.'

'Neb's...betrothed?' Menefer gasped, astonished. It took her a moment to recover, then remembered. 'Yes, Ned mentioned he had met someone called Sarem!'

She invited the woman into her day room. 'I...I'm afraid, uh...are you aware of Neb's—'

'Yes, I know,' the woman interrupted, her sad eyes suddenly glistened with held-back tears. 'We met when he came to our village, to visit a nearby quarry. We became friends and planned to be betrothed once he had made arrangements with his family. He returned to Akhet Aten, promising to return. When I had not heard from him, I came here, then, found the house in ruins, I learnt of the...attack. A neighbour told me what had happened. I was devastated. I was told you were here, at the North Palace, but when I came to visit you, you were away, at Ipet-Isut...'

Menefer was curious. 'Why did you wait so long, almost four years before coming here?'

'A lot has happened since then. I was at his burial, and hoped to meet you there...but did not see you...'

Menefer could not give Sarem the true reasons for her absence and just explained that certain circumstances prevented her from attending.

The woman nodded, 'I can understand. It must have been a shock. My life too, was empty. I could not settle. There was so much trouble; I became restless, left home and roamed all over the Two Lands, travelling to many great cities to trade.' She gestured. 'When Smenkhare became Pharaoh, and No-Amun had once again become the seat of government, I, as many other merchants had been doing, decided to return, to trade. I have family there,' Sarem continued, 'I am now weary of travelling and wish to settle and start a new life. Akhet Aten was one of the stops on my journey, and I decided to seek you out.'

She explained she was a maker of sweetmeats and other delicacies, and had great skills in making these for banquets and other special occasions.

'That was how Nebaten and I met. He had quite a sweet tooth.'

'Yes, I know. You will do well in No-Amun and should find great favour with Queen Tiye. She has a honey-mouth as well, and is very fond of cakes and sweets. I know the superintendent of her household well. His name is Huya. Ask for him at the palace and tell him I sent you.'

'I will do that, thank you.'

'I too, will be going to No-Amun…soon. Perhaps, we will meet up again.'

'That will be good. I'll be looking forward to it. When?'

'As yet, I do not know, but probably would not be too long.' Menefer did not tell her the reason. That would be revealed in good time.

Sarem's visit ended all too soon.

'I am so happy we met,' she said, as she took her leave. 'You were most helpful with your suggestion. I will certainly contact Huya, thank you. I am very grateful.'

Sarem was not to know it then, but her return to No-Amun was to have dire consequences.

***

As Sarem had expected, merchants and other tradespeople, flooded back into Egypt, heading for No-Amun. With a new Pharaoh on the throne, the fear of bandits eased, and No-Amun, once again, became the hub of trade. All were certain of making their fortunes in the "new" Egypt. A continuous stream of caravans crossed the Eastern desert from the sea, and foreign ships awaited berths to unload their wares. This port had not been this busy for many a year. But, with so many people and goods arriving, and with the exotic cargoes brought in, came something else, much more unwelcome.

Among the skilled labourers and builders streaming in to help repair the many neglected temples and other buildings, were also scores of *hupsu*, unskilled workers seeking employment.

Rakhmet, called to a worker's village where a disturbance had been reported, arrived with some Medjay to restore order. Instead of friction, he found the villagers in panic. 'What is the trouble? Why have we been summoned?'

'Captain Rakhmet, our foreman has died.'

'Why call on the Medjay? People die every day. It is not our concern. This is something you can handle yourselves!'

'Lord, the foreman shared a dwelling with other men, from the Great Waters to the East. Two had died, then the foreman became sick and also died. Since then, two more in the same house, had became sick.'

They took Rakhmet to the house where the men were being cared for. A foul stench greeted him as he entered the dwelling. He had seen this before, a long time ago. Some villagers, who had escorted Rakhmet into the dwelling, were immediately ordered out.

'Everyone out! Get everyone away! These men have the plague!'

The men scrambled out relaying Rakhmet's words. Shouts of "plague" quickly spread.

Rakhmet informed Horemheb who quickly investigated and the two hurried to the Palace to see the Vizier, Lord Nakht.

'The plague? Are you certain? Could it not be some other malady?' Nakht asked hopefully.

'I have seen the plague before. When Akhet Aten was being built, a worker from across the Great Waters to the East brought the disease. Hundreds died, including the Pharaoh's second daughter. The men I saw this day, had similar swellings on their necks, and weeping sores. They will be dead in a few days.'

'How can we stop it, or prevent it from spreading?'

They summoned Kafre, the physician from Buhen, who had been appointed as court physician.

'Strong incense must be burnt in the chamber,' he advised, 'and honey smeared on the sores. Those who had not been affected should rub soured wine over their bodies at bedtime.'

This treatment was immediately initiated, but people continued to get sick and die. A few days later, Rakhmet returned home to find a concerned Istar cradling their son, Menet. 'He is ill. Her tear-stained cheeks and wide-eyed look, showed her fear. 'He suffers from headaches and chills and has a fever. I treated him with everything you mentioned, *imeru* and willow bark, but it is not helping.'

A cold fear suddenly gripped Rakhmet. He sent for Kafre, and also a message to Horemheb. Horemheb and his wife, Amenia, arrived soon after the physician.

'I am not certain, but I don't think it is the plague,' Kafre said after a quick examination. 'There are no black patches on his skin, no swelling under his arms or groin. It will pass.'

Everyone sighed with relief. They had expected the worst. Then Horemheb was summoned to the military quarters, some of his men had also developed symptoms.

Days passed. Horemheb and Amenia often called on Rakhmet and Istar to check on the boy's condition but Menet did not improve. He developed severe coughs and started coughing blood. Alarmed, Rakhmet summoned the physician again. He burnt incense, recited incantations and applied more medication. They even tried an ancient remedy—Menet was fed a cooked mouse. The bones of the animals, placed in a linen sachet, was then tied to a cord around the boys head, Then Istar too, became ill!

***

'The Plague?' Nefertiti asked, shocked. She had been visiting her daughter, Queen Ankhsenpaaten at *Per nesu*, when Kheruef, the Chief Steward brought her the news. 'How bad is it?'

'Many had already died, Majesty. Most of the victims were among the *hupsu*,' Kheruef's voice dropped. 'I have learnt that Captain Rakhmet's wife and child had also died.'

'Oh no!' she called out, distressed. 'Can anything be done to stop it?'

222

'Thus far the disease is contained in Waset, Majesty, but it could spread.'

'Is it not ironic, Kheruef,' Nefertiti remarked. 'That this curse has descended upon the very city where Amun had been reinstated? We have had one calamity after another since then,' she became agitated. 'Aten is taking revenge and is punishing its citizens. We must not allow the illness to spread.'

'Yes, Majesty,' Kheruef dared not mention that it had happened here, in Akhet Aten, once. 'Apparently workers from Feka had been brought over. One was infected and spread the disease.'

'Why did we bring in workers from that country? Do we not have enough *hupsu* here in Egypt to satisfy our needs?'

'We do, Majesty, but Queen Tiye was impatient to have the restoration of buildings completed and had these workers recruited.'

'Tiye, always Tiye!' Nefertiti spluttered, clenching her fists. 'That accursed woman is blight on the land. Wherever she goes, calamity follows.' She paced back and forth, then turned and gestured, 'Have the borders closed immediately. Let no more workers or merchants enter the country, not until this disease is halted. Examine all returning countrymen closely! We need to be more vigilant in future.'

Kheruef agreed. He also suggested they restrict travelling in the land. 'We had already taken the precautions, Majesty, of not allowing any boats from Upper Egypt to land here. The border, just north of the Ninth Nome, has been closed. Soldiers had been posted and will not allow anyone through'

'Well done, Kheruef,' Nefertiti remarked. 'We cannot allow this terrible sickness to spread.'

But boat had docked at Pu Khent-Min in the Ninth Nome and some travellers had already embarked in the port city. Determined passengers, aware of the blockade, travelled overland where there were no patrols. They found a route along the hills of the eastern desert, and from there, entered Akhet Aten.

Kheruef, who had already anticipated they might try that route, sent word to taverns in remote villages, to be wary of strangers and informed the Medjay there, to detain them.

*We can, but I hope they don't have families there,* he thought to himself, *relatives or friends would certainly shelter and conceal them.*

# Chapter Twenty-Nine
## Tiye

Tiye, surrounded by her attendants, was relaxing on a couch at her favourite place, her pavilion on the banks of the pleasure lake. The two royal barges had been burnished to a mirror sheen. She nibbled on another of the delicacies she had acquired, while gazing dreamily at *The Aten Gleams,* rocking gracefully on the water, and contemplated another leisurely cruise around the lake. A flock of ducks circled the barges, then noisily, settled in the water nearby.

*That new maker of sweetmeats really knows her trade,* the queen thought, as she popped another sweet into her mouth, bit on it and grimaced. She had suffered toothache for many years and chewing was very painful.

She was thinking about asking the woman to make the delicacies a little softer, when a sharp headache suddenly made her wince. She grasped her head where the pain occurred, and found her right arm a little numb. She rubbed the side of her head, pinching her eyes shut, but when she opened them again, the vision in one eye had blurred.

She called to her maid to summon her litter, but found her tongue to be heavy and unresponsive and her speech slurry. She stretched out her hand to alert Bakamun and started to rise, but collapsed back onto the couch with a cry. Her right leg had gone lame.

Alarmed, Bakamun, fearing her mother had contracted the plague, rushed to her aid. Hastily, they took Queen Tiye back to the palace.

*** 

In Akhet Aten, unease reigned as the news of more deaths, closer to the city, reached the inhabitants. The superstitious, including Queen Nefertiti, blamed the young Pharaoh's rejection of the Aten, but Lady Mutnedjmet scoffed at this latest gossip.

She and Queen Nefertiti were playing a half-hearted game of "Hounds and Hares", a variation of senet, but neither could concentrate on their moves.

'Mutny, I was wondering…we keep getting reports of the disease creeping closer, but, what if the messengers *themselves* are bringing it here.'

'There is no fear of that. News is being called to one another across the border. There is no physical contact between them.'

'I hope you are right, but there is talk that the very air we breathe can carry the evil. People go about the streets with their faces wrapped in cloths soaked in wine and oils.'

A knock on the door made both Nefertiti and Lady Mutny turn. Menefer entered and bowed. 'Your Majesty…it is Princess Setenpenre. She is ailing!'

Alarmed, the Queen rushed to the nursery, followed closely by Lady Mutnedjmet who called out for Menefer to summon Pentu.

The physician arrived within minutes and examined and tended the eleven-year old.

'She has a fever, weakness and a cough. I gave her some milk and honey for the cough. And… Your Majesty, I know it is against the Royal decree, but I placed a talisman, an *Udjat*, the Eye of Horus, on her chest.'

Horus, the god of healing and protector against evil, was the son of Amun, the banned one, but for now, that did not matter. 'Yes, yes anything that will help, Pentu. We must get my little one well.'

Pentu chanted some magical incantations, burnt offerings and recited a prayer. 'I have done all I can here, Majesty. She is resting,' he said after an hour. 'I have here, the sap of *Imeru*, mixed with that of a camphor tree. Rub her chest with this ointment every few hours. It will relieve the fever and soothe the chest pains. I will now go and make a sacrifice at the temple.'

Menefer feared for herself and especially for Messu. Hentaneb, the nurse, had also taken ill and had been sent home. Messu had been with the princess, who in turn had been with their governess, Hentaneb.

Menefer took over the nurse's duties but feared that she too, might be infected. Messu, much younger than either Tutankhaten or Hiknefer, enjoyed playing war games with the two older boys. She decided to avoid contact with the boys and advised Messu, Tutankhaten and Hiknefer, a friend, to play outside.

The two older princesses, Sherit and Nefer busied themselves with more grown-up tasks, threading beads and seeds for bracelets or fashioning ornate collars. Nefertiti had gone to the children's quarters to be by Setenpenre's side. Menefer, temporarily freed from her duties of tending to the princess, was left to amuse herself.

She had been mending more of Messu's garments, and so engrossed in her work, she did not hear Hatiay's soft knock. She looked up, only when he knocked a second time. At the request of Queen Nefertiti, he had come to enquire about her own health. Menefer assured him she was well, then she asked about the servant, Hentaneb.

'I am afraid she had died, Mistress Menefer,' he answered gravely.

'What?' Menefer gasped.

'It was the dreaded illness, as we had feared. A member of Hentaneb's family arrived a few days ago…from Waset. He avoided the border patrols by travelling the long way round, slipped across the border, then sought shelter with them, but died shortly afterwards. He had been ailing, and had infected several persons along the way.' Fearing her family would be punished for breaching the queen's command, Hentaneb kept quiet about the incident and continued to look after the princess, but she herself had been infected and had, unknowingly, carried the disease into the palace.

***

Smenkhare stared out across the wide balcony to the east where the river was glittering in the morning sun.

'Merit,' he said, without turning around, 'News had reached me that Aziro the Ammonite is taking advantage of our situation here, and causing more trouble. He is threatening Aki-Izzi, Lord of Katna.'

Concerned, he sighed deeply, turned and gestured. 'It seems Aziro wasted no time to test my tolerance and power…like a jackal or hyena that snaps at a new-born calf to judge the mother's defence. I've dispatched funds and troops to fight him. I'm due to meet an assembly presently to discuss it.'

Frustrated, he swung his arm in an arc. 'But…with the crisis of the disease, the soldiers are fully occupied to try and keep order. Most of the Medjay had deserted.'

'Most are blacks, from Kush,' she nodded. 'Not the bravest of souls, I hear.'

'They are good fighters…when they can see the enemy,' Smenkhare turned to his wife and gestured broadly. 'This is different. Fighting an unseen enemy is beyond them. They had never before experienced a disease like this, and like us all, are frightened. They are a very superstitious people.'

'Your Majesty,' Lord Nakht interrupted. 'An urgent matter, Majesty.'

'Yes, Lord Nakht. I know—the meeting with the officials. I am on my way.'

'No, Your Majesty, it is Queen Tiye—'

Smenkhare swore angrily. 'If she wants to see me over some trivial matter, tell her to wait. I am in no mood for her petty requests at this time!'

'No, Your Majesty…' Nakht cleared his throat. 'She ails—'

Smenkhare and Merit looked startled. 'The plague?' Merit asked, alarmed.

'No Majesty. The lame sickness. She can no longer walk and her speech is slurred.'

'I will go to her.' Merit headed for the door.

'Wait, Merit. Is it wise?'

'The laming sickness is not catching. I will be all right.'

\*\*\*

Queen Nefertiti was not told of Hentaneb's actions for fear of reprisals against the servant's family for harbouring an illegal visitor. Three days later, after Princess Setenpenre became ill, she died.

A week later, fifteen-year old Princess Neferneferuaten ta Sherit, known as Sherit, also followed her sister to the Land of the West.

The Royal family mourned and wept and the plague continued to spread. The barriers they had imposed were ineffectual, as people continually sought ways to by-pass them.

Pentu was concerned that Hentaneb might have infected others in the Royal household. With the assistance of Menefer, who had been cleared, set about screening all others.

\*\*\*

Queen Merit, shattered by the news of the deaths of her two sisters, wept for them. She tried to hide her puffy eyes and tear-stained face with heavy make-up. She finally emerged from her quarters, but the black kohl eye-liner could not disguise her red eyes.

'I am afraid, Smenkhare,' she sank heavily into a chair. 'Visitors are barred from Entering Akhet Aten. We will not even be allowed to attend the burial of my two dear sisters.'

'It is not for another two months,' Smenkhare tried pacify her. 'The disease might be over by then.'

'But people are still dying all around us. There is no sign of this scourge easing.'

'It looks grim, Merit!' Smenkhare took her into his arms. 'The physicians and priests are doing all they can.'

'I am beginning to believe the rumours. *We* are the cause of this catastrophe. We turned our faces away from Aten and he had now cursed the land.'

'No, dear Merit, that is not so. Remember, the plague struck before. When the city of Akhet Aten was being constructed, in honour of the Disk, the people claimed it was because we were turning away from *Amun*. These are conflicting rumours. Which ones are we to believe? It is an ill wind that brought the disease. Religion is not to blame.'

Smenkhare wished to remain by Merit's side to comfort her, but he had arranged yet another audience with his advisors and officials. 'It pains me to leave you at a time like this, Merit, but other matters, just as pressing, await my attention.'

Merit looked up in surprise. She pulled away from Smenkhare's embrace and sat down. 'Other matters? Something more serious than this...this catastrophe? Well, I will not detain you, then. I will go and see how Tiye is doing.'

As Merit headed for Queen Tiye's quarters, Smenkhare suddenly felt light-headed and stumbled.

'Your Majesty!' Nakht called out, concerned, and assisted Smenkhare to a couch.

'I am...fine, Lord Nakht.' He brought his hands up to his head, and Nakht summoned Kafre, the physician.

'Rest, Your Majesty,' Kafre advised him. 'You had been over exerting yourself during these troubled weeks.'

'There is too much to do, Kafre. I will have enough time to rest once this plague has gone.'

He dismissed the physician and tried to brave the weakness that overtook him, but his health did not improve. He developed a fever, and within a short while, he too started coughing blood.

\*\*\*

The news quickly reached Nefertiti of Smenkhare's death.

Hatiay, who had brought her the news, was waiting for an emotional outburst from the queen, but Nefertiti had had her share of weeping. After the recent deaths, the infants, then Akhenaten and two princesses, she just stood, stunned. She tilted her head back, closed her eyes and rubbed the back of her neck. Her helmet suddenly felt too heavy for her slender neck.

With a pained expression, she removed it, dropped her head and stared at Hatiay for a long moment, then under her breath she repeated, again, what many others had said these last months. 'We are a cursed family, Hatiay. Just how many more will follow?' She closed her eyes again and shook her head slowly.

'Majesty, there is more news…'

'More? Not my daughter!' Nefertiti suddenly looked at him, fear in her eyes. 'Queen Merit? Has she also…?'

'No Majesty, it is Queen Tiye!'

A look of disdain appeared on Nefertiti's face and she sat down. She knew the Dowager Queen had been stricken by the lame sickness, but Tiye was still ruling the Southern Lands. 'Do not tell me she has already announced Pharaoh's successor!'

'No, Your Majesty, Queen Tiye's condition had grown worse. She is now completely lame and helpless…'

Nefertiti's eyes grew wide. She was told the queen had been improving.

'Queen Tiye's had lost her ability to speak.'

Hatiay could not be certain, but he could have sworn he saw a twitch, a hint of a smile, appear at the corners of Queen Nefertiti's mouth.

# Chapter Thirty
## More Funerals

Two months later, the plague started to abate, but not before it had claimed a few more victims. One month after Pharaoh Smenkhare's death, Amenia, the wife of Horemheb, was struck down, and Hiknefer, the young Nubian prince, too, fell ill. Fortunately, he was one of the lucky ones and managed to recover.

Smenkhare had been embalmed and preparations for his funeral were under way, but Queen Nefertiti, still in deep mourning for her two daughters, remained in Akhet Aten, for her daughters' burials. The scourge had not yet disappeared, but two members of the Royal family, Queen Ankhsenpaaten and Lady Mutnedjmet, accompanied by Menefer and Messu, decided to brave the risk to travel to No-Amun to attend Smenkhare's burial.

***

Two barges approached the city. The Royal barge was steered towards the western docks and the oarsmen lowered their oars to slow its progress. Menefer and Messu, in the boat behind the Royal vessel, stood on the deck, as their vessel was also manoeuvred to follow. How different everything had turned out. This should have been a time of joy. She should have been arriving for her wedding and a future of happiness, but it became a time of sorrow…instead of celebration, she now attended a funeral.

She stifled a sob, but could not hold back her tears. Three times the gods had intervened in her happiness. She remembered the words of the sooth-sayer, all those years ago. *Great sorrow awaits you*! She already suffered much sorrow. Is this what the seer had meant? How much more suffering awaited her after the loss of Rakhmet, the deaths of her mother, her father, Nebamun, and now Smenkhare?

On their left, the temples of Ipet-Isut and Ipet-Resyt came into view. Menefer wiped at her eyes, composed herself and gazed towards the great pylons and obelisks. How she wished she could tell Messu, it was there where he was born, but he must not know…yet.

'Are we going there?' ke asked when he saw her staring at the great buildings.

'No, we will be going to the western side of the city. The funeral will be in a valley behind those hills,' she pointed.

'What's a funeral?' Messu asked.

She patiently explained, 'A funeral is a ceremony to bid farewell to someone who had died.'

'Like a festival?' he asked, hopefully.

'Something like a festival, but not a happy one.'

'Will there be tumbrils and dwarfs?'

'*Tumblers* and dwarfs,' she corrected him. 'No.'

'But I like tumbrils and dwarfs,' he replied, disappointed.

She laughed and explained that this was a serious and sad festival and people did not make merry. This explanation seemed to satisfy him.

'Did we know him?'

'Yes, we knew him very well. You met him, once. One day, when you are older, I will explain all.'

***

Menefer and Messu were given their own quarters at Malkata Palace. It was some time before they were finally invited to see Queen Meritamun. The queen tried to be cheerful and pleasant for their sake, but, still deep in mourning, she would gaze pensively out, over the balcony, into the distance. It was obvious the queen was distracted and forlorn. Often, she did not hear when they spoke to her. Menefer decided to withdraw and allow her time to reflect.

The morning of the funeral, Menefer and her son were roused early. They were directed to the landing place where mourners were already milling around, awaiting the arrival of the funerary barge. Kheruef approached.

'Menefer, you and Messu will be with this group.' He escorted them to where officials and court favourites had assembled. Horemheb, still in mourning for his wife, joined them.

'Horemheb! I am so glad to see you.' The Commander looked tired and had dark rings around his eyes. She introduced him to the wide-eyed boy, 'You know my son, Messu? Messu, this is the Great Commander Horemheb!'

'Not exactly *great*,' he answered, modestly. 'He is a fine looking boy.'

'Horemheb, I heard about Amenia…I'm so sorry. I wish I had known her better. She sounded like a wonderful woman.'

'Yes, she was. She disregarded her own safety to care for others. Throughout the epidemic, she tended the ailing, took them food, and bound their wounds…'

The barge with the coffin arrived and Horemheb excused himself to see to his men. 'I will return once the procession starts.' He left.

Ay had performed the "Opening of the Mouth" ceremony. The procession had crossed the river and started for the tomb. An Ox-drawn sled, carrying the coffin accompanied by the sounds of gongs, flutes and sistrums, chanting and wailing, led the mourners to the Valley of the Kings.

The mourners followed the long procession of ox-drawn vehicles, priests and priestesses and the inevitable crowd of professional mourners casting dust upon their heads, much to the annoyance of Messu.

'I wish they would stop. I'm getting dust in my face.'

'Hush,' Menefer scolded. 'It is part of the ceremony. They are paying their respects.'

Horemheb hurried over. 'My guards had been given their instructions. Would you mind if I walk with you?'

She was pleased to have his company. 'No, I don't mind at all. I'm delighted to have company.'

'Yes, it would be a rather a long and tedious walk without someone to talk to.'

After they had travelled for over an hour, Messu was showing signs of fatigue. 'I'm tired. When will we get there?'

'It is not too far now,' Horemheb answered, but he did not really know exactly how far they still have to go.

Messu nodded, licked his lips, then again complained about the dust from the mourners getting into his mouth.

'Are you thirsty?' Menefer asked and Messu nodded, licking his lips again.

Water carriers and food sellers, vendors of fly whisks and lotions to keep insects at bay, lined the way or were rushing back and forth along the line of mourners. She was about to call one, when Horemheb intervened. 'No need. I have water here.' He removed a water bladder from his sash and handed it to the boy who greedily gulped down some of the liquid.

'They do good business during these processions,' horemheb gestured. 'Refreshments are not supplied to the mourners along the way and it is some time before the feasting would begin.'

'They certainly seem to be doing well,' Menefer remarked, looking around, 'and knowing the needs of the people, probably raised their prices.'

'I do not really blame them if they do. They are just trying to earn a living,' Horemheb explained. 'Probably only trying to retrieve what they had lost in trade, during the epidemic.'

'Yes…and probably with families to feed,' Menefer said, looking at Messu.

'Not all, at least, not one I know of,' he pointed. 'Like her, for instance. She has no one to care for, and is doing rather well on her own.'

Menefer looked around, but did not see to whom Horemheb was referring.

'That one there, leading the ass with bundles strapped to its back,' he waved her over. 'She does a brisk trade in delicacies which she makes herself, and is sure to please you, Messu.'

'I know her!' Menefer exclaimed in surprise as she recognised the woman hurrying over.

'Sarem!' Menefer called out and smiled.

Sarem was equally surprised. They exchanged greetings.

'You know each other?' Horemheb asked, equally amazed. Menefer explained when and where they met as Sarem steered the donkey towards them.

'Your suggestion was most helpful, Menefer. Queen Tiye loved my wares, and through her patronage, I was able to build quite a good reputation. I acquired regular clients, including Commander Horemheb, here!' She offered them some of her wares, eager for them to taste, but she refused payment.

Both Menefer and Horemheb insisted they reward her. 'How will you make a living if you give away free samples?' Horemheb scolded.

'I will have a container-full of these, Sarem,' Menefer requested. 'There is a long day ahead of us, and Messu is always hungry.'

Sarem filled a small reed basket for her, then after reluctantly excepting payment, and exchanging parting words, went off to find more customers.

In due course, they reached Smenkhare's *House of Eternity* and the mourners crowded around the entrance. The tomb had been hastily prepared to receive the young king.

Menefer had shed many a tear at Smenkhare's passing, but the end of seventy days, while the body was being prepared, she had recovered from her shock and sorrow. She had been dry-eyed since they left Akhet Aten, but now, at the final moments before the burial, tender memories of Smenkhare again overwhelmed her and she wept inconsolably. Messu, not comprehending her sudden change of emotion, just stared at her, puzzled.

Horemheb drew her close to comfort her and, after a while, she wiped at her puffy, red eyes and straightened up again. 'I'm so sorry,' she said, dabbing at her face.

'Do not be. It is natural to shed tears for a friend. I believe you were close to him?'

Menefer nodded, and then noticed an unknown weeping woman caressing the coffin. 'Who is she? She appears very distressed.'

Horemheb turned to look. 'That is Mutemwaya, Smenkhare's mother.'

With a start, Menefer realised she had never even given her a thought. Mutemwaya had been confined to the Royal House of Women ever since Amenhotep III's death and they had never met.

Menefer and Messu approached her, and she gently touched the woman's arm. Mutemwaya turned a tear-stained face towards them.

'Lady, you know me not, but I am—'

'Menefer?' Mutemwaya looked at them and managed a smile. 'I know of you... He told me of you and my...your little son. I asked about you and someone pointed you out at the landing place that is how I knew you.' She bent down and hugged the startled Messu.

'He has his father's eyes,' after a long moment, staring at the son of her son, she turned to Menefer again. 'I... I am so glad we finally met,' she went into another spell of weeping, excused herself and hurried away.

Horemheb approached Menefer again and nodded towards the coffin.

'It was meant for her, you know... The coffin. It was fashioned for her and is...was in the likeness of Mutemwaya, but had been hastily altered,' he gestured towards the tomb. 'Even this burial place...was built for Queen Tiye.'

Some decorations, done in haste, were not really befitting a king, but many craftspeople had died during the plague, and those that survived had to make do. An outer coffin, which had being fashioned in wood and covered in gold, had not been finished in time, and was abandoned.

Menefer nodded. She had been aware of it. Smenkhare's death was so sudden, there had been no time to have anything done, not even fashioning a coffin for him. She was about to say something, when the priests started chanting and the funeral ceremony began.

Horemheb had to leave Menefer and Messu to be with his guards. Royal and privileged mourners walking behind Queen Meritamun, followed the coffin into the tomb. The passage, too narrow, in places for Queen Tiye's chair and its bearers, compelled her to remained seated, outside. The remaining mourners would also remain outside. Only a selected few were allowed to enter. Menefer looked around, as if searching for someone.

The chanting priests and priestesses were preparing to follow the cortège inside and she was about to approach one of them when Lord Nakht hurriedly over to her.

They greeted and she expressed her appreciation for him arranging passage for her and her son. 'Lord Nakht, could I ask a small favour of you?' He nodded and she explained, 'Could you place a personal item in the tomb for me?'

'Why not do it yourself? You and your son are to follow Her Majesty. It was His Majesty's last request,' he replied. 'He must have regarded you and the boy very highly.'

'More than you realise, Lord Nakht,' she said as he lead her through the crowd.

Just before entering the tomb, she glanced up and her eyes met those of Djenna. She was standing with those who were to remain outside. Menefer nodded a greeting, but Djenna turned her head away, a scowl on her face. She only turned her head back, once her friend had entered the tomb with the Royals. 'What makes *her* so special?' Djenna muttered under her breath.

The narrow, confining passages, made the tomb hot and stifling. Pungent odour of smoke from oil lamps, candles and burning incense, could not disguise the smell of stale perspiration.

They proceeded along a sloping corridor through several rooms, and finally entered the burial chamber. The flickering oil lamps and torches in the enclosed space, made the room even hotter and Messu griped again.

'Shh,' Menefer whispered a warning. 'It is our duty to attend. Do not complain. Be respectful.'

They had lowered the coffin into the stone sarcophagus and removed the lid for the final libation, revealing the wrapped body of the king, wearing a silver death mask. The inlaid eyes stared sightlessly at the ceiling where the painted image of the star-bedecked Sky Goddess Nut stretched out her arms protectively.

Queen Merit placed a bouquet of corn flowers on the body, then Queen Ankhsenpaaten added some flower petals. Then Bakamun leaned over and kissed her brother's funerary mask. Meritamun beckoned for Menefer to approach. Menefer removed a scroll of papyrus from her tunic and tenderly placed it at Smenkhare's feet. It was a scroll containing a poem…the poem Akhenaten had written to him all those years before.

The High Priest Ay poured a final libation over the body, the coffin was closed and the heavy stone lid of the sarcophagus lowered into position. The priest recited a final solemn prayer and the mourners filed out of the tomb. Then servants, carrying funerary furniture and other items, entered, and placed the items in the tomb. They left and the entrance was sealed.

Pharaoh Smenkhare would rest, in a second-hand coffin, in a hastily decorated, discarded tomb, for all eternity.

# Chapter Thirty-One
## The Boy King

The plague finally abated and went, and the people started to repair their shattered lives. Queen Ankhsenpaaten begged Nefertiti to return to *Per nesu* and the queen eventually relented, but she missed her Southern Palace. *Per nesu* held too many unhappy memories and she had felt ill at ease there.

She and Lady Mutnedjmet were in the day room. Mutnedjmet had just returned from No-Amun, which Nefertiti still referred to as *Waset*, and they had been discussing the funeral. Mutny fiddled with some lotus blossom in a bowl on one of the tables while Nefertiti, sitting on a couch, watched her.

'Well, Egypt now has four widowed queens, and no king. Ay wished Merit to name Smenkhare's successor, but she was too distressed. He pressed her to do so immediately, nevertheless.'

'I imagine he would,' Nefertiti answered. 'Did he…make any suggestions?'

'Not directly,' Mutnedjmet waved a lotus flower in the air, 'but he did hint she considers someone with experience in State matters, like himself…'

'I guessed he would. Our dear father is eager to take the throne, but I told him Tutankhaten now has precedence.'

'He is a little young, don't you think?' Mutnedjmet placed the flower in the container, then carefully adjusted the arrangement.

'I suppose you are right.' Nefertiti shrugged then added, 'but he can be guided.'

'Yes, but,' Mutny frowned, picking up another lotus bud, 'by whom? Ay?'

'I could do it. I can take over until he comes of age. Hatshepsut did it when her stepson was about the same age.'

'But then she took control and continued to rule, even after Thutmose came of age,' Mutnedjmet mused.

Nefertiti turned on her sister, sharply. 'I am *not* planning to seize the throne, Mutny.'

'Not yet!' a man's voice answered from the door and both women turned as the Ay entered the day room.

'Father! I have not seen you since your return.'

'I think it will be a wrong decision, Nefertiti! I overheard your discussion. About the boy!'

'He *is* the son of Akhenaten!'

'You had planned to have him crowned, right from the start, did you not? Your opportunity to be the power behind the throne?'

Nefertiti glared at him, angrily. Mutnedjmet could see an altercation coming, quickly made an excuse and left the scene.

'He *is* next in line, father!'

'And at nine years old, and ailing, he would be easy for you to manipulate,' Ay added, sarcastically, 'as you had accused Tiye of doing.'

'How dare you compare me with her?' She jumped up, her fists balled by her side. 'Tiye and I have nothing in common.'

'A dowager queen, trying to recapture her former glory after the death of her husband? And advisor to a young reigning king?' He looked her up and down. 'That describes you both!'

'Be careful, father! If you wish to remain Vizier, you should curb your tongue!'

Ay lifted his head slightly and stared at Nefertiti defiantly. 'Are you threatening me, Nefertiti?'

'No, it is not a threat, it's a warning!'

'You told me once, Akhenaten had changed, but it seems, not just he. You too have changed. You too want power, and now you have the means to attain it.'

'And you, father? Have you no such ambition?' She sat down again and glared at him.

'And if I do? You forget, daughter, one of my parents was of Royal blood.'

'In Mitanni, yes, not here. You have no claim to the Egyptian throne.'

'Unless I marry a Princess Royal… Meritamun and Ankhsenpaaten are now widows, and the thrones of both Upper and Lower Egypt are vacant. I can rule there, and perhaps Tutankhaten here, in the Lower Lands.'

'Marry Merit? What about my mother? Will you make her a concubine then, or secondary wife in order to marry Meritaten?'

'It will be for the good of Egypt. She would understand…and Merit is now called Merit*amun,*' Ay softened his approach. Nefertiti has the power to grant him his one desire and he did not wish to antagonise her. 'Nefertiti, be reasonable. Tutankhaten is much too young. You need someone on the throne who will rule Kemet fairly, someone with experience, and who will keep the welfare of the people in mind.'

'*I* too, have the welfare of Egypt in mind. It is my duty to do so, but what about you? Do you not wish to rule for the sake of gaining power and authority, or for ambitious self?' Nefertiti kept her voice calm and composed.

'No, of cause not. That is what *you* want, is it not?'

Nefertiti tried to control her anger and leaned back on the couch. 'I had always kept my personal desires to myself! I had never interfered with the rule of the land.'

'Yes, you did! You had influenced Akhenaten. Only, when he turned against you, you had wished him dead, remember?' Ay smiled wryly.

'What!' Nefertiti gasped.

'Had you forgotten already?' He took a seat opposite her and leaned forward, speaking in a low voice.

'You wished it was in your power to smite him, remember?'

'I was angry. I did not mean—'

'A bit late now to regret your utterances, dear daughter. It was spoken and it was done.'

'Was done? You mean… Akhenaten was killed? *Murdered*?'

'On your wishes…'

Nefertiti clasped her hands to her face in shock. 'Father, no!' She rose slowly, unsteadily, moved her hands up to her temples and rubbed them. 'This…this is too much to comprehend. I have a headache. I'm going to my bedchamber.'

'You can not! You have a duty to perform,' he smirked. 'Egypt before personal desires, remember? I assure you, Nefertiti, the Two Lands will be in better hands if I rule.'

'I will think upon it, father. I will make the announcement of my decision at the next council meeting.'

***

A hush fell over the assembly as Queen Nefertiti entered. Everyone anticipated the announcement of Smenkhare's successor with apprehension.

'You are all aware of the crisis in the Two Lands.' Nefertiti addressed the assembled high officials with a hint of emotion in her voice. 'The plague had not only decimated the population, but…it had also taken from us many members of the Royal family. My two young daughters and our king, Pharaoh Smenkhare,' she paused and looked around at the expectant faces. 'Kemet is without a ruler and one must be chosen immediately.'

A hubbub of voices agreed with her. Nefertiti raised her hand for silence. 'That is why I called this assembly.' She gazed around at the expectant faces in the hall. 'There is only one eligible, in Akhet Aten. He is right here at *Per nesu*.' She glanced at her father.

'One of us, Majesty?' Ay looked at her eagerly, feigning surprise.

'Yes, Lord Ay, he is here. Only one person can be considered as the next Pharaoh. To legitimise his claim, I have decreed he is to marry Queen Ankhsenpaaten, the widow of Pharaoh Akhenaten. The wedding will take place immediately, and the coronation will be arranged at the most auspicious occasion as calculated by the stars. I will now call forth the one who will sit on the throne of Egypt.' She glanced towards Ay again. He straightening up and took a step towards the dais.

She clapped her hands and signalled. Everyone turned and looked towards the door as Pentu entered, escorting a boy.

'People of Towy,' Nefertiti called out. 'Bow down and pay homage to your next Pharaoh, King Tutankhaten!'

***

Once again, discontent spread throughout the land. The young king, under the influence of Queen Nefertiti, a worshipper of Aten, would rule Upper and Lower Egypt. A very real fear that the worship of Amun would once again be outlawed made the people tense. Queen Nefertiti had anticipated strong resistance to her choice. She feared reprisals against the young king.

Menefer and her son moved from their quarters at the Northern Palace, back to the city and were given lodgings in the *per-hempt*, the House of Women. Both had been close friends with—and well liked by Tutankhaten. Queen Nefertiti, remembering Menefer's uncovering of Lord Tutu's secret dealings with the enemy all

236

those years earlier, was pleased. She needed the young woman's assistance to keep the young king safe.

'He needs someone close by; someone he can both trust and confide in, someone to watch over him. Trust no one, Menefer,' Nefertiti warned. Rumours had spread that both Pharaoh Akhenaten and Senpa's baby had been murdered, and Ay's suspected involvement, concerned her greatly.

'I dare not accuse anyone, but we must be wary. Respected officials, close friends…even family, could be the enemy.' The Queen paused to make her statement sink in, 'It is said that it is easy to betray an enemy by making him your friend. There are enemies of the Royal family here at *Per nesu*, feigning friendship. Be wary! I have assigned food tasters, but there is a constant risk from other quarters.'

Menefer agreed to be vigilant.

***

For Tutankhaten, the child of a concubine, to claim the throne, his marriage to Queen Ankhsenpaaten, a Royal Princess, would be necessary. She was almost twenty years old, and he was nine!

They were married amidst great splendour and celebration. During the feast, a chieftain from Punt arrived. He had been delayed and had missed the ceremony, but had hoped his gifts, two dwarfs and a tame cheetah, would please the young king. Dwarfs were very popular and entertaining, and were sure to please him but, by the time the chieftain arrived, King Tutankhaten had disappeared.

Alarmed, Queen Nefertiti feared the worst. Their enemies would target the boy. She ordered an immediate search. *Per nesu* and the palace were searched from corner to corner but Tutankhaten could not be found.

'Where is he?' Nefertiti asked Senpa, anxiously.

'Where is who, mother?'

'Your husband! Tutankhaten!' she snapped.

'Oh! He took his sling and he and Messu went bird hunting.'

'Hunting? During his wedding feast?'

'He is only nine, mother,' Ankhsenpaaten sounded indifferent.

'He should be here, with his guests!' Nefertiti waved her arms in exasperation.

After a lengthy search, they found him outside the palace grounds by the river. 'Tutankhaten, we've been looking all over for you. What were you doing there? You should not leave the palace grounds!' Nefertiti scolded once he returned.

'I was bored,' he answered casually. 'I thought a king could do anything he wanted.'

'Yes, but you cannot wander off by yourself. It is dangerous.'

As he was led back to the feast, he told her about the hunt. She smiled indulgently down at him. At his age, hunting seemed far more exciting than a newly wedded wife.

***

Planning the coronation, a much more serious matter than a wedding, took place months before the event. Lord Nakht had been recalled to Akhet Aten to calculate the most promising date for the event. The young king had to be instructed in the rituals of the ceremony, and had much to learn and remember. After a lengthy practice of the ceremonial speech, the frustrated Tutankhaten ran, crying, to his quarters.

Later, Menefer found him and Messu playing by the lake. Both were covered in mud. 'Messu! You are filthy. What have you been up to?' She started wiping away the grime with a kerchief.

'We've been playing soldiers. I slipped in the mud and Tut helped me out.'

'Well, you are both needed at the palace. Go and clean up. You cannot go into the hall looking like that!'

The two boys ran off and Menefer returned to lake to rinse her mud-covered kerchief. She saw a movement in the corner of her eye and was about to chastise Messu for disobeying her, when she saw Khay coming towards her.

'I was hoping I'd find you here,' he said.

'Khay, I thought you were in Waset.'

'I was, but came back for the coronation. After your...friend's death, there was no more need of me, there, anyway.'

'My friend?'

'Smenkhare!'

Menefer stood up, wrung the water from the kerchief and looked at him askance, wondering where this was leading.

'You are still unmarried, Menefer. I think, as we will be seeing a lot of each other now, it might even develop into something...'

'Khay, I told you once before. I do not wish our relationship to develop into anything more...'

'Oh, but I think it will. I have a document that will change your mind.'

'Document? What document?'

'One with Smenkhare's seal, one in which he acknowledges your *adopted* son as his...your son, and of *Royal* blood!'

She stared at him, bewildered.

'I know all, Menefer. *You* bore Smenkhare a son. You went away to birth him, then returned and claimed him as being a *foundling*.'

Menefer was speechless and did not know how to answer him.

He continued, casually, 'The people are again restless. They fear Nefertiti's influence to persuade the young king to abolish Amun. Disorder will start all over again.' He paused and watched her wince.

'What has that to do with me?' Menefer's voice trembled slightly.

'Here is my proposal. The boy needs a father, and I am available. If you wed me, I will—'

'I will never marry you, Khay!'

'Let me finish! If you wed me, I will keep your secret, but refuse...' he paused and sneered. 'Who knows? I wonder who might be interested. There are many who want to replace Nefertiti's pawn, that sickly young king. Someone who could be introduced in the ways of Amun. Like his father, Messu could be that person...*your son* could take over the throne!'

Horrified, Menefer stuttered, 'That's…that's treason, and…and is also extortion!'

'I told you once, I will have you, no matter what it takes.' He folded his hands in a gesture of defiance. 'I will do whatever is necessary.'

'And I will do what I can to prevent you!' She took a menacing step towards him.

He looked at her scornfully, and folded his arms across his chest. 'In the end, you will *beg me* to come to you!'

'Never!' She turned on her heels and marched away.

'Remember, Menefer…' he called out after her. 'I have the document…in a safe place!'

*** 

Segi, the Mute, had found Menefer crying in her bedchamber and summoned Lady Mutnedjmet who came to investigate. 'Why, Menefer, whatever is the matter?'

Menefer composed herself, wiped away tears and explained about Khay's threat and the document.

For a while Mutnedjmet sat, in deep thought, biting on her thumbnail. 'Exposing you and Messu could be serious. He is right…there are some who will stop at nothing. These people will do anything to gain control of the…of gaining control of the present situation.'

'I wish I knew what to do, lady Mutny. I have no desire to marry the scribe.'

Mutnedjmet patted her hand. 'Do not fret. We will think of something. In the meantime, get yourself involved in something to ease your mind. Senpa is designing a *tchama*, a chair, for the coronation. She wanted a throne that will outshine that of Akhrnaten's, but she needs assistance. Why don't you go and see her?'

Menefer thanked her and headed for Ankhsenpaaten's day room. She found the young Queen poring over some crude designs on wafers of slate. Senpa, pleased to see Menefer, immediately got her involved in the project.

After some hours of designing, re-designing and modifications, Senpa clapped her hands in delight.

'That is it, Menefer. It is perfect. I will summon craftsmen immediately to fashion the chair.'

It took almost two weeks of labour to fashion the throne, but Khay's threat hung over Menefer like a dark cloud and she could not rid herself of her fear.

The *tchama* was brought to Queen Ankhsenpaaten for her approval, and both Menefer and Senpa were delighted. It had been crafted in costly timber and gilded. It had two lion's heads at the front and armrests in the shape of winged serpents, each wearing the crowns of Upper and Lower Egypt. The leg braces were carved in the traditional *sma,* interweaving of lotus and papyrus reeds to represent the unification of the Two Lands.

The backrest depicted Ankhsenpaaten anointing Tutankhaten. It was fashioned from intricately carved and polished pieces of precious and semi-precious stones.

Tutankhaten was called to come and see the wonderful chair, but was less than impressed with it.

'It looks uncomfortable. I prefer my curved cow-hide stool.'

Senpa shrugged and with a wry smile, told Menefer he was in a grumpy mood and not to take any notice.

'I don't like being king. There is too much to learn and remember.'

'Everyone has to do things they don't like at one time or another.'

'Why can't they find someone else to be king? I'd rather go outside and play.'

'Who?' Senpa sighed. 'There is no one else.'

Tutankhaten pointed at her. '*You* can be queen, like uh…Queen Shupset…uh…'

'Queen Hatshepsut,' Senpa corrected him as she caressed the polished surface of the chair, 'I have no ambition to rule. I seek no power.'

Tutankhaten suddenly burst out giggling.

'What is so funny?'

'You,' he sniggered. 'I think you will look funny wearing a *nemes* head-cloth and khabes, as Hatshepsut did.'

Senpa and Menefer laughed with him.

'You are right. I don't think a beard, ceremonial or otherwise, will be very becoming.'

***

'My, don't you look fine?' Menefer adjusted Messu's tunic and surveyed her son proudly. She turned him around and inspected him from all sides, then fussed with his plaited *Lock of Youth*. The curl at the end of it had become a little unruly, and she wet her fingers to reshape it.

Segi tapped on the door and signalled that the ceremony was about to start. She took Messu by the hand and hurried to the palace.

In the crowded courtyard, they had to wait patiently to enter the Great Hall.

'Mother, who's that man? He keeps staring at us?'

She looked in the direction where Messu was pointing. It was Rakhmet. He quickly turned away. 'Oh…' she hesitated a moment. 'It's…it's someone I knew, a long, long time ago.'

The Great Hall of the Palace was packed. Menefer and Messu were again allocated to the area reserved for high court officials. Standing close to them, were Lord Sethi and his wife. As they exchanging greetings and small-talk, Queen Tiye arrived, carried in, in her sedan chair.

'I don't see Bakamun or Queen Meritamun,' Menefer nodded towards the queen.

'They decided not to attend,' Sethi mentioned. 'They had decided to remain in No-Amun. Meritamun had been very depressed since Smenkhare's death and her health had become delicate.'

The crowd hushed as the Royals entered. Tutankhaten's leg was troubling him again and he walked with a cane. Tutankhaten and Ankhsenpaaten took their seats on the thrones on the dais as the High Priest Meryre, entered. He performed the coronation ceremony, and after the *Sekhemti*, the double crown of the Two Lands, had been placed upon Tutankhaten's head, he turned to the people.

'Hear me, O people of Kemet and all our vassal countries. Behold. Look upon thy ruler Per-O Tutankhaten, Neb-Khephrure, Lord of Diadems, Lord of Towy, the Two Lands. King of upper and Lower Egypt. Life, prosperity and health, may he live forever and ever and may his reign be a long and peaceful one.'

Tutankhaten, looking very uncomfortable, adjusted the heavy crown and ceremonial beard, then noticed Messu in the front row. He grinned widely and waved. Messu waved back and a few of the guests sniggered.

Meryre stopped and glared at the King for this breech in protocol. Tutankhaten quickly composed himself, the priest cleared his throat and continued, 'May his reign be long and peaceful,' he turned toward the queen, 'And to his Great Royal Wife, Queen Ankhsenpaaten, life, prosperity and health. May she live forever and ever.' He turned to the crowd and commanded. 'Kneel before thy king!'

There was a rustle as all, but Tiye, went onto their knees. The hall, packed tight, made it somewhat difficult for some. At a signal from Meryre, Tutankhaten, a little unsteady, stood up. Meryre handed him his walking stick, but he waved it aside and, picking up the crook and flail symbols and folded his hands across his chest.

'Rise!' Meryre ordered and rustling sounded around the hall as the people rose. In a quavering, high-pitched voice, hardly audible at the back of the hall, Tutankhaten cleared his tightening throat, as he prepared to deliver his first public speech, the one he had so much trouble with remembering.

'I, Neb-Khephrure, Tutankhaten, vow to be a fair king. To rule with compassion, to protect and expend...' he hesitated and Senpa whispered something.

'To protect and *extend* the boundaries of the lands of Egypt and to slay my foes without and axe, and shoot the arrow without a bow...uh...without *drawing* a bow.'

'Hail Pharaoh Tutankhaten!' Meryre shouted as Tutankhaten resumed his seat, and the crowd took over the cheer.

'Hail Pharaoh Tutankhaten!'

# Chapter Thirty-Two
## Poison

Visitors crowded the marketplace. Messu gaped open-mouthed at all the stalls. At one, a baboon, with the most wonderful colours on his behind and face, was doing tricks. At another stall, a man demonstrated spinning toys, and wooden monkeys that danced when he pulled a string.

In a clearing, a dancer entertained the crowd, gyrating and writhing her body sinuously to the beat of the music of sistrums and drums. The delighted young men in the audience clapped their hands in rhythm. The dancer had tattoo markings on her belly and thighs, identifying her as a priestess of Hathor. These women were practiced in the art of entertaining men in all the pleasures of the flesh.

A little further on, some naked dwarfs were performing to a crowd, and children squealed with delight at their antics.

'Can I have one?' Messu asked.

'Have one what? A dwarf?' Menefer shook her head. 'No Darling, we cannot afford it.'

'But Tut has *two*!' he insisted.

'Tutankhaten is a King, Messu, Pharaoh of the whole of Egypt. Dwarfs are very highly regarded and costly. Only the very rich can afford them.'

'One day I will be rich,' he sighed. 'Then I'll have one, too.'

'Come, let's look at other stalls,' Menefer suggested and started to move on.

'Can I stay to watch?' he begged.

'Only if you promise not to wander off by yourself,' he nodded, and she relented. 'Very well. Stay right here. I will return shortly.'

She continued browsing among the stalls within sight of her son.

'Menefer!' A voice behind her made her turn around.

'Commander Horemheb!' They exchanged greetings. 'What are you doing here, Commander?'

'We were posted back to Akhet Aten, for the coronation.'

'No, I mean, here, at the marketplace?'

'Oh. Yes, I came to see Sarem. She too, had decided to move back. There is more business here, in the city where Pharaoh resides.'

'Don't tell me you are courting her,' Menefer asked slyly.

'No, I came to order some more sweet-cakes.'

'I did not think you were such a honey-mouth, Commander.'

'Not usually,' Horemheb laughed, 'but they had been Amenia's favourite, and, I too had grown fond of them.'

He escorted her over to a stall where Sarem was and she and Menefer hugged. After catching up on news and gossip, Horemheb picked up a platter. 'Taste some of these little cakes. They are the ones I mentioned.'

At Sarem's insistence, Menefer took one and took a tentative bite, then popped the rest into her mouth. 'They are delicious, Sarem,' she said, chewing. 'How did you make them?'

The confectioner laughed. She shook her head and her wavy hair cascaded over her shoulders in curly locks. 'That I cannot reveal, but I used minced dates, carob and honey, plus some secret ingredients.'

Sarem offered her a platter-full for Messu, but refused payment.

'You must stop giving away your profits,' Menefer laughed and dug into her tunic. She removed a fold of cloth containing a few deben of copper and insisted on paying for them.

'I hope you have enough of those ingredients, Sarem,' Horemheb reminded her. 'I need a sufficient quantity for the feast.'

Menefer looked at him, puzzled, 'A feast?'

'For Princess Nefer. She will celebrate her seventeenth birthday soon and will leave for Babal, with her husband, Prince Nijmat, shortly afterwards.'

***

A tremendous amount of work needed to be done to set up a new Government. New overseers had been appointed, new laws were drafted and old ones amended. A small army of scribes was needed to transcribe the many documents of which copies had to be made for the officials of the many nomes.

Nefertiti and Mutnedjmet had been busying themselves in the dayroom. Nefertiti had been studying a document, and looked up. 'The religion of the disk should be the religion of the land, not just this nome!'

Lady Mutnedjmet, who had been altering one of her garments, looked up at her sister. 'Nefertiti, why not leave this matter be? We are now at peace. A change again, could cause nothing but grief.'

'Mutny, The King is a worshiper of Aten! It is only fitting we follow. Did you forget what happened when Smenkhare ruled? He turned to Amun and immediately after the restoration, plague broke out. It caused the death of my two dear little ones, then Smenkhare himself.' She became sombre. 'It was an omen…a warning from Aten.' She gazed out beyond the balcony towards the south. 'My poor Merit is still residing in that city. She is ailing, and Tiye has the lame sickness.'

She turned to Mutnedjmet, sharply. 'Does that not prove Amun is a blight on the land?' Her expression changed to one of determination. 'No. We must make thing right lest another calamity befalls us.'

Mutnedjmet tried to talk her out of her decision, but Nefertiti persisted. 'My faith in Aten had waned… I had neglected my duties to the Disk after Akhenaten's death.' Nefertiti raised her hand, dramatically, then made a fist. 'We turned our faces away from Aten and paid a terrible price. I must lead Egypt back to the true faith, away from calamity. I can do this through Tutankhaten. My way is very clear.'

'I think you are making a big mistake, Nefertiti. If you stir a calm pond, it will only make the waters murky.'

Nefertiti could not be swayed. 'Tutankhaten is young. He represents Aten's rejuvenation, its rebirth,' a strange look came over Nefertiti. A look of enthusiasm and dedication. 'I will commission Menefer to fashion a likeness of the young King. He will emerge from a lotus-bud, just as the Sun emerged forth from the ancient waters.'

'Please, Nefertiti. Do not become as Akhenaten had been, follow his ways and—'

'Do not regards me as another Akhenaten, Mutny,' Nefertiti shouted, turning on her. She slammed the document down on the table. 'I shall not persecute my people the way he had done! I shall show them that Aten is good. Aten gives life…*is* life! I shall rule with kindness and compassion. I shall—'

'Nefertiti, listen to yourself. You are talking about *your* people, when *you* rule! *Tutankhaten* is King! *He* rules, not you. You are beginning to sound and act like Tiye.'

'You too? You dare compare me with that woman!' furiously, Nefertiti sprang up, tipping her chair over. 'I am nothing like her! She manipulated Akhenaten for her own benefit. I have no such ambitions. Tutankhaten is young and inexperienced. He needs a guiding hand and that is *all* I am giving him. Do not *ever* suggest anything different!'

Mutnedjmet looked down at her hands and rubbed at a non-existent mark, then without a word, she rose and went to her own quarters.

***

The arguments between Nefertiti and Mutnedjmet continued and, as Nefertiti's ambitions intensified, the rift between them grew wider.

Nefertiti even became impatient with Tutankhaten. When the Viceroy of Kush came to see him on an important matter, and the appointed time approached, the king was away again, this time playing a game of hide and seek with his two dwarfs and Messu. Tutankhaten's personal servant, Khares, eventually located them and ordered the king back to the palace.

Nefertiti was waiting. 'Ah, Pharaoh. You finally decided to honour us with your presence!' She was annoyed. 'Just look at your garments! They are soiled!' She turned to servant. 'Khares, get a cloth and bowl and clean His Majesty.'

'Now, young man, you have a duty to preform!' she scolded, while Khares was cleaning him. 'I do not want this to happen again! Egypt depends on you, understand?'

He nodded reluctantly. Official duties were boring. He would rather be playing with his friends

After attending the audience between Tutankhaten and the Viceroy, Nefertiti went to the garden to study more documents. She was sitting on a bench under a shade tree when Ay approached. She rolled up the document and looked up. Ay took an arrogant stance, arms folded.

'Nefertiti, why was I not invited to the audience with the Viceroy? As Vizier I have the right—'

244

'You no longer have those rights, Ay.'

'What?' Ay moved his arms akimbo, the fly swat dangling behind. 'Why?'

'You are like a banner on a pylon pole. You change direction with every change in the wind.'

'What do you mean?' He swished at an annoying fly.

'You were High Priest of Min before Akhenaten came to the throne, then switched to Aten to gain favour. When Smenkhare ruled in Waset, you were observed worshipping at the Temple of *Amun*!'

'I was not worshipping, merely paying my respects…'

'By giving offerings? That was not a fitting thing for a priest of Aten to do! You have been relieved of your post! A new Vizier had been appointed to King Tutankhaten's court,' she paused, 'Ramose!'

'Ramose?' Ay spluttered and took a step towards her. 'Where does that leave me?'

'You can always go back to Akhmin, to the priesthood of Min, or share as *Overseer of the Royal Stables* with my dear half-brother Seti.'

'The stables? Me?' he straightened up, indignantly. 'I was *Fan bearer to the King's right.*'

'That king is now dead…by *your* hand, Ay.' She waved the rolled up document at him. 'You may, of course, one day, continue to serve as Vizier to Akhenaten—when you join him in the hills in the east.'

She settled back, and tapped the rolled papyrus into the palm of her left hand. There was a sardonic smile on her face as she watched his storm off. Her revenge for Akhenaten's death tasted sweet.

***

Several days later, Menefer was taking some garments to where her laundry was usually done. Khay was returning from the records storehouses, studying one of them.

He was engrossed in the document, not looking where he was going and they almost collided. 'Oh…uh, I beg forgiveness. How nice to see you again, Menefer! I noticed Messu is growing up fast.'

'Yes, he will be six years old, soon.' She was uncomfortable talking with him. 'Sorry, but I cannot tarry. I have things to do.'

'He really needs a father around, at that age,' Khay ignored her urgency to leave. 'It is not fitting for a woman to fend for herself and a child.'

'I will manage.' She tried to pass him, but he stepped in front of her.

'You're trying to avoid me, Menefer. Is there someone else?'

'What do you mean by *someone else*, Khay?'

'First there was Rakhmet, then Smenkhare and now Horemheb!'

'Horemheb?' she exclaimed, surprised.

'I saw you two in the market place getting all cosy.'

'There is nothing between myself and Horemheb. We are just friends.'

'Just friends? Like you and Smenkhare were?'

He saw her blanche. 'You are not to see him again.'

'What?' Menefer was getting angry. Her voice rose and she gestured dramatically. 'I will see whomever I please, Khay. You will not control my life!'

'You are mine! I demand it.'

'You have a nerve!' she sneered. 'Keep your nose out of my business. Go and feed yourself to the crocodiles.' She turned away abruptly and stormed off.

'What can I do, Lady Mutny? He is persistent. Constantly pestering me. How can I stop him?' They were in Mutnedjmet's day-room.

'I wish I had it in my power to assign him to some lonely outpost,' Mutnedjmet sympathised, 'somewhere, with only serpents for company.'

'Whom do you wish to banish there, Lady Mutny? Me?' Horemheb joked as he entered and caught the tail end of the conversation

'Horemheb, what a surprise. We were just discussing Khay, the scribe. Menefer has been having a lot of trouble with him,' Mutny explained.

She told him about Khay's harassment and the scribe's determination to marry her, but did not mention the incriminating document. Horemheb might start investigating and uncover Menefer's secret.

'He is obsessed with me—determined to have me as his wife. He has been making threats,' Menefer added.

'That soft bellied son of a desert scorpion.' Horemheb pounded his fist into the palm of his hand. 'His back will taste the sting of my whip.'

'Please, Horemheb. Let him be. Do not harm him.' She feared Khay would avenge himself on her and her son.

'You plead for that Son of Seth?' he was puzzled, then, after a brief moment, nodded. 'Very well, I will not hurt him, but he needs to be warned.'

The following day, Khay was walking along the pillared walkway of *Per nesu*. Horemheb approached him and grabbed the startled scribe by the shoulders, lifted him and banged him against a pillar.

'Scribe, I do not like to waste words, especially on swamp slime like you, so I will make it short. Leave Menefer alone if you value your hide!'

'Do not threaten me, Commander,' Khay swallowed hard, frightened, but he was confident of his hold over her. 'I can cause a lot of trouble for her—and her son.'

'If you harm her or the boy, I'll come after you!' Horemheb emphasised his words by thumping him into the pillar.

'I won't need to do a thing,' Khay answered calmly, grabbed hold of Horemheb's arm and tried to wrench himself free. 'All I need do is let certain people know the truth of her and her son...and *they* will do the rest!'

'What do you mean?' Horemheb lowered Khay who then proceeded to straighten his twisted collar.

'For one thing,' Khay smirked, 'there are people, opposed the new decrees who would relish the truth about her and her *adopted* son,' he emphasised the word "adopted". 'Did you know he is *her* son...of her *own* body!'

'Her...own?' Horemheb was momentarily taken aback, but quickly recovered. Khay was only trying to wriggle out of the confrontation by outrageous statements. 'Even if it were true, an unwed mother will not be harmed...not in this nome.'

'What if I produce a document, *with a Royal seal attached*, revealing the father is of Royal blood?'

'Of… Royal blood?' Horemheb gasped. 'Who…'

'The father of Menefer's son is Smenkhare!' Khay casually smoothed his tunic.

Horemheb was stunned. His mouth gaped open and Khay could see his remark made a deep impact.

'Yes, Horemheb. Messu has Royal blood, and I have proof! Do you realise what will happen if the news reaches the *wrong* people?'

Horemheb flung Khay off the walkway. 'Get out of my sight, Scribe!' Khay got up and dusted himself off as Horemheb marched away, angry and bewildered.

'You will pay for this, Horemheb!' Khay called out after him, seething with rage. 'By Amun, you will pay dearly!'

***

Khay wasted no time in confronting Menefer again. The evening temple ceremony had ended and he waited for her in the garden where she would pass. She saw him immediately she entered the garden and felt uneasy.

'What do you want, Khay?' she demanded.

'Is Horemheb your new lover?' he asked bluntly.

'What? Horemheb?' She stopped and stared at him. 'What gave you *that* idea?'

'It was Horemheb who sent Rakhmet away,' Khay used his fingers to mark off each situation. 'It was Horemheb who took you home after your accident. It was Horemheb who accompanied you in the funeral procession,' Khay's eyes narrowed. 'It was Horemheb you met at the marketplace, recently, where he purchased some sweet-cakes.'

'Are you *spying* on me now?'

'It is true, is it not?' He smirked. 'Why else would he warn me off seeing you?'

Menefer was furious. 'There is *nothing* going on between us!' she shouted, stormed past him and headed for her chambers.

'You cannot keep avoiding me, Menefer,' he called out after her, 'Sooner or later, you will be mine and Horemheb will not be there to shield you!'

***

Princess Neferneferure's farewell feast was being held in the Great Hall of the Palace. Most of the city's *mariannu*, the nobility, attended to pay their respects and express their good wishes to the princess and Prince Nijmat, who will soon be leaving for Babal. Horemheb, Lady Mutnedjmet and Menefer joined them.

Khay was watching from a little distance. When it seemed the Commander would be occupied for a while, he unobtrusively left the hall.

Tears kept welling up in Princess Nefer's eyes as she embraced her family and friends. She will most probably never see any of them again once she had left, and had mixed feelings, eager to start her new life, but sad to be leaving everything and everyone she knew and loved.

Mutnedjmet tried to lighten the mood, and enthusiastically extolled the merits of her new country. 'Do you realise, Nefer, you will be going to live in a fabled land of wondrous palaces. The city is right on the trade routes of all those incredible gems stones…and fabrics to swoon over.' She moved her hands in a floating gesture. 'Some so sheer and light, it is rumoured they are woven by spiders!'

'And, Your Highness,' Horemheb added, 'you must taste their amazing foodstuffs.' He looked about him and called a servant girl to bring them over, 'I have some sweet cakes, made in the fashion of those in Babel. Would you care to taste some?'

Nefer, having the honey-mouth of youth, eagerly tried the delicious looking balls. They were rolled and dipped in honey. She was greatly surprised by the taste. 'Yes, Commander, they are lovely.'

'Thus far, they had proved very popular with the guests,' Horemheb said, pleased. 'If word gets around, it would surely improve my friend, Sarem's business, greatly.'

Ramose, the new Vizier, escorted the Viceroy from Babal around the Great Hall. 'And here, Lord Yussuf, is part of Princess Neferneferure's dowry…a chariot, clad in electrum and inlaid with lapis lazuli…and over here—'

'Ah yes. Magnificent!' he then inspected a chest crammed with rhino horns. 'These are much prized in my country. They make excellent handles for daggers and scimitars.'

Ussar, the Viceroy's associate staggered over. He had a little too much to drink and was unsteady on his feet. 'Yussuf,' he slurred. 'You musht try this Egyptian emmer beer. It'sh much better than that made by the women in Babal.'

'Yes, Ussar, and also much more potent. Have something to eat as well, before you fall down.'

'But ish… (hic) …is it not the Egyptian custom to become completely intoxi… (hic) …toxicated?'

'That is true, Lord Yussuf,' Ramose laughed. 'It is a compliment to the host.'

A servant girl, carrying a platter of Horemheb's sweets, walked past and Ramose stopped her. 'You *must* try some of those little rolled titbits.'

Yussuf took one and tasted it. 'I am familiar with these, Lord Ramose. They are also made in my country, but these are quite delicious. There is another flavour that I cannot immediately identify. I must take some home to my wife, in Babel.'

'Commander Horemheb,' Ramose called out. 'Lord Yussuf is quite taken with your rolled sweetmeats. He would like to take some back.'

Horemheb walked over, smiling. 'Certainly. I am glad you like them and, it seems, so do many others.' He noticed the platter to be almost empty. 'I have more in my quarters. I will send someone to fetch them.'

'Oh, no, Commander. We do not wish to treat ourselves from your personal store.'

'It is no problem, Lord Yussuf, a friend will gladly keep me in good supply.' He turned and clapped his hands for the Royal Messenger who was standing close by, 'Sentu, Lord Yussuf would like some more of these treats. I have another platter in my quarters. They are on a table by my sleeping couch. Bring them here.' He turned back to the guests. Sentu bowed and left for Horemheb's residence.

Horemheb's quarters were in the military barracks. There were no guards about, as Khay had expected. There was no need. The rooms were very sparsely furnished with just the basic necessities. Nothing of value was kept there. After a short search, he found what he had been looking for…the tray with the sweet cakes he had seen Horemheb purchase.

He opened a small phial and dripped some greenish liquid on some of the sweets. 'Your honey-mouth will cost you dearly, Horemheb,' Khay remarked under his breath.

As he left the Commander's quarters, Sentu hurried past him. Khay appeared flushed and wide-eyed, but Sentu paid no heed to the scribe, fetched the tray and presently returned with the delicacies.

***

The Viceroy was conversing with Vizier Ramose, and Ussar, clasping yet another cup of emmer, stood swaying on his feet nearby. Horemheb approached them.

'Lord Yussuf, the delicacies have arrived.' Horemheb held out the tray. 'Regretfully, these are the last of my personal stock, but I can arrange for more to be made, if you wish. You said you wanted to take some back to your wife?'

Both Lord Yussuf and Ramose helped themselves to the sweets.

'Thank you, Commander. These taste better than those from home. Perhaps, my wife will be able to duplicate them, if she can identify that other elusive flavour.'

'I will have them for you, before you leave.'

Horemheb offered some to Ussar, but he declined. 'No thank you, but I *will* have another cup of your emmer,' he hiccupped again, 'that ish very good. In my country, if a person makesh bad beer, he or she is severely punished, sometimes compelled to drink only his, or her own brew for the resht of his life. What a pun—' he burped loudly and giggled. ''Scuse me…what a punishment!'

Suddenly, Ramose gagged.

'Lord Ramose, what ails you? You look quite ashen faced!' concerned, Yussuf took hold of the Vizier's shoulder.

Ramose started to gurgle then he collapsed. Horemheb rushed over and helped him to a couch, then beckoned for a servant. 'Quick! Summon the physician. Make haste!'

Pentu arrived shortly afterwards, then sniffed at the sweet Ramose had been eating.

'It is poison. Quick, get me some fresh milk.'

The milk was administered but Ramose did not improve.

'It is the Commander!' Ussar shouted, suddenly frightened into sobriety and pointed at Horemheb. 'He brought us those sweet cakes. He tried to assassinate the Viceroy…with poison!'

Yussuf turned angrily on his assistant.

'Ussar, you have brayed enough this night! Do not make yourself more of an ass than you already have. The sweets we had consumed earlier, were fine. It was those from Commander Horemheb's personal supply that had been tampered with.'

He turned to Horemheb. 'Commander,' Yussuf declared, sombre voiced, 'whoever poisoned them, wanted to harm *you*. Someone wants *you* dead!'

# Chapter Thirty-Three
## Aten Returns

The death of Vizier Ramose caused quite a stir, and when it was revealed that Commander Horemheb had been the target, worried Nefertiti. Was Horemheb's food poisoned by mistake? All the Royals were present at the feast. They could have been the target. Her fears, for attempts on Tutankhaten's life, were renewed. Security, tightened and all foods or drink to be consumed by Royals, were tasted. Tutankhaten was forbidden to leave *Per nesu* or the Palace without a heavy personal guard. Even Messu and the dwarfs were searched before they could approach the king.

The tampering with Horemheb's private foodstuffs, an attempt on his life, remained a mystery. Why would anyone want to kill the Commander? He had no enemies. Although strict with his troops, he was respected and well liked by the men. Sarem was a suspect. Did she have a grudge against him? After lengthy cross-questioning, the distressed lady was proven innocent.

Sentu came forward and mentioned his encounter with Khay, the scribe, around the barracks. Khay was summoned and questioned. There was no evidence against him, but he was detained while investigations continued. The scribe became agitated and concerned.

'Why am I being detained, Mahu? I have done nothing wrong,' Khay lamented. 'Why are you not investigating more serious crimes?'

'More serious?' Mahu, the chief of the Medjay, asked. 'What could be more serious?' He was suspicious of detainees who always try to blame others.

'I heard of a plot against the royal family. There are rumours of a usurper being trained to rule in the stead of the boy-king, and of a secret document.' By diverting the Medjay's attention away from himself, Khay assumed he would escape suspicion.

'Interesting,' Mahu answered. 'Tell me more.'

'I know nothing more. I've only heard of these rumours…'

***

A new vizier had to be appointed but Nefertiti could not decide between Usermontju, who had been secondary Vizier under Ramose, or General Nakhtmin.

'Nakhtmin!' Nefertiti pondered. She heard that name before, but where? 'Nakhtmin…' she repeated his name. 'It sounds familiar,' Nakhtmin, who had been stationed in the Lower Lands as Commander-in-Chief of the military, was summoned to Akhet Aten for her final decision.

Tutankhaten instantly took a liking to Nakhtmin. In the short time, he had been in *Per nesu*, he enthralled the boys with his tales of bravery and exciting adventures. Nefertiti was finally persuaded, on Tutankhaten's insistence, and Nakhtmin was appointed Vizier, and Horemheb, Commander-of the-Armies, was promoted to the higher rank of Commander-in-Chief.

Menefer also thought the name Nakhtmin sounded familiar. For days, she was trying to remember, and it nagged at her. Then it came to her! Was this not the same Nakhtmin, Lady Mutnedjmet had once been married to? She decided to go and ask her about it.

Mutnedjmet had a visitor. 'Forgive me Lady Mutny, I did not realise you had company.'

'Come in,' Mutnedjmet invited. 'Commander Horemheb was just leaving.'

'Yes, I must attend to my duties,' Horemheb stood up and started for the door. 'We will meet again, soon.'

Menefer nodded. 'I heard about that dreadful incident at the feast, Commander, had the culprit been captured?'

'No, not yet. We will continue to investigate, but in the end, he will be caught! Stay in peace, Lady Mutny, good day, Mistress Menefer.'

Once the two women were alone, Mutnedjmet said something that surprised Menefer. 'I think Horemheb is courting me!'

'The Commander?' Surprised, Menefer took a seat close to Lady Mutnedjmet.

'Yes. I went to find out about his well being after the poison attempt, and he said he was touched by my concern, then asked if he could return the visit. I was flattered and consented. I've always admired the man.'

'I am glad. He must have been very lonely since his wife's…uh, since the plague.'

Mutnedjmet nodded and leaned back, resting her arm on the armrest carved in the form of an antelope and idly caressed the carved horns on the head.

'Now, Menefer, you came to see me about something?'

'Uh…oh yes. I wanted to ask you about our new Vizier, Lord Nakhtmin…is he…?'

Mutnedjmet smiled. A fleeting hint of pain crossed her face and she turned her head away. After a long moment, she turned back to Menefer. 'Yes, it was Nakhtmin I had wed, all that time ago.'

She paused again. 'I have not seen him…or our children since…since we separated, but now we will most probably encounter each other often.' She shrugged. 'It will be awkward, but our former union is now in the past.'

Menefer shrugged and nodded. She knew what it would be like, to forget the past and go on with one's lives, as it was with her and Rakhmet. What has passed, should remain in the past.

*\*\*\**

Menefer was on her way to her quarters, when Horemheb called out to her. He had been waiting for her in the garden since his meeting with Mutnedjmet. He looked around furtively to make certain they would not be overheard, then led her to the high wall surrounding *Per nesu* at the far side of the garden.

'Menefer, I heard some interesting, but disturbing news…' Horemheb's voice was hushed. 'I want you to tell me the truth. It has come to my ears that…that your son, Messu is of Royal blood…'

'Khay!' Menefer burst out. 'Did he tell you?'

Surprised, Horemheb nodded. 'Yes.'

Fear suddenly surfaced in her wide eyes. She hesitated.

'You can tell me, Menefer. I will not reveal any of this. I will protect you and the boy as if you were my own family.'

Menefer dropped her eyes and nodded. 'Yes. Messu is my own son. His father is…was Smenkhare,' she looked up, 'What else did he tell you?'

'He tried to scare me…threatened to expose your secret with a document, a letter with Smenkhare's seal, and about a rebel plot to use your son to remove and replace Tutankhamun. That scribe is dangerous. He is in custody at the moment, suspected of the poisoning incident.'

'What am I to do?' Tears welled up in her eyes, making them glisten in the filtered sunlight coming through the trees. 'If he produces the letter, they will believe him about the plot and Messu would be in danger!'

Horemheb rubbed his chin thoughtfully for a moment, then, almost to himself, replied, 'He is using intimidation to get his way. It would not surprise me if he is capable of other criminal deeds. When I confronted him for threatening you, he threatened to make me pay dearly for interfering. It would not surprise me to learn *he* had indeed poisoned the sweet cakes.'

***

Menefer had been working on a clay likeness of Tutankhaten for Queen Nefertiti, and was nearing completion. It was one of several the queen had commissioned. The afternoon grew late and Menefer decided to suspend work for the day. She washed her clay-covered hands in a shallow bowl of water, then reached for a wet rag to cover the sculpture to keep it damp, when a familiar voice made her spin around.

'Greetings Menefer.'

Surprised, and a little peeved, she managed a half-hearted greeting. 'Rakhmet! Greetings. I heard you were back.' She wrung out the rag and draped it over her work.

'Yes. Permanently, I hope.'

'That's nice,' her voice was cold and aloof as she tucked the damp cloth carefully around the clay figure. 'Did you come here to renew our friendship?'

'No, Menefer. I am here officially…to investigate a disturbing matters.'

She did not look at him. 'I know nothing of the poison affair—if that's what you're—'

'No, not that. Queen Nefertiti fears for King Tutankhaten's safety. There is talk of the overthrow of the king.'

'Overthrow?' She wiped her hands dry, unaware of smudges on her face, where she had earlier brushed a lock of stray hair from her eyes. 'Why are you telling *me*? What has that to do with me?'

'Mahu, the Chief of the Medjay, asked me to investigate. You assisted in a previous plot. You helped expose the plot against Pharaoh and I thought you might assist again.'

'I will do what I can to help, but…where do I start?'

Rakhmet seated himself on a bench and lifted the cloth covering of the sculpture to have a look. 'Your position at court—your close contacts with officials—I was hoping you might hear something.'

She moved the sculpture out of the away. 'I will try, but where do I start?'

'There is, apparently, a letter, with Smenkhare's seal upon it.'

Menefer stiffened, then spun around staring at him. Blood drained from her face, she suddenly felt light-headed and grabbed the edge of the worktable for support.

'Menefer, are you all right? You look pale!' He reached out to steady her.

'I'm—I'm fine.' She managed to compose herself. 'I need to know more if I'm to help you.' She sat down on a bench opposite him and nervously fiddled with the edge of her tunic.

'In this—supposed document, Smenkhare claims to have a son. I must find out if there is such a document, and the names of the persons mentioned, at any cost.'

'What will you do then? I mean, when you find it?'

'If it's true, and the child is being groomed to replace the king, all those concerned will probably be tried for treason and put to the sword.'

'Kill a child?' Menefer responded, alarmed. 'That is—rather drastic!'

'Menefer, you know I am neither an Aten worshipper nor a child killer, but I am a professional soldier. As a *follower of His Majesty*, I am bound to protect him and what he stands for. I have sworn allegiance to the king and bound by my duties. This child could be a threat to the crown. If anyone is using this information to stir up rebellion and threatening the king, that person could be sent to the natron mines for life.'

'I see,' Menefer's voice was soft, almost a whisper. She had grown pale and was trembling. 'I will try and help—wherever I can.'

'Well, as I said, they are only rumours and too many ifs. It might lead to nought, but I would appreciate if you can find out what you can,' Rakhmet thanked her and left.

A moment later, Lady Mutnedjmet entered, beaming. 'I just saw Rakhmet leave. That is wonderful. Well, he made the first move—probably wants to continue your relationship again. Are you going to give him a second chance?' Mutnedjmet noticed her distress.

'Menefer! You look pale and you're trembling. What happened?'

'Oh Lady Mutny, I…we are in serious trouble.'

She quickly explained what Rakhmet had been ordered to do. 'He said this child might secretly be groomed to take the King's place and if found, he will be put to death!'

'What?' Mutnedjmet gasped. 'Dear Isis, that is unbelievable! Perhaps, I should talk to Rakhmet. Explain everything. I am sure he will understand.'

'No!' Menefer reacted, horrified. 'He once tracking down a rebel, his best friend, and his friend was executed. He is too dedicated in his duties. We cannot risk it. What can I do? I—I'm confused and scared. What if someone *is* secretly grooming Messu?'

'Horemheb told me he is aware of the situation. Perhaps he can help. In the meantime, do nothing foolish. Do not even mention anything to Messu—lest this secret instructor, if there is one, hears of it!'

\*\*\*

Horemheb pondered this new development for a while. 'What you told me sounds very serious. The scribe is behind this. He has done nothing illegal—yet, so I cannot take action. Confronting him will not help. He most probably has the document in safekeeping somewhere. Coercing him will only aggravate him and force him to act. Who knows what a rebel group is capable of, should that scroll fall into the wrong hands...' he let the sentence hang.

'What about Menefer and the child? What can we do to protect them?' Mutnedjmet sighed and spread her hands, concerned. 'If someone is grooming the boy, who could it be? We don't know whom to trust.'

'If the situation gets worse, I have a suggestion, but I don't know if you will agree to it,' Horemheb addressed Menefer.

The two women looked at him, expectantly.

'I will go and consult Lord Sethi. He is Messu's guardian and protector. Perhaps he can help.'

\*\*\*

'I can arrange for him to enter a military school,' Sethi suggested, 'he will then be under my protection.'

'That will not really protect him. He will still be within reach!' Mutnedjmet was still concerned.

'No, not here—well away from Akhet Aten. There is a very good military academy at Avaris. He will be safe there, much safer than anywhere in this nome.' Sethi glanced at Menefer who had not said anything yet. 'Menefer? What do you think?'

'Perhaps you are right,' she agreed. 'Messu will be excited at the idea. He had always wanted to be a soldier.'

'Good, but let us not act too hastily. All this might blow over soon.'

\*\*\*

Queen Nefertiti, already upset over the death of her Vizier, but angry at the news of the attempted murder of Horemheb, had Nakhmin and Mahu, the chief of the Medjay summoned.

'Mahu, word reached me that the Royal Scribe had been imprisoned in connection with this incident. Has he revealed anything yet?'

'No, Your Majesty. He claims no knowledge.'

'Have the scribe brought here. I want to hear what he has to say!' Nefertiti ordered.

'Your Majesty,' Mahu seemed uneasy. 'Uh—I have been instructed to await the return of Commander Horemheb. He is investigating the…'

Nefertiti jumped up angrily, clasping the armrests of her chair. 'Horemheb does not rule Egypt! Have the prisoner brought before me immediately!' She sat down again.

Once they were all present, including Horemheb, Khay was escorted into the Hall of Audience and the scribe immediately fell to his knees before the queen.

'Majesty, I am innocent!' he cried.

'Scibe, I was informed that you were seen leaving the barracks the night of the poisoning of Ramose, and you are suspect of the attempt to poison Commander Horemheb.' Nakhtmin folded his arms and glared at him.

Khay denied the accusations. 'Why would I need to harm Commander Horemheb?'

'The commander mentioned that you and he had "words", is this true?' Nakhtmin asked.

'Commander Horemheb was furious because I was courting the sculptress Menefer, Majesty,' he glanced slyly in Horemheb's direction. 'We had a slight altercation, yes, and it was probably misconstrued that I had a grudge against him.'

'Slight altercation, Scribe? Tell us all about it,' Nakhtmin demanded.

'He warned me to stay away from the lady Menefer, and threatened me with bodily harm, Lord.'

'And if you did not, what would he have done?'

'I am the injured party here, Lord. He threatened to *come after me,*' Khay grinned. 'Perhaps it is *I*, who should lay charges.'

'Charge Horemheb? One of the most powerful man in Egypt?'

'Lord. I have something he wants, and therefore I am a threat,' Khay was suddenly feeling in command and this gave him confidence and false bravado.

'Oh? And what might *that* be, Scribe?'

'A letter Lord, a scroll!'

Nefertiti sat up, suddenly very interested. She had heard the rumours, and the mention of the scroll was significant.

'Scroll?' She glared at him.

Suddenly, Khay realised he had revealed too much.

'It is nothing, Majesty, just a letter.'

'You threatened Commander Horemheb with a letter?'

Khay acknowledged in a meek voice. 'Yes Majesty, but I no longer have the document. It was taken from me by rebels…' he lied.

'Taken by rebels? How do you know they were rebels?' Nefertiti asked.

'I know some of them, Majesty. They have been spreading ill words against Aten and they knew I had this document, Majesty.'

'Why is this document so important?' she demanded.

'It is—' he looked about him, terrified. 'It is a letter, dictated by Pharaoh Smenkhare. It contains information that could harm the crown, Majesty.'

A murmur from the assembly spread around the chamber and Nefertiti gasped. 'Harm the Royal family? Smenkhare's letter can do that?'

'Yes, Majesty. The rebels heard of it and forced me to hand it over. They wanted to use it for their plans against the Aten, Majesty.'

'How did these rebels know you had such a letter?'

'I don't know, Majesty. I am a loyal subject and would never…'

'Why did you not report this matter?' Nefertiti interrupted.

'I feared for my life, Majesty. 'I know these people. They will stop at nothing to achieve their goals.'

'Oh? You know these people? How is it you know the rebels?'

Flustered, and his eyes showing white, Khay tried to untangle himself from his own lying words. 'I…I overheard men talking…on the boat, when I came from No-Am—uh—Waset, Majesty. I assumed they were radicals.'

'Will you be able to recognise them?'

'No, Majesty, I don't know any of them,' Khay wrung his sweaty hands and wiped perspiration from his forehead.

'But you said earlier, you know them, scribe!'

'I…I know *of* them, Majesty, not any of them, personally.'

Nefertiti tapped her fingers on the armrest. Her eyes narrowed. 'Mmm…I was also informed you might be involved in the poisoning of Vizier Ramose!'

Khay went pale and shook his head, slowly. 'I, involved, Majesty? I…I was not even present.'

'Sentu *saw* you leaving Commander Horemheb's quarters!' Nakhtmin approached Khay and poked his finger into his chest. 'What were you doing there?'

Khay broke down. He was not accustomed to being interrogated and could not think straight.

'Yes, yes. I was there. I only wanted to frighten Commander Horemheb. It had never been my intention to harm him—or anyone else.'

Nakhtmin saw Khay's distress, knew he was flustered and getting into a panic, so he pressed him harder.

'Now tell us again, about these rebels. You said you knew some of them. Name some!'

'I…I only know one name, lord. I think he was called Barak.'

'You first claimed you did not know these people, yet now you say one is named Barak? What information does the letter reveal that can cause harm?'

Khay looked about him fearfully. He had already given them vital information, had incriminated himself, and his lies had driven him into a corner. He became stubborn and refused to say any more.

'Mahu, take this man and persuade him to reveal more,' Nakhtmin ordered.

Khay prostrated him before the Queen, quivering. He knew of the methods used to persuade prisoners and begged for mercy.

Khay was taken to a chamber in the barracks. His wrists were tied behind his back and the rope passed through a metal ring fixed to the ceiling. Two Medjay took hold of the end of the rope and pulled, forcing his arms backwards and up. The pain was excruciating and Khay screamed.

'No! Please stop! I will tell all!'

A shaken Mahu revealed Khay's confession before the Queen.

'Smenkhare has son?' Nefertiti was stunned.

'Yes, Majesty, the son of the sculptress Menefer. He is King Smenkhare's son,' he exclaimed. 'This boy is the usurper to the throne.'

For a long moment, Nefertiti sat stunned, contemplating. *Smenkhare and Menefer had been seen together frequently*, she recalled. *They had been rather close and then Menefer's absence for nearly nine months afterwards, then her return just before the child was found...yes. It is all clear now.*

Nefertiti summoned Rakhmet. She knew he was fiercely loyal, and, as he and the sculptress had once been friends, he would know where to find her.

'Apprehend them both. Menefer and her son,'

Rakhmet was as stunned by the news as Nefertiti had been. He had no wish to cause either any harm.

'We need proof, Your Majesty!' Rakhmet, concerned and fearing for Menefer and Messu's safety, tried to stall. 'We have just the scribe's word.'

'Very well, find that document!' she ordered. 'If this proves to be true, they will both be charged with treason!'

# Chapter Thirty-Four
## Menefer Flees

'The queen had never been this harsh,' Horemheb said when he heard of Queen Nefertiti's orders.

'She's become paranoid lately,' Lady Mutnedjmet sighed. 'She trusts no one. She imagines an assassin lurking in every corner. The rumours of Tutankhaten being overthrown had truly disturbed her. Then she learnt that Menefer's son, is the illegitimate son of Smenkhare,' Mutnedjmet threw up her hands in despair. 'She wants all threats to the throne, removed.'

Horemheb placed his elbows on the armrest of the chair, and rested his chin on his laced his fingers, deep in thought. After a while, he straightened up.

'I can only suggest that Menefer and her son disappear, leave for another city and start a new life there.'

'Where will she be safe? How will she fend for herself and the boy, alone among strangers?'

Horemheb brightened. 'Lord Sethi suggested the boy to be sent to Avaris, in the Delta. He is from there, is he not? Perhaps, he has family there who could look after them both. Sethi is an honourable man and is fond of them both.'

Lord Sethi was asked to come and see them. Menefer, Horemheb and Lady Mutnedjmet, met him in the garden, where they could not be overheard.

'The boy is very special to me,' Lord Sethi said, after they explained the situation. 'The orders for Menefer's arrest, sounds very serious, so Her Majesty must certainly feel threatened.'

'She had even banned Lord Ay, our father, from *Per nesu,*' Lady Mutnedjmet replied. 'She distrusts him as well.'

Sethi turned to Menefer, 'As I mentioned before, the boy will be safe in Avaris, but you too, need to leave. As I suggested before, perhaps we should adopt him? My wife would be pleased, and I will take great care of him. Are you willing to have Messu fostered by someone else?'

Menefer did not welcome this idea before, but now she hesitated.

'You will not be losing a son. He will always be yours, but as my adopted son, the boy would be safe. I have been away for many years from Avaris, and there would be no questions asked. I was a Judge of high standing there. Avaris is in the *Blossom of the Nile,* and Messu would love hunting in the marshes. It is also much cooler there than Akhet Aten, lush and green. I miss it and would not mind going back. Akhet Aten had become rather...unstable. Will you consent?'

Menefer was still hesitant and Sethi continued.

'I could claim to be the boy's *real* father and can documents drawn up so there can be no dispute.'

This was a very big decision for Menefer. 'Lord Sethi, It is not so much the adoption that concerns me, I know it is for his safety, but, being separated from my son—'

'I might be able to help there,' Mutnedjmet interrupted. 'As Lord Sethi suggested, you too, must leave Akhet Aten. Menteret's parents live just upstream from Avaris—in a village called Djane.' She turned to Lord Sethi. 'Menteret is the High Priestess of Ipet-Isut, and assisted with Messu's birth. She knows everything, and her parents would love to have Menefer there.' She addressed Menefer again. 'Ever since Menteret left home, they had been complaining that the house seemed bare with just the two of them there.'

'Djane is but a short distance from Avaris, a mere two hours away by boat. I have been there a few times,' Horemheb added. 'You could visit each other often.'

Menefer was finally convinced. It seems the best solution. Lord Sethi was not that old, just fifteen years older than her and it would not be that improbably that he could have sired a son...and his wife would be pleased to have Messu in her care. She had already expressed that desire, before.

'You must make haste, Menefer. Do not pack. No one must see you with your belongings or they will become suspicious,' Horemheb advised. 'I will send them to you, later. The caravan of Prince Nijmat and Princess Neferneferure leaves at dawn on the morrow. I will arrange for you and Messu to accompany it.'

Later, Menefer explained the situation to Segi, her mute servant.

'I will send for you the moment I am settled,' Menefer promised. 'But for now, it must appear that we are still in the area. You must carry on with your duties as before.'

Segi was in tears, when she heard of Menefer's plans, but nodded. She hugged and kissed her and Messu, wiped her face and bravely went about her chores as if nothing was amiss.

***

'Can I go and see Tutankhaten first?' Messu asked, hopefully.

'No!' Horemheb warned. 'Talk to no one. Should anyone ask, you are going to the marketplace to shop, understand?'

'But my toys and sling and things—!' he looked disappointed.

'They will be sent to you later. Hurry!' Horemheb urged. He removed a bundle from a bag. 'You and Messu will be disguised as servants of Lord Yussuf. He is expecting you. Here, put these on.' He gave them the garments and two wigs to wear, wrapped in linen.

'But this is a *girl's* wig!' Messu held up the hairpiece, annoyed.

'Pretend you are playing a game, in disguise. From now, you *are* a girl. If anyone asks, you two are sisters, for a while anyway, until you are well clear of the fifteenth nome,' Horemheb instructed.

Dressed in wigs and the garments of those of Babal, Menefer and Messu managed to leave *Per nesu* without being recognised, and were escorted to Lord Nakht's house where they would stay overnight. Susmaat was waiting.

'My, don't you look pretty?' Susmaat, who had been told of the ploy, said, looking at Messu.

He quickly explained that they were disguised, and they were only playing a game.

The soldiers came to Menefer's quarters that very afternoon, burst into her bed chamber and started ransacking the place. One of the soldiers, Amnet, drew his sword and started jabbing it into cupboards and under the couches.

'Put your sword away, Amnet. We are not to harm either of the two.'

'She is the daughter of that carver of stone images, Haram. They had images of the forbidden ones in their workshops and she probably is also a follower. She and her son are a threat to the king and Aten. We took care of her family and I am not prepared to let her, or the boy escape!'

Segi, who had been hiding behind some drapes covering an alcove, inhaled sharply at the threat. Amnet spun around and pulled the covering away.

'Where is your Mistress?' Amnet approached her and grabbed her by the hair. Segi clawed at his face and her nails left three scratches. Furious, Amnet struck out, thrusting his sword upwards and into her ribcage. With a sobbing grunt, Segi staggered backwards, grabbed at the drapes, and pulled them down on top of herself as she crumbled into a corner.

'You fool!' Haram shouted. Why did you do that?'

'You are the fool,' Amnet spat at him. 'You called me by my name. She could identify us and would have told them what was said.'

'She could not speak, idiot. She was mute!'

***

The next morning, the caravan was ready for departure. Food and water had been loaded for the long journey north. It was the moment Nefertiti had been dreading. Her little Nefer was leaving, and she would probably never see her again. She wished she could keep her daughter close, but she knew this was not to be. Neferneferure was to marry and leave home, but it was necessary. Her daughter needed a husband and Egypt needed allies in Asia.

The day before and throughout the night Mother and daughter had spent a tearful time together. Little Nefer longed to see Menefer before her departure, but Nefertiti could not mention she had ordered the arrest of her and her son. The princess had been fond of them both and the queen had no wish to upset her daughter who was leaving Egypt forever.

All too soon, the time arrived for the parting. 'Go in peace, Little One, may your life be a long and happy one.' Nefertiti hugged and kissed the girl.

'Stay in peace, Mother. May all the troubles in Egypt fade away and happiness return.'

***

Well before dawn, Menefer and Messu had, as instructed, gone to join the caravan at the Eastern wall of the Great Temple outside the city. Horemheb was waiting for them and gave them final instructions. He wore a cloak as not to be recognised.

'Menefer, I have some bad news. Soldiers went searching for you,' he whispered, 'your servant, the Mute, had been killed.'

Stunned, Menefer gasped, but suppressed an outburst of grief as not to draw attention.

'Hurry!' Horemheb urged. 'They are still searching for you. The caravan is preparing to leave.'

One of the camel drivers came over and made the camel kneel. It had a hawdaj, a canopied seat wide enough for two and the driver beckoned for them to climb in.

'Are we going to ride on these strange animals?'

'Yes. Get on,' Horemheb ordered. 'Speak only to your driver. He had been instructed to care for you. Here is a pouch with silver and copper deben. This should be enough to sustain you for quite a while.'

'You will travel north through the desert, over the low lands to Bastet,' Horemheb explained, as they mounted the beast. 'Then the caravan will continue east, to the narrow land-bridge that connects Egypt with Aamtt and travel through the wilderness of Feka towards Assur, then on to Mitanni and Babal.'

'Are we going to Babal?' Messu asked, eagerly.

'No. I am only telling you this in the event someone should ask. It is to deceive anyone who might be listening. You will leave the caravan at Bastet where someone will meet you, and together you will travel to Djane. At Bastet, more travellers will join the caravan, and hopefully, in the confusion, no one will notice you are no longer with them.'

'What happens when we reach Djane?' Menefer asked.

The person who will meet you in Bastet will take you to the home of Sena and Khames. Lady Mutny had sent a speedy messenger ahead who will arrange everything. Lord Sethi will meet you in Djane, to take Messu to Avaris.'

With shouts and whistles from the men, clanking bells and groans from camels, the caravan started on its journey.

'You seemed to have thought of everything, Commander Horemheb,' Menefer said as they started to move.

'I hope so. I also paid passage for a woman and boy to travel to No-Amun by boat. That should send anyone on the wrong trail should anybody try and track you. Farewell. I wish you well.'

***

Presently, more guards arrived at Menefer's quarters to find them gone and their belongings intact. Then they discovered the body of the servant. She had most probably been killed by her mistress, to prevent her telling where the fugitives had gone. Slaves were not regarded as important, and her death was ignored.

Enquiries revealed that a mother and son had left for Upper Egypt that morning. Immediately, a chariot was dispatched to Zawty, the next port to the south, to intercept all boats and arrest and bring the fugitives back to Akhet Aten.

The caravan was also searched when it reached the border of the fifteenth nome, but no one with Menefer, or her son's description were found. Menefer and Messu's faces were veiled and no soldier would dare unveil an Eastern woman.

The caravan started its trek north again. After several more hours, Messu started to complain.

'When are we going to camp?'

'It is late afternoon. It will not be much longer.'

'Can't I walk? I'm tired of riding on this animal.' He squirmed, trying to make himself more comfortable.

'But you were so excited when we started?'

'Yes, but now my back hurts from the swaying.' He stretched and twisted his torso. 'I miss Segi. She always rubbed my back when it ached.'

'Lie back on the cushions. We have another two weeks of this, so you had better get used to it.' Menefer dared not tell him of the servant's fate.

They rode along in silence for a while, then Messu turned to his mother again. 'In school, Khay told me I am very important and will become powerful one day. What did he mean?'

'Khay? The scribe?'

'Yes. He said I will have my own palace and my very own army—and can even have my very own dwarfs!'

'Really? What else?'

'He said I would learn how to command and give orders. He said Aten was bad and Amun was good—but I thought Aten was good, Tutankhaten said he was.'

'Well, he will no longer teach you things like that. Soon you will go to a military school and learn to be a soldier.'

'I'll like that. I want to be a soldier when I grow up.'

Menefer heard that military school was not all that pleasant for young recruits and they were often beaten. Young men were warned against following this profession and she once tried to talk Messu out of it, but, as the son of Lord Sethi, he would escape the brutality. This comforted her.

By talking of the new adventure they are experiencing, and planning their future, it would make the journey seem shorter. It also took her mind off the recent death of poor Segi. She was so much more than a servant. Segi was a dear and loyal friend, and Menefer would miss her dearly. She would also miss the company of Lady Mutny. How will she cope without the cheerful conversations they used to enjoy, and Lady Mutny's welcome advice and assistance? Mutny was only about ten or fifteen years older than Menefer, but she was like a second mother to her.

Menefer sighed, and adjusted her wig. She too, hated wearing the wig as much as Messu did and longed for this uncomfortable journey to end. But it was necessary. Their lives depended on it. Then she thought of Little Nefer who still had many long weeks of travel before her and did not envy the princess her destiny, but with trouble once more brewing in Egypt, she should be must safer.

*** 

Bastet, the seat of the cat goddess Bast, was a busy trading centre. The caravan approached the caravanserai, on the eastern side of the city, close to the river. They would camp here for two days to obtain more supplies, and where other travellers would join them for the trip through the wilderness of Feka. The "Land of Turquoise" was notorious for bandits, and it was safer to travel in convoy, rather than attempt it alone.

They found a clearing large enough for the camp. The unpacking and tethering of the camels were, as usual, accompanied by groans and complaints from the animals.

An elderly man, thin, and with grey hair, approached the caravan leader who directed him to Lord Yussuf who then summoned Menefer and Messu. They walked over to where the two men were waiting.

'Mistress Menefer?' The elderly man enquired.

Menefer nodded. 'Yes.'

'You are to come with me.'

Menefer thanked Yussuf for his kindness for allowing her and her son to travel with them.

'It had been a pleasure to assist,' he replied.

The man beckoned her to follow him, turned and started walking towards the city. He then gave her a bulging fabric bag. 'You will need it later. Some of your garments—from Horemheb. The rest of your things are at the house.'

'Thank you, but what about our camel?' Menefer hesitated. 'Should I summon the caravan driver?'

'Everything had been taken care of,' Yussuf assured her and they took their leave. 'I bid you a pleasant journey and a joyous life,' he called out as they parted. 'Peace be with you.'

She and Messu followed their escort for some distance until they were out of sight of the caravan travellers. 'I am Khames,' he said. I could not introduce myself earlier, as your destination must remain secret. My name is well-known here in Bastet, and I did not wish anyone at the caravan to know you accompanied me. It is now safe for you and your son to change into your own garments.'

'Finally!' Menefer replied with relief. She was as eager as Messu to discard their disguises.

'It is very kind of you to meet us, Khames, but I had expected you to send someone younger. It is a lengthy journey for you to come all this for us, and must be very tiring.'

'I am a merchant and often travel to Bastet,' he explained. 'It is no trouble. I have several asses waiting at my usually lodgings in the city.'

In the city, they retrieved the animals and immediately set off on the final lap of their journey. Travelling by donkey was no more comfortable than by camel.

They reached Djane late that afternoon and Menefer and Messu were glad their trip was finally over. Sore and stiff, they alighted at a modest, but comfortable house. A mud-brick wall enclosed the dwelling and a delightful garden with many fruit trees and flowerbeds. An elderly, heavy-set woman emerged, wiping her hands on her skirt. She smiled broadly and Menefer immediately saw the resemblance between her and her daughter, Menteret, the High Priestess.

'Welcome Menefer, and you too, little one.' She approached and hugged them like family who had been away for some time. 'We received the news about your coming several days ago,' Menefer liked her immediately.

Sena ushered them inside. She showed Messu to his room. He was delighted to discover all his toys and his favourite sling had been brought from Akhet Aten. Sena tugged his Lock-of-youth playfully. 'I believe you will soon be going to a military school, young man?'

'Yes,' he replied. 'I'm going to be a soldier.'

'I hope we are not inconveniencing you in any way,' Menefer said.

'Of course not!' Sena explained. 'We have the rooms, why not use it! You are both welcome to stay with us for as long as you wish!' she turned and gestured. 'Now, Menefer, this way to your room.'

They made their way to the rear of the house. Messu tagging behind. He was in unfamiliar territory and wanted to know where his mother would be.

'I cannot understand why you did not travel by water,' Sena remarked. 'A boat trip would have been so much faster and more comfortable than riding on those swaying beasts.'

'Commander Horemheb thought it would be safer to travel through the desert,' Menefer explained.

'Oh, yes, of course. We were not told the whole story, but we are aware that you were in some kind of danger.'

They reached the room and Sena helped Menefer unpack her garments. She groaned softly as she stretched to hang a tunic on a wall-peg.

'Oh, please.' Menefer reached up and helped her. 'Let me do that.'

'It is no trouble,' she said. 'It had been lonely since Menteret and the other children left home. It pleases us greatly to have young people around again.'

Khames, who had seen to the asses, joined them.

'I'm going away, soon. I'm going to live with Lord Sethi,' Messu told him. 'I'm going to be his adopted son.'

'Yes, I am aware of that,' he laughed softly. 'Sethi is a greatly respected judge in Avaris. I am glad he is back with us.'

'Come,' Sena invited. 'You must be famished. I have made something special for you, and cakes,' they returned to the main chamber.

'Cakes! I love cakes!' Messu exclaimed.

'Khames is a merchant,' Sena told him. 'He travels around the country a lot, even to islands in the Great Green Sea. Many areas have local dishes, and whenever he finds one he likes, he learns the process for preparing them and teaches me. I have learnt to make many a great variety of dishes already.'

Menefer immediately thought of Sarem. 'I have a friend, called Sarem, who did the same thing. Perhaps Khames had encountered her at some time.'

'No—I do not know anyone by that name,' Khames pondered a moment. 'Oh, that reminds me, the courier who brought your belongings, also mentioned something about a scribe, the one who had apparently tried to harm you?'

'Oh—yes. Khay,' Menefer answered, her eyes wide with fear. 'Does he—does he know where we are?'

'No, no. Nothing like that. He had confessed to several crimes, the attempted poisoning of Commander Horemheb, an attempted kidnapping and his association with rebels. I was told he had been punished for his crimes—he had his head cut off.'

'His head!' Messu exclaimed, horrified. 'Yuck!'

'Khames!' Sena scolded. 'No gruesome news like that in front of the child!'

Khames shrugged and pulled a face, then quickly changed the subject. 'Messu, we have a goat and ducks in the yard. Would you like to go and feed them?' Excited, Messu agreed and was given a container with barley. He rushed outside where the birds were kept in pens with the goat tethered nearby.

Once Messu was out of earshot, Khames continued in a low voice. 'Apparently, at first, the scribe was to just have his nose cut off, but he angered Her Majesty by threatening her with a document that could "*break the back*" of the Royal dynasty. He told her he would hand it over only once his sentence is cancelled.'

'Yes,' Sena added. 'Then Queen Nefertiti replied "*Very well, I will cancel that sentence. We will not remove your nose, but your head, instead!*" He was executed soon afterwards.'

'That was not the end of it,' Khames added. 'Several rebels suffered the same fate. During an evening ceremony to the Sun, rioters openly denounced the Aten and demanded Nefertiti restore Amun. On commands from the queen, archers were ordered to shoot into the crowd. At least a hundred people were killed—innocent as well as guilty. Her Majesty seemed to have become very cruel, lately.'

***

As Akhenaten had done before, Nefertiti too, had banned the worship of Amun. Once again, those who disregarded the Royal ruling, were persecuted. Renewed outbreaks of violence occurred in Akhet Aten and angry mobs surrounded the palace, demanding the retraction of the queen's decrees. Even some of the soldiers have joined the rebels. Horemheb had been visiting his troops in Abedju, a city just north of No-Amun, when word reached him of the trouble.

'We must hurry back to Akhet Aten, Captain Sekhem,' Horemheb announced to one of his captains. 'The Royals are in real danger. We will take two loyal companies from here to restore order.'

'Are we now to fight our brothers, Commander?'

'It is our duty, Captain. The Royals must be protected.'

'Nefertiti? We did not pledge loyalty to her.'

'No, we fight to protect the king. He is our Pharaoh, our God. We have all pledged to protect him and, anyone opposing us, whether a brother soldier or not, will be removed—by force, if need be.'

'We stand beside you, Commander. We must protect the king! I will assemble two companies immediately,' Sekhem agreed. 'We march on Akhet Aten!'

# Chapter Thirty-Five
## Death of a Queen

Anxious to get to Akhet Aten, Horemheb and his troops sailed all that day and well after nightfall. The boats were guided only by moonlight shining on the water, and an occasional oil lamp flickering from inside a peasant's hut on the shore. They arrived late at night. Rebel forces had been attacking Royal soldiers and guards, and they had to be wary.

Lit torches illuminated the palace and they approached the city.

'There, Captain,' Horemheb pointed to the faint outline of a trading vessel, moored at the jetty, just visible against the docks. The men manoeuvred their crafts carefully to berth behind it, trying not to make too much noise. The troops disembarked and waited, silently, for their orders.

An alert guard noticed the movement of the men on the docks. 'Halt! Who goes there?'

Horemheb identified himself and the Gatekeeper apologised. 'I did not recognise you in the dark, Commander, or knew that you had returned.'

'I am back, as you can see.' Horemheb did not bother to elaborate. 'How are the Royals?'

'It is quiet now, Commander, but *Per nesu* is surrounded and rebels are roaming around the King's Way. They are demanding Queen Nefertiti relent her powers. They want an Amunist Pharaoh.'

'And the troops? Can they not disperse the rebels?'

'There are just a handful of loyal guards left. Most of the Medjay had deserted and joined the rebels. Captain Rakhmet and just a small battalion, about two hundred, are barricaded inside the walls.

'I have brought reinforcements. We will try and get the Royals to safety. Is there a way in?'

'Yes, Commander, through the Palace courtyard and across the bridge of the *Window of Appearance*.'

The gates to the courtyard were opened and troops silently entered into the Palace courtyard. Horemheb found Rakhmet in the *Hall of Audience* at *Per nesu*.

'I have brought two companies, five hundred men in all. We came as quickly as we could. Are the Royals safe?'

'For now, yes, Commander. Troops are stationed outside the main hall. Queen Nefertiti is in a bedchamber next to the old nursery. Pharaoh and the queen are in the bedchamber where Akhenaten used to sleep.'

'And Lady Mutnedjmet?' Horemheb was concerned for her safety as well. He had grown very fond of her.

'At the Northern Palace. She and Queen Nefertiti had a quarrel and…'

'Yes, I know. Send word to her. Tell Lady Mutnedjmet to dress in the garb of a soldier, then arrange the same for Queen Nefertiti and escort them to the boat.'

'Disguised as soldiers, Commander? Will that work?'

'Yes. It is dark and no one will scrutinise every soldier's face.' Horemheb knew this ploy had worked once before. Menefer and Messu had managed to escape in disguise, and he decided to try the strategy again.

'Yes, Commander,' Rakhmet sent a messenger to the Northern palace.

'We need to get Pharaoh and his queen to safety first, then we can worry about Queen Nefertiti.' Horemheb left and Rakhmet went to wake the young Royals.

Tutankhaten, roused from his slumber, yawned, sleepily.

'Forgive me for waking you at this late hour, Your Majesty, but we fear for your welfare. We have come to take you to safety.'

In the dim light of an oil lamp, Tutankhaten looked around. 'It is safe here, Rakhmet, safer than the North or South palaces.'

'No Majesty, I mean away from Akhet Aten. More rebels are arriving daily.'

'But they will recognise us the moment we leave,' Tutankhaten, still stubborn, objected.

'You will be in disguise, Majesty. We have brought soldier's garb for you to wear.'

Tutankhaten was immediately interested. He loved pretending to play soldiers.

'But, he is too young to be taken for a soldier,' Queen Senpa commented, 'and I can never be mistaken as a male.'

'We have cadets as young as His Majesty…and it is dark. No one will suspect you are female.'

Tutankhaten eagerly accepted the plan. He and Queen Ankhsenpaaten were dressed in the uniforms of cadets. Tutankhaten made fun of his queen when he saw her. 'You look funny, Senpa. Wearing a cap instead of a wig.'

'So do you, but you better remove that gold band around your *lock-of-youth*. A cadet will not be wearing anything that costly.'

Dressed as cadets, and accompanied by several others of the same age, they blended in quite easily. They then made their way to the landing place. Shortly, Lady Mutnedjmet arrived, also dressed in a like manner. Horemheb met them in the Palace courtyard, told them briefly of his plan and gave them last minute instructions.

'But, are you not coming with?' Lady Mutny asked, disappointed.

'No. The rebels know me too well. I will make my presence known at *Per nesu*, they will then assume I am still guarding Pharaoh.'

Rakhmet arrived and informed Horemheb that Queen Nefertiti refused to leave. 'We cannot force Her Majesty. There should be enough guards to protect her if she wishes to remain, but we must make haste and depart soon. By morning we must be well away from the city.'

'We? Are you to accompany us?' Lady Mutnedjmet asked.

'Yes. Come,' Rakhmet started towards the jetty.

Horemheb wished them a safe and speedy journey, then, alarmed, he saw a band of rebels on the jetty, curiously watching the activity on the pier.

'Quick!' He looked around and saw one of the gatekeepers with a bladder, a container for liquids, strapped around his waist. 'Hey you, soldiers, what have you there?'

The soldier paled visibly in the dark. Beer was not allowed while on duty.

'Wa…water, Commander!' he lied, but Horemheb knew soldiers better than that. Night duty in cold weather, was always more pleasant with something to warm their insides. He took the water bag, removed the stopper and sniffed.

'Emmer! I thought so.' He turned to the soldier, 'For once, I am glad you disobeyed the rules.'

The soldier sighed with relief.

Horemheb called out softly to Tutankhaten and Ankhsenpaaten.

'Quick, you need to drink a big mouthful,' he whispered. 'Both of you.'

Senpa took a big swallow, but Tutankhaten did not like the sour, watery porridge-like drink, but was urged to drink anyway. Grimacing, he managed to down a few mouthfuls.

'Now Your Majesty,' Horemheb whispered. 'You need to act drunk.'

'Where do you think you are going, Soldier?'

'I am Khem,' Mutnedjmet answered in her best deep voice. 'I am an officer from Zawty. We are taking home a friend who had a little too much to drink.'

'Why not let him sleep it off here?'

'He has been given leave to visit his family in Khmun, an hour's journey down river. They are expecting him.'

'This time of night?'

'Yes. It was urgent,' Mutnedjmet lied. 'His…mother is dying, and he needs to be there.'

'So why did he celebrate with emmer?' The rebel was still suspicious.

'Distress!' she answered. 'He was so overcome with grief, he, uh…drank too much… to dull his sorrow!' she cringed at her own feeble lie.

The rebel's attention was on Senpa and did not give Lady Mutny or Tutankhaten as second glance. He leant over and sniffed the "cadet's" breath.

'He will not get a good welcome home in that condition!' the rebel laughed. 'And you, boy, much too young to be drinking,' he said, gesturing towards Tutankhaten then waved them on. 'Get going!'

They boarded the vessels where Rakhmet had been waiting. The mooring ropes were loosed, the current caught the boat and it immediately started drifting down steam. Once they were clear of the city, they dispensed with their disguises, although Tutankhaten wished to continue wearing his uniform. Mutnedjmet asked Rakhmet, who had been talking to the pilot, where they were being taken.

'We are heading for Khmun, Lady Mutnedjmet. The cadets will disembark there but we will continue north, to the "Blossom of the Nile" and the city of On.'

'Blossom of the Nile?' Tutankhaten asked.

'The Delta. It is known as the "Blossom of the Nile" because it resembles a lotus bud. That is where the Nile split into many separate branches. The course of the river changes frequently in the Delta and often new channels are created. An experienced pilot is essential to guide the boat. Just south of the river's first branching, at the city of Mennufer, a few hours away, we will pick up such a pilot. Our destination is the city of On, on one of the eastern canals.'

'Why On?'

'We will be safe there, Your Majesty,' Mutnedjmet assured him. 'Aten is also worshipped there.'

'How long will we have to remain?' Tutankhaten was concerned. He had to leave his pet cheetah and the two dwarfs behind and will have nothing to entertain him.

'Hopefully, not long, Majesty,' Mutnedjmet promised. 'As soon as order is restored and Akhet Aten is, once again, safe, we will return.'

They did not know it then, but none of them would ever set foot in Akhet Aten again.

***

Tutankhaten gaped as they passed strange buildings to the west of them.

'Those are tombs of some of the early Pharaoh!' Senpa explained, pointing at some pyramids. 'I learnt about them… but I thought they were bigger.'

'These *are* smaller ones, Your Majesty. There are three across the river from *Ast-t Tem* that are many times bigger,' Rakhmet explained. 'They reach almost to the sky!'

'Ast-t Tem? Is that near On?'

'It *is* "On", Majesty, also known as Iunu, the City of the Sun, or City of Seers.'

'Is it alongside the Nile as well?' Tutankhaten was curious. They would remain there for some time and he wanted to know as much as he can about the place.

'No, Majesty. It is well inland, but there is a canal from the Nile to the city. We will travel up this waterway.'

***

The following day they arrived and, as it was very rare for a Pharaoh to visit the city. The people of On turned out in force to welcome King Tutankhaten, and the banks of the canal were lined with cheering crowds. At the jetty, a large delegation of dignitaries awaited the Royal party.

The boat was rowed alongside the rickety wooden landing place, and secured. Tutankhaten and his queen, still dressed in comfortable plain tunics and sandals for the journey, were helped off the ramp. Both felt very conscious of their simple outfits, compared to the magnificent, elaborately decorated garments of their hosts.

'Welcome, Your Royal Majesties.' A man stepped forward and bowed low, the crowd followed his action, 'I am Aa-mu, Vizier of Iunu.' He wore a short wig of tight curls, the traditional leopard skin cloak of office and carried a golden staff, topped with the head of Seth. He straightened and gestured about him.

'We had been expecting you, but I regret we had but little time to decorate the city in your honour.'

'We are pleased you can accommodate us on such short notice, Lord Aa-mu,' Tutankhaten replied. Queen Senpa gave her boy-husband a sideways glance and smiled. He had been rehearsing the speech all the way from Mennufer and delivered it flawlessly.

'We are honoured that you have chosen Iunu to be the dwelling place of Your Majesty's court. We have no palace, Majesties, but I would be honoured if you accept my house for your pleasure. It had been prepared for you.'

Tutankhaten accepted his offer graciously. 'We thank you, Lord Aa-mu. We are sure to be comfortable there.'

They escorted the Royal party to waiting chariots to transport them to the dwelling. Along the way, the people cast flowers in their path.

Amazed at the large number and diversity of blooms, Queen Ankhsenpaaten called over her shoulder. 'Where did all these flowers come from, Lord Aa-mu? I had never seen so many varieties.'

Lord Aa-mu waved his driver to steer closer to the Royal chariot and called back. 'Your Majesty, the climate here is much cooler and wetter than that of the South. We have extensive gardens, and many varieties of flowers and fruit trees, not found in Akhet Aten, are grown here.'

The house and it neighbouring areas was very much to the liking of Tutankhaten. Vast papyrus marshes, lush grassy plains and groves of palms surrounded them. The city was peaceful and no strict guards were needed to accompany him everywhere. After years of restrictions, close surveillance, and fear for his safety, he could now, finally, relax and explore without concern.

\*\*\*

Six months had passed since the king and queen had fled Akhet Aten. The violence in that city escalated and rebels vented their anger and frustration at the city buildings, obliterating the Royal names and images of the Disk. Many of the soldiers and Medjay had joined them. The remaining faithful were outnumbered, helpless and could do nothing. Horemheb tried his best to make peace, but, this time, his speeches fell on deaf ears. All the promises made to them, had been broken. The people felt betrayed and demanded the return of Amun. 'We will cease our aggression when Nefertiti revises her decrees,' they answered, but Nefertiti remained stubborn and determined.

Fearing assassination, she no longer attended the Ceremony of the Sun at the temple—in fact, there were no more ceremonies. It had become too dangerous to venture outside the palace walls without a strong guard. She decided to return the Northern Palace, away from the city and its dissidents. Her own palace, well away from the noise and the rabble, seemed much safer, and she had her own temple within the palace walls where she could worship.

Dressed in a battle uniform and body protection, wearing her familiar blue-green helmet, and surrounded by a squadron, five companies of ten chariots, with her half-brother, Seti, as master of the horse, and led by Commander Horemheb, she retreated to her own palace.

\*\*\*

270

From her balcony, Nefertiti watched the destruction of their once-proud city. With Horemheb out of the way, the rebels had broken into *Per nesu*. Dismayed, she looked on as peasants carried off much of the gilded wooden furniture. Even her gold-covered sleeping couch with its lioness-headed carvings, was loaded on a cart to grace some lucky peasant's hovel.

Fortunately, Horemheb had the forethought of salvaging King Tutankhaten and Queen Ankhsenpaaten's furniture and belongings, and had them shipped south, to the safety of the Malkata Palace in Waset.

Akhet Aten was now at the mercy of the rioting mob. Horemheb, who had returned to the Great Palace, watched helplessly as chaos reigned.

'The city is ailing, Pentu.'

'But this is one ailment I am unable to cure, Commander Horemheb,' the former physician, shook his head sadly.

'Lord Pentu. You must depart and join His Majesty in On. His future is in your hands, and you and Vizier Nakhtmin must guide him on the correct path. I will remain here and, hopefully, with loyal troops, restore order.'

'You too, ought to leave, Horemheb. The city is in ruins. There is nothing to protect any more. One cannot destroy what is already destroyed.'

Every building and temple associated with Aten had been plundered. The beautiful wall paintings by Thutmose, Ipuky and Nebaten were destroyed or defaced. Citizens of Akhet Aten left in droves, never to return. The city became derelict and the people of neighbouring villages scavenged the ruins. The beautiful tiled floor that once graced Queen Nefertiti's *Per nesu* quarters, had been removed and now covered the floor of the home of a *tche-t*, a peasant.

A merchant, who had shipped in blocks of costly *Aabu* stone for the construction of an elegant home, abandoned them, and fled. The stones were later cut up by farmers and used to make grinding stones for wheat.

The marketplace had been abandoned. Goats scavenged around deserted stalls and around the double row of sphinxes in the courtyard before the small temple.

The only signs of bustling activity were at the docks were ships arrived and departed continuously, transporting people and their possessions, away from Akhet Aten, to safer cities or villages to the north and south.

Just sixteen years after Akhenaten had made this his capital, the once splendid city of Akhet Aten, the City of the Sun that was to have lasted *forever and ever*, had become a pile of rubble and a virtual dwelling place for crows and vermin!

\*\*\*

Faithfully, Nefertiti kept making offerings to the Disk in her private temple. She alone attended the morning and evening prayers. Greatly distressed at the desertion of her family and the damage wrought by the people, she begged Aten to intervene. Every morning and every evening, she would beseech the god to curb the violence, to end the senseless destruction.

'Oh Mighty Aten, Oh shiny Disk, how could this have happened? Thou art the Giver of Light, the Giver of Life! Why could the people not see thy glorious wonders, but instead destroy wherever thy name appears? Hear my prayers, Oh Aten. Bring again, the peace and love we once enjoyed in thy city.'

She interrupted her prayer and turned as Ahmose entered the temple. He had once been Akhenaten's personal servant, but had since served Nefertiti.

'Ahmose, it pleases me to see you. Everyone else had deserted Aten. Have you come to join me in worship?'

He did not answer, but approached and stopped next to her.

She turned again towards the huge gilded carving of the Disk, then made a mental note to reward Ahmose later for his service to her and his devotion to Aten. She finished her prayer and looked up at him again, smiling. His expression was grim.

A cold fear gripped her heart and thoughts of Ay flashed through her mind. He had been furious when she had chosen Tutankhaten to rule instead him. Ay and her half-brother, Seti, would stop at nothing for their own gain. Tutankhaten had become an obstacle. Pharaoh had fled and she could not protect the boy-king from her father's ruthless ambition.

'What is it, Ahmose?' Alarmed, she stood up and searched his sullen features. 'Did something happen to Pharaoh Tutankhaten?'

He said not a word, but instead, reached for her throat. Startled, Nefertiti staggered back and bumped into the altar, scattering the fruit and flowers she had laid on it as an offering.

His strong hands encircled her slender neck and he squeezed. Nefertiti grabbed his wrists and tried to break his hold, but his grip was firm. Her eyes rolled back and her face reddened. Frantically, she clawed at his arms. The blue-green helmet, the one she had worn for her portrait bust, fell off her head and bounced on the decorative tiled floor. Her legs sagged, and Nefertiti crumpled to the floor. Only then, when her slack and lifeless arms dropped to her side, did Ahmose relaxed his grip. She fell forward, hitting her face on the floor and lay still, alongside her helmet.

Ahmose straightened up and looking down at Queen. Nefertiti. The *Beautiful Ones has Come*, was gone.

He glanced up at the image of the Disk. 'This is your doing, O Hated One!' he muttered, turned and left the temple.

***

Several days later, a vessel from Akhet Aten arrived in On. On board, were the Vizier Nakhtmin, Pentu the physician and Commander Horemheb, who had decided, after all, to accompany them. There was no longer any need for any of them to remain in the stricken city.

They went to see the king and queen.

'Your Majesties,' Nakhtmin was nervous as he faced the Royal couple. 'I have grave news from Akhet Aten.'

'My mother… has something happened to her?' concern showed on Senpa's face.

'Yes, Your Majesty. It is my regret to inform you, Queen Nefertiti is dead!'

Tutankhaten and Ankhsenpaaten were both shocked. Senpa felt faint and sat down, her fingertips lightly caressing her bowed head.

Pentu rushed over to assist her. 'Quick!' he demanded. 'Get me some fresh cow's milk and powdered carob. Stir a little honey in the mixture. It will help Her Majesty regain her strength.' A servant girl hurried off to prepare the medicine.

Lady Mutnedjmet had learnt of Horemheb's arrival and went to meet him. She entered the chamber and came face to face with Nakhtmin. Startled and shaken, like a child caught stealing honey-cakes, she did not know what to say to him.

'Greetings, Mutny,' he said, in a friendly, but emotionless voice. 'It has been a long time.'

'Why are you here?' She managed.

'I have some grave news. Your sister, Queen Nefertiti, had been killed!' His answer was blunt.

'How… how did she… how did it happen?' she asked anxiously.

'Mutny,' Horemheb went over and placed his hands on her shoulders. 'Do you really wish to know?'

'She is my sister, Horemheb. We were close, once. Yes. I want to know the truth.'

'She was assassinated. Strangled… in her private sanctuary.'

Mutnedjmet did not cry, but her eyes started to glisten and she turned away. 'Oh, how dreadful… thank you for telling me, Horemheb.'

'We *must* bring peace to the land, quickly!' Nakhtmin hurried off. 'I will seek out Lord Aa-mu. Together we might come up with a solution.'

***

After much debate, the two Viziers approached Pharaoh with their suggestion. The king immediately accepted their proposal. He had been thinking about it for some time and Senpa was in agreement. A feast day was arranged where their Majesties would proclaim a matter of great importance.

A dais had been constructed, high enough, for the king and queen, seated on their thrones, to be in full view of the public. The ceremony was being performed by the High Priest, Pawah of On, in full regalia of his office. Most of the people of On attended, but no one was sure what it was all about, only, as far as everyone was aware, an important announcement.

Immediately after he presented and paid tribute to the Royal couple, Pawah turned to the people and held up his arms for silence. 'People of Iunu, because of the great strife in Akhet Aten, we, of On, had given sanctuary to Their Majesties, and therefore, on behalf of Pharaoh, the title *"khenu—The Place where the King and his court reside"* has been bestowed upon our city.'

A huge cheer went up from the crowd and Pawah again had to silence them. 'The people have been discontent. The sole worship of Aten had brought nothing but sorrow upon the Two Lands. Their Majesties had, therefore, decided that the decrees be withdrawn. All people in Towy, the Two Lands, will be allowed to worship any gods of their own choosing…'

More cheering followed, and Pawah had to restore order once again. 'His Majesty has chosen, as the god of State, to be *Amun.* Therefore, as per the custom, Their Majesties' names will be changed accordingly. Henceforth Pharaoh is to be known as Tutankh*amun*, and the Queen will be called Ankhsen*amun*!' More cheers from the crowd immediately followed.

When silence and order was again restored, Pawah continued, 'As a tribute to our great city, and the kindness shown to him and his Great Royal Wife, by the people of On, His Majesty had also chosen to honour us by an additional title to his name. Hereafter he will be called—*Neb Kheperu Ra, Lord of On*.'

The cheering crowds went wild, and shouts of "Long live King Tutankhamun and Queen Ankhsenamun!" went up all over the city.

It was year four of the reign of Pharaoh. He was only thirteen years old and his queen, twenty-two!

# Chapter Thirty-Six
## Return to No-Amun

A year had passed since Tutankhamun and the Ankhsenamun fled Akhet Aten. The violence and discontent had ceased and the country, once again enjoyed peace. Commander Horemheb and Lady Mutnedjmet were married a few months earlier and Tutankhaten and Ankhsenamun were anxious to return to Akhet Aten.

The Vizier, Nakhtmin, was sent to Akhet Aten to assess the conditions there, and to determine how long it would take to restore the damage. Tutankhamun eagerly awaited the results and immediately upon his return, Nakhtmin requested an audience.

'When can we go back, Lord Nakhtmin?'

'Your Majesty, the news is not good. Akhet Aten has been destroyed. It is a city of the dead and would take as much effort to restore it, as to rebuild it. We can never return.'

Disappointed, Tutankhamun slumped onto a stool.

'The Malkata palace in No-Amun is being been prepared for Your Majesties. All your furnishings and personal items had already been taken there.'

'It will be good to see Merit again,' Senamun exclaimed. 'We have not seen one another since... Smenkhare's burial.'

'When can we leave?' Tutankhamun asked, anxious to be back.

'Not for at least four months, Majesty. There is still more to be done to make Your Majesty comfortable.'

'But I'm bored. There is not much of a garden here, the house is small...'

Ankhsenamun, now called *Senamun* for short, entered and overheard his complaint. 'We all have to make sacrifices, Tutankhamun. Why not go fowling again? You love hunting.'

'Yes, I do, but... this place belongs to someone else. I feel... unsettled here.'

'I agree, Majesty. You need to rule from your capital,' Horemheb acknowledged. 'No-Amun is the city of Amun and your people await you. We must have your court settled. You now have control of the Two Lands and would need a council, soon. A priest of Amun, from Mennufer—'

'Menefer? Is she here?' Senamun interrupted. She had not been paying much attention and only the one word caught her attention.

Horemheb smiled and corrected her, 'No, Majesty, *Mennufer*, the city of Ankh Towy. A priest from there would be arriving soon to instruct Your Majesties in the ways and worship of Amun,' he paused, 'Would Your Majesties prefer being tutored here, or at the temple?'

'Do you know where she is, Commander Horemheb?'

'It is a *he*, Majesty. A priest—'

'No, I mean Menefer... the sculptress—and her son Messu.'

Horemheb hesitated. Dare he reveal her hiding place? He was certain Tutankhamun had been aware of the threat to his throne.

'I know not, Your Majesty. They had both, just... vanished.'

Tutankhamun went over and patted Senamun's hand. 'I too, miss her. Perhaps one day...'

*\*\*\**

The Royal couple were schooled in the duties of Amun. It was very different from what they had been used to. Images of the god were all around them. They had to place offering before these images, and muttering incantations whenever they passed, and as the earthly representatives of the god, the Royal couple had to perform endless ceremonies. The months went by quickly and the time came for the Royal Court to move to No-Amun.

Merit was excited to see them again but her mood had become very melancholy. She mostly kept to herself and only rarely joined her sister and family. Queen Tiye, too, remained in her quarters. Unable to communicate or move around freely, she shunned company.

Once established in Malkata, and to show his gratitude and establish his beliefs in Amun, Tutankhaten immediately commissioned the construction of another temple. Peace reigned, but not everyone was content.

Lord Ay, demoted to Master of the Horse, was in command of the stables and Chariots at Malkata, but was greatly displeased with his position. He had been ranting and raving ever since leaving Akhet Aten.

'I was once *Fan bearer to the King's Right,* High Priest and Vizier,' he complained to Seti, his son. 'Look at me now! In command of *beasts*...overseeing the removal of animal manure!'

'It is still an honourable title and high office, Father,' Seti reminded him.

'*I* should have followed Smenkhare to the throne, not that...that son of a concubine!'

'He is the son of Akhenaten and has every right,' Seti had heard the same lament a hundred times already.

'I was the father of a *Queen*! Surely, that would entitle me to a higher office than *this*!' he waved his arms contemptuously about the stables. 'Tutankhamun is weak... sickly! Why did he not die as an infant?' Ay sagged visibly and shook his head slowly. 'He will not make a good ruler, Seti. Mark my words! He knows nothing of leadership.'

'Well, he is Pharaoh and we must serve him, and you are a priest of Amun. At least that has prestige!'

'Prestige! Bah! What do you know of prestige!' he pointed an accusing finger at his son. 'You have never experienced power, *real* power!'

Then two more tragedies befell the Royal family. Queen Merit, who had never recovered from Smenkhare's death, pined away and died in her sleep. A year later, Queen Tiye had another seizure of the laming sickness and she also died.

As the Eighth Year of the reign of Pharaoh approached, a grand parade had been planned. Seti, who had been giving some last minute instructions for the Royal procession, had the horses groomed and caparisoned, and the chariots bedecked in wreaths of flowers and ribbons. Tatty ostrich feather plumes on the head ornaments of the horses were replaced with newly dyed ones. All the brass fittings had been burnished. Everything was in readiness for the parade.

Seti was walking back to their house when he met up with Ay, who had just returned from the temple. Tye, Ay's wife, had prepared a sumptuous meal for them that evening. Famished, Ay looked forward to the meal, but a short distance from the house, they stopped and Ay looking about him furtively, making certain no one was within earshot.

'How would you like to have *real* power, my Son?'

'But I already have. I am in command of—'

'No, I mean, to be the most powerful man in the Two Lands?'

'But only Pharaoh has that power. There is no other more powerful.'

'That is exactly what I mean! Pharaoh is almost seventeen and there is still no heir to the throne. If something should happen to him—'

'He is still very young, father. Give them a few years. He is yet to—'

'Let me finish!' Ay shouted then lowered his voice again. 'If something should happen to the boy, *I* will be next to claim the throne, then, when my time comes to go West, *you*, as my heir, will be Pharaoh!'

'But Father, Tutankhamun had already declared Horemheb as *rpat,* crown prince, if he has no sons…'

'He is a commoner, Seti. Just because he married Mutnedjmet does not make him *that* royal. They could easily be… removed.'

Seti looked stunned. For a long moment, he did not answer but stared at his father incredulously. 'Are you saying what I think you are?'

'Removing an obstacle to achieve one's goal is not as difficult as you think. It has been done before…that drink I gave you to take to Akhenaten…'

'Father! You had me *poison* him? He was my friend!'

'And a hindrance. The whole country wanted him gone, including Nefertiti. We all benefited from his demise. Smenkhare's parting proved a little more difficult, but it was finally achieved.'

'But Smenkhare died from the plague…how can you—'

'Yes, it was risky, getting an infected person to his chamber, but by promising him I'd care for his family, it worked.'

'You committed *murder* for your own gain? And what did it get you? No where! A secondary priest in a dilapidated temple!'

Ay started walking again and Sethi followed. 'Not for long, my Son. With your help, it will not be long!'

***

Tutankhamun had been poring over some documents when Nakhtmin approached. 'Your Majesty, it is the middle of the month of Mesore, season of Shomu...'

'I am aware of the date, Lord Nakhtmin. Why tell me?'

'Majesty, in fifteen days it will be the month of Thoth, season of Akhet...the day of Upit.'

Tutankhamun uttered an expletive. 'The Upit festival! I had forgotten. Thank you for reminding me.'

'Also, Your Majesty, Lord Pentu had asked me to mediate for him. He wishes to be relieved of his post of Second Vizier. He wants to return to the task for which he had been trained...that of Physician.'

'Let him make the request in person. Thank you. You may go.' Nakhtmin hesitated.

'Is there anything else?'

'Yes Majesty, you had ruled for over eight years and as yet Your Majesty had not given instruction for the building of Your Majesty's... uh... House of Eternity. May I suggest Your Majesty consider having plans drawn up.'

'I know, I know. Everyone keeps reminding me of Smenkhare being buried in Tiye's abandoned tomb. I will see to it presently.' Tutankhaten waved a hand of dismissal, then looked at Nakhtmin, but the Vizier still did not make any moves to depart, 'Anything else?'

'Your Majesty, I have taken the liberty and arranged for Maya to consult with Your Majesty on the matter. He is waiting without.'

'Maya? The Royal Treasurer?'

'He is also the Overseer of *Per-neheh*, Majesty, the Royal tombs.' Tutankhamun sighed.

'Oh, very well. Send him in.'

\*\*\*

More time passed. Pentu, who had been restored as Court Physician, approached Tutankhamun.

'You wish to see me, Pentu?'

'Your Majesty...it is a delicate matter, but, Your Majesty needs an heir...and I have come to suggest...'

'Oh for the sake of Nut! There is plenty of time for that. I am but sixteen years old.'

'And a grown man, Majesty. One cannot delay such matters.'

'We have been trying, Pentu, without success. The Gods are not to be hurried, we need to be patience.'

'I have prepared some *meseh* for Your Majesty. To make Your Majesty strong and virile.'

'Oh, no, not the powdered, dried member of a crocodile again, Pentu. Is there no other way?'

'It is a well-known and proven potion, Your Majesty.'

'It has not worked on me, and I have taken it three times already.'

'May I then suggest Lord Nakhtmin, Your Highness?'

'What? Have him dried and powdered?' Tutankhamun laughed.

Pentu did not appreciate the joke and continued seriously. 'No, Your Majesty. He is a priest in the temple of Min. Perhaps an offering to the god of fertility may help?'

'I will think on it, Pentu. Now go!'

Tutankhamun talked it over with Ankhsenamun, then summoned the Vizier and explained the situation. Pentu's treatment had no effect and suggested Nakhtmin make offerings.

'I have done so, Majesty,' Nakhtmin explained. 'Pentu had already told me. I have been burning offerings in the temple for some time, but Min remains silent. May I suggest we approach Susmaat, the wife of Lord Nakht?'

'Susmaat? What can she do?' Senamun asked.

'She is now Tawi, Majesty,' he replied. 'The Chantress of Amun. Perhaps we can offer together, to both Min and Amun.'

The joint offerings were made which pleased the Royal couple. Several months later, to their delight, Queen Senamun discovered she was with child. The grateful Tutankhamun immediately ordered the building of yet another temple, dedicated to Min.

***

Lady Mutny had again joined the Order of Mut. She had to attend the frequent ceremonies at the temple, and like Tutankhamun, was occupied with duties, and could not keep the queen company all that often. Senamun was lonely and longed for Menefer's presence.

'I really miss her, Mutny. We were such very good friends.'

'What about the orders against her? Would she not be arrested should she and her son return?'

'My mother is dead, Mutny.' Senamun removed a lotus bud from a bowl, sniffed at it and walked over to the balcony. To the east, the river glittered and a sparkling wake followed a fishing craft as it drifted down the river.

'Her orders no longer apply. Anyway, I cannot believe Menefer would have tried to have her son replace Pharaoh.'

'Neither do I, but we need to find that document. It will always be a threat. The city is in ruins, so I guess the document is also lost.'

'Had all the vaults been searched? All the storage rooms in the magazines?'

'Yes. We found clay tablets, still in their baskets, but not that papyrus document.'

'Wait—I just remembered something!' Senamun turned from the balcony and gestured excitedly. 'Remember when Menefer uncovered those letters that convicted Lord Tutu?'

Mutnedjmet nodded, wondering what that had to do with Smenkhare's document.

'After the trial, she told us that Khay had a secret compartment. It was hidden at the back of one of the alcoves. Perhaps he had hidden this document there.'

'You knew of this all the time?'

'Yes, but I kept quiet,' Senamun confessed. 'I dared not mention it at that time. I did not want my best friend and her son condemned.'

They summoned Horemheb. He explained that all the vaults were thoroughly searched.

'There are...were several rows of mud-brick walls with niches built into them,' she explained, hopefully. 'The furthest wall, away from the doorway, also had these alcoves or niches. There is a secret chamber in one of them, the very last one at the bottom. It has, or had, a loose mud brick. This brick concealed a hidden compartment.'

'We will search again,' Horemheb promised. 'Perhaps this time, we will have more luck.'

Like all the other public building in Akhet Aten, they found the magazines complex in ruins. Horemheb had searchers climb all over the remains of walls and they tried to distinguish the vault from the rest of the rubble. Finally, after a search, they found a few remnants of walls with built-in niches. Horemheb was notified and he made his way to where the rear wall would have been. The wall had toppled, but a few sections were still intact, including the bottom row of alcoves, covered in broken mud bricks and sand. Baskets of clay tablets lay scattered all around, covered over by sand. He ordered people to dig to uncover the niches. The brick, covering the secret compartment, had broken. Behind it, barely visible under the sand and rubble, they found the secret compartment—and a papyrus scroll!

Whoever destroyed the building, either missed it, could not read, or they deemed its contents unimportant.

Horemheb straightened up and unrolled the scroll. It turned out to be the document he had sought, and yes, the rumours were true. In it, Smenkhare claimed Messu to be of his own loins. His son. The document was a request for Menefer and the boy to join him and his queen in No-Amun, and for her to become his secondary wife.

Horemheb signalled to the other soldiers that he had found the scroll and they returned to No-Amun.

\*\*\*

Tutankhamun and Senamun studied the scroll. Its implications were disturbing, but neither wanted Menefer or her son to be harmed. They had the document placed in a secure location.

Several months later, Queen Ankhsenamun gave birth to a stillborn daughter. Distressed, she wept. 'Will I never give birth to a healthy child, Tutankhamun? This is the second child I have lost. I am cursed.'

'No, do not say that. It is ill to think of such things. We will try again'

'What if...what if it never happens? What about your heir?'

'Think not of such things, Senpa. I have made Horemheb *rpat*. That should be enough.'

'I'm concerned about Ay,' Ankhsenamun looked troubled. 'He is craving to rule. If...when we have a son, *he* will of course take precedence, but if not...I was warned to be wary of Ay. He is ambitious and has his eyes on the throne. We cannot let that happen.'

Tutankhamun disliked Ay as well. 'I will give it some thought. There is always Nakhtmin. I could include him, but I'm not promising anything. I do not believe you are cursed. We are young. You will bear more children.'

'I was actually thinking of Menefer's son, Messu. He is of royal blood. Perhaps… Horemheb found the scroll, perhaps he could find them as well,' Senpa sighed. 'I will ask him the next time I see him. I miss Menefer. She was a good friend.'

***

Preparing another trip to *Djan Net,* Khames had been loading the asses when a chariot approached. Surprised, he watched as it drew up in front of his dwelling and a high-ranking officer alighted.

'Is this the house of Khames, the Merchant?'

'Yes, Lord,' Khames touched his forehead with the tips of his fingers and bowed in respect of this important man.

The driver dismounted and tied the reins to a gatepost. Respectful and apprehensive, Khames beckoned him inside.

'Please my Lord, be seated,' he invited.

The officer sat down. 'The sculptress, Menefer. Is she here?'

Sena entered and joined her husband who turned and looked at her, suddenly fearful.

'I… I don't know, Lord…why?' Menefer's whereabouts had been a secret, and he was wary.

The officer, noticing her reluctance, replied. 'She is in no danger. I am a friend.'

'She…she lives here, yes, Lord, but is away at the moment. She has a stall at the marketplace.'

'Please send for her,' the officer answered curtly. 'I will wait.'

Khames hurried to the market and told Menefer she had a visitor. They both returned to the house.

'Horemheb!' Menefer almost rushed over to hug him but restrained herself. She introduced Horemheb to her hosts and both bowed low in awe. Everyone had heard of the Great Commander Horemheb.

'It has been a long time,' Menefer said as they sat down. She was honoured, but curious why the Commander would pay her a visit.

After pleasantries, Horemheb then explained that he was passing through on military matters, and made a detour to tell her the news.

'Menefer, King Tutankhamun and Queen Ankhsenamun wish you to return to the Palace.'

'They want to see me?'

'Yes, the queen is very eager to have your company again. They directed me to scour the country while inspecting military stations.'

'It is a ruse!' Menefer exclaimed, alarmed. 'They consider me a threat!'

Sena and Khames looked at each other, bewildered. They knew Menefer and her son had to flee from Akhet Aten, but assumed they were in danger because of the violence and rioting. They had never been informed of the true reason.

281

'Why would you be a threat to them?' Sena asked.

As the rebellion had been crushed and the threat to the throne dissolved, Horemheb decided to inform them.

'I know you are honourable people, and I trust you will keep Menefer's secret, therefore I will tell you…Menefer's son, Messu, was believed to have been a threat to the throne,' Horemheb explained. 'He is the son of Pharaoh Smenkhare!'

'Oh!' Sena flung her hands up and clasped her cheeks. 'Oh my! That dear little boy a…a *prince*? I… I never suspected!'

Horemheb explained briefly. 'During the troubles in Ahet Aten, rebel forces had planned to groom Messu, to replace Tutankhamun, but the rebellion had been dissolved, Queen Nefertiti is dead. Tutankhamun is firmly on the throne and Messu is no longer a threat to him.'

'And they want me to return to the Palace?'

'Both of you. Messu as well!'

'Messu is in Lord Sethi's care…' Menefer stalled.

'I'm on my way to Avaris now, on military matters. I will speak with Lord Sethi, if you are willing. It is Messu's destiny, and this move will be to his benefit…Sethi will understand!'

Menefer hesitated and Horemheb put her at ease. 'Believe me, Menefer. I will never put you, nor your son, in any danger.'

***

Ay paced up and down in his quarters, troubled. Word had reached him, through an informant in the palace, that Messu and Menefer had been invited to Malkata. Because of Nefertiti's erstwhile warrant for the arrest of the boy and his mother, he had been made aware of Messu's blood-ties to Royalty. The boy could be proclaimed as Tutankhamun's heir and it concerned him greatly. Seti sat and watched his agitated father.

'Incompetence!' Ay shouted. You had more than one opportunity to rid us of Tutankhamun and you did nothing! As Pharaoh's chariot driver, you could easily have arranged an accident. Now this—other boy is arriving and my chances for the throne is becoming more distant.'

'I am not a murderer. Pharaoh and I have become friends and I cannot bring myself to do him any harm.'

'You are weak, Seti. It looks like I will have to do everything myself.'

'I did your evil deed for you the last time, remember! It was I who, unknowingly, took the poisoned food the Akhenaten! Were you also involved in the death of the child? Princess Ankhsenpaaten Ta Sherit?'

'No, that was a natural death. In any event, it was a girl-child and no threat. As for Akhenaten, yes. I am the one who put the stuff in the food. I knew you would not soil your hands and probably would have disposed of the meal had you known what it contained!'

'We must all enter the Hall of Judgement one day,' Seti reminded him. 'We will all face the Scales of Anubis, when the Feather of Ma-at is weighed against one's heart. I wish not to be devoured by Ammut.'

'Osiris will understand,' Ay justified his crimes. 'My actions had always been for the sake of Egypt!' he stopped and slapped his fly swat against his leg, thinking. 'If Pharaoh has no sons, this boy, Messu, will surely follow him to the throne and our claims would mean naught. We must not let this happen. If you do not have the ambition to rule some day, or the stomach to achieve our goal, then I will find someone else, but, Seti...' he turned on pointed a finger at his son. 'That boy and the King must be removed.'

He clenched his fist and shook it at the sky. 'I *will* rule, by Nut! One day, I *will* sit on the throne of Egypt!'

# Chapter Thirty-Seven
## Menefer's Sacrifice

*'The Land is sick. O Amun,*
*My prayers and sacrifices are not accepted.*
*The curse of my father rests heavily upon me.*
*I have rejected his decrees, O Amun,*
*I beseech thee to hear the hymn written for thee.*
*It is sung in all thy temples throughout the land in thy honour.*
*The sun of him that knew thee not, has set, O Amun,*
*But he that knoweth thee, he shineth.*
*The forecourt of him that assailed thee is in darkness*
*While the whole earth is in sunlight.*
*Whoso putteth thee in his heart, O Amun*
*Lo, his sun hath risen.*
*He that hath restoreth thy dwelling is here,*
*To make offerings to thee for thy reward.'*

Tutankhamun finished his prayer and placed offerings of a freshly slaughtered goat and a basket of the choicest fruit upon the altar, then, accompanied by the chanting of priestesses, the strumming of harps and shaking sistrums, he left the temple and returned to the palace.

He found Senamun in the common room. She had been studying the scroll. She smiled as he entered and he took a seat across from her.

'I have recited my prayed and made offerings,' he said, and shrugged. 'It is all in the hands of the gods, now.'

'You have done as much as you can. While you were away, I thought about Messu…if Menefer had wanted him to replace you, she would have done so, well before now. It has been almost nine years since your coronation!'

'You are right. We need not be concerned. Horemheb said Menefer was willing to return, but she is wary. She wants assurance no harm would befall her or her son. I will make her that promise. I will have a letter drawn up assuring her safety.'

After the scribe had written the document, Tutankhamun summoned Rakhmet, gave him the scroll and instructed him to escort the sculptress and her son to No-Amun.

\*\*\*

Menefer's day at the marketplace had been prosperous. It was the second to last day of summer, the twenty-ninth day of Athyr in the season of Akhet, the day of the Feast of Bastet. Menefer had prepared for this day and had fashioned about two hundred images of various sizes, of the cat goddess. Every single one had been sold and her purse was heavy. Khames, away on one of his trips, had left Sena at home, as always. When Menefer arrived back at the house, an unfamiliar chariot was tied up at the gatepost. It was neither that of Lord Sethi, nor Horemheb.

*Who could the visitor be?* She wondered. Then Sena came hurrying towards her. 'Menefer, you have a guest. He is awaiting you in the family gathering room,' Sena seemed nervous and apprehensive.

Menefer entered from the bright sun and it took a moment for her eyes to adjust to the dim interior, but she immediately recognised his voice.

'Menefer... You have not changed a bit, after all these years!'

A chill gripped her. Her immediate thoughts were of the orders he had once been given. 'Rakhmet! You will not lay one finger on my son!'

He walked over to her, reached out and tenderly took her by the shoulders. Menefer cringed and stepped back.

'I am not here to harm you...nor your son,' he dropped his arms. 'I would never have done so...even at the command of Queen Nefertiti.'

'How did you find me?' Menefer was still wary.

'Horemheb gave me the instructions.'

'Horemheb? He would *never* betray me!'

'No one betrayed you. The king and queen want your friendship, nothing more. I am to escort you.' Rakhmet reached out for Menefer's hand. 'You sound hostile, Menefer.'

She pulled her hand away. 'What do you expect? You are skilled in breaking vows,' her voice was cold. 'You returned to Akhet Aten with a *wife* in tow when we were still betrothed, then you had your best friend executed and then I heard you were seeking us to put my son to the sword!'

'Pardon me,' Sena interrupted. 'I am preparing *mesit*, will you join us for the meal, Captain? It is but a humble one, a stew, bread, goat-cheese and emmer.'

'Thank you, Sena. I am sure our...*guest*...is hungry,' Menefer answered coolly.

Rakhmet turned to Sena. 'Yes, that sounds good, thank you. Commander Horemheb told me you are a wonderful cook.'

Sena returned to the *rekhes*, the cooking place, and Rakhmet turned to Menefer again.

'Allow me to explain. I will start at the very beginning.' He again took her by the hand and escorted her, reluctantly, to the couch where they sat down. 'About Istar... I was alone in Buhen, far away from friends and family, then I received a letter saying that you were seeing that scribe, privately. You had been seen kissing him! I wrote, asking for an explanation, but you never answered.' He shrugged and spread his hands wide. 'What was I to think? All I heard was about your frequent meetings with this man.'

'That is not true,' she sounded upset. 'I sent many letters, and *mine* were never answered! Whoever told you about my meetings with Khay had... had misunderstood! It was a request...from Lord Nakht! It was an official matter.'

'Yes, regretfully, I learnt about that later, much too late. The other matter, about your son aspiring to claim the throne… I never believed you had such ambitions for him. Commander Horemheb explained everything. There is no longer a concern. Queen Nefertiti is dead.'

As they talked, everything started to become clear. They had both been under a dreadful misconception. Baka, the Commander of Buhen, eager for Rakhmet and Istar to become more than friends, and wanting a good marriage for his daughter, had most probably intercepted their letters. He had mentioned, several times, that no suitable husband was available in Lower Nubia.

All correspondence to or from Buhen had gone through his hands, and it would have been easy for any letters, not in agreement to his plans, to "disappear". The ones Rakhmet did receive, those unfavourable to Menefer, had all come from Djenna. Menefer had always known, that Djenna would stop at nothing for her own gains. She had wanted Rakhmet for herself and wrote those damning letters, but Djenna did not realise that, instead of returning him to her, she drove him into the arms of Istar.

Rakhmet should have expected nothing less from her, but at that time, he had been hurt, physically and emotionally, and could not think clearly. Istar's father had also used Rakhmet's loneliness and vulnerability to manipulated him, making him believe Menefer had been unfaithful, and then swayed him to marry his daughter.

Rakhmet and Menefer understood and forgave each other for their mutual distrust and misunderstandings. Since then, both had suffered great losses, endured great heartache and emotional anguish—Rakhmet, through the deaths of his wife and son, and Menefer, the loss of her family and Smenkhare.

Sena could not help but overhear much of the conversation. When she went to call them to the meal, she saw their tender embrace and her heart warmed to them both. She silently withdrew to the cooking place and she wept quietly with joy, by herself.

Some time later, Menefer peeked into the room and, beaming with happiness, told her about her and Rakhmet's reunion. Wiping her eyes, Sena hugged them both.

*** 

Menefer and Messu were taken to their quarters the moment they arrived at Malkata. Menefer had been organising her chambers, when Lady Mutnedjmet arrived. After affectionate greetings and lengthy exchanges of news and gossip, Lady Mutnedjmet told Menefer she had joined the priestesses at the temple of Amun. 'I am now a Chantress, a *Singer of Amun*,' Mutny explained proudly. 'I chant prayers during the Ceremonies of the Oracle.'

'Oracle?' Menefer showed immediate interest.

'Yes, Queen Senamun often consults *The Voice of the Oracle*, the priest who performs the ceremony. Why don't you accompany her? I am certain she would be glad to have your company.'

'Oh, yes. I would love to!' Menefer exclaimed.

As soon she and Messu were settled in, they went to see the king and queen and were welcomed like members of the family.

Messu and Tutankhamun immediately went into planning their next fowling hunt. Menefer was anxious to know about Smenkhare's letter, but did not know how to broach the subject. They had been discussing all that had occurred since they last met, when Queen Senamun reached into a decorated wooden box and handed Menefer a papyrus scroll.

'Here is something that should have been delivered to you a long time ago. It is yours now, to do with as you wish.'

Delighted, Menefer thanked her and took the document. It was the very first time she had seen the letter from Smenkhare, and her eyes filled with tears as she read it, then pressed the document to her bosom. It was like holding a part of him, once again—imagining she was embracing him. 'Thank you again, Your Majesties. It means much to me.'

***

Senamun was pleased Menefer could accompany her to consult the Oracle. Tutankhaten always scoffed at the seer's predictions, but she knew Menefer had faith in them. They were taken to the temple in carry-chairs.

Maids, carrying flowers, fruit and other offerings, followed close behind. People in the streets, accustomed to seeing the Royal Family visit the temple, bowed and touched their foreheads in respect.

At the temple gate, they were met by a number of priestesses dressed all in white, each with a lotus bud affixed to the front of their perfumed, braided-hair wigs. Lutes, drums, flutes and sistrums, accompanied their chanting.

A youthful-looking priest came forward and escorted the Queen inside. Menefer followed close behind. Entering from the brightness outside, the temple seemed dark, except for a few flickering oil lamps that illuminated the bases of the mighty columns.

'The altar is ready, Your Majesty.'

Lady Mutnedjmet stood with her back to the altar and faced a huge statue of Amun. She was chanting a hymn. The image of the god, standing with one leg before the other, as in a stride, wore a cylindrical crown. Two symbolic ostrich feathers, called *Sawaty,* rose from the back of the headpiece with a disk of the sun in front.

Perfume, of burning incense, permeated the hall, from braziers on either side of the statue.

Senamun's maids handed her the offerings which she placed, carefully, one by one, on the altar. The priestesses struck drums and rattled sistrums as each item was offered.

Wearing a cowl, the "Voice of the Oracle", emerged from the gloom.

The young priest, who had escorted Senamun and Menefer, turned and saluted him.

'Oh Seer of Tomorrow, give us the words we seek,' his voice was not yet that of a man, and broke on some words. The queen smiled, and glanced at Menefer, amused. Oblivious, the priest continued. 'Draw from the Infinite Realm of Nut, Goddess of the Sky… Shu, who blows his breath across the Land of Ra, who rides

287

his boat above the earth. They see all, hear all, know all. Reveal to our Brother the secrets we seek. Reveal to us thy words of wisdom.'

He turned to the queen. 'Speak, Majesty,' the young priest commanded. 'The Voice of the Oracle listens.'

'I wish to know the future of the Royal Family,' Senamun asked. 'Will there be an heir?'

'One deben of silver will answer all your questions,' the priest promised.

The queen deposited the silver on the altar. The *Voice of the Oracle*, raised his arms wide and answered in a strange voice. 'She who wears the crown will carry the seed of the crown, but he who wears not a crown will be mightier than those before.' He lowered his arms, turned and walked back into the gloom.

'The Oracle has spoken,' the young priest replied. 'There is no more!'

'But...but...?' Senamun stared after the departing Mystic, then turned, disappointed, to the young priest. 'It is so frustrating when he speaks in riddles!'

'The Oracle always speaks thus, Majesty. We can but try to interpret his words.'

As they were leaving the temple, Senamun explained, 'my interpretation is...I will bear a child. He is not yet wearing a crown, but will do so when he is full-grown, he will be a great king...a greater king than all those before!' Senamun's explanation seemed feasible. 'I will have a son, who will one day, be a mighty ruler of Egypt!'

'Yes, that sounds true, Majesty,' Menefer agreed, and remembering the prophesy she had once received. It had been just as vague.

\*\*\*

'Again, you did not eat your lettuce, Tutankhamun. What ails you?' Senamun lifted the platter.

'I told you. I do not like lettuce, Senamun!' He sat toying with his food, then pushed the plate away.

'But you *must* eat it,' Ankhsenamun insisted, and placed the platter before him again.

'I am not a hare. I don't eat leaves!' He pushed it away again.

'You know very well why you have to eat it.'

'Yes, yes.' Tutankhamun pouted like a stubborn child, 'It is to make me virile, to have sons. Everyone keeps telling me that. Lord Nakhtmin, Lady Mutnedjmet, Menefer...and you! Am I not virulent enough? Have I not proven it by siring a child?'

'Yes, but it was stillborn, Tutankhamun.' Her voice was tender and caring. She stood behind him and placed her hands on his shoulders. She spoke close to his ear. 'We need a strong, healthy child, one that will grow to adulthood. A son to carry your line.'

'And these leaves will do that?' He flicked the bowl with the back of his fingers.

Senamun straightened up, and asked in a more intimidating voice. 'Would you prefer a *meseh* potion?'

'No. The powdered member of a crocodile is…unpleasant, most distasteful,' he sighed deeply. 'Very well… I will eat the leaves, but am doing it under protest, and only if I have it with honey cakes or date bread to veil the taste.'

'I don't think all those honeyed things are good for you,' Ankhsenamun smiled patiently.

'Oh? Do you know any unwell bees?' Tutankhamun smiled slyly.

***

Messu and Tutankhamun both attended the Royal military school. Kings had always led their troops into battle and it was necessary to be well versed in battle devices and tactics. They both loved the mock battles and hunting. Both were skilled in using the bow and arrow, but Messu preferred using the curious Nubian bow Rakhmet had given him.

The time had come for Tutankhamun for advanced training, mastering the skills of spear, bow and arrow from a speeding chariot.

Messu was still too young for this exercise and complained bitterly. Now ten, he considered himself a man, but everyone still treated him like a boy. After much arguing and begging, Tutankhamun finally relented.

'Very well, but if you get hurt, Messu, do not blame anyone but yourself!' Tutankhamun warned.

'I will steady you with my arm, Young Master,' Ranefer, his chariot driver, suggested. 'Lest you to fall and hurt yourself.'

'No. I can balance quite well on my own, thank you!' Messu answered, miffed.

'The terrain could be rough. You had not had much experience there,' Ranefer insisted, but Messu was determined not to be coddled.

Also present was Hiknefer, Tutankhamun's boyhood school classmate. As a Nubian Prince, also had to learn the art of combat. His charioteer was one of Ranefer's best pupils. Seti, the Overseer of the Royal stables, was driving Pharaoh's chariot.

For their exercise, instead of stationary targets, Horemheb had arranged a hunt. Gazelle frequented the scrubby desert east of No-Amun. Small patches of acacia and tamarisk grew along the banks of wadis, the dry river courses originating in the eastern mountain ranges.

Several experienced officers, driving their own chariots, accompanied the cadets. The officers had no need for drivers. They will not join in the hunt themselves, but were merely to protect, observe and instruct the young soldier.

The party had been travelling east for about two hours when a small herd of antelope was spotted. The animals were on a ridge, warily watching the approaching invaders. They pricked their ears, swivelling them forward and side-to-side to pick up any suspicious sounds.

Horemheb waved to the charioteers to spread out and move in upon them downwind in a wide arc. They slowed their pace and cautiously approached the herd, keeping the cover of the trees between them and the animals.

Seti and Tutankhamun were on the southern flank of the arc, Messu and Ranefer on the north and Hiknefer in the centre. The chariots approached with caution, the half circle was closing in on the nervous herd and had almost surrounded the herd.

Then, on a signal from Seti, they charged. The gazelle scattered in all directions, some heading for the open spaces between the chariots. This was what they had anticipated and aimed their bows and arrows.

Suddenly and without warning, a lioness charged out of a small scrubby bush. She had been stalking the antelope and the charge of chariots had flushed her from her hiding. She fled, taking a course between Hiknefer and Tutankhamun's vehicles.

Seti had swung his chariot to his left in pursuit of some gazelle, inadvertently crossing almost directly, the path of the fleeing lioness. The wheel of the chariot hit a ridge of sand and both riders were flung upwards and forwards. Sethi held onto the reigns and landed back on the platform, but Tutankhamun, holding the bow and arrow, went flying over the rail and landed heavily in the sand. The impact winded him. Frightened by the sudden appearance of the lioness, Seti's horses veered away to the right. Seti did not make a great effort in halting their progress. This accident, exactly what his father had wanted, was not of his doing, but should anything had happened to the king, he would be blameless, he thought, as he tried to reign in the horses.

Hiknefer, seeing Tutankhamun fall, directed his charioteer towards the King. The lioness, confused by the thundering horses on either side, first weaved back and forth, then darted away from Hiknefer's approaching chariot, and heading directly towards the young king. Tutankhamun raised himself on an elbow and stared in horror at the fast approaching lioness.

Hiknefer levelled his drawn bow, but did not dare to shoot as he might hit his friend, now almost directly in front of him. The lioness, also badly frightened, saw the prostrate man in front of her, and leaped.

Tutankhamun fell down, clasping his arms over his head for protection. The lioness sailed over him and disappeared into the shrubbery.

Hiknefer leaped down and helped his friend up into a sitting position. 'That was too close, Your Majesty!'

'Yes.' Tutankhamun, his face pale from the excitement and breathing rapidly, grinned. 'But it was thrilling, was it not?'

Everyone at court heard of the incident later, and Tutankhamun, retelling of the event, recalled the childhood stories he used to listen to, about the brave lion hunter. 'I could have killed the lion,' he boasted.

'Or, could have been the *lion's* kill!' Ankhsenamun muttered under her breath.

*** 

In their own quarters, a pleased Ay confronted Seti. 'That was a very good effort!' Lord Ay clapped his hand on his son's shoulder. 'It almost worked. Almost the perfect accident.'

Seti did not tell him it was not planned, that it *had* been an accident, but, instead, just nodded and smiled.

'Better luck next time, my son,' Ay assured him. 'Another opportunity will yet arise.'

Menefer had been as disturbed about the incident as Queen Ankhsenamun. 'Dreadful, Your Majesty. It could have been disastrous, not just for the Royal Family, but for the whole of Egypt. What if…what if…'

'Do not dwell on *what ifs* Menefer. We must make certain such a thing never happens again, but the king has resolved to learn all about warfare and there is nothing we can do about it. It is his duty, he said, to lead his army when war does break out.'

'War? But, during the conflicts in the Eastern countries, neither Pharaoh Akhenaten nor Smenkhare deeded to—'

'Tutankhamun is determined not to remain here. If the trouble escalates, he is steadfast to be there, to lead an army…but let us not talk of conflict, I have better news,' Ankhsenamun grabbed Menefer by her shoulders. 'Guess what? I am again with child!'

'What?' Menefer gasped, surprised.

'Your suggestions worked, Menefer. Remember when you told me to find a couple with a large family?'

Menefer nodded.

'I learnt of just such a couple. Paye, the Overseer of the Royal chambers and his wife Repyt have been blessed six times by the gods. They have three sons and three daughters. We borrowed their head-rests, as you directed, and slept on them for six weeks.'

'It is a well-known solution, Your Majesty. I am glad it worked. Was His Majesty pleased?'

'I have not yet told him. I was about to, when we received the news of his accident. It distressed me so much, I had completely forgotten, but will tell him tonight. Your advice made it possible.'

Menefer was just as excited by the news as the queen. With another child on the way, and hopefully, a boy child, that nagging, self-incrimination she had felt, would disappear. She had seen the queen watching Messu, at play or when he and the young king was going hunting in the reeds, and she was aware of the queen's longing to have a son of her own. Messu's presence would always be considered a disquiet.

If only there was a way she could prove that her fidelity, that her son would not be a threat. Then Menefer made a decision. There was a way. It would set her own mind at ease, and dispel this mistrust forever.

***

Tutankhamun was overjoyed with the news. 'Let us pray that, this time, a healthy child will be born.'

'A healthy *boy*-child,' Senamun added. We must give offerings to all the gods. At the altars of both Amun, as well as Min.'

'And I too will make offerings!' Menefer said. That evening, she accompanied the Royal Family to the temple of Amun. After chanting some prayers, the king and queen placed their offerings on the altar.

It was Menefer's turn, and both Tutankhamun and Ankhsenamun looked on curiously, as she stepped forward. She did not carry anything to offer.

'Oh Amun, I offer you my most prized possession. On behalf of Their Majesties, I wish you to accept this meagre gift. Grant them their dearest wish. Grant them the healthy son they both crave, Oh Great One.'

She reached inside a fold of her tunic, removed a scroll of papyrus, and placed in on the flames.

As the papyrus caught fire, it unrolled, the queen recognised it and cried out. 'No, Menefer! Not the document!'

'It is done, Your Majesty. Let the flames consume the testimony that binds my son to the Royal House. He will henceforth be known only as the son of Lord Sethi. With this sacrifice, may your wishes come true, and prove to Your Majesties that neither I, nor my son, have designs on the throne. May I, with this act, prove my fealty. Messu and I are both loyal subjects to Your Majesties and will remain so. Always.'

Ankhsenamun hugged Menefer tearfully. 'That was an unnecessary, but noble thing you did, Menefer. I…*we* appreciate your gesture.'

'We had always believed you to be loyal and true,' Tutankhamun added. 'Now, because of your great sacrifice, beyond any doubt, you have proved it. We will never believe any insincere words against you. You and Messu will forever be our truest friends and subjects.'

# Chapter Thirty-Eight
## War

Tutankhamun had been summoned to the council chambers for an urgent meeting and had to cancel his fowling trip to the marshes. Messu was disappointed, but realised the king had more serious issues. The trouble on the eastern borders of Djahi had escalated. Simyra and Autha were now in the hands of the enemy, but Amurra, who had sought to break free from Egyptian rule, had not succeeded and had renewed its onslaught in Djahi.

Horemheb, troubled, addressed the matter. 'Your Majesty.' He waved an arm in the general direction of the Middle East. 'The Semitic people of Djahi, the *Habiru*, had, up to now, been neutral, but had now joined the enemy. The Hittites, if not actually assisting, are backing them!'

'Horemheb is right,' Nakhtmin added. 'Khatti had had designs on Mitanni and Mesopotamia for a long time. Mitanni is the buffer between the enemy and their target. Shubbiluliuma covets the land between the Euphrates and Tigris rivers.'

'Mitanni has been linked to Egypt by the provinces of Djahi. Now this link is broken and Mitanni is cut off. The Hittites can overrun them and advance on Babal,' Horemheb explained. 'During the last thirteen years of his reign, Pharaoh Akhenaten had ignored Djahi's calls for help, and they had now defected. If we do not act now, Egypt will lose more of its allies, and should they also join the enemy, we are lost! All our dialogue for reconciliation had gone unheeded.'

Tutankhamun was concerned. The reluctance of both Akhenaten and Smenkhare to act, had left Egypt in a sorry state. 'The Egyptian armies had been idle since the rule of the third Amenhotep, and their lack of training concerns me.'

'Once, the sight of an Egyptian army would have sent the kings of Amurra fleeing,' Nakhtmin remarked, 'but now the sons of Abdeshirta had come to despise us and had grown bolder.'

'What can we do?' Tutankhamun asked.

'It is time for Egypt to show its teeth, Your Majesty. We *must* act. And soon! Too long have we tarried. The enemy is getting aggressive and growing stronger. We must strike, and strike hard!'

'Yes, I agree, Commander Horemheb.'

'We cannot afford a war now, Majesty,' Maya, the Royal Treasurer, interjected. 'The coffers are empty. Our building projects and all the restorations had eaten into it…and our soldiers are unprepared!'

'We cannot afford *not* to, Lord Maya!' Horemheb responded. 'The longer we wait, the more we stand to lose! Have we not lost enough of our Asian territories?

No! I say we attack them now. Take them by surprise and drive them back. Force them into submission and regain the lands we have lost!'

'I agree.' Tutankhamun looked at Maya. 'We must do this. We will surprise them. They will not expect it.'

'But, Your Majesty, you are but a mere—'

'A mere boy, a cripple? Is that what you are saying? I am your king, Lord Maya, and I will lead the troops,' he made a sweeping gesture, 'I will fight alongside them!'

\*\*\*

'Oh Menefer, I am frightened…all this talk of war!'

They had come to the lake pavilion to relax. Two handmaidens were strumming lutes, but Senamun was anything but soothed by the music. She paced back and fro across the raised tiled floor.

'Is it that serious, Majesty?'

'Yes. You once told me things always happen in threes. Tutankhamun already had two chariot accidents… What if he should have a third? He is not very steady on his legs, as you know, and often uses a staff for walking.' The queen gives a helpless shrug.

'The king wants to take up arms himself. He plans to lead his armies into battle, but his only experience had been that one hunt…and he was almost killed by a lion. The Asians are experienced fighters and are excellent bowmen. They have been fighting these wars since before I was born.'

'But what about our battles in Nubia and Kush?' Menefer recalled Rakhmet being sent there to quell unrest.

'Scuffles. Against barbarians, primitive peoples. People who had never encountered a well-trained, organised army. This is something must bigger, much more serious.'

'What other options have we, Majesty?'

Ankhsenamun did not answer Menefer's question. She watched as some egrets circled the papyrus swamp, calling out in raucous croaks as they landed. On the lake, the two pleasure boats that had once glided across the placid waters were gone. They had both been buried with their owners, to enable Queen Tiye and Pharaoh Smenkhare to enjoy them in the afterlife. Now only a reed skiff, fishing for the palace table, was using the Royal Pleasure Lake. The pleasant day had been marred by the looming war.

'Why do men always want bloodshed?' The queen sighed. 'Greed and power…it seems they hunger for that, and the women and children suffer for it.' The queen's condition was just beginning to show, and she absent-mindedly caressed her growing belly.

Menefer, about to make a comment, saw Messu coming down the path and called out. 'Messu, what brings you here?'

He approached the pavilion, bowed and saluted the queen. Ankhsenamun acknowledged with a nod and a smile.

'Mother, guess what! I am to join the troops, with Commander Horemheb!'

Menefer suddenly sat erect, clasping the edges of the couch with both hands. 'You mean, go into war? No!'

Messu frowned, his hands on his hips. 'Why not?'

'You are much too young!'

'I am *almost eleven*, mother. Tutankh…' he glanced at the queen. 'I mean, His Majesty, King Tutankhamun, was only *nine* when he married and—'

'Marriage and war are two different things, Messu. I will go and talk to Commander Horemheb!' Menefer got up. 'I will not have you trotting off to war!'

Messu rolled his eyes skyward, bowed to the queen, and scowling, turned and left.

***

Menefer and the queen had been busying themselves stitching infant garments. The birth was still many months away but they decided, by keeping busy, to keep their minds off the coming conflict.

Horemheb had been invited to join them at his earliest convenience, and he arrived, covered in dust. He tried to brush it off, but his tunic, damp with perspiration, caused the dust to remained put.

'Your Majesty!' He bowed. 'I came as quickly as I could. You wished to see me?'

'There was no need to hasten, Commander. It was not urgent. Mistress Menefer wanted to talk to you.'

Horemheb turned to Menefer, slightly annoyed at being called away from his troops for something trivial.

Menefer put her stitching down. 'Horemheb, Messu said he was to join your troops in battle. Is that true?'

'It would be a beneficial exercise for him. He is very eager to become a good soldier.'

'But he is still too young. Why the request for him to join?'

'He asked *me*!' Horemheb slapped his hand to his chest. 'I merely consented.'

'But going to war? Messu knows nothing of battles! Men get killed…cannot he learn to fight without going into war?' She looked pleadingly at the Commander.

'One cannot learn to swim before going into water, Menefer—'

'I agree with Menefer,' Queen Ankhsenamun lowered her stitching and looked at Horemheb. 'Even His Majesty has no experience. It will take years of training to ready them—'

'Your Majesty, we do not have years.'

'But, to send an untrained army into battle…that is suicide!'

Horemheb took a deep breath, trying to sound patient.

'Your Majesty, the Asians too, think we are untrained and unskilled. They will not expect an attack. We hope to surprise them by striking first, and without warning.'

'But…' Ankhsenamun was still concerned. 'The king is still a beardless youth, and Messu has barely reached manhood. Are we going into battle using children as soldiers?'

'Neither His Majesty, nor Messu will be in any danger, Majesty. His Majesty will be under my protection all the time. I will personally see he does not reach the front lines. Seti will be his charioteer and is the best, and Messu will be lucky if he even gets to *see* the battle. He will be the responsibility of his father, Lord Sethi, and as a cadet, he will remain in the camp. He will be assigned to preparing uniforms, laying out weapons and help treat the wounded.'

'But have we not physicians to do that?' Ankhsenamun asked.

'They will treat the badly wounded, Majesty. Lesser wounds will be seen to, and bound by cadets.'

\*\*\*

Horemheb once again sought audience with the king, who then summoned other councillors and military heads to attend. 'Your Majesty, the Asian armies are on the move,' he declared. 'We had alerted all the armies from the *sepatu* of the Two Lands, and they are ready. I need your approval to announce our march north.'

'What about civilian conscripts? Or do we have enough voluntary soldiers?'

'No, Majesty,' Rakhmet answered. 'We need many more. All males between fifteen and sixty had been called upon to serve. Young cadets, from age ten, will be used in the camps for menial duties. Only the infirm will be excused, and those whose services are needed here, to keep peace during the armies' absence.'

'Very well. When do we march?' Tutankhamun answered.

'In three weeks, Majesty. All craftsmen had been kept busy the last months, making weapons, but we need many more arrows and spears.'

That night sleep would not come to Tutankhamun. He tossed and turned on his sleeping couch until well past the midnight hour. Ankhsenamun, who had noticed his restlessness, rose and came to him.

'Are you unwell, my lord?' She leaned over and touched his shoulder.

'I am fine. It is just the excitement that is keeping me awake. Go back to sleep.'

'I understand. It is a great undertaking.'

'It might be many months before I see you again,' he turned toward her.

She stroked his face then bent over and kissed him. 'I will be waiting, no matter how long it takes. I just pray the gods will smile upon us and bring you back safely.'

'And victory…' He looked up at the decorated ceiling. 'We need to be victorious.'

\*\*\*

For several days, boats had been travelling north past No-Amun, loaded with troops, private armies and mercenaries. They had come from Pu Khent-min, Yebu, Kush and Nubia, all heading for Theb-en, where they will camp to await the arrival of the rest of troops. These splendid blacks were renowned for their fighting skills, but were also apt to desert whenever the opportunity arrived. They had to be watched constantly.

In No-Amun, an air of excitement and apprehension reigned. In the pre-dawn, torches were lit. Their flickering lights reflecting off the glistening bodies of the men. They had been assembled into ten battalions of about five hundred soldiers each. These were subdivided into companies, two hundred and fifty strong, and five platoons of fifty men each. Then the chariots and horses were loaded onto barges while the troops stood at attention, awaiting their orders to embark.

With great fanfare, the gates of the palace swung open and Tutankhamun, dressed in full battle gear and wearing a blue leather helmet, rode his chariot, steered by Seti, ahead of Commander Horemheb, Lord Nakhtmin and Lord Sethi. They passed the cheering battalions and headed for the Royal barge where they alighted and boarded the vessel.

Their chariots would accompany them on the barge, but the horses were taken to another vessel.

On deck, Tutankhamun, with his hands clasped behind his back, stood and looked back towards the Malkata Palace where, on a balcony, the distant figures of the Queen and Lady Mutnedjmet were just visible.

'They look splendid, Mutny. Even in this light,' Senamun gazed towards her husband and Horemheb, illuminated by flickering torches.

'Yes, may this dawn also be the dawn of a new, more powerful and victorious Egypt,' Mutnedjmet agreed.

'My feelings are so mixed... I am proud and excited, yet I also fear for their safety.'

'As are all those wives, mothers and sisters down there. They all feel exactly the way we do, Senamun,' Mutnedjmet sighed. 'It is the lot of all women, but Horemheb had promised to *guide His Majesty's footsteps* all the way. You need not be concerned, His Majesty will be safe.'

'May they both return, safely,' the queen added. 'Where do they go from here?'

'To Theb-en, in the delta. To await the armies from the other provinces before they march north.'

Watching the departure, from the far end of the docks, was Ay. He spotted his son, Seti, on the dock and approached him. 'I thought you had left already.'

'I will, very soon, Father. My task, that of seeing to the loading of the horses and chariots, is done, and I am about to embark. Well, war has finally come to Ke-met!'

'Not exactly,' Ay responded. 'War had not *come* to us; Egypt is taking it to Asia.'

'You know what I mean. It had been threatening for years, and now it has come. We are at war...my division is ready for departure and I will be leaving soon.'

'You will be missed, my son. May you be safe and return unharmed. But before you go, I just wanted to ask... have you given and more thought to... what we discussed?'

'You surely do not wish me to go ahead, do you? With that plan of yours? It is risky. If I am discovered, I will be executed. My body will not be brought back to Egypt for burial and there would be no afterlife for me, do you realise that?'

'It is perilous, I know, but these are risky times. If one wishes to succeed, one has to take risks.'

'*I* am taking the risks, Father, but *you* stand to gain by it.'

'I already explained. If you succeed, we will both gain in the end.'

'*If?* …You think I might not?'

'I meant *when,* of course. You *will* succeed!'

'I hope so, Father. And I hope it will be worth it in the end.'

'It will. Believe me, it will! Now, go in peace, my son. May you be victorious… in *all* your undertakings.'

'Stay in peace, Father,' Seti saluted, turned and marched away.

From the balcony, Queen Ankhsenamun and Lady Mutnedjmet watched as the last of the boats departed. Menefer too, watched from the end of the wharf. She saw Rakhmet, instructing his men on board one of the vessels and remembered how, once before, she had come to see him sail away. That parting had changed her life and brought her much sorrow. Now again, he is sailing away. What sorrow will this one bring? What calamity lies ahead?

The mooring ropes were unfastened and rowers pulled at their oars. Slowly, the last craft moved from the dock, then caught in the current, it joined the other craft as they made their way downstream. The sun was just rising above the eastern horizon.

# Chapter Thirty-Nine
## Enemy Territory

In the third month of Khyak, of the season of Akhet, in the ninth year of Tutankhamun's reign, the Egyptian army was marching through Djahi to make war on Amurra. It was early autumn, but the weather was much cooler than Egypt, this far north.

Marching at the head of the troops and leading the Amun division, under a horned-sun disk banner, were Pharaoh Tutankhamun and Horemheb, Commander-in-chief of the armies. Both were in full battle dress. Affixed to the front of Tutankhamun's war helmet, were the two symbols of Royalty and power, the golden head of Nekhbet, the vulture goddess, and Buto, the golden uraeus, a cobra with flattened hood. Across Pharaoh's chest were draped the golden wings of Isis, acting as both protective symbol and body armour. Straining at their decorative yokes, the horses too, were splendidly caparisoned in leather and gold. From their heads fluttered richly dyed ostrich feathers and colourful ribbons that bobbed as they pranced.

Behind the King and their Commander, marched the troops. They were classified by their weapons—spearmen and archers. They also carried battle-axes, clubs and short dagger-like swords. Their uniforms were simple, short linen skirts with narrow leather aprons for protection; they wore no helmets, but carried cowhide shields.

Standard-bearers of each division, held aloft long staffs, with the symbol of each, fixed to the top. Rakhmet, heading the second division, had been promoted to General and proudly wore the uniform of his new rank and a war helmet. With his troops, under the sacred *Amakh*, the Eye of Horus banner, they were an impressive sight.

The third and fourth divisions, that of *Khnum*, under the Ram's head banner, and Sobekh, under the banner of a crocodile, was headed by Lord Sethi and Lord Nakhtmin respectively, and the fifth, the *Ankh* division, under Lord Huy, Viceroy of Kush.

As the army marched through villages and cities, people came out in droves to stare in awe. Never before had they witnessed such a splendid army.

For the benefit of the gaping crowd and the disciplined troops, Pharaoh was placed at the head of the troops, but, as Horemheb informed him, his position in the First Division was for the procession only. During the battle, and for his safety, Tutankhamun would be placed with the fifth, the Ankh, division.

'You are moving me to the fifth division? Why?' Tutankhamun was most displeased. 'Horemheb, you are still treating me like an immature boy!'

'Your Majesty, we will be in the front line. I plan to use the Amun division as bait. It will be much too dangerous for Your Majesty. I have taken an oath to protect Your Majesty's person.'

'I object! I came here to fight. For my people, for Egypt. I will not be used as a lucky charm, a talisman, or just for show!'

Horemheb smiled. 'It will be much more than that, Majesty. There *will* be fighting and the fifth division *will* be involved. The Horus division will be the lure, to draw out the enemy.'

'But if I cannot be with you, place me in the second division, I will be a better temptation,' he gestures to his uniform. 'With all this regalia I am festooned with, I will be a greater draw.'

'It is too much of a risk, Majesty. I cannot take that chance.'

'Horemheb! Who has the greater power, you or I?' Tutankhamun demanded.

'Your Majesty, of course.'

'Then, as I outrank you, I demand to be in the first division where I belong, under the banner of Amun!'

Horemheb protested, but Tutankhamun was determined.

'Very well, Majesty. As you command!' Horemheb was not happy with this decision, now he will have an additional plight to concern him, and he will have to revise his strategy. Tutankhamun had just doubled his task.

***

Lady Mutnedjmet and Menefer were enjoying the late summer sun at the lake pavilion, watching ducks darting in and out of the reeds. Menefer had always found peace and relaxation here, but Lady Mutnedjmet looked upset. She had received a letter from Horemheb, and it disturbed her. Menefer was about to ask her about it when Queen Ankhsenamun joined them.

Mutnedjmet quickly rolled up the papyrus and placed it in a basket, but Ankhsenamun had already seen it. 'Bad news, Mutny?' she asked as she took a seat.

'Horemheb is concerned. His plans to keep Tutankhamun safe, had been thwarted. His Majesty insists on fighting in the first division, in the front lines.'

'He did?' Senamun looked surprised. 'I too received a letter…from Tutankhamun, but he made no mention of the change of plans,' she sighed and absent-mindedly reached out for a juicy fig. She did not eat it, but merely toyed with the fruit. 'I'm afraid, like most other young men, he just wants excitement without considering the risk to his person. Like them, he thinks he is indestructible. I fear he will undertake unnecessary risks.'

'Horemheb promised to protect him, Majesty, and I am certain he will.'

'I hope he can persuade the stubborn king to change his mind. There is still time before they reach their destination, but it will take more than a week for word to reach us…he might be injured and we will not even know it.'

'Majesty, do not dwell on what might be. They will all return to us safely. Keep your heart free from ill thoughts. Remember your condition. As they say, a happy mother will have a joyful child; a distressed mother will have a child of sorrow.'

'You are right Menefer,' Senamun agreed. 'You certainly have a wealth of these sayings. Where do you get them from?'

'From my mother, Majesty. She had one for almost every situation.'

Lady Mutnedjmet changed the subject to other, more pleasant things. 'The child is due in the month of Phamenat, in the season of Proyet, is it not?

'No, probably a few weeks later, the first week of Pharmuti.'

'That would be wonderful,' Menefer added. 'It will be cold, but surely fortunate to be born during the time of Nut's Feast of Heaven and the Festival of the Lights of Neith. It is a very good omen.'

'I hope you are right, Menefer,' Senamun nodded, hopefully. 'I sincerely hope you are right.'

*** 

The Amorites had heard of the approach of the Egyptian army and had retreated north, well into Amurra, the area known as Retjnu, the northernmost frontier of the Egyptian Kingdom.

The Egyptians had been marching for about a month. No one had tried to intercept them or shown any aggression thus far.

The troops had travelled roughly parallel to the coast almost all the way, then veered inland, bypassing Pursath, the land of the Philistines. These were a troublesome people occupying the stretch of land along the coast south of a mount called Carmel. These people, originally from one of the islands in the Great Green Waters, had settled this area about the time the third Amenhotep came to the throne.

At Autha, the soldiers stayed over for a brief well-needed rest and to purchase supplies and additional weapons. The Phoenicians, the people from Khor, were well known for their excellent weaponry. The city had been under siege by the Ammonites, but they had withdrawn when they heard of the approach of the Egyptian army.

The citizens were grateful, and from them, Horemheb learnt that the Amorite army had headed inland in an easterly direction, towards Temesqu, beyond the mountains. He set off in pursuit.

'I fear the enemy might try to reach Khatti to seek assistance from the Hittites,' Horemheb remarked, concerned. 'If that happened we would lose the chance of dealing the blow we had hoped would annihilate Aziro's "liberating" army.'

'That means, we will not be able to bring Amurra and Khor under Egyptian rule!' Tutankhamun added.

'Yes, Majesty, we must therefore make haste.'

The midday sun blazed down and Tutankhamun looked up into a cloudless sky. They had left the coastal plain and the day was unusually warm for the time of the year. 'Is it my imagination, or does it seem hotter here than Kemet?' He brushed the back of his hand across his perspiring forehead.

Horemheb glanced at his young king. Dust from the red soil clung to him and left smears where he wiped his damp face. Even the kohl around his eyes had been smudged giving him a comical appearance. The Commander smiled at Tutankhamun's grime streaked face. 'It only seems thus, Majesty. It is the clamminess,' Horemheb explained. 'Damp makes the air seem more uncomfortable than the dry heat of Kemet. It will be much cooler when we reach higher ground away from the coast.' He pointed ahead towards the distant mountains shimmering through the haze.

Tutankhamun pondered the remark a moment. 'That is not very reassuring, Commander. In the open, it would have been impossible for anyone to approach us without being seen, and it looks like the mountains are heavy forested. We could be ambushed there.'

Surprised, Horemheb looked at him. 'Your Majesty is quite correct, but...'

He looked up as two figures approached. He shielded his eyes and squinted. They were the two scouts he had sent ahead. The scouts approached, breathing heavily after running for several hours.

'There is a village up ahead at the foot of the mountain,' one scout gestured. 'The chief there, told us of a large Amorite army that had passed their way just a short time ago, heading towards Temesqu.'

'The army is about eight thousand strong and has about two thousand chariots,' the second scout added. 'From the villagers, I learnt that there seemed, apart from Amorites, to be a large number of Khorru and Hittites present.'

'Well done.' Horemheb was pleased and sent the scouts to refresh themselves. Once they had gone, Horemheb muttered, 'So, Khorru and Hittites are involved. I suspected as much!'

'Will we besiege the city?' Tutankhamun asked. He had heard of Temesqu and was eager to see it.

'No, I do not relish the idea, Majesty,' Horemheb scratched his cheek. 'Our quarrel is with Aziro, not the people of Temesqu, but I will send eyes and ears into the city to determine their next move.'

The scouts were given food and drink from the supply wagon, to much grumbling and resentment from the soldiers. No food or drink were supplied to them during the march and were only available during the overnight camp. Each soldier had to carry his own rations of water and bread while marching and they were careful not to overindulge.

'Why are they treated thus?' one muttered. 'We are burdened like asses. Our necks and shoulders are sore like those of pack animals. We are denied food from the supply wagon, yet these scouts need not carry packs and are treated and pampered.'

Fortunately for them, Horemheb was not aware of their discontent, for they would surely have been reprimanded.

***

The army had marched alongside the Litani River from the coast, but because of the hilly countryside, the river followed a winding course and, what would have been a two-day march, stretched to several. The river made a sharp bend from the north, which they reached late in the afternoon on the third day and a camp was set up on the western bank. They would need to find a shallow area where they could cross,

Most soldiers were amazed and confused when they first saw the river. The Nile flows from south to north, so *downstream* always meant "north", but here a river flowed in the opposite direction and seemed, to them, that it was flowing backwards. How can that be? They had crossed several rivers on their march, which flowed into the sea from the east to the west, but this one, flowing south, had them puzzled. Superstitious rumours quickly spread until Horemheb, annoyed at their fear-provoking, tried to explain that water flows from the high mountains to lower coastal areas, which here, happens to be different to Egypt. Most accepted his explanation, but a few still believed that it was unnatural and they were facing supernatural forces.

Chariot horses had already been unharnessed and fed when the wagons, trailing behind the marching soldiers, were drawn together in the middle of the camp. The oxen and asses were untethered and allowed to graze. Messu and the other cadets were kept busy, helping with the unpacking and setting up the sleeping quarters for the officers, cleaning and laying out their battledress and armour. It was not a task Messu relished.

While the tents and sleeping pallets were unloaded and set up, meals were prepared. As usual, camp followers, women who saw to the needs of the men, helped with these tasks.

After the meal, Horemheb had called a meeting to start planning their strategies, when a disturbance outside the tent halted the proceedings.

Angrily, he flung open the tent flap. 'What is the meaning of this? Who is making the racket?' A man, tied at the wrist, was being dragged, stumbling, towards him.

'Lord Horemheb, a Khorru spy had been captured within the camp,' a soldier explained. 'We need your permission to deal with him.'

'No! I am not a spy,' the frightened man protested. 'I came to your camp freely!'

'For what purpose?' Horemheb demanded as the man was forced into a kneeling position. The man hesitated.

'Come now. What brings you here?' Horemheb asked, impatiently, as Tutankhamun and other officers peered out of the tent.

'I… I am a deserter, Lord.'

A low murmur swept through the gathered officers.

'He has come to do the King harm!' Nakhtmin said.

The man ignored him, looked first at the king, then at the assembled officers, then back at Horemheb.

'You are the Overseer of the *Mesha*?'

'Yes, I am Horemheb, Commander of the Armies.'

'I ask for asylum, Lord. I…' He hesitated and looked around at the officers again.

'Leave us!' Horemheb dismissed the guards with a flutter of his fingers and beckoned the man inside and he and Pharaoh seated themselves again. The man prostrated himself and Tutankhamun ordered him to rise, then ordered Horemheb to continue. 'You say you deserted?'

'Yes, Lord, I am a simple man, a *hupsu,* a labourer. The *mariannu* are our overlords and we must obey them. When they summoned us to fight on the side of the Amorites, we had no choice but to leave our homes and families. I did not wish to fight the people of Djahi. They are like my brothers, I fled.'

'How is it you were captured in our camp? You must have known we are Egyptians!'

'Lord, the Egyptians are not my enemy. In my city, we still worship the gods of Egypt. Ask any man if it is not so. I came here to seek food. That was where I was captured… at the food wagon.'

'We cannot feed those who do not serve us,' Tutankhamun folded his arms and scowled at the man, '… and we do not keep prisoners.'

'Majesty, I can earn my keep. I can mend weapons.'

'Weapons?' Horemheb showed interest. 'Doing what?'

'I worked at a place where iron is cast, Lord.'

'You know the secret of making fire hot enough to melt iron?' Tutankhamun too, was now curious.

'Yes, Majesty.'

Tutankhamun looked at Horemheb and lifted his eyebrows, but Horemheb was still suspicious. 'How can we know you have not been sent to sabotage our weapons on a pretext of mending them?'

'If that is so, Lord, my life is in your hands.'

This man could be most valuable. The people from Phoenicia, the land known as Khor, had guarded the secret of producing and maintaining high heat for a long time. The Egyptians had purchased many iron weapons from them, but had not been able to duplicate the smelting process. Horemheb looked at Tutankhamun who nodded his approval.

'Very well, Khorria,' Tutankhamun consented. 'You may remain with us; on the condition you teach us your skills.'

'And, to ensure you do not betray us and cause mischief,' Horemheb added, 'we will seek out the whereabouts of your family. If you lied to us, they will be taken to Egypt in bondage…and you will lose your head.'

The man knelt down in gratitude and kissed Tutankhamun's sandal. 'Thank you Lord, I will serve you faithfully,' he turned to Horemheb to repeat the gesture, but Horemheb quickly pulled his feet away.

'Have you any knowledge of the Amorites' plans?' Tutankhamun, elbows on the chair's armrest, and resting his chin on his intertwined his fingers, looked at him.

'No Majesty, a *hupsu* is not informed of anything. We merely take orders, but just before the Amorite army left, I overheard a soldier mention that they were heading for a camp on the bank of the Litani River…on the road to Qatna.'

'Qatna?' Horemheb asked, surprised. 'Are they then not heading for Temesqu?'

'No, Lord.'

'If he is correct, we have been misled!' He turned to Tutankhamun, 'The villagers fed us false information!'

After a lengthy interrogation, the man gave them more information on the location of the camp, the number of troops and chariots and he described their weaponry. The man was fed and provided with accommodation, but he was still kept under guard.

'We had almost walked into an ambush,' Horemheb told the officers, 'but now we will surprise *them* instead!'

After thinking about it during the night, and because of Tutankhamun's presence, Horemheb had to revise his plans slightly. Instead of the Horus division being the lure, as he had originally planned, the Amun division would be the trap instead. He explained his strategy the following morning. 'We will advance north, towards the enemy, with the Amun and Horus divisions in front, as planned. We will march together, but then the Amun division will stealthily slip away, a small number at a time, and reassemble inside the forested area. His Majesty will be in my protection in this division…'

An outcry followed this announcement. 'Commander Horemheb, the king in the front division?' Rakhmet enquired, alarmed. 'But I understood…'

Horemheb nodded towards Tutankhamun. 'His Majesty insisted.'

There were further protests, but Tutankhamun silenced them. 'That is what I decided, and we will hear no more of this, General!'

Horemheb continued. 'Hear out my plan. Lord Sethi will lead the third division. General Rakhmet, your division will proceed parallel to the river, with two-man and three-man chariots in the lead. I want you to be as visible as possible—you will be the lure.'

There was an exchange of opinions among the commanders.

'Silence!' Horemheb called out. 'You can discuss this later,' he looked around. 'The third and fourth divisions…'

Sethi and Nakhtmin looked up expectantly for their orders.

' Lord Nakhtmin, you will travel, fully visible, as much as possible., along the mountain foothills, then head for the forests, and Lord Sethi, travel along the Litani River, two or three hours behind the second division. Hold your banners high.'

'March through the forests, Commander?' Nakhtmin was puzzled.

'It will become clear later,' Horemheb explained.

Each of the divisions had about two thousand five hundred men including charioteers and chariot archers. In addition, divisions three and four included smaller units of private soldiers from various *sepatu* or provinces, each with their own leaders and banners. The *Unit of Life,* led by Huy, under a banner of an *Ankh,* the *Unit of the Kheper* with a scarab their symbol and the smaller units, the *Squad of Faith* under the Feather of Ma-at, and the mercenary soldiers under the *Djed* symbol, had altogether, nine hundred to a thousand men each. There were eight divisions in all.

Horemheb bent over a tray of sand on the table and with a stick, drew a rough map of the area. 'This is the source of Litani River. Lord Sethi, when you reach this place,' he drew a crude line and indicated their route, 'we will reach a plain, then head for the Arenth River, here, then the third and fourth divisions will lower their banners. Those who watch, should not be able to identify the one from the other. The fourth division will then follow the river.

'The third and fourth will follow the Arenth for two hours,' he gestured as he talked, 'then the third will head for the mountain range here, the fourth division will continue along the river, along the route the third division would have taken.'

Tutankhamun had been studying the crude map and had followed Horemheb's plans carefully. 'It's a bit confusing, Commander,' he observed, 'with the banners lowered, and the units crossing back and forth.'

'Exactly, Majesty,' Horemheb beamed. 'That is my plan. With the two divisions continuing to switch sides, I am hoping, any scouts observing these manoeuvres, would also be confused. Hopefully, they would soon not be able to tell whether they are seeing two separate units, or the same one. I had watched gazelle do this often when they are chased by a lion, changing directions and criss-crossing each other's paths, bewildering the predator.'

'Mmm. You think it will work on people?' Huy asked.

'I hope so,' Horemheb straightened. 'When you camp tonight, the third and fourth divisions will, as the Amun division, remain concealed as much as possible. Cooking fires are banned. The wheels of the chariots and the horses' hooves are to be bound with strips of cloth to dull their progress in the event the ears of the enemy are sharp.'

He explained his strategy further, and that the fifth division, the Ankh division under Huy, would march well behind the Horus division, followed by the three other divisions. The last division, the Djed Division with the mercenary soldiers, will march at the rear and the camp followers and wagons, loaded with provisions and extra weapons would follow well behind. Food and water would not be available during the battle and each soldier would have to carry extra rations and course blankets, as it will start getting colder.

Horemheb turned to Tutankhamun. He looked concerned. 'I urge Your Majesty, once again, to please reconsider. Your Majesty wanted to be seen by the enemy and the fifth division will be visible…and comfortable. These last divisions will be the only ones to have camp fires and hot food.'

'No. I will bear the same hardships as the soldiers. I will not have special treatment!'

The soldiers within earshot quickly spread the word. Tutankhamun was immediately taken to the hearts of the men. 'Pharaoh demands that he eats cold rations and sleeps in the open like the rest of us *Hupsu*. He is one with us!'

The Amun division veered away, and as planned, keeping concealed, made camp in a forested area. They had passed the source of the Litani River and reached the Arenth River when Horemheb noticed Tutankhamun shivering slightly.

'You need to dress warmly, sire,' He called out and waved towards to distant mountains, the peaks already covered in snow. 'It can get chilly in these mountains.'

'It is the first time I have seen snow,' Tutankhamun nodded. 'I would like to see it up close. I believe it is quite beautiful.'

'It is too early in the season for it, here, Majesty, but I believe it to be very cold.'

They kept the conversation light and casual, but as the distance between them and the enemy grew shorter, their talks became more strained. Scouts had been sent ahead, and everyone scanned the horizon and the edges of the forests. They were now well into Amurra and every bush could conceal the enemy.

They were approaching yet another wooded area when the two scouts appeared, racing back to meet the troops. Horemheb held up his arm and the column halted. The scouts were excited and even before they could be understood, their gestures indicated that the enemy was close.

The Amun division reached a rise, which overlooked the valley towards the east. Aziro's camp could be seen in the distance. A lazy column of smoke was rising from cooking fires, and a few men casually went about their business. They seemed oblivious to the Egyptian army.

The Horus division, as planned, camped in the open valley where scouts would be able to see them and report the number of troops and chariots to their commanders.

The progress of the third and fourth divisions, trying to find suitable paths through the forests and riverside woods and shrubs for the chariots, proved to be difficult. They sought rest under cover of trees and constructed a wall of shields. The animals were herded inside for protection, then the soldiers made themselves as comfortable as possible. Sleep, for many, did not come easy. It was cold and damp in the mountains. Giant cedars, pine and oak trees covered the slopes of the mountains and extended well onto the valley floor. The forests were also the dwelling places of wolves and bears. Every little noise was foreign to the Egyptians and whenever they were roused from their slumber, would cast their eyes around in the dark, expecting an attack from man or beast.

They woke the next morning to another foreign phenomenon. Fog. It was especially thick in the mountains. Many had never experienced such a sight. The enshrouding clammy blanket hung silently and heavily about them, obscuring their vision. The rising sun appeared as a dim orb through the grey cloud mass, and many declared this to be an omen of catastrophe.

'Look!' one whispered fearfully, and pointed to the insipid disk in the sky. 'Ra has deserted us. The sun is no brighter than the moon. This will surely be a day of calamity.'

Others who had experienced this before, tried to allay the fears of the superstitious, but many were not convinced. The Nubians turned their eyes to the sky, moaned, and looked about for ways to escape back to their families and familiar surroundings. The fear of the unknown, hungry wolves and bears, animals, not found in Africa and awaiting to attack any lone traveller, was much more terrifying than the wrath of their superiors. Duty and fidelity convinced most of the soldiers to remain, but a few did manage to desert.

Finally, the mist cleared and the sun came through again, bright and warm. Those who spoke of doom were made to feel foolish, and a number of those who had deserted, returned shamefaced. The Egyptians needed all the men they could get and the deserters were forgiven. They ate a hasty meal of bread and onions, washed down with water, rolled their pallets and continued on their way through the forest.

Far ahead of them, Horemheb's scouts brought news of the enemy camp. They had camped on a hill, at the southern tributary of the Arenth River, about half a day's march north-east of where, under cover of trees, the second division had camped.

'The Amorites are preparing to march north-west towards Qatna,' the scouts informed Horemheb.

'We must intercept them before the reach the city for reinforcements,' he remarked. 'They are aware of the second division's position, but will not expect us. We will cut them off. Let us hope the surprise will be in our favour.' The camp was struck immediately and the order was given for the march. 'We will see battle before this day is done, Majesty,' Horemheb warned.

Tutankhamun, suddenly very afraid, could only nod. He shivered again, but time, it was caused by pre-battle nerves.

# Chapter Forty
## The Battle

As Horemheb had predicted, the Amorite scouts were deceived. They had reported the advance of the second division, and had assumed it to be the first division and reported the numbers of men and chariots to be far less than they actually were.

The enemy's mountains scouts and those along the river, observing the third and fourth divisions, had assumed seeing only one division. Their report mentioned the second division, and the third division seemed to be marching irregularly, continually crossing from the mountains to the river, then back and guessed they were searching for a hidden enemy, stationed there for an ambush. The Amun division, well north of them, had not been detected.

'Commander Horemheb is a fool!' Imar, Amorite General of the Methen division, remarked. 'He approaches like a goat, leading his flock to sweet grass, not heeding anything in the way.'

'… Or he is very cleaver,' Aziro answered. 'Maybe that is just what he wants us to believe… But we will beat him at his own game. I have arranged a little welcome for him.'

'I heard Pharaoh accompanies the general, but thus far, we had not detected him. Perhaps their king, a mere boy, has been placed safely at the rear, with the food wagons!' Imar laughed.

Horemheb, still hidden, had deploy just north-west of the enemy camp. 'I need a messenger to take orders to the third and fourth divisions.' He looked around for a volunteer.

A man stepped forward, 'I will go, Commander.'

'Good. The third and fourth will form two horns, one under Commander Sethi, the other under Lord Nakhtmin. Each horn will have its own chariot marshals with several squadrons of five companies,' he gestured and indicated where he wanted them to go. 'They are to proceed to either side of the enemy, who will target the Horus division, there,' he pointed. 'The enemy will spread out and their flanks would turn for defence. We will then surprise the enemy by coming from the north and draw them toward us. We will engage them in battle, then the two horns would close in.' He closed his arms into an embracing gesture. 'They will be virtually surrounded and we must make certain their retreat to Qatna is foiled.'

The messenger nodded, was made to repeat the orders, then sent off to repeat it to Commander Sethi and Lord Nakhtmin. Horemheb waited until he was satisfied they had received their instructions.

As expected, the enemy attacked the Horus division. The fourth and fifth divisions at the east and west appeared. One horn moved around to the south-west, and the other, closed from the south-east. Then the insignia of Amun was raised. Unit commanders ran up and down the ranks giving orders, then with a crack of a whip, the rustle of thousands of feet, wheels grinding against rocks and leather squeaking against wood, the army, in block formation ten abreast, the first division advanced from the north-west from the forest.

The surprised enemy quickly changed tactics. 'So, they tried to deceive us!' Imar observed. 'We will deceive them, instead. I have prepared a little surprise of my own.'

Suddenly, with blares of trumpets, ram's horns and beating of war drums, an Amorite chariot unit charged at the Amun division unexpectedly, followed by a unit of infantry, from a small forest from the east.

The Amun division split and prepared to face this new threat. They quickly formed two rows on their flanks. The men knelt and pressed their spear shafts into the earth with the spearheads forming a formidable barrier against the advancing chariots. The third and fourth row of archers took their positions behind the kneeling men and waited for the order to attack.

The fourth division of Sobekh had been delayed and third division, instead of closing the pincers or the horns, now had to swing north-west to defend themselves. Horemheb's strategy had not worked.

There was confusion in the ranks. The Egyptians now had to defend themselves on two flanks thereby thinning the defensive lines. The Horus division seemed to have a battle raging on three flanks—to the north, east and west.

The Amorite chariots split and veered away and charged at the thin defensive line of the Egyptians, then swerved away at the last instant as the archers released volleys of arrows. The second wave of Amorite charioteers, using ropes and whips, lashed at the embedded spears of the Egyptians, snaring many of them, and some soldiers, in rope nooses, and dragged them along, leaving gaps in the defensive lines. A third wave followed immediately behind and broke through the gaps where the enemy infantry poured through. The Egyptians had no time to regroup and only a few of their arrows hit their targets. The surprise of the attack and the confusion that reigned caused a devastating blow to the Egyptians.

Horemheb looked on helplessly as Egyptian chariots started giving chase to the Amorites' chariots, which fanned out. He had given no orders for this manoeuvre. The Egyptians pursued the enemy for a distance, but veered towards the advancing infantry, which quickly retreated back into the trees where the chariots could not follow.

The enemy chariots circled around and were now between the Egyptian vehicles and their division. By the time the Egyptians realised their mistake, they had been cut off. As they turned to face the Amorite chariots, more enemy infantry emerged from the forest and attacked them from the rear. Many brave men were lost.

Aziro watched the battle from a rise. 'This is an easy victory,' he gloated. 'The Egyptians fell into our ambush readily. We will crush Horemheb this day, capture their young king and march on to Egypt.'

After the first wave of attack, the Egyptians retreated and regrouped and hastily planned a new strategy. Horemheb was very concerned for his young King, as they were now in the midst of a battle.

'They had grown weak from lack of battle experience,' Aziro laughed. 'Our troops had surrounded them.'

'What about the divisions still approaching from the south, Lord?' Imar enquired.

'I have sent troops south to deal with them.' His boast was cut short as a cheer from the embattled Egyptians made him turn and he uttered an oath.

He did not realise that another division had been approaching. The division of Sobekh, led by Nakhtmin, delayed by heavy mud, had managed to march all the way around without being detected and suddenly emerged from the forest, east of the Amorites. The Amorites were now cut off completely, and caught between the Egyptian forces.

Aziro's division, which had attacked the Egyptians from the south east, suddenly turned toward the new thread, that of Sobekh and the fifth, the *Ankh* Division, charged from the south. The Egyptians had marched close to the river. Behind them, the sixth, seventh and eighth divisions arrived, the Egyptian infantry and the private mercenary troops of the Djed division, armed with arrows, spears, slings axes and clubs, joined in the melee.

The retreating Amorites were now, in turn, trapped between the divisions who had joined up with each other and were advancing, in a closing arc. The combined Amun and Horus divisions were in the centre and attacking the enemy from within.

It was now the Amorite army that was fighting on all fronts. The heavy-wheeled Amorite chariots found it difficult to make sharp turns, whereas the lighter Egyptian vehicles could charge, loose their arrows and spears, then veer away quickly before the Amorites could retaliate.

As they charged past, Huy's Khnum chariots sent wave after wave of arrows into the Amorite ranks. They charged into a chaotic, seething mass, trampling the terrified infantrymen.

Horemheb and an Amorite prince were engaged in close combat and the two chariots were racing along side by side. Too close for spears or bow and arrow, they were compelled to using swords. The Amorite was clearly at a disadvantage. His charioteer battled to manoeuvre his ungainly vehicle when an arrow struck Horemheb's driver in the neck and he fell from the vehicle, mortally wounded. Horemheb grabbed the reigns to control the chariot. The Amorite prince, seeing Horemheb's disadvantage, took this opportunity to retreat. Horemheb gave chase and his lighter vehicle and soon caught up with the fleeing heavier chariot of his foe.

The prince saw Horemheb approaching fast. As Horemheb drew level, the Amorite slowed his chariot slightly and veered towards Horemheb's chariot. Horemheb immediately realised what the Amorite was trying to do. The thin-spoked Egyptian vehicle, although faster, was also flimsier than the heavier and sturdier Asian one. If the Amorite's wheels locked onto his, his wheel could easily be dislodged or shattered.

Horemheb grabbed the driver's whip and urged his horses on, to try and outdistance the Amorite's but the terrain was uneven and he had to concentrate to manoeuvre around obstacles which the enemy vehicle took with comparative ease.

As the two vehicles again drew close, the prince readied his scimitar to strike. Horemheb lashed out with his whip and with a sharp backward flick, wrapped it around the enemy's forearm. With a jerk, he pulled the prince off balance. The prince, struggling to regain his balance, released his weapon and grabbed hold of his driver to steady himself. Horemheb veered his chariot to the left, away from the enemy. The struggling driver, unable to manoeuvre his vehicle quick enough, struck a ridge and tipped over, flinging the prince and the charioteer to the ground. The prince rolled some distance, winded.

Horemheb spun his vehicle around and saw the prince's chariot tumbling empty and out of control behind the horses. The prince scrambled to his feet and groped for his weapon as Horemheb, with spear at the ready, raced towards him. The prince slashed at Horemheb's horses as they thundered past. Horemheb cast his spear and struck the prince in the chest.

Horemheb scanned the seething mass of fighting men and racing chariots for Tutankhamun. He had taken an oath to protect the king, and this was his main objective now. There were heavy losses on both sides.

Tutankhamun, who had been kept well away from the front, was trying to reach the battle, but Seti, under strict instructions from Horemheb, tried to keep him back. 'The king must be kept safe at all times,' Horemheb had warned, 'or your hide will be forfeit.'

The battle raged for several hours and both sides were tiring, but Tutankhamun, not having had a direct hit and feeling frustrated, could but shoot his arrows over the heads of his troops hoping it would find its mark.

Elsewhere, Rakhmet was trying to get past two other chariots, whose warriors were engaged in hand-to-hand combat. He was suddenly attacked from behind and narrowly escaped a spear-thrust, but managed to slash at his attacker with his sword. He grabbed his spear and hurled it at the enemy, but his chariot jerked and the spear thudded into the chariot-guard next to the man. Before the man could counter-attack, he was hit in the temple by a stone from a sling. He collapsed, bleeding from the wound. Rakhmet's charioteer found an opening and they lurched forward towards a fresh target.

Tutankhamun, who had become frustrated by Horemheb orders, again urged Seti on. 'I have not yet shot an arrow at a target. I command you! Get closer!'

'But, Your Majesty—'

'There! That chariot… Faster, I want a clear shot!'

Seti veered the chariot towards an Amorite vehicle ahead and closed in. Tutankhamun raised his bow and loosed an arrow. The Amorite, hit in the arm, turned to face the king. Tutankhamun drew his short sword. As they pulled alongside, he raised the weapon, but his chariot-wheel clipped the enemy's, tilted, and swerved violently. The young king lost his grip on the guard-rail. He felt a hand against his back as he was flung off the platform. An Egyptian chariot, immediately behind him, trying desperately to avoid the fallen king, was too close, and the thundering horses and one wheel of the vehicle ran over the king.

Rakhmet saw him the fall, forced his way to the king's side and leapt off his chariot. He used his shield to protect the fallen king as chariots rushed by and fighting men milled around. Seti, still holding onto the reins, called upon other charioteers to form a barrier around Pharaoh and to summon the physician, then he too, rushed over and stood over Tutankhamun, sword at the ready to keep the area clear. Seti was searching the crowd for the physician, when an arrow struck him in the neck. He clutched at the shaft, toppled forward and lay still.

***

The Amorites had broken ranks and were milling in confusion, running into one another and getting into each other's way. Some managed to shoot of their arrows and flung spears, but only a few found weapons their marks.

The trapped enemy found a break between the Horus and Sobekh divisions and managed to retreat back to their camp. They were on the run with the Egyptians in hot pursuit.

Horemheb, not realising Tutankhamun had been injured, searched among the fighting soldiers for sight of Pharaoh's blue helmet, then noticed the king's caparisoned horses and golden chariot, hemmed in by several stationary chariots. He forced his way towards them and saw the guard of soldiers. A chill went through him…*had the king been killed?*

He jumped off the platform and raced to where Rakhmet was cradling Tutankhamun in his arms. The King's leg had been broken above the knee and badly gashed. Blood was flowing freely from a wound on the left side of the king's head, ran down over Rakhmet's arm and dripped to the ground.

Rakhmet looked up as Horemheb approached and nodded imperceptibly. 'His Majesty is still alive…'

Nufer, the physician from Buhen, who was in the division of Khnum, had been summoned, but it took a while for him to reach the king. After a brief examination, he cleaned and bound the leg and the king's head. The wounds were treated with *Imeru*, a balm made from an aloe plant and honey, which he spread on a dressing of linen. 'It is bad. His leg seems to be broken, but it is not a fatal injury. His Majesty will recover,' he told the officials. 'Take him to a safe area, but carry him very carefully.'

The enemy had dispersed and returned to their camp while the Egyptians were assisting and comforting their wounded, retrieving the weapons and loading the dead onto chariot platforms. A way was cleared through the milling confusion and Tutankhamun was taken to one of the four-wheeled carts, given a potion and made as comfortable as possible on a pallet of straw to avoid the vibrations of the moving vehicle.

It was the custom that the right hand of every slain soldier was cut off and taken back to the camp. Scribes, accompanying the troops, then had the grisly task to tally the number of hands and record the enemy casualties for posterity. One of these scribes was a crippled ex-soldier, a man named Batu, a friend of Rakhmet.

The king's vision was blurry and his skin felt clammy. His stomach could not retain the medication that was administered and he vomited.

In spite of his injuries, Tutankhamun was nevertheless more fortunate than other wounded. Seti, his charioteer, was in a bad way and he, with other serious wounded, were slung over the backs of asses. Those able to walk were helped along by friends or makeshift supports, and faced a long painful march back to Egypt.

Many died before reaching Kemet and were buried in shallow graves. Only those, whose families could afford it, had their bodies prepared and taken back to Egypt for burial. To be buried in a foreign land was a thing the Egyptians abhorred. One of those who had died and was being taken back home, was Seti, the son of Ay.

***

The Egyptians did not pursuit the fleeing Amorites, and the Amorites did not regroup to attack, so a stalemate was reached. Neither army officially claimed victory, but the Egyptians, who would never admit it, would proclaim victory on their return, but Phoenicia, ancient Khor, which had been annexed by the Amorites, had been lost to Egypt.

At the camp, the cadets had been kept busy tending the wounded, administering ointments and binding wounds. Squeamish as first, but under command of his superiors, Messu had to force himself. He learnt how to shave around headwounds, extract arrows from shallow wounds, stitch together open cuts, and apply tight bindings to stop bleeding. On several occasions, he threw up, but slowly became hardened, and got used to getting blood on his hands. That night, bloodied and hungry, he sank down next to a patient, exhausted, and fell asleep. He had to be shaken awake to cleanse himself and eat, before being allowed to go to his own pallet to rest.

Tutankhamun had a restless night. All that night, Nufer, the physician, watched over the king. Pharaoh had developed a slight fever and kept muttering in his sleep. 'I was pushed...' Tutankhamun repeated several times.

'Who, Your Majesty?' Nufer asked. 'Who pushed you?'

'My enemy. One of our own wants me dead!'

Nufer tried to find out what the kings was talking about, but Tutankhamun made no sense. 'He is not coherent, Commander,' Nufer explained.

Seti, his charioteer, had died and Horemheb could only find one witnesses to establish what had happened. The man, whose chariot struck the king, was questioned.

'I am sorry, but it all happened so fast. The King's chariot struck the enemy's. His Majesty lost his balance. His driver tried to steady him, but he fell before my chariot. I could do nothing to divert or stop.'

Satisfied at the explanation, Horemheb did not pursue the matter further. It had been just an accident. Pharaoh's injuries, although bad, were not considered life-threatening.

'A broken leg is serious, but not fatal, Commander,' Nufer reassured him, 'but we need to get His Majesty back to Egypt. Winter is approaching fast.'

He gave Tutankhamun a preparation to make him sleep, and Horemheb ordered their return to the Two Lands as soon as possible.

314

They broke camp and started the march back to Egypt. More men died along the way and had to be buried, but that did not interrupt their march. It was a painful and long journey, made even longer by Tutankhamun's wagon that had to be moved slowly and carefully to minimise a bumpy journey. The tired and injured also hampered their progress and the journey was painfully slow. The king had regained consciousness but suffered severe pain. Every jolt of the vehicle, even slight ones, caused him to cry out.

Several thousand people, captured soldiers and civilians from enemy villages, were taken into bondage. The army also had to replenish their food stocks from plundered enemy villages. What they could not take, was destroyed, leaving no means of livelihood for the old and infirm left behind.

In Egypt, the news of their "victory" preceded them and the people from all over the provinces came to honour the soldiers as they passed through the villages and cities. Flowers and palm fronds were strewn along their way and a great cry went out as they passed.

'Hail Per-O! Amun has given him strength. He had lifted his hands and smote the rebels of Amurra so that Aziro fell before him. Praise to King Neb-Kheperu-re. May he live forever and ever!'

Tutankhamun, propped up in the wagon, nodded and smiled to his people. He was pleased. Akhenaten never had such a reception as this.

'Once I am back in No-Amun, I will show my gratitude. I will commission a great monument to be built in honour of this battle, Horemheb, and your name will be glorified. In ages to come, men will see the stellae and know of this victory.'

The journey to No-Amun took much longer than their march north, much longer than had been anticipated. The extended journey did not help the king's injury. The leg did not heal and his condition grew steadily worse. Nufer was concerned.

He shook his head. 'Commander Horemheb, the king must get treatment and rest soon. If not...' he shrugged and did not finish the sentence, but Horemheb understood what he meant.

# Chapter Forty-One
## Together Again

Cheers and chanting, drums and horns greeted the returning troops all along the riverbank, as they sailed towards No-Amun. Horemheb and Rakhmet stood on the deck and watched their approach to the city.

'What will you say about the battle, Commander?' Rakhmet asked, concerned. 'We had the enemy on the run, yet we abandoned the attack. We could have destroyed Aziro forever!'

'My concern had been for His Majesty. What good is victory if we lose our king? Although we did not smite him, Aziro will know we can defeat him, he will be wary and never again test the armies of Egypt, so, in that sense, we did win the battle. It will thus be written.'

'But Pursath and Khor had been lost to us…'

'Yes, but what is more important,' Horemheb wags his finger, dramatically, '…most of Djahi had been saved. Remember that!'

Bearers carried Tutankhamun to the palace where he was made him as comfortable as possible. His leg, still extremely painful had become badly swollen. Both Pentu, the former physician to Akhenaten, and Nufer, who treated the king after the battle, took turns in ministering to him. His bedchamber had been darkened so that the bright light would not hurt his eyes. Incense and herbs were burned in all the braziers to ward off bad spirits and demons, but the acrid smoke made him feel light-headed.

Ankhsenamun remained at Tutankhamun's side constantly, fussing over him like a mother hen over her chicks. Although his condition had not improved, he insisted on fulfilling his commitments.

'My lord, you must rest. Let your leg heal,' Ankhsenamun pleaded.

'I have duties, Senamun.'

'They can wait!' Senamun insisted. 'Lord Nakhtmin can take care of all that.'

'There are things Lord Nakhtmin cannot do for me…you are with child. He cannot go to the temple to make offerings on my behalf.'

'I will go to the temple for both of us. Rest your leg.' She sat down beside him on the sleeping couch and, while she bathed the wound on his head, chanted a magical rhyme that mothers often crooned to sick children.

*'Disappear O Demon, who comes in the darkness,*
*And enters with your nose behind you and your face turned backwards,*
*for that which you had come for, will escape you!*
*Did you come to embrace this man?*
*I will not permit you to embrace him.*
*Did you come to harm him?*
*Did you come to take him away?*
*I will not permit you to take him away from me...'*

The magical chant did not really help to ease the pain, but her voice soothed him and he drifted off into a fitful sleep.

It hurt Senamun to see her young husband like this. Her love for him had grown strong and she could not bear to leave his side, even for a moment, but he depended on her to make the offerings in the temple and she must do it. To have a male heir was their most urgent objective.

***

'The Upit ceremony is due. It is also almost the tenth year of my reign,' Tutankhamun shifted, making himself more comfortable. He grimaced painfully. 'The ceremony is an important one. I must honour those who proved their valour during the battle.'

Tutankhamun's leg had grown worse and black patches appeared on his feet. The queen, very concerned, tried to delay him. 'The ceremony can wait. You must let your health improve.'

'No, Senamun. These men risked all for our country. I must endure the torment to reward them.'

'Very well, but then I will summon Pentu to relieve the pain,' she clapped her hands and gave the orders. Pentu appeared a moment later with the potion.

'This is what you gave me yesterday, physician. It did not help. I need something stronger,' Tutankhamun waved the mixture away.

'It is the strongest I have, Majesty.'

Tutankhamun reluctantly drank the concoction and grimaces. 'Why does medicine always taste so foul?'

'The worse it tastes, Majesty, the more potent to drive away the evil.'

The queen had wanted the ceremony to be held in the king's chambers, but he refused to listen. 'It is not fitting to perform such an important task from a sleeping couch.' He beckoned Ipay, the Royal Butler, to approach, 'Help me onto the carry-chair.'

Against Ankhsenamun's advice, Tutankhamun was carried to the Hall of Audience and placed on his throne.

When all had assembled, Kheruef entered and tapped his staff three times. 'All kneel. His Royal Majesty, Lord of Towy, King of Upper and Lower—'

Tutankhamun, impatient and in pain, stopped him as he started his customary recitations of Royal titles. 'Enough! They all know who I am.' He called out, 'All rise,' in a lower voice, he again addresses his Chief Steward, 'Now, Lord Kheruef, get on with it!'

Kheruef, momentarily bemused, cleared his throat. 'Commander Horemheb, Overseer of the Armies!'

Horemheb approached and bowed.

'Commander Horemheb, you have shown great courage before me during the battle.' Tutankhamun beckoned for Horemheb to approach and knelt down, 'For you bravery, I present you with the Golden Beb, the pectoral of honour.'

Without rising from his seat, the king placed the wedge-shaped, golden pendant around Horemheb's neck.

'You are hereby also granted land to the south of the city of No-Amun, from the stellae of Amun at the foot of the mountain to the village of Ptah, and all the land down to the banks of the Nile. You are granted peasants from the villages on this land to toil for you and till your lands. You will also receive a hundred head of cattle and a house. In addition, you will hereby have the titles of "*Chief Commander*", "*Scribe of the Soldiers*" and "*Overseer of the Fields of the King*". It is decreed. Let it so be written let it so be done.'

Horemheb rose and backed away, holding his palms forward, in the Royal salute. The next to be honoured, was Rakhmet.

'Captain Rakhmet, for valour and outstanding performance during the battle, you will receive the Golden Beb.' Rakhmet came forward, knelt, and received the pectoral. 'From this day onward, you will have the title of "*Overseer of the Buildings of Amun*" and promoted to "*Commander of the Southern Armies*".'

Lord Huy, Viceroy of Kush was granted lands to the east of the Nile, from the second cataract to the temple of Ptah in the south, and east as far as the Oasis of *Tshesen*. Lord Nakhtmin received the Golden Beb and the office of "*Fan bearer on his Majesty's Left*".

After receiving his pectoral, Nakhtmin stepped down from the dais. Suddenly, a horrified outcry came from the assembly. Tutankhamun had collapsed.

Pharaoh was taken back to his bedchamber. In extreme pain and a halting voice, Tutankhamun summoned Lord Ay and addressed him from his couch. 'Lord Ay, Queen Nefertiti had wronged you deeply. You have always been a faithful and competent Vizier. It seems I am not able to perform my duties for a while. As the father of the mother of Queen Ankhsenamun, it is my wish you take over my tasks—for a while. You are hereby to act as my regent until I am able.'

Overwhelmed and pleased at the sudden promotion, Ay thanked the king profusely. He had all but given up hope of achieving his former status. The death of his son had been a great blow and he feared all his plans had been for naught, but once again, his hope had been renewed.

'You will continue the ceremony of the *Open hand*, and afterwards attend Ankhsenamun for the temple offerings, but take care, she is with child and I do not want her to tire.'

'I promise to look after Your Majesty's affairs and Her Majesty's well being. I give you my oath, Majesty, I will see to *everything*!' He smiled, satisfied. Everything is working out fine.

Ay left and Senamun approached Tutankhamun. Once they were alone, she kissed him, then proceeded to rub his temples. He had an exhausting day and drifted off into slumber.

'Rest, dear husband,' she whispered. 'Sleep well, my Lord.'

***

Menefer's stay with Sena and Khames had made her long for a house of her own. Their quarters at the palace were comfortable, but they did not have the freedom and cosiness of a home. Since the document that tied Messu to the Royal house had been destroyed, and as a commoner, they could live elsewhere, and the king and queen granted her a house close to the palace.

She had been preparing the evening meal when the front door opened. 'You are early today,' she called out without looking up.

'Am I?' a man's voice answered.

Startled, she turned. 'Oh, Rakhmet…! I thought it was Messu!' Still holding the ladle she had been using, she hurried to the gathering room. 'Any reason for the visit?'

'Do I need a reason, other than just wishing to see you?' He laughed and greeted her warmly.

'We still need to celebrate your promotion. When shall we arrange—'

He took her by the shoulders and looked earnestly and deeply into her eyes. 'No, it is not a time for celebrations, Menefer. Pharaoh's condition is worsening. He is unconscious.'

'Oh dear…yes, the queen told me he was not mending.' The ladle was dripping sauce on the floor. She ran her finger over it and stuck her finger in her mouth. 'Thanks for coming all this way to tell me. Please sit. I'll be with you in a moment,' she started turning towards the cooking area.

'Uh, no, that's not the reason for my visit. I came to talk of…other things.' He looked at the floor, twisting the edge of his tunic nervously. She stood, watching and waiting for a response. He looked anxiously about the room, trying to think of the right words to explain his visit.'

'What is it?' she asked, again wiping the dripping ladle.

'I have been trying to build up the courage to talk to you,' he sat down.

'Why do you need courage?' She waved the ladle around. 'Am I more fearsome than facing the Amorites?'

'That was different. I could defend myself against them…but facing you is…hard.'

She had never seen him so nervous. 'The Great Commander of Southern Armies grows pale when confronted by a frail woman holding a dripping ladle!' She laughed, placing the ladle in a bowl.

'Do not make fun of me, Menefer. It is difficult enough to try and form the words I wish to say…'

'Just say it, Rakhmet!' She came over and sat opposite him.

'It's about us… I brought you great anguish after my return from Buhen. I wish to make amends…to—uh—'

'You want us to try again?… Start over?'

'Yes. Menefer.' He was relieved she had uttered the words he could not. 'I have been such a fool…to have believed those things Djenna said in her letters…would you allow me to repair what I have done? To mend the bond between us? I will punish those who had caused it all.'

319

'Yes, Djenna had caused a lot of grief…for everyone, but she is gone. She moved away after Queen Tiye's death. Let her be.'

'Not her, Baka, the Commander of Buhen. As *Overseer of the Southern Armies,* I now outrank him. He was the cause of all that trouble. He did it for his own advantage. I will strip him of his command. I will have his nose cut off—'

'No. He has suffered enough when his daughter and the son she bore, died.'

Rakhmet nodded.

'Then leave it be, for the sake of their memory. Let the past stay in the past. We had both experienced happiness and tragedy since then. Let us not continue with hate and vengeance in our hearts—I will not have a husband who would do someone injury.'

Rakhmet looked up, delighted. 'Husband? Then…you agree we can again be…?'

Menefer nodded.

He rushed over, took her in his arms and kissed her passionately. For a long moment, they stood there, locked in each other's arms. They would be together again… at long last.

Messu cleared his throat. 'Well, what a sight to come home to…my mother in the embrace of a man.'

Menefer and Rakhmet spun around and faced the door. Both were smiling. 'Messu, I have something wonderful to tell you. Rakhmet and I are to be wed!' Menefer blurted out.

'Is this not a complete change-around?' Messu was puzzled.

'I've always had strong feelings for him,' she tried to explain.

'Yes, I know. Hate!' Messu gestured. 'I remember well, the venom in your voice whenever you spoke his name.'

Rakhmet and Menefer loosed their embrace. 'Love and hate are closely related,' Menefer tried to justify herself. 'One can change.'

Messu shrugged. 'I do not understand, but I guess it can happen!'

'Then you approve?'

'Yes, I suppose so…but I will remain the son of Lord Sethi!' Messu emphasised, concerned about his future with his adopted father and career in the military. He feared, by Rakhmet becoming head of the family, his position would be terminated, especially since he had been promoted and, not yet thirteen. He will soon be able to join the academy to train as an officer. He had grown tall, and looked a little older than his age.

'You were legally adopted and will remain Sethi's heir,' she turns to Rakhmet. 'It seems my son is well in control of his own destiny.'

'The life of a recruit is not easy,' Rakhmet warned. 'In the military, we have a saying, "*A young man has a back and listens to the person who strikes it,*".'

'I have heard all that before. I have also been told by my father, Lord Sethi, "*He who perseveres and can endure, can attain status and a future secure*".'

'True, but you will have to work hard at it.'

'I know and am prepared.'

Messu walked to the *rekhes* to find something to eat, stopped and turned, and as an afterthought, added, 'I wish you both much happiness.' He turned, noticed the mixture in the bowl, and reached over.

'And stay away from the food!' Menefer scolded. 'We will have *mesit* soon. I am preparing the meal now and do not want you to spoil your appetite.'

She turned to Rakhmet. 'You are staying over for the meal, are you not? I have enough prepared.'

'Yes, I would like that,' he answered. It had been many years since he had last been part of a family.

Messu returned and sat down next to his mother. 'When is the big day?'

Menefer and Rakhmet looked at each other. 'Soon. Very soon,' Menefer answered. 'The Feast of Isis is in a few months, the ideal time for a wedding, don't you think?'

Rakhmet readily accepted.

'I will start making the wedding arrangements almost immediately,' she said. 'I don't want anything to come between us again. The sooner we are wed, the better.'

But, once again, fate would decree otherwise.

***

Shortly before his thirteenth birthday, Messu started his training as a junior officer. As he had expected, and because of his ability to read and write, he was singled out for more extensive training.

'We can break in horses and teach monkeys to dance,' his instructor told him, 'but I will teach you to make *others* dance.'

After four weeks, Messu was presented with an armband, a sign of authority over the other recruits.

Proud of his new rank, he wanted to go home and boast about it, but discipline was strict and he was not allowed leave. Even if he could have returned home, Menefer would not have been able to see him. She had been summoned to Queen Ankhsenamun side.

Queen Senamun needed someone close, someone in whom to confide. She could not call upon Lady Mutnedjmet. As Horemheb's wife, and her duties at the temple as priestess, she was kept very busy. Senamun summoned Menefer.

The king's condition had confined him to his own quarters and the queen was fretful and apprehensive. The time of the birth of her child was drawing close.

'Majesty, you must relax more,' Menefer tried to calm her. 'You are doing yourself and the unborn child harm. There is no point, agonising over the future. Your distress will only make it worse. It is in the hands of the gods.'

'I know, Menefer,' Senamun lamented. 'I cannot shake this dread I feel. Tutankhamun's condition troubles me severely. We must go to the temple to pray and burn offering.'

'Your Majesty, we have been there twice already, this morning.'

'We must go again,' Senamun insisted.

Heavy with child, she had to be helped up and down the temple steps the third time that day. She was at prayer once again when she suddenly called out in pain. Menefer alerted the priestesses who called for her carry-chair, and she was taken back to the palace.

The *meskhen-t* stones had been kept in readiness in the birth-chamber. The mid-wife, kept on duty at all times, had been alerted. Even before the queen arrived back at the palace, the chamber had been prepared. Religious artefacts to aid the birth, had been assembled and the incense burners lit.

The queen arrived and they started dressing her in the birth-garments, but she went into labour before she was ready. Her maidservants assisted her onto the birth stones and the baby was born soon after.

'Is it a boy?' the queen asked anxiously. The entire Kingdom had been waiting and praying for a male heir.

Menefer shook her head. 'A girl!' Her expression remained grim and the queen knew immediately something was wrong.

'Is she…was she…also stillborn?'

Menefer dropped her head and nodded, tears glistening in her eyes. Ankhsenamun's wail of despair echoed through the corridors, startling the servants. The guards glanced about wide-eyed. They had all guessed the reason.

Pentu was with Tutankhamun when the physician was summoned to the queen's side. Leaving Kafre to tend to the king, Pentu found Her Majesty greatly distressed.

'Please, Pentu!' she begged. 'The king must not learn of this. He is not strong, and the news would surely kill him. Promise me you will not tell him!'

'You have my oath, Majesty,' Pentu promised.

***

Tutankhamun's leg had turned black, and was oozing and produced a foul-smelling odour. Sweet smelling oils, strong herbs and fragrant woods were burnt to mask the smell and drive away the demons, but did not really help. Those that entering the room had to breathe with restraint. The king had also developed a fever and his head and body was being bathed with wet linen to try and keep him cool.

Ay entered the chamber and glanced at Pentu. 'Any changes in His Majesty's condition?'

'His Majesty is…resting. He is as well as can be expected,' Pentu answered cautiously. 'We are doing all we can to make him comfortable.'

'Good, good. We are all praying for his recovery.'

*Another dead child…an ailing king, and he had been given the power as regent,* Ay thought*. It would be but a small step to seize the throne once the king has passed. Seti son had done well*, he thought. What a pity *he had died so close to their moment of triumph.*

'Alert me immediately of any change in his condition,' Ay said and left the chamber, suppressing a smile.

Tutankhamun woke after a restless sleep and immediately enquired after the queen. 'Any word about the queen, yet, Pentu?'

'Her Majesty is resting, Majesty,' the Physician answered with the usual vague and standard description.

The king grimaced from the pain, and forced himself not to cry out every time he moved. 'I wish to see her.'

'Your Majesty, the queen had a very restless night and I gave her a sleeping draught,' Pentu was nervous and cautiously asked, '…shall I awaken her and summon her to Your Majesty's side?'

'No. Let her sleep. I shall see her when she wakes.'

Pentu sighed, almost audibly, with relief. His lie had saved him from an awkward situation.

The king closed his eyes again. 'I will have some more of your pain-killing potion, Pentu.'

'Yes, Majesty,' he poured a measure of the bitter liquid into a cup.

'But this time,' Tutankhamun added, 'add more honey. Your cures taste awful!'

'Yes, Majesty,' Pentu obliged. There was little else he could do to ease the king's suffering.

# Chapter Forty-Two
## Desperation

'When can I see her?' Tutankhamun asked. 'I wish to see the Queen.'

Queen Ankhsenamun, not wishing him to know she had lost the child, devised a way to conceal the truth. She had Menefer fashion a padded belt to wear under her garments. Her ailing husband would never suspect anything amiss.

The King drifted in and out of coherency. One minute he would be lucid, the next he would talk gibberish.

Kafre was attending him when the queen, accompanied by Menefer, entered his bedchamber. Both were struck by the odour from his weeping leg. The wound had been smeared with a mustard and honey-mixture and bound in clean linen, but the fluid that oozed from the wound had seeped through the cloth.

'Clean and bind his leg again,' Ankhsenamun commanded. 'He cannot be left thus.'

'Yes, Majesty.' Kafre immediately attended the leg again, although he had cleaned it but a moment earlier.

'The queen...is she here?' Tutankhamun tried to lift his head.

'I am here, Lord,' she approached and wiped his fevered brow.

'I see...your time has not yet...come. When do you think...?' His breathing was shallow and speech difficult.

'I do not know, My Lord,' the queen lied. 'These things cannot be predicted. The physician thinks stress is delaying the birthing.'

'Do not be concerned for me. You must take...care of yourself above all.' He turned to Menefer, 'How is Messu? Well, I hope?'

'He is fine, Majesty. He has already been promoted,' Menefer answered.

'Good. Good. Give him this...' Tutankhamun reached over with difficulty.

'Allow me, Majesty,' Kafre passed him the container.

Tutankhamun opened it and removed an object, which he gave Menefer, a ring in the form of an asp. 'A token of my friendship and affection...and one of good luck...to ward off evil.'

'Thank you, Your Majesty. He is sure to treasure it.'

Suddenly, the Kings startled everyone by shouting at invisible demons hovering about his bed. 'They are about me! Bring my sling, quickly! I must drive them away...'

He clutched at the Queen, then called for the baby's hood and tippet he had fashioned in anticipation of the birth. It was made of fine linen and studded with gold bosses. 'The cowl... I want the cowl...' His mind had once again wandered. 'The child will be here soon...the cowl must be readied.'

'It is, my Lord,' Ankhsenamun took his hand in hers and kissed it. 'Everything is in readiness, do not fear.'

Tutankhamun seemed to calm again and sank back on the couch.

'If it is a…a male child, as soon as he is old enough, we will go fowling in the reeds.'

His head sank back onto the headrest.

'I… I am very tired. I will rest for a while, now.'

A moment later, Kafre whispered that the king was asleep. Menefer rose to leave.

'I will remain by his side, Menefer. You go and rest,' the queen suggested. 'It has been a fretful day…and you too, physician. I will tend my Lord during the night,' Kafre bowed and saluted, and he and Menefer left quietly.

Some time after, the king lapsed into a coma, the *Sleep of the dead.* Kafre was again summoned. The news spread, and the people of the Two Lands prayed and burnt offerings for the king to awaken, but this was not to be. For three days, he remained thus, moaning and whimpering. The queen, ever at his side, bathed his perspiring, fever-ridden body. She would not rest or leave him, even at the urgings of Kafre, Lady Mutnedjmet or Menefer.

'I must stay with my Lord,' she said. 'If he wakes, he must find me by his side.'

On the eve of the fourth day, the king calmed. He stopped perspiring and his brow cooled. He appeared to be improving and the exhausted queen, resting her head upon his couch, finally allowed herself to sleep.

She woke the next morning with the sun already well above the horizon. Another bright sunny day, the first day of the month of Payni, the season of flowers.

She looked at Tutankhamun. He was still sleeping. The king had not had a good rest since his return from the battle, almost four months ago, and she was careful not to wake him. He looked so peaceful, with a slight smile on his lips. Careful not to wake him, she stretched carefully to ease her cramped and stiff limbs.

*He's getting better*, she thought to herself. *He's finally going to get well.* She leaned over and kissed his cheek tenderly. It felt cold.

Tutankhamun was dead. He was just eighteen years old!

***

Lord Ay sought out Queen Ankhsenamun. She was in the pavilion by the lake, with some maids in attendance. She had been weeping and her eyes were red and puffy. It had been just hours since the body of Tutankhamun had been taken to the *House of Skin* for the embalming process, and she already had a stream of solemn visitors expressing their condolences. Many more were expected, but weary of them, she had to get out of the palace for a while. There were too many memories. It was peaceful here at the lake. It had been Tutankhamun's favourite haunt. He used to spend every leisure hour here, content to hunt waterfowl in the reed marshes.

In her mind's eye, she could see him, there, on his skiff, armed with his sling or throwing stick, searching for a plump bird for the table. He had never been a very good hunter, but occasionally by sheer chance, he did kill a bird, and boasted about his skills for weeks afterwards. She smiled to herself and wiped yet another tear from her cheek.

'Your Majesty,' Ay approached and bowed deeply. She beckoned him to sit. 'My deepest regrets for Your Majesty's…and all Egypt's great loss.'

Senamun nodded her understanding.

'Majesty, I will continue to perform the tasks His Majesty had entrusted upon me during his illness. Your Majesty is in mourning, and should not be called upon to handle matters of State. With Your Majesty's permission, may I conduct these affairs until a decision is made?'

'Decision made? What decision, Ay?'

'An heir, Majesty. All Egypt is waiting to know who will succeed…and may I add, Majesty, in the entire Kingdom, no one is more qualified—'

Ankhsenamun straightened up, her hands gripping the side of the couch. 'Lord Ay! They had not even started the embalming of the King and you are already claiming the throne!'

Ay coughed nervously. 'It seems…unfitting for me to have mentioned it so soon, Majesty, but it is necessary. In just over two months, by the time of the sealing of the tomb, a successor *must* be named.' Then, with a courteous bow, Ay turned and marched away, smiling.

Senamun and Menefer were in the queen's day room, busying themselves with their usual decorative stitching of garments. It gave the queen something to do, to keep her mind from her sorrow. A lute-player had been strumming the instrument softly in a corner. The soothing music had always calmed Senamun, but this time she hardly noticed it. For the umpteenth time, she turned to Menefer and again bemoaned her lot. 'Why Menefer…why did this happen? He loved life…He was so young…'

'Majesty, our fate is in the hands of the gods.'

'Our family is cursed. The gods still seeking vengeance for Akhenaten's rejection of them. First, my sister died when that accursed city was being built, then my first child, then Akhenaten, Smenkhare, my younger sisters, my mother, two more of my children…and now my dear Tutankhamun…all taken. Why?'

Menefer remained silent. Nothing she could say would answer the queen's questions, the questions everyone always asked at a time like this.

'Seventy days…just seventy days…'

'Majesty?' Menefer lowered her stitching and looked up.

'Seventy day…the embalming period and preparations for the burial would take seventy days.'

'Yes Majesty,' Menefer nodded, but not certain why the queen mentioned it.

'That is the time I have left. I must then announce a successor. It is the custom. I have to name a successor during the funerary feast… Pharaoh heir!'

'Who will it be, Majesty? Chief Commander Horemheb? He was named *rpat* by His Majesty.'

'Probably. He is not of noble birth, but his marriage to Mutnedjmet has strengthened his claim…but Ay has also laid claim.'

'Lord Ay?'

'Yes. He is of noble birth. His mother was a Mittanian princess and his father, a noble at the court of the third Amenhotep. As the father of my mother, he claims the title Father of the god,' Ankhsenamun paused a moment, 'Tutankhamun made him regent during his illness and he was able to do an excellent job and for that the council respects him…but the only thing…' Senamun hesitated again. 'The only thing is… he has to marry me!'

'Marry? Lord Ay?'

'Yes. To ascend the throne, he has to marry a Princess Royal!' She hesitated, then, in a quavering voice, she continued. 'Menefer, I have no desire to marry him. He is sixty four years old!'

'But Lord Ay is already married. What of Lady Tey!'

'She will become a secondary wife.'

'Your Majesty, why not rule alone…as Queen Hatshepsut had done?'

'I already thought of that, but Ay told me *Power is not for the faint hearted.* He is right. I have not the desire nor the strength to rule.'

'Then why not marry someone else, a prince from another country, perhaps?'

'I thought of that, too, but there are none. The last eligible prince married my younger sister, years ago.'

'What about King Shubbiluliuma? I believe he has several sons.'

'Shubbiluliuma? But he is our enemy. I cannot make an enemy a king of Egypt!'

'Hittites fought with Amurra against us, Majesty, but King Shubbiluliuma had never actually declared war on Egypt, he had merely given assistance to the Amorites. He had always declared his neutrality. Let him now show it.'

Ankhsenamun thought long on this proposal. 'Yes,' she finally admitted. 'This could be to Egypt's advantage. We will have a powerful ally. You seem to know a lot about politics, Menefer.'

'I learned much from Rakhmet, Majesty.'

'Rakhmet? You are together again? This is great news, why did you not mention this before?'

'The king was ill, Majesty. It did not seem fitting to mention my personal feelings.'

'Perhaps you are right,' she paused again, then came to a decision. 'Your idea, by marrying a son of Shubbiluliuma, might be the solution. I will do it. I will write to him!'

The Queen summoned Rakhmet. 'Rakhmet, I have an important mission for you. You and a delegation are to travel to Khatti, to city of Hattusa. Seek an audience with Shubbiluliuma, the Hittite king, and explain the situation. You will carry an official letter with my seal. She explained the situation briefly.

'Make haste, Rakhmet. I need an answer by the time of Pharaoh's burial. Time is short. How long is the march to Hattusas?'

'It took us a month to march to Khor, Majesty. Hattusas is about another fifteen days beyond, forty-five days. A delegation will not make it back in time. But if I travel alone, I will be able to travel much faster.'

'It is too dangerous, going alone. You will be going through enemy territory.'

'I can do it, Majesty. I can travel there and back in just under half that time by chariot.'

'Very well, then do so, Rakhmet, and may the gods go with you!'

A scribe, versed in the *words of the mouth of the Hittites* drew up the document. Rakhmet wrapped the dried and baked tablet in fabric and after loading some provisions for the journey, bade Menefer and the Queen farewell and set off for Hattusas.

'Pray that his journey be successful, Menefer...for my sake as well as for Egypt...if he fails, I know not what I will do!'

*** 

Rakhmet's journey took him through the very lands he had travelled earlier on the way to battle. He drove the horses hard and had to change them frequently. He had also lost time, more than once, when he took a wrong road and had to backtrack. The people were now wary of Egyptians, but as he was not wearing battledress or uniform, they treated him courteously.

Sixteen days later, exhausted and grimy, he reached Shubbiluliuma's remote capital, built on a series of barren hills, and surrounded by high mountains. His first sight of the city was the immense city-wall, with watchtowers that ran across a massive sloping structure, every twelve steps, resembling a pyramid. In the middle of the sloping edifice, a huge gate-way faced south. Two bearded human-headed animal figures guarded the gate, each wearing a tall cylindrical crown.

An inner wall, even more massive than the outer one, ideal for ambushing any enemy that somehow managed to penetrate this far, guarded the city from within. On a high hill, in the centre of the city and also surrounded by a defensive wall, stood the fortress-palace of the king. Huge timber-and-bronze gates led inside.

He requested an audience with the king even before he had cleansed himself or had something to eat. His mission, was more important than nourishment or appearance.

'What does he want?' King Shubbiluliuma, suspicious of the Egyptian, asked. 'They probably want me to withdraw my troops from the Mittanian border. They have as much chance of that as asking for snow to fall on their lands! Let him wait!'

Several days passed. After repeated requests from an anxious Rakhmet, an audience was finally granted. He was escorted into the throne room and bowed deeply before Shubbiluliuma. The king, an imposing, powerful man whose presence could easily strike terror into the hearts of anyone, awaited him and nodded. A shock of dark curly hair rimmed his head, capped by a tall cylindrical crown, similar to the guardian sphinxes at the gate. A tightly curled beard framed a scowling face, and thick eyebrows met in the middle of his forehead. They shaded his dark, intense eyes whose gaze seemed to penetrate the very soul of those he beheld and made him even more menacing.

'Well, Egyptian? I have been informed you have a request from your Queen Dakamun?'

'Yes, Your Majesty.' He explained that his mission was very urgent. 'Her Majesty, Queen Ankhsenamun, whom you call Dakamun, sends her greetings and wishes you well. She also wishes Your Majesty a long and—'

'Never mind the niceties,' Shubbiluliuma silenced him with a quick gesture. 'What is the reason for your visit? You have a letter?'

Rakhmet unwrapped the tablet and held it out towards the king. Impatiently, he signalled to a scribe to read it. The scribe took the letter and cleared his throat.

*'My husband, Neb-Kheperu-re has died. I have no sons. There is no heir to the throne of Egypt. Never shall I pick a servant of mine to make him my husband. Thou have many sons, they say. If thou send me one of thy sons, he shall become my husband and king of Egypt. I am afraid.'*

'Such a request has never before been put to me,' Shubbiluliuma replied, apprehensive. 'She wishes to make my son, king, but it appears being King of Egypt is not too healthy a prospect…they seem not to live to a great age.' He shifted his weight. 'I value my sons and have no wish for them to follow the way of your kings so swiftly. How do I know this is not a ploy, a trick to lure my son away and use him to coerce me into submitting to your demands, to retract my armies from Mesopotamia?'

Rakhmet had to restrain himself from showing his anger. The king had virtually accused him and his queen of lying. He explained the queen's dilemma once again.

'I need to contemplate the request. An answer cannot be given lightly. I will have an envoy accompany you to No-Amun. I will give you my decision upon his return.' He summoned his chamberlain, Lord Hattu-zitis, 'You will accompany the Egyptian, speak to the queen. Verify her request, and bring me back the details.'

'Your Majesty, the situation is critical,' Rakhmet pleaded. 'Queen Ankhsenamun *must* announce an heir by the time of the funeral of our king, and the time is short.'

'Then you better make haste! Go!'

No amount of persuasion could change Shubbiluliuma's mind and the protesting Hattu-zitis was in no hurry to leave. 'It is well past noon and I proposed we wait till morning.'

'We leave within the hour!' Rakhmet insisted. 'We must make haste…by the orders of King Shubbiluliuma!'

The chariots were harnessed and equipped and the two men departed on their long journey south.

\*\*\*

The travellers arrived back in No-Amun thirty-two days after Rakhmet had left on his mission. Already late in the evening, they went immediately to the palace. Hattu-zitis protested that he had not eaten since midday, but Rakhmet ignored him and asked to see the queen.

'Her Majesty has already retired, Commander,' the guard replied.

'Rouse her! It is most urgent!' Rakhmet ordered.

The guard hesitated, but another command from Rakhmet sent him scurrying to her chambers. They were immediately summoned to her day-chamber. The queen was in her sleeping garments when she received them. She found no need to dress as the anticipated news from Shubbiluliuma was more important.

'Welcome, Lord Hattu-zitis,' she replied when Rakhmet introduced the emissary, bade them be seated and immediately sent a maid to bring food for the tired and hungry men. While they ate, Rakhmet told her, in detail, of the Hittite king's demands. Senamun, almost in tears, again summoned the scribe, then dictated another letter.

'Rest well tonight, Lord Hattu-zitis, Rakhmet,' she told them. 'I regret the inconvenience, but the matter is grave. You must leave in the morning.'

They were given quarters in the palace to rest. After the day's long journey, Hattu-zitis immediately prepared to retire, but Rakhmet wished to see Menefer first.

'Rakhmet! How wonderful to see you. Was your undertaking a success? Is the prince—'

He took her into his arms. 'The mission is not yet over, Menefer. I must depart again at dawn. We have but this one short moment to be together.'

'You need your rest, then. You have another very long journey ahead.'

He tried to persuade her to be with him for a while, but she ordered him to bed. 'Now, sleep, Rakhmet! I want to hear no more from you!' She spoke the way she used to with Messu when he wanted to stay up.

He protested, but exhaustion soon overtook him and she left the room. When she roused him just before dawn, he felt as if he had hardly slept. He stretched, yawned, hastily gulped down the meal she had prepared for him, then went to meet up with Hattu-zitis. They set off again, this time accompanied by Hanis, the queen's emissary, to support Rakhmet's story. Shubbiluliuma *had to* be convinced.

Rakhmet suffered another delay. One of the wheels of his chariot, hit a rock and was badly damaged. Both wheels had to be replaced as the new one, slightly smaller than the original, unbalanced the vehicle. Eighteen days later, the party entered Hattusas.

Rakhmet and Hanis bowed and Hattu-zitis prostrated himself before his king, then they rose on command. The king waggled a finger for Hattu-zitis to speak.

'Your Majesty, I have been to the Egyptian court and saw things with my own eyes, and heard with my own ears the position there. It is as the envoy had said. The queen is being compelled—but has no desire—to marry her Vizier, Lord Ay is an old man. The queen is young and comely. She must announce Pharaoh's successor within twenty days! It is, as Commander Rakhmet had said, of the utmost urgency, Lord! She has sent another letter.'

Hanis handed the letter to the scribe.

'Your Majesty, the queen was distressed when she dictated it and—' Rakhmet started to explain.

'No speeches!' Shubbiluliuma silenced him, then impatiently turned to the scribe. 'Read the letter!'

The scribe started to read.

'*Why did thou say, "They wish to deceive me?"*' he read. '*If I had a son, would I humiliate my country of my own accord to write to another country thus? I did not write to another country, but to thee alone. They say thee has many sons. Give me thou one of thy sons to me. I will take him for my husband and he shall furthermore be King of Egypt.*'

The scribe stopped, waiting for a response.

'Is that the end of the letter?'

'Yes, Lord.'

Shubbiluliuma sat thoughtfully, leaning on the arm of his throne and twirled a strand of his beard. 'Um... yes!' He tapped his lip with his forefinger. 'Maybe an alliance with Egypt could benefit both Empires.'

After another few moments, he suddenly sat up and slapped the armrest of the throne. 'Very well. Summon Prince Zannanza.'

A few moments later, a handsome young man appeared. His pale face, surrounded by a halo of black curly hair, had a fuzzy hint of the beard he was trying to grow. Rakhmet judged him to be a little older than King Tutankhamun had been, probably nineteen or twenty years old.

The prince had been informed of the circumstances and no explanation had been necessary. 'Majesty.' The Prince looked troubled. 'I am aware of the situation and your decision. You wish me to go to Egypt, perhaps forever? Never to return? Have I no say in any of this?'

The King's severe expression suddenly changed and he became a compassionate and caring father. He put his hand on his son's shoulder.

'Understand this, my son, your older brothers would all be considered before you. When I die, the choicest lands in Khatti would go to them. You will be given a much smaller region to rule. Mursil, as the eldest, will, one day be supreme ruler of this country and you will always be subservient to him.' He patted his son's shoulder tenderly, 'But if...when you marry this Egyptian queen, you will be a king.' He spread out his arms in an encompassing gesture, 'Not just of a small province, but a mighty Kingdom...you will be Pharaoh of Egypt! We could be allies and bring a long sought-after peace.' The King straightened up and once again became the commanding figure he represented. 'You leave for Egypt on the morrow.'

Mursil had been standing on one side, observing his father. As a future king, he often attended these gatherings to gain experience. Now he stepped forward and excited, clasped his brother's forearm in a gesture of admiration.

'Father's reasoning is sound, Zannanza, do you realise the potential powers that awaits you?' He clapped his brother on the shoulder. 'You would become king before any of us, of a Kingdom as mighty as that of our father.'

Others came forward to wish the young prince well and congratulated him on his good fortune. The thoughts were like strong wine to Zannanza. His head swirled in anticipation and he now looked forward to the wedding.

'Assemble a great caravan,' he ordered. 'As befitting a future King of Egypt!'

'Forgive me, Your Highness, 'Rakhmet intervened. 'The journey is of the utmost urgency. We need to travel light and with speed. The caravan with your belongings could follow after our departure.'

'Yes, you are right, Commander,' the Prince reluctantly agreed. 'I will take just a few things and fifty of my personal guards.'

Rakhmet, still concerned, explained, 'With that many travellers, even at their fleetest, we might still arrive too late. We need to maintain a steady pace. For speed, the number of guards will need to be drastically reduced.'

'Why? Each will keep up with the rest. Those that lag, will be left behind,' Zannanza insisted.

'It is not their speed that concerns me, Your Highness. The horses will tire and must be changed frequently. There are places where this can be done along the way, but they have only a limited number of fresh and rested beasts in readiness.'

'Ah, but have you not heard of our horses?' Zannanza boasted. 'Their stamina exceeds any other. They are specially trained.'

Rakhmet, not convinced, continued to object and in the end, they reached a compromise. Zannanza reluctantly, agreed to cut the number of his guards drastically, a move that would cost them dearly.

# Chapter Forty-Three
## Anguish

'What is this?' Ay asked, furious. He had just learnt of Rakhmet's mission. 'Why have I not been told of this?'

Lord Nakhtmin answered, surprised, 'I thought you had been informed, Lord Ay.'

'No! This is the first I've heard of it. You say she actually *begged* the Hittite king for one of his sons? She would let a *Hittite* sit on the throne of Egypt?'

Nakhtmin nodded.

Ay paced back and forth in the Audience Hall, fuming. His face red with anger, he kept swatting at his leg with the fly whisk. The mid-spring heat, already upon them, made him most uncomfortable.

'Hyksos had once sat on the throne of Egypt and for three hundred years we were ruled by foreigners.' He waved the fly whisk dramatically. 'We were a conquered land. When they were finally driven from the Two Lands, we vowed never to let that happen again, yet now our queen is offering that very throne to a *Hittite?* Like it was a…a garment or a honey-cake!' He stopped and glared at Nakhtmin. 'When did this take place?

'They left here about a month ago.'

'Hmm!' Ay rubbed his chin. 'Thirty days…it's about a month's journey to Hattusas and back, or, say thirty-five days if they are delayed.' He did some rough calculating, 'They should then be back in about week—ten days from now. The king's funeral is to be in twelve days time, so they should arrive back about…Uh…in about two or three days from now, well before the funeral, unless—'

'Unless, Lord?'

'Uh…oh, nothing, Lord Nakhtmin. I was just pondering…' Ay hurried from the room.

*\*\*\**

'We are making good progress, Lord Hanis. We are half a day ahead already. We shall reach No-Amun with several days to spare.'

Hanis and Rakhmet were driving their chariots alongside each other at the head of the column, and managed to keep a good pace.

'Good, General Rakhmet. Yes, the young prince handles his chariot well, but he did not changed his horses for fresh ones. Surely, they will weary?'

'Those are Arabi horses, specially trained animals,' Rakhmet explained. 'He insisted in bringing them all the way to Egypt and assured me the horses have great endurance. When they are paced, they can canter for twelve hours with just an occasional rest. They seemed to be as he had claimed.'

They rode in silence for a moment. 'Did you know the Hittites are excellent horsemen? A man named Kikkuli, a master horse trainer, had a method unmatched by any other country. The animals are fed oats, barley and hay three times a day. Have you observed how the prince's horse-master scrubs them with warm water every time we rest.'

'Yes,' Hanis nodded. 'The prince treats his horses better than we treat some of our slaves. He unharnesses and grooms the horses himself.'

*** 

They were nearing Egypt in good time and everyone's spirit rose, including Rakhmet. His mission had succeeded, even with the delays caused by Shubbiluliuma's suspicion. He started making plans that, once they are back in No-Amun, he would request a long break from duty. He and Menefer would then be wed, and perhaps spend a leisurely week or so together, alone. They both certainly deserved it, he thought and smiled to himself.

Presently, they arrived at the well in Gatchai, their last overnight stop before reaching Egypt. Rakhmet, exhausted but content, alighted from his chariot. It had been a long and punishing journey and the end was nigh.

The travellers unharnessed and fed the horses, set up camp in a sheltered area, surrounded, but well away from some boulders, and finished their evening meal. They were making ready to retire, but the horses seemed nervous. Their whinnies and trampling alerted the guards, who immediately armed themselves. No wild animals had been encountered thus far, but there were lions about. Prince Zannanza's immediate concern was for his precious stallions and he hurried over to where they had been tethered.

A dark shape moved amongst the boulders. Hattu-zitis, the Hittite chamberlain, rose to warn the prince, cried out and fell forward, an arrow protruding from his back. The rest of the party immediately grabbed their weapons and shielded themselves as more arrows thudded around them.

'Bandits!' Zannanza shouted and raced back to the group.

In the early evening darkness, they had difficulty seeing anything. Whoever had shot the arrows, remained hidden, concealed by the boulders. Rakhmet realised the area was lit by the camp fire and they were easy targets. He quickly kicked sand over the flames.

The men formed a tight circle facing the boulders, their only protection were their shields held in front of them. Hanis looked around. There was no sign of the two sentries they had posted on the boulders.

The men had no idea how many bandits were about. One would appear suddenly, loose his arrow, then duck behind his cover, then another would appear elsewhere, shoot and vanish. One by one, the guards were hit, some mortally, others wounded, but were again targeted as they tried to crawl to safety.

Then one of the bandits rose from behind a boulder almost immediately in front of Rakhmet. He took aim, and they made eye contact.

'Sothis!' Rakhmet cried out cursing the name of the assistant to the Royal treasurer, but before he could utter another word, an arrow struck him in the back. He reeled around, clutching at the shaft protruding from his body, then another arrow struck him and the world went black.

***

The body of Tutankhamun had been embalmed and was being readied for the final rites. It had been wrapped in the finest of linens. On his fingers and toes were placed golden stalls and each digit individually wrapped.

Tutankhamun, who had been so desperately trying for a male heir, had become a follower of the god Min, the god of fertility, and, as a symbolic gesture to that deity, the young king's member had been wrapped in an erect position, in the manner of the god, to enable him to be virile in the hereafter.

One hundred and forty-three gold and jewelled ornaments, amulets and charms were placed within the folds of the linen. A portrait mask, in the image of the king and fashioned of beaten gold, wearing a *Nemes* royal headdress, was inlaid with lapis lazuli, obsidian and quarts. It had been placed over the head. On his chest was placed a broad golden collar encrusted with gemstones—green feldspar, carnelian, lapis lazuli and obsidian.

Just as Smenkhare before him, Tutankhamun was taken across the river to the temple of *Ipet-Isut.* Ay and Mutnedjmet performed the ceremony to notify the gods of the coming of their earthly incarnation, and executed the ceremony of the *Opening of the mouth.*

Tutankhamun's body rested in a coffin of solid gold, covered with a jewel-encrusted lid in the likeness of the king.

*Renpet*, the time of flowers, had arrived. Just before the lid was closed, Queen Ankhsenamun placed a garland of blue cornflowers and May-weeds on the body, together with a poem she had written for the young king.

'*I am thy wife, O great one— do not leave me!*
*Is it thy good pleasure, O my brother, that I should go far from thee?*
*How can it be that I go away alone?*
*I say, "I accompany thee, O thou who didst like to converse with me,"*
*But thou remainest silent and speakest not!'*

The lid was closed and the coffin placed in a second coffin of gilded wood. Both were then lowered inside a third coffin, the gilt-covered wooden coffin, once fashioned for Smenkhare, and abandoned all those years earlier. It had been quickly refashioned with Tutankhamun's name.

The three coffins were lifted onto a catafalque, then taken back across the river to the western bank on the funerary barge, where the queen, her ladies and Menefer, were waiting.

On reaching the western bank of the Nile, the women mounted carry chairs for the trip to the tomb. Menefer had been invited to share the queen's transport. They followed behind the ox-drawn sleds transporting the coffins, furniture, and all the other trappings of a Royal burial. Priests and priestesses followed, and behind them walked the professional mourners. Other mourners of rank, followed.

They travelled in silence. Menefer did not wish to disrupt the deeply mourning queen in her grief, so she busied herself with private thoughts.

Being carried was much more comfortable and less tiring than her journey to Smenkhare's burial. Her thought turned to Messu. He was one of the guards on duty. This time he would not even be able to quench his thirst along the way. She felt sorry for him, but she knew the importance of discipline. He had chosen his profession and had to abide by their rules.

Then Ankhsenamun broke the silence by sighing deeply. 'I loved him so, Menefer. I really loved him with all my heart.'

'I know, Majesty. You were well suited for one another...'

Senamun sighed again, '"*He tormented my heart with his voice. It fluttered whenever I thought of my love for him. Whenever he was near, my heart would not act sensibly and leaped from its place*",' she quoted. 'That was another poem I had written for him.' Then she turned and gazed into the distance behind them, 'Where could he be?'

'He is now in the realm of Osiris...' Menefer started to explain.

'No, I mean Hanis, the envoy I sent to Khatti.'

The queen's mind was wandering, from the memories of Tutankhamun to her present predicament. Within a few hours, she would need to announce the successor to the throne. It concerned Menefer as well. Rakhmet should have been back days ago. Why is he taking so long? Both women prayed in silence for the arrival and outcome of the mission.

They continued to the Valley of the Kings in silence.

***

At the tomb, the oxen were unharnessed. The sled, containing an alabaster chest that held the King's internal organs, was taken inside followed by the dismantled shrine, later to be erected inside the chamber. As they took the sled inside, Menefer noticed something unusual. Isis, protector of the liver, had been placed at the front of the sled, where Selket, protector of the intestines should have been. Had this been deliberate, or an error, perhaps because of the haste of preparing the funeral? This is surely a very bad omen. The cold fingers of fear clutched at her heart again. Calamity is surely to befall them this day.

The sled with the king's body, inside its nest coffins, was next. Nobles, in a final act of respect, dragged the catafalque.

The tomb of Tutankhamun appeared very modest compared to those of earlier Pharaohs. Sixteen steps descended steeply down to the doorway of a sloping passage, which led into a series of chambers.

On her way down the stairs, the Queen faltered and Menefer had to assist her. They passed through the first of the chambers, the largest, where the furniture would be placed. A large wooden chest had already been positioned. A painted war scene on it, depicted Tutankhamun's battle with the Amorites, his last battle.

The mourners had to wait in this chamber while the heavy nest of coffins had been taken into the burial chamber and lowered onto a magnificent quartzite sarcophagus. Its four corners were carved in the likenesses of the four goddesses, Nephtys, Neith, Selket and Isis, their wings outstretched, embracing the sarcophagus protectively. This time, Menefer noted, the goddesses were placed correctly.

Ankhsenamun turned and anxiously looked towards the entrance.

'Is anything amiss, Majesty?' Menefer asked, puzzled.

'No sign of Rakhmet yet. I posted men along the way to alert us as soon as sight of the convoy should appear.'

Menefer could not think of reassuring words or anything else to say.

Ay announced that all was ready, and a way was cleared for the queen. They entered the burial chamber. The walls were decorated with paintings, one wall depicted Tutankhamun's funerary cortege, another, Ay performing the *Opening of the Mouth* ceremony, yet another of the king embracing Osiris.

The queen stifled a sob and fell on the coffin, weeping. Menefer leaned over to comfort her, then noticed two other tiny coffins in the chamber. They were not those of sacred animals, cats, baboons, crocodiles or hawks that were often buried with the deceased. These contained the bodies of two babies, Tutankhamun and Ankhsenamun's two stillborn children would accompany him into the next world.

Fortunately, Ankhsenamun did not see them, but continued stroking the coffin tenderly. She murmured softly, 'Farewell, my dear, sweet Lord, my love. Wait for me in that land of green reed marshes where you can go fowling forever-more. I will be joining thee there, soon, and we can walk together, hand in hand along the banks of the river, and smell the sweet fragrance of blooms in the land of the eternal flower season.'

After libations were poured over the body and incantations chanted, the mourners were escorted out, and the sarcophagus lid eased into place. Because of the cramped space, movements were restricted. The heavy stone covering slipped from the grasp of the men, fell and broke in half. The workers looked at one another in horror. It was surely another evil omen.

Last prayers were recited and four golden shrines, one fitting inside the other, were erected inside the already crowded crypt. The remaining priests had to squeeze their way out of the chamber, then a great shroud, of blue fabric and studded with gold medallions, was draped over the shrine.

The priests left the tomb. The burial chamber was sealed behind them, and two life-sized images of the king, each holding a spear, placed on either side of the sealed doorway. Then the rest of the funerary equipment, the king's clothing boxes, weapons and chariots, were carried inside. Among Tutankhamun's treasured items, together with his costly jewellery; earrings and finger rings, were his most treasured possessions, a simple sling and a few pebbles.

\*\*\*

'What lies in store for Egypt now?' Queen Ankhsenamun murmured as they walked over to the pavilion, erected for the funerary feast. 'What fate awaits the Two Lands? Oh, where can Hanis and Rakhmet be? Did they succeed in their mission, and if so, when is the Hittite prince coming?'

'I too, am concerned, Majesty. Something must have delayed them.'

'We can but hope and pray they are well and safe.'

Well past mid-afternoon, despite the heat of the day had reached its peak, Senamun shivered from anticipation and uneasiness. The banquet started and ritual songs and dances were performed. The mourners feasted while a blind harper sang a song.

*'Rejoice, and let thy heart forget that day when they lay thee to rest.*
*Cast all sorrow behind thee and bethink thee of joy,*
*Until there comes that day of reaching port,*
*In the land that loveth silence.*

As the song ended, Ay turned to the queen. 'The time has come, Majesty, to make the announcement.'

'Not yet. Just another hour, please, Lord Ay.'

'Very well, Your Majesty,' he replied impatiently. 'But the hour grows late and Your Majesty *must* make a decision!'

For the hundredth time that day, Ankhsenamun turned her face toward the east from whence the expected news would come. 'Where can they be?' she whispered again. 'I cannot delay the announcement much longer. Everyone is getting impatient.'

The afternoon wore on.

After some time, Ay stood up. This time he did not address the queen directly, and called out in a loud voice so everyone could hear. 'Your Majesty, the time has come to announce to the people, the successor to the throne. We are all aware Your Majesty had approached King Shubbiluliuma for one of his sons as a husband, to rule over Egypt...'

There were gasps and murmurs from the crowd. For most, this was the first they heard of the queen's desperate pleas to a foreign, an *enemy* king, for help. An unprecedented move.

Ay smiled smugly. He wanted everyone to know how far Queen Ankhsenamun would stoop to avoid marrying him, and he continued, scornfully. 'It is obvious that the Hittite King had rejected your Majesty's offer!'

Ankhsenamun lowered her head, hurt, and Ay's spiteful words stung deeply. He had embarrassed her before her people.

She rose slowly and a hush fell over the crowd as all eyes turned towards her expectantly. 'Lord Ay speaks the truth,' her voice broke, but she continued, 'I had sought to marry a Hittite prince, but it had been an attempt to cement ties with Shubbiluliuma. No one likes war. Egypt had suffered a great loss in the battle against the Amorites. I, as well as many others, had lost someone they loved. Many had suffered and is suffering still,' she paused to murmurs of agreement. 'Do not condemn me for my action. By my deed I had hoped Egypt would gain a powerful ally, to ensure it would end hostilities forever. I had desired for a lasting peace between our two countries.'

The Queen looked around the crowd and, in the late afternoon sunlight, Menefer noticed her cheeks were glistening with tears.

'But, as Lord Ay had said, no word has reached me yet. The envoy I sent to Hattusas had not returned. My mission had failed and therefore I have reached a decision. I have chosen someone among my own people, someone of noble birth and great wisdom, to be Pharaoh's heir.'

Ankhsenamun's voice faltered and for a moment, it seemed as if she would swoon. She cleared her throat, regained her composure and spoke again. 'I…I therefore ask Lord Ay to be my consort…to be my husband and to become the next King of the Two Lands!'

# Chapter Forty-Four
## Back from the Dead

No word reached Egypt from Rakhmet or Hanis. With a heavy heart and no other option, Queen Ankhsenamun wed Lord Ay, and sat, head bowed, during the ceremony.

'Lift your spirits!' Ay ordered. 'We have guests and they should not see you thus!'

'Yes, My Lord,' she answered and forced a weak smile.

Immediately after the ceremony, preparations were made for Pharaoh's coronation. The Royal couple and court officials were in the midst of planning the event, when a guard entered and announced that a messenger had arrived, asking for an audience with the queen.

'Bid him enter,' Ankhsenamun answered. 'I will see him presently, in the antechamber—'

'No!' Ay interrupted. 'We will not be disturbed. I will see him on the morrow.'

'But he wishes to see *me*, Lord. We could meet in private—'

'*I* am Pharaoh!' Ay insisted. Your business is my business. We will not be disturbed. The messenger can wait!'

'Yes, My Lord,' Queen Ankhsenamun sighed and turned to the guard. 'Inform the messenger,' the guard saluted and left.

Well into the following day, the queen was finally able to grant the messenger an audience. Menefer, who had been keeping her company, excused herself and left the chamber for the queen to hear the message in private. He had just started to deliver his news when the queen halted him and summoned Menefer to return. 'You should hear this also, Menefer. It concerns both of us.'

From the queen's shocked expression, Menefer immediately realised the messenger had brought bad news.

'Please repeat your message,' Senamun commanded.

'Your Majesty, Mistress Menefer, the news I received concerning General Rakhmet and Lord Hanis, is grave…they, and their entire party, had been slain.'

'Rakhmet? Dead?' Menefer covered her face in her hands.

Queen Senamun now had to comfort Menefer. 'What happened?' The Queen asked the messenger.

'The convoy, including Prince Zannanza of Khatti, and his personal guards, had camped at the well of Rabata, just off the caravan route in Gatchai and were attacked by bandits. A merchant caravan, arriving at the well several days later, discovered the bodies. None survived.'

Both the queen and Menefer were devastated by the news.

'Please, arrange for the bodies to be brought back to Egypt, for burial.'

The messenger bowed and was about to leave, when Ay entered. 'No. We cannot spare the cost of such an expedition.'

The queen was stunned. 'But…but why? Surely it's—'

'By the time a retrieval party reached the place, wild animals would have been at the bodies. Vultures had, by now, already decimated the remains and none would be recognisable,' Ay was adamant and replied coldly. 'There would be no point in bringing them back.' He then shrugged, unsympathetically, 'Most were Hittites, after all!'

'Rakhmet and Hanis were Egyptian! Surely they deserve burial in Egypt!' Ankhsenamun objected. 'Rakhmet was an officer and my friend, and Hanis a loyal court official. We owe them this one last courtesy.'

'No!' Ay was adamant. 'Leave them be. We have neither the funds, nor the facility to identify anyone from a pile of bones!'

'You are right, My Lord,' Ankhsenamun answered meekly. 'But, what about the bandits, can we not seek them out, punish them for this dreadful crime?'

'How can we? We know not the land of Gatchai. These robbers strike, then vanish like shadows, leaving no trace. No, I fear they will never be known!'

The queen lowered her head, disappointed, and nodded. A sly smile curled her husband's lips. His plans had worked well. With one stroke, he had rid Egypt of the Hittite Prince, and not only gained a young wife, but also the throne of Egypt.

*\*\**

Menefer visited the queen in her day-chamber at the far end of Malkata, and found the queen in tears. Queen Senamun seemed pale and troubled and clutched a little effigy of Tutankhamun.

'Your Majesty, what ails you?'

'Oh, I feel so miserable, Menefer. My spirits are very low.' She beckoned Menefer to sit beside her, put the figurine down and clasped Menefer's hand in both of hers. 'I'm so sorry, Menefer… I always seem to be bemoaning my own lot when you too had suffered a great loss.'

'We had both lost dear ones, Majesty, since…since then. Three years had passed but Your Majesty still grieves. We can but look ahead to—'

'It is not just the loss of my beloved Tutankhamun I lament, but my life has become a burden…it is no longer a joy.'

She released Menefer's hand, reached over and removed something from an ornate box. 'I wish you to have this.' She held out a gold ring, a scarab of lapis lazuli with gold wings that wrapped around the finger. 'I had it fashioned for Tutankhamun, but it had not yet been completed when he…when he left us.'

'Your Majesty, it is too costly…'

'I no longer have any use for it.'

'Thank you, Majesty. I will wear it all my life. It is a most wonderful gift.' Menefer put the ring on her finger and Senamun again picked up the little figurine of the king and stroked it tenderly.

'I pray to Osiris daily…'

'Osiris? The god of the Underworld!'

'I miss my husband…my *true* husband. To Ay, I am no more than a maidservant. I have now been lodged here…' she spread her arm wide. 'These quarters were once occupied by Djenna, Queen Tiye's Robe Mistress.'

The name brought back a flood of memories and Menefer wondered whatever became of her friend after Queen Tiye's death.

Senamun slouched back on the couch. 'I pray daily, for Osiris to reach out and take me to his bosom so, once again I can be with my beloved.'

'Oh Majesty, no!' Menefer cried out in alarm. 'Do not ask for such things! His Majesty, King Ay is an old man. How many years has he left? He might…' she left the sentence unfinished.

'I know. I thought of that too, but then what? Marry Lord Nakhtmin? He had been named as Ay's heir, you know? But he is not of Royal blood and can only secure the throne by marrying me.

'Oh, Menefer, if only you had not destroyed that letter… she paused, then had another thought. 'Do you think, perhaps I can ask Shubbiluliuma to send another of his sons?' She laughed a humourless, bitter laugh. 'As you had once suggested, I cannot rule on my own and Ay made it quite clear that I have no head for politics and matters of State.'

Ay's personal steward arrived with a message from the king. Queen Ankhsenamun's presence was required in the king's bedchamber.

Senamun sighed and rose slowly. 'I must go. My Lord has summoned me to his bed and I must obey. We will talk again, soon…but, will you to do something for me?'

'Anything, Highness.'

'When I was awaiting the birth of Akhenaten's child, a bowl of flowers was brought to my chamber, remember?'

'Yes, I do. Oleander flowers. A plant from across the Great Green Waters to the North.'

'Can you get some for me…to remind me of…happier days?'

'Yes, Majesty. I know where to get some of them. I will have some sent presently.'

***

Menefer woke from a nightmare with a start, covered in perspiration and could not get back to sleep. She tossed and turned for hours, then finally gave up.

It was still dark and the morning star had not yet risen. She got up and went to the *rekhes*, the place where food was prepared, then stirred some honey in a flagon of *emmer*, a draught prescribed for her many years earlier by Lord Pentu, the physician, that should bring about sleep. The potion had little effect. Dawn came and she was still awake. A flock of ibises flew by, called to each other on their way to their early morning feeding grounds. Only then did Menefer drift off into slumber.

A loud knocking startled her and she sat up, disorientated for a moment. The urgent knocking came again and she got up to answer the door. It was the Queen's maid.

'My lady, come quick. Her Majesty wished to see you urgently.'

Menefer hurried to the palace and the queen's quarters.

Senamun was lying on her sleeping couch. She looked tired and there were dark circles around her eyes. She had obviously also spent a sleepless night. Her garments, the same clothing she had worn the day before, were dishevelled and creased. 'I am glad you could come.'

'Your Majesty, are you unwell?' Menefer asked concerned. The queen indicated to a chair and Menefer sat down. 'Shall I summon Kafre?'

'No, no,' Senamun said with a tired gesture. I no longer have need of physicians.'

*What an odd thing to say*, Menefer thought. Ankhsenamun paused and seemed to grimace as if she were in pain. 'Menefer, I have made arrangements…you will be provided for, for as long as you live.'

'Your Majesty, there is no need—'

Senamun interrupted, 'I will be joining my beloved soon and… I want to do this for you.'

A sudden dread came over Menefer. 'Your Majesty, what has happened? Did you…'

The Queen's speech had become slurred and she kept wiping her mouth with the back of her hand. 'I have taken a potion…made from Oleander leaves.'

'Majesty, no!' Menefer jumped up and fell to her knees before the Queen. 'Please, let me summon Kafre. Save yourself.'

'What for, Menefer? To be bedded by an old man? To be treated no better than a servant?' She reached out for Menefer's hand. 'Dear friend, you have known me for a long time. Surely you…understand…it is better thus…'

The Queen's voice faltered, she clutched at her chest and closed her eyes. 'The people don't need me…they need…a king who…who…'

Menefer pressed the Queen's hand to her tear-stained cheek. Senamun looked up, but her eyes were glazed.

The Queen squinted and blinked a few times as if her vision was failing. 'Rakhmet was a good man… I'm so sorry…for your loss. He died in my service. May…you find…happiness…'

The Queen's hand, still pressed to Menefer's cheek, suddenly relaxed and she slumped sideways on the couch. Queen Ankhsenamun was dead.

\*\*\*

Menefer never knew such loneliness existed. It had been several months since the queen's death, and she was depressed. Everyone she had been close to was gone. Messu, now eighteen, no longer visited her as much as she would like. Lady Mutnedjmet and Horemheb had their own lives to live and she saw them only on rare occasions.

Queen Ankhsenamun's wishes were honoured and she was well provided for, but she needed something with which to occupy herself. She busied herself with her sculptures and talismans, which she sold at the marketplace. There, she often met up with Sarem, the maker of sweet cakes and delicacies. During their meetings, Menefer could forget about all the sorrow and heartache of the past.

'Oh, Sarem,' she lamented. 'I feel so guilty about sending the queen that wretched plant. If only I had an inkling—'

'Do not blame yourself. The queen had been very depressed. Her life had been shattered and she wanted to go to that place where she could be with the young king again. I too, felt like that when Nebaten died, and I am sure you must have felt the same misery when you learnt of Rakhmet's fate, did you not?'

'Yes, you are right, Sarem, but we managed to overcome our despair. Why could Queen Senamun not do the same?'

'Would you be happy, living with someone like Ay, and old man who used you for sport only, then cast you aside, like a soiled garment, when he was done?'

'You are right.'

'Senamun wanted a way out of her misery. If you had not provided her with the means, she would have found it elsewhere. Misery breeds like clutter. If you don't tidy up quickly, it seems to grow worse.'

This was one bit of advice Menefer had never heard before. It made Menefer feel much better and she cheered up.

That afternoon, after a busy day at the market, Menefer arrived home a little earlier than usual and decided to do some cleaning up. She had become slovenly and the cooking place was a mess. Soot and ash from the fireplace had not been removed for quite a while, and, as Sarem had warned, clutter breeds.

She was in better spirits than she had been for quite some time. She donned some old and worn garments and proceeded to sweep up the muck. Food had spilled onto the mud-brick floor, making the task a difficult one, but she did not mind. Her mood finally changed for the better. She was humming to herself and did not hear the approaching footsteps behind her.

'Mother, I hardly recognised you…covered in grime from head to toe!'

'Messu! What a surprise,' she pushed a stray strand of hair from her dirty forehead with the back of her hand. 'Your visits have become rather scarce.'

'I wanted to surprise you, but now, I am surprised…and embarrassed.'

'Embarrassed? Why would you be embarrassed? You've seen me cleaning house before,' she straightened up and stretched her aching back.

'This time I brought someone with me…someone I wanted you to meet, but—'

Then Menefer noticed the attractive girl standing behind her son. Messu turned and steered the girl round in front of him. 'Sitre, believe it or not, but this charwoman is my mother.'

Menefer did not know how to react. 'This is most embarrassing. Messu, why did you not warn me…?'

'I'm pleased to know you,' Sitre stepped forward and kissed Menefer on her grimy cheek. 'Do not be embarrassed. My mother always says "*A woman always groomed, is, as a housewife, surely doomed*".'

'That's just like my mother,' Messu laughs. 'Often covered in flour and always has an old saying at the ready for almost every situation.'

Menefer wiped her hand on her skirt. 'Excuse me a moment, I will go and clean up.'

'Hurry back,' Messu said. 'We have something to tell you.'

A while later, Menefer reappeared. She had cleansed herself, groomed her hair and donned a clean tunic. Messu and Sitre were already seated and Menefer made herself comfortable.

'My, you certainly scrubbed up well,' Messu teased.

Menefer ignored his remark. 'Now, what is it you wanted to tell me? You are finished with your training and will be moving back?'

'Sitre and I are betrothed!'

Menefer was taken aback for a moment. 'Really? Why did you not tell me before? I could have arranged for a feast…'

'No. I care not for these celebrations. We just decided to do it. Pledged our troth…with her parent's consent of course, and Lord Sethi's.'

'But I—'

'No mother,' his expression changed and became more serious, 'You, of all people, know very well the folly of delaying. Too much can go wrong, so we decided not to put it off. We will marry as soon as possible.'

'It is a life-long commitment, you know! Are you certain…?'

'We have known each other for some time and we care much for each other.'

'We had even consulted a seer,' Sitre added. 'She predicted that, together, we will "*Create a radiance that will be known for a hundred times hundred years*", whatever that means, but we were assured it was a good prophecy.'

Menefer was pleased. Sitre reminded her of herself, in many ways. She gave the couple her blessing. 'I wish you all the joy and happiness you wish yourself. This day is certainly the best I've had for a very long time. Nothing can improve on it,' she hugged and kissed them both.

She turned as a chariot pulled up in front of the house. 'That must be Horemheb,' she said as she walked to the door. 'He sometimes pays a visit, but usually not at this time of day.'

The driver, dressed in the garb of a desert dweller had his face covered in the manner of the Bedu. He stepped off the platform and removed his face covering.

'Oh, by all the gods!' Menefer cried out weakly, and clutched at the door jamb, quivering.

Alarmed, Messu rushed to his mother, then recognised the visitor and hastened to greet him. 'Rakhmet! You…you're alive!'

'It's been a long time.' Rakhmet clasped Messu in greeting, 'You have grown!' Rakhmet remarked, then with outstretched arms, approached Menefer.

She rushed into his arms and they embraced. 'I thought…we were told you had been killed!' she wept against his chest as he held her close.

'I nearly was,' he whispered in her ear.

'But how? …Am I dreaming? Is it really you?'

'I am here, Menefer. I have come back.'

'How I had wished, prayed, that the reports were false, but as the weeks, months…years went by…'

Rakhmet tethered his horses to a trough where they could drink and feed, then went inside where Messu introduced him to Sitre. 'Commander, meet my betrothed, Sitre, and Sitre,' Messu gestured with both hands, 'this is Commander Rakhmet.'

'I have heard much about you, Commander, including your…death.'

Rakhmet laughed. 'Fortunately, it had been only a rumour.'

Everyone waited, eager for an explanation, and while having a mug of emmer each, he told them his incredible story, how he survived the massacre, his loss of memory, living with the Bedu and his life as a trader.

'We were trading in the city of Theb-en, in the Delta, when word reached us of the death of Queen Ankhsenamun. Upon hearing the queen's name, my memory started to return. I remembered the massacre…and the face of one of the attackers, a face which I could not identify before and then I remembered… I knew one of the men that had attacked us!'

'You recognised one of the bandits?' Messu asked, surprised.

'Yes, our attackers were *not* robbers, as we thought, they were Egyptians, *deliberately* sent to ambush and kill us. Fortunately for me, they did not do a thorough job and I was left for dead.'

'Who…who is he?' Messu asked.

'I will reveal his name in due time. No one must know I am still alive. I don't want anyone to be forewarned until I face him—and others responsible. I vowed to avenge the slaughter of my convoy. That is the reason I came here in disguise. I trust you will keep my secret?'

All pledged not to mention a word. It would ruin Rakhmet's plans to learn the names of all those guilty, but both Rakhmet and Menefer already had their suspicions.

# Chapter Forty-Five
## Retribution

Menefer's house had a room with a bathing cubicle and Rakhmet could cleanse himself of the grime of his journey. The cool water he poured over himself was most refreshing. While living with the Bedu, water had been scarce and they could only bathe whenever they reached a city or passed close to a stream.

It had been a long and hot journey from Theb-en. He had left before dawn the day before and had hardly stopped to eat. After a hearty meal, fatigue overtook him and he kept dozing during their conversation and Menefer urged him to bed. He fell asleep almost immediately and slept till late the next morning.

Well rested and fed and still wearing the garments of desert dwellers. He needed someone, someone with authority as a witness, for what he had planned. Rakhmet went to see the most fitting person, a judge, Lord Sethi.

Lord Sethi was just as surprised and delighted to see him as Menefer and Messu had been. Once again, Rakhmet had to re-tell his tale, but this time, he mentioned the assailant he had recognised, by name.

'Sothis?' Sethi asked, incredulously. 'Lord Maya's assistant?'

'Yes.'

'Years ago, I did notice he had acquired several foreign horses,' Sethi remarked, 'but did not pay much heed.'

'I wish to see those horses…and Sothis' chariot,' Rakhmet said, frowning.

Sethi and Rakhmet accompanied by two guards, went the stables where Rakhmet carefully inspected the horses, then the chariot. They then proceeded to the workplace of Lord Maya. He had once been General of the Army under Akhenaten, then later, he became Superintendent of Construction, and *sab*, Minister of Finance under Tutankhamun. Sothis was in his service.

When they arrived, Rakhmet removed his face covering. Lord Maya was astonished at seeing Rakhmet alive, and, once again, the story had to be related. It was becoming tedious, Rakhmet thought.

Lord Maya listened intently, as Rakhmet described the horses and chariot in the stable. Maya summoned Sothis.

Sothis arrived presently and upon recognising Rakhmet, he visibly paled. 'Commander Rakhmet! But…but I thought—'

'Yes, Sothis. I'm still alive, no thanks to you and your *bandits*!' This time, Rakhmet had no need to retell his tale.

'Commander Rakhmet…let me explain… I had nothing to do with—'

'I *saw* you, Sothis!'

'Commander, it was not my doing.' He wiped his perspiring brow.

'Let me guess…you were forced into this,' Rakhmet replied calmly. 'You were pilfering from the Royal Treasury. I know all about it. Ay's son, Seti, caught you and told me about it, years ago!'

'You were helping yourself from the treasury funds?' Lord Maya gasped. 'I had wondered why some of the coffers did not tally.'

'Lord Maya, His Majesty, King Tutankhamun, wanted a tomb constructed but we had trouble getting workers…we had to pay them a little extra.'

'As overseer to the construction, I know about the cost of the worker's payments. There was still a shortfall.'

'Was it a case of *two deben for them and one for me*?' Rakhmet scowled. 'After their payments were made, you had a tidy sum for your own coffer, is that not so?'

'No, Commander!' Sothis was sweating and there was desperation in his eyes.

'You have a fine house, Sothis,' Maya reminded him. 'Much better than many of the other court officials of your rank. Explain!'

'I am… frugal with my saving, Lord Maya,' he swallowed hard.

'And all your fine and costly furnishings…?'

'I… I managed to find workmen who were willing to work cheap…'

'You have a chariot fit for a *mariannu*. Do not tell me you found a chariot builder who can work cheap!' Rakhmet sounded sarcastic. 'If so, give me his name as I too would like one, mine had *disappeared* after the attack,' he paused, watching Sothis sweat, 'and your horses, they are Hittite horses, are they not!'

'Hittite horses? What makes you think they are Hittite Horses? Did they speak to you in the *words of the mouth of the Hittites*?' Sothis asked, trying to be flippant.

'Do not take me for a fool, Sothis. I had been to Khatti. I had seen the way their Master of the Horse trained them. These horses have a special gait. Only Hittite horses—*your* horses—are trained that way! And that chariot, the one you pointed out as being yours—it had been renovated, but it is *my* chariot.'

Sothis looked incredulously at Rakhmet. What makes you so certain?

'The wheels. They too, are from Khatti! One of my chariot wheels had been damaged during my journey, but both had to be replaced. I examined the wheels on this chariot carefully and recognised them immediately!'

Trapped, Sothis lowered his head and it seemed about to weep. 'Yes…yes. I admit it. I will tell all,' he inhaled sharply, almost a sob, 'I borrowed from the treasury… I was planning to replace it but was found out. Seti, Pharaoh's son, discovered it and told his father. Pharaoh Ay was Vizier at the time. Ay said he would waive my crime if I served him and do his bidding when he needed it. Some time later, after the death of the young king, when Commander Rakhmet and Lord Hanis left for Khatti, he demanded I gather a company to execute this foul deed, threatening to take my wife and children into bondage if I refused. I had no choice.'

Sothis prostrated himself before Lord Maya and weeping, asked for forgiveness.

'Pharaoh? He's above the law and cannot be prosecuted,' Sethi whispered to Rakhmet. After a moment in thought, he decided that, at least, the killers could be punished. He had to have a detailed account of the confession for evidence and decided to continue.

'What exactly did he ask of you?'

Sothis swallowed hard. 'Ay did not want Queen Ankhsenamun to marry Shubbiluliuma's son and was to stop the enemy prince from entering Egypt. *If I was a loyal Egyptian*, he said, *I would gather a crew and waylay the caravan.* The entire convoy was to be killed as well as the Hittite prince and I was to make it look like a bandit attack. If I did this, I would be a hero.'

'But you overlooked one important thing, Sothis. Bandits would have stripped the prince of his costly robes and jewellery.'

'We are not robbers, Commander. We took the horses and the chariots, yes, but we cared not for looting the dead.'

'You said you were not a robber, but you *are*. You robbed Her Majesty of a future husband, by killing the queen's envoy, you robbed his family of a husband and father, you robbed King Shubbiluliuma of his son, and nearly robbed me of my life!'

'What was your reward for your vile deed?' Sethi asked.

'I was given the house and furnishings you mentioned, and was also allowed to keep the horses and the chariot, Lord. The other chariots were sold and the horses divided among the others in my group.'

After more questioning and some persuasion, Sothis revealed the names of the other men involved.

'Commander Rakhmet, I have heard all I need to know,' Lord Sethi replied. 'I have enough evidence to condemn them all.'

'Mercy, Lord Sethi! Forgive me… Commander Rakhmet… Spare me!'

'You ask for mercy, Sothis? Like the mercy you bestowed on Prince Zannanza and the others, like the mercy you showed me?'

The other accomplices were all rounded up. Sothis was to be sentenced to death. All the others would be sent to the quarries and Natron mines for the rest of their lives.

There was one remaining person to be dealt with but, as Lord Sethi had mentioned—Ay was above the law and could be charged. For fear that Lord Sethi would intervene, he did not mention his next move. He had sworn an oath to avenge this deed. He would deal with this man, himself. Privately.

***

Getting into the Malkata palace, wearing his foreign garments to confront Pharaoh Ay, would be difficult, so Rakhmet changed into his uniform. He approached the palace gate where Minares, once Scribe of the Gate at Akhet Aten, had been assigned.

Minares had grown old, and at fifty-four, was looking forward to his retirement and a life-long allowance from Pharaoh for his services. He was dozing in his small booth just inside the gate. Rakhmet called his name softly. Minares awoken from a dream, startled. He thought it was a spectre, the *ka* of the Commander that appeared before him. He nearly fell over backwards, terrified and covered his face with his hands, moaning.

'Minares!' Rakhmet called again. 'I am alive. You are not seeing a spirit.'

The scribe slowly opened his hands and, with one eye, peered at the vision before him through his fingers.

He lowered his hands slowly and reached out to cautiously touch Rakhmet. 'It *is* you! You have returned form the dead!'

Rakhmet hoped he would not have to repeat his tale of escape again, but fortunately, Minares did not question him. 'Minares, I need to get into the palace undetected. Can you help?'

Eager to help, Minares agreed and escorted Rakhmet to a passage, used by servants, at the rear of the palace. The corridors were not decorated like those of the rest of the building, and all manner of cleaning items cluttered the passage.

Rakhmet made his way to where the corridor opened into the Audience Chamber. It was empty. He was just preparing to make his way to Pharaoh's day-room, when Ay and his Vizier Lord Nakhtmin. Entered. Rakhmet quickly concealed himself behind the open door.

'You have been ordered to remove all references of Tutankhamun from public buildings, but I believe you have overlooked some.'

'Yes, Majesty. Those at the temple at Ipet-resyt had not yet been done. I will arrange for that task presently. It there anything else, Majesty?'

'Not as this moment. See to it. You are dismissed.'

Lord Nakhtmin saluted and walked away.

Ay watched him for a moment, then crossed the chamber towards an opposite door. He had just attended the council and was dressed in the regalia of his office and wearing the *nemes,* the striped cloth headdress. He no longer had his ever-present fly swat, and instead, carried a golden staff topped with the head of Horus.

Rakhmet drew his sword, stepped out from behind the door, and silently closed it. Ay turned at the sound of footsteps but before he could call out, Rakhmet clamped his hand over his mouth. 'Silence, if you value your life, Ay!'

Ay nodded, wide-eyed as Rakhmet removed his hand.

'You dare to lay hands on me?' Ay squinted at his assailant, not recognising him. His eyes had dimmed over the last few years. 'I am Pharaoh. I will have you...' he looked closer, then recognised the man who had clamped his hands over his mouth. 'You!'

'Yes, *Pharaoh*!' Rakhmet spat out the title, making it obvious that he had no respect for the man's position.

'But how...how did you esc... You were declared dead!'

'You were about to say "escape"? Yes, I escaped... to avenge those you had massacred!'

'Commander Rakhmet! You accuse me of murder? Me?' Ay straightened up, appearing offended. 'I am *Skhai-t*, Pharaoh of Egypt.'

'It is not beneath a Pharaoh to kill!'

'I killed no one!'

'Whether you committed it yourself, or had it done, is the same. Your hands are stained with the blood of Hanis, Prince Zannanza and all his party, as surely as if you loosed the arrows that killed them.'

'It was for the sake of Egypt,' Ay shrugged. 'Ankhsenamun was preparing to put a *Hittite*, an *enemy*, on the throne of Egypt!' he spread his hands in an arc, 'We *could not* let that happen. Anyone...anyone who is loyal to the Two Lands, would have done the same!'

Ay started to back away from Rakhmet towards an opposite door.

'You are going to pay for your deeds.' Rakhmet stepped forward, blocking his escape. 'I made a vow you will—'

'This is treason! You will be fed to the crocodiles for this. Lay down your arms!' Ay commanded, then shouted, 'Guards! Guards!'

Rakhmet took another step towards him and drew back his sword.

'Do not come closer…stay back or…or…'

'Or what *Majesty*?' He sneered. 'Have me killed—again?'

'I warn you…uh…uh…' Ay clutched at his chest, his face contorted in pain. 'Uh… I, uh…' With a strangled gurgling sound, he sank down to the floor.

Rakhmet suspected Ay of putting on an act, feigning illness, hesitated for a moment, then sheathed his sword and bent down to examine the prostrate Pharaoh.

Suddenly, the door behind him burst open. Horemheb, Lord Nakhtmin and a number of guards stormed in. Startled, Rakhmet spun around.

Rakhmet had not thought of cautioning Minares to keep his arrival undisclosed and the excited Minares had spread the wonderful news of his return. It quickly reached the ears of Horemheb who immediately realised what Rakhmet had in mind, and rushed to the king's assistance.

'Don't, Rakhmet! If you harm Pharaoh, or make any threatening move, I will be compelled to kill you!' Horemheb warned. Rakhmet stepped back. Horemheb approached and knelt by the fallen Ay. The King gurgled and reached up weakly. 'My…chest… I…uh…' he grimaced in pain; his eyes turned up towards the ceiling and glazed over.

After a brief examination, Horemheb turned to Lord Nakhtmin. 'Pharaoh is dead!'

A stunned silence followed, and they looked at Rakhmet, accusingly. 'Seize him!' Horemheb commanded and Rakhmet was restrained.

Kafre was summoned and after a thorough examination, declared that it had been a seizure of the heart. 'He had not been touched. There are no marks on His Majesty's body and the cause of death had been natural. Rakhmet had not harmed Pharaoh.'

'You are very lucky, Commander, but you *did* come here to kill him, did you not?'

'Yes. It was he who had ordered the massacre of my party. Ay had directed the killings.'

Once again, he retold the story, this time in greater detail. 'I made a vow to avenge them all. The others involved are already in custody.'

'Yes, Lord Sethi informed me, that's how I realised your intention. It was fortunate for you that the gods had intervened. Had you succeeded, I would have had no option but to have you executed!'

'I know. I was prepared to die for that.' Rakhmet looked on as Ay was taken away to the *House of Skins,* and shook his head. 'His Majesty's heart was heavy with evil… Sobekh will feast well in the netherworld.'

'And, once again, Egypt is without a king!' Lord Nakhtmin observed.

\*\*\*

An emergency council was summoned to the Audience hall. Nakhtmin addressed the assembly. 'A new "Father of the Two Lands" must be chosen, as soon as possible,' he paused, then picked up a scroll and read from it but hesitated.

'Who had been chosen?' everyone asked. 'Who will be our next Pharaoh?'

Horemheb silenced them. He took the scroll from Nakhtmin, 'In this document, Pharaoh Ay had named Lord Nakhtmin as heir!'

There were agreements as well as objections from the gathering.

Meryre held up his hand for silence. 'I agree with Pharaoh's decision, but Lord Nakhtmin is not of royal blood. As is the custom in the Two Lands, to enable him to rule, he will need to marry someone of royal blood, but there is no one.'

Then Horemheb spoke. 'There is another of royal blood. I know not how many of you are aware that Messu, the adopted son of Lord Sethi, is of the loins of King Smenkhare.'

There were exclamations of surprise and acknowledgement, but Meryre, former High Priest of Aten, silenced them and spoke up. 'Many are aware of this, but there is no proof. Royal births must be witnessed and recorded.'

'There *was* a witness. Menteret, the High Priestess of Mut was present at his birth.' Horemheb reminded him.

'She witnessed a birth, an illegitimate birth. There is no proof that the child was of Royal blood,' Meryre persisted.

'I was told there was a document—that had the seal of King Smenkhare.'

'Produce this document, then we'll decide.'

'Alas, it had been destroyed,' Horemheb replied. 'Messu must be chosen. There is no one else,' Horemheb protested. 'There is no one else.'

'What about Lady Mutnedjmet?' Meryre asked. 'She is the *daughter* of Ay, and last remaining Royal.'

'Yes, that is correct.' Nakhtmin spoke up, 'and Horemheb, *you* are married to that lady...'

'That means naught!' Horemheb added. 'Just because—'

'Yes, it does! His Majesty, King Tutankhamun had designated you, Horemheb, as *re-pat*, the crown Prince. I witnessed the document myself.'

'It was a title of honour, it does not mean—'

'It means much! As consort of the Royal Lady Mutnedjmet, you are next in line, Horemheb.'

There was an instant hubbub of agreement. 'Horemheb for Pharaoh!' Others took up the cry. Soon everyone was chanting. 'Hail Pharaoh Horemheb!'

The court debated and argued well into the night and finally an agreement was reached. The vote was unanimous. Only one person was qualified to sit on the throne of Egypt, and that person was Horemheb!'

# Chapter Forty-Six
## Hail Pharaoh!

All of Egypt rejoiced. The people of the Two Lands, greeted the announcement that Horemheb would be Pharaoh, with much feasting and merriment. Well liked, he had proved himself a fine leader and would be a mighty king.

Horemheb received the double crown of Egypt on the ninth day of Shomu, in the season of Payni, and given the additional titles of Djeserkheprure Setenpenre Horemheb Meryamun, *Chosen of Ra, Beloved of Amun.*

Garlands of fragrant blooms welcomed him as he made his first public appearance.

'Hail Pharaoh Horemheb, hail his great Royal Wife, Queen Mutnedjmet!'

Mutny leaned over to her husband and, above the cheering, had to speak up in order for him to hear. 'Impressive titles!' She smiled.

'Impressive names do not make superior rulers,' he called back. 'Akhenaten too, had impressive titles, but he was a fool; Ay became a tyrant; Smenkhare and Tutankhamun tried, but both were too young and inexperienced.'

'You will be a great ruler, Horemheb. You know how to command and the armies love you… the two things none of your predecessors ever had.'

'Let us just hope my reign will be a peaceful one.'

That evening, during the coronation feast, Horemheb summoned Nakhtmin, Rakhmet and Meryre and spoke about Ay's involvement in the massacre of Prince Zannanza and his convoy. 'I want peace to reign. To keep it that way, it must never be known that Ay had set out to waylay the Hittite Prince. If Shubbiluliuma should hear that Egyptians had murdered his son, it could start a war, the likes of which we had never know. Let the massacre remain as it had been accepted, a bandit attack.'

They all agreed. Publicly, Horemheb announced that Ay's connection had been just idle gossip, but privately, Horemheb loathed him and systematically, commenced destroying Ay's monuments. He even had Ay's sarcophagus smashed, usurped his funerary temple at Djamet, The *Place where four of the Ancient Gods are buried,* for his own use, and had Ay's name erased, and on the back of a colossal statue, had Ay's name replaced with his own.

\*\*\*

Shortly after the coronation, Rakhmet and Menefer were wed.

'This day had been long in coming,' Lord Sethi announced as he hailed the bride and groom. 'It is certainly the longest betrothal I have yet come across in all my years as judge…over twenty years! I wish you both the joy, health and prosperity you deserve, and may your future be a happy and fruitful one. May you enjoy your lives together, forever and ever.'

Messu rose and added. 'I speak also for my wife, Sitre. We are in accord with Sethi, my father. Rakhmet, Mother, you had both waited a very long time for this event, so may nothing ever separate you again.'

Rakhmet rose. 'Thank you, Lord Sethi, Sitre and Messu, or should I call you by the name you are now known at court… Paramessu? You have become quite an accomplished charioteer already, and your appointment as *Master of the Horse* is quite a move up the ranks.'

'I am so proud of you Messu,' Menefer added and kissed him. 'To receive plumes for your horses from Pharaoh himself is a great honour.'

'Enough of speeches,' Rakhmet interrupted. 'Let the feast commence.'

The newly weds were pleasantly surprised when a messenger from the palace arrived with a gift from Pharaoh and his queen, a scroll with a certificate, granting them a large area of land in Pu Khent-min, in the ninth *sepat*. They also received an invitation to visit the palace.

Menefer had not been at the palace since Queen Ankhsenamun's death, and looked forward to seeing Queen Mutnedjmet again. Mutnedjmet was just as happy to see Menefer and they embraced as befitting long-lost friends.

'Menefer, I'm so happy for you! After all the trials and hardships, you and Rakhmet are finally wed.'

As the queen escorted Menefer to a seat, Menefer saw a familiar figure standing in a doorway. Djenna had been watching the show of affection and the two erstwhile friends just gazed at one another.

The queen noticed Menefer's stare. 'Oh, yes, Djenna is now my *Mistress of the Royal Robes*. During my time as priestess, I had been obligated to wear simple garments, but I am now again at court, and Djenna had been a great help in choosing and organising my wardrobe.'

Menefer and Djenna, both feeling equally awkward, nodded frosty greetings, but Queen Mutnedjmet, tried not to notice the coldness between them.

'After Queen Tiye's death, poor Djenna had been languishing at a market stall, stitching garments for the *mariannu*, but those snobbish nobility did not appreciate her fine sense of elegance,' she beckoned Djenna closer. 'But fortunately, I heard about it, immediately came to her aid and offered her this position.'

Mutnedjmet, aware of Djenna's role in separating Menefer and Rakhmet, relished in demeaning her on Menefer's behalf. Djenna felt humiliated but forced a smile. All she had set out to achieve had resulted in naught and had never married. But Menefer, plain Menefer who had had so little ambition, had won the heart of Rakhmet and had become the queen's best friend. Djenna was envious.

'Djenna, dear, did you know Rakhmet and Menefer had married? Pharaoh had granted them land, including a small village from which they could demand toil from the peasants, and Messu had been appointed as Pharaoh's chariot driver! He is sure to achieve greatness one day.'

With a stiff smile, Djenna congratulated her, then made her excuses and retreated to her quarters.

The queen had shamed Djenna, and Menefer felt sorry for her old friend, thinking about the good times they once had had together. Mutnedjmet spoke, but Menefer did not hear the queen's question.

'Menefer… I asked if you had heard from Ipuky yet?'

'Forgive me, Majesty. My mind had wandered. No, I have not heard from him for some time, but I believe he is living in Mennufer.'

'We must try and contact him. Pharaoh has many building projects planned. He wants several pylons constructed at the Great Temple of Ipet-isut. Lord Maya has been sent to Akhet Aten to retrieve and use the *talata*t blocks from ruined monuments for the purpose.'

'It seems everyone is dismantling Akhenaten's temples and buildings, to use in other projects.'

Mutnedjmet sighed. 'Yes. A great pity… Akhet Aten had been such a beautiful city.'

Building projects were not the only things Horemheb had in mind. He called another meeting of counsellors and High Officials but grew impatient with the lengthy Royal introductions before each session. 'Let us get on with business!' He glared at the assembled group. 'There had been a gross abuse of power since the start of the reign of Akhenaten. Too many people in High Office misused their powers for gain. This is going to stop!'

Ipi, the Royal scribe since Tutankhamun, was summoned and commanded to make notes, to be known as *The Great Edict of Horemheb*.

'There had been an over centralisation of State Power and privileges in the hands of a few officials. This will no longer be the case. I will appoint judges and regional tribunes to all the *sepatu* in the land. These provinces will all abide by the same laws, and no longer by individual regulations.'

A murmur rose from the assembly. Many would lose out on the lucrative incomes they had enjoyed thus far.

'I am also reintroducing local religious authorities and will divide legal powers between Upper and Lower Egypt, and between the Viziers of No-Amun and Mennufer. I will re-establish order of the Two Lands and curb abuses of State authority. I am also going to reform the army. I call upon the commanders of the Armies, Commander Nakhtmin, Commander Rakhmet, Commander Huy, Lord Sethi and Commander Sekhem. You will see me afterwards for the necessary arrangements.'

More murmurs followed and Horemheb clapped his hands for attention. 'The priesthood of Amun had been restored after the demise of Akhenaten, but they are once again forming a stranglehold of power. These priests are again trying to gain supremacy. That was one reason why Akhenaten had turned against them, but I will not permit that to happen again. I will therefore appoint priests that had come from the armies.'

Another hubbub rose from the crowd. Meryre, the High Priests stepped forward. 'Your majesty, may I speak?'

Horemheb nodded and signalled for him to continue.

'Does that not seem a bit drastic, Majesty? Appointing priests from the army?'

'Meryre, I am not appointing soldiers as priests. I am talking about priests who had once been soldiers, who had once served under me. They are disciplined, will be loyal and not try and dictate to me or impose on my rule. These priests will confine their control only to spiritual matters and not interfere with the State!'

Most of the assembly seemed to agree with that decision. In the past, priests had grown wealthy by intimidating local authorities. Horemheb was determined this would not happen again.

'Lord Maya,' he addressed the Royal Treasurer. 'As Overseer of the *Place of Eternity*, you are responsible for preparing and maintaining the last resting places of the rulers of Egypt. They had been neglected, so you will organise a workforce and repair the tomb of Thutmose the Fourth. It had been disturbed and badly damaged by tomb robbers. Tutankhamun's tomb had also been violated, but fortunately, the robbers had been caught and were duly executed. The tomb had been repaired and must be re-sealed, the passageway filled in and concealed. I also wish to have a second tomb constructed. My original one is not a suitable one for a Pharaoh'

Maya nodded. His new Pharaoh is certain to leave his mark on the Two lands.

'And lastly…' Horemheb paused and his expression softened, to a more compassionate one. 'Because my Great Wife, Queen Mutnedjmet, is unable to bear me an heir, I must decide on someone to take my place…when the time comes. I have therefore chosen Lord Sethi to be my heir. As Judge and Commander of Armies, he is greatly respected, the most qualified to make decisions and to mediate should disputes arise. Let it so be written.'

\*\*\*

The years passed. In the twenty-fifth year of his reign, Horemheb was preparing for Upit, the New Year festival. His rule had been fair and peaceful, but, for the last twelve years, since Mutnedjmet death, a lonely one. He had not married again, and occupied himself with revising Egypt's laws and reforms that had made the Two Lands prosperous.

Menefer and Djenna had once again reconciled their differences. It had taken a while, but they had decided that there was no point in continuing their hostilities. Djenna had lost her beauty. The years she toiled at the marketplace, stitching garments for the wealthy, had taken its toll. At sixty, her skin had become leathery and wrinkled and her hands were calloused. In contrast, Menefer, only a year younger, had grown old gracefully and looked years younger than her friend.

'This is surely a proud day for you, Menefer,' Djenna said and they made their way to the palace for Pharaoh's Upit ceremony. 'Last year, your son was appointed Commander of the Fortress and Controller of the Nile Delta, and today, once again, he is to be honoured by Pharaoh.'

'Yes, Messu is very fortunate,' Menefer agreed.

Djenna gave a one-shoulder shrug. 'But what is success? Unless it brings him riches.'

Djenna's old pessimism is showing itself again, Menefer thought, but said nothing. After all, can Djenna be anything else?

'My father had been honoured thus, once. He became Vizier and Fan-bearer on the King's Right, but it did not make him wealthy.'

'Success is achieving your goals, Djenna, not the wealth you accumulate.'

'Well, *you've* certainly been successful. Provided for, for the rest of your life by command of Queen Senamun; a husband who is honoured and respected at court, and a son who had achieved great esteem. What else can he accomplish to outdo that?'

Menefer grinned. 'I have not told you this, Djenna, but there *is* something! Messu's son, Seti, is soon to be a father!'

Djenna stopped in her tracks and stared, amazed. 'You? Becoming a *great-grandmother*? But your grandson is still a child...'

'Seti is almost nineteen years old, about the same age when Messu became a father. Can you believe it? What else can a mother...or grandmother hope for?' Giggling, they continued on their way.

A vast crowd had already formed around the canopied dais when they entered the palace courtyard.

Rakhmet, Messu and his family had arrived earlier and were waiting for them. Menefer introduced Djenna to her grandson, Seti and his wife Tuya, whose condition was clearly visible. They were discussing the coming happy event, when Meryre mounted the dais. A hush fell over the crowd as he lifted his arms.

'People of Egypt, kneel. All hail Pharaoh Djeserkheprure Setenpenre, His Majesty, King Horemheb Meryamun, Lord of Diadems, Lord of the Two Lands, may he reign forever and ever.'

Horemheb signalled for everyone to rise. 'People of the Two Lands, it is once again Upit, the Feast of the New Year, a time to rejoice. As per the custom, those who had served me well and faithfully during the last year, will be rewarded.'

Huy, Viceroy of Kush, received the title of *Fan-bearer to the King's left*. Lord Maya, the Royal Treasurer, received a golden *Beb*, land and cattle, the land being measured by as much as he could cover on foot in one day, to the west of Iunet.

Then Messu was called. He stepped forward and he too received a golden *Beb*. After being given the title *General of the Two Lands,* he was about to return to his family when Horemheb halted him.

'One moment, Messu,' Horemheb addressed the crowd again. 'As you know, I have no offspring. Lord Sethi had been named as my heir, but because of his recent death, a new successor must be chosen.' He looked about the crowd. All the faces were turned to him expectantly. 'Four other kings, including myself, had all ruled without a male issue. I do not wish that tendency to continue. I have to be certain my successor would be more fruitful,' he paused for effect, 'Egypt needs a king who could continue the dynasty.'

He made an elaborate gesture towards Messu. 'The son of Lord Sethi, Messu, has a son, and *his* son's wife, too, is with child. This surely indicates a future and fruitful dynasty. Messu has served me well and is compassionate and trustworthy. I therefore, name Messu, the son of Lord Sethi and lady Menefer, to be my heir!'

Deafening cheers greeted his announcement and an awed Djenna had to shout to be heard above the noise. 'Menefer! Your son...to be...*Pharaoh*? Magic... I am dumbfounded.'

Menefer was just as surprised. 'This...this is completely unexpected!'

'Unexpected, Menefer? Why would you be surprised? After all, he is of Royal blood.' Rakhmet had purposely mentioned this for Djenna's benefit.

'What do you mean, Royal blood?' Djenna asked, puzzled. 'Messu is adopted. He has a high rank, but surely not… *Royal*?'

'Yes, Djenna.' Rakhmet smiled smugly, relishing his every word. Finally they could get back at Djenna for the wrongs she had done them. 'Messu is Menefer's true son…her own flesh and blood,' he paused to watch her expression.

'I… I had always suspected it…but that does not make him Royal!'

Rakhmet grinned, 'Messu is the son of *Smenkhare*. He is a prince!'

'What…? What are you saying? Is that true?' Stunned, Djenna stared at Menefer, her eyes large and disbelieving.

Menefer nodded, 'It is true, Djenna. Why did you think I had been under Royal supervision ever since Messu's birth?'

Djenna's mouth opened and shut in amazement. 'Why…why did you not tell me, Menefer? Me, your best friend.'

'Djenna, you know very well you cannot keep a secret… I dared not take that chance.'

Djenna had not been hurt by Menefer's remark. She had been told often enough that she was a gossip.

'You and Prince Smenkhare! The news really astonished me. I would never have guessed…'

Then Djenna suddenly recollected something. 'The prophesy…the one told you by the seer, remember? During the Pageant of Empire… Did it not foretell this?'

'Now that you mention it, yes,' Menefer tried to recollect the words. 'The seer said something like—I will *walk in the shadows of five Great Houses,* five pharaohs… Akhenaten, Smenkhare, Tutankhamun, Ay and Horemheb. *And from you, shall come forth a light that will cause a shadow that will overshadow them all.*'

'That's it. I remember now,' Djenna brightened, realising the meaning of those words. 'Overshadow them all! That means your son will be greater than… Oh, by all the gods, it's…it's truly magic!'

'Yes, magic!' Menefer smiled and looked at Rakhmet.

He leaned over to Menefer, grinning. 'Requital is sweet, is it not?' he whispered and she grinned back at him.

***

# Epilogue

Pharaoh Horemheb ruled for another four years and was succeeded by Messu. At his coronation, and as custom dictated, he added the name of Ra, the God of State, to his name, and Messu became *"Ra Messu"*— Ramesses, the first Pharaoh of the nineteenth dynasty. His grandson, Seti's son, was named Ramesses II, also known as Ramesses the Great. The Pharaoh, scholars believe, to be the Pharaoh of the Exodus.

# Ancient Egypt

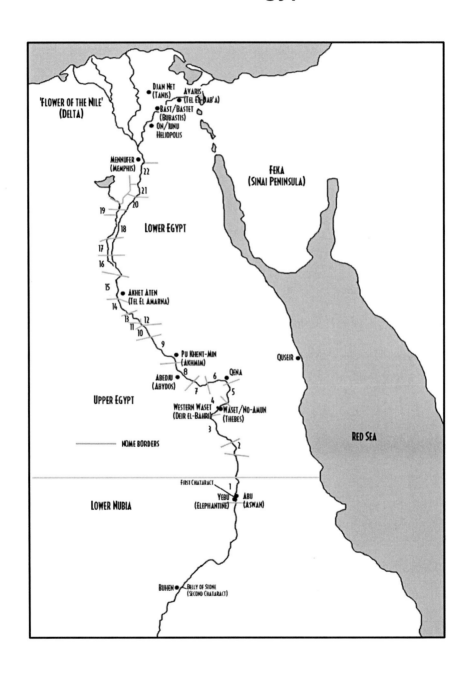

# Akhet Aten

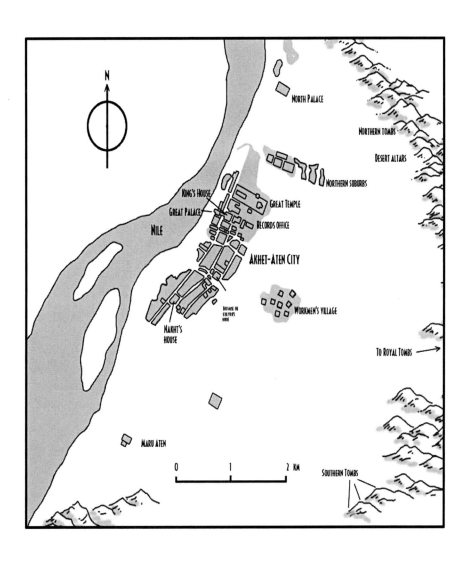

N

NORTH PALACE

NORTHERN TOMBS

DESERT ALTARS

NORTHERN SUBURBS

KING'S HOUSE

GREAT TEMPLE

GREAT PALACE

RECORDS OFFICE

NILE

AKHET-ATEN CITY

THE HOUSE THE
SCULPTOR'S
HOUSE

WORKMEN'S VILLAGE

NAKHT'S
HOUSE

TO ROYAL TOMBS

MARU ATEN

0       1       2 KM

SOUTHERN TOMBS

# Akhet Aten City

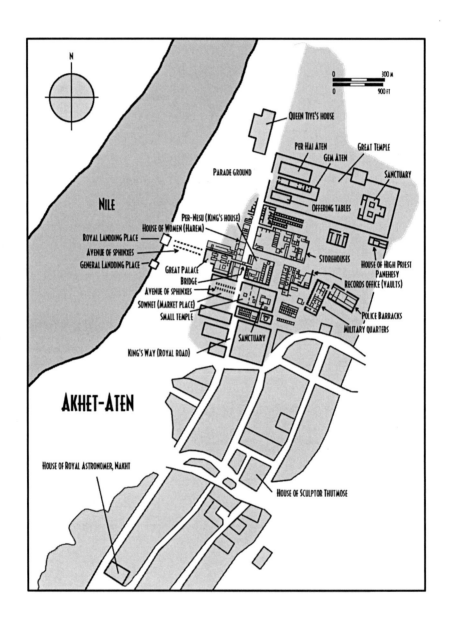

**Queen Tiye's House**

**Per Hai Aten**  **Great Temple**

**Gem Aten**

**Parade ground**  **Sanctuary**

**Offering tables**

**Nile**

**Per-Nesu (King's house)**

**House of Women (Harem)**

**Royal Landing Place**

**Avenue of Sphinxes**

**Storehouses**

**General Landing Place**

**House of High Priest Panehesy**

**Great Palace**

**Bridge**  **Records Office (vaults)**

**Avenue of Sphinxes**

**Sownet (Market place)**

**Small Temple**  **Police Barracks**

**Sanctuary**  **Military quarters**

**King's Way (Royal road)**

**Akhet-Aten**

**House of Royal Astronomer, Nakht**

**House of Sculptor Thutmose**

# Egypt and Eastern Mediterranean

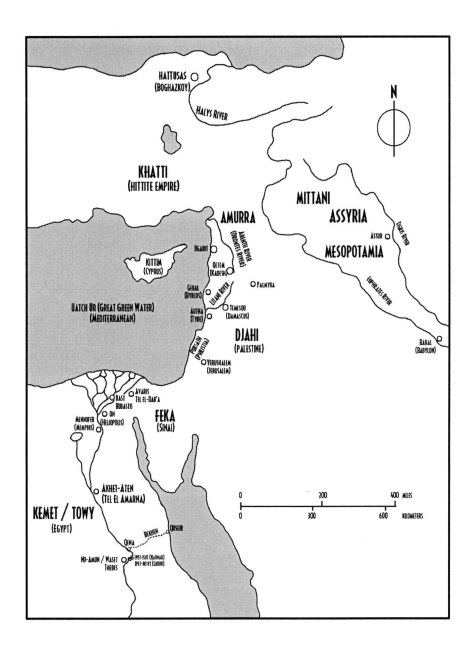

# Historical Characters

| | |
|---|---|
| Ahmose | Akhenaten's personal steward |
| Akhenaten | Pharaoh of Egypt (formerly Amenhotep IV) |
| Amenhotep III | Father of Amenhotep IV (Akhenaten) |
| Ankhsenpaaten | Third daughter of Akhenaten. Married Akhenaten, then Tutankhaten, (later changed name to Ankhsenamun). Married Ay after death of Tutankhamun pleaded with Shubbiluliuma to send one of his sons as a husband. (A.k.a Dakamun) |
| Ankhsenpaaten ta-sherit | Daughter of Ankhsenpaaten by her father Akhenaten – Died an infant. |
| Apay | Royal Butler. Also served Horemheb. |
| Ay | High Priest, Vizier, father of Nefertiti and Mutnedjmet |
| Aziro | King of Amor (Syria). Commander General of Amorites |
| Azna | Viceroy of Khatti |
| Bak | Chief Sculptor and Master of Works of Akhenaten |
| Baketaten/Bakamun | Akhenaten's sister, Daughter of Queen Tiye |
| Dhaba | Smenkhare's personal servant, later Tutankhamun's then Ankhsenamun's |
| Hanis | Queen Ankhsenamun's envoy to Shubbiluliuma |
| Hatiay | Overseer of the Royal Household. Nefertiti's steward |
| Hentaneb | Royal nurse to princesses |
| Hiknefer | Tutankhaten's boyhood friend – Nubian prince |
| Horemheb | Commander of the Armies, later Pharaoh of Egypt |
| Huy | Viceroy of Nubia |
| Huya | Superintendent of Queen Tiye's household |
| Imar | General of Methen troops (under Aziro) |
| Ipi | Royal scribe |
| Ipuky | Sculptor, Court artist under Akhenaten |
| Kafre | Physician at Buhen |
| Khares | Personal servant of Tutankhamun |
| Khay | Royal Scribe under Akhenaten |

| | |
|---|---|
| Kheruef | Chief Steward |
| Khiya | Lesser wife of Akhenaten, Probably mother of Tutankhaten |
| Mahu | Chief of Medjay (Police) |
| Maya | Royal Treasurer under Horemheb |
| Meketaten | Second daughter of Akhenaten. Died early |
| Menteret | High Priestess of the temple of Mut |
| Meritaten | Eldest daughter of Akhenaten and Nefertiti. Married Smenkhare. Died soon after her husband. |
| Meryre | High Priest of Aten |
| Messu | Paramessu. Son of Sethi. Pharaoh Ramesses I, first king of the 19th Dynasty. |
| Mutemwaya | Secondary wife of Amenhotep III, mother of Smenkhare |
| Mutnedjmet | Sister of Nefertiti. High Priestess of Mut. Later, wife of Horemheb |
| Nakht | Royal advisor, Astronomer, Royal Chancellor and Chief Justice and Vizier under Akhenaten |
| Nakhtmin | First husband of Mutnedjmet. Commander-in-chief of armies and Vizier under Ay |
| Nebamun/Nebaten | Artist, sculptor |
| Neferu | (Nefernefertuaten ta Sherit) Fourth daughter of Akhenaten |
| Neferneferu | (Neferneferure) Fifth daughter of Akhenaten. Married Prince Nijmat of Babylon |
| Nefertiti | Queen of Egypt, wife of Akhenaten |
| Nijmat | Son of King Burnaburash of Babylon. Husband of Princess Neferneferure |
| Panehesy | High Priest of Great Temple of Aten |
| Paramessu | See Messu. |
| Pawah | High Priest of On |
| Paye | Overseer of Royal apartments, husband of Repyt. (Had three sons, Nebre, and Mahu, and three daughters) |
| Pentu | Royal Physician to Akhenaten, later Vizier to Tutankhamun |
| Pernefer | (He who washes the hands of the King) Master of Akhenaten's household |
| Ramose | Vizier under Tutankhamun |
| Ranefer | Akhenaten's chariot driver |
| Ribbadi | King of Byblos, assassinated by Aziro |
| Sekhem | Captain of soldiers at Abedju |
| Setenpenre | Sixth daughter of Akhenaten. Believed to have died from plague during the 14th or 15th year of Akhenaten, together with her sister Neferu. |

| Sethi | Judge. Troop Commander from Avaris. Father of Paramessu |
| Seti | Son of Ay. Overseer of the Royal Horse and Chariots (Royal Stables) |
| Shubbiluliuma | King of the Hittites |
| Sitre | Wife of Messu (Queen of Pharaoh Ramesses I) |
| Smenkhare | Son of Amenhotep III and Mutemwaya, Akhenaten's half-brother. Co-regent. Died soon after Akhenaten. |
| Sothis | Assistant to Maya, Royal Treasurer |
| Susmaat | Wife of Nakht. (Later called Susmaat Tawi), Temple Singer of Amun |
| Tey | Wife of Ay, Mother of Nefertiti |
| Thutmose | Royal Sculptor. Sculpted the famous bust of Nefertiti |
| Tiye | Dowager Queen, wife of Amenhotep III. Mother of Akhenaten. |
| Tushratta | King of Mitanni, Akhenaten's ally. |
| Tutankhaten | Later named Tutankhamun. Son of Akhenaten and Khiya, a secondary wife. |
| Tutu | Foreign Official of Akhenaten. (Is thought to have been involved in treasonable activities, in league with Shubbiluliuma and Aziro) |
| Zannanza | Son of Shubbiluliuma, slain on route to Egypt |

# Fictional Characters

The following characters are entirely of the author's imagination.

| Asi | Rakhmet's boyhood friend |
| Asti | (Egyptian) Name the Bedu gave Rakhmet |
| Baka | Commander of Buhen |
| Batu | Soldier that caused trouble during a royal feast. |
| Djenna | Menefer's childhood friend. |
| Istar | Baka's daughter, wife of Rakhmet |
| Kenti | Lord Tutu's servant |
| Menefer | Rakhmet's betrothed, Artist who becomes tutor to royal children. |
| Menet | Son of Horemheb and Istar |
| Rakhmet | Officer in the Royal guard. Menefer's betrothed |
| Sarem | Nebamun's would-be betrothed. Manufacturer of sweetmeats and delicacies. |
| Segi | Mute slave girl. Mefer's servant. |

In this tale, Menefer is the daughter of Thutmose and Mutnames, and the sister of Ipuky and Nebaten/Nebamun, but this is purely fiction. Thutmose and Mutnames both existed, and were husband and wife, and Ipuky and Nebamun, both sculptors, share a tomb near Beir el-Bahari, but there is no evidence that they were related.

Lord Nakht, the Royal astronomer, scribe and priest, and his wife Susmaat were both real, and are depicted in a remarkable life-like statue-group, but Djenna, Menefer's friend, being the daughter of Lord Nakht and Lady Susmaat, is fictional.

The narrative of Messu being the son of Menefer and Smenkhare is also pure fabrication.

The real Paramessu was not of royal birth, but was born into a noble military family.

Other incidental characters, not mentioned in the above list, including the Bedu (chapter one), the are all fictional, and were created for the story.

Many incidents involving historical characters, had been devised for dramatic purposes only, and are in no way connected to historical events. No evidence exist on the causes of deaths of most of these figures, but in a few instances, there are speculations that Akhenaten was murdered, Tutankhamun died of injuries, and some of the princesses died during a plague epidemic. There is also evidence that Queen Ankhsenamun was very unhappy after her marriage to her grandfather, the Vizier, Ay, as her letters to King Shubbiluliuma indicated, and as she had died just a few years after the wedding, there is speculation that she took her own life.

# Meanings Of Ancient Egyptian Words

## A

| | | |
|---|---|---|
| Aabu stone | – | Granite |
| Aft | – | Couch with cushions. Bedstead like the Sudani |
| Afen-t, afen-tu | – | Headcloth(s) |
| Amakh | – | Eye of Horus |
| Ankh | – | Life, symbol of life |
| An-tiu | – | Dwellers of the Eastern Desert |
| Apir | – | Mercenary soldier |
| Atur | – | 10 kilometres |

## B

| | | |
|---|---|---|
| Ba | – | Soul |
| Ba-ti | – | Black Land (Egypt) |
| Beb | – | Metal pectoral or breastplate |

## D

Deshret       –       Red Crown of Lower Egypt, also Red Land (Nile basin)

## E

Emmer       –       Millet beer

## H

Habiru       –       Hebrews
Hupsu       –       Labourer

## I

Imeru       –       An unknown substance from an ancient medical papyrus (Aloe?)

## K

Ka       –       Double (as in spirit)
Kalasiris       –       Sheath dress
Kamp-t       –       'Word of the mouth' (language)
Kemet       –       Egypt
Khabes       –       Beard (ceremonial)
Khepersh       –       Royal war helmet
Khenu       –       Any Egyptian city where the king and his courtsides.
Kheri heb       –       'He who has charge of the festival' Title of the priest
Kohl       –       Eye paint

## M

Metcha-t       –       Letter, writing holy script
Meti-u       –       Plural of above mariannu –Upper classes, nobility
Medjay (m'tchaiu) –       Police, town guard (usually blacks from the Sudan (Kush)
Mena       –       Nurse
Mes       –       Child, son, baby
Mesh       –       An amulet worn by women to obtain labour
Meseh       –       A drug made from the member of a crocodile (Aphrodisiac)
Mesit       –       Evening meal, cakes of the evening
Meska       –       Bull skin in which dead are wrapped to effect resurrection
Meskhen-t       –       Pair of stones (bricks) upon which women squatted during childbirth
Mesq-t       –       House of skin (Mortuary) for mummification
Mes or mesu seru       Child or children of nobles

| | | |
|---|---|---|
| Met-t mut | – | Death sentence |
| Metu ra en Kamp-t | – | 'Word of the mouth of Egypt' (Egyptian language) |
| Metu ra en Kamp-t | – | 'Word of the mouth of Egypt' (Egyptian language) |

## N

| | | |
|---|---|---|
| Nechit | – | Painting in colours |
| Nefer | – | Beautiful |
| Nekenu | – | murderer |
| Nemau sha | – | 'Those who traverse the sand' (Nomads) |
| Nemes | – | Striped royal headdress or head-cloth |
| Neshu-t | – | Hair in its natural state. Undressed hair |
| Nesu | – | King |

## P

| | | |
|---|---|---|
| Per | – | House |
| Per-hemt | – | House of Women (Harem) |
| Per-neheh | – | House of Eternity (Tomb) |
| Per nesu | – | King's house |
| Per-O | – | Great House (Pharaoh) |

## Q

| | | |
|---|---|---|
| Qerf-t | – | Head cloth |

## R

| | | |
|---|---|---|
| Rekhes | – | Cooking place, kitchen |
| Renpet | – | Spring |
| Rpat | – | Heir, Crown Prince |

## S

| | | |
|---|---|---|
| Sab | – | Master Scribe, master Policeman (Title of Minister of finance) |
| Sbau | – | Place of learning. Classroom |
| Segi | – | Mute |
| Sekhemti | – | Double crown of Upper and Lower Egypt |
| Sekh shat | – | Writing for documents (running writing) |
| Sutenu | – | White Crown of Upper Egypt |
| Shenti | – | Loincloth |
| Shesmu | – | Judge, assessor |
| Shesp | – | Sphinx |
| Shu | – | Feather, wind, air |
| Sistrum | – | Rattle, musical instrument |
| Skhai-t | – | Crowned One |

| | | |
|---|---|---|
| Sma | – | Lotus and papyrus intertwined, Sign or symbol of unity of the Two Lands (lotus – Upper Egypt, Papyrus – Lower Egypt) |
| Sopet | – | The star Sirius |
| Sownet | – | Market |
| Sunu | – | Physician |

## T

| | | |
|---|---|---|
| Tche-t | – | Peasant |
| Tchama | – | Coronation chair (Throne) |
| Tef | – | Father |
| Tjaty | – | High Priest |

## U

| | | |
|---|---|---|
| Udjat | – | Eye of Horus |
| Ur ser | – | Great One, Prince |
| Upit | – | New Year's Festival |

# Magical Charms Placed On A Mummy

Udjat or Amakh (Eye of Horus)
Djed pillar
Ankh (Symbol of Life)
Kheper (Scarab) Used in Akhenaten's name

# Place Names – Ancient Egyptian / Modern

| Ancient name | Modern name |
|---|---|
| Aahes | Nubia (Head of the Land of the Bow) |
| Aamtt | Western Asia |
| Abedju | ('Jjeni' in the Ta-wer nome) Abydos |
| Amurra (Amor) | Canaan, N/W Syria |
| Ankh Towy, Mennufer | (Life of the Two Lands) City of the |
| Great | White Wall) Memphis |
| Akhet Aten | Amarna, Tel El Amarna |
| Arenth | Orontes River |
| Arabi | Arabia |
| Assur (or Ashar) | Assyria |
| Autha | Tyre |

| | |
|---|---|
| Avaris | Tel el-Dab'a |
| Babal | Babylon |
| Bast | Tel Basta, Bubastis |
| Belly of Stone | Second Cataract |
| Djahi | Palestine |
| Djamet | Medinet Habu |
| Djan Net | Tanis |
| Feka (Turquoise Land) | Sinai Peninsula |
| Gatchai | Gaza |
| Gebal | Byblos |
| Gebtu | Qift, Koptos |
| Hattusas (Hattusha, Khattusa) | Boghazkoy |
| Ipet-isut (Northern Ipet) | Karnak |
| Ipet-resyt (Southern Ipet) | Luxor |
| Iunet | Dendera |
| Iunu | See On |
| Jjeni (in the Ta-wer nome), Abedju | Abydos |
| Kemet | Black Land (Egypt) |
| Khatti | Hittite Empire (Part of Turkey) |
| Khenu | (Name given to any city where the king and his court resided) |
| | |
| Khmun | Hermopolis |
| Khor | Syro-Palestine |
| Kush | Sudan |
| Mennufer | See Ankh Towy |
| Methen | Northern Syria |
| Mitanni (Mithna, Nahrin) | Northern Iraq |
| No-Amun (No), Waset | Thebes |
| On, Iunu | Heliopolis, City of the Sun (Suburb of modern Cairo) |
| | |
| Pars | Persia (Iran) |
| Pu Khent-Min | Akhmim |
| Punt | Somaliland |
| Pursath | Country of the Philistines (Philistia) |
| Retjnu | Phoenicia |
| Temesqu | Damascus |
| This | Girga |
| Towy    (The Two Lands) | Egypt |
| Uatch Ur (Great Green Water) | Mediterranean Sea |
| Uainn | Greece |
| Waset / No Amun | Thebes |
| Yebu (Abu) | Elephantine (Aswan) |

# REFERENCES

Egyptian tales – Late Egyptian Stories – A Gardiner
Illustrated London News, Sep 5 1931
       Nefertiti alive after separation – p367
       Oedipus and Akhenaten –Velikovskyp
       Amenhotep III wearing woman's clothing – p34
       Ay siding with Nefertiti, his daughter – p96
       No-Amun (Residence of Amun), Waset – p23
       Queen Tiye represented as a winged sphinx – p28-29
Son of the Sun – 'The City of the God' – Savitri Devi
       Akhet Aten – chapter IV
       Amarna letters – p223, 229 - 238
       Map of Middle East – p40
       Poem of hate against Akhenaten – p274
The Cult of the Immortal – Ange-Pierre Leca
       Funerals and mummification – p195
       Hathor – Tattooed Women; Priestesses, women of ill repute
       Punishments – p61
       Pregnancy out of Wedlock – p56
       Rites of Mummification
       Sickness & Health – p56
The Last Journey – William MacQuitty
       Embalming Tutankhamun – erect penis
The Lost Pharaohs – Leonard Cottrell
       Akhet Aten – Palace garden zoo – p192
       Ankhsenamun's Letters to Shubbiluliuma – p191
       Carrying chair – made of sesnedjem-wood and sheathed in gold
       Contradictory views – p218
       Amarna letters – p187, 188, 200
       Nefertiti's Disgrace – p216
       Pageant of Empire – p194
       Royal quarrel – p189-190
       Smenkhare's Mummy in Queen Tiye's tomb – p 216
When Egypt ruled the east – George Steindorff and Keith C. Steele
       Akhet Aten – p207-212

# BIBLIOGRAPHY

An Egyptian Hieroglyphic Dictionary – E. A. Wallis Budge
Atlas of Ancient Egypt – John Baines and Jaromir Malek
Cult of the Immortal, the – Ange-Pierre Leca
Curse of the Pharaoh, the – Philipp Vandenberg
Digging up the Past – The Egyptian Empire – David Down
Egypt – Gods, Myths and Religion – Lucia Gahlin
Egyptian Mythology – Paul Hamlyn
Egyptian Mythology – Richard Patrick
Egypt, the World of the Pharaohs – Regine Schultz and Matthias Seidle
Illustrated London News – Oct 10, 1936
Lost Pharaohs, the – Leonard Cottrell
Mysteries of Ancient Egypt – Lorna Oakes and Lucia Gahlin
Nubian Twilight – Rex Keating
Oedipus and Akhnaton – Velikovsky
Son of the Sun – Savitri Devi
Tutankhamun – The Last Journey – William Macquitty
Voices in Stone  – Ernst Doblhofer
When Egypt Ruled the East – George Steindorff and Keith C. Steele
Women in Ancient Egypt – Gay Robins

## INTERNET

Ancient Egyptian Festival Calendar
Ancient Egyptian Quarrying – Medicine
Angelfire.com/realm2/amethystbt/Eankhesensuman – Ankhesenamun
Egyptian Wedding Traditions
Egyptmyway – Map with Ancient Egyptian city names throughout the Nile Valley
eMedicineHealth – Gangrene
Geographia.com – The Bedouin Way
Health AtoZ – Gangrene
History of Ancient Egyptian Writing – Marie Parsons
Horemheb, the Last King of Egypt's 18th Dynasty
kikkulimethod.com – Horse trainer
King Ramesses I, Founder of the 19th Dynasty
Lib.utexas.edu/maps/middle East and Asia/Syria – Map
Matt & Andrej Koymasky Home – Biographies – Smenkhare

Music and Dance of Ancient Egypt
Oriental Institute Map Series – Egypt
Party time in Ancient Egypt – Ilene Springer
Ramesses/I
Rediscover Ancient Egypt – Tehuti Research Foundation – Maps
Sekhmet and The Art of Ancient Egyptian Medicine –
Syria Gate – All about Syria – Geography, climate
The Ancient Egyptian Calendar – Vol II No 3
Timeline 3300 to 1300 BCE
Wedding Customs of the Past and Present
Wikipedia, the free encyclopaedia – Ramesses
Wikipedia, the free encyclopaedia – Tiye
Wikipedia, the free encyclopaedia – Tutankhamun